NORTH T.

JOSEPH GORDON

MINERVA PRESS
MONTREUX   LONDON   WASHINGTON

NORTH TERRACE
Copyright © Joseph Gordon 1995

ISBN 1 85863 330 3

First Published 1995 by
MINERVA PRESS
10, Cromwell Place,
London SW7 2JN.

Printed in Great Britain by
Ipswich Book Company Ltd., Ipswich, Suffolk.

NORTH TERRACE

A NOVEL ABOUT LOVE AND HATE, LIFE AND DEATH AND
OF CAMPUS LIFE IN THE CITY OF ADELAIDE
1952–1956

Set me as a seal upon your heart
As a seal upon thine arm;
For love is strong as death,
Jealousy is cruel as the grave;
The flashes thereof are flashes of fire,
A very flame of the Lord.
Many waters cannot quench love,
Neither can the floods drown it:
If a man would give up all the substance
of his house for love,
He would utterly be scorned.

Song of Songs 8: 6.

Foreword

In *North Terrace* I set out to write a record of student life, concentrating on the extracurricular and private lives of students, against a background of lectures and examinations. My first task was to find those students. I couldn't incorporate real people, students that I once knew, into my novel for several obvious reasons. I had to create and original group of students to live their lives in my story.

I got my first character from an anecdote told at a departmental luncheon. I sat opposite the head of the local CSIRO laboratories. This Fellow of the Royal Society was the life of the party, a W.C. Fields of a man. He told us that the Government Printer had recently been approached by a young lady, who wanted to buy exam papers. When he refused to take money, she offered him something better than money! For some reason, he didn't continue the story, so I don't know what happened next. The story and the characters took over, in that part of one's brain that creates stories. The novelist creates a hero, heroine or a villain. These creations have to behave in character, but they have their own destiny. They take control of the writer. He can only guide them on the roller-coaster ride to the end of the novel.

There is a mixture of actual events and fiction in *North Terrace*. As the characters are creations of the mind, anything that they say or do is fiction. One family in *North Terrace* is the richest family in Adelaide. I have no idea who held that distinction at the time. I did not write about them. If they had offspring at the university, nobody told me.

I used the memories of the time I spent at Adelaide University to tell the story, but I also used these memories to eliminate all characters that might resemble real people. If any Adelaide reader sees any likeness to a real person and to their personal life, this is purely coincidental. I describe certain college sporting results. My characters were not the actual participants, so don't look for them in the relevant college magazines.

Included in the book are details of world and local events. I think a novel about student life should mention important world events, especially those that may effect their lives. Two Australian events stand out, the Petrov case and the Orr case. The defection of the Russian, Vladimir Petrov, destroyed the Labor party and its leader, Dr. Evatt. The dismissal of Professor Orr, on a flimsy charge of sexual misconduct with a student, aroused students and staff at universities all around the world.

Life at the University of Adelaide was wonderful. It was a pleasure to be educated by competent and dedicated lecturers and professors. They spared no effort to make the acquisition of knowledge an enjoyable experience. There was plenty to do between lectures, when we needed a break from the books.

SOUTH AUSTRALIA

ADELAIDE AND RENMARK

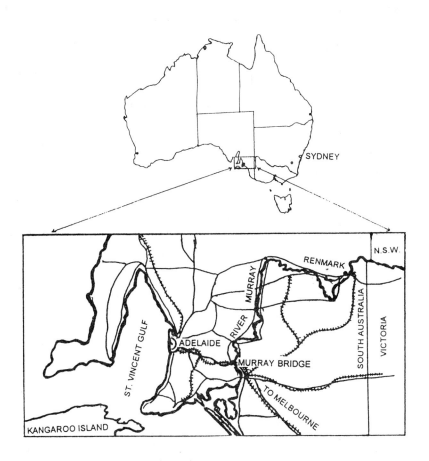

ADELAIDE

PLACES OF INTEREST IN NORTH TERRACE

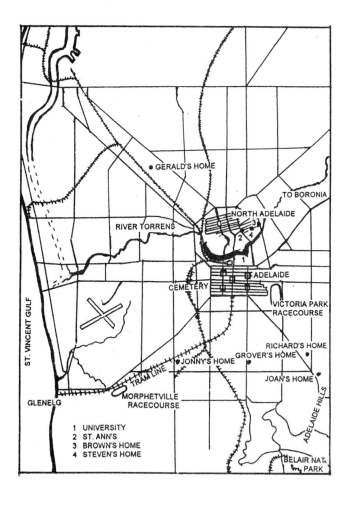

THE UNIVERSITY OF ADELAIDE

1952 - 1956

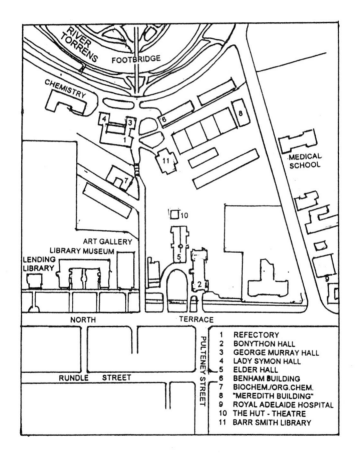

1 REFECTORY
2 BONYTHON HALL
3 GEORGE MURRAY HALL
4 LADY SYMON HALL
5 ELDER HALL
6 BENHAM BUILDING
7 BIOCHEM./ORG.CHEM.
8 "MEREDITH BUILDING"
9 ROYAL ADELAIDE HOSPITAL
10 THE HUT - THEATRE
11 BARR SMITH LIBRARY

Chapter One

March 1952

There is a thin line between a practical joke and a stupid prank, between frolic and folly. What began as a game on that March dawn was in fact a cruel bullying act with terrible consequences. If only the instigator had been brought to account for his action, the subsequent tragedies of 1956 would not have happened, but the one witness didn't want to get involved. That was *her* tragedy.

In all probability the big man responsible for the 1952 calamity should not have been at the university. He wasn't a good student, his talents were elsewhere; but he had matriculated, his mother had paid the fees, so he was there. He had failed twice; something that would have discouraged any normal person, but not this man. He was now a senior, repeating his first year. It made him feel superior to the know-nothing Freshers. Then, there were all the freshettes, last year's schoolgirls in the prime of youth. The problem was that he wasn't the only bull in the pasture. The big man had an irrational hatred for one of them, a young man who had done him no wrong. This hatred would bring calamity to both of them, to that one witness and her family.

The University of Adelaide, like the city of Adelaide, was a quiet, placid place in 1952. This was the backwater capital of South Australia, a 'City of Pubs and Churches', a sleeping beauty far from Europe recovering from the second world war, dreading a third, far from London that was mourning the death of a king, anticipating the coronation of a second Elizabeth, far from the United States at the end of the Truman presidency. Sydney was four days flying time from London and Adelaide, another four hours away by DC-6 or Convair 240.

The university sits behind many of the public buildings on North Terrace, Adelaide's most impressive street, with only the old Administration Building and the new Bonython Hall facing the city. If it wasn't for the sign, one mightn't know that there was a university tucked away there behind the grass, the trees and the flower beds. On the other side of the street with brick-red tramcars moving up and down, office blocks were beginning to crowd the skyline, which for a hundred years had seen numerous church spires in this city of a square mile. Post-war prosperity and Premier Tom Playford had brought wealth to the state, and it was beginning to show on the skyline. Adelaide was awakening at a pace commensurate with its Mediterranean climate.

It is a short walk from North Terrace to the River Torrens, but it's like entering another world. You walk down the roadway, between the Art Gallery and the Administration Building, down the red-brick steps beside the Barr Smith Library, also red-brick, with massive columns at its entrance, past the Refectory, eating hall and centre of student life.

In 1952 the Refectory was the only spacious room for student use. In that last week of March, Orientation Week, there was a blackboard and another notice board, telling new students what the student societies offered, urging them to attend meetings and join faculty clubs, sports clubs, religious or political societies. A couple of students in black gowns were moving in and out of the Union office and the *On Dit*, editorial office, offering help and advice to the eighteen-year-old Freshers. The grounds were full of Freshers, wandering around the paths and gardens with copies of the Orientation Week *On Dit*, the student newspaper, or the student handbook, getting their bearings in a world so different to the schools that they had recently attended.

The sky, high above the plane trees with their autumn leaves, was a brilliant blue, with wisps of feathery clouds, white as milk. Outside the Union Gates an occasional car passed between the campus and the Torrens, that modest stream dammed into a lake, set in parks and gardens, the principal garden in this garden city. The lake-river separates the lecture theatres and the laboratories from the playing fields and residential colleges in North Adelaide, a short walk from the river via the University footbridge.

Students and office workers come down to eat their sandwiches near the footbridge, a frail-looking structure on a cantilever arch of iron, painted green. Set in a bend of the river, it is one of the quietest spots in this serene city, and one of the most beautiful, with a variety of tall trees, yellow in their autumn colours, dropping their leaves into the placid water, where ducks and black swans float to and fro searching for food.

White gulls soar or strut on the grass, clustering near lunching couples, hoping for a free feed and fighting for it when it comes, their beaks and webbed feet red, the same colour as the bricks of the university. One gull was the bully here, cautiously sidling up to the sandwich eaters, chasing away other birds that came too close. When a morsel was tossed to them, there was a scramble, and bully-bird was so busy chasing others away that most of the time he missed his chance and another bird took it and swallowed it, head up, at a safe distance. They were almost human.

Who would believe that this island of serenity, this bend in the river, could be the scene of tragedy twice in two years? For years students had regarded the river bank and the muddy water as their playground. An annual tug-of-war was held across it, with the losing team being pulled into the murky water, and who knows how many students were thrown into it and survived? Then, one tragic night during a student initiation, one young man lost his life, a terrible loss of a gifted person at the start of his adult life, a cruel blow to his family and devastation for those responsible.

The only one to profit from this tragedy was the gutter press who, not satisfied that the legal processes would do what had to be done, proceeded to print regular condemnations of student behaviour. Not much was happening in Adelaide or on the campus, but *Truth* had to be published, and its readers read the rubbish, probably believing what was printed. Month after month, student immorality and irresponsibility featured in the pages of *Truth*, alongside tall stories of film stars' sex lives, rapes, murders, and busty girls in bikinis. *Truth* hadn't gone topless in 1952.

Adelaide on the surface was a very moral city, the wowser capital of Australia. *Wowser* is Australian slang for killjoy, guardian of other people's morals. But there were brothels in Sturt Street, drunks in the city parks, and a gutter press full of filth for people to read in spite of the wowsers. There was adultery and premarital sex and there was the Kinsey Report on the Human Male. There was no sex education in school and no contraceptive pill in the pharmacies.

Students, if they were diligent, might see the inside of the magnificent mock-Gothic Bonython Hall on graduating. The other opportunity was when they were ushered in to be welcomed by the

Vice-Chancellor and other dignitaries, parading like peacocks in their coloured academic robes. It is said that the hall has a sloping floor so that it could never be used for such frivolity as dancing. In a city and a university lacking good halls, this great edifice was regarded by the student body as a luxurious waste of money, a beautiful, seldom-used monument, an architectural bowl of wax fruit.

Among the students arriving in their grey suits, white shirts and old school ties were Gerald Fisher and Richard Flynn, ex-Adelaide High School students, and Jonny Marco, an ex-college boy. Jonny was observed by a Goliath of a man, an older student, Louis Brown, frowning as he recognised the youth. None of the trio noticed Bully Brown.

Waiting to go into the hall, they heard the approaching sound of music. Turning they saw a girl drive up in an open red Mercedes and park it outside the Elder Hall, its radio the source of the melody. Gerald and Richard had to jump onto the grass to get out of her way, to the music of Mitch Miller and the rich tone of Guy Mitchell singing, *Truly, Truly Fair*. She turned off the motor and the music stopped.

"That's truly, truly fair!"

It was Richard who spoke, but it was Gerald, closer to the car, staring at the lovely driver, who got the blame. Later he couldn't remember if he was looking at the driver, or the interior of the only car of its kind in Adelaide. It didn't matter, she looked up and caught him. For a second he was looking down at a pair of sparkling hazel eyes, a face ringed with jet black hair, then down the front of her dress, a dark valley between two sun-bronzed hills. Gerald averted his eyes, but not before taking in the scenery.

"You're a cheeky boy." She smiled at Gerald and gave him a wink. Then she swivelled her body around, pushed open the car door, showed the boys her sun-tanned legs and got out of the car. Putting on a wide white sun-hat, she was about to walk away when an attendant ran up and told her to park on the lower level. Off came the hat and back came the voice of Guy Mitchell as she switched on the engine. Off she roared.

Richard called after her, "Don't go away. I was listening to that."

Six minutes later she and the hat reappeared, joining the Freshers entering the Hall. Richard commented to Gerald, "That's Joan

Meredith of Meredith Beer. She has to wear an umbrella hat to keep the sun off her tits. Thinks the sun shines out of her arsehole. Look at the way she wiggles her bum, the sexy bitch. She can park those high heels under my bed any night."

They were only a few feet behind her and Gerald was sure that Miss Meredith could hear what Richard was saying, but if she did she didn't show it.

The social reporter of the *Advertiser* had seen Joan and was making a bee-line for her with a camera-man in tow. She stopped her and a smartly-dressed brunette with long hair, Evelyn Robertson. A few seconds later Joan stopped talking to the reporter and looked about her to see if there was a man to include in the photo. Her eyes fell on Gerald watching the proceedings.

She called over to him, "Come here, cheeky boy. We need a man over here."

"Who? Me?" No woman had ever called him a man, no woman with a come-hither voice like Joan's. It was one thing to admire Miss Meredith from a distance, but Gerald found her summons disconcerting. He hesitated.

The reporter woman took his arm and he joined the two women. They were both the same height, two inches shorter in their high heels than Gerald's five feet eleven inches.

"You don't mind having your picture taken for the *Advertiser*, do you? You're all first-year students? Good, come over to the cameraman and I'll get your names while he takes the pictures. How are you, Joan? Any news for your favourite reporter?"

"Ring me up tomorrow at ten. I don't want to be late for today's pep talk. Better still, come and have a beer with me at the new flat. I have to tell you about our pre-Ball party."

Richard stood next to Jonny Marco and watched, as the photographer sandwiched his friend between the two beautiful girls. It was warm and Joan's perfume was overpowering. Gerald felt uneasy. None of them noticed the towering bulk of Louis Brown, hovering like a rain cloud on the periphery. He had come to get a look at the new talent, the freshettes, eighteen-year-old fresh fields to conquer. Joan Meredith had caught his eye as the photographer was catching her image. At this stage Evelyn Robertson meant nothing to him.

"That's it, girls. Try to keep the hat out of the boy's face, Joan. Smile boy, you're not getting married."

They all laughed, and the photographer got his picture. He took another and a third. Then the three of them went under the stone arch, past the massive polished wooden doors, and took their seats in the magnificent hall, Gerald again sandwiched between the two young ladies.

He didn't pay much attention to the speeches. There was too much to distract him. He gazed up at the stone arches above the upper balcony, and the ornate Old English ceiling, like a heavily-iced inverted cake of immense proportions. It would be another three years before he would be permitted to see the inside of this magnificent building again, if he didn't fall by the wayside as some students must.

This thought didn't enter Gerald's mind as he tasted this new wondrous world of academic splendour. He might have been in Oxford or Cambridge, it was so grand. That wasn't all, he was sitting between two lovely ladies, ladies who in the coming years were to play major roles in his life. This he didn't know, as from time to time he sneaked a look at each of them.

Joan Meredith, whose perfume was far too strong, made him think of a buxom barmaid. She was a little more than medium height, but nothing else about her was medium. He'd heard other boys at school extol the wonder of the Meredith tits. As he took sideward glances at them he wondered if her dressmaker had had to work overtime making the dress, which fitted her like a glove, with two B-17 gun turrets at the top. There was enough of Joan visible to prove that in the words of the song, 'everything she had was absolutely real'. He wondered what she would look like in a bikini, with the beach inspectors removing her from their domain.

Gerald Fisher wasn't obsessed with sex, but he couldn't take his mind off Joan Meredith's mammary splendour that afternoon, or whenever he saw her again, which was the effect that Joan had on most men, the effect she wanted to have, with the help from her dressmaker. Of all the ladies in the hall, only Joan, daughter of Meredith Beer, dressed like a lady at a cocktail party; the rest, like Evelyn Robertson, wore smart conservative suits or simple dresses. Joan's big sun-hat was far too big for her own lap and it brushed against Gerald's leg. Every time she wiggled, which she did quite often, the brim rubbed against his thigh. It was little wonder that he remembered little of the speeches. But then, *who* did?

He was so taken by Joan and the stimulation of her sun-hat that he didn't pay much attention to the other girl sitting next to him. Evelyn Robertson wore a smart grey suit with short sleeves and a high v-collar, a little too hot for the warm autumn weather outside, although it was suitable for the chill in the big stone building. Later Gerald recalled that she did have a nice profile, almost classical. Schools in Australia were not co-educational and Gerald, although he had taken out a few girls, had never had a girlfriend, had never even kissed a girl. He wondered what it would be like to kiss the slim beauty next to him or the buxom one, and he blushed at what else he thought. He felt hot under the collar, under Joan's sun-hat too, and was glad to get out of the hall.

'I'd better pay better attention in lectures,' he thought as, without saying a word to either of the two women, he strolled down to the Union. 'Girls are too damned distracting, but what the hell — it sure beats a classroom full of boys. I think I'm going to enjoy going to university.'

By contrast, Evelyn Robertson listened to every speech, taking in every word, like a believer at a Billy Graham crusade. Gerald was awed by the surroundings, Evelyn was overawed. She felt like Anna at the King of Siam's palace. This was the happiest day of her life, the day she'd been looking forward to ever since her father had brought in the paper to show her that she'd been awarded a Commonwealth Scholarship and had asked her if she was going to accept it. He didn't want her to go to the city, but left the choice to her — a first in the Robertson household.

Yesterday she had said good-bye to her father and travelled down on the early train with her mother, who had taken her to the Women's College in a taxi. Her new high heels were a bit of a bother; she had had to get used to them when her father wasn't around. He didn't approve of high heels. Now her feet hurt. After saying a tearful good-bye to her mother at the station she had had two hours to kill, so she spent it in Rundle Street getting to know the department stores. On her first visit to the city, four years earlier, she had only seen the gardens and the churches.

The girl from Renmark had enjoyed her earlier visit, but there had been a scolding when she'd laughed at a couple of drunks, followed by a lecture on the evil of drink. Dad had repeated that talk at the train station yesterday, but she wasn't convinced by it. Renmark was proud of its wines, South Australia was proud of its wines. Evelyn had tasted wine. She didn't see why her father had to lecture her about it.

Evelyn didn't like concealing things from her father. She loved him, it was Father who had helped her with her studies; without him she wouldn't have got her scholarship, and without it she wouldn't be going to university. It was sad leaving home; she was the only student from her class to do what she was doing. Her father had wanted her to find a respectable job and a husband. But how could she do that if he wouldn't even let her go to parties or go to the pictures?

She used to visit her class-mate Deirdre Williams on Saturdays, to sneak over to the picture-house to see Humphrey Bogart and Alan Ladd, or listen to the 5DN hit parade (when they should have been studying) to sounds that would have been considered sinful in her father's house — songs of love and kissing and holding close. Deirdre confided to her friend after the finals that she was called 'the girl who's never been kissed' by the students of Renmark Boy's High School. She wondered if it was a compliment or a criticism. It was a fact that no young Renmark man had put his lips to hers. They, like Evelyn, were too frightened of her father.

It wasn't that Evelyn had been unhappy in her puritanical home. She didn't want to break loose and indulge in whatever had been forbidden to her, but she was going to go to parties and dances and to the pictures now that she was away from father. And if a boy wanted to kiss her, it wouldn't be a sin to let him. She would tell all this to her mother, like the way she'd told her all about the pictures she had seen. Mrs Robertson enjoyed life through the eyes of her daughter.

After the lecture, Evelyn didn't leave the hall with the others. She went down the aisle and sat in the front row, with all the hall to herself and her shoes beside her on the polished wooden floor. She remembered the professors in their gowns of black and red and gold, picturing herself standing up on the stage, with the Chancellor handing her her degree and her father watching way back in the hall, where she had been. He would be proud of her on that day.

She was almost locked in the Bonython Hall. At the last minute an official saw the diminutive figure and called out through the echoing hall, telling her to leave. The Bonython Hall had to be closed. It wasn't there for students to sit in. Evelyn put on her shoes and joined the other undergraduates sitting on the Union lawns. No one spoke to her, everyone seemed to know somebody else and not her. She didn't mind, just to be here was divine. She was intoxicated with her new freedom. Later she walked across the narrow green bridge to her new home, St Ann's, the women's residential college.

Gerald found himself a vacant table in the Refectory, sitting down to read a copy of the student paper, *On Dit*. He had scarcely opened the paper when he felt a slap on the back as Richard Flynn sat down next to him.

"What the hell are you doing here, Gerald? I thought you'd be off with the beer heiress, having a suck on those wonderful tits of hers, you cheeky boy."

"Joan Meredith?"

A rhetorical question, Gerald *knew* who he meant.

"Gerry boy, you had it made. Didn't you see that 'Come on to my house' look she gave you? All you had to do was slip your hand under that sun hat of hers, and by now you'd be in it up to your balls."

"You're kidding, Richard. She'd probably have screamed, and got me thrown out of Bonython Hall and the university as well."

"Where have you been all your life? Greg Smith banged Joan Meredith at the school ball, in the prefects' room, and he wasn't even her partner. She's had more bangs than you've had breakfasts."

"You don't really believe that story, do you? That's just boys' talk. Have *you* gone to bed with her?"

Gerald leaned over the table, lowering his voice as he spoke, which was strange as there wasn't anyone near them.

"No, but I might, sooner or later. The beeress is in three of our classes, so it won't be hard to get to know her. You and I are going to be classmates of Miss Meredith Beer, one of Adelaide's most famous institutions, like Victoria Park racecourse, or the head waiter at the South Australian Hotel. They say she has lager in the right tit and bitter in the left, enough to get a fellow completely pissed, and buttocks like jelly on springs."

"That's no way to talk about a fellow-student, Richard."

"You don't *fancy* her?"

"I find her a little distracting, that's all. Like Jane Russell in *The Outlaw*, a bit hard on the fly-buttons."

"Good, I was beginning to worry about you. Joan Meredith does it on purpose, she's a prick-tease, but unlike other prick-teases she shags! *That* is common knowledge."

"Who'd marry a girl like that?"

"*I* would, half of Adelaide would if they had a chance, for that body of hers and her bank balance. Rich bitches like Joan don't have to care about their reputations. Miss Meredith and her brother will inherit millions and, what's more, she's beautiful, bloody beautiful — brainy too. She got distinctions in Leaving Honours Chemistry and Physics. She's the perfect woman."

He threw Gerald's *On Dit* six feet into the air and caught it again, almost falling off his chair as he did.

"Richard, if the stories are true, she's a nympho. Could a woman like that be faithful to her spouse?"

"Probably not. So what, if he caught her at it he'd get a bag of money as a divorce settlement. You wouldn't marry her for love, you'd do it for the sexual ride of a lifetime. She's probably incapable of love. I wouldn't marry her right away. I'd have the honeymoon first, show her who's boss, and if I survived the experience, I'd get her so pregnant that no one else would be able to get near her."

Richard laughed, his laughter echoing through the Refectory. Other students looked to see what was so funny.

"I wish you well. When do you intend to start your assault on this tower of infidelity, Richard?"

"I don't know. What about the Fresher's Welcome, next week? But it's *you* that needs a woman, Gerry, not me. If you don't feel up to Joan Meredith, would you like me to fix it for you with the other girl who was sitting next to you?"

"The brunette? She looked quite sweet. Don't tell me that she bangs, too?"

"All girls bang. It's just a matter of lighting their fuse. It's just that they don't like to advertise the fact, not even town bikes like the Meredith woman. Regarding the brunette, she must be a country girl. I've never seen her at a dance or any other social gathering, and I would have noticed a good-looking woman like that. You coming to the Commencement Ball?"

Gerald felt embarrassed. He wanted to go to the ball but hadn't asked anyone.

"No, Richard. Not unless you can get me a date. I don't want to take the girl next door. I've been out with her twice and it was a big mistake. I think she likes me, but I don't want to get involved. At the school ball she was all over me and I didn't know what to do. I didn't know how to react to her. I couldn't wait to get her home."

"You could have got in some practice, you certainly need it. All the girl wanted from you was a kiss and a cuddle, *not* a baby, for God's sake. She must know you're a student and not a good catch. Pity you didn't come to the party. I didn't get home until the crack of dawn. And I had dear little Dawn, before dawn."

"You taking Dawn to the ball?"

"No, she broke it off."

Gerald wanted to ask *what* exactly she had broken off, but thought that it wasn't such a good joke.

"After what you did to her, I'm not surprised," he said.

Richard looked at his best friend. For a second he thought he was joking, but he knew that he wasn't.

'He doesn't know the first thing about women,' he thought as he answered him.

"On the contrary, Gerry. She wanted to make it a regular thing. She got very broody and lovey-dovey, as women do after a good shag, and started to talk about wedding bells. She even asked me what we would call our children."

"So what did you say you'd call them?"

"'Bastards!'" I said. I'm not getting married until after I graduate. I thought it was a good answer, all things considered, but dear Dawn had no sense of humour and hit me. Then she put her pants back on and went home. Women! Give them an inch and they think they're a ruler."

"An *inch*?"

Richard recognised that as another of those rhetorical questions. He joined in the joke.

"OK, six inches. We had a good thing going, Dawn and I. Why did she have to spoil things by talking of marriage? I told her I'm going to be a student for the next three years. She asked me if I wanted her to wait. It was a hard decision. Imagine if after three years of making love I changed my mind. I wasn't ready to make that kind of commitment. I'm going to miss her."

"Is making love to a woman *that* good?"

"You bet! It sure beats pulling the pud."

"Aren't you afraid of getting a girl pregnant?"

"Of course I am. That's why I only shag pretty girls who I could live with, if my little rubber friend failed me. I also buy the best English brands of *French Letters*. I'm too young to get married and I don't know if I'd have the nerve to ask a girl to have an abortion."

A puzzled look came over Gerald's face. He didn't want to show his ignorance but wanted to know the meaning of that word, so he asked his friend, "*What's* an abortion?"

"You don't *know*?"

"I know it's an obscene word. I've heard it and I've read about women having abortions in *Truth*. A girl died last year in Melbourne, and the woman she went to in order to have an abortion got fifteen years in Pentridge. They said that it was a botched job, but didn't say what it was."

Richard gave his friend a short lesson on contraception and the crime of artificially terminating a pregnancy. He explained to him that the doctors are allowed to do it when a mother's life is in danger.

"They say that some doctors perform illegal abortions, but they're hard to find and take a lot of money for doing it. I hope I never have to call on their services."

"That's one worry that I don't have, Richard. I'm having trouble finding a partner to take to the Commencement Ball."

"I'll ask my sister. I don't think she'll mind. She's between boyfriends and would do anything to go to a university ball. I know I can trust you with my sister, especially as I'll be driving the car. Come and have a game of table tennis with me. It's too early to go home."

"Where?"

"In the basement of the George Murray, near the toilets."

"I haven't been there yet."

"It's a place you should know. The writing on the wall is quite literary, not like the graffiti on the school dunny wall."

The corner building near the footbridge housed the George Murray Hall. They went out through the Union entrance to go there, passing Evelyn Robertson who was still sitting on the grass. She recognised the young man who had sat next to her in the hall, "cheeky boy", as Joan Meredith had called him. They didn't notice her.

In the basement the two Freshers relieved themselves against the porcelain, reading the student graffiti as they did. Gerald wasn't impressed. Only 'Stand close, the next man may have bare feet' made him smile.

'There aren't any Henry Lawsons or Banjo Patersons in this lot,' he thought. 'More like Ezra Pound.' Gerald wasn't an admirer of Ezra Pound.

In the locker room next to the toilet block a well-worn table stood with a torn net across its middle. A big man with big ape-like arms, was just putting the finishing touches to a smaller, inferior player and making a lot of noise in the process.

"Out! Eighteen - five. Can't you put the bloody ball on the table?"

He smashed viciously at the next ball and missed.

"Eighteen - six."

Then he served a ball, which his inept opponent missed. Grunting like a pig, he reminded Gerald of Napoleon, the head swine in *Animal Farm*.

"Six - nineteen, you serve. Two more points."

He was right. The first serve missed the table and the second was high. Louis Brown, big Louis Brown, demolished it. As the ball smashed against the lockers, he held up his arms high above his head.

"The Brown Bomber wins again."

"We'd like to play," said Richard.

"Good. Who'll play *me* first?"

"We want to play each other."

"First you have to beat me."

"Why?"

This man was beginning to annoy Richard.

"Winner plays on. That's the rule."

"Who made the rule?" Richard asked.

"Let's forget it," said Gerald, tugging at his friend's coat-sleeve. He didn't like the look of Bully Brown.

"It's the rule of the place. I've been here two years, I should know."

"Alright, big boy. I'll play you and then I'll play my friend."

He had the gleam of the Pied Piper in his eye. The reason for this gleam would soon become apparent.

"First you'll have to beat me, Fresher."

This upstart was treating him like last year's garbage. Brown didn't like him at all, or his friend for that matter.

"Stop wasting time, Fatso. Play for service."

For ten minutes Richard let the man he had just insulted dictate the pace, as big Louis Brown smashed ball after ball at him. Richard stood a yard back from the table and returned every ball with cool efficiency, forcing the bigger man to make errors and expend a lot of energy. Finally, down six - seventeen, Louis Brown, sweating like a pig, slowed down and tried to hit the ball short. Richard raced to the table, angling the ball across the net for a winner. Then he too changed his game, returning each service with a smash, finishing off Brown twenty-one - six. This done, he turned around and, with his back to the loser, called out, "Brown, be a sport and piss off. You're sweating like a sow in heat. I wish to play with my friend."

Louis Brown left the room without replying. Richard had beaten and humiliated him, reminding him of a similar humiliation that he had suffered almost three years earlier, inflicted by one Jonny Marco. That runt didn't even know what he'd done. He'd seen that runt today for the first time since that humiliation. Louis Brown had come to look at the new crop of women. Instead he had seen Jonny Marco and Richard Flynn. Flynn had insulted him, but Jonny hadn't, and yet he hated both of them.

Meanwhile the two friends had the table in the locker-room to themselves. Gerald couldn't get over the way his friend had thrashed the bigger man.

"That was great, Richard. I can't play you. I'm not in your class."

"Neither was the Brown bummer, was he? I can't stomach Louis Brown. He was one of the biggest shits in that posh college he went to. Ask any of the guys who went to school with him. There's something about him, something nasty. I'd stay away from him if I was you, he's bad medicine."

"So why did you tell the big bastard to piss off? He'd kill you if you ever got into a fight with him."

"I don't know. It felt so good when I was beating him that I just couldn't resist saying that. It did the trick, didn't it? Brown's a bully. He had a habit of picking on other boys. The younger kids hated him. Remember Ray Jones — he left college and came to Adelaide High because of Brown's bullying? Just because he was big, he was a little better at sport than smaller boys, so he acted like king of the castle; but I saw him come a cropper once or twice. The bugger stayed on an extra year at school to captain the footy team, but in the all-important intercollegiate match he missed the simplest of marks in the last quarter, and some little kid scooped it up and scored. Instead of being the captain of the winning team, he was the one that lost the game. What a come-down. They carried the other kid off, shoulder-high, with all of the younger kids cheering although their school lost. Bully Brown had lost, that's what mattered to them."

"What's he like at other sports?"

"I think he won the shot putt and the broad jump. He's big and strong. That gave him a hell of an advantage. He was last leg of the relay team and got the baton a yard ahead of the other team. Then this little fellow came running like the wind and was just ahead at the tape. Boy, was that extra year at school a waste of time. It probably helped him get into uni. He must be a dumb bugger or bone lazy, probably both. I saw his name in our Botany class. He should be in third year by now, not doing Botany 1."

Richard gave one of the battered bats to Gerald and went to the far side of the table.

"OK, Gerry, we've got the table now, do you want to play a game?"

"You'll beat me twenty-one to nothing."

"I'll give you a lesson if you like."

They played for half an hour, Richard instructing his friend all the time, hitting the ball back to keep it in play. Then two more students came down and asked to play.

"First you have to beat me, house rules."

"Brown made that rule. Where is the big shit, anyway? An hour ago he was ruling this room. We couldn't get a game."

"I beat him and told him to piss off."

They didn't believe him. It showed in their faces. "You told Brown to piss off? You're game."

"Bully Brown belongs in the toilet with all the other brown things, not with decent people like us."

Richard and Gerald went up the stairs and started to walk up to North Terrace.

"Thanks for the ping-pong lesson. I feel that I've learned something."

"That's what you're going to university for. What say we play every morning? Can you get here at eight?"

"Sure, I can get a lift with Dad and save the tram fare."

"Good, we'll get a few others to join us and in no time you'll play a good game. You might even beat me some day."

"*And* Brown?"

"Within a week, if he ever shows his face in the basement again."

"Won't it interfere with our studying?"

"Of course not. If a fellow can't study, play a little sport, have an occasional beer and shag an occasional girl, he has no right to be at a university. Did you see the way I had Brown running from one side of the table to the other?"

Louis Brown didn't play table tennis after that and didn't forget the insult, minor as it was. That wasn't his nature. Like an elephant, he remembered Richard in that part of his memory he reserved for those who humiliated him. It took time, but he got his revenge — not on Richard, but on Gerald who hadn't said a word to him.

He went to have a beer at the Richmond Hotel, where he met Joan Meredith coming out of the lounge with some of her friends. She recognised him.

"Hello, Louis. How's the football?"

He couldn't tell if it was a genuine question, which it was, or if she was making fun of him, which she wasn't. She didn't know him well enough to want to make fun of him.

"I play Rugby now."

"You need a shower, Louis."

He was sweaty, he smelt like an animal, or like a man after a night in her bed might smell.

"I've just come from a game."

"Rugby?"

"No. I'm thirsty. I came up here for a beer."

He couldn't tell her he'd worked up a sweat playing ping-pong.

"Come back to my place, Louis. I've got a fridge full of beer. You can have a shower too."

Louis went with Joan. It was a royal command. It was an invitation he had day-dreamed about after seeing her in front of the Bonython Hall earlier in the day.

The following morning, as Brown was just getting home, Gerald's father woke him up at seven and gave him the morning paper, something that he'd never done before.

"You're on page three of the *Advertiser*. Who's the sheila with the big hat?" (Both of them knew that he wasn't referring to her hat.)

"She's a fellow student, an heiress. Her father owns Meredith Foods, Meredith Mills and Meredith Beer. They also have a lot of land in the south-east. You should see the sports car she rides around in. Richard says it's the only one like it South Australia. I've never met her before yesterday, or the other girl in the picture, if you must know."

"The skinny one?"

He sat up in bed and looked at the picture. There he was between the two women, his fellow students for the next three years. It was a good picture of Joan, but not of himself or the other girl.

"The picture doesn't do much for her, but she's quite pretty."

"Well, you stick to the one with the money and the big — hat."

"I'll stick to getting a degree, if you don't mind, Dad. Now can I get some sleep. I don't have to be in until ten."

"Alright, son. I just wanted to show you the paper. I thought you might want to see it."

"Thanks, Dad, but don't make a habit of it."

Gerald didn't go back to sleep, but looked for a while at the picture on page three, remembering the Meredith tits, recalling what Richard had told him about her. These were not suitable thoughts for a young man alone in bed, under his warm Onkaparinga rug, so he cast an eye over the other headlines. The war was still on in Korea and General Ridgeway, Supreme Commander of US forces in the Pacific, warned that Russia was planning action against Japan. Gerald wondered if this was fact or fantasy, if World War Three was coming, atomic World War Three. There was an article about the possibility of talks about having truce talks in Korea. He thought of the neighbour's son who had volunteered and was somewhere over there. What a silly bastard to volunteer for a war! There were troubles in Persia with someone called Dr Mossedeq. The British were annoyed because Mossedeq had nationalised the oilfields. The British were also having it out with the Egyptian police in the Canal Zone. It was all very confusing, even in this right-wing newspaper. There was a new Danny Kaye film at the Regent, *On The Riviera*. He made a mental note to see it.

He got up and cut out the photograph. Unlike the girl with the big hat, he hadn't had a photograph in the papers before. It wouldn't be the last time.

In Renmark Mr Robertson showed the picture to his wife over the breakfast table. He wasn't pleased. But it wasn't his daughter who had soured his morning mood. It was the other girl in the picture.

"Look at that woman, dressed like a whore with her chest uncovered. No decent woman should expose herself like that. Evelyn showed a lack of good sense to be photographed with her. I hope our daughter doesn't associate with tramps like that. I'm not sure that we did the right thing sending her to live alone in the big city."

Mrs Robertson looked at the picture. Miss Meredith *was* over-exposed, but she *did* have a good figure. She wondered whether it aroused her husband, and what he really thought. Her daughter, she knew, had just as good a figure, but that was for a husband's eyes only when her wedding day came. Evelyn's mother looked at her daughter's shoes in the picture, but here was nothing to worry about. It was too indistinct for her husband to see the high heels.

When Wesley Robertson went to work, she cut the picture out of the paper, put it in an envelope, and sat down to write a letter to go with it. Then she went out to the neighbour's and asked her if she'd seen Evelyn's picture. The woman cut out the picture and gave it to her. Later in the week she got a letter from her daughter, who sent her another copy. She put it in the top drawer in Evelyn's room. She was missing her daughter. It was lonely without her, not to have her come home after school or from her holiday job.

Evelyn's mother was glad that her daughter was in Adelaide. She respected her husband, but she knew that her daughter's future would be happier away from him. He was a hard man to live with, a man who thought that he knew the will of God and inflicted it on his family, restricting their activities and limiting their circle of friends. Evelyn had an inquiring mind. For her mother, her daughter's escape to Adelaide had been a red-letter day.

Chapter Two

April 1952

Although there were no lectures in the first week of April, the University was a hive of activity. Evelyn, Joan, Gerald, Richard and Jonny attended almost every day. They went on the campus tour, including the impressive Barr Smith Library with its huge reading room lined with books beneath high windows, and attended the preliminary lectures of the various subjects for which they were enrolled to study. The young men played a lot of table tennis. Louis Brown looked in on them, but when he saw Richard, he went back upstairs.

The shy girl from Renmark wandered around the city. She went to the Curzon Cinema and, sitting by herself, saw a risqué French film, blushing as she read the sub-titles in the dark. They spoke too fast for her Leaving Certificate French with its English, 'French Without Tears' pronunciation. It was about a young woman who had a boyfriend at the start of the war and everything to live for. Then the hostilities began and she was seduced by a French soldier in a bombed building, after which she became the mistress of a series of German soldiers. When the village was liberated, she was dragged into the town square, had her head shaved, and escaped lynching by the skin of her teeth.

Evelyn felt sorry for the girl, as was the film-maker's intention, especially when her former boyfriend returned from a prison camp to seek her out. It looked like it might have a happy ending, but he hit her, calling her a whore and a host of other names that were lost in the translation. The girl was more sinned against than sinner. The film with its carnal scenes and brief nudity was one experience that she couldn't share with her mother.

The millionaire's daughter went everywhere, but unlike Evelyn she was never alone; if she wanted company, she picked up her telephone and called one of her many boyfriends. Louis Brown had just joined her *entourage*. He gave her his night tour of the campus, including the unlit area across the river on the slope overlooking the University Oval. Joan pretended that the place was new to her, accepting his offer of a quickie in the open air. She didn't enjoy it. The grassy slope was for the under-privileged who didn't have what she had: a flat with a private entrance.

One preliminary talk stuck in their memory, long after they'd forgotten what the others were all about. One of the younger professors concluded his talk with a bit of advice.

"One word of warning to the men. I know the aim of a university is to enlighten, but you are here for one important purpose: to get a degree and a good one. Sooner or later you'll have to support yourself and a wife, etcetera. Some of you may have scholarships, most of you, and you'll lose them if you don't pass your exams. So stay away from the fair sex. Save it for the summer vacation or when you've got your degrees. There's nothing worse for studying than a love affair."

"Or the lack of it!" Richard, who was at the back of the hall, commented quite audibly.

The professor chose to ignore the comment and the laughter generated by it.

"Now, to the ladies. What I said *also* applies to you. Keep away from the girls — sorry, the men."

'That's what they call a Freudian slip,' thought Gerald, who had just finished reading a paperback book on Sigmund Freud, his life and his teachings.

"Frankly, from a purely materialistic point of view, it's a waste of time having you young ladies here. I grant that you can be most ornamental, but quite a few of you — the majority, if the past is any guide to the future — will marry and drop out before you finish your degree. If you do graduate, which employer is going to bother to take you in and train you, only to have you disappear to have a baby and never come back? What you are doing here is to take a place and a scholarship from some young man seeking a serious career. Now that I've said that, don't think you'll be discriminated against in my department. You'll be treated as equals and get no less teaching, or favours, or special consideration — which may or may not be the case in other faculties."

Joan Meredith put up her hand.

"Do you have a question, Miss Meredith, or are you drying your nail polish?"

Joan, unflustered by the comment and the resultant laughter, spoke for all the ladies in the lecture-room.

"I have a question, Professor."

"I'm glad to hear that, Miss Meredith, it shows the right attitude. Feel free to ask questions if you have them. I'll remain after the lectures specifically for this purpose. Now, Miss Meredith, your question?"

"I read in the papers last week that Dr Malan in South Africa intends to legislate special anti-black laws. Do you think that such anti-women laws would be a good thing at Adelaide University? Would you restrict women to secretarial jobs and to cleaning toilets?"

"I'm afraid that you've misunderstood the meaning of what I've been saying. I was just stating facts, not offering an opinion. Personally I deplore the loss of female brain-power when clever women spend much of their lives working in the home. Where would we be without Madame Curie's discoveries?"

'Without the atom bomb,' thought Evelyn, but she was too shy to speak out loud.

"Employers feel the same. It's in your hands, ladies. Perhaps your generation will change things. It's no secret that most of the women on the campus are more interested in changing the letters before their name, than after it. It will be interesting to see how many of you get your BSc, and how many your Mrs. I'll wager that a few of you may even get both.

"I suggest that you attend lectures in something less gaudy, Miss Meredith — a high collar, for instance. When I lecture *I* want to be the focal point. Call me vain, but that's what I want. I also want only ladies in the three front rows. If any couples want to hold hands, do it down on the river bank. Please don't tell that to *Truth*. They might try to get me dismissed for promoting immoral acts.

"The first lecture is at twelve on Tuesday next. We start at ten past the hour and we don't admit late-comers. Please sign the attendance book as you come in. Any student who has an unsatisfactory attendance record will be warned, and if he doesn't buck up, he may be excluded from the finals. That applies to practical classes too. Do your drawings in class and not from textbooks or other students."

That night, that fatal night, the Science Association held their annual Fresher's Welcome in the Lady Symon Hall. Until 1951, this was called 'Initiation Night', an evening of fun and games with the object of breaking the ice and letting students, new and old, get to know each other. Older students in lab coats or academic gowns subjected the students to a little harmless humiliation and horseplay, which made them feel part of the place.

'Initiation' became a dirty word at Adelaide University with the accidental death of a student, so this year's welcome consisted of a few speeches and dancing to records, followed by tea and biscuits. It was not a success. It was a definite flop, a bad start to the year's activities. Most of the male students congregated together and didn't ask the young ladies to dance, so it was left to the few committee members and older students to try and rescue the situation. They couldn't dance with everybody and the male students decided to be collectively difficult, so they served refreshments early. (The committee decided there and then to go back to the old-type welcome for the following year.)

Louis Brown turned up at the welcome. He wasn't a Fresher and he wasn't a committee member, but that didn't matter — the committee needed all the help it could get. Brown played the piano for a while. He played well. It made a change from the records, but even his proficient playing couldn't save the evening as no one seemed to know the words to the songs. He joined Joan on the almost-empty dance floor. He hadn't seen her for a couple of nights.

Jonny Marco asked Evelyn Robertson for a dance. He, like Brown, was a good dancer. Evelyn silently thanked Deirdre for teaching her to dance, a skill her father thought unnecessary for her education. It was wonderful to be held in the strong grip of a man, to move across the floor to the liquid voice of Nat King Cole — wonderful, but frightening. Evelyn had not been embraced by anyone other than her mother, not since she'd been a baby. She felt her nipples hardening when their bodies touched and wondered if he felt them too. He didn't, the padding in her bra kept them under control. Jonny just felt the full roundness of her breast against his shoulder. He liked what he felt. Evelyn was slightly taller than her dancing partner, but she didn't mind this. There was something masterful in his step, like Fred Astaire or Sammy Davis Junior. She didn't want the music to stop. The moment, like the song, was *Unforgettable*.

Gerald watched, annoyed with himself for not asking one of these two lovely women to dance. He'd been introduced to both of them on his first day by that photographer woman. It would be easy to talk to them again, but Big Brown and little Jonny had both beaten him to them. He didn't want to dance with any other girl in the room.

Most of the other Freshers didn't mix and get to know one another, the object of the welcome. As people began to leave, Gerald was drinking his tea and wondering if all social evenings would be so dull, when Joan Meredith separated herself from Louis and came to speak to him.

"I've got something here for you, Gerald Fisher."

She had the sweetest honey voice and a smile that matched it. He wondered what she could possibly have for him. He hoped that it wasn't Louis Brown. He thanked God that she'd stopped calling him 'cheeky boy'.

"Here's a photograph from the *Advertiser*."

"Thanks, Joan. I already have a cutting."

Joan took an eight-by-ten glossy photograph from a white envelope and put it in his hand. There she was, as pretty as a peacock, with the other two in attendance — like the Queen Mother wearing that hat of hers, with her daughter and son-in-law behind, a Royal trio.

"Would you like me to sign it, Gerald, as a memento?"

Then she noticed the other person in the picture and called out to Evelyn Robertson, who was talking to a short smartly-dressed young student, whose face was familiar.

"Here's Evelyn. Evelyn, I've got a photo for you."

Gerald noticed that Joan had interrupted a conversation that the two were having. The interruption seemed to bother the young man, as Joan, with Brown by her side, elbowed him away from Evelyn.

"How much do I owe you, Joan?" they asked together. Evelyn laughed. She looked lovely when she laughed.

"Have it on me. I always get a set from the papers whenever I'm photographed, even if they don't publish it, which is very rare indeed. Otherwise I'd have to go down to the newspaper office almost every other week. I have drawers full of newspaper photos. Would you like to see inside my drawers, Mr Fisher?"

Gerald wasn't used to her manner of talking and blushed at the *double entendre*. So did Evelyn. They'd soon get used to her and would become quite worldly wise in a matter of months. (Later

Richard, who was listening, asked him why he didn't look her straight in the face and say, "Yes, Miss Meredith, I would like very much to get inside your drawers.")

"We're having a party at my house. Would you two like to come along? This one was a disaster, wasn't it?"

"I have to be back by eleven-thirty. I'm staying at the women's college," Evelyn replied. She looked about her for her former dance partner, but he was short, so she couldn't see him in the gathering crowd.

"I'd like to come, but I don't have a car," said Gerald.

"We'll fit you in somewhere. Come along."

Gerald watched as Evelyn frowned, wondering why, not knowing that she wanted to resume her interrupted conversation with Jonny Marco. But he wasn't standing there anymore. His place had been taken by Brown, who was hovering near them like a big brown bear around a pot of rich honey, Joan Meredith. All around was confusion, with people getting into cars or racing for last trams. Evelyn gave up looking for Jonny and joined the tram race.

There was no room in the red Mercedes, but Gerald and Richard managed to get into a Holden full of people, six of them in the back and another four, including the driver, in the front. They both had girls they had never met before on their laps. Between them sat the boy who had been talking to Evelyn Robertson.

"I'm Jonny Marco," he said, out of the corner of his squashed face, and the other five in the back introduced themselves. Gerald recalled that both the face and the name meant something to him, but he couldn't remember what. On the way there, it came to him — Jonny Marco had topped the state in maths. *That's* why he knew the name.

The Mercedes raced out in front of them and they lost it well before they were out of Frome Road. It was a twenty-minute drive to the Meredith Estate in Glen Osmond, and they arrived five minutes after Joan, together with another two cars. Louis Brown arrived last, in his Morris Ten. He looked absurd as he unfolded himself out of it, like a huge pocket knife being opened.

About twenty-five of them poured into Joan's flat, which had once been servants' quarters, at the back of the house. Louis, who had been there before, at once made himself at home, bringing out bottles of beer from the well-stocked fridge, playing *mein* host. He handed

Gerald a glass and called out to all and sundry, "The toilets are down the hall, mates, so don't go chundering on the floor if you can't take your beer, and don't piss on the lawn. Joan's only just moved in down here so don't mess up the place. The beer's always free at Chez Meredith for those of us who know how to drink."

It was warm in the flat and the beer was nice and cold. Gerald downed his glass quite quickly.

Brown came up to him and slowly refilled his glass.

"That was terrific. Do you boat race?"

"I don't follow," Gerald replied. "No, I don't row."

He realised as soon as he spoke that he'd said something amusing. Brown laughed and elucidated, "Boat race! Chugalug! Knock it down! Wait till I get your glass refilled."

He filled his glass with beer, then he put his full glass up against Gerald's. He knew he was Richard's friend and wanted to humiliate him.

"Someone says 'GO', and we see who can finish first. That's what a boat race is."

Several people said "GO", and Brown was away. Gerald tried his best, but the first glass had filled him up and the big man won by half a glass. He felt bloated and he tried to bring up gas quietly. Brown belched loudly.

"Any other takers?"

He repeated his triumph against another of the Freshers. Joan laughed loudly. "That's what I like to see. Good old Meredith beer going down the hatch. Daddy has to sell a lot of that stuff to fill the Mercedes with petrol."

She opened the fridge to show everybody the beer. It was filled wall to wall with brown bottles. It was obvious that Joan didn't use the flat for cooking.

"There's a water shortage, Joan," Louis answered, "and what comes out of the taps ain't worth drinking. As long as Adelaide water tastes like gin's piss, your father will continue to rake in the money."

Someone put on a record, and soon everybody was dancing. Joan pressed her head against Louis's shoulder; he held her very close and slowly moved his hand down the back of her dress to her waist, pressing her willing body hard against his. As he started to feel lower down her back, she whispered something into his ear, and a wicked grin spread over his face. Five minutes later the two of them slowly and separately disappeared. The click of a door being locked could distinctly be heard between records.

Richard noticed and mentioned it to Gerald.

"It looks like the Brown Bomber scores tonight, lucky bastard. Gerry-boy, I have just left the competition for Miss Meredith. If she'll go to bed with that shit, she'll sleep with anyone. *La Belle Dame Sans...*"

For a second he thought for the right word.

"...discrimination."

"You're only jealous."

"You *bet* I am, and I'm disappointed with that woman."

"I wonder what Freud would have made of Joan Meredith. Would you have gone with her to the bedroom if she'd invited you in?"

"I'll tell you, Gerry, if and when it happens. I probably would, out of curiosity. What do you think, Jonny?"

Richard spoke to the short stocky man with smart Latin features, who Gerald had first met in the back of the Holden.

"I think 'good luck' to Brown if he's on the winning side. Last time that I met him he was on the losing side."

Richard and Gerald both wondered what he meant by that. It left an impression on their minds that was cemented there after what happened at the Commencement Ball.

"You don't think much of Brown?" Gerald asked.

"That's right. I don't think of Brown at all. As a schoolboy he thought he was the greatest sportsman since Don Bradman — which was bullshit. He was all piss and wind, didn't have any stamina, couldn't last the distance. When his team were doing their final laps of the oval, Bully Brown was in the showers."

"Were you two at school together?"

"No, thank God, but I have played against him. Just because you play for one college doesn't mean you can't have friends in rival college teams. Brown wasn't one of them."

"You're a footballer?"

"Don't you know anything, Gerry? He was voted 'best and fairest player' in the school teams last year, *and* the year before," Richard answered for Jonny. "He's scored more times than Joan Meredith. Jonny's been asked to try out for the varsity team. He'll make it too. You two talk, I see a girl that I'd like to know better."

"Aren't you a little small for a footballer?"

"I play rover, or in the front pocket. I can run fast and get away from the man marking me, or turn quickly. Between you and me, it can be infuriating for the bigger guys, but what the hell — we little guys have to do what we can. *I* look after myself."

"What do you do?"

"I was always one of the smallest guys in the class, I got pushed around, so when I was eleven, after some bully bloodied my nose, I went to a gym and took up body building. Later, when my hormones hit me, I started to lift weights at the Italian club. It took a long time, but now no one pushes Jonny Marco around. I'm thinking of taking up Judo."

Gerald wondered what Freud would have made of Jonny. Was sport sexual sublimation? If it was and it worked, perhaps he should take it up? Poor sex-starved Gerald couldn't keep his mind off that woman in the bedroom who had given him her photograph to take home.

"What's Judo?" he asked Jonny Marco.

"It's a Japanese sport, like Jujitsu. Some of the soldiers who were in the Occupation Forces brought it back and it's starting to take on here."

"Why were you pushed around in school?"

Jonny took a deep breath and continued, "Because we were Italian. We were not only the enemy, we were the *cowardly* enemy. Did you know that dago tanks had ten gears, four forward and six reverse? What is the shortest book in the word? It isn't *Australian Cultural Gems*, it's *Italian War Heroes*. Do you know, my family were in an internment camp in two world wars?"

"How come?"

"We're from Trieste, on the border of Italy and Yugoslavia. Before the First World War we were part of Austria. My family were living in Egypt at the time to get away from the Austrians. Come the war, we were Austrian nationals, so the British had us interned. After the war we were given the choice of Italian or Yugoslav citizenship. Italy was an ally of the British and our people were Italian-speaking, so we became Italian. Who the hell had heard of Yugoslavia? It was a new entity, full of mad Serbs and Croats who started the war. We took Italian citizenship. Comes the second world war, Italy joins Hitler, and in we go again. Wouldn't you know it!"

Gerald was fascinated. He had only known Jonny for half an hour, but already felt an empathy with him. Would he join Richard as one of his closest companions?

"I was six at the time. We were shipped to Australia to a camp in NSW. It was a bit of luck as it turned out, as we were able to stay after the war, but at the time it seemed like the end of the world for my parents. God, we're lucky to live in Australia. Egypt today is no place for foreigners, and Trieste's been divided. My parents spoke English and my father was a qualified French teacher, so he managed to get a job here in Adelaide at one of the colleges. Having a father for a teacher didn't help my popularity at school, even if he is the best French teacher in the state. I concentrated on sport, and by the time I finished school I was probably the most popular Italian in Adelaide."

'What a guy!' thought Gerald. 'What a family! Look how they've managed to adjust when the cards were stacked against them.'

"What are you going to major in, Jonny?"

"Pure and Applied Maths. I've got several exemptions, so I'll be doing mainly second-year subjects this year."

"Didn't you get a prize last year for maths?"

Jonny nodded.

"I like maths — maths and footy, those are my two loves."

"No women in your life?"

"Oh, I have a few friends. To tell you the truth, being in the first team makes it easy to get a date, but like the good professor said, I'm not interested in getting too involved. Girls and study don't mix. Which reminds me, what happened to that girl you were talking to with Joan? Why didn't she come to the party?"

"Evelyn Robertson? She had to get back to her college."

For those at Joan's party the social at the Lady Symon Hall had been a bore, but not for Evelyn, not for the country girl who'd never danced with a member of the opposite sex, the girl who'd never been kissed. She caught the second-last tram up the hill and got ready for bed. The walk to the tram and the wait had been twice as long as it would have taken to walk home, but she didn't want to walk by herself across the dark oval.

She undressed and put on her flannel nightie, thinking of the young man who had danced with her. He had also asked her to the Ball, but she'd been too surprised to answer, before being dragged away by

Joan Meredith. It was nice of Joan to ask her to a party, and she wished, like Cinderella, that she could have gone. Tomorrow she would see Jonny Marco and tell him that, OK if he didn't mind taking a country girl who didn't have a ball-gown to the ball, she would love to accompany him. What would she do if she didn't find him? What if he asked another girl at the party tonight? She wished that she hadn't hesitated. Then a couple of students came into her room to chat with her and she put Jonny in another corner of her mind. Slowly but surely, she was making friends in her new environment.

Jonny wished that he'd used his head and walked the Robertson girl back to the college and not come to Joan's party. There was something about Evelyn that attracted him — her freshness, her country innocence, something lacking in *this* party, at *this* residence. He had watched the Brown go with Joan and had heard the door being locked. He was filled with disgust. But he was also envious. He wouldn't mind a romp in bed with the lovely daughter of the beer millionaire.

Behind the locked bedroom door Joan led her partner towards the bed. There was no point in playing coy with him, they both knew what they were in the room to do. This wasn't Brown's first visit to Chez Meredith, to Joan's bedroom. She undressed in the dark, pulled back the bed-linen and plopped onto the bed. Then she called out to Louis,
"Get a move on, big boy. I've got to get back to the party."
Louis did as he was told and was soon groping his way to her, over the sheet, wondering why she, a single girl, needed a double bed. When she felt, once more, how heavy he was, she was glad that the bed was built for two. Bed was better than a rough blanket on the sloping grass. That was for the birds.
"You don't mind if I go on top, do you, Louis? You're probably twice my weight. You're more than I can stomach."
"It's your bed, Joan, we'll do it any way you want." He slid one hand under her soft skin and drew her to his hairy body. He felt her warm eighteen-year-old breasts, freed at last of dress and brassiere, smooth and round and soft in his hand, then he buried his face between them, as he'd done with many a young woman. Then they

moved closer, she feeling his erection with her hand, he seeking the place to put it.

"You're a big boy, Louis Brown."

"Don't you think I should put something on it, like we did at the oval?"

"I've got my Dutch thing in. Besides it isn't the dangerous time. You just hold it until I get on top. We don't want to give you a fracture, do we?"

She slid crab-like over him until she felt the tip of his penis pulsing and probing the soft mound between her legs. Manoeuvring slowly, she opened her legs. She was moist, very moist, so that her partner slipped up into her as she moved down, sitting up as she did, like a rodeo-rider.

"Hold my shoulder," she requested. Those were the last words spoken as they both began to move, making animal sounds and sighs, unheard by the party-goers in the next room.

It was over quickly, too quickly, as Louis felt the world bursting in his loins. Joan felt his huge intruder pulse again and again, the sheer force of it made her climax too, a few seconds after him. She wanted him to continue to roll over and crush her to the mattress but it wasn't to be. Brown just lay there, like a dead whale. She lay down on him, sexually satisfied, but emotionally empty.

'There must be something more to this love-making,' she thought. 'There should be love, not just making it!'

She rolled her exquisite body off his and lay beside him. They once more became aware of the music playing in the other room.

"I'm going to rest for a minute, Louis. Then I'm going to wash that muck out of me and go back to the party."

They said nothing about what they had just done, Joan feeling that something was lacking from their intimacy. She knew that whatever it was — warmth or emotion — there had been no tenderness, no love between them, just the physical act of mating. She felt nothing for this man, and he didn't seem to feel anything for her. Well, at least he didn't pretend like other men did. He would do until a better man came her way.

She got up and went to the shower. Louis thought of the other women he had had. This one was one of the best. With her obscene wealth, she wasn't just another conquest, she was a woman to be cultivated — he would even marry her if that's what she wanted. He was out of his depth, but he didn't know it. He had left a bigger impression on her mattress than he had on her mind. In the shower she was washing him out of her body and out of her hair, like Mary Martin in *South Pacific*.

Joan put on a fresh dress and went back to Louis. She didn't give a damn what the others thought about her, she knew that men boasted about what they did with her, especially those that weren't doing it any more — that they called her a bike that any man could ride. At first, it had upset her — so much for honour among boyfriends — but it didn't stop them coming back for more, the bastards. Now she no longer hid the fact that she liked a good shag. It was her way of making her ex-lovers jealous, to make them pay for their verbal infidelity. Conventional morals were not for her, she was a member of the house of Meredith, not a refugee from Europe or a great-grand-daughter of an Irish convict.

"I'm going back to the party, Louis. You can have a little sleep if you want — just lock the door when I go out."

"Joan, want a little more fun tonight?"

"It *was* fun, perhaps again some time — not tonight."

She was hedging her bets, not sure whether she wanted to be intimate with Brown or not on a future occasion. She didn't know that Louis meant something else by 'fun'.

"After the party I want to have a little initiation ceremony with Jonny Marco. It's against university rules, so we have to do it secretly. I need you to get him to join in."

"Tell me about it."

Joan was always interested in something new and forbidden.

Gerald was still talking to Jonny when he noticed their hostess returning to the room, wearing a fresh dress, looking as pretty as a picture.

He whispered to Jonny, "I've heard stories about girls that do it, but I didn't believe half of it until tonight. How can she go into her bedroom with a man, with all these people here?"

"Hormones, Gerald, hormones. Haven't you got any? She's obviously got more than her share. Don't tell me that Miss Meredith doesn't send them running through your loins?"

"I suppose so, but a woman like that scares me. I think I'd faint if she spoke to me again."

"Well, you may just do that. She's coming this way. This *could* be your lucky day."

Gerald held his breath, but it was Jonny that the approaching apparition addressed.

"Hello, Jonny, how is the best and fairest tonight? Let's see if you dance as well as you handle a football."

Jonny accepted the challenge. He was a good dancer. She smelt of *Lux* and *Chanel Number Five*, not of Brown and banging as Jonny had expected. After a couple of minutes, Joan complimented him.

"I think I'll give you my vote, for best and fairest here tonight."

"What about your previous partner?"

Jonny wasn't afraid to speak his mind.

"He was feeling a little tired, so I put him to bed."

Neither was Joan.

"Brown never had much staying power."

"I bet you have." She felt the muscles of his back and shoulders. "Jonny, you've got muscles like Kirk Douglas. Take off your shirt and give us a look at them."

He thought of telling her to do likewise, but was too much of a gentleman. He changed the subject.

"You smell very fresh tonight, Joan."

"I've just had a shower. You can have one, if you wish."

She thought of the water splashing off those shoulders. It made her think of a rocky mountain stream. She also wished Louis would hurry up and vacate her bedroom. She would have loved to take this young man in there. He was so much more sexy than Louis Brown.

"Thanks for the offer," he told her. "I don't feel the need for a shower just now."

"Some other time. I suppose we'll see a lot of each other now that we're fellow students."

Jonny went to have a beer. He thought about Joan and what she seemed to be offering him, of seeing a lot of her. One thing stuck in his mind, preventing him from playing along with her. Joan had gone into her bedroom with Brown less than half an hour ago. As sweet and fresh as she was, he wasn't interested. As beautiful and sexy as she was, he wasn't having any — not after Brown and at a party, advertising what they were doing! Still, it was a difficult decision. He'd never had an offer like this one. In any case she might just be playing with him. Another time, another place, he might play mouse to her cat, to her pussy. It would be a nice diversion from study, and a feather in his cap, to root the richest girl in Adelaide.

Later they put away the Xaviar Cugat, stopped the dancing and listened to Ruth Wallace records. Richard told Gerald and Jonny that these were banned. They were Joan's latest acquisition, smuggled in from the US. When he heard the lyrics of *Long Playing Daddy* and *Davy's Dinghy*, Gerald understood why they were banned. It wasn't that they used bad language or that she sang about sex, it was that each verse had a second meaning, made crystal clear by the impish voice of the singer. When she sang about a naval engagement, it wasn't at sea. Soon everyone was splitting their sides laughing. The few couples on the couch left off smooching and sat up, as it wasn't easy to laugh and pet at the same time. They played each record several times. Gerald was learning more in this night than he'd ever learnt from his Freud book. Parties with his school friends had never been like this.

Brown came out of the bedroom rubbing his eyes, wakened by the commotion. He was about to say something, but Joan put her hand in front of his mouth, so he sat down and listened.

It was late and Gerald wondered how he'd get home. Would he have to catch the first tram in the morning, or would he get a lift? It was too far to walk home as they were on the wrong side of town, in the foothills. He was lucky, for when the party broke up at five o'clock, the driver of the Holden took a car full of party-goers right around Adelaide to everybody's house. Nobody noticed Jonny Marco leaving the party.

Jonny got into the back of Brown's old Morris Ten. He couldn't understand why Joan got into the front of the car and why they stopped outside the gates of Morphetville Race Track. They got out of the car and asked him to do so too.

"Brown, what are we doing here?"

He didn't like the look on their faces.

"We're going to have a little fun."

"I'd rather you took me home if you don't mind, what I need right now is a little sleep. You should have stopped a couple of miles back."

"Joan and I want to see how brave and strong you *really* are. I'm going to tie you to the tram line. The first tram will be here in twenty minutes. Do you think you can untie yourself in that time?"

"That's mad. That's schoolboy stuff. I thought you'd grown up, Brown. I guess I was wrong. Now can we go home?"

"I told you, Joan, he's yellow. He's a little Italian yellow-belly. Come, I'll take you home."

Jonny was hurt by Brown's insult. Joan said nothing and her silence seemed to say, "He's right, Jonny, unless you prove that he's wrong." She meant nothing to him, but he knew he was a better man than this lover of hers. He bit on Brown's baited hook, he wavered.

"What happens if I do?"

Joan whispered to him, "You can *shower* at my place."

The way she said 'shower' gave it another meaning.

Brown stood by, Hemingway-like, as Joan pulled in this fish for him. It was *too* easy. He felt like telling her to throw him back and try again.

"Not tonight, Joan, I'm too tired," Jonny told her.

"Whenever you want."

It wasn't the prospect of showering with Joan that hooked him, but proving to her that he was more of a man than Bully Brown, that big bastard who was rooting her.

"And if I *can't* untie the rope?"

Louis Brown took an axe out of the car. It shined in the darkness, reflecting the light of a distant street lamp. All he lacked was a blindfold and chopping block to create the illusion of the executioner.

"Don't worry. I'll cut the rope in a second and free you. Are you game? We only have nineteen minutes left."

"Quickly, then. No fancy knots. Joan, you keep track of the time."

Joan kissed him, a fair maiden to her knight-in-shining-armour kiss, as Louis Brown tied his legs together and then his arms. He slipped another rope under both rails and though the space between Jonny's arms around his prostrate body, then twice around his ankles, before pulling it tight and tying it to the other end of the rope. One whack of the axe, and Jonny could scramble free. Then they stood back and watched him struggle with the rope binding his hands.

"You've got sixteen minutes," she said and went to where Louis Brown was standing a few yards back.

"I don't like this silly game, Brown. Let's stop now. If he wants, I'll keep my part of the bargain. He's probably a better root than you are. This is stupid and dangerous. Go and cut the rope."

"He's in no danger. This isn't a race day. He's tied to a siding. The other two tracks are the up and down lines."

Brown was beginning to see the foolishness in what he was doing. In his wish to have a little innocent sport with this little nobody, he was losing his newly acquired bed-friend to Jonny. That wasn't the object of this dawn patrol. Joan was showing too much concern for the little wop.

"That's clever." She smiled, looking at the three tram-tracks. "Do you think he knows?"

"Of course. Any fool can see. We've done this lots of times before that guy went and got himself drowned and they banned initiations."

"*I* didn't notice that it's a siding. You'd better tell him, Louis."

'Damn her!' he thought. 'Why is she so interested in him? Typical woman, goes from man to man like a silver dollar. What am doing wrong?'

He answered Joan, "Cut him loose and spoil the fun? One guy, two years ago, shat his pants. It's frightening when one of those monster trams goes past. You'll see."

"Tell him, Brown, that it's on another track."

"Don't be silly," he told her. 'Stop giving me orders, you bitch!' he said to himself.

"Tell him, or I'll go over and untie him."

"Shit!"

"Tell him."

"Alright."

Louis Brown went over and whispered to Jonny Marco, "Get a move on, wonderboy. Time's running out."

Jonny looked at Bully Brown with a look of contempt. He was proving to Joan that he was the better man.

"I'll soon have my hands free. How long have I got?"

'Why am I doing such a stupid thing?' he thought as he flexed his hands and felt the rope loosen slightly. 'Why did I let that bastard sucker me? Because he called me a yellow-bellied Italian? I should have punched him in the guts and walked home. Five thousand students at the university, and I have to play silly-buggers with these idiots. I should have made a bet with him and taken the bastard's money.'

Brown answered his question, laughing as he did, "I'd say you have a minute. I can see its lights now." Jonny turned his head and saw a flicker of light way down the track. The Glenelg tram was approaching. "It's early. Cut the ropes, you bastard."

"You'll make it, Jonny. Keep trying."

"Cut the bloody rope. Stop fooling around."

Louis Brown, trying to suppress a laugh, went back to Joan who hadn't noticed the approaching tram.

"Did you tell him?"

"Yes."

"So why is he telling you to cut the ropes?"

"He's acting the part. He's not only a good footballer and a brain, he's an actor too. This is terrific."

Brown had him scared. He had achieved his purpose. This was going to be great.

"Cut the ropes," his accomplice told him again. "I don't like your kind of fun. My God, the tram's coming early! You made a mistake, Louis. Why is Jonny screaming 'Cut the ropes'? *Do* something."

She pushed him. She didn't move him an inch.

"Shut up, Joan. You're spoiling the fun. I wonder if he'll shit himself too."

"He doesn't know! You bastard! He doesn't know!"

Joan ran to Jonny and called out to him, "The tram's on the other track! The other track!"

Jonny didn't hear her. All he heard were the vibrations in the rail next to him. His whole mind was filled by the sight and sound of the approaching giant. He was petrified and couldn't get his hands free. He was going to die if Brown didn't axe the rope. Then a blackness covered his eyes and there was no bright light.

Chapter Three

April 1952

When trams were taken out of service in the late 1950s, the only line to remain was the Glenelg line. Part of the enjoyment for children, on a day at the beach, was and is a ride on the Glenelg Tram. The double carriages, in brick red with a yellow stripe down the side, are fast, very fast.

On this morning, the first day of April, the tram left the Depot in Angus Street, trundled slowly into Victoria Square, and, without stopping at the terminus, moved south along King William Street, doors tightly closed and steps folded up. The highly-polished wood shone in the light of the square and the wires above crackled with the blue sparks of the overhead trolley-wheel. On the outward run it didn't stop to pick up passengers, but it didn't pick up speed until it passed South Terrace and entered the parklands. Here it took off like a charging bull, pausing only at the end of the field to cross another road, and went hurtling on to the seashore. It was now an express train, gates closed on the roads as it drew near, with bells and lights flashing on unguarded crossings. It crossed the railway on a long bridge, moving in a straight line towards the racecourse and the three students.

Jonny watched the flickering light grow in size until it blinded him, as he struggled with the rope holding his hands. He couldn't think, he didn't know what he was doing, and the rope just seemed to tighten. Why didn't they cut it? He couldn't see anyone or anything except the blinding light. He gave one last pull and blacked out. No one will ever know what went through his mind in those last seconds, when he was sure that the tram was going to cut him down.

The driver didn't see the other two. He saw something lying on the siding and focused his eyes on it for a few seconds. By the time that he realised it was a person, he was only a second away from the spot. He sounded his horn and, as he flashed past, tried to look back at what was there, but the angle was too acute to see anything. He pressed on, making a mental note to report the person, or body, on arrival at Glenelg in a few minutes. It might be a drunk sleeping it off. What a *silly* place to sleep.

Joan got to Jonny first. She saw that his eyes were closed, so she shook him. He didn't move. Louis put down the axe and started to untie the rope at the feet of the silent student.

"Silly bugger's fainted," he said. "Let's get him home. Did he shit his pants?"

"He's not breathing! Get him off the rails. We'll have to revive him."

She put her head to his chest. "His heart's beating. Quick, get him off the rails."

They removed him from the track. Brown slapped his face. "Stop fooling around. Don't play possum, Marco. Get up." Joan put her mouth to his and blew air into his lungs. She'd seen this done when someone almost drowned in the family pool. Her accomplice stood by, not knowing why Joan was kissing him. He didn't realise that her actions could save their necks. If she failed, the charge might be murder. Manslaughter was the best that they could expect.

"Stop playing around, Joan. We have to get out of here before that tram comes back or the police come."

As far as she was concerned, Brown wasn't there. She continued with the resuscitation until she heard Jonny cough, and he started to breathe unassisted. She lifted his head into her arms and started to cry.

The gravity of the situation suddenly dawned on Louis Brown. He came over and asked Joan, "Is he alright?"

"I don't know. He's breathing and his heart is beating, but he's still unconscious."

"Do you know where he lives?"

"No. We'd better get him to a hospital, Brown."

"Let's get him into the car."

"You didn't tell him! You let him think the tram was on his track. How *could* you? You're a *bastard*, Louis. Don't you ever invite yourself to my place again. You're not welcome there."

"I was good enough to do you tonight."

"You were *pathetic*. You should stick to rugby if you can last the distance. What about ping-pong? Wait until I tell my friends, my *real* friends, about what you did to that boy tonight."

"What *I* did? It was you who convinced him to do it, to 'shower' in your bathroom, with all that that includes."

Joan glared at him by the dawn's early light. "You wouldn't *dare* say a word?"

"No, but Jonny will. We'll have to stick together, just in case he decides to talk about it. We'll have to make sure that he doesn't talk."

A dreadful thought entered her brain.

"You're not thinking of killing him? I won't get mixed up in that. I saved his life, in case you don't remember."

"Joan, I'm a practical joker, *not* a killer. We just have to tell Jonny when he comes around that we're sorry and ask him to forgive and forget. You should be able to find a way to do it, before or after a shower."

He laughed a wicked laugh.

"Or in the shower? Use those big tits of yours to gag him. He won't talk when you remind him why he agreed to be tied down."

"I *hate* you, Brown, you big shit. I'll get you for this. You're dealing with a Meredith. Wait till I tell my brother. Steven will know what to do with you."

Jonny, still in her arms, stirred.

"I think he's waking up. How soon do we get to the hospital, Brown?"

When the big double tram arrived at the beach terminus, the driver told the conductor what he had seen at the Morphetville siding. Then he opened the doors, and as the few early morning passengers got in out of the cold he stepped down and telephoned the police.

"I'm the motorman from the Glenelg tram. I want to report that I saw a body lying beside the tracks beside the racecourse. He might be dead, or drunk, or injured."

"We'll send a car at once. Just where is the body?"

"About fifty yards from the crossing, on the siding. You can drive to the spot. It's near the entrance."

"Can someone show us?"

"We have to keep to our schedule, but we'll be back there in fifteen minutes. I'll stop, if you want, right at the spot."

"Good. We'll go right away and, if we find someone, we'll look after him. If we can, we'll wait for you. If the person needs medical help, we'll get it for him."

As he neared the crossing on the return journey, the motorman slowed down and peered through the window. The sky ahead was already light, making it was hard to see in the shadows ahead of him. Finally, as he slowed down for the stop, he saw the black police car. He got out and went over to the driver.

"Did you find him?"

"No. Is *this* the place?"

"He was on this siding here, give or take a few feet."

"You must have woken him if he was a drunk. Silly place to sleep."

"If it had been the other line, officer, I'd have killed him, cut him into pieces."

"There's another possibility. Today is the first of April. This *might* be someone's idea of a joke."

"Do you mean someone lay down to play a joke on us?"

"That, or they put a dummy on the line."

"They'd have done that on the main line, to make me think I'd run over a real body on the line."

"Who knows? They're probably watching us right now. I'll have a look around the area."

"And I'd better go. These passengers want to get to the city. Damned university students, I bet. That's the stupid tricks they get up to."

He got back into the tram and soon it was on its way to the city. The incident was soon forgotten. It was not connected to subsequent events.

Joan was sitting with Jonny propped up against her in the cramped back seat of Louis Brown's car. He moved his eyes and arms, looked about, but said nothing. Meanwhile Louis stopped the car at a public telephone and went inside. He quickly found Jonny's address in the book, returned, and started to drive off.

"Who did you ring?"

"No one. I wanted to see where the nearest hospital is."

He was lying to her.

"Take him to Royal Adelaide."

"He lives near here. I'm taking him home."

"Do you want to go home, Jonny?"

Jonny nodded. They drove up to a house, close to where South Road crossed the tramline. Before Joan knew what was happening, Louis had pulled Jonny out of the car and was helping him up the path to the house. Jonny pushed him away, steadied himself, and walked to the front door. He opened the screen door, fumbled for his key, and let himself in. "

Louis got into the car, started it, and turned to Joan.

"See, he's *fine*. Tomorrow he'll be joking about it. "

"We were wicked to do that to him, Louis. He might have died and then both of us would have ended up in jail. "

"Me, *not* you. You're a Meredith. You'd have got off and left me to take the rap. "

'That's a funny thing to say,' she thought, 'after I told him to tell Jonny he wasn't in any danger.'

"I'd have been finished socially, the girl who offered her body as a bet and got a fellow student killed. If this ever gets out, I'll have to go interstate. "

"It *won't* get out. It's you and me against Jonny. "

"Jonny won't tell. He's a man, not a rat like you. I should have seen that earlier this evening. "

"If you like him so much, why don't you marry him or have him move in with you?"

Louis said this as a joke, but to Joan it was no longer a joking matter. Giving Jonny the kiss of life had affected her, had touched that spoiled heart of hers.

"I could do a lot worse *if* he'd have me. "

"Have *you*? With your body and your money *I'd* have you. *Any* man would have you. "

"Well, I wouldn't have any man or any rat like you. There's a taxi. Put me off. Don't you ever talk to me again, Bully Brown. "

Joan got in the taxi and arrived home just as the day was dawning. Her bed, she thought, still smelled of Louis, so making a decision to have it changed that day, she put on a night-gown and got into the spare bed. Tired as she was, she found that sleep didn't come quickly as it usually did. She had Jonny on her mind, and the events of the previous half hour running around in her brain.

'What did we do to you, Jonny? What kind of a person am I? Are you alright? Why didn't you say anything? Will you come and take that shower with me, or do you think that I was in that horrid joke with that bully?'

This was the first time that a male had kept Joan Meredith awake, *without* being in bed with her. She was just eighteen, but used to late nights, alcoholic drink, and men. She started having sex long before the age of consent. Nothing bothered Joan Meredith. She was a girl at the threshold of life, pretty, intelligent, rich, obscenely rich, without a care in the world.

Love, Joan had made with many men, but she had never been in love with any man. She felt some, many in fact, attractive, even satisfying in bed, but felt little for any of them. She didn't feel any emotion, any love, even for her parents or her older brother, Steven. She knew how to act the part, and kiss and hug her parents whenever she thought she should, which was at every meeting. They looked like an ideal loving family, but their emotions, like beauty, were skin deep.

This morning, the first day of April, was probably the first time that something got to that young heart of hers. It was Jonny Marco. As she thought of him, she succeeded in blotting out the memory of Louis Brown and all the other men she had ever known. She gradually forgot the horror of the tram racing out of the darkness and Jonny screaming. She remembered the boy with the muscular frame who danced with her and sat with her in the car, his head in her arms. She remembered giving him the kiss of life. Was it maternal instinct, or the *need* to be loved and needed by a man? Who can tell? Joan Meredith felt something for Jonny Marco that she had never felt before. Thinking of him, she drifted into sleep. Louis Brown also slept soundly. As for Jonny Marco, he lay in bed as still as a statue, eyes open staring at the ceiling, listening to the sounds of the early morning, reliving the nightmare of the life-threatening tram.

At noon, feeling very restless, Joan got up and found Jonny's phone number in the book, then she went back to her bed and telephoned that number.

"Can I speak to Jonny, please?"

"Who's calling?"

"Joan Meredith." She omitted to add, daughter of Charles Meredith of Meredith foods, or granddaughter of Sir William Meredith, founder of Meredith Mills and the brewery, or that her ancestors were founders of the State of South Australia, the only state not settled as a convict colony. This was no time for ostentation.

"Jonny's resting. Can he call you back, Joan?"

Joan gave her phone number to Mrs Marco and wondered if the lady knew who she was. Then she lay back on her bed and thought about Jonny. They had a date tonight, a nebulous kind of date, but nevertheless a date. She had promised him to have him over for a "shower" *if* he took part in that macabre dare, and they both knew what that meant. She was prepared, eager to keep her promise, and looking forward to it. She showered, dressed, and went up into the big house. Her mother was busy writing letters.

"Good morning, Joan. Not going to the university today?"

"No, mother. Lectures don't start until next week."

"So, what did you do yesterday?"

"Can we talk later? I'd like to have breakfast."

The less said about last night, the better.

"Breakfast? I've arranged to have lunch sent up in another half an hour. If you can't wait, ring for a snack."

"I wouldn't mind a cup of coffee and a bit of toast."

Mrs Meredith pressed a button, and a minute later a servant appeared in the doorway.

"You called, Mrs Meredith?"

"Yes, Gwen. Please bring us a pot of coffee and some buttered toast, and remind cook that we'll be eating at one."

"Yes, Mrs Meredith."

"Now, Joan, tell me what you did last night. When we came home, there was quite a party going on."

"Did we disturb you?"

"No, we couldn't hear you upstairs. I thought you said that you were going to a university welcome."

"It was rather dull. All the boys were either too shy or taken. I invited some of the crowd back here afterwards and we had our own party. It didn't break up until five."

"Isn't that rather late for a weeknight?"

"We're still on holiday, Mother!"

"Who was there? Anyone that I know?"

"Only Maureen Fitz-Williams, who was at school with me. The others were all science students."

"So you're making lots of new friends. That's nice."

The coffee and toast arrived, Mrs Meredith came and sat next to her daughter. She noticed a serious look on Joan's face. Was she growing up or just tired? Time would tell. Mother didn't know that her daughter had had almost every sexual experience possible, except rape and childbirth.

The front door bell rang, and Mr Meredith was let in. He had a front door key, but he always rang the bell. He greeted his wife and daughter with hugs and a kisses, joining them in the sitting room. Ten minutes later, Steven Meredith arrived. He was tall and handsome, like his father, and they were both taller than the two ladies. Father and son were very much alike, as were mother and daughter. Mother and progeny all had jet-black hair, like Jonny Marco.

When they had made their greetings, Mrs Meredith pressed the bell again, and, when Gwen reappeared, she told her that they were ready for lunch. They all moved into the dining-room and sat down at a table that was far too big for the four of them, so they bunched together at one end and ate their four-course meal in silence. There was no beer on the Meredith table, but fine South Australian wines from the family vineyard in the hills to the east of the city.

South Australia, the last of the states to be settled, is proud of the fact that it alone was not a convict settlement and was established by free men. The Merediths claim to have descended from one of the men who landed in 1836 with Governor Hindmarsh on the *Buffalo*. Wisely disdaining the lure of the 1851 gold rush, Norman Meredith bought copper shares and made a fortune growing wheat to meet the needs of the gold rush, investing in land at Gawler and Port Adelaide. Later the family bought land in the south-east near the border, which, although it had a modest rainfall, was known as the hundred-mile desert. When, in the 1930s, trace elements needed for cultivation were found to be lacking, this became valuable grazing land.

It was Sir William who bought the mill and the brewery that bears the Meredith name, and added the winery when he married Eva Strauss, the grand-daughter of a German immigrant who made fine wines. He kept the Strauss label for the bulk standard wines and fortified plonk, but added the Meredith name for the special bins of fine "sherry" wines and white table wines that English wine snobs belittle.

During the second world war Sir William's son, Charles, produced millions of cans of corned beef and mutton for the Allied forces in the Pacific. It wasn't very tasty, but it was meat and filled many an empty stomach in a foxhole, and could be traded for fresh food where this was available. One or two Meredith cans even stopped sniper's bullets in the jungles of New Guinea. In 1945 Meredith bully beef, dripping, and canned processed peas, were among the food that graced British tables, together with canned Christmas pudding, which was eminently edible.

Back in Adelaide, VJ Day was celebrated by the biggest barbecue ever held at the Meredith estate. Although meat was still rationed, every worker that day took home some special cuts in addition to the normal pilfering, and no one asked where the rump steaks and lamb chops came from. Meredith's VJ Day barbecue, for those who managed to get an invitation, was the talk of the town — more important than the scientists' new atom bomb that had brought the war to an end so suddenly.

Joan Meredith remembered the day well. Big brother Steven came home on special leave from Darwin. His colonel was a foreman in Meredith Mills, and Sergeant Steven Meredith not only got a four-day leave pass but a place on a plane to Adelaide and a flight back, which thousands of worthier soldiers wanted, but didn't get. Steven was supposed to tell his father who got it for him, but it slipped his mind in all the celebrations and making up for lost time with the Adelaide women. Six months later, in April 1946, he was home again, and he joined the first intake of returned soldiers at a university recovering from its war effort.

Steven Meredith didn't live at home. He was established in an eighty-year-old house in North Adelaide. It had once been the home of a leading legislator, a relative of his grandmother. It had historic value. He lived alone most of the time, but slept alone on rare occasions. It wouldn't do to install a mistress in the house, but if a young lady sneaked out in the early hours of the morning or spent a weekend at the old house and nobody knew, *what* did it matter? One weekend in 1950, the young lady had been his sister. They did it out of curiosity, rather than filial affection, but Steven wasn't the first man to have sister Joan in his bed — not by a long way.

On this warm autumn day Steven joined his family for lunch, after an absence of a fortnight, the longest time since he had moved out of the house. He'd just come back from Surfer's Paradise, where he'd spent his days water skiing, and his nights "shaggin' sheilas" in his hotel suite, well away from his home town, its social photographers and their wagging tongues. He'd spent this April morning back at work.

"What's new, Steven?" his father asked, "How are the bugs?" (Steven had a Master of Science and was doing his doctorate in Bacteriology.)

"Fine father. How's the beer and bully beef?"

"Couldn't be better. The cold weather hasn't arrived and everybody's thirsty. The English are still buying every can of beef and meatloaf we can make, when we can get the tinplate. We're considering sending frozen sides of beef and lamb, but there aren't any suitable freezer ships. Would you believe it, the war's been over six years and Europe still can't feed itself. I suppose they never will.

"The grapes are good this year. Your mother and I will be staying at the winery next week. It's the height of the crushing season. The warm weather's making the grapes all ripen at one time. We'll be working round the clock."

'That's a laugh,' his daughter thought. 'What's this "we" business? I can't see a Meredith getting his hands dirty picking grapes. Counting money, perhaps, but not picking grapes.'

She picked herself a bunch of lady-fingers from the fruit bowl and holding above her mouth, sucked grape after grape down into her mouth, like Bacchus in *Fantasia*.

"You coming with us, Joan?" asked Mrs Meredith.

"No, Mother, the term starts next week and I'm rather busy. There are a lot of parties that I must go to, and I still have to buy my books."

'And if no one's here, I can swim naked in the pool with whoever strikes my fancy,' she told herself.

"You can buy all your books at the WEA just down from the Administration block. That won't take more than half an hour," said Steven.

"I want to attend meetings, and there's the Ball on Saturday. Besides we're all going to Hardy's winery in a couple of weeks with the Science Association to see how the wine is made."

"So why are you going? You've seen wine made every year, ever since you could stagger."

"I'm going for the company. To be with my fellow students, Steven."

"*You* go on a bus? That'll be the day?"

"I used to go to school by bus, if you haven't forgotten, until last year. By the way, I noticed your car outside the hospital last night. What happened?"

"Nothing, I was seeing a sick friend."

"At *five* in the morning! By the nurses entrance! What did she have, early morning sickness?"

"Joan!" Her mother was indignant. "Keep a civil tongue in your head. Just because you're about to start university, you don't have to talk like a lout."

"Mother's been reading *Truth* again, Steven. Do we have it delivered in a brown paper wrapper? I wouldn't like it known that we get *that* paper in this house."

"Steven, I told you that I don't like you going out with nurses," Mrs Meredith continued; "I don't want a nurse as a daughter-in-law. You don't know what they might come in contact with in the hospital."

"Mother, some nurses come from very good families. It's a respectable profession and an important one. Look how nice they were to you when you had your gall bladder removed."

'That was a good fortnight,' he said to himself. 'All the nurses came to see the *Queen Mother* in her private room, hoping a little of her money would rub off on them, and the *heir apparent* was able to take a few willing ones to his house on the hill where none of them would ever mistress be.'

"Name *one* nurse from a good family, Steven."

"If you mean a rich old South Australian family, I can't — but then I don't know all the nurses in Adelaide."

"Liar!" said Joan.

"Shut up, Joan, when your betters are talking," he shouted at his sister, before resuming his conversation with his mother.

"I can't ask every girl the colour of her blood and her father's money. As for eligible Adelaide ladies, forget it. If we Merediths restrict ourselves to marrying within our little circle, we'll be inbred like the Russian Royal family and have bleeders for descendants. If I decide to get married, which is a big IF, I'll marry whom I like, when I like, and irrespective of race, colour or creed."

"What about Lil, the abo from the cookhouse at the station? The station-hands swear by her."

"Joan, keep out of this! Being a Meredith heir is an impediment to a man's love life. Take a girl out twice and some little reporter writes snide comments in the *Sunday Mail*. Take out any simple girl, and I don't know if she likes me for myself or the Meredith money."

"Or your modesty!" Joan was enjoying this lunchtime *tête-à-tête*. "Perhaps we could put you on the Bob Dyer *Pick-a-Box* show or send you to America where everyone's rich and you'll be like everyone else."

"Steven," his father asked, ignoring Joan, "I realise that finding a suitable wife may be of concern to the ladies, but what I would like to know is: when do you intend to join me in the running of the businesses that we have? I can't run the mill, the brewery, *and* all the other interests, without help. What about it, Steven?"

"I don't know, Father. Do you *really* need me?"

"Yes. When do you expect to finish your doctorate?"

"My PhD? Next year. Then I intend to go overseas."

"Good idea. You should see the world, and while you're about it go and see a few breweries and factories. Go to the States — that should broaden your education. Then come back and help me run the businesses."

"No, Dad. I want to go to America and do academic work, research, and come back and find a place at a university."

"Here in Adelaide?"

"Wherever I can get it — Adelaide, Sydney, Melbourne, even Perth, or Canberra. Perhaps with the CSIRO."

His father thought for a few minutes, then spoke. "In Bacteriology? Why not Food Science?"

"There's no such faculty or department."

"Well, there ought to be."

"In the agricultural colleges there might be, but not at any university."

"Steven, I have an idea. Let me think about it for a while and talk it over with some people that I know. I think it's about time that we had our name on a university building, like the Barr Smiths and the Bonythons."

"Buildings are expensive these days, father. The university does need a theatre, by the way. Probably more than it needs another library."

"Next year, when you get your doctorate, do you want to continue with bacteria? Have you ever considered doing academic work in Food Science?"

"I said there's no course here, Father, and no place to work in that field in any Australian university."

"Not *now*, but there *might* be. We'll discuss this later in the year. I have some research of my own that I want to do. Now that the universities are getting more money, there'll be some changes made — you'll see."

"Who's giving the money?" Joan asked, "Meredith foods? Will we have to sell the Mercedes and rent my flat?"

"No, sister dear. Meredith foods could fill all the vacant lots at the uni with buildings and still declare a dividend. Why don't you sell the businesses and invest the proceeds, Dad? We could go on living as we always have, happily ever after."

Steven didn't see the point of making more money. When he reached the age of twenty-one, his father had given him shares in Meredith companies and he received half a million in dividends every year. He paid more in taxes than he banked. He could shower his girlfriends with diamonds and minks if he wanted to, without touching the capital. The truth was that he liked spending money for himself, but hated spending it on others. But a girl could live for a month on the money he gave her for a night in his bed. He wasn't being generous, he wanted to keep such relationships on a strictly business only level, with many happy returns.

"I'm doing it for you, Steven, you and your children, and your children's children. You should be proud of what I've done, and your grandfather, and his father too. It was tough going at the start when the first Meredith landed at Holdfast Bay."

"We call it Glenelg, Dad, and we all know that the first settlers went broke and had to be bailed out in the bad old days," said Joan. "Why isn't there a Meredith Street or suburb named after our illustrious ancestor, Norman, who brought us out of the land of bondage, free men, and not slaves like the rotten Tasmanians and New South Welshmen?"

"Well, I for one am glad that the Merediths are at last giving, if that's what you have in mind, Dad. When I see what some of my colleagues have to live on, I can't look them in the face. I share a lab with a guy who gets a three-hundred-pound-a-year grant and thinks he's lucky to get that."

"Son, Meredith foods give employment to over a thousand people, thousands more indirectly, and we pay millions in taxes. That doesn't mean that we don't donate to worthy causes. I'll ring Sir Mellis today and go and see him. I don't want to say any more now until we settle something."

After lunch Joan returned to her flat, to her thoughts about Jonny and the horror of the early morning. She wanted to make amends for her part in it, but how could she? She decided that the first thing she would do was to break her date for Saturday's Commencement Ball and ask Jonny to be her partner instead, even if it meant using her car. Joan had a weird idea that the best thing she could do for a man was to go out with him or into bed with him. It wasn't such a weird idea, the weird part was that she thought that she was doing him a favour. She regarded herself as a commodity; in the same way that her father traded shares and her brother dealt in women, she dehumanised herself without knowing it.

She didn't break her date. Maybe Jonny wouldn't want to be her partner. Maybe he already had a partner for the ball. She had seen him playing a lot of attention to that country girl.

Joan had to know if Jonny was feeling better and to ask him not to tell anyone about the dawn stupidity.

She telephoned to his house. Mrs Marco again answered.

"Jonny isn't taking any calls."

Joan could plainly hear the worry in her voice.

"Tell him that Joan Meredith wants to talk to him. Tell him that it's important."

She was ordering the woman to get her son. It was the Meredith way of talking. Mrs Marco went and quickly returned to the telephone.

"I told him, but he didn't say anything. He just looked at me and sat there. He's not himself today."

"*Please* ask him to ring me. Do you want my number?"

"It's still by his bedside."

"Is Jonny alright, Mrs Marco?"

"I don't think so. I've never seen him this way. He's usually so talkative, but he hasn't said a word at all today. He got up and got dressed, ate the breakfast that I made for him and went back to his room without saying a word."

Remembering what she and Brown had done to him, Joan felt a tremor of fear. Jonny Marco was still feeling the shock of the cruel trick played on him.

"I want to come over. Do you think he'd mind?"

"How can I tell? He doesn't say anything. I'd like you to come over. You sound very sweet. He might speak to you and snap out of it. I'm alone with him — my husband's at work and I'm so worried."

"I'll be right over."

"Are you a friend of Jonny's?"

"A recent friend. I'm starting uni next week, and also doing Science. I've seen Jonny play football."

"Yes, Jonny's a good footballer. We go and watch him whenever he plays, but I don't understand anything about the game. He's going to play for the university."

"I know."

"He's a real dinky-die Aussie, not like his parents. What could have happened to make him so strange today?"

Joan felt rotten. She couldn't tell the woman what she knew. She couldn't tell anyone. Later she wished that she had, when it would be too late for Jonny or the others, and too late for herself.

"I'll come over right away."

Twenty minutes later Mrs Marco heard a noise and looked out of the front window, as Joan Meredith pulled up in the red sports car and gave the engine one last rev. before she turned it off. She always did this. It attracted attention. Pretty as a picture, she opened the gate in the Cyclone fence and walked down the stone path to the modest brick house, with its terracotta tiles and steel-framed windows. It was like most of the houses along Anzac Parade, all the way down to the bay, solid working-class, each with a well-kept garden. There were rose bushes around the lawn, two large poplars near the entrance, yellow, waiting for the first winter winds to rob them of their leaves. It was everything that the Marco family could wish for, but to the young lady it was all a little pokey and so unlike her friends' houses in Unley Park or Glen Osmond.

Mrs Marco looked at the car, looked at the young woman coming down the gravel path and thought that Gina Lollobrigida was coming to see her son. If this thing of beauty couldn't snap him out of his mood, then nothing could. Crossing herself, she praised God that help had arrived.

When she opened the door to let Joan enter, she saw that she wasn't quite as tall as the film star and not quite as beautiful, but as pretty a girl as she'd seen in real life. Her imperious manner on the phone belied her appearance.

"You must be Joan Meredith. I'll call Jonny."

She led Jonny out and he came, slowly and silently. At first, when he saw who was at the door, he frowned and stood there without any expression on his face. Joan felt very uneasy, but as she watched him that warm feeling towards him returned. Could it be love? If it was, it was a new experience for Miss Meredith.

Mrs Marco took her son into the living room at the front of the house and sat him down in a lounge chair. Joan followed silently. Closing the door behind her, Mrs Marco went and busied herself in the laundry, not wishing for an instant to pry on Jonny and his visitor.

When Joan was sure that his mother had gone, she went and sat close to Jonny and spoke to him, her voice trembling with uncertainty. Gone was her superior manner.

"Hello, Jonny. I'm here to apologise for what happened this morning. I pleaded with Brown to tell you that you weren't in any danger. I didn't know what he was doing or why he was doing it. I still don't know. *What* has he got against you, Jonny? Everybody likes you, Jonny Marco. I've never met you before, but I've heard about you. You're a popular guy, Jonny. I'm sorry for what I did and I want to make it up to you. Alright by you, Jonny?"

The young man sat like a dummy. Only his breathing and the occasional winking of his eyelids indicated that he was alive. No words came to his mouth. Joan had no way of knowing if he was hearing her words, but she continued, hoping that he was.

"*Please* forgive me. I'll do *anything* if you'll only forgive me. I'll keep my part of the bargain — just say that you forgive me."

There was no reply, not a movement as he sat looking through her at the wall.

"Jonny, I like you. Forget the bargain — it was a stupid bargain to make. Come with me to the ball on Saturday night. Let's be friends, real friends. We're going to be students together, we should be friends. This has nothing to do with what we did to you this morning. Jonny, I really like you — you're a man, not like Brown, that overgrown schoolboy."

That same frown appeared momentarily and was gone. Had she imagined it? She continued her pleading, "Please tell me that you'll come to the ball, Saturday night. Please tell me that you'll even go to the pictures, if you don't want to go to the ball. I don't have to go to the ball. What about tonight? Say something, Jonny."

She realised that she was raising her voice, so she lowered it again. S he was getting nowhere with Jonny and she was beginning to get upset.

"Jonny, I'm really a nice person when you get to know me. Jonny, I need you. I need you to forgive me. I need to know that you're alright. Tell me at least that you don't hate me. I couldn't bear the thought of you hating me."

Joan started to cry. Jonny too wanted to cry, to say something, to give her a sign, any sign — but he couldn't. His vocal cords wouldn't move. He couldn't move them. He felt as if he were outside his body, a spirit looking in on himself, a spectator unable to control his faculties. It was as if he really was dead, and was watching himself from heaven. Then he heard a noise and he was filled with fear.

Joan saw him react, the look of fear in his eyes. It was a look that would haunt her for the rest of her life. Then she heard what caused it as the sound of a passing tram disturbed the quiet of the suburban street. Jonny stood up his face filled with horror, his brow wrinkled, eyes open and rapidly moving, his nostrils wide and his mouth open as if silently screaming. He raced out of the room. Joan called out to his mother, and they both went to his room to find him lying on the bed with his head under the pillows. His knuckles were white as they pressed the pillow to his ears. Joan knew what had frightened him, and that she had to tell his mother to remove him from the sound of the trams, but how could she explain it without telling the whole story? She was letting him down and she knew it, but she didn't tell his mother what was the matter with her son.

'My God,' she thought, 'what *have* we done to him?'

She went over to Jonny, took away the pillow, and held him as she'd held him in Brown's car. A warm tear fell on his face and startled him. She kissed him on his cheek. He wanted with all his might to respond, but he couldn't. Joan wiped her eyes and left him sitting on the bed.

"Jonny, please ring me tonight or tomorrow."

She took hold of Mrs Marco's arm, and they both wiped their tears as they went back to the kitchen. There was a bowl of green peas on the table, and she started to shell them. Joan helped her.

"Jonny's not well, Mrs Marco. You have to call a doctor, or take him to see one."

"*Why* doesn't he talk?"

"I don't know, Mrs Marco. He needs help and he needs it badly. Something's bothering him. Have you any relatives out of the city where he can stay?"

She knew that the sound of the Glenelg tram, so near to the house, was terrifying him. She would have gladly let him stay in her flat, but how does one offer such a thing? She couldn't just say to his mother, "Jonny will be staying in my flat and sleeping with me. I'm going to see if sex therapy will restore to him the use of his tongue. That and some swimming. No, he won't need his swimming costume."

For a moment she thought of asking Mrs Marco to bring him out to the car, but didn't. Later she realised that not telling the woman about the trams had been a terrible mistake, but although she was a clever young woman, she neither had the sense nor the guts to tell her. She knew that Jonny was sick, but not how sick. What does an eighteen-year-old spoiled girl know about the human mind? What do doctors, even great doctors, know about the human mind, especially the traumatised mind? Maybe if Joan had told the family or the doctor the cause of Jonny's trauma and maybe if he'd seen a psychiatrist or been hospitalised, they might have got to the bottom of his illness and been able to help him, but they called in the local GP. What happened after that was inevitable.

As Joan drove home, she recalled the words from the play that she had had to study at school, the words of Ophelia:

> "*O, what a noble mind is here o'erthrown!*
> *O, woe is me, to have seen what I have seen, see what I see.*"

Chapter Four

April 1952

Joan didn't call Jonny, but she did jump with anticipation whenever the phone rang, and it rang frequently. He didn't call, and every person that did received a cool answer. Some noticed it, some didn't. The hours leading up to Saturday night were tense as she couldn't get Jonny out of her mind. She wanted to ring up again and find out if Jonny was better, but she knew in her heart that he wouldn't be, so she didn't. And she didn't tell the family what had happened to their son.

'Perhaps,' she thought, 'he has a girlfriend of his own and will turn up at the ball with her.'

When her original partner rang to ask when to pick her up, she didn't put him off. She wanted to go with Jonny, but failing that she wanted to go to the ball.

Her partner was an old friend, a third-year Law student, an ardent admirer of hers, one of many who would have gladly taken her for his wife, irrespective of her family money and her soiled reputation. He called for her in his father's big black Humber, which looked like a funeral director's car. Joan insisted on driving to the ball in her Mercedes. He didn't like it, but he knew from experience not to argue with Joan. On the other hand it would give him an excuse to return to her flat, which would be much more comfortable than the back of the Humber, spacious as it was.

At the Refectory, Jonny was forgotten. Joan began to enjoy herself. There were two big bands, one playing dance tunes and a jazz band that played Dixie and really got the couples going. Several couples could jitterbug, and the floor was cleared for them as other dancers watched and clapped. Joan was with the jitterbuggers. Only the clarinet could be heard above the noise.

Most of the men wore dinner jackets, but there was a sprinkling of dark suits. The ladies, on the other hand, were very colourful in their fashionable evening gowns.

It was a warm night and the Refectory doors were open, with tables for the dancers filling the pathways around the sunken lawn under the colonnades. No alcoholic drinks were allowed; those who wanted something stronger than lemonade brought it in kitbags and hid it under the tables, or had their drinks in or near their cars, in contravention of the university and state bylaws. Consuming liquor in the vicinity of a dance hall was an offence in South Australia. It was a very respectable, well-run ball, a credit to the student organisers.

Jonny too packed a kitbag and put on his best suit. His mother heard the door close and saw him leave the house from the front window. When she saw him in his best suit, it made her feel better. He was going to see a girl. She wondered if it was that pretty Meredith girl who had come to see him and had left her phone number.

It had been a terrible four days for Mrs Marco. She'd called the doctor who had come over late in the day, a few hours after Joan's visit. Jonny didn't say anything to the doctor, who tried to engage him in conversation, listened to his chest, and looked into his eyes. Finally, he gave Mrs Marco a prescription for a barbiturate.

"Get him to take this and go to bed at nine, and ring me in a few days. If he's not better, I might have to send him to a specialist."

"What do you think is wrong, Doctor?"

"Beats me. I've never had a case like this. Anything unusual happen to him?"

"Not that I know of, Doctor. He's supposed to start university next week. He went to a welcome last night, looking forward to it, perfectly normal, said goodbye to me, kissed me before he went. He woke up this morning and hasn't said a word all day. Sometimes he goes and buries his head under the pillow. I *can't* understand it."

"I'm not a specialist of mental disorders, but your son may be on the verge of a breakdown. The fear of the unknown, the new way of learning, the change from school may be weighing on his mind. He should rest. As soon as he gets into the new routine he'll forget his fears. If he doesn't, you'd better take him to a specialist."

"Thank you, Doctor. How much do I have to pay?"

"Don't pay me now. It's half a guinea per visit and we send out the account at the end of the month. Send a cheque in the mail or bring it to the surgery, whichever is convenient. Call me if there's any change for the better or any other change."

Jonny took the tablet before going to bed, and he didn't hear the Glenelg Trams again until he woke up in the morning. He stayed in the house three more days and said nothing to his family or the many friends that came to visit. What thoughts passed through his mind nobody knows. He didn't communicate with a living soul.

When he left the house, Mrs Marco rang the doctor. His wife answered the telephone.

"The doctor is just going out. Is it very urgent?"

"I don't want to see him. I just want to tell him about my son. He's been sick these last four days."

Dr Vaughan came to the telephone. "What is it, Mrs Marco?"

"My son, Jonny. He got dressed and went out tonight."

"That sounds promising. Where did he say he was going?"

"He didn't say. He just put on his best suit and went."

"Probably got a date with a girlfriend. Just what he needs. Call me on Monday and tell me how he's getting on. I wouldn't worry any more about him, he seems to have snapped out of it."

Mrs Marco put down the phone, feeling relieved. Dr Vaughan went to the theatre with a troubled mind. This Jonny Marco patient was beyond him. He felt that he should have sent him to a specialist.

Jonny walked away from the house, away from the tramlines to the highway that led from the city to the beach. He stood watching the traffic for a few minutes, thinking. He turned towards the sea, took a few steps and stopped. Changing the kitbag to his other hand, he set off in the direction of the city. He walked quickly. In a hour he had crossed the bridge at Keswick, the parklands that surrounded the city, and was walking purposefully down West Terrace, past the cemetery. He slowed down near the New Adelaide High School, hesitating as he had to cross the tramlines, then crossed quickly when he saw that no trams were in sight. He strode up Hindley Street where there were no tramlines. The occasional trolley-bus didn't bother him.

At Morphett Street he stopped once more before turning north to walk across the rail bridge. In the middle he looked down at the station. The Express was leaving for Melbourne and its two huge Mountain Class engines startled him. He ran across the bridge and didn't stop until he reached the quiet of the gardens, down by the Torrens. Finding a bench by the water's edge, he peered at the black water before him. The nearest light was twenty yards away and the nearest person at least a hundred. He was all alone.

Jonny rested for about ten minutes, picked up the kitbag and walked along the water's edge past the "Popeye" boat landing stage, past the bandstand, walking under the city bridge, past a couple of drunks who were just starting out on their bottles of cheap fortified Strauss wine, past the boats for hire, and approached the University Footbridge in the bend of the river. It was ten o'clock when he put his kitbag at the southern entrance of the bridge. No one noticed him arrive and none of the couples walking about the lawns or boozing in the parked cars paid any attention to him, as he walked up to the Union entrance of the Refectory.

In those days, before the addition of the bookshop, the Refectory portal was uncluttered. Jonny stood in this entrance and looked at the happy crowd within, silently taking in the scene. He might have been looking for Joan, he might have been looking for Louis Brown, maybe for no one. Joan was at the other end of the room, having her picture taken by the *Advertiser* photographer for the Monday papers. The *Mail* had gone to press, and she'd already been photographed for tonight's edition at a pre-Ball dinner party.

Richard, who was dancing near the door, noticed Jonny and spoke to Gerald who happened to be nearby.

"Look at Jonny Marco. He looks like John Wayne at the saloon door looking for a fight."

"When did he arrive? Who's he with?"

"I don't know. I didn't notice him before. I haven't seen him since that party at Merediths."

"He looks as if he's in a daze, like he's had too much to drink. Fancy Jonny Marco getting drunk."

They went on dancing and forgot Jonny for the moment. They moved down nearer the band, past Louis Brown, past Joan Meredith who recognised them from the party and greeted them. When she saw them, she remembered her party and Jonny. She didn't see him come to the ball. If she had, she would have spoken to him and what happened next might not have happened. Then someone shouted from the other end of the large room, "Someone's pushing Brown's car into the river."

Several people cheered and others rushed out to see what was happening. Louis Brown didn't hear his name mentioned. Gerald told Richard, who hadn't heard the shout, and they both raced out leaving their partners. This was too good to miss. They arrived at the gate just in time to see a short stocky figure manhandle the back wheels of the small car over the curb, move over to the steering side and then disappear together with the car down the sloping path. No one went near him, but they all followed and stood by the lamp post at the top of the slope. The car went down quickly and Jonny let it go halfway, watching as it toppled over the bank, rolled onto the driver's side and quickly filling with water, disappeared under the muddy waters. A cheer arose from the multitude who just stood and watched. Some of them went down to the waters edge and some started back to the ball.

A few of them tried to speak to Jonny, but he just brushed by them.

"Brown'll kill you, Jonny," a voice called out.

Gerald took his hand. "Why the hell did you do that, Jonny? Are you crazy?" His hand was cold as death. There was no smell of booze on his breath.

Jonny pulled himself away and walked back up the path, up to the footbridge, picked up his kitbag and walked slowly, a solitary figure, to the middle of the bridge. No one went with him, not knowing what he was about to do. The watchers saw him stoop down and open the kit bag, but didn't see what he was doing. The next thing that they knew was that Jonny, half stooping, climbed over the railing and, still in the stooping position, fell into the black water below. As he hit the water a mixture of screams and cheers went up from some of the watchers. Others looked on silently, not knowing what was happening. Then there was silence as the waters closed over Jonny, and large circular ripples raced to the shore, reflecting the light of the lamp high up where the people were watching. As the wave hit the bank it could be heard clearly moving along the shore away from the bridge, a series of dull thuds breaking the silence. The watchers crowded down by the water's edge.

"What the hell is he doing?"

"Why doesn't he come up?"

"He's fooling around. Where's he coming up?"

"He's drowning! I'm going in!" somebody shouted.

"Me too."

Gerald and Richard were among the first to strip to the waist, kick off their shoes, and join the half a dozen young men swimming out to the middle, diving down into the dark shallow water. Richard was the first to touch Jonny, but couldn't pull him up. He surfaced and called to the others.

"He's down here. Help me pull him to the surface."

Three of them pulled as hard as they could, each on an arm or a leg, but they couldn't get Jonny up. They consulted at the surface.

"He's caught up in some rope that's holding him down. Anyone got a pocket knife?"

Someone raced down to the bank with a knife, giving it to Gerald. He told people on the bank to call for an ambulance and then swam back to cut the rope holding Jonny under the water. They pulled the lifeless form out of the river and tried to get the water out of his lungs. A medical student took charge and was trying artificial respiration when the ambulance came from the nearby hospital. But Jonny had been under the water for over five minutes. The rope he had tied to the weights to hold himself down had prevented the swimmers from saving him. It was clear to the would-be rescuers, the medical student and the ambulance men, vainly trying to fill his lungs with oxygen, that Jonny was beyond their help. It remained for the doctors at Royal Adelaide Hospital to declare him dead.

Evelyn wasn't too upset about missing the ball. She kept an eye out for Jonny during the remainder of the week, but he didn't come to any of the meetings or to eat in the Refectory. She saw Joan coming and going, but the beer heiress didn't notice her. On the other hand Gerald and Richard invited her to join them when they came across her sitting alone in the Refectory. No one asked her to the ball and she didn't ask anyone how to get in touch with Jonny. It is interesting to speculate whether her voice calling him on the telephone could have restored his sanity.

She thought of him that evening. Most of the St Ann's students went to the ball, and the others congregated in groups and chatted. Evelyn was just about to go to bed when the first of the girls returned from the ball, terminated prematurely by Jonny's death. The girl was crying. She told the girls, who poured out of their rooms, a short version of what had happen down by the Torrens. She didn't tell them the jumper's name. Evelyn found that out the next day.

One of the last persons to see Jonny Marco being carried into the ambulance was Joan Meredith who, when she heard that Jonny had jumped off the bridge, raced out and pushed her way to the front of the crowd just as they were placing him on the stretcher. She listened to the voices in the crowd as he was lifted into the gaping doors which quickly closed behind him. The ambulance sped off, siren screaming. She heard several people say that Jonny Marco was dead. Joan ran to her car and drove off, leaving her partner standing and staring. He got a lift home. Louis Brown and his lady friend had to go home by taxi. Louis's car went to a scrap yard when it was pulled out of the Torrens the following day.

A car pulled up and a cameraman got out together with a reporter. They quickly got to work taking pictures and asking questions. They photographed the muddy boys and the girls in party dresses. The next copy of *Truth* would be a beauty. They were sure that this was just another student prank that had gone wrong. Then four or five big students grabbed them and hustled them towards the gate. They both were sure that they too would find themselves in the river.

"You're on university property, without permission. Hand over the film."

They searched the photographer, exposed all the film that they found on him, then dropped his camera and the two reporters out in the street. They drove away as fast as their wheels would carry them.

Blankets were brought for the wet boys and they walked up to the nearly empty Refectory. The bands were packing up their instruments. A bottle of Chateau Tanunda Brandy was brought from one of the cars and passed around. The police arrived and started asking questions. The first thing that they wanted to know was who threw the boy into the river. It took them some time to understand that this was not the case, and they settled down to hear the witnesses' stories.

"Where's the boy's partner? Maybe she can help us."

Nobody came forward. Gerald spoke up, "I don't think he came with a partner. I saw him at the doorway for the first time a few minutes before it happened. I told Richard here that he looked rather funny. I'm sure he'd just arrived when we saw him. He was alone."

"You two are wet. When did you go into the water?"

"When Jonny jumped off the bridge and we saw that he wasn't coming up. We expected him to come up."

"Yes, we expected him to come up."

"Did you know that he was going to jump?"

"No, I don't think anyone did."

"You say that you had to cut a piece of rope that was holding him under the water in the mud."

"Yes, when we got him out, we found that it was tied around his waist."

"What was it tied to?"

"I don't know. Something heavy. It's still down there at the bottom, under the middle of the bridge."

"We'll look for it in the morning. Are you two friends of the dead boy?"

"We only met Jonny the other night. Everybody knew him, he was great at sports."

"A good swimmer?"

"Probably. That's why we felt sure he would come up and swim out. Jonny could take care of himself."

Gerald said this with conviction, although he knew Jonny was dead. What he had done was completely out of character.

"You say that he took something out of his kitbag before jumping. What was it?"

"We couldn't see. Whatever it was it's probably in the mud at the bottom of the river."

"Well chaps, it looks like a case of suicide. Did he leave a note or tell any of you that he was going to do it?"

"I had a chat with him the other night," said Gerald. "He was looking forward to starting uni. He was a bright boy with everything to look forward to. He didn't seem like a guy about to kill himself."

"What about a girl? Perhaps his girlfriend left him."

No one could answer this question. Then someone spoke, "I saw him writing something on the blackboard just before he went over to Brown's car."

The blackboard was brought in. A circular patch had been cleaned in the middle of a large notice about the ball. In this patch there were three words: YOU ARE FORGIVEN.

They looked at the sign but nobody spoke. The police officer asked them what it meant, but nobody knew. All of Jonny's actions, the writing, the pushing of the car and his final death leap, suggested that he had lost his sanity.

Richard drove his wet friend home and returned with his sister and his own companion. His route took him through the square in the centre of the city. It was late. The clocks on the Post Office and Town Hall towers were close to twelve. In Victoria Square the trams were leaving on the last trip to Glenelg. They would resume again at noon. On Sunday there were no morning trams to disturb the living. They would never frighten Jonny Marco again.

Chapter Five

April 1952

The next day Joan spoke to her father, "I have something to ask you, Dad."

"Whatever you want, Princess. How was the ball last night? You were home early."

"Haven't you heard the news?"

"There aren't any papers on Sunday, only the *Mail* and that goes to press on Saturday. It doesn't have last night's news. What happened?"

"A boy jumped off the footbridge and died. It'll be in the papers tomorrow. I came home early as I was so upset. He was such a nice boy."

Charles Meredith put a piece of fried tomato into his mouth, swallowed it and answered.

"Sounds terrible. What did you want to ask me?"

"The boy was here last Tuesday night. It was a small party. I don't want the press to make anything of it. It might be embarrassing and I don't want it in the papers."

"But, Joan, you're *always* in the papers. Only last week your picture was on page three."

"That's another thing. The *Advertiser* took my picture for tomorrow's paper. Be a dear and ask them not to use it. I don't want it in the same paper as Jonny."

"Did this boy kill himself because he was in love with you or something silly like that?"

"No, not because of me."

"If you know the reason you should tell the police."

The last thing that Charles Meredith wanted was a scandal, but more than that, he didn't want his daughter involved in anything illegal.

"Dad, I'll tell the police about the party. Nothing happened at the party. I just don't want it mentioned in the papers, that's all. You can see to it. They need Meredith advertising, so they'll listen to you."

"What shall I tell them?"

"At present, just not to put my picture in the paper. If the police interview me, I'll warn you and you can pull a few strings to keep the family name clean."

"Who was this boy? How are you involved?"

"A boy that I met for the first time on Tuesday. He must have had a breakdown and killed himself. I went to see him the other day to try and help him. It didn't help, I'm afraid. I even asked him to partner me to the ball last night, but he wasn't interested. He was too ill, I suppose."

Meredith was amazed. A man wasn't interested in Joan. What was wrong with him?

"He *must* have been ill! What do I tell the police?"

"You're a friend of Captain McInnes. Ring him and ask him to have a chat with the investigating officer so that he'll be discreet and not tell the press about the party."

"McInnes is a busy man."

"He'll have time for you, Daddy."

"If nothing happened at the party, *why* bother him?"

"Because we all had a good time, we drank beer and the party ended at five. We listened to banned records that Mother brought back from the States last year. Do you want all that and whatever else they care to print in the papers?"

"No."

Joan had a point. Diana shouldn't have smuggled in those Ruth Wallace records.

"Dad, whatever happens I want you to believe in me. I liked this boy and I tried to help him, I really did. I didn't succeed, that's all."

"Don't worry, Joan. I believe you."

Charles Meredith didn't know that his daughter was not being honest with him.

Later in the day, Louis Brown telephoned.

"I have to see you, Joan."

"If you can borrow a car, come over. I'll give you ten minutes and then you can clear off, or I'll set the dogs on you. I don't want to see you, but I suppose that I have to. Remember, ten minutes and not a second more."

When he arrived half an hour later, Joan didn't admit him into the flat, but walked with him to a seat in the grounds, close to the swimming pool, a secluded place.

"Make it quick, Louis Brown."

She hated this man now and it showed in her voice.

"We have to talk, Joan. Our stories have to match."

"I intend to tell the truth."

"You *do*, Joan, and I'll say that you did it with me. You tell on me and I'll tell on you."

This is what Joan had expected him to say. Louis Brown was running to form.

"Our lawyers will make mincemeat of you."

"Your lawyers will tell you to shut up and pay me to shut up too."

"What do you want from me?"

"Well, I wouldn't mind another shower, but I'll settle for your silence. After the party we took Jonny home and there was nothing wrong with him. I won't tell about the sex at the party — we just danced and listened to a few records. I won't mention the kind of records or the beer. I'm sorry that he's dead. It was an accident. I didn't think this would happen."

Joan was furious. She was used to men treating her with respect, even those who, like Brown, had had full use of her body. This was one bad dream that wouldn't go away.

"You killed him, Bully Brown. You're a murderer."

"If I am, so are you. You helped me."

"I didn't know what you had in mind. You used me to hurt Jonny. Why, Louis, why?"

Louis knew why, but he wasn't telling this girl, this rich harlot. From the moment he noticed Jonny Marco on the university lawns, he'd wanted to do something to him, something humiliating. Now with Johnny lying dead in the City Morgue, Louis knew what a terrible thing he had done. He wished it hadn't happened.

"I had my reasons, but they're pretty stupid now. I didn't like him and I wanted to humiliate him. I didn't want to hurt him."

"Hurt him! You destroyed his mind. I saw him the next day. He was a shell of a person. He had a complete mental breakdown."

"You and he were together the next day? You kept your part of the bargain?"

"Why shouldn't I? Do you think that I'd cheat him? I'm a Meredith, not a Brown."

Brown forgot about the dead student. He wanted to know about Joan's liaison with him.

"How was it? Was he alright at the time. Was it before or after he had his breakdown?"

"Don't talk like an absolute fool. He didn't take up the offer. If he had, who knows? He might be alive now. As far as I know, he never uttered another word to a living soul. You killed him, you bastard."

"*We* killed him."

"I tried to stop you. I asked you to tell him. I told you to cut the rope. I'll tell you one thing, Bully Brown. He was a man, a real man, which is more than you'll ever be."

"I was a good enough man for you the other night. I was good enough to shag you, or have you forgotten that?"

"You were a mistake. I can see that now."

"You seem to make a lot of mistakes, Miss Meredith."

Joan slid down the seat, and mustering all her might gave him a whack in the face that knocked him off onto the grass. He got up holding his jaw. His chin had been gashed by one of her rings.

"I asked for that, I'm sorry."

"Louis, you're a slimy bastard, but you've got me by the short hairs and I know it. I'll keep our secret for as long as it suits me, but I'll get my own back on you. I don't know how, or where, or when — but I will."

"You can't do anything to me, even if you and your bloody family own half of Adelaide. You can't touch me. If I decided to blackmail you, I could do very well out of this. I'll write a letter to your dear father and tell him what a tramp you are."

"You do and I'll see that you pay for what you've done to Jonny. I'll see myself shamed and you in jail before we part with a penny. You asked me to support your story. I agree. Now you'd better go before I change my mind."

"Well, I got what I wanted. I wasn't really going to blackmail you. Remember, Joan, we drove him straight home."

"Don't forget that I caught a taxi."

"Forget it. They won't check that. All they want to know is why he killed himself. They won't ever suspect what we did to him."

"But they'll want to know why I visited him."

"Make up your own story. Make it believable or the press will have a field day."

"No they won't. They need the Meredith ads. We also own shares in one of them."

"We roughed up a *Truth* reporter last night. He tried to take a picture of the boys who went into the river after your friend. We exposed all of their films."

"Bully for you! When are you going to stop hurting people?"

"Don't take it that way. I think Jonny was crazy. Did you see what he wrote on the blackboard?"

"No."

"*I forgive you*. What could he have meant? Perhaps he thought that he was Jesus Christ and could walk on water."

Joan was horrified. The bastard was making jokes! Jonny was dead and Brown was making jokes! But she had learned something: Jonny *had* forgiven her. It was cold comfort.

"You'd better go, Brown. Get out!"

"What did he mean?"

"Get out. I said, get out!"

Joan was hysterical now. He got up to go, then turned to face her again.

"Can I have a shower first?"

Joan tried to hit him again, but missed. Then, not having a car, he walked down the gravel path and up to the Glen Osmond tram terminus.

Joan Meredith lay on her bed and wept.

"Poor Jonny, poor Jonny. Why didn't you say something? Why? Why didn't you ring me? I'd have looked after you. I'd have kept my part of the bargain. I didn't want to be forgiven. I wanted you to live. Why, oh why, Jonny?"

The questions were never answered. They couldn't be. Jonny didn't know why Brown had done what he did, and afterwards he couldn't help himself. All he could feel was the tram coming down at him and death with it.

Later in the day, the friend that she had stood up the previous night called, and Joan apologised for her behaviour, explaining that the shock of the drowning had distressed her, as it indeed had done. He came over to see her, thinking what a sensitive girl she must be. He had to pick up the family car which he'd left there. He also wanted to spend the evening with her, but she wasn't in need of that kind of comfort, so he had to wait a week before he too shared her bed and shower. She slowly put Jonny out of her thoughts, but not completely. He remained forever deep in the recesses of her mind. She couldn't look at the footbridge or at a Glenelg tram without remembering what they had done.

Lectures started on the following day, Monday the seventh of April. The blackboard next to the Student's Union no longer bore the message from Jonny. Where it had been there was a new notice:

WE REGRET THE DEATH OF A YOUNG STUDENT, JONNY MARCO. THE LOSS OF SUCH A YOUNG AND PROMISING STUDENT IS FELT BY ALL OF US. HIS PASSING FROM OUR MIDST HAS IMPOVERISHED US. WE EXTEND OUR SYMPATHY TO HIS FAMILY.

WOULD WITNESSES TO THIS TRAGEDY AND ANYONE WHO MIGHT BE ABLE TO HELP THE POLICE IN THEIR INVESTIGATIONS PLEASE CALL IN AT THE UNION OFFICE. A POLICE OFFICER AND A SOLICITOR WILL BE AVAILABLE FOR THE NEXT TWO DAYS TO HEAR WHAT YOU HAVE TO SAY AND TAKE STATEMENTS. DO NOT GO DIRECTLY TO THE POLICE OR GIVE INTERVIEWS TO THE PRESS.

WE ALSO WISH TO THANK THE STUDENTS WHO ASSISTED IN THE RESCUE AND RESUSCITATION ATTEMPT.

That afternoon a second notice board was set up. Where welcome meetings had been announced, there was now one large notice giving the time and place of the funeral.

Gerald Fisher and Richard Flynn were having tea and scones in the Refectory, when Joan Meredith came in. She must have been looking for them. She made a bee-line for their table.

"Have you boys made your statements?"

"No, we're going as soon as we get this into us," said Richard. "Have a scone, they're terrific."

"No thanks. I have to watch my figure."

"You leave that to us, Joan. Gerald, move over and let the lady sit down."

"I want to come with you when you make the statements."

"Why? What did you see?"

"Nothing special. I just want to tell them about the party last Tuesday."

"Why? That's not important," said Gerald, but as he said this he wasn't sure. Jonny had come with them in the Holden, but he hadn't left with them. Gerald wondered how he got home from Joan's party.

"It *might* be. I think they ought to know, and be told by us and not have them come and ask us about it later. Did Jonny say anything that may have indicated that he was sick or suicidal?"

She wanted to shift any suspicion from herself. That meant she would have to remove any suspicion from Brown too.

"I had a long talk with him," said Gerald. "He didn't seem sick or suicidal to me. He told me his family history, very fascinating it was too, and what he wanted to do at university. He sounded alright to me, not like a guy who was going to kill himself."

"How did he get home?" asked Richard. "He didn't go in our car, unless he was at the bottom of the pile."

"Louis Brown drove him home. If you see him, tell him to come and make a statement."

'Brown probably drove him crazy,' thought Richard, but didn't say it. Brown and Joan were more than close friends, he mused. He'd seen that at the party.

"Try not to mention the naughty records or the beer. It isn't relevant and I don't want it in the press, if you know what I mean."

"That's alright, Joan."

The three of them went into the Union office, where they were interviewed by the police officer in the presence of the other man, a recent law graduate who was there to protect the students' interests. Gerald told his story first, from the time that he noticed Jonny until he was carried away in the ambulance. Richard had little to add, the two of them had been together all the time. Joan listened quietly at first but soon started to sniffle, then sob, and finally cried. Her tears were genuine, very genuine. Finally, the officer turned to her.

"Well, Miss Meredith, it's your turn. Do you think that you can tell us what you saw?"

"I didn't see Jonny at all Saturday night. I got to the ambulance just as they were lifting him into it. It was horrible." The last words were sobbed out.

"You needn't have come, Miss Meredith. You could have spared yourself the anguish."

"It's not about Saturday night that I came. There was a party at my place last Tuesday, after the welcome. I invited some of the crowd. I didn't pick and choose them, just whoever was close at the time. The welcome was a bit of a flop, you know."

"Jonny Marco was there?"

"Yes, and so were we," said Gerald, pointing to Richard.

"Go on, Miss Meredith."

"I rang Jonny the next day, but his mother said he was ill, so I went to see him."

The policeman knew this. He had spoken to Mrs Marco and knew that Jonny's strange behaviour began the morning after the Science Association welcome. He wanted to know if Jonny was alright the night before, if his illness was caused by something that happened at the welcome. But the two people who could supply this vital evidence had made a pact of silence to deny him the all-important information.

"I know about your visit, Miss Meredith, his mother told me. Why did you go to his house?"

"Because he was ill. I wanted to help him."

"Why did you ring him?"

"I wanted to talk to him."

"About what?"

"No particular reason. I danced with him the night before; he seemed like a nice person, so I rang to have a chat with him."

The policeman wasn't satisfied.

"Do you usually ring boys that you've only met once?"

"I have done before. I don't ring every boy that I meet, only the interesting ones."

"So why did you ring Jonny?"

"I told you, because he seemed like an interesting person."

"Did he seem to be alright at the party, Miss Meredith. Can you shed any light as to why he did what he did?"

"He seemed to be perfectly normal at the party."

"And you saw Louis Brown drive him home?"

"Yes."

"At what time?"

"A little after five. Just as it was getting light in the sky. He left ten minutes after the other guests in that small car of his. Have you spoken to him?"

Joan was amazing herself at the ease with which she was lying to the police. It hurt her, because she wanted them to know what Brown had done to Jonny Marco.

"Yes, he told us that he drove straight to Jonny's home and that Jonny didn't speak to him on the way home, except to thank him and say good-bye. He said that he didn't seem to be insane or distressed. Whatever happened to the boy must have happened overnight. Did he have a lot to drink at the party? Was he drunk?"

"We all had a few beers, but nothing stronger. I don't think that Jonny had more than a glass. We had soft drinks too. Everybody expects a beer at the Merediths'. We were all over eighteen, so we weren't breaking the law."

"We have no objection to you drinking, Miss Meredith, just as long as all the car drivers didn't have too much."

"They didn't, *nobody* did," said Gerald, helping her out. He didn't mention that Brown and a few others had done some pretty heavy drinking. Richard backed him up, "That's right officer. I can swear that Jonny wasn't drunk and I don't think anyone else was either."

"I'd like the names of the others at the party, please."

They helped Joan write out the list and went out into the roadway, each deep in contemplation. Richard spoke first. "Tell me, Gerry, why do I have a Brown taste in my mouth? Why was Jonny happy and healthy at five o'clock in the morning and out of his mind eight hours later? Do people go mad in their sleep? Why did Jonny choose Brown's car to push into the river — just because it was easy, or was he trying to say something? Everywhere we put our noses they come up Brown."

"Do you have to talk about it like that?" said Joan, and they could see that she was still very distressed. They remembered how Joan and Louis Brown had disappeared into the bedroom at the party. Richard knew that he had been tactless, as Joan obviously liked Brown. He didn't know what really had happened between them. This wasn't the way to get into her good books or an invitation back to her flat. He offered to buy them all drinks.

On his way back to the table with the bottles he noticed Evelyn Robertson sitting by herself. He suggested that she join them. Evelyn was pleased to do so — she knew no one in Adelaide other than her college companions of a week.

Ten minutes later Joan got up to go. Richard asked her for a lift, as he lived on that side of town. She was still upset by his comments about Brown, but she took him all the same, not saying a word to him all the way home. They left the other two sitting together.

"I'll walk you to the college. I can catch a tram home from North Adelaide." Gerald wanted to get to know Evelyn Robertson better. He had been admiring her in the glossy picture that Joan had given him. She was prettier in the flesh. She had a lovely smile.

"Sure, it's a nice day for a walk." It was nice to have a man walk her home.

As they crossed the footbridge Evelyn shuddered. There were a couple of boats down there, with men in them poking with sticks and putting down grappling hooks. In the boats they could see a small heap of assorted rubbish including a bicycle frame and some trays from the cafeteria.

"What are they looking for, Gerald?"

"I suppose whatever it was that held him down. Must have been something heavy."

He saw the look of horror on Evelyn's face, and putting his arm around her to comfort her he hurried the frightened girl off the bridge. They didn't look back.

"I didn't see you Saturday night," he said.

"I wasn't there."

"That was a pity."

"I should have been there. I was talking to Jonny at the welcome and he asked me if I wanted to go with him. Then Joan Meredith grabbed me before I could accept and showed me the pictures, and you all got into cars, and I didn't see Jonny any more. I so much wanted to go and I didn't know what to do. I've never been to a ball. Do you think that he killed himself because no one would go with him?"

"You didn't say no to him. He must have realised what happened and would probably have called you, if something hadn't prevented him. They say he was taken ill during the night, what was left of it."

"I didn't know what to do. Why didn't I say yes, instead of taking that stupid picture? I must have hurt him."

"Evelyn, now you're being silly. If every man killed himself every time that a girl didn't say yes to him, there'd be no men left in no time. He asked me where you were at the party. I told him that you had to go back to college. If he'd been alright, I'm sure he'd have rung you."

"Do you think he came looking for me at the ball?"

"No. He was ill. You weren't the cause. I had a long talk with him at the party and he was in a good mood."

"Thanks, Gerald. You've taken a load off my mind. I didn't really think it could have been because of me, but I had to tell someone. Are you going to the funeral tomorrow?"

"Yes, I noticed that they've cancelled first-year practical classes so we can attend. What a way to start uni! Tell me, what's it like at St Ann's?"

"It's nice and clean and the rooms are nice. The food is fair, not quite home cooking, and it's very strict. We have to be in early at night and we can't have men visiting in any part of the building, let alone the rooms. It's a senior boarding school. They call it St Trini-Ann's."

"So why don't you stay at home?"

'That's a laugh,' she thought. 'Gerald doesn't know that my own father is twice as strict as the college head.' She replied, "I'm from Renmark. I was lucky to get a place here."

Gerald thought quickly, 'This lovely lady is from the country. She almost certainly hasn't a boyfriend down here. I have to ask her out before someone else discovers her.'

"Would you like to go out next Saturday night? There's a new Danny Kaye film at the Regent."

He had chosen the right bait. She too was a fan of Danny Kaye, and dying to make the most of being away from father by going to the pictures whenever she could.

"Do you think you can get tickets?"

"I can try. If not, I'll find something else."

"I think there's a good movie at the Piccadilly. That's not too far from the college. We could walk there."

'What a good idea,' thought Gerald. 'They have double seats in the back row, perfect for getting to know a lady.'

The Piccadilly was one of the newest picture theatres in Adelaide, North Adelaide, and was the latest thing in interior design. As a boy, he had lived nearby and waited each week for the matinée with the Buck Rogers or Flash Gordon serial. But would Evelyn want to cuddle in the back row? Better stick to the Regent and Danny Kaye. He was pleased with his walk with Evelyn. She seemed to enjoy his company, as he did hers.

Just before the college they came to a row of old houses. Evelyn pointed to one of them.

"Joan Meredith's big brother lives there."

"How do you know?"

"Everybody knows. It's a famous house."

"Because it belongs to Joan's brother?"

"No, because it was built for someone important in the last century. At the college they all talk about Steven Meredith. He's a bachelor you know, rich as Midas."

"The Merediths are all richer than Midas *and* just as miserly, they say."

"This one has girls over almost every night, they say. He's a lecturer at the uni."

"And a lecherer at home."

"So they say."

"The Merediths seem to be over-sexed."

"Do you find Joan Meredith attractive?"

"Joan is every man's dream and nightmare combined. Don't tell this to anyone, Evelyn, but she frightens me. Look what happened to Jonny."

She looked at him with that same horrified look that she'd had on the bridge. He wished he hadn't said that.

"Joan? *What* did she do to Jonny?"

"I don't know. She and Brown know something and are keeping it a secret. I'm sure Brown is at the bottom of this and so does Richard."

"But that's *terrible*."

"Well, it's up to the police to find out what. Don't tell anyone what we think. I suppose that we ought to be silent unless we know what really happened. You, Richard and I will have to be the three wise monkeys: see no evil, hear no evil, and speak no evil."

"If they did anything to Jonny, they should be punished."

"I doubt if they will be. What could you do to make a gutsy guy like Jonny become mad overnight? If they really did do something, it must have been terrible. On the other hand, we *could* be barking up the wrong tree."

Inside the fortification of the women's college, Evelyn asked one of the second year girls, "Who's Louis Brown?"

"He's the guy who lost his car in the river last Saturday night."

"I know that. *Who* is he?"

"A big gorilla with a big mouth and not much grey matter. He failed Botany 1 for the second time last year, and both his second-year subjects. I didn't think that he'd be back this year. I think his parents send him here to keep him out of trouble. It must cost them a pretty penny to keep him here. I think he's a member of the rugby club. He's quite cool at the piano and quite a charmer. He asked me out once, but I told him that I had a boyfriend, which at the time was a lie. Stay away from him — he's bad medicine."

"Thanks for the advice. I've just been asked out by a nice boy, one of the boys who tried to save Jonny Marco. I think he likes me. Have you heard anything really bad about Louis Brown?"

"No. He doesn't go out with St Ann's girls, or to tell you the truth *they* don't go out with *him*. Ask at the Children's Hospital down the hill. *Why* all the interest?"

"He was at Joan Meredith's party last week. I was invited, but couldn't go because of the curfew here."

"Very wise. You don't want to get on the wrong side of the Head here, not in the first week, not in any week. Getting in after curfew is almost impossible, so don't try it at St.Trini-Ann's. Better to stay out all night and sneak in at breakfast time. But that's risky too. What did you hear about Brown?"

"Nothing definite, just suspicions. My friends were talking about him. I thought I'd ask some of the girls."

"Don't, if you care what the other girls think of you. And stay away from the Browns of this world."

It was good advice and Evelyn remembered it. It was a pity that she didn't take it.

The Warden of the Union, a gentle man who had recently been appointed to the post to see to the welfare of the students and be around when they needed to talk to somebody, went with the President and Secretary of the Union to see the bereaved family. They did their best to comfort Jonny's poor parents, a hopeless task. Back at the university, he spoke to as many of Jonny's fellow students as he could contact, and a large number turned up for the funeral the following day. Gerald, Richard and Evelyn had lunch together before taking the bus to the cemetery.

This was the first time that Gerald had been to a cemetery. As they passed down the roadway it came as a shock to him to see the row upon row of marble and granite tombstones, each with its name and inscription, and to realise that under each and every one there was a dead person. The sight of the open earth and the fresh brown soil waiting to cover the coffin also affected him profoundly, that and the sight of the coffin itself, made of dark wood, polished like the sideboard in his parent's living room.

Then, for the first time, he saw Jonny's parents. Dressed in black and supported by friends and relatives, they made their way into the graveyard, broken people. Mrs Marco noticed the group of students, recognised one or two as old friends of Jonny and looked for a few seconds for the Meredith girl who had tried to help. She couldn't see her, and her thoughts returned to her dead son as she listened to the words of the priest.

The Marcos were Roman Catholics, and at first there had been an objection to burying a suicide in the cemetery proper. The family doctor and the Warden of the Union were able to convince the priests that Jonny's death was due to sickness — sudden, unknown, and catastrophic. The facts were clear. He had taken some of his weights with a piece of rope attached in the kitbag, and tied this to his waist before jumping. But he had been mentally disturbed and acting abnormally for four days. No one questioned Brown's story that he had driven Jonny straight home. All that could be said was that Jonny Marco took his life in a state of insanity. *Why* he did remained a mystery.

The cemetery lies on the side of a hill in the Western Parklands. Half a mile away at the bottom of the hill there are railway goods yards, with the main train line running through, up to the hills, and on to Melbourne. From time to time a steam engine disturbed the solitude of this desolate hillside, passing by or shunting in the goods yard. The wind rustled the leaves of the poplar trees as the priest read on and the mourners wept. They were an isolated gathering in the middle of the city. Gerald closed his eyes, reliving the events of Saturday night, seeing in his mind's eye the small figure clutching the weights, and climbing over the rail before falling like a stone into the blackness below. It was a memory that he would often recall, asking the question: *why?* What was the reason?

Gerald was shocked back to reality by the thud of the first sods of earth hitting the coffin lid. He, like most of the congregation, had tears in his eyes. Evelyn, standing next to him, had tears streaming down her cheeks. She looked at him with reddened eyes and he took her hand to comfort her. She squeezed his hand and gave him a quick smile. They both felt a little better.

The three of them didn't take the bus back to the university, preferring to walk. At the cemetery entrance they noticed Joan Meredith's car a short distance from the gates, with the roof closed. Richard noticed it first.

"That's *funny*," he said. "I didn't see Joan at the graveside. Did either of you?"

"No. We're almost the last here. I didn't see Brown either — not that I expected to see him."

"Joan's sitting in the car," said Evelyn. "Do you want to say hello to her?"

"No," answered Richard and they kept walking. Evelyn was glad — she too was overawed by the rich girl. She wanted to be alone with her new friends and not share them with the other woman. Joan saw them go and was relieved to think that they hadn't seen her. She waited until all the mourners had moved away, before she got out of the car.

They walked through the parklands, dry with the stubble of the summer before for the winter rains, past Adelaide High, their old school. Gerald had taken Evelyn's hand at the graveside and still held it. They turned into Hindley Street, following the path that, unknown to them, Jonny had taken on his last walk. They walked past the old houses facing onto the street, with no gardens in between, and the warehouses and businesses in the old part of the city. They didn't turn at Morphett Street, near the fish market as Jonny had done, but continued down Hindley Street, towards the city shopping centre and into Rundle Street. This part of the city was alive with people and traffic, comforting after the loneliness of that windswept hill.

At Angus and Robertsons, they looked at books. Evelyn bought *The Caine Mutiny* and Richard *The Cruel Sea*. Gerald didn't have money for books. What with the Commencement Ball and his coming date with Evelyn, he was into next week's allowance.

It had been a long walk and they were all thirsty. Stopping in a milk bar, they sat down and ordered milkshakes. The place was full of school students in their distinctive uniforms, chattering like monkeys. It reminded them of how they were just a few months ago and it made them feel a little superior. Two boys recognised Gerald and Richard and came over to talk. Gerald remembered that he had to do something.

"You two wait here. I'm popping down to the Regent to get tickets for Saturday night. Keep your fingers crossed."

"Saturday night? You haven't got Buckley's chance. It's sold out for eight weeks for Saturday night," Richard told him. "Go to a matinée."

"I *might* be lucky. I'll be back in five minutes."

Gerald pushed through the thick glass doors of the Regent into the cool lobby, and went up to the ticket office.

"Two tickets for Saturday night, please."

The girl looked at him in amazement, as if he was a loony escaped from Parkside.

"We're sold out until June for a Saturday night."

"No cancellations?"

"I'm afraid not. You could try just before the show, but you'd have to be very lucky."

"Thanks anyway."

As he started to walk to the door, he suddenly had a bright idea. They kept tickets, he'd been told, for VIPs, so why not have a go? He went over to the commissionaire, an impressive portly man in a blue uniform, with lots of braid and buttons, standing inside the entrance, beside a four-foot smiling cardboard face of Danny Kaye.

"Where's the manager's office?"

He was unsure of what to say to the manager, but he went slowly to the door that the commissionaire pointed out to him. He didn't see the man walk over to the ticket office. Before he reached the door marked MANAGER, he heard the man calling him.

"Excuse me, sir. What do you want with the manager? Can *I* be of service?"

"Mr Meredith of Meredith Foods sent me to get some tickets. I was just going to ask the manager if he could find some."

"I think we might find them without bothering the manager."

He spoke to the girl for a few seconds. Gerald's plan was working!

"We have the tickets. They were set aside. The girl didn't know that you wanted the tickets for Mr Meredith."

"*My* fault. I should have told her."

Back at the milk bar he held the tickets.

"Front row, balcony. Right in the middle."

"*How* did you do that?"

He told them. They never lacked good tickets after that. But they were expensive tickets, the best in the house. They would make a hole in his meagre savings.

At about this time the sun was setting over the sea, sending long shadows over the land. The lone figure of Joan Meredith could be seen weeping among the shadows of the tombstones, over the flowers she had added to those already on the fresh grave. As the sun dipped into the distant sea she got into her car and drove slowly home. It had taken a young man's death to make a human being out of this spoilt young woman, this society princess.

Chapter Six

April 1952

Gerald was surprised at how fast they got down to work once lectures started. From the first day he filled page after page with lecture notes. Chemistry and Physics mostly covered material that he'd learnt the year before, but Botany and Zoology were completely new and interesting to him. Lectures started at nine with Physics or Botany, followed by Practical classes. Some days there was a break until twelve, which they usually spent in the Barr Smith library. Just before their noon lecture they went for a quick morning tea, with hot scones, butter and jam, taking lunch at one, eating on the lawns or inside the crowded Refectory on wet days. As Gerald, Richard and Evelyn took the same four subjects, they spent a lot of time together.

Evelyn usually raced back to the college for a hot lunch and raced back for the afternoon practical classes. Her family money, her self-assurance, and her ravishing looks assured her a place at the Refectory equivalent of the Captain's Table. These were not just *university royalty*, they made campus life interesting, publishing *On Dit*, organising debates and the myriad activities that relieved the tedium of study.

Botany practicals were held after the morning lecture, and here they learned to examine thin sections of plants, which they had to cut with a very sharp razor. Richard got into hot water the first day, when sharpening the razor he turned the blade the wrong way, cutting the razor-strop into two equal pieces. They placed their one-cell-thick slices of stems and leaves and roots on slides under the microscope and attempted to draw what they saw. They soon learned to draw what they were *expected* to see and the way they were expected to draw it.

"Cells are drawn as complete rounded entities and not like a series of joined or not joined match sticks. Draw the cell walls, not houses of cards."

In the first few weeks they used their erasers more than their pencils. In Zoology they started by looking at, and drawing, all kinds of microscopic animals. None of them had ever learned drawing, but they gradually improved and managed to make reasonable copies of what they saw. The Biology laboratories in the new red-brick Benham

Building were large, well-lit, and uncluttered, facing the tennis courts in front and the river behind.

In contrast, the Chemistry lab was like a factory. Instead of sitting on stools they stood in front of smelly black benches, with rows of reagent bottles in front of them, and gas and water pipes above. In the Biology labs it was mostly quiet, but in the Chemistry lab it was all noise, chatter, and smells. There were a couple of Kipps generators in the fume cupboard and the smell of H_2S often filled the room. Once a week they crowded into the lab and feverishly learned how to analyse simple chemicals. Then still smelling of the lab, they joined the five o'clock office crowd, racing home to dinner and a night of study. There were text books to read and lecture notes to decipher. Gerald soon found out that if he didn't copy up his lecture notes within a day or two, there were things written down that he no longer understood. Some of the lecturers spoke fast so they had to scribble in note form and use their memory to decipher the scrawl.

Gerald left the house every morning at seven forty-five, travelling to the city with his father. He and his friends played a little table tennis before the nine o'clock lectures and sometimes at other breaks. They ate lunch at the same table or on the same patch of grass, at the same time with the same friends.

As he didn't have a driving licence, Gerald and Evelyn had to take the tram to the picture on Saturday night. What did they care? They had the best seats in the house! As the lights dimmed they settled down in the soft red velvet seats and enjoyed the Newsreels, the travelogue and, just before the intermission, the Tom and Jerry cartoon. Gerald bought a packet of "Fantales" and they read the stories of the film stars from the wrappers as they chewed on the soft chocolate coated toffee and waited for the main feature. Beside the stage a lady played on the Wurlitzer Organ tunes from musical comedies, the ornate proscenium arch ringing with music. Then down she went, and the curtain parted for the MGM lion, preceding the master of comedy, Danny Kaye.

It was a great movie with Danny playing, as he so often did, twin roles. Gerald wondered if he got twin salaries for doing that. There were lots of pretty girls, lots of laughs and terrific dance scenes. But, as usual, it was the songs and antics of Danny that made the show — what with *Ballin' The Jack* and *Popo The Puppet* and the title number,

Who Could Ask For Anything More? They got back to St Ann's just before the curfew and he ran up the hill only to see the last tram disappear down O'Connell Street. Gerald didn't have money for a taxi, so he walked the three miles home.

He set off at a brisk pace, trying to remember the words of one of the songs in the film, *The Rhythm Of A New Romance*:

> *"It's not the beat, beat, beat, of a jungle drum,*
> *that makes my heart start to dance.*
> *But the urge to merge,*
> *that begins to surge,*
> *when I start to feel the rhythm of a new romance."*

He couldn't remember the next part and decided to buy the record. He remembered the last few lines:

> *"So if the world looks flat like Columbus found,*
> *when you strike new ground,*
> *then it will look round, and dance,*
> *to the rhythm of a new romance."*

Gerald felt that it would be a song to remember, one that would be a special song with a special meaning for Evelyn and himself. As he crossed the parklands he remembered as much as he could, the words of the title song:

> *"If you look, you'll see the people of Pari playing on the*
> *Riviera.*
> *When there's ice and snow,*
> *it's nice to Nice to go,*
> *Where the moon, Clare de lune, is clearer."*

It was a quarter-to-one when he turned off the main road into the quiet, faintly-lit street leading to his house. He quickened his pace as he was so close to home and a fresh cold wind had sprung up. He didn't notice the couple sitting in the parked car, perhaps they were too low down. Just as he was passing, someone lowered the window a little and flicked out a lit cigarette butt. It arced in front of him like a rocket and made a shower of sparks as it hit the roadway. He stopped, startled. Then he heard the springs of the car start to move rhythmically. He took off down the road, as if he'd seen a ghost.

When he got home he realised how silly he'd been, but he was glad to get under the covers of his own bed in his own room.

The next day he got up at eleven and went to have a late breakfast. On the table there was a newspaper, placed there specially for him to see. He just had to glance at the headline to realise that last Saturday's tragedy was being raked over by the *Truth*, poor dears, who had to wait a whole week to publish their venom.

STUDENT KILLED AT UNIVERSITY

The death of first year student, Jonny Marco, at the university last Saturday night has all the markings of a student stunt that went wrong. The public is sick of irresponsible behaviour by these privileged louts, and has the right to know the truth about this new victim; how he died and to see that those responsible are punished. Why did this fine young man in the prime of his life, topple to his death from the footbridge in what this paper thinks was another irresponsible ceremony of initiation that went wrong? Was Jonny Marco thrown off the bridge or was he made to jump by bullying older students during a drunken orgy of dance? Was he drunk or drugged? The police say "No". How can the public be sure that the *post mortem* was not carried out by ex-students who could not be relied upon to give results if they were unfavourable to their friends? Who dared him and who helped him in what we believe was a Houdini attempt at an underwater escape? Was the plan to have this unfortunate boy escape and swim underwater, faking a drowning? Did the perpetrators want to shock the onlookers and have the police drag the river as a joke? These questions have to be answered. When we are dealing with privileged students, anything is possible. We have evidence that alcohol was consumed in parked cars along the roadway that night. We have handed the bottles to the police and we hope that they apprehend those responsible for this breach of public order. One of our reporters was savagely attacked by a mob of beer-crazed students. His camera was smashed and he

had to fight them off to escape a fate similar to that of
the deceased. The police did nothing, stating that the
students were within their rights when they assaulted
our staff members, claiming that we were trespassing
at the time. Since when can a section of the
community commit all kinds of crimes not a mile from
the State Parliament and get away with it? Is the
University a part of Adelaide or a foreign body in our
midst? Where, we would like to know, was the
university warder? Was he not appointed to stop this
kind of thing? He is in receipt of a fancy salary, so
why wasn't he doing his job that night? If he isn't able
to do the job and keep his charges under control, let
the police police the university and bring these law
breakers to heel.

The reference to the warder was a sting in the tail of this article,
being a deliberate misspelling of the word warden, or student
councillor, and *not* jailer as the paper wished to intimate. The insult
was a particularly vicious one, angering the student body and those
who knew the man referred to in the article.

Gerald was furious.

"How could they write such a mixture of lies and venom? What
have the university and the student body done to them?"

He only read the paper on rare occasions, usually the most sordid
sections. They were especially sordid in the days when most papers
were very respectable. *Truth* made headlines of murders, rapes and
divorce court details, the goings-on of film stars and the famous. The
latest in swimwear and tight sweaters was a regular feature, especially
bikinis, that would have got their wearer sent off any Australian beach
from Surfer's Paradise to Rottnest Island and certainly at Glenelg or
Semaphore.

Until this Sunday morning Gerald had regarded *Truth* as a
harmless somewhat amusing diversion, but today he felt that he, as a
student, had been soiled by the scandal-rag. He went to the living
room, paper in hand, where his parents were reading the *Mail*.

"Do you want the comics?" his mother asked.

"No thanks, Mom, I found *them* on the kitchen table and I wasn't
amused."

"I thought that you'd be interested," said his father, looking up from the sporting pages. "I noticed *Truth* down at the shop when I went for the *Mail*, so I bought a copy."

"Well, you wasted your money. There isn't a shred of truth in it. I'm ... mad." He didn't use bad language in front of his mother — *that* privilege he left to his father.

"You're not mad at me, son. I just bought it because I thought that you'd want to see it."

"Thanks, Dad. I'm glad you bought it, but mad at the Bs that printed it, and at the thousands of people who'll read and believe that rubbish. It's a complete pack of lies and wicked insinuations. I was there and there's not a shred of truth in the whole article. You know that I was one of the boys who tried to rescue Jonny Marco. Who gives them the right to publish lies like that, Dad? They ought to be made to eat their words. A complete retraction is the least that they should make."

"You'll never see that. Firstly, they don't say anything, they just ask a lot of questions and suggest answers. I've never seen anyone win a court case against them and they've upset a lot of people over the years. Who's going to sue them and make them eat their words — a lot of students who, let's face it, aren't even named in the article? They could write a lot worse than that and still avoid an action for libel. For that you'd have to prove that it's not only false but malicious. *What* does it matter? *Who* takes them seriously?"

"Plenty of people do. What gets my goat is what they said about the warden. That's pure character assassination, making fun of a decent person."

"Yes, I know that, but students do play pranks and act the fool a lot."

"Why shouldn't they? This town needs livening up. It's more like a cemetery than a modern city. I had to walk home last night when I missed the last tram."

"The tram drivers need their sleep too, you know. How would you like to work late Saturday night? How was the picture?" his father asked, changing the subject.

"Terrific, Dad. You two ought to go and see it. I want to go again when it comes to the local. Dad, I want to get my driving licence so I don't have to walk home after the pictures. Alright by you?"

"Alright? I told you to do it when you turned seventeen."

"Will you teach me to drive?"

"Just as soon as you get your licence. You can get the pamphlet with the questions near the university, and sit for the test there, too. Then you can learn to drive."

That same morning Mrs Meredith also read the offending article. She showed it to her husband and her daughter, who became hysterical upon reading it, tearing the paper to shreds as she ran down to her flat to weep.

"Really," said Diana Meredith. "You ought to do something, Charles. They shouldn't be allowed to publish such scurrilous lies as this."

She didn't know that it was Joan's guilty conscience that sent her down running to her flat, in tears.

"I couldn't do anything if I wanted to. I don't have any shareholding in the paper and I'm not a friend of the editor. I know the people at the respectable papers."

"What if they write about Joan's party and say it, too, was a drunken orgy? That poor boy was at the party. Charles, I don't want them writing lies and innuendoes about our daughter. You don't know what they'll say."

"So *what* do you want me to do, Diana?"

"You know lots of people. You'll think of something."

Mr Meredith went to his office early the next day and made a few phone calls. The first was to Captain McInnes of the city police. They were old friends, having been fellow officers in the First AIF in France. Before his father handed him control of the companies, he had often lunched with McInnes at the RSL club, and now they were both members of the exclusive Adelaide Club on North Terrace. He arranged to met him there for lunch.

When he arrived, they ordered drinks and he told him what was on his mind.

"Jack, it's about that article in yesterday's paper. Have you read it?"

"I had to speak to someone in the Premier's office about it. I told him, and I'll tell you now, that as far as the police are concerned it's a load of rubbish. Is that why you asked me to have lunch with you?"

"My daughter saw it and was most upset by it. She's just started university, you know, and she met the boy a few days before he killed himself. Terrible thing. He was a fine boy, so I've heard."

"You've heard correctly, Charles. I've seen the officer handling the case and he can't understand what got into the boy. No one else seems to have been involved. He just tied weights to his body and jumped. Must have been crazy. Well, he didn't leave a suicide note, so we'll never know why he did it unless someone comes forward and tells us."

The waiter came with the menu, which they knew by heart. They ordered the consommé.

"Jack, he was at a party at our house a few days before he jumped, one of Joan's parties."

"Yes, she told us."

"Well, I don't want false accusations and allegations made about her, the kind I read in yesterday's *Truth*."

"Will there be?"

"That's just the trouble, Jack, you can't tell. Do me a favour and find out if there's likely to be. Ask your officers, they usually know who's sniffing around, and let me know. I want to quash this before they try to blacken the Meredith name."

"What makes you think that they will?"

"Jack, they had a few beers at the party and it ended quite late. We both know that there's nothing wrong with that, but it could be blown up out of all proportion by the people who wrote yesterday's article. They could pillory my daughter and her friends. The editor's got a grudge against students. If I wait until it's already on the news-stands, the damage will be done and no amount of apologies, or even winning a libel case, will repair that kind of damage. If something's afoot, *I* want to nip it in the bud if you get what I mean."

The head of the South Australian Police ordered roast beef and horseradish sauce, as did his host, then waited for the waiter to leave before answering:

"Well, I don't think that there is any press activity, Charles, but I'll ask the boys. I'll get back to you if I find out anything."

"Thanks, Jack. I must have you and the wife over to dinner soon."

Mr Meredith received assurances from the editors of the dailies, that they weren't planning to write anything about his daughter and her party. Jonny Marco's death was old news, why rake over it? Later he received a call from the officer in charge of the case.

"Mr Meredith, this is Detective Sergeant Williams. Captain McInnes asked me to call you. He probably told you that we've finished our investigation on the Marco death and are closing the file. We know that no one pushed the boy or in any way influenced him to jump. As far as we can conclude, he decided to jump and took the weights from his home for that purpose. As for his reasons for doing so, we have no idea. From that point of view the whole thing is unsatisfactory, but the coroner concluded that he was suffering from a mental disorder and, as we have no evidence of anything criminal in the case, we're closing the investigation. Your daughter's party and what went on there is of no concern to us. It seems to have been a pretty harmless get-together."

"Thank you."

"One thing more, the reporter that the students tossed out of the university that night has found out about the party and is asking questions about it. I thought that you ought to know."

"Oh, I don't like the sound of that."

"Well, they don't go to press until the weekend, so they might decide that it isn't worth printing."

Mr Meredith didn't ring the paper. He sent a messenger boy to the paper's editor, asking him to meet him the following morning. The editor came. When Charles Meredith summoned, people came.

"Good morning, Mr Meredith. I got your message. How can I help you?"

"Arthur, I've known you ever since you got your first job as a reporter for the *News*. I think you interviewed me once or twice. You should never have left the paper and gone over to the thing that you're editing now. I'm not at all impressed by your paper, Arthur, it's a scandal rag and a disgrace to the community."

"*I* don't make policy, Mr Meredith. There's a demand for our paper and the pay is a lot more than that of a reporter on the *News*. Now, you didn't call me over just to tell me that you don't like my paper. You could have told me that in your note."

"Saturday's paper was a pack of lies."

"I am sorry to hear that. I thought that we made a good point. The boy's death was a mystery and all the students are refusing to talk to our reporters. I'm sure that if we get to the bottom of the mystery, we'll be doing the community a service."

"Shouldn't you leave it to the police? The students co-operated with them. There is no law that compels them to speak to reporters."

"The police are closing the case without getting to the bottom of it. We think that that's irresponsible."

"But you're bringing up a lot of questions that are irrelevant. Why are you creating a mystery where there isn't one?"

"Because mysteries sell newspapers."

"Why are you dragging my daughter into it?"

This shocked the editor of *Truth*. The last thing he wanted was to antagonise Charles Meredith.

"*Are* we?"

There was concern in his voice.

"I believe so. Your reporter is asking a lot of questions about her."

"I'm sorry, I didn't know that."

"Well, he is. If you have anything that you think you must print, you ring me and tell me. It's a free press, but I expect you to do the decent thing and warn us. But let me warn you too, *if* you print any lies or innuendoes about my family and libel us, I'll break your paper and sue you for enough money to close you down. You know that I can afford the best solicitors; you're not dealing with snotty-nosed students, you're dealing with Meredith. Remember what I said, and let me know today if you still intend to write about my daughter's party."

The millionaire stood up as he made his point, and the editor was forced to look at him from an inferior position.

"I will, Mr Meredith."

"Good. Meredith Foods has always had a good relationship with the press. There's no reason why we shouldn't have one with *Truth*."

The Meredith face was now wreathed with smiles.

"Yes, Mr Meredith. No reason at all."

Back at the editorial office he summoned the reporter responsible for the Jonny Marco article.

"Are you writing an article on Joan Meredith, about a party at her place or something?"

"Yes, Arthur. A real humdinger. I think it could take up all of page five. Do you want it for page one? Drunken sex orgy leads to Jonny's suicide. I'll go and get it for you, if you like. That Meredith girl is a real beauty . It's a pity that we can't feature her on page three in a bikini."

"Do you know who she is?"

"Yes, she's the beer heiress and the town trollop. They say she bangs like a battleship."

"Be careful what you say, and cancel the article. Her old man's too damned influential for us to tackle."

"So how are you going to fill page five?"

"We're putting in a full-page beer ad for Meredith beer. Take this note to the advertising manager."

On the fifteenth of April President Truman hosted a ceremony in Washington at which forty-nine nations signed a peace treaty with Japan, ending World War Two in the Pacific. On the twenty-second, thirty-five million TV viewers in the United States watched as an atomic bomb was detonated in the Nevada desert.

On the second of May BOAC began the first scheduled service from London to Johannesburg, with a jet aircraft, the Comet. The Orson Welles film *Othello* won the Grand Prix at the Cannes Festival on the tenth of May.

Chapter Seven

May 1952

Thanks to the planning of Colonel Light and those that followed him, Adelaide entered the motor age with broad streets. At the start of the fifties there was a demand for cars that the manufacturers and importers couldn't meet. The new Holden plant at Woodville was producing thousands of all-Australian cars, but there was a waiting list of over a year for these. The Toyotas, Hondas, and Mazdas were a thing of the future. Driving was a pleasure on the open Adelaide roads for those lucky enough or patient enough to buy a car.

Cars may have been difficult to come by, but getting a driver's licence was unbelievably easy. South Australia used to issue driving licences *without* requiring the applicant to pass a test, or, for that matter, to have ever sat behind the steering wheel. Such an applicant was Gerald Fisher.

Now that he had a girlfriend he wanted to be able to drive her to parties and outings, to picnics in the hills, to the beach in summer, and not have to rely on lifts from friends or on last trams. The Motor Registry Office was near the university on North Terrace, so he went and got a questionnaire, learned the answers, and presented himself for the examination. He answered correctly eleven of the thirteen questions, paid seven shillings and six pence, and was issued with a driving licence. Now all that remained was for him to learn to drive.

The Fishers owned a Morris Minor 1000. Gerald's father and elder brother both used it, mostly in the evenings and weekends, so the car wasn't often available. The first Saturday after he'd obtained his licence his father sat him behind the wheel and gave him a lesson for an hour, after which he showed him what was under the bonnet, how to check the water, oil, and battery. He even taught him how to change a tyre. Sunday morning he gave him another lesson, after which he told him to learn by himself.

"Gerald, I could sit next to you and give you another six or seven lessons, but I haven't the time and it makes me nervous. You take the car when it's available, drive about the back streets here for a few weeks, and then when you think you want to try yourself in traffic come and tell me. We'll go for another drive together when you're ready. Just let me know when you're going to take the car."

Three weeks later Gerald drove his father down to the Outer Harbour and back, passing through Port Adelaide in the busy Saturday morning shopping crowds. The following day he was allowed to take the car, having satisfied his father of his ability. On the way there was a hill with a level crossing at the bottom, so he took the long way around North Adelaide, beside the golf course. It took him a little longer, but he didn't feel confident about hills.

Arriving at St Ann's, he asked to see Evelyn. She had to be sent for, as he wasn't allowed inside the building. Evelyn was surprised to see him.

"Gerald, how did you get here?"

"I've got the car. I'm taking you for a drive."

"Where are we going?"

"Firstly to Richard's and then we'll see how much time we have. I'm getting a little practice driving. I have to have the car back by one."

It was a bright sunny winter's day, cool and crisp. They drove slowly around the parklands skirting the city, past the Botanic Gardens, past the playing fields of Prince Alfred College, and Victoria Park Racecourse, to Richard's home at Glenunga. Richard was sitting in pyjamas and dressing gown having a late breakfast. They joined him, had a cup of tea with him, then he got dressed quickly, and they sat around listening to records. Richard's father had a fine collection of early jazz 78s, 30s swing, 40s Bebop, and the latest Benny Goodman and Count Basie records. There were funny records — Spike Jones, Danny Kaye, and Stanley Holloway; and popular dance records — Guy Mitchell, Ella Fitzgerald, Carmen Miranda, and Frankie Laine.

"They're my sister's," Richard told them. "She buys all the dance records. I think we ought to get a new gramophone and start a microgroove collection. Then we can get classical stuff which lasts almost half an hour and you don't have to change the record every three minutes."

"But what about all these old records? How will you play them?" Evelyn asked.

"Simple. You have two needles — sapphire needles — bloody expensive but they last for years. That's another thing, you don't have to change or resharpen needles all the time. If I pass the finals, Dad's promised to buy me a radiogram for my room. We'll probably be doing our National Service next summer, Gerald, old pal. Looking forward to Nasho?"

The look on Gerald's face told him that he wasn't, a fact that he already knew.

"Like a dental appointment. Most of the guys who did it last year say that the whole thing's a big joke and a bloody waste of time. Did you see the article in *On Dit* and the reply to it from Canberra? It said the meat was full of maggots, and that was the only thing fresh on the menu. Most of the time was spent doing nothing or marching and being put down for being university students. When the yellow red peril comes swarming down though Indonesia, a mob of half-trained boys aren't going to stop them."

"What makes you think that they're coming down?"

"Because they're so many of them and Russia is arming them. Korea is a mess, the French are fighting a war in Indo-China, the British in Malaysia, and the Indonesians are half Communist already. The whole area's going Communist, like Eastern Europe, and we're sitting on enough land to settle millions. I tell you, Richard, we're in trouble. We can't defend ourselves. And now we're in ANZUS we could be in a war at any tick of the clock."

"So where do we go — England, the United States, or South Africa? How would you like to work in the diamond mines? Did you ever see that film *Rope Of Sand* with Corinne Calvert? The kids at school went ga-ga over her. Let's go to South Africa."

"If it's Corinne Calvert you like, you'd better go to Hollywood, or Paris, or the Riviera," said Evelyn. "She was in the film with Danny Kaye. It's a pity that you boys will be busy next summer. I thought that you might like to come fruit picking in Renmark."

"We'd love to, but Bob Menzies needs us to defend the White Australia Policy and to keep the Communists out. They'll probably have us unloading ships or digging coal if they have more strikes in the summer. That's where the Commies are — in the Trade Unions."

"I don't care what they get us to do, Gerry, as long as they feed us properly, no maggoty meat. It's not until December so let's worry about it after the exams. I wouldn't fancy doing Nasho and having to sit for a supplementary exam at the end of it."

"Are you crazy, Dick? You'll be getting distinctions, not a supplementary. I know that if I failed, I'd have to find a job for a year or give up all together. My father wants me to get a degree, but he's not going to pay for me if I lose my scholarship."

"Me too," said Evelyn. "Going to college is costing my parents a packet. I couldn't show my face at home if I didn't pass. Dad didn't want me to study. If I were to fail, I'd be stuck in Renmark for ever."

"We fail! But screw your courage to the sticking place, and we'll not fail..., to quote the Scottish play."

"*Macbeth, Richard*?"

"You mustn't say it, Evelyn, and it isn't anything to do with the University Professor who wrote the Organic Chemistry book. Not even an ancestor, as our Scottish chief's wife was too busy washing her hands and attending to bloodspots to have any children."

"I hope you know your *Animals Without Backbones* and your *Black's Flora*, as well as your Shakespeare."

"Black and Flora I have yet to meet, Evelyn, but *Animals Without Backbones*, must surely mean Louis Brown."

"Do you have to talk about a fellow student that way, Richard?"

Evelyn didn't like Richard sounding off about his pet hate. He often talked about Jonny's death and his suspicions. It was too horrible to contemplate that one student had driven another student to his death and Evelyn didn't want to hear about it. Richard continued, "The fellow is not a student, but an idle bastard, and if the likes of him ever gets a degree from Adelaide University, then they ought to fly the Jolly Roger from the Bonython Hall. The only place for Bully Brown in this university is in the medical school, in a tub of formalin."

Evelyn turned to Gerald, "If you have to get the car back by one, we'd better be moving."

Richard had upset Evelyn by his blunt manner of talking, the way he'd annoyed Joan Meredith, but by the following day she would forget what he had said to had upset her, and they'd all be friends again. For the present she wanted to take her leave of him.

On the drive back to the city she was quiet, but her spirits soon recovered. They drove down King William Street as the first Sunday trams were coming out of the sheds into Victoria Square. There were very few cars out, a few people returning from church or going to visit relatives for Sunday dinner, and families or couples enjoying the sunshine in the park down by the city bridge. They stayed outside the college for a quarter of an hour and he kissed her for the first time, the first time he had kissed any woman other than his mother. It was also a first for Evelyn. They both wanted to stay there, continuing to kiss and hold each other, but it was broad daylight and neither wanted to be seen, especially by the college head.

Evelyn went in to her three-course dinner of watery vegetable soup, roast beef with the vegetables boiled to death, and canned pears with thick custard. Gerald drove up the main road across North Adelaide, down the dreaded hill into Torrens Road, arriving home in plenty of time for dinner. Their food was much tastier than college food and the house was full of the smell of roasting lamb, which they ate with baked potatoes and pumkin from Mr Fisher's garden, followed by preserved peach halves from his tree. Gerald wanted to ask his mother if he could invite Evelyn for Sunday dinner. Then they could study together in his room and who knows, he might even get in a little kissing in private. He relished the idea, as he relished his mother's roast lamb and baked potatoes. Now that he could drive, his love life would not be restricted by such things as last trams and getting lifts — only by the St Ann's curfew, the needs of the other two drivers in the family, and his call-up in January.

The relationship between Gerald and Evelyn was subject to a lot of strain, mostly because she lived in the college and because they were both timid, inexperienced people. Other girls may have found ways of staying out late or all night, but not Evelyn. Gerald managed to get the car only every third or fourth Saturday night, and Evelyn went home to Renmark every holiday. He got into the habit of parking the car around the corner from the college, away from prying eyes.

Sometimes, when the weather was fine and sunny, they walked in the Elder Gardens watching the families and children feeding the ducks and swans, while the ever-present gulls flew and flocked about them eager for food. Once or twice, when he didn't have the car, they took a boat out on the lake, but they only rowed downstream away from the footbridge and the bend in the river. That section made them shudder, being spoiled for them, as it would always be, by the death of a colleague.

Whether it occurred to Evelyn's parents that their daughter was totally unprepared for life as a young woman away from home, they failed to do anything about it. Her mother told her that one day she would get married and feed her babies with milk from her breasts, which wasn't news to her. Her friends on a farm had told her that. When Evelyn began having periods, her mother told her that this was because she was capable of having children. She also told her that when she married, her husband would — she didn't explain how — put his seed inside her womb to unite with her seed making a baby, and that this must not happen until then. She picked up some additional information from her girlfriends.

One of the college girls loaned her a thin book on sex education. It had passed through many hands and was rather torn. Some pictures were missing. Books on sex education were sold by mail order from companies that advertised in *Man*, a magazine not read by Mr Robertson. Evelyn's mother wouldn't have known where to get such a book. Her husband would never have wanted his daughter to read such a book.

Evelyn read and reread the book. It answered some of the questions that she would like to have asked her mother, but it made her think of many more that it didn't answer. It didn't explain the feelings the book aroused in her, or the feelings she felt when Gerald touched her, or when they kissed. But the book did cover two topics that she had heard of but didn't understand: contraception and abortion — words never mentioned in her parents' home. Evelyn wondered what it would be like to make love to a man, then she put the notion aside. She had no intention of marrying before she got her degree or sleeping with a man before marriage. She wondered if Gerald would be that man; would they still be friends in three years time?

If the students thought that first term was difficult, then second term was worse. In Botany and Zoology they filled notebooks full of facts about plant and animal families and had to commit all this to memory. Their ability to reproduce this information in the finals would be the difference between passing and failing. Unlike Chemistry and Physics which they had studied in school, these two subjects required hours of swotting, committing facts to memory.

While they learned quite a bit about plant and animal physiology, ecology and evolution, the biggest section of both disciplines was classification, from the smallest micro-organisms to the tallest trees, and the most complex flowers and animals including man, the most complex of all. Many of the plants and animals they had never heard of, and were introduced to them from slides, pictures displayed in the practical classes, or real specimens if available. They learned out about Australian native plants, especially the eucalypts and wildflowers.

In Zoology they learned how all classes of animal life reproduced — some, like the many parasites of man and animal, leading very complicated sex lives. They learned about fertilization and development of the embryo, comparing the different kinds of animal development. Not being medical students they didn't cover human biology in any detail.

In practical classes they dissected dead animals. After opening up, examining, and drawing the inside of a frog they had to clean and mount the skeleton of a Queensland cane toad, *Bufo marinis*. It was big, ugly, poisonous, and smelled awful when Gerald boiled it in his mother's kitchen. It took a long time before the skin and flesh could be removed from the bones. Many of these were small and easily lost. Gerald had to rescue part of the toad from the cat — in fact rescue the cat from the dead toad which had enough poison in its skin to kill an army of cats. No bones were lost or broken. These he bleached with peroxide, then slowly and carefully, with the aid of *Tarzan's Grip*, stuck them together like a miniature of a museum dinosaur on a piece of black cardboard. This was one of a number of projects and essays that kept them busy.

The next big dissection was that of the dogfish, neither dog nor fish, but the Port Jackson shark, the most benign of the sharks that used to frequent Sydney waters, their population having been reduced by shark meshing, pollution, and the needs of first-year science and medicine students. Most of the specimens were about eighteen inches long, but Richard grabbed a huge fish about twice this size, thinking that a big fish must be better to work on. They set to work cutting into the formalin-soaked fish.

Formalin must be one of the nastiest-smelling chemicals, used to plague students of Zoology and Anatomy. You can almost feel the object gloating at you in front of your watering eyes. If ever an invention were needed, it is a gas mask for the use of students. Pity the poor cadaver in the medical school being dissected by second and third-year medical students, but pity more the students who, for two years, have to spend hundreds of hours in this teargas atmosphere, leaving the anatomy room with the smell of their toil on their hands and in their hair, like last night's cigarettes. *Truth* wrote editorials about lazy over-privileged students, having a good time at the public expense. Had the editor spent a few hours in a dissecting room, he would have written something different, assuming that he could see the paper through watering eyes.

One doesn't get used to the smell of formalin, one suffers it. So Gerald and Richard and the others did what was expected of them — cut into the soft cartilaginous bone of the dogfish, baring the blood vessels and the nerves, to the satisfaction of the demonstrator, drawing what they saw. Richard's drawing had a wicked smile, but his dogfish got its revenge on him by being tough, so tough that he broke six scalpel blades during the two sessions and had to work twice as hard as the others.

"Serves you right for being a hog and grabbing the biggest fish," Evelyn commented.

"I made a mistake. I forgot that we weren't supposed to eat it. I like fish and at home I always grab the biggest. You can't spare me another blade can you? I'll buy some more at Fauldings tomorrow. I can't go to the city smelling like Caliban, fresh from the cesspool."

"I smell of horse piss," said Gerald.

"You're lucky. You and Evelyn both smell the same. My girlfriend won't let me near her until I get the smell of the dogfish off my hands. It's ruining my love life. The trouble is, after I think it's gone other people can smell it. I had to eat in the kitchen last night. My Mom makes me undress in the laundry when I come home, and the other day the tram conductor asked me to vacate the non-smoking area. He said I was worse than a dozen fags — cigarettes, that is."

"I get noses turned up at me, too. They can't work out if I've pissed myself or invented a new form of booze."

"Have you noticed that Joan's using a double amount of that perfume of hers to smother the smell?"

"Yes," said Richard, "the combination of *Allure*, dogfish, and formalin is like champagne and shit. It's disgusting. Be a sport, Evelyn, and put the dear girl wise to herself."

There were excursions in the early spring. The Botany excursion took them by bus up into the Mt Lofty hills, where they noted the vegetation as it changed from foothills to slopes, sunny or shaded, and on into the dryer mallee area, with its stunted trees, where the wide Murray river meanders down to the sea a few miles to the south.

As soon as they set out in the bus, out came the Union Songbooks. They started with the traditional *Gaudeamus Igitur*, and moved on to folksongs, *Botany Bay* and *Click Go the Shears*, with songs from America (*The Streets of Larado*), France (*Alouette*), and a special favourite *The Foggy Foggy Dew* too lewd to be broadcast on the ABC. Another favourite was about the Prime Minister:

> *There'll always be a Menzies*
> *While there's a BHP,*
> *For they have drawn their dividends*
> *Since 1883.*
> *There'll always be a Menzies*
> *For nothing ever fails,*
> *So long as nothing happens to*
> *The Bank of New South Wales.*

and so on.

They followed this with *The Red Flag*, and *Lilian*:

> *Lil was a girl, she was a beauty,*
> *Lived in a house of ill reput-ee,*
> *She drank deep of the demon rum,*
> *And she smoked hashish and opium.*

and *Caviare*:

> *Caviare comes from the virgin sturgeon,*
> *The virgin sturgeon's a very fine fish.*
> *The virgin sturgeon needs no urgin',*
> *That's why caviare is my dish.*

> *I gave caviare to my girlfriend.*
> *She was a virgin, tried and true.*
> *I gave caviare to my girlfriend,*
> *Now she does what I want her to.*

After a break, while the lecturer told them the purpose of the trip and pointed out some trees and plants that they should note, they got back in the bus and started singing again:

I've shares in the very best companies,
In tramways, tobacco and tin,
In brothels in Rio Janiero:
My God, how the money rolls in.

My cousin's a starting price bookie,
My mother sells synthetic gin,
My sister sells sin to the sailors,
My God, how the money rolls in.

There were six verses in the book, but when they were finished, someone added a seventh, in a short solo:

My uncle manufactures French letters,
My cousin pricks holes with a pin.
My auntie arranges abortions:
My God, how the money rolls in.

Gerald hadn't heard that verse before, and burst out laughing, until he remembered who was sitting next to him. He looked sideways at Evelyn and was relieved to see a smile on her face too.

They stopped for lunch in the mallee scrub, among dry stunted trees, each with three or four trunks at odd angles. The boys lit a campfire in the sandy soil and boiled the billy, while some of the country boys, agriculture students, went out looking for rabbits to shoot with a .22 rifle. Seeing nothing live to shoot at, they took pot-shots at some tin cans instead. Gerald had never held a gun before. At the third attempt he hit the tin some fifty yards away. He won ten pounds that the boys had put together for the first person to hit the tin.

"Beginner's luck," he commented as he showed the tenner to Evelyn.

"Now I'll have to pay for the beer."

He had liked the feel of the rifle and the thrill of hitting something with it.

On the long slow drive back to Adelaide the country boys and a few other rowdies got together at the back of the bus with a few bottles of beer and wine. Everybody joined in more singing, with the boys at the back singing "rugby songs" at the top of their voices, starting off with *Roll Me Over In The Clover*, and proceeding to the *Ball Of Kerimore*, *Charlotte The Harlot*, and *Nancy And The Deacon*.

Most of the boys knew the songs, but most of the girls had never heard songs like this before. Gerald didn't join in — it wasn't the thing to do in front of his girlfriend. Finally she said to him, "If you want to go back and join Brown and the others, don't mind me. I know you guys like to drink and carry on. Go and enjoy yourself."

"I'm enjoying myself being here with you. Carrying on with Brown is not my idea of fun."

"Who would you like to carry on with?"

"That's a silly question."

"Would you like to carry on with Lana Turner, or Rita Hayworth, or Joan Meredith over there?"

"Evelyn, I'm a one-woman man — why would I want to carry on with anyone but you?" he whispered in her ear.

"You're sweet," she whispered back, kissing him on the ear. He felt that the whole bus was watching them and his ears turned crimson. The boys at the back were now singing:

> *Life presents a dismal picture,*
> *Dark and dingy as a tomb.*
> *Father has an anal stricture,*
> *Mother has a fallen womb.*

"Do you know the words, Gerald? I can't quite make them out. Isn't that *Deutschland Uber Alles*?"

"It isn't, just the same tune. If I'm not mistaken, this song appears in James Joyce somewhere, so it's quite literary. Some of these rugby songs are known all over the world, some are local. Mind you, they haven't got to the really crude ones yet."

"Well, let's hope they don't. My mind has been broadened enough this afternoon. If my father heard me listening to those songs, he'd wash my ears out with Lifebuoy soap."

"So you don't want me to teach you the words?"

"Next year perhaps, when I'm a little older. Some of them are quite funny, that one about Nancy and the Deacon, 'despite the fella's urgin' remained 'the village good-girl'. I almost had an accident when I heard that line. Who writes these songs?"

"I don't know. I've never seen them in print. They're part of our oral heritage."

The Zoology excursion was more sedate, the class being smaller and free of agricultural science students. It took place on the reef and shoreline of Port Noarlunga, where the Onkaparinga River reaches the sea. They all fitted into one bus, which took them to the water's edge, where a boat ferried them out to the exposed reef at low tide. The date and time had been carefully selected, so that they went out as the tide was ebbing, had two hours to look into the rock pools and collect specimens, returning with the boat as the water began to rise. Half the group stayed on the shore and did similar work on the rocks to the north of the beach. Early in the afternoon, the boat picked the party off the reef and took them to the shore group. It was an ideal day for the excursion, with a calm glassy sea and an overcast sky. They all wore hats and shirts over their swimming costumes to protect them from the sun, but it was a long day and they did get a bit burnt on exposed places.

Back at the lab the lecturer asked them what they had seen and learned on the trip, where each type of animal life existed, from the big black cormorants, commonly called shags, looking for fishes stranded in the pools, to the small black snails that clung to the rocks and corals at the water's edge and the crabs, anemones, and tiny fishes that inhabited the pools or crevices. Then the motley band went home to hot baths and to write their essays on the day's discoveries.

Gerald studied most nights until midnight, listening to classical music on 5CL and the weekly Jazz hour with Kym Bonython. He developed a liking for Count Basie, Hoagy Carmichael and the Modern Jazz Quartet. His father couldn't understand how he could study with the radio on, but it helped him stay awake. When the local stations went off the air and he wanted to work on, he tuned in to one of the all-night stations from Sydney. He only heard an occasional word, but it kept him company. Without it he found himself falling asleep, unable to concentrate. He also made notes as he read the prescribed textbooks, as this activity prevented him from dozing.

Chapter Eight

July 1952

June and July are winter months in Adelaide, with frequent cold fronts that bring rain and Antarctic air in behind them. In the Barr Smith reading room there were hot pipes for the students to warm their feet on, to induce them to stay in the room and read. The trees in the circle between the library and the footbridge were bare and the damp lawns free of students. Some days were crisp and crystal clear with bright sunshine without a breath of wind. It was on such a night that the Annual Science Association Dinner, at ten shillings a head, was held in the dining-room of the main railway station, also in North Terrace.

About a hundred and twenty students came to the dinner, together with staff members invited as guests. Before the meal they crowded into a small room, sipped sherry and nibbled at savouries until all the guests arrived. The dining room with its high ceiling seemed to dwarf the party as they entered it. It normally accommodated five times as many diners, travellers waiting for trains. The meal was fair average quality, better than the usual fare served daily to train travellers, and there was a more than an adequate supply of wine. They had a clear soup, whiting in bread crumbs, garnished with lemon and parsley, beef and vegetables with canned fruit for desert. It was probably as tasty as the food served across the road at the South Australia Hotel, where the important people ate, provided they wore a tie; the head waiter was very particular about ties. (His patience was stretched to the breaking point in July 1951, when half a dozen students came to dinner wearing dinner jackets and an assortment of elaborate ties. All that was lacking from their attire was *pants*: their gaiters and longjohns were displayed under their coat tails. *The Expedition To The South*, as it was called, was photographed by the papers, giving Adelaide a good laugh.)

Here at the Station there was sherry before the meal, sauternes with the fish, claret with the beef and port with the fruit — all local Tintara wines.

Between courses there were speeches. There were plenty of good and humorous speakers in the faculty, and as both speakers and audience were well wined they were accompanied by much laughter and clapping. After the last speech they sat in silent awe as Professor Emeritus Sir Kerr Grant recited Kipling's poem, "If", which he had recited every year at the conclusion of his physics lectures. K.G. and his "If" recital were an integral part of campus tradition. Then they crowded around the piano and started singing while they finished off the rest of the wine. To begin with, they stuck to the well-known university songs, keeping away from the lewd ones, and then went on to some of the recent pop songs. Louis Brown played the piano, and played it well.

Gerald spoke to Richard, "What's the matter with Joan Meredith? She seemed to be enjoying herself. As soon as we came over here to the piano, she took her coat and left with that 'someone isn't using Amplex' look on her face. *That's* not like Joan."

"Perhaps she's going to another party."

"No, I think it's because of that certain party playing the piano."

"Brown?"

"Yes, Richard. It's the same in Botany practicals. You know how Brown walks around telling everybody what to do, giving us the benefit of having failed the course twice. If he comes anywhere near her, she turns green and looks the other way. He doesn't talk to her either."

"So they had a lover's quarrel. She's going out with a third-year law student. A vast improvement on Brown."

"Anything is an improvement on Brown."

"Don't cry for Brown. His type attracts girls like flies. Watch it, Gerry — while we've been talking he's been making eyes at Evelyn. With Joan gone home she's the prettiest girl in the room."

"She was before Joan left, Richard. I'd better join her, or she'll feel neglected. Brown can't do anything with both hands on the piano."

Louis Brown was playing some recent pop songs, and one of the usually sober professors — but now far from sober — was singing like a schoolboy.

"I wanna sing speedboats. Speedboats are a-coming..."

Louis Brown played *Shrimp-boats*, *Riders In The Sky*, and *Mule Train*. Then the caterers hinted that it was getting late, so they stood as steady as they could as Brown played *God Save The Queen*. They collected their hats and coats, the professor's wives collected their husbands, and they proceeded slowly out into the station, some still singing, to the amazement of the people waiting for late trains. Next day was a Friday and there were lectures to present or attend.

Just as they were setting off for the tram Louis Brown spoke to Evelyn.

"Do you need a lift home?"

"I was going by tram with Gerald. Have you got room for both of us?"

"Where does he live?"

"Kilkenny."

"That's a bit far, but I can see *you* home, Evelyn. Where do you live?"

"North Adelaide, St Ann's College."

She didn't comprehend what he was saying, that he didn't have room for Gerald, no matter where he lived. He wanted her company exclusively, much the annoyance of her companion.

"It's on my way home. Hop in the car."

"Good. I can catch a tram from there," Gerald added, not wanting Brown to take his girlfriend home. "I'll come as far as the college."

Brown didn't like this, he only wanted to take Evelyn by herself, but he reluctantly agreed and the couple got into the back of the Ford Prefect that his mother had bought him to replace the sunken Morris Ten. They made themselves comfortable, Gerald with his arm around Evelyn. The big man watched jealously in the rearview mirror for a few seconds, then drove them the short trip to the college without saying a word. They thanked him and he drove away. He swore as he drove up the hill. Fisher had outmanoeuvred him.

'The bastard,' thought Gerald. 'He's after my Evelyn.'

"That was nice of Louis to give us a lift," she said.

"He shouldn't be driving. He drank a lot tonight. We all did. We're lucky he didn't drive us into the Torrens. I hope he gets home alright." That was a lie.

"Why," asked Evelyn, as they walked arm in arm to the college gate, "must you associate a drive with Louis with falling into the river? Because of Jonny Marco? Why don't you like Louis Brown, Gerald?"

"Nobody likes *Bully* Brown."

"Don't be silly. He was the life of the party tonight."

"He played the piano. I don't have to like him because he plays the piano. He has certain character flaws that do not make him likeable. He's a bully and a sadist."

"What evidence do you have of that?"

"The word of boys who were in college with him, and something much worse that we suspect him of, but we don't know how he did it."

"Of causing Jonny Marco to jump off the bridge. *That's* a dreadful accusation that you can't prove."

Evelyn didn't know why she was defending Brown. Was she playing Devil's Advocate, or was it something else? Louis had spent the evening watching her from that piano, looking up and down her figure like a farmer assessing a filly at a fair, like the men in the French movie that she'd seen at the Curzon. There was something frightening about Brown. She listened to Gerald as he answered her.

"He drove him home from a party and was the last person to see him sane. So he didn't push him off the bridge, but he must have done something. We don't know what he did or why, but we're sure that Brown did something."

"What could he have done?"

"I don't know."

"Good. Louis is generous enough to give a boy a lift, like he gave us a lift tonight, and you make him into an ogre. Who have you discussed this with?"

"Only with you and Richard."

"Yes, Richard. Anyone else?"

"No, but Joan Meredith knows something. She was very friendly with him — in fact they were more than good friends at the party, if you get what I mean."

"I *don't*."

Gerald was amazed. Hadn't Evelyn heard anything? Didn't she know about Joan?

"You know Joan's reputation. I wouldn't have believed it if I hadn't seen it with my own eyes. She and Brown went into the bedroom for half an hour, openly, not furtively. If you don't believe me, ask some others at the party. I'll give you the names."

"I believe you."

"Well, you know how extrovert she is and how talkative."

"You like her, do you?"

"I'm not going to let the fact that she's a bit of a trollop worry me. As long as she doesn't do it on the street and frighten the taxi-drivers, that's her concern. Yes, I like her, but it's you, Evelyn, that I love. Getting back to the lady with the millions, whenever Brown appears she makes a face like she's just trodden in dog droppings. She's been doing that ever since that party. We noticed her do it tonight. Did you see her waiting the day Jonny was buried, outside the cemetery? Brown wasn't at the funeral either."

"After Jonny pushed his car into the river? What do you expect?"

"That's another thing — *why* Brown's car?"

"Because it was the only pushable car."

"No, because Brown hurt him. I wonder what he did to hurt Joan Meredith?"

"Joan Meredith shouldn't make faces at Louis. She's a no-good tramp."

"Because she does what comes naturally?"

"Yes, and so is her brother. They're both notorious, rich, and promiscuous."

"You don't believe in sex before marriage?"

Gerald had never expected to ask Evelyn that question.

"I think that a girl should save herself for her husband, and a man for his wife."

"Fine! The rich Merediths are promiscuous. Louis Brown also isn't a decent person."

"Why?"

"Because he too doesn't match up to your standards. He was Joan's lover last March!"

"I only have your word for that."

"Don't believe me. Think what you want, but don't accept lifts from Brown, *not* when you've had a drink or two."

"Yes, Gerald. Now, hadn't you better go? You'll miss your tram."

Gerald didn't want to leave her this way. They were on the verge of a tiff. That was the last thing he wanted.

"Not until we've said goodnight."

They kissed and he held her close. They both felt that hundreds of eyes were watching them, when there were none. They both felt that the preceding conversation had somewhat soured the evening. Gerald resolved to keep Brown out of future conversations with his girlfriend.

Evelyn went up to her room to study, her concentration troubled by thoughts of Gerald, Louis, and the memory of Jonny Marco. She felt a restlessness that made her uneasy. The restrictions of college life were getting to her.

"This is more like a convent than a university college. I bet that the men's colleges aren't like this."

Gerald walked up the hill to wait for the tram in the cold night air, thinking about Evelyn. He felt a change in his feelings towards her. Until tonight he'd enjoyed her company, holding her close and kissing her good-bye at every meeting, but the intrusion of a possible rival had made him madly jealous and possessive. He felt a sudden fear at the thought of losing her, and she became much more precious to him. He wanted to possess her and never leave her. He wanted to marry her and make love to her, but he didn't know the first thing about love making. He didn't know what to do when kissing and cuddling weren't enough. What did Evelyn *want* and what would she *permit*? Would she stop seeing him if he tried to do something? Should he ask her or just try? He had only recently kissed a girl for the first time, *this* girl. He knew what he wanted to do, but he believed that nice girls didn't do that. It was a mistaken idea and he would pay dearly for it. He decided to talk to Richard. They met at eight the next morning.

"Grand dinner last night, Richard. I wasn't sure you'd be here for table tennis."

"I need a bit of sport to clear my head for lectures. How's your head, Gerry?"

"My head's alright, it's my heart that bothers me. I think I'm in love, Richard."

"Then your head is not alright. But don't worry, you'll get over it."

He was about to serve the ball, but put it down. Gerald had something on his mind and Richard was all ears.

"Richard, I really think that I'm in love with Evelyn."

"What have you two been up to?"

"Nothing. Not like you and your girlfriends. Evelyn's a good girl. How does a guy know *when* he's in love, Richard?"

"You hear a little voice whisper in your ear, 'You're *in* - love'."

Gerald wasn't in a mood for Richard's joke.

"That won't happen to me, not for a long time."

"Why not? You love the girl, so give it to her. If you don't, someone else will. Have you kissed her yet?"

"Of course I have."

"Well, there's some hope for you. The question now is where, and when? Her place is out of the question, it's too risky — so what about yours?"

"What! With my parents at home?"

"Don't they *ever* go away?"

"Not very often, and then they take the car. How would I get her to my place and back?"

They had the place to themselves. Richard was in his element, lecturing his friend about sex.

"Fetch her by tram, or taxi. Don't do it on the cheap. You have to create a big impression on her. According to Christopher Fry, you must do it with clean sheets and a well-polished floor."

Gerald remembered the quotation. He had been with Richard when they listened to *The Lady's Not For Burning* on the ABC. He was more concerned, at this time, to the reference to the aphrodisiac moon and the rising birth-rate.

"I can imagine the scene, Richard. 'Please submit quickly. My parents have only gone to the pictures, my brother's out with his mates, they might return any minute.'"

"Take a blanket to the university oval, join the mob."

"In the middle of winter? Perhaps I should take a tent?"

"Now you're really thinking, Gerald. The August holidays will be upon us soon. Wait till then."

"No good. Evelyn goes back to Renmark every holiday."

"So you go too."

He was walking around the table, bat in hand, gesticulating.

"I can't until she invites me. Her parents are quite strict, so the invitation won't come quickly, and they'll probably watch her like a hawk."

"Tell her you'd like to meet her parents. Get her to invite you. Have her out at your place. Then she'll have to invite you back."

"It isn't the same. A meal at our house, compared to a visit to hers. I don't even know if she feels the same way about me as I feel about her."

"Well, there's only one way to find out. A full frontal, physical approach. Show her how much you desire her."

"And if that doesn't work?"

"Doesn't work! Man you've been seeing the girl for five months. *That's* what she wants, what they all want, whether they know it or not. If that doesn't work, there's one last resort. Appeal to her motherly instinct and her pity."

"How?"

"Undo your buttons, whip it out, put it in her tender little hands and burst out crying. If that doesn't work, she's nothing but a hard-hearted bitch and you're better off without her."

"Richard, how often do you get your face slapped?"

"Quite frequently, but I get my end in frequently, too."

"Don't you feel bad about seducing girls and not marrying them?"

Richard protested, "I do not *seduce* girls. If I think a girl wants more than just a bit of fun, I back off, like I did with Dawn. She wanted to get serious, but I didn't, so we parted. We parted friends. Believe me, it wasn't easy, I miss her. I've got three years of study ahead of me and I can't contemplate marriage in the near future, and she didn't want to wait."

"Why couldn't you continue as you were for three years?"

"I don't know. I don't think that she, or for that matter any other girl that I've met, would have played second fiddle to my studies."

"But Evelyn would?"

"Yes, Gerald, I think she would. Don't forget that you're both students and you're studying the same subjects. It's an ideal arrangement. Make the most of it. And remember, faint heart never won fair maidenhead."

At about this time another fair maid, Joan Meredith, was in the basement of the corresponding building, the Women's Union. Checking to see that she was alone, she took out a lipstick and wrote on the wall of the ladies' washrooms:

BROWN HAS VD

She wrote a similar message in the toilets of the Botany Department, the staff toilets in the medical school, and the nurses quarters — places calculated to do maximum damage to Louis Brown's sex life. She was sick of that "we have a sordid secret" Pyecraft look that he gave her every time he saw her — that made her sick inside. He might have got away with murder, but she could still make his life miserable. Joan often thought of how she could hurt Louis Brown. This impulsive act would not be the last one. He would know she was responsible — if and when he found out.

Before the walls were cleaned, hundreds of women had read the message and told others about it. Brown was a well-known person in student circles, and quite a few students discussed the red message, wondering who had written it and why? Within a fortnight it was a big joke. The only person who didn't know about it was Brown himself. Girls stopped going out with him, some even went for check-ups, as the story spread, with embellishments that Louis definitely had VD and had given it to so and so.

Oblivious to the rumour, Louis Brown had entered his nomination for the position of Science Representative on the Student Representative Council. As he had a small group of friends, he had a chance of getting elected in a faculty where only a few of the students voted. A week after Joan had scribbled the messages she persuaded a friend of hers who worked on the student paper to put a comment in it.

When the next edition of *On Dit* came out, in the gossip section, *The Gleanings of Glug*, there was the comment:

BALSHAZZAR'S FEAST

On the sixth of July last, the Grand Hall of Babylon echoed to the raucous row of wine-filled students and their teachers, filling their bellies with rich meats and their brains with alcohol. Bacchus was idolised at this sinful gathering and there were voices raised and loud music. This evening of unbridled debauchery did not go unnoticed by the one that seeth and knoweth all (we do not mean the Vice-Chancellor). While the gluttonous participants were sleeping, an unseen hand was writing on the wall, on many walls, in letters of blood red, in the lime that normally covers the nether regions of our edifices. As it is written in the Scriptures: *"You have been weighed in the scales and been found wanting. An evening with Bacchus, a night with Venus, and the rest of your life with Mercury."* Well, L.B., it is said by Confucius that he who sleep with carpenter's daughter, likely to get circular sores. We hope that you have seen the light, the blue light.

To the worried young thing that wrote to us, asking if Koch's bacillus was the infective agent in VD, our answer is in the negative, depending on how you spell Koch. We wish to remind all students and LB that free medical counselling is available, and that they should take advantage of this service. Those who have not had their TB X-ray and Mantoux tests should attend to this, as it is compulsory. Good health to you all.

Gerald read the paragraph to Richard as they ate their lunch in the Refectory.

"L.B? Could that be Brown?"

"It is. A sign in the Lady Symon dunny says he has VD."

"How do you know? You don't piss there."

"Some of the girls told me. No, I haven't seen it for myself if that's what you think."

"Well, that's going to put him out of action for a while and spoil his prospects."

"For which particular girl?"

"Not for any girl. Of getting elected to the SRC. Who'll vote for him after this gets out?"

"Gerald, it *is* out. I've known about it for a week. There's a meeting in the George Murray Hall and he's speaking on his own behalf with the other science candidates. It'll be a scream. Let's go."

"I promised to wait here for Evelyn. She should be here any minute. Don't say anything to upset her, if you can help it. Don't say anything about LB having VD."

"Why not?"

"Because she thinks we dislike him without a reason — so as far as I'm concerned, I don't talk about him. I don't think I'll go to the meeting for that reason."

Just then Evelyn arrived back from lunch.

"Come and sit with us," said Richard, holding a chair out for her.

"We'll be late for the election meeting."

"I think I'll skip it, Evelyn. Do you want an orange drink from the machine? It's giving free drinks again."

"I want to go to the meeting. Aren't you coming?"

The boys got up and they all went to the George Murray Hall. Gerald was, on the one hand, keen to see Brown get heckled, but not keen to be with Evelyn when it happened. Brown was the third of four candidates who spoke. The meeting was orderly until then, rather dull in fact. As soon as he got up, someone called out, "Give the man a big clap." This brought the house down. Others called out, "clap", and Louis Brown, thinking that this was a sign of his popularity, smiled, enjoying himself but not the joke.

After he finished, one of Joan's friends called out, "Louis Brown, have you seen the writing on the wall?"

"No I haven't. I don't follow the question." A look of puzzlement replaced his broad grin.

"Are you positive?"

This also brought the house down. Brown stood on the stage, knowing that they were making fun of him and that he was missing the point. He answered the question, "If you were listening to what I said, you would have known that I do have positive plans for the benefit of students and science students in particular."

Again the hall was filled with laughter and Brown felt acutely embarrassed.

"What are they laughing about?" asked Evelyn.

"Don't you know?"

"No."

Gerald told her about the writing on the washroom wall, and showed her the paper. Thanks to the book she had so recently read, he didn't have to explain its meaning of VD.

"That's dreadful. He shouldn't be allowed on the campus."

"*If* it's true."

"It *must* be true. You said it was written on the wall."

"Evelyn, you're supposed to be a fair, rational person. Are you going to believe the scribble on a lavatory wall? Where's your sense of fair play?"

"*Who* would write such a thing if it wasn't true?"

"A girl that he had hurt, a rejected lover. Brown has a lot of enemies."

Suddenly Gerald knew who had put up that message. He wondered if Joan Meredith might have VD.

"Like you and Richard?" asked Evelyn.

"No, we aren't his enemies, but we aren't his friends either. This must have been someone with a real grudge, or a girl that he infected who wants to tell the world. Whoever did it must have had a good reason."

"Do you suppose that he knows?"

"He didn't before the meeting, but I'm sure he's finding out right now. He'll have to either admit it or prove it isn't so. But it's his business, not ours."

He was glad that she hadn't taken Brown's side. He hoped that she believed the story. Gerald was worried that the big man wanted to take his Evelyn away from him.

After the meeting Brown's friends told him of the graffiti and showed him the article in *On Dit*. He went to the office and demanded an apology. The editor agreed to publish a statement to the fact that Brown did not have VD, if and when Brown could prove it. He went straight away to the medical officer, and two weeks later there appeared a letter in the paper stating that LB didn't have the said disease and never had. But the damage was done. Very few people read this letter and Brown was not elected to the SRC. He wasn't invited to parties and had to look further afield for female company. He no longer smiled when he saw Joan Meredith. He knew that she had written the words on the wall and he hated her, as he had once hated Jonny Marco, but this time he had a real reason for his hatred. Joan, however, was rich and her family wealth gave them power. Louis couldn't take out his spite on her.

The same day Evelyn happened to use the toilets in the Botany department and saw the red scrawl. She knew that handwriting. It was Joan's. Gerald had told her that Joan had been Brown's lover. He had also hinted that Brown had driven a fellow student out of his mind. She didn't know what to believe.

Chapter Nine

July 1952

On the eighth of July an unusual edition of *On Dit* went on sale. Students were startled to see the following headline:

THREE NAKED WOMEN RUN AMOK IN BARR SMITH.

Eagerly buying the paper, they read on:

> We wonder if, but for that headline, you dirty-minded crowd would have bothered to read further into this paper. What a shame it is that we find it necessary to descend to the level of a certain Adelaide publication to stir you more-than-senseless-things into something which has a vague resemblance to life.

Under the article was a drawing of a tombstone, inscribed: IN LOVING MEMORY OF ADELAIDE UNIVERSITY. DIED MANY YEARS AGO. The drawing was labelled *"The University of Adelaide, as it is today."* Next to this was a picture of two similarly-inscribed tombstones, labelled *"The University of Adelaide, as it is proposed."*

The editor's purpose was to create interest in a meeting called to discuss the holding of an annual procession at the end of the term. In 1951 the procession had been cancelled.

Other startling headlines read: FIRE GUTS BONYTHON, and SRC BOMB PLOT REVEALED IN TIME. The editorials read THE SEX LIFE OF SOCRATES and ARE DUCKS PROMISCUOUS? The paper must have had some effect on student apathy, as at a meeting held on the twenty-fifth it was unanimously agreed to hold a procession in 1952 and to collect money for the Crippled Children's Appeal. July also saw an appeal for World Student Relief, to help students in Eastern Europe, India, and in Chinese and Japanese universities, where living conditions were appalling and textbooks almost unobtainable.

Charity begins at home. The National Union of Australian University Students decided to establish a fund to create scholarships and send Australian Aborigines to university, a project which eventually helped Charles Perkins become the first genuine Australian university graduate.

A meeting was held to launch the fund, at which the students were reminded of what the white Australians had done to the people who lived here before the arrival of the First Fleet. It was a sorry tale of killings and legal discrimination of an entire race that was given the minimum of an education and menial work, far away from the centres of population. Most students at the university had never seen a native Australian Aborigine. Most aborigines had never seen a high school, let alone a university.

After the meeting a group of students went around the grounds collecting money for the appeal. Most students gave. They came upon Louis Brown in the middle of the crowded Refectory and asked him and his friends to contribute.

"Not *another* bloody appeal? Last time it was for the Indians and the Chinese. We should have sent them French letters, not books. There's too many of the bastards over there. What's it for this time, *more* bloody foreigners?"

"No, Mr Brown, it's for full-blooded dinkum Aussies, a scholarship to send an Aborigine to a university."

"You've got to be kidding! To study, or be studied?"

The canvasser was beginning to regret asking Louis Brown for a contribution.

"Are you going to contribute — yes or no?"

"Stuff it, mate, it's a waste of money. You can't educate a black feller. They're monkeys, not human beings. Haven't you heard of the White Australian Policy?"

"Yes, and I'm not proud of it."

A crowd had gathered, including a couple of students from Tonga, black students. Brown didn't see them or he mightn't have said what he said next:

"Well, I'm proud of the White Australia Policy. I don't want to see slant-eyed yellow bastards and black monkeys living here, touching our white Australian women. I'm white, W-H-I-T-E, all over my body and I'm proud of it."

One of the Tongans stepped forward. He also was a big man, black as night, with cherry-red lips and a gleam in his eyes. He stood face to face with Louis Brown and it looked for a moment that he was going to hit him. Then he spoke to him in a soft, cultured voice.

"So your name is Brown and you are white? My name is Matthew White, W-H-I-T-E, and I'm a black man, Mr Brown. I'm black and

I'm *proud* of being black. I'm black all over. No, that isn't quite correct, my arsehole isn't black, Mr Brown, it's brown, B-R-O-W-N, brown — just like you."

Several students clapped as Matthew White and his friends left the Refectory.

July also saw the end of the monarchy in Egypt, the ousting of the comical King Farouk by a group of army officers led by General Naguib.

"Soon there will only be five kings left," he said, "the kings of England, Hearts, Diamonds, Clubs, and Spades."

There was more trouble in Persia with anti-American riots and the formation of a new government under Mohammed Mossedegh, the man responsible for nationalising the Anglo-Iranian Oil Company.

Australia's Frank Sedgeman won Wimbledon, with a seventeen-year-old Maureen ("Little Mo") Connolly winning the woman's title.

The Helsinki Olympic games were also a July event, with gold medals for several Australians, including sprinters Margorie Jackson and Shirley Strickland. Hungarian women swept the pool in the swimming events. Emil Zatopek, winner of the thousand metres in London, made it a triple this time, winning the five thousand and ten thousand metre races, and the Marathon — the first time he ever ran one! His wife, Dana Zatopek, took the Gold medal for the Javelin, setting a new Olympic record.

The Minister of Interior in the Menzies Government sent a cable to the team manager asking that they play *God Save The Queen* at medal ceremonies and not *Advance Australia Fair* as they had been doing.

Gerald and Evelyn went to the York Cinema to see the *African Queen* with Humphrey Bogart and Katharine Hepburn. They also attended a Youth Concert at the Town Hall, where Henry Krips conducted the South Australian Symphony Orchestra in a performance of a Mozart Overture, Beethoven's Seventh Symphony, and Khatchachurian's Piano Concerto. She kept the programme to show her father.

In the Chemistry Laboratory Joan Meredith played an old laboratory joke on Richard. She got him to place a big rubber bung on his forehead, and, placing a large funnel down his trousers top, told him he had to drop the bung into the funnel. In this position he couldn't see the funnel, or Joan pouring alcohol into it, drenching and cooling his genitalia.

In the last week of term the students not only attended lectures but they also got their posters and floats ready for the procession. This was held on the last Friday, during the office lunch break, at a time when most of the city workers could watch and contribute to the appeal.

A convoy of decorated trucks and cars left the gate next to the Bonython Hall and proceeded, after a police inspection to remove indecent signs, across North Terrace into Pulteney Street, turning into Hindmarsh Square, then down Currie Street, King William Street, North Terrace, and back to the Union via Frome Road. The favourite of the large crowd was a rickshaw cart with a pot-bellied man wearing a bathing costume, sunglasses, and a fez, like the recently-deposed king of Egypt, under a large banner labelled "FORSOOK". Other floats dealt with the Olympic Games, Rum Jungle Uranium ("We want the RUM not the URANIUM"), National Service, "the Goodside of Woodside", and the student enemy *Truth*. An army of students went among the crowd collecting money for the crippled children, but most of the onlookers kept their hands and their money in their pocket, as at the end of the parade the total collection was a mere one hundred and thirty-seven pounds. Procession Day had been re-established.

In the afternoon the annual Men versus Women rugby match was held. To make it a fair game, the men had to wear leg-length sacks with the end cut out for their bare feet and were only allowed to tackle with one hand. Rugby, it wasn't, but a free-for-all, with whoever managed to get the ball being manhandled or woman-handled by the other team and a lot of loose play. It's amazing what a rugby player can do with one hand. If a man looked likely to score, he was penalised, so that the women's team won as usual.

A special Procession Day Paper was published, full of alarming headlines, a parody of *Truth*. Page one was headed:

SOUTH AUSTRALIA SECEDES FROM COMMONWEALTH.

SA troops fighting on Victorian Border. The Premier, Thomas Playford will announce the secession at a special meeting of the Legislature to be held this morning...

Page three was reserved for sex and sensation:

TERROR IN THE CITY. GREEN SEDUCER AT LARGE

This told a ridiculous tale of women in fear, and of the police searching in vain for a man disguised as a pot plant, of an Irish priest who was an associate of two prostitutes, Miss Wanda Lust and Miss Harlot O'Scara. Next to this was a picture of Miss Wanda Lust, an over-endowed and under-covered beauty, with the caption *"Local entertainer says there was absolutely nothing at all between us."*

There was a Social page, making fun of the Adelaide papers, a page of bogus ads and a STOP PRESS. This told of a man in New Guinea who was arrested for desecration, for selling the ashes of cremated natives in cans labelled "Instant Man", with forty-three bones in every cup.

The paper was distributed along the path of the procession and seemed to cause more astonishment than amusement. It is probable that one or two office girls went home that night avoiding anything green, and wondering if their boyfriends would be sent to fight the Victorians.

Gerald and Evelyn did not ride the floats that year, but walked next to Richard's float collecting money. In the evening they went to the end-of-term Procession Hop, an informal dance held in the Refectory to round off the day's activity. Evelyn was particularly affectionate to Gerald that night, with good reason. The next day she went back home for the two-week August holiday. With exams in November, they both spent much of the holiday studying. They missed one another, counting the days till they would be reunited.

A sixteen-year-old Harrow schoolboy became King of Jordan on the eleventh of August. In July 1951 his grandfather, King Abdullah had been assassinated in Jerusalem. King Hussein's father was mentally ill and unable to rule.

In September US carrier-based planes raided an oil refinery in North Korea, at Aoji, only twelve miles from the Russian border. Richard Nixon, Eisenhower's running mate for the November presidential election, successfully defended himself against charges that he'd misused political funds. He is remembered as a supporter of Senator Joe MacCarthy.

On the first of October US troops shot and killed fifty-two Chinese POW's in a prison camp riot. The inmates were celebrating the third anniversary of the Communist rule in China.

Chapter Ten

November 1952

Third term was a time of intense study, culminating in November exams. The lecturers had to complete the set courses and went at it, hell for leather, right up to the final date for lectures. Practical classes were also intense, with the students getting their results and drawings up-to-date as practical books contributed marks, and an unsatisfactory book could fail a student. It was during a Botany practical that Louis Brown came to see Evelyn Robertson.

"Can I borrow your practical book, Evelyn?"

Before she could answer, Richard replied for her. "What for, Brown? You've had three bloody years to fill in a book, and you act as if you know more than all the bloody demonstrators, and probably the professor. Why do you want Evelyn's book?"

"I missed a class last term, when I was sick."

"Did you hear that, Gerald? Don't tell us what sickness you had, not in front of Evelyn here."

This annoyed Evelyn and her sense of fair-play. She had seen the retraction published in *On Dit,* stating that Brown was VD-free and that he'd never had the said disease.

Gerald fired the next salvo. "If you'd done the work like we did, instead of telling the rest of us what to do, and stayed away from the ladies of Sturt Street, you wouldn't have got sick and so wouldn't have to copy from our books."

"Listen to me, Gerald Fisher. All that talk about me last term was a pack of lies. I suppose it was you who wrote those messages on the wall?"

"*Me?* In the *womens'* toilet? You flatter yourself. I wouldn't write about you in the mens' room. Now, if you don't mind, some of us come to these classes to work, don't we Richard?"

"Yes, Gerald. Brown, be a good chap and get your Brown nose out of here. Come and see us in January, we won't be needing the books then."

"But you might," mocked Gerald.

All this time Evelyn, to whom the request had been made, said nothing, watching the other three as a spectator, with no sign on her face of what she was thinking. When Brown left, she spoke her mind.

"How could you speak to a fellow student like that? He asked me for my book, not yours."

"We wanted to save you the bother of speaking to the turd," said Richard.

"Yes, he's got a hide, wanting to copy your work."

"That's not fair, Gerald. He just wanted to catch up on a class he missed."

"So why didn't he do it last term?"

"I've helped you with things you've missed."

"Only when I didn't finish in time. Brown never does anything in practical class, except disturb those sitting near him. Ask anyone. He's going to fail again and probably never come back again."

"I'll drink to that, Gerald."

Evelyn, obviously annoyed, got up and went down to where Brown was sitting. She gave him her book.

"Bring it back next class, Louis."

"Thanks, Evelyn."

Then he went home to copy the work that he hadn't bothered to do in class, as he hadn't bothered to do the two previous years that he'd done the course.

Richard gave Evelyn a lecture when she returned.

"You are *so* gullible, Evelyn Robertson. I bet you didn't even look at his practical book and see if he's telling the truth. I bet you just handed it to him. Go and copy the lot, cheat, steal my work. Perhaps you'd like to write his exams for him."

"Thank you, Richard. That was spoken like a true Christian. Do you agree with your friend, Gerald?"

He had never seen Evelyn so agitated. He didn't feel that Brown was worth a row with his girlfriend, so he adopted a compromising position.

"They're your notes, Evelyn. I just hope you get them back. If you want to be kind to stray dogs, that's your business — just make sure that you don't get bitten."

"Helping Brown is a waste of time," said Richard. "He couldn't get a degree from a thermometer."

The two boys laughed, and at the other end of the room Brown heard them. He knew that they were laughing at him. For the next two weeks he copied Evelyn's notes, borrowing them after practical classes. She was the only person in the class prepared to do this. Joan

Meredith made a point of snubbing him, and as she was a popular girl in the class many others followed suit. Richard and Gerald mocked him when he came to borrow Evelyn's book, so he was glad to get out of the Botany laboratory. Brown wasn't very bright, but he was clever enough to find a way of making the boys pay for their mockery. He was also making himself very agreeable to Evelyn Robertson, the Achilles heel of his mockers, the only person in the class that treated him like a human being.

Some lecturers were boring, some interesting. The lecturer in Chemistry was entertaining. Dr Pennycuick had, over the years, given the same lectures week after week, with modifications from year to year. He told little chemical jokes, recited little chemical poems, and made *big* chemical bangs in his lectures.

One morning, during the lecture, he asked his assistant to open the tap over a bell jar full of hydrogen, which was sitting over two bricks, and to ignite the hydrogen, which burned like a bunsen burner *above* the apparatus. Then he explained that being a light gas, the hydrogen flowed upward out of the tap.

"But what is happening *inside* the bell jar? As the hydrogen escapes upwards, air is replacing it, making an explosive mixture and causing the upward pressure to drop."

He had timed this statement well, and as its implication sank in, the flame, without the pressure of the gas to keep it up, fell inside the bell jar. The resultant explosion lifted it off and back onto the bricks. It also lifted all the students off their seats, especially the girls in the front rows.

The concluding lecture of the year was a special one, with special jokes and poems. In 1952 it was especially special as Dr Pennycuick was retiring. The staff and students crowded the Rennie Lecture Theatre, two to a seat, sitting on the steps and standing at the back. There were flowers on the demonstration bench, balloons and bunting. A contraceptive filled with hydrogen, two foot in diameter, hovered above with a sign attached to it.

Evelyn was squashed against Joan Meredith and asked her, "Where did they get such a big balloon, Joan? I've never seen such a big balloon."

"At any non-Catholic pharmacy."

"Since when do they sell balloons at a chemist shop?"

"They keep them under the counter, in brown paper, like the Modess. Do I have to draw you a *picture*? They stop you from getting in the pudding club. Strong, aren't they?"

Evelyn got the message. She realised how little she knew about sex, what married people did in bed and how they practised contraception. She wanted to ask someone like Joan or one of the girls at the college to tell her more, perhaps to loan her another book on the subject, but she was too embarrassed to ask. She would have to learn by experience, the way that most young women found out.

The lecturer entered the lecture theatre, to be greeted by cheering and clapping, to deliver his last lecture. The older students moaned at his jokes and puns, cheering at the poems. After he finished, a representative of the students thanked him for having made the course so enjoyable and gave him a present from the students and staff. The big contraceptive balloon was released. Rising up above the campus and, catching the breeze, it floated off in the direction of the city.

On the third of October Britain's first atomic bomb was detonated on Australian soil, at Monte Bello Island, forty-five miles off the coast of West Australia. Later tests were carried out in the desert, north-west of Adelaide.

On the twenty-seventh Gerald's father told him of the death of Billy Hughes, ex-Prime Minister of Australia. Gerald knew that he was a controversial figure, but didn't know why. He asked his father.

"Gerald," he told him, "you young people have a good life now. It was different thirty years ago when Billy Hughes was Prime Minister. I was a kid in 1915 and we were at war, a war that many Australians felt wasn't their concern. Others were for compulsory conscription, sending boys your age to fight in France. It split the country and it split the Labor Party. There are a lot people of Irish descent here who had no love for the British. You know what happened in Ireland during the war?"

"They revolted, didn't they?"

"Billy Hughes was for conscription, so he and his supporters left the Labor Party (who were mostly against it), and formed an anti-Labor party. They held a referendum for conscription and lost. They held a second, and lost it again. A lot of people got upset by what he wanted to do and what he did. Someone threw eggs at him in Queensland and hit him. Conscription was a mistake. I'm glad we threw it out. We sent plenty volunteers to that useless bloody war. I hope you *never* have to fight in a war."

On the fifth of November Dwight Eisenhower was elected the thirty-fourth President of the USA, with Richard Nixon his Vice-President.

As a second-year chemistry student, Louis Brown was asked to help out with the first-year practical exams. He watched as the demonstrator prepared the unknown solutions and compounds that the students had to analyse, and helped with the labelling, checking, and dispensing of the samples on the benches. His job was to fill the reagent bottles and replace them on the shelves. Passing one bench, he noticed Richard's name next to that of Gerald's. Quickly looking about, he peeled off the labels on the bottles and reversed them on the two adjacent benches. They would now both have the original numbers, but samples different from that given to them. They would fail for sure. He finished his work and went away to gloat, as the students filed in for the exam.

He met the trio entering the laboratory.

"Good luck, boys. Good luck, Evelyn."

"Thanks, Louis," only Evelyn replied, the boys being too bewildered by this strange, friendly gesture.

"There," she told them. "If you're nice to people, they're nice to you in return."

"It must be a hard exam," replied Richard.

"How would he know?" said Gerald. "No one would trust him with the exam paper. He'd sell it for ten pounds a copy."

Evelyn frowned, and they all forgot about Brown.

Each student received a bottle of chemicals to titrate and calculate the concentration of its contents, with a second sample to analyse and determine what salt it was. There were four different sets of samples, each labelled with a number, arranged so that adjacent students weren't working on the same samples and couldn't copy or compare notes. They set about the task silently, amidst the hissing of the bunsen burners and the clanking of reagent bottles, as they went through the set sequence of tests to determine the nature of the unknowns and carry out the confirmatory tests. With the exam over, they crowded by the exits, comparing results to see who had the same unknowns as they had. Richard, Gerald, and Evelyn all went to lunch pleased with themselves, but the two friends had the wrong answers on their exam papers, and Brown felt pleased with his morning's work.

It was lucky that their papers were near the top of the pile and that the demonstrator in charge was curious to see how the exam went. He noticed that Gerald Fisher, who he knew to be a good student, got the wrong answer for his unknown salt sample and that his answer corresponded to a different unknown. He took the list and found that the same was true for the quantitative sample. This had to be some kind of mix-up. He looked at other results until he found Richard's. The *same* thing. He knew them both and that they worked side by side. The careless buggers had got their bottles mixed. They'd have to sit again in March.

Then he had another thought. Suppose the labelling was *wrong*. He went into the lab where the bottles were being cleared away and together with another demonstrator found the samples that the two candidates had used. It took them ten minutes to realise that one of the bottles was wrongly labelled, and another half an hour to check the rest. A meeting was held of all the demonstrators, at which the one who had labelled the bottles got a flea in his ear. No one knew of Brown's part in this; he went home annoyed that he hadn't succeeded, but pleased that he hadn't been found out. The two boys got good marks in the exam and the incident was forgotten. They were unaware of it.

Examinations were held in a number of different halls in and around the university. One of the last exams was Botany I, held in the Elder Hall on the twenty-fifth of November, a day to go down in University of Adelaide history as "Fanny Day", a day when the Vice-Chancellor lost his sense of humour and, sick of being the butt of student pranks, called the police. It was the day that the students perpetrated one of the greatest pranks in student history and became the envy of student pranksters the world over.

Built in 1900, the Elder Hall was the site of the Music Faculty, its ceremonial duties having been taken over by the Bonython Hall for those two days in the year that the hall was used. Set back from the ro badehind a circular driveway, a lawn and tall poplar trees, it was a rather drab building, grey in colour, Florentine Gothic in design, with a steeply sloping slate roof, topped by a number of small ornate spires and a large one in the middle.

During the early morning of the twenty-fifth, when the student body was either studying or had put their books away for the night, a band of students left their studies and took up paint brushes, ropes, and "Fanny". Early on the following warm sunny morning, an early bird, on his way to work, noticed something strange on the tallest spire high above the Elder Hall. It looked like a woman, a nude woman, perched precariously with her back to the ironmongery at the highest point of the building. The absence of any hair or arms soon made it clear that it was only a shop dummy, but silhouetted against the sky its true nature was not apparent to the crowd that had gathered on North Terrace. Someone alerted the university authorities who then became aware of the "footprints".

The first ones led away from the Vice-Chancellor's cottage just up from the Union Steps. They were three foot long, yellow in colour and led from the cottage gate to the front of the Bonython Hall, stopping on the way at the men's lavatory. One print was inches away from the seldom-trod carpet of the hall. The prints then went back to, then up the side of, the Elder Hall and down the other side. Some agile roof walker had even painted one on the slates, halfway up the roof. They returned to the residence from whence they had started.

It was as if some huge inhabitant of the residence, some abominable snowman, had taken a nocturnal walk and, King Kong-like, had scaled the Elder hall, leaving a damsel in distress tied to the very top. Nothing was ever found out about the "thing" that did this, apart from his shoe size. To the inhabitant of the residence, the VC, this was not only an act of vandalism, but a personal insult. Several brave, young, foolish men had risked their necks to make this day not just another dull day. The VC made a hasty decision and called in the police.

Gerald arrived at eight, intending to get in a little table tennis before the exam, which was set down for nine. Richard met him at the entrance to the building and dragged him in the direction of the tennis courts.

"Come and see what they've done. This is fabulous."

"I thought we were going to play table tennis."

"Look, you can see it from here. On the Elder Hall."

They were standing in front of the Botany Department, beside the tennis courts, where the Union Theatre now stands. Gerald followed

Richard's gaze, saw the dummy and couldn't understand what he was seeing.

"It's a dummy, dummy! Her name is Fanny. You should see the crowd up front. Come up and join in the fun. We've got to go there for the exam."

They joined the spectators standing beside the poplar trees, where they could see the dummy clearly. They listened to the other students.

"That's Fanny. She's got no arms."

"Yes, she's been a student here longer than Louis Brown."

"She's prettier."

"She's got more brains."

"How did she get there?"

"I think the VC took her up on one of his nocturnal strolls, looking for courting couples. He left his footprints. See them on the side of the building."

"I heard someone saying that they used a helicopter."

"In the middle of the night, in this graveyard! They'd wake up half of Adelaide. I think they used a trained cat."

"Have you ever tried to train a cat?"

"Or a giant gorilla."

"No, not a gorilla. The roof would have caved in."

Evelyn joined them ten minutes before the exam was due to start. They showed her "Fanny" and watched the expression on her face, first of disbelief, then of amazement as she worked out what was on top of the spire. Then they took one last look and joined the others streaming through the doors of the building that all the city was watching.

They were no sooner inside than a roar was heard outside, followed by cheering. It was still a few minutes to the start time, so they ran out, to see a huge black flag with the Skull and Cross bones that had suddenly risen to the top of the flagpole on the Bonython Hall. University officials, who had been gathering and wondering what to do about the dummy, raced to all the exits, hoping to catch the culprits. They found that the lock had been broken and went up the tower looking for the flag raisers. A concrete slab had been placed over the trapdoor and when the officials finally succeeded in getting to the flagpole, they found that an alarm clock had been set to start a device that raised the flag. Whoever had placed it there had probably left by scaling down the wall. If they were out there watching, they were really enjoying themselves.

The students went back inside and the exam got under way, ten minutes late. Meanwhile a one-hundred-and-twenty-foot fire ladder was brought in, the biggest that the fire brigade possessed, but it was well short of the mark and the university had to call in a professional steeplejack. Exam finished, Gerald and his friends handed in their papers and went out to see what was going on with "Fanny". She remained high on her perch as she had been all morning, like the figurehead on a sailing ship.

"I'm sick of studying," said Richard. "Let's go to a matinée."

"Alright by me. You coming, Evelyn?"

"I was going to have lunch at the college."

"Have lunch with us. Then we'll get a milkshake in Rundle Street."

"What's showing?" asked Gerald.

"*La Ronde*, at the Curzon."

"We saw it two weeks ago, Richard."

"Well, what about a psychological Hitchcock thriller, *Spellbound* with Ingrid Bergman and Gregory Peck? It started last week at the Mayfair. It's supposed to be terrific."

"It's a possibility. Isn't there anything lighter?"

"What about the *Lavender Hill Mob* with Alec Guinness?"

"Just what the doctor ordered. They say it's a scream."

After the pictures they went back to the university and were just in time to see the steeplejack bring "Fanny" down from her perch. It cost the authorities fifty pounds, but as the newspapers commented the next day, that was a small price to pay for a day's entertainment.

As to who took part in the rag, and there must have been many, it was thought that engineering students played a part. No one was ever charged with having any part in the night's work, the names of those involved remaining a closely-guarded secret known only to a select few. The police got as far as deciding that "it must have been a group of undergraduates". Fanny kept her mouth closed and returned to the university the following year to take part in undergraduate ceremonies and the 1953 annual procession.

Gerald and Evelyn walked slowly in the lengthening shadows through the gardens to North Adelaide and the college. They found a park bench almost hidden by trees, sat holding each other close, kissing and cuddling as they had often done on this secluded bench. Term was coming to an end and they would soon be separated.

"This time next week, I'll be in Renmark, Gerald."

"And a month after that, I'll be in Woodside. We aren't going to see much of each other this summer. Do you have to go back home so early?"

"Yes. Why don't you come and see me?"

"Where could I stay?"

"I'll ask Mom, but I've never asked before so I don't know what she's likely to say. You could stay in a boarding house. Lots of people let rooms in the summer."

"It would have to be after Christmas when I stop working. Do you think you could find me a room from Christmas to the second of January? My call-up's on the third."

"I'll try to find something. I'm working in the cannery labs until the end of February."

"I'm going to miss you, Evelyn."

"You'll be so busy marching and learning to shoot, and you'll make lots of friends. In no time it'll be the new term and we'll be back together. I'm glad I've got a job. I won't have time to mope and miss you."

"You *won't* miss me?"

"Of course I *will*, Gerald, don't be silly. If I had to stay home with Mom, I'd go mad. I'm just glad that I'll have something to do with myself."

"I'll come and see you when I have leave."

"There, it won't be so bad. I'll write to you."

"When are you going home?"

"On the fifth, two days after our last exam."

"I want you to come and have dinner with us on the fourth. I want you to meet my parents."

"Thanks. I'd love to come. Thanks for taking me to the film. I'd better go, or I'll be late for dinner."

"I needed a bit of comedy after that bloody exam."

"Gerald, when you come to Renmark, try not to say words like 'bloody'."

"Everybody says bloody. It's the great bloody Australian adjective. C. J. Dennis wrote a poem with bloody in every line. Bloody is as Australian as meat pies."

"Well, my parents don't say bloody, so when you're at my bloody place, I want you to mind your bloody language. I want them to think well of you, so don't talk like an undergraduate when you're with them."

"I *am* an undergraduate. Would you prefer me to talk like a soldier? If you think bloody is bad language, you've never heard real men talking."

"I've heard them talking when I wasn't supposed to, and I'm sure my parents have too. They're Methodists, strict Methodists, and they don't approve of smoking or dancing and alcoholic drink either, so if we go to a dance, don't say anything. I want you to get on with my parents."

"Didn't you ever go to a dance in Renmark?"

"Once or twice and I felt like I'd committed a sin. I smoked a cigarette once and I felt sick. I prefer dancing."

"Do you feel sinful dancing with me?"

"I don't believe in sins like they do. I've changed a lot this year. I'm not the country girl that I was a year ago. I used to try and live up to my parents' values, but no more. I wonder what I'd be doing now if I hadn't won a scholarship?"

"Well, you did, and I for one am very glad you did."

Exams over, Gerald and Richard had two free days and the weekend before they started work. Richard got the car and they spent Thursday afternoon at the Glenelg Beach. The sun was warm, the water cool and clear, and the beach almost deserted as schools were not yet on holiday.

"Pity you boys can't come to Renmark this summer. Dad tells me that there are plenty of jobs at the cannery. Everybody's working a lot of overtime and making good money."

"Will you be making good money?"

"Not as good as the men."

"What are you going to do with the money?"

"I don't know, Gerald. I've never had much money to spend. I might buy myself some clothes. I need a dress for dances, and some shoes. It'll be a change to buy my mother a present for her birthday without having to ask Dad for the money. What are you going to do with your wages?"

"You'll see."

"OK, surprise me. What about you, Richard?"

Richard was doodling pound signs in the sand.

"Normally I'd spend it having a good time, but as the army has other plans for us I suppose I'll be able to buy a few microgroove records. I'm getting a radiogram for Christmas if I pass the exams. Listen to us! We haven't earned a penny and you've got me spending it. What if we get the sack on the first day, Gerry?"

"I can't afford to get the sack. I need the money."

"Your father's cutting your allowance?"

"No, but I need the money."

"Got a girl into trouble?"

Richard saw by the expression on both of their faces that this remark had embarrassed both of them. It wasn't the kind of jest one made to a young man in front of his girlfriend, and not at this stage in their relationship. He changed the subject.

"I don't know why the army wants us. We'd be better off working along with the other scientists who are developing bigger and better weapons and more efficient methods of killing people. In the next war they won't use soldiers, just little men in white coats pushing little red buttons. The side with the best scientists and their hand on the button first will win."

"Sorry to shatter your illusion, Richard, but a war is being fought right now, in Korea, without atomic bombs or red buttons."

"So why are they testing the bloody things all the time? The Yanks have just let off an H-bomb that made the Hiroshima bomb look like a fart."

"What does a fart look like?" Gerald asked. "They're testing H-bombs because the Russians have them I suppose, or because it's good for business."

"You can say that again," said Richard. "There's more money to be made in guns and bombs than Meredith makes from his beer. If I'd had shares in copper and lead when the Korean War broke out, I wouldn't have to go to work next week. And what about uranium? We ought to hire a geiger counter and go prospecting for uranium."

"My father showed me a bit in the paper last month about Krupp, the owner of the factory that supplied the Germans with arms. They just let him out of jail where he served six years for war crimes. Would you believe it, he's getting a fifty million pound payment — compensation for war damage to the Krupps plants? Our prisoners who spent four years in Japanese hell camps — those that weren't murdered or starved to death — got the princely sum of thirty-two pounds each. Who says crime doesn't pay?"

"Mom's brother was captured in Malaya," said Evelyn. He died on the Burma-Siam Railway. Mom says a prayer for Uncle George every time she goes to church. He's buried somewhere over there so she can't even visit his grave. When you come to Renmark, you'll come to church with us on Sunday, won't you, Gerald?"

"Why not? When in Rome, do as the Romans do. Do your parents know that you don't go when you're in Adelaide?"

"I sometimes go."

"Is that what you tell them? Your 'sometimes' seems to me to be once or twice a term."

"It isn't a lie." Evelyn felt caught out, as if her father was listening, "If Dad asks me the exact dates, I'll tell him. I only go when I'm at home because I'm expected to. I don't go because I want to go."

"Are you an atheist, Evelyn?"

"No. I just don't believe in church-going and all the rigmarole. That doesn't mean that I don't believe in God. My parents enjoy their church-going and I go to please them. I believe that people should behave decently — in charity to the poor and doing unto others as you would be done by them. I thank God that I live in Australia and not in an atheist country like Russia, or in a war-torn country like Korea."

"What I don't understand," said Gerald, "is why, if there's only one God, there are so many religions, especially Christian religions? Why didn't the church prevent Hitler taking over Christian Europe? There's nothing like a world war for encouraging atheism. My parents only go to church for weddings and funerals. What about you, Richard?"

"Mom goes, but not Dad. I used to go with her, but I haven't been for ages. My sister goes with her, still."

"Well, we're all atheists."

"No, Gerald," said Richard. "Just a bit wishy-washy, that's all. Atheists say there's no God. I don't think we'd even be classed as agnostics, those who don't know, sitters on the fence. We're just run of the mill bush-Baptists, non-church-going Christians. What I don't like about religion is the way they try to attribute human attributes to God, like calling him 'he'. Why God the father?"

"Would you prefer God the mother, Richard?"

"No, Evelyn, and not king, or queen either. Creator, yes, by definition, but nothing else — no heaven, or hell, or angels, or all the other mythological claptrap."

"No Trinity, no Christ?"

"When I look at the miracle of nature, the complexity of living things and the beauty in creation, I think that that's enough. As for the rest and life after death, well, I suppose that I'll just have to wait and see. What the hell are we going to do all day in heaven?"

Evelyn brushed the sand off her legs, "If my father heard you say that, he'd make me promise that I wouldn't associate with you, and I'd get a lecture about meeting the wrong people at university."

"Tell him not to worry. You're in safe hands at St Ann's. As long as you're there you'll never get corrupted."

The boys recalled the words of a well-known University song, a parody of a Noel Coward number, and began to sing:

"Don't send your daughter to the Shop, Mrs Worthington,
Don't send your daughter to the Shop.
She's been wisely taught at boarding-school
That ignorance is bliss,
That petting with boys and other such joys
Are things that she'll never miss.
She's been sheltered
And doesn't engage in risqué talk.
Believes the yarn about the stork
And drinks but ginger pop.
So be sure, Mrs Worthington,
Keep her pure, Mrs Worthington.
Don't send your daughter to the Shop."

"Change the name to Mr Robertson," said Evelyn, laughing, "Why do they call it 'the Shop'?"

"It means the Degree shop, Evelyn, it's what they call Melbourne University. It was written there. I'm going for another swim. You coming?"

As the three of them went down to the placid water, Richard took a good look at Evelyn. It was the first time that he had seen her in a swimsuit. She was young and ripe and had a good figure. She was ready for love-making, he thought. 'They seem happy and very much in love, but they're so young and innocent, like Romeo and Juliet. Tonight they are going to be separated for the summer. I wonder if they make love — I doubt it. They wouldn't be here with me if they did. They'd be spending the last day in some secret place. *That's what I'd be doing if my girlfriend was going away.*'

He wanted to tell his friend to stop dallying and do it tonight, but he didn't find the opportunity or the right words. At four-thirty they took Evelyn back to St Ann's.

"I'll be ready at half past five, Gerald."

"Good, I'm just going to have a look at the shops."

He kissed her good-bye and Richard dropped him off in Rundle Street.

"Where are you two going tonight?"

"I'm taking Evelyn to dinner at my place. She's meeting Mom and Dad."

"And then you're going to meet her parents after Christmas. Gerry, are you hiding something from me?"

'Perhaps they are making love,' thought Richard.

"No, but I'm going to look and see how much engagement rings cost. Want to park the car and have a look with me?"

"And spoil a good day? When are you getting engaged?"

"We're not. But I'd like to, before we start Nasho."

"Why?"

"Because I'm in love with her."

"And she loves you?"

"Yes."

"So what's the hurry? Are you frightened that she'll forget you over the summer holiday?"

They both knew that this wasn't possible.

"No, but the idea of being separated from her makes me ill. If we were engaged, I'd feel better. I'd know she'd be waiting for me. I think Evelyn would feel better too if we settled something between us."

"Evelyn wants you to commit yourself? Is that her idea?"

"No, it's just a feeling I have."

"Gerald, do what you want. I hope you'll both be happy."

"You think I'm mad, don't you?"

"No. You're in love, and all lovers are mad."

"You think I'm making a mistake?"

"No, I think you've chosen the nicest girl in Adelaide, or Renmark to be precise."

"So *what* am I doing wrong?"

"Nothing."

"So why are you less than enthusiastic?"

"Gerald. Evelyn's the first girlfriend you've ever had, and you seem to be the only boyfriend she's ever had. You're both so young and inexperienced."

"We can't help that."

"You know something, Gerry. I've been making love to girls ever since I was seventeen, and I've been in and out of love a few times. I envy you, you're in love with a girl who loves you, and I bet you haven't made love to her. I'm an old man at nineteen and you are enjoying love in a way that I never knew it. I wish *I* had a girl like yours. Hold on to her. I would if I were you."

Gerald looked at engagement rings. He wondered if he'd get enough money from his summer job to buy one. Then he walked down King William Road and over the bridge to meet Evelyn. Just before the City Bridge he passed the Army Parade Ground with its barracks building, a reminder of his coming National Service. If it hadn't been for Nasho, he could have spent his holidays picking fruit, his evenings with his love. He swore to himself.

He thought of the last war — World War Two — of the bombing and the killing, and the atrocities. He thought of the German death camps with their gas ovens and piles of bodies. He thought of the Japanese, how they bayoneted twenty-two Australian nurses, leaving them dead or dying in the surf, how they cut off prisoners' heads with their Samurai swords. He thought of Tojo, who tried to commit suicide before he was hung, and of the emperor that they didn't hang. He thought of the Korean war, dragging on into its third year, with each side accusing the other of atrocities, and of the new ANZUS Treaty that committed Australia to the defence of South-East Asia. All he wanted to do was to finish his Science degree and be left alone to be with his girlfriend. 'What is the point of training to be a soldier? Only madmen want wars. Why can't the politicians do the fighting?'

Chapter Eleven

December 1952

When Gerald arrived home with Evelyn, his father was already there and everyone was ready for dinner. He introduced her to the members of the family, quickly showered and dressed. Then they all sat down to eat. The Fishers usually ate their main meal in the evening, but tonight Mrs Fisher excelled herself. There were candles and flowers on the table with the best linen tablecloth and serviettes.

They started the meal with pea soup made from fresh peas from Mr Fisher's garden, followed by rump steak and vegetables. For desert Mrs Fisher opened a bottle of her preserved pears and served them with whipped cream and passion fruit from the vine that grew on the garage wall.

"My father loves gardening too, Mr Fisher," Evelyn commented, when Gerald told her about the fruit they were eating. "He works in the cannery at Renmark."

"Evelyn's got a summer job there."

"When do you start work, Gerald?"

"Tomorrow, Dad. They wanted us to start last Sunday, but we only finished our exams this morning."

"Good. It'll keep you out of mischief. Lucky no one was killed putting that dummy up the spire last week."

"Don't you admire their guts, Dad?"

Mr Fisher swallowed a mouthful of potato and told Gerald what he thought of the "Fanny" stunt.

"Guts! Lucky their guts weren't spread over the roadway. And their brains - *if* they have any!"

"The VC called in the police. They have a list of suspects."

"Yes? Are *you* on their list?"

"Yes, I suppose I am, and a few thousand students, all the student body, except for the inmates of Evelyn's college who were all safely tucked into bed."

"Just as long as it wasn't you, my boy."

"I was here studying, Dad, or sleeping."

After dinner Gerald's parents went out to visit friends, and his brother took the car. He promised to bring it back by ten-thirty, so Gerald could drive Evelyn back to college.

Gerald was now all alone in his own house with his girlfriend. This was what he'd been wanting for months. They stood in the lounge room, listening to the sound of the car moving away and the noise of the cooler on the wall outside. Gerald decided that it wasn't needed any more so he turned it off. The venetian blinds were closed and privacy was theirs for a few hours.

'What do I do now?' he thought, wishing that he'd asked Richard for some opening gambits.

Evelyn was also apprehensive. 'What is Gerald going to do and how am I going to respond? We won't be seeing each other for a long time.'

Gerald knew what he'd like to do. He wanted to ask her into the bedroom and all that that invitation meant, but he couldn't just say, "Come to the bedroom. We've only got a couple of hours."

He felt that such a suggestion would be turned down and he was probably right. Evelyn loved Gerald, but she still had a romantic idea of saving her virginity until their wedding night. She was also frightened of getting pregnant. They sat together on the sofa, chatting awkwardly for a few minutes. Then Gerald put on a record, and they got up and danced. Nat King Cole brought them close together, the nearness of their bodies arousing their feelings. When the record stopped, they forgot about dancing and lay on the sofa as close as in the dance, kissing slowly and then passionately, with an intensity that surprised them both. Evelyn put her head to his chest and listened to his pounding heart.

Slowly Gerald unbuttoned one of her blouse buttons and then a second one. She let him, surprising both of them. Then he kissed the space he'd exposed between her breasts just above her bra. She took his head in her hands and kissed him on the forehead. They were both feeling strange, intense sensations. Emboldened by her response, he unbuttoned her blouse completely and started caressing her round breasts, feeling them soft and warm and inviting though her cotton brassiere. Evelyn felt faint; she was just about to ask him to undo her bra when he decided by himself to do this and sought out the means of freeing her breasts from their prison. As he undid the clasp at the back he wondered how on earth she managed to get her hands back there to do and undo the infernal device.

Had Gerald been experienced, he would have raced her off to bed, there and then, and in all probability Evelyn now would have gone.

But he dallied, kissing and cuddling his new found friends, her wondrous breasts, while she sighed and revelled in the sensation of a lover touching and kissing them for the first time. Her whole body tingled with delight and she wished he would never stop, a wish they both shared. He didn't know it, but she was his and he could do whatever he wanted with her. When he put his mouth to her taut nipple and gently sucked on it like a baby, the sensation was too much. She told him first to stop and then to continue, tears coming to her eyes.

"I love you, Gerald," she repeated over and over and he kissed her on the mouth, telling her how much he loved her. He turned off the light and they caressed for almost an hour. Now, more than ever, he wanted to make love to her that very night. He looked at his wristwatch.

"Wouldn't it!" he thought out loud, "It's almost ten. My parents will be home soon. I don't want to take you back to the college."

"I don't want to go, Gerald. I want to stay here with you for ever."

She wanted him, but she didn't know what she wanted, or how to tell him.

Gerald had a brief vision of his parents returning. He could tell them that they were going to bed and see if they were broad-minded. Perhaps if they just went to bed, they'd think he'd taken Evelyn home. Without the car? That wasn't likely. If only he had a lock on his door, he could sneak her out in the morning, back to the college for breakfast or she could go there to collect her luggage for the trip back to Renmark. But he didn't have a lock on the door and his mother was bound to peep in to say "good-night".

"What are you thinking about, Gerald? You look worried."

"I'm thinking that my parents will be coming home soon, and I don't want them to come. I won't see you again until after Christmas."

Evelyn sat up and covered her breasts with her bra. She was beginning to feel that she'd done something wrong, that she shouldn't be doing this before she was married to Gerald.

"Gerald, help me do it up. It's easier that way."

"So soon? I was just getting to know them."

"*Please*, Gerald. There'll be other times."

"Alright, but it's against all my instincts. You have such beautiful breasts, Evelyn. Tell me, do you wear a brassiere to bed?"

"Of course not, silly."

"What do you wear?"

"Guess."

Gerald felt light-hearted for all his frustration. "I know," he sang, "a silken nightie in the summer when it's hot, warm pyjamas in the winter when it's not, but sometimes in the springtime and sometimes in the fall, you slip between the sheets with nothing on at all."

They both joined in the chorus:

"Glory, Glory for the summer when it's hot,

Glory, Glory for the winter when it's not.

Glory for the springtime and glory for the fall,

When she slips between the sheets with nothing on at all."

Now that Evelyn was back in her bra and with her buttons done up, their passion had subsided but not their desires. They went into the kitchen to have a drink. They were still there drinking tea and eating biscuits when Mr and Mrs Fisher and Gerald's brother returned.

They drove back to North Adelaide silently, neither of them wanting to be separated from the other. They kissed and caressed each other near the college, Gerald sliding his hand inside her blouse to feel her breasts, soft and warm, their nipples hardening in response to his touch.

"You'll come and visit me, Gerald?" There were tears of joy wetting his cheek.

"After Christmas, if you like. We'll have a little holiday together before I go to Woodside."

"Can't you come earlier?"

"I've got this job here, and you've got yours there. There weren't any December jobs in Renmark. I asked, but there weren't any."

"Until Christmas, Gerald. I love you."

"I love you, Evelyn."

Evelyn was late getting in and was reprimanded. It didn't worry her, as it was her last night in college until next year. She went to bed and thought warm thoughts about Gerald.

"Why couldn't we spend this last night together? We love each other. It can't be wrong to make love. I know he'd marry me if I got pregnant, but we'd take precautions. We can't go on like this wanting each other so much and not fulfilling our love. Gerald's sensible, he'll be careful. We have to be, we can't afford to set up house just now. It wouldn't be a sin to give him what he wants, what I want too. Gerald, alone in his own bed, thought similar thoughts.

The following evening, as Evelyn helped her mother do the dishes, she confided in her, "I'm in love, Mother."

"With Gerald?"

She nodded. Her mother noticed something radiant in her smile. Evelyn had written a lot about Gerald in the past few months.

"And is Gerald in love with you, dear?"

"Yes, it's all we say to each other these days."

"Are you considering getting married and leaving the university? Are you, Evelyn?"

"Neither, Mother. We can't afford to get married."

"Would you, *if* you had the money?"

"I told you, Mother, Gerald hasn't even asked me."

"So how do you know that he wants to marry you, Evelyn — that this isn't just a student romance?"

Evelyn looked at her mother. She was upset by her remark, but only for a moment. It was a fair question.

"I know Gerald's feelings, Mother. I'll tell you one thing: I don't think we'll get married before we finish studying, but if we do, I'll get my degree and so will Gerald. That's another thing, Mother. We've been over the exam papers. We did well, Mother, all three of us."

Mrs Robertson knew about Richard.

"It's been a wonderful year, Mother. I've studied well, I've made lots of friends, and I'm in love. Thank you and father for doing this for me."

The following day, Thursday, the fourth of December, Gerald started work. He had breakfast with his father and they caught the tram together. He glanced at the headlines in the *Advertiser*. Eleven Czech leaders, leaders of the Communist party, were executed for "Treason, Titoism, and Zionism". Gerald wondered what kind of crimes were Titoism and Zionism? Another headline told of French troops fighting to retain a small fortress town fifty miles from Hanoi. It was good to be living in Australia and not in one of those trouble spots.

He met Richard at the department store and they went together into the personnel office. Richard went to work on the counter where they sold Christmas tree decorations and cards, whilst Gerald was sent up to the fifth floor to Parcel Dispatch, where he joined a team of permanent and temporary staff wrapping and addressing goods for local and country delivery. It was three weeks before the holiday and all of them were kept busy. As fast as he wrapped the parcels, trolley loads were wheeled into the dispatch room. They worked from eight-thirty to five-thirty, with a ten minute break for morning and afternoon tea and an hour for lunch. Gerald became an expert at wrapping and tying up parcels.

That evening he wrote to Evelyn, receiving a letter from her the following Tuesday. Their letters had crossed, the Christmas mail taking a long time. He received several letters before the holiday and there was no hint in them of what was to follow in January. They were happy letters in which she told him of her love and how much she hated being separated from him.

Instead of eating in the store's canteen, Richard and Gerald strolled down from Rundle Street to the university, where they ate their sandwiches with friends on the lawns.

Meanwhile, in the red brick buildings, the staff were busy marking exam papers and assembling the results. Meetings were held and the examination results finalised for posting and publication.

Ten days after starting work, as they went to lunch, Richard said to him, "Guess who was in the store today?"

"Tom Playford, Don Bradman, Moey Mackacky? Don't play guessing games, if you don't mind, Richard."

"Joan Meredith, in a huge sun hat and a summer dress so low that it would make a baby hungry. She was just passing by on her way to buy some presents when she noticed me, so she stopped to have a chat. I sold her some decorations for their Christmas tree. I wouldn't mind getting into her stocking on Christmas Eve."

"She should hang up her bra — it'll hold more presents."

"Gerry, I *do* believe you're growing up. She asked about you. Did she come and see you?"

Gerald frowned. It was boring work he was doing.

"No. It's 'staff only' where I work."

President-elect Eisenhower visited the troops in Korea in the first week of December. On the tenth, Albert Schweitzer received the Nobel Peace Prize for 1952. On the fifteenth, Christine Jorgenson returned from Copenhagen to New York after sex-change treatment. The former US soldier sold her story to *American Weekly* for thirty-thousand dollars.

On Tuesday the sixteenth, the examination results were due to be posted. During the lunch break the boys went down to see if they were out, but they weren't. At four, Joan Meredith came into the shop to seek out Richard.

"Dick, the results are out."

"You haven't seen mine by any chance?"

"I did make a few notes, but first ask me how I did."

"Hurry up, stop teasing and tell me."

"I passed all four, with a distinction in Botany. You and Gerald both got distinctions in Physics and Chemistry. That girlfriend of his got four passes, one distinction."

Richard's eyes lit up. He smiled from ear to ear.

"Evelyn? That's great! I can't wait to tell Gerry."

"I'll tell him. Where does he work?"

"On the fifth floor. Shoppers aren't allowed up there."

"I'm not just a shopper. My father owns twenty-five percent of this bloody store."

Joan took the lift to the fifth floor, walked right past the PERSONNEL ONLY sign and into the Dispatch Office.

"I want to see Mr Gerald Fisher," she told the Dispatch Manager. She spoke to the manager like a man requesting a shoe-shine.

"Who do you want to see?"

He was amazed by the woman's effrontery, and more so by her dress.

"Mr Gerald Fisher. There he is, over by that trolley."

She waved to Gerald.

"I'm sorry, Miss, but employees are not allowed visits while they are at work. You'll have to wait until five-thirty, when he finishes."

"In a pig's eye, I will. I have important information for him. Are you going to let me see him or do I have to call the Manager?"

"I'm only following company rules. If you don't go, I'll call the Manager and have you removed."

"You do that, my rude man, and see who ends up on his arse in Rundle Street — you or me. My father's a director of this emporium. Will you please get out of my way."

"What is your name, Miss?" Her manner had him flustered.

"Meredith, and I'm the daughter of Charles Meredith and grand-daughter of Sir William Meredith."

She stood there, as bold as brass, waiting for him to cower as most flunkies did when she told them who she was.

"I'm sorry, Miss Meredith. Be quick. We've got a lot of parcels to get out before closing."

'Spoilt bitch,' he said to himself. 'I wish I were your father so I could tan your hide.'

He had other wishes, as she passed him and he watched her cute backside in motion.

He left the two of them to talk.

"What are you doing here? Do you want to get me fired?"

"You won't get fired. Besides, I could get you a better job at the brewery or Meredith Mills. Gerald, you passed with two distinctions, Physics and Chemistry."

"Terrific. I went down at lunchtime, but they weren't posted then. I've been so busy here that I forgot all about it. How did Evelyn do?"

He wanted to hug and kiss her, but the manager was watching them. He knew he had done well, but it was great to have it confirmed.

"She passed, with one distinction. Thanks for asking how *I* did."

Gerald realised that he'd made a *faux pas*. He apologised.

"Sorry, Joan. How did you do?"

"I came fifth in Botany and I passed the rest."

"Terrific! Thanks for calling. I'd better get back to work. I feel great. Have you seen Richard?"

"Yes, he got the same pass as you. I'll pop down on the way out to say good-bye to him."

As she went, Joan thought about Gerald. 'Pity he's so gone on that Evelyn girl. He's rather cute. Rather innocent, like she is. Not at all like his friend, Richard. They're a sweet couple, Gerald and Evelyn, but if she were to let him go, I'd soon cure him of his innocence. But that isn't likely to happen.'

Later the Dispatch Manager spoke to Gerald.

"Would you like to work overtime today, Mr Fisher?"

"Not today. I just got my exam results. We've got a bit of celebrating to do."

"What about the rest of the week? Could you work until eight the rest of the week?"

"Sure. I could do with a bit of extra money."

"Are you a friend of the young lady who was here earlier?"

"Joan?" He decided to tease the Manager. "She's a fellow student, that's all. She wants to marry me, but she'll have to wait until I finish my studies and I've got a job. Don't mind Joan, her bark is worse than her bite. She certainly knows how to dress, doesn't she?"

'Undress!' thought the manager, but didn't say it. It was unnerving to have a VIP like Gerald working under him, a Meredith future son-in-law.

At five-thirty Gerald and Richard raced down to the university noticeboard to see the results for themselves. There were only a handful of students now, so they could read the lists and see how their fellow students had fared.

"Look, Richard. Louis Brown actually passed Botany I. Must have been Evelyn's influence. He's got a supplementary exam in Bacteriology. That'll spoil his holiday."

"The bugger must have worked this year."

"He bloody-well copied Evelyn's botany prac book. She felt sorry for him."

"I'd watch that bastard, Gerry. That bastard's got his eye on your woman."

"Don't worry about Evelyn, Richard. She's out of town."

"So will we be, Gerry, in two weeks time. Let's go up to the Richmond Hotel. I feel like getting pissed."

"We'll have to hurry. It's almost closing time."

Up at the Richmond bar they met up with a few of their friends. The place was full of men getting their bellies full of beer before closing time, with a sprinkling of students and university staff. They were lucky to get served before the six o'clock call of "Time Gentlemen, please. Finish up" was heard and everybody downed the last of the cold amber liquid, as the bar closed for the day.

"That was nice of Joan to come and see us, today," said Gerald. "She threatened to have my boss fired if he didn't let her speak to me. I told him that she's my girlfriend. He was so polite to me afterwards. I want to ring Evelyn and tell her that she's passed. Where can I call Renmark?"

"You could go to the GPO, but you might as well go home. We can't celebrate with the pubs closed."

"I miss her, Richard. I haven't seen her for two weeks."

"Get used to it, Gerry. We'll be in the army for three and a half months."

"We'll get leave. I'm going to Renmark on every leave."

"That reminds me of what Adam said to Eve when he had to go back to the army."

"What did he say?"

"'Eve, I have to go back to the army, leaves up.'"

As soon as he got home Gerald put in a call to Renmark.

"Evelyn, the exam results are out. We both passed."

"Thank God. When did you find out?"

"Today. Joan Meredith came to the store and told us."

"Gerald, you're not seeing her while I'm away?"

"Evelyn, I'm counting the days until I can come up to Renmark and see you."

The was a pause. Evelyn had bad news for him.

"Gerald. There's a problem. I inquired with all the guest houses and hotels. There isn't a room to be had in Renmark, for love nor money, not until the fifth. There are at least a hundred students here from the uni. Louis Brown is up here. It's the fruit-picking season and the holidays. T here isn't any room. I asked everywhere."

"Couldn't I stay with your family?"

"I asked Mom, but her sister and their family will be here until early in the new year. She's the one whose husband was killed by the Japs. She'll be sleeping in my room and the boys will be in the sleep-out. We'll be sleeping two to a mattress."

"I'd like that."

"I know you would, so would I."

Evelyn amazed herself by what she had said, but it came from her heart.

"Why don't you come down here?"

"Where would I stay?"

"Here, at my place."

"My father wouldn't agree."

"Haven't you any friends or relatives in Adelaide?"

"No."

"So when do I see you?"

"I'll come down for a day, after Christmas. I'll talk to Mom and then I'll write to you."

"Come down for a couple of days. I'll find you a place to stay. I'll ask the neighbours."

"I'll write. I love you, Gerald."

"I love you too."

He said this mechanically, as he put the phone down, disappointed that he wasn't going to go to Renmark to see her and not knowing when he'd be with her again. He had been so full of joy when he called her, but now he was so let down. He wanted to celebrate, but there was no one to do it with. He rang Richard, but he was out. He thought for a moment of ringing Joan Meredith but he quickly dismissed the idea. He went into the living-room where his parents were listening to the radio, to the Colgate-Palmolive play.

"Dad, I feel like having a beer. Like to share a bottle with me?"

"Sure, Gerald. I'll drink to your pass."

"What about you, Mom?"

"I'll have a shandy. There's lemonade in the fridge."

Gerald went to get the beer. There were two bottles of Meredith Bitter in the fridge.

"Why am I surrounded by Meredith wherever I go?" Even the lemonade was a Meredith brand.

Later he thought of Joan Meredith as he lay in bed. He felt a little guilty, so he tried to think of Evelyn and that last evening spent with her in the living-room, the night that should have lasted for ever.

On the twenty-second, Evelyn gave her father a letter to Gerald for posting. He usually put the family mail in with the office mail which was taken to the post office every morning. Unfortunately the letter remained forgotten in his briefcase, and it wasn't posted until after the holiday. On this occasion there was no intent to hamper her communication with Gerald.

Meanwhile the rush to wrap parcels at the store was over. On Christmas Eve Gerald was sent to the decorations department and joined Richard, selling. There were few customers, most of the public having shopped early. Just before lunchtime the personnel manager came to see them.

"I need you two in the warehouse next week. You're both good workers and I have to replace staff on holidays. We're transferring stock for the January sales. Are you available in January? I could use you during the sales, too."

"We're being called up for Nasho, I mean National Service, on the third. Aren't we finishing today?"

"No, your job application says until the thirty-first."

"I forgot. Does it matter?"

"I need you boys. Don't you want the money?"

"I'll stay. Gerald here has to go to Renmark for a couple of days."

"I'm not going now. Evelyn couldn't get me a room. I can work until the end of the month."

"Good. Do a good job, and we'll put something extra in your pay packets and save you places next summer. See you after Christmas. Stay sober and drive carefully."

The man wondered who Evelyn in Renmark was. He'd been told that the young man was Meredith's future son-in-law. How many girlfriends did this mild young man have?

"Why aren't you going to Renmark?" Richard asked.

"The place is full of fruit pickers and cannery workers. Evelyn tried all over town. Her house is full of bloody relations. She's coming down for a day."

"And a night?"

"No, damn it."

"How are you two getting on?"

"Considering the distance between us, terrific. I'm bloody frustrated. I don't know how I'll last until April."

"The army will see to that. Plenty of exercise and fresh air. They put bromide in the tea to stop you getting randy. I'd drink it if I were you."

"It's terrible being away from her. When I knew that I'd see her every day, I took her for granted, but the prospect of not being with her all summer is just too much. I should have failed my medical."

"Boy, you *have* got it bad. You need a wild weekend with Joan Meredith."

"All I need is a few hours alone with my Evelyn. You can stuff Joan Meredith."

"Your words, not mine but I couldn't have put it better. The only cure for the lovesick is to find another woman."

"I don't need a cure. Soon I'll be with Evelyn. I can wait. I'll get her to stay down here for a few days after Christmas. I wish we could get married when she's down here."

"They don't have married accommodation at Woodside. Where would you live next year?"

"It was just a wish. I can't afford to get married. But we could get engaged. I'd have to ask her father first."

"No you don't. You ask Evelyn. She isn't the frightened chicken that she was when she came to Adelaide. If she says 'yes', then you tell her father. The old bastard probably wants her properly wed. I gather he's a tyrant, so she'll be well shot of him."

'Maybe we could get married and move into my room until we graduate,' thought Gerald, but he didn't tell anyone. It was only a passing notion. He hadn't even proposed to Evelyn, but he would before he went into the army.

Chapter Twelve

December 1952

Gerald attended a party at Richard's house on Christmas Eve. He danced with plenty of girls, drank more than he usually did and spent the night — or what was left of it — sleeping on a sofa in Richard's room. Richard wasn't there. One of the girls at the party had invited him to spend the night with her, and he tiptoed into the room after seven. Gerald heard him and sat up.

"What time is it?"

"Go back to sleep, it's early."

"I can't sleep. It's hot and this sofa's too hard."

"I told you to take the bed."

"What have you been doing?"

"I've been doing a blonde physio, from Handorf, pure German stock. I couldn't keep my *hand orf* of her. She gave me a massage that I'll never forget. I've never had a massage like that in my life. Someone ought to open a massage club in Hindley Street and have the girls rub you. It's the best overture to shagging that you could imagine. It could be quite a business."

"Not in Adelaide."

"There's nothing as relaxing and stimulating as a good rubdown. You massage your woman and she'll do anything, and I mean *anything*. Start with her neck and shoulders and go where the mood takes you. When are you seeing your woman?"

"I'm waiting for a letter. She's coming to Adelaide later in the week. I think I'll get dressed and go home. I can't sleep, and you look as if you could do with some."

All this talk about making love had unsettled Gerald. He needed to sublimate.

"There aren't any trams, Gerald."

"Shit, I forgot."

"I'll have a few hours shuteye and then I'll take you."

Gerald got dressed as soon as his friend went to sleep. There was some cake left over from the party and some flat lemonade. He made a breakfast of this and wrote a note to Richard:

I'm walking home. I'll be there before you wake up. It's
only a three-hour walk. It'll be good practice for Nasho.

Thanks for the party. See you at work.

It was a warm sunny morning, just right for a hike. Gerald made good time walking down the gentle slope of Glen Osmond Road. By nine he was halfway across the city, walking down a deserted Pulteney Street towards the Bonython Hall. There was a service at Scots Church, but apart from this there were few people in the city. He crossed over North Terrace. The university was closed, so he walked on under the canopy of trees, past the Public Library, the Museum, and the stone wall surrounding Government House. He turned into King William Road out into the sunshine, down the road to the City Bridge.

Gerald stood for a few minutes looking down at the water and the gardens, remembering the times that he'd spent down there in a boat with Evelyn. He set out again, passing St Peter's Cathedral at the edge of the gardens as the morning worshippers emerged. At Montefiore Hill he stood under the outstretched arm of Colonel Light, looking over the roof of the Adelaide Oval at the city beyond. He had stood there with his parents when they lived in North Adelaide, and with Evelyn, looking at the same view. He recalled watching numerous cricket matches down there, tests played against England or Sheffield Shield matches. As a kid he'd collected empty bottles under the scoreboard, watching Bradman, Miller, and Sid Barnes make mincemeat of the English bowling, and Lindwall and Miller make kindling of their wickets. The Fourth Test would start soon, but he'd be at Woodside this year. Australia would soon be defending the Davis Cup too, down below at Memorial Drive.

The sun was now mercilessly hot. Gerald moved into the shade, turning his back on the city and bronze statue of the man who had planned it. He set off again at a brisk pace past Aquinas College towards Wellington Square. He crossed the square with its huge pine trees, frightening a family of magpies, magnificent birds, as he passed. The magpie, jet black and brilliant white, doesn't like intruders, especially in the nesting season, when it swoops at and frightens passers-by. Today Gerald, walking quickly, did the frightening.

Gerald's parents were having a late Christmas morning breakfast when he strode into the house, hot and sweaty. The radio was on in the kitchen, playing *I Saw Mummy Kissing Santa Claus* for the umpteenth time. The last two miles down Torrens Road had been mostly in the sun and Gerald was tired.

"Where did you come from, Gerald? Where did you sleep last night?"

"At Richard's place, Dad. I left just after seven and walked all the way."

"From Glenunga? You must be mad."

"Richard was sleeping, and I was wide awake and restless, so I decided to walk."

"You're barmy, boy."

"I wanted to get home. Did Evelyn ring?"

"No, were you expecting her to call?"

"I hoped she might. I want to know when she's coming down. There won't be any mail now for two days."

"I thought you were going up to see her this week."

"There's nowhere for me to stay. Mom, can she stay here for a couple of nights? I can move into Bill's room and she can take my room."

"I suppose so. What will her parents say?"

His mother didn't know it, but she'd hit the nail on the head. Her father wouldn't let her stay with a boyfriend.

"She's not a baby, Mom. She's been staying at St Ann's all year."

"Don't you go getting the girl into trouble," his father added and then wished he hadn't.

"Dad, Mom, we love each other. I want to marry Evelyn as soon as we finish our studies."

He didn't have the guts to suggest getting married *before* that time. He couldn't get married and expect his parents to support him and Evelyn.

"Have you proposed and has she accepted you?"

"No, but she told me she loves me. We can't get married now, but we *can* get engaged."

"Gerald, are you *sure*?" his mother asked. "Evelyn's the first girlfriend you've had."

"And the last, mother. We haven't discussed getting engaged or getting married, but when you're in love as much as we are, you know how you both feel. I'll ask her next time I see her."

"What's the big hurry, son?"

"Because I'm going away to do my National Service."

"You think she won't wait?"

"No, I think she'd feel happier if we were committed. I know that I would. When I come back from the army, we can get engaged. I want to spend my wages on an engagement ring."

"It's your money. If you're planning to get married as soon as you graduate, you'll need every penny you can get."

"So, we'll have to rent a place. I'll find holiday jobs and we'll save between now and then. When we both have degrees, we'll earn good money."

"You'll get a better start than we did," said Mrs Fisher. "We met during the depression when jobs were scarce. We couldn't get married until your father found work. Then we lived with his folks for two more years until we could afford a place of our own. Now that there's full employment, overtime, and good wages, we're doing alright."

"Yes, son. You get your degree, find yourself a place to live and we'll help with the furniture — but *not* until you've finished your studying. You're young and you can wait. Don't do anything silly. Young people in love can be silly sometimes."

"Dad, Evelyn and I are both serious about our studies. Neither of us had any intention of falling in love when we started going out together. Getting our degrees means a lot to both of us. We won't let our feelings affect our futures, I promise. I want to get a job in a scientific company, like Fauldings or perhaps the CSIRO. I might stay and work at the uni, but I doubt if we could get married on that."

Gerald went to his room and tried to read a book.

"*What* a way to spend Christmas! The person that I want to be with is two hundred miles away. I could ring and speak to her. It'd be great to hear her voice. Oh, what the hell, she'll be here in a couple of days. We ought to become lovers. We should have, that last time, when we were alone in the house together. Everybody else is doing it, why not Evelyn and me?"

He got up, moped around the garden, and then walked down to the school oval. Some boys were hitting a cricket ball and were glad to have another player. Gerald hadn't played since leaving school. He joined in, taking his turn fielding, bowling, and batting. He forgot his loneliness and how much he was missing Evelyn. By lunchtime he was in a good mood, having built up an appetite for the festive Christmas dinner. He showered and joined the others at the dinner table.

The air cooler had been turned on most of the morning. It consisted of a big drum of wire and dried seaweed, revolving in a water tray behind a big fan. It cooled and humidified the hot dry Adelaide summer air, but was very noisy, so you had to shout to make yourself heard. Mr Fisher's parents, his sister and her family had joined them for dinner. It was a noisy gathering. The dining table was extended, and lovingly laid.

Mrs Fisher had a big oven but it took all of her skill and organisation to cook the chickens, the leg of lamb, and the heapings of vegetables. As usual, it was all crisp and tasty, being quickly consumed together with beer and Barossa Pearl. The pudding was full of raisins, sultanas, and dried fruit, with threepenny bits strategically placed, so that there'd be one in every slice. Everybody ate and drank too much, and they sat bloated at the table, swapping yarns for an hour after the dinner. At four they had a cup of tea, and the guests left. They all helped with the clearing up and dishwashing, going out at five-thirty for a drive to Semaphore Beach.

Mr and Mrs Fisher and their two sons walked along the hard sand by the waters edge, past piles of brown dry seaweed, shells, bits of crabshell, and clear blubbery dead jelly fish, then out on the wooden jetty, where they watched the sun set, blood-red, into St Vincent's Gulf. It was an outing that they often took on hot days. There was usually a breeze over the water. The whole place smelt of salt water, fish, and seaweed, but to all of them it was as refreshing as *eau-de-Cologne*. They walked about the amusement park and the main street, where the train rang a bell as it puffed up the middle of the road into Semaphore Station.

It was late when Gerald got to bed. He lay awake wondering how Evelyn had spent Christmas. He rightly guessed that she'd been to church with her parents to please them.

The twenty-sixth, Boxing Day, was another holiday. The next day Saturday, and Sunday, Proclamation Day, there were no mail deliveries and no news from Evelyn. On the twenty-ninth, Mr

Robertson posted his daughter's important letter. The same day Evelyn received a letter from Gerald. In it he reminded her that she'd promised to come down and see him before he went into the army. She'd written to him. In her letter she'd told him of her plans to keep that promise. Now he wanted her to spend a few days in Adelaide.

She asked her mother, who told her to ask her father. She did and he said "no". She told him that she was going down for a day. He asked her if she had the train fare. She said that she did, from her wages. He consulted the railway timetable and told her what train she had to catch. She said "yes" to him, but she was annoyed. It wouldn't have hurt him to let her spend three days in Adelaide. If Gerald had suggested that they run away and get married that day, she would have accepted. She had mixed feelings towards her father: love, anger, and annoyance at being treated like a piece of his property. But, above all, she was afraid of him. All her life she had been afraid of her father. Two more years and she'd be out of his house, probably a married woman. She had a man in Adelaide who loved and desired her, who, she knew, wanted to marry her, even if he hadn't proposed to her. He had said that he loved her more times than she could remember. He had written it in all of his letters, as she had in hers, her letter which her father hadn't posted when he should have.

These were long frustrating days for Gerald. If there was a train or if he could have borrowed a car, he would have gone to see Evelyn. Instead he waited for news from her. On the twenty-seventh he and Richard worked at the store, moving trolley-loads of summer clothing in from the warehouse for the sale.

"Richard, let's drive up to Renmark after work. I want to see Evelyn."

"Your car or mine?"

"It'll have to be yours. I'll never be able to get ours. We'd be away overnight."

"Gerry. I get pretty free use of the car, but I don't think I could get it for a drive to Renmark, especially at only a couple of hours notice."

"You could ask. I'll buy the petrol."

Richard rang home and came back quickly.

"My folks are using the car tonight. I managed to get it for a drive tomorrow. I have to have it back by seven."

"That rules out Renmark. I'll just have to wait for Evelyn's visit. She'll probably be here for New Year's Eve."

"There's a party at Joan Meredith's. We can crash it."

"We couldn't do that. We're not invited."

"Everybody crashes parties on New Year's Eve. It's not as if we don't know the woman. She'll think it a compliment if we crash her party. You can bring Evelyn."

"*If* she turns up."

"She'll turn up."

Chapter Thirteen

December 1952

Evelyn arrived on the thirty-first of December at the railway station in North Terrace. Her train arrived at eleven but Gerald wasn't there to meet her. This wasn't surprising, the letter which her father had mailed two days before had only just been delivered and there was no one at home to read it. She called his home number, and when nobody answered, rang Richard's house. His mother told her that both boys were still at work.

"I thought they were finishing work on Christmas Eve."

"The store kept them on."

"I was supposed to meet Gerald at eleven."

"You could go and see him at the store."

Evelyn had written. She hadn't expected him to be working. She walked up North Terrace, located the store in Rundle Street and went to see the personnel manager. She told her story to the manager's assistant and that she had to see Gerald urgently, as she had a train to catch at five-thirty back to Renmark. Normally he wouldn't have done anything to help her, but Gerald was a friend of the Merediths, requiring special treatment. The man located the department where he was working and he was called to the phone.

"Mr Fisher, there's a young lady to see you."

"Evelyn? Is it Evelyn Robertson?"

"I think so. I'm putting her on."

"Evelyn, where are you?"

"I'm in the personnel manager's office."

"Great. I'll be right down. Why didn't you write?"

Evelyn wondered if and when her father had posted the letter. She hoped that he hadn't opened it. There were things written in it that he wouldn't have liked.

"I *did* write, Gerald. It must be the mail. I should have written earlier. Why are you still working?"

"I'll come down now and we can go to lunch. I'll tell you then."

They strolled down North Terrace and sat together on a park bench. Embracing, they held each other close.

"I expected to see you at the station. I rang your house and nobody answered. I should have telephoned yesterday."

"I'd have come to the station. Am I glad to see you! Where are you staying?"

"I'm not staying. I'm catching the five-thirty train."

The smile disappeared from his face.

"But tonight's New Year's Eve."

"Where can I stay? The college is closed."

"You can have my room. I asked Mom and she said that it would be alright. Besides, we're all going partying and we'll be up all night tonight. We're invited to at least four parties. Richard's got the car. We're going to crash the party at Joan's tonight. I'm so glad you're here. It's going to be the best New Year's ever."

"Gerald, I *have* to go home tonight. Can't we go somewhere and be by ourselves?"

She wanted to hold him close, have him caress her. She could see that he was upset.

"Why? *Why* do you have to go back?"

"I told my father that I'd be on the five-thirty train, or rather, *he* told *me*. He made me promise. There aren't any other trains until the second of January."

"I start National Service on the third. Please stay these last days with me."

"What'll I tell my father?"

"That you missed the train. It'll be the truth."

"And where will I tell him I slept?"

"At a girlfriend's house."

"Gerald. He isn't a fool. He knows that I came down to see you. He posted my letter to you."

"The one I didn't get? Tell him you slept at my place."

"He won't like that."

"He'll get over it, which is more than I will if you catch that damn five-thirty train."

He hadn't seen her for three weeks. Five hours was too little time. Where could they go?

"Gerald, Dad won't let me do that. He'd stop me from coming back to college next year."

"You're kidding."

"I'm serious, Gerald. Dad's old-fashioned. If he knew I drank wine and danced at parties, and kissed and cuddled with you, he'd probably take the strap to me."

"At your age?"

"Maybe not the strap. I've never given him reason, but if I don't turn up tonight there'll be hell to pay."

"Please do it for my sake. I want to be with you before I go away."

"Me too." She thought for a minute before continuing. "Gerald, I'll tell you what I'll do. I'll ring up and tell them I'm staying with a girlfriend. I just hope that Mom answers the phone."

"Ring up just after the train leaves."

"Dad will know I missed it on purpose."

"Evelyn, you're a big girl. You're nineteen, for Christ's sake. Many women your age are married and having babies. I think it's about time you began sticking up for yourself."

"You can talk. You're a man. You don't need your father's money to keep you at college."

"Yes, I do. My parents aren't rich. They've had to skimp and scrape all their lives. I'm almost twenty and they still have to feed and clothe me. Dad doesn't mind, as long as I pass my exams. If I failed, I'd have to go to work and study part-time. And pay my own way."

"There isn't much chance of that. You did alright this year. Besides, you live in Adelaide, so it doesn't cost your Dad too much. My father has to pay college fees."

"Wouldn't it be cheaper if you rented a room?"

"My father likes me being in college. He knows that I can't stay out all night or invite men to my room."

"I don't think that I like your Dad."

Gerald knew that he wanted to know this man's daughter carnally, that there was a conflict of interests. But he wanted to marry Evelyn, he loved her, and she loved him. Her father would have to surrender his daughter to him sooner or later. Why not *tonight*?

"He's alright. He doesn't want anyone touching his daughter, putting his little baby in the family way."

Evelyn was surprised how easily these words came to her lips. Nine months earlier, when she took the train down to Adelaide to start her studies, the thought that that she might have a sexual relationship would never have occurred to her. Now it was a question of when to sleep with her boyfriend, and how to prevent her father from finding out about it, and how to prevent a baby. That, she didn't want.

"Tell your father that I too don't want that to happen to his daughter, not until we're married. You will stay, Evelyn, won't you?"

"I'll think about it."

He had never asked her to marry him. They both took it for granted that they'd get married.

"Please stay."

"Alright, Gerald, I'll stay."

His eyes lit up and Evelyn felt happy for him, for herself, too.

"I'll see you after work. I'll get off early. You go out to my place. Mom should be home by two o'clock today. She'll lend you anything you need. Try and get some sleep. You won't get any tonight."

"I haven't even got a toothbrush."

"I'll buy you one. I have to go to the chemist."

He wondered if she'd know what he wanted to buy at the chemist, something without which there'd be no love-making.

"What'll I wear tonight?"

"Come as you are. You aren't trying to catch any boys tonight."

"Only you."

"You've already done that. I'll see you about five, five-fifteen. I love you, Evelyn."

By four-forty Gerald was on the tram heading for home and his love, with a new toothbrush and a packet of Durex in his pocket. Tonight was going to be the night they'd both been waiting for. Gerald wondered if they'd make it to the party or just stay home alone, while his parents and his brother went out to celebrate, or would he sneak in with her into her bed in his own bedroom in the early hours, or find a bedroom at one of the parties. First he would ask her to marry him, probably as soon as he got home, and then when she said "yes", as he knew she would, it would follow as night follows day, that they would consummate their love. He also had a big pay packet in his pocket. He would spend his savings buying her an engagement ring.

He arrived home, running from the tram stop, and burst into the house. The first person he met was his mother.

"Hi Mom, where's Evelyn?"

"She rang a few minutes ago. She's at the station."

Gerald's plans fell down, like the shards of a broken window. Evelyn had chickened out. Gerald felt as if a cricket ball had hit him in the *solar plexus*.

"No, Mom! What did she say?"

"She's going to ring again in five minutes, just before her train leaves. She went back to the store to say good-bye but she just missed you."

"Shit!"

"Gerald, please don't swear."

"She promised me. She promised me she'd stay. I won't see her again for months."

The phone rang. Picking it up, Gerald heard Evelyn's voice. He didn't hear what she said because she spoke so quietly.

"Why aren't you here?" He asked.

He was upset. It showed in his voice.

"Gerald, I *couldn't* do it. I haven't got the strength to stand up to my father."

"Why, Evelyn, why?"

"You don't know him, Gerald."

"Is there a train that I can catch? I want to be with you."

"Not after five-thirty."

"I'm coming to get you. Don't catch the damn train. I'm coming to fetch you in the car."

It hadn't occurred to him that the car wasn't home yet.

"I can't, Gerald. My father told me to catch the train. It's going in five minutes."

"To hell with your father. I need you, Evelyn. I love you, Evelyn. *Don't* catch the train."

"Gerald, please don't make it difficult for me."

"God, Evelyn, don't you understand? Doesn't our love mean anything to you?"

He was saying the first thing that came into his head in an effort to keep Evelyn in Adelaide.

"I'll see you soon."

"No you won't. You haven't made the slightest effort to see me. You kept me away from Renmark with that story about the town being full. I'd have come and slept under the stars to be with you. Then you said you'd come and be with me, and all we had was half a hour on a bloody park bench. I've got to go into the army. If you didn't want to come and be with me, why did you have to lead me along?"

"Gerald, it isn't like that. I want to stay — I can't."

"Cut the bullshit, Evelyn. I'm coming to pick you up. If you love me, you'll be there."

"Gerald, I love you. I'll make it up to you. Gerald, there isn't much time."

"Don't hang up. Talk to me until the train goes."

"I've got to go, Gerald."

"You do, and it'll be the end for us."

It was a stupid thing to say and he didn't mean it, but he was clutching at straws. He was an insane marionette, with his hormones pulling his strings.

"No, it won't. We've got a lifetime ahead of us."

"Stay with me!"

"I can't."

Gerald was mad. He began to shout without thinking, to say more things that he didn't mean to say, words that he couldn't take back.

"Damn you, Evelyn. Go to your bloody father. Thanks for a lovely visit."

"I didn't expect you'd be at work. Gerald, they're calling my train."

"Go back to your bloody father. Damn you, you make me sick. I wish I'd never set eyes on you."

He slammed the phone down, and went out to the garden. Then he remembered the terrible things he'd said. "What must Evelyn be thinking? *What* have I done?" He quickly returned to the telephone and picked it up again, but Evelyn was off the line. He kicked himself for being a bloody fool. For an hour he hoped against hope that she'd ring back, and when she didn't, he cried, sitting there in the late afternoon sunshine. She was on the train to Renmark. He went inside and lay on his bed, his face buried in his hands. He'd said words that he'd never meant to say, and yet it wasn't fair. She should have stayed with him.

"I'm sorry, Evelyn. I didn't mean what I said," he sobbed. Then he tried to think what to do. He decided to telephone her, but he'd have to wait until tomorrow. He didn't know when she'd get home, only that it would be late.

Evelyn put the receiver on its hook and stood for a moment stupefied. Then she slowly moved onto the platform and walked to the train like an automaton, not knowing what she was doing. When the door closed and she was seated in an empty compartment, she broke down and cried. 'What have I *done*?' she thought. 'Why am I on this train going back to my mean father and leaving Gerald hating and cursing me? I shouldn't have come to go away like this. I've spoiled everything. I've spoiled our love. Gerald doesn't love me any more.'

Two things that Gerald had said turned over and over in her mind: "It'll be the end for us" and "you make me sick, I wish I'd never set eyes on you". They hurt her as the speaker had intended, but she wasn't to know that he regretted his words as he said them, that he was as full of remorse as she was. One thing she knew: it was a mistake to be on that train. Later, she remembered this day and the worst decision she had ever made. She hadn't eaten anything since leaving home, and the conversation with Gerald made her feel quite ill. She sat all alone in her compartment looking listlessly out of the window as the train slowly passed under the Morphett Street Bridge and turned south. She saw the cemetery up on the hill where she'd seen poor Jonny laid to rest. That had been a sad day too. The train gathered speed, passing under Anzac Parade and the Glenelg tram line, starting the long winding climb up into the Mt. Lofty Ranges.

They stopped at Mt. Lofty to change engines. Evelyn considered getting off the train, but while she was hesitating it started up again and didn't stop until Murray Bridge. She didn't get out with the other passengers for refreshments. In her misery she didn't feel like eating. She lay down across three seats and fell asleep, not waking until the train was almost at Renmark. Every year as long as she could remember she'd spent New Year's Eve at home, and had never stayed up to see the new year in. Her father didn't believe in New Year's Eve. Meanwhile, the distance separating her and Gerald was widening.

Richard rang at seven. Gerald told him that he wasn't in a party mood, but he didn't tell him why, or what he had done to the woman he loved. He wanted to ring Evelyn and take back the nasty things he'd said to her, but he knew that she wouldn't get home until God-knows-when. At ten o'clock his mother persuaded him to go to town. He decided to ring Renmark the next day. He went with his parents to join the crowd celebrating in King William Street in front of the Town Hall. The building was outlined in lights, as it would be for the coronation and again for the postponed Royal Visit. A large crowd gathered late in the evening, dancing and merrymaking. Just before midnight they played *Auld Lang Syne* as hundreds of people joined hands and danced. Midnight chimed and 1952 became 1953. As they were in the city Gerald went into the GPO and placed a call to Renmark. An angry Mr Robertson told him that Evelyn was out. The Fishers went home, had one last drink to welcome in the new year, and then went to bed.

Evelyn was a mess by the time she reached Renmark. Her face was muddy from dirt and crying. She was dusty from the swirling desert dust that crept in and covered everything in the train, smudged with soot and cinders from the engine.

There was no bus at the station. Her father knew she'd be on the train; why wasn't he here? Evelyn was glad that he wasn't at the station; she didn't want to see him. Crossing the river bridge she shuffled slowly and sadly down the deserted highway. There seemed to be a party in every fourth house with loud music and plenty of laughter. She envied them their joy. She wondered if Gerald was getting over his disappointment. Had he gone to the parties as planned? Did he *really* mean it when he said that he was sick of her? Was he even now finding himself a less-distant girlfriend? Was he partying with Richard and Joan? She decided that she must telephone him the moment she got into the house. Would he be home or would he be out trying to forget about her? Then she noticed a familiar face. Someone had stopped his car and was looking at her. It was Louis Brown. He was on his way to pick up his latest conquest, a local girl.

"Hello, Evelyn. Where are you going?"

"I've been to Adelaide. I'm on my way home."

"Hop in the car, I'll drive you there."

Forgetting earlier warnings, she accepted the lift.

If she'd been to Adelaide she must have been to see her boyfriend, Flynn's friend. By the look of her, it hadn't been a happy meeting. Louis had had his fill of the local girls, but this one was different. What a prospect! Gerald Fisher's girl alone and looking miserable, on New Year's Eve! What a crime! What an opportunity not to be missed! He didn't ask her to the party immediately, but walked her up the path to her house. Mr Robertson was waiting for her in the living-room. He was sure that she'd missed the train, and frowned when he saw that he was wrong and again when he saw Louis Brown. What was his daughter doing in that man's car?

"Where's Mom? I want to talk to her." She wanted her mother to call Gerald for her to tell her that she was sorry, to find out if he'd meant what he'd said. She wanted her mother to comfort her in her misery. She didn't want to be with her father. It was because of him that she'd lost Gerald. It was all his fault.

"Evelyn! I thought that you missed the train."

"No such luck." There was that 'I don't trust you, Evelyn' tone in his voice — damn him. "The train left on time and arrived on time. Why don't you look at your timetable?"

"Your mother's gone to sleep. I suggest that you go to bed too. You look awful."

"I feel fine," she answered defiantly.

"Why did you go to Adelaide, anyway? You can get anything you want here in Renmark."

'Oh, how wrong you are, Daddy,' she thought. 'How wrong you are.'

He turned his attention to the man who had just helped Evelyn out of his car, like the perfect gentleman he wasn't.

"Who's this man? Did he come with you from Adelaide?"

"This is Louis Brown. He's here picking fruit during the summer. He's a fellow student of mine."

"Pleased to meet you, Mr Brown. What are you doing here, so late at night?"

"I gave Evelyn a lift from the station."

"So, what are you waiting for?" His rudeness was beginning to annoy Evelyn, who had obeyed him at great cost to herself and hated him at this moment, as no child should ever hate a father.

"I thought Evelyn might want to go to a party to celebrate New Year's Eve."

'Louis doesn't know that we don't believe in New Year's Eve in this house,' she thought. 'He's put his foot in it.' She was about to tell him politely, "No thank you, Louis" but her father beat her to it.

"We don't believe in such celebrations, Mr Brown. Evelyn's tired and going to bed."

Her annoyance with her father had reached breaking-point. She quickly and foolishly announced, "I'll be right with you, Louis. Can you wait until I clean up and put on a dress?"

"Sure."

She had shocked her father. He didn't want her to go with this man. He didn't like the look of him.

"Evelyn, it's after eleven."

"I know, Dad. I'd better hurry."

"Who's giving the party?" he asked Louis.

"Mainly students from Adelaide, in the packing shed."

"Will there be alcoholic drinks?"

"I don't think so," he lied.

"And dancing?"

"No. We'll just sit around singing songs and drinking orange juice," he answered facetiously. Mr Robertson didn't know whether he was or wasn't telling the truth. He didn't like this Louis Brown.

While Evelyn was showering and putting on her best dress, her father lectured Louis Brown on morality, with 'what's wrong with the youth of today'. Louis couldn't believe his ears. The man was against drinking, and smoking, and swearing, and mixed dancing (was there any other kind?). He was also against other things that he couldn't bring himself to mention, and Louis gathered that this included kissing and touching. Louis's habits included all of the things that this man despised. He listened attentively, agreeing with him like the liar he was, all the time thinking how he was going to seduce his daughter. What would the man say if he knew about the bottles of beer in the car, the cigarettes, and the contraceptives in his wallet?

As they left he told his daughter, "Be back by twelve."

"Don't wait up," she told him, still annoyed with herself for catching the train as he'd insisted she do. In the car she remembered that she hadn't telephoned Gerald. She decided to write him a letter.

Arriving late at the party, Louis brought in a kitbag with bottles in it, mainly beer. There was also a bottle of gin, but he kept it wrapped in a brown paper bag. He asked Evelyn to dance and soon her father was forgotten. He was a good dancer. She was thirsty and he gave her an orange drink with a thimble-full of gin in it. She didn't notice the taste so he gave her a second one with two thimbles in it.

"This tastes a bit off," she said, but drank it all down, just the same.

"It's canned juice. You're probably used to fresh."

At midnight, like the gathering in the Capital, they too danced *Auld Lang Syne*. She was a little light in the head from the gin, but everybody was kissing everybody else and it was a great party. Brown too kissed her on the lips, a little too friendly, she thought, and then they danced slow. He held her closely and his body felt so nice and cuddly next to hers. She had a few more glasses of "orange juice". The strange taste seemed stronger and her head ever so light. She was now drinking one-quarter gin three-quarters orange juice, and for the first time in her nineteen years she was under the influence.

At half-past twelve she said to Louis, "Louis, I think I'd better go home. I can't hold my head up. I'm so tired. Sorry to be such a pain in the neck. It's such a great party, but I feel so funny."

He gave her another drink. Afterwards, he realised that it was a mistake. It was the drink that broke the camel's back.

Louis didn't drive her home, not that she knew where he was taking her. He drove half a mile past her place to a road that ended by the river bank just out of town, but far away from the prying eyes of the townsfolk. There was a landing stage there, but no one used it at night. He'd been there several times with one of the local girls. That girl he'd dumped tonight in favour of Evelyn — or Gerald Fisher's girl, as he thought of her. He hated Gerald and Richard, and so seducing Evelyn was a delightful way of getting back at them for humiliating him in Botany classes. He'd soon have a story to tell them when he got back to Adelaide.

Evelyn knew that she wasn't home, but didn't have the slightest idea where she was. She knew they'd stopped and were sitting in the dark, but not much else. In the morning she wouldn't remember any of this. Louis put his arm around her, drawing her close to him. It felt so comforting. Louis had given her enough gin to make her half-drunk in his opinion — a quarter of the bottle. He didn't know that she normally didn't touch drink apart from the Science Dinner and a few occasions when she'd had a small beer with Gerald, nor that she hadn't eaten anything but tea and toast at five that morning. She had a strange feeling in her head, a stranger feeling growing in her stomach, and a very strange look on her face. She pouted her lips as he drew her to him and he too pressed his lips together, closing the gap for a kiss. As he did, he began to unbutton her dress.

He got the wrong signal from her. Her lips were tightly closed, as she felt an irresistible force rising inside her. It wasn't desire, it was *vomit*. Her stomach, rebelling against the way it had been abused, was expelling the vile gin. Evelyn was too drunk to move away or put her head out of the car window, and Louis was holding her tightly. She couldn't speak. Her tight lips were trying to hold back the inevitable, but they failed. The pressure was too great. They opened and the dam burst over the two of them. Gin, orange and gastric juice went everywhere — from the ceiling of the car to the leather seat and carpeting, over the back of the seats into the rear section. Evelyn continued, drenching both of them in the sickly fluid and dampening any remaining desire that Louis had for the poor sick girl.

Louis backed out of the car dragging Evelyn with him. She fell flat on her face, wetting the dust with her soaked dress. He helped her up, supporting her, wet and muddy, while he tried to think what he could do. He remembered her father, probably waiting in the sitting room counting the minutes. He could see the house from where he was standing. There was a light lit on the front veranda. He'd better get her home as fast as he could.

He had a rug in the back for 'shagging under the stars' and a beach towel. He wiped himself down and her too, feeling her limp womanly body under her wet clothes and cursed himself for what he was missing. He wrapped her in the rug and drove back to the Robertson house, arriving at a quarter to two. There was a light on in the living room and as he stopped he saw her father come to the front door. He assumed, and was correct in this, that the man was furious.

'I can't put her to bed,' he thought. 'It's just as well that he's here to take her off my hands.'

Louis Brown helped the semi-conscious girl out of the car and carried her to the front door, still wrapped in the rug.

"What do you mean by bringing my daughter home at this time and *why* are you carrying her?"

"Evelyn took ill, Mr Robertson. She was violently sick and went outside to throw up and must have tripped up."

"Why are you so messy? Were you sick too?"

"No, it happened when I was helping her. I think she's better now that she sicked up. She's very weak. I think she passed out on the way home."

"I'll wake my wife and she'll look after her. Put her down on the seat."

Louis put Evelyn down and supported her until her parents returned.

"Look at her," her mother cried out. "She's got dirt all over her face and her dress is ruined. What happened?"

"It must have been something she ate on the train."

He convinced the mother, but not the father. He was smelling something and not liking what his nose was telling him. It was the smell of liquor that he'd smelt so often on town drunks. He said nothing, dismissing Louis politely, his politeness hiding what was going on in his head. His daughter's behaviour had exceeded his wildest nightmares.

"You'd better go, Mr Brown. We'll take care of our daughter. Thank you for bringing her home."

Then he went inside and to bed, leaving his wife to look after Evelyn. Tomorrow she'd have some explaining to do. Mrs Robertson bid good-bye to the smelly stranger, turning her attention to her daughter. She took her to the bathroom.

Chapter Fourteen

January 1953

Most of Australia slept late on the first day of 1953, but not Mr and Mrs Robertson, in spite of their being tired after the night's disturbance. He was in a foul mood and his daughter was in for it when she decided to get up.

The phone rang at nine-thirty. Mr Robertson picked it up, thinking it might be that man who had brought his daughter back in a state of drunkenness. It wasn't Louis Brown. It was Gerald, who had been waiting all night to make this call.

"Hello, is that Mr Robertson. My name is Gerald Fisher. I called last night. I'd like to speak to Evelyn."

"My daughter is asleep. Ring back this afternoon."

"Would you tell her that I called. Please tell her I didn't mean what I said yesterday."

Mr Robertson didn't answer. He just closed the phone. He told no one in the house the content of the conversation.

Evelyn woke at about ten-thirty with a terrible headache. She wanted to call her mother to come and give her an aspirin, but felt too weak. When she tried to sit up, it was worse and her stomach ached. Her cheek was scratched, how she couldn't recall! She couldn't recall anything. She remembered being on the train, meeting Louis Brown and leaving for the party, but the rest of the evening was hard to remember. She wondered why she felt so bad and what she'd done the previous evening. She recalled the row with Gerald and lay there as still as she could, thinking about what he'd said and feeling sorry for herself. She cried a little, a bad omen for 1953.

An hour later, when her mother peered around the door, she still hadn't moved. She raised a hand to indicate that she was awake, and her mother came to the bedside.

"Are you alright, Evelyn?"

"No, mother. I've never felt so bad in my entire life. I can hardly lift my head."

"Come to the kitchen and I'll give you a cup of tea."

"I'd rather stay in bed. I feel so weak."

"I'll bring it to you. You were sick and ruined your new dress."

"The red one that Daddy calls immodest? He'll be glad."

"Yes, Evelyn, the red dress."

Mrs Robertson wasn't worried about the ruined dress — that was the least of her worries.

"What happened? Why was I sick? Who put me to bed?"

"Evelyn. I was asleep when you came back from Adelaide. Your father woke me up in the middle of the night and I found you covered with vomit and mud, semi-conscious on the front veranda. You went to a party and some young man brought you back, sick as a dog."

"Mother, I still feel sick as a dog. I vaguely remember meeting Louis Brown and drinking canned orange juice that tasted strange. Don't tell Dad, but there was music and dancing and I was having a good time."

Then her face lost its smile as she remembered the visit to Adelaide.

"Mother, I had a row with Gerald and he said such nasty things because I didn't stay, and it's all my fault because I was mean to him for not staying, and now I've lost him. He told me he's sick of me."

"Write to him when you're feeling better. He'll forgive you if he really loves you; if not, you'll get over it. Evelyn, did you drink alcohol last night?"

"No, Mother. I only had orange juice, tinned orange juice. I think it was that that made me sick. I wonder if anyone else was sick?"

"Your father is convinced that you were drunk."

"Mother, there was beer at the party and I danced. But I didn't drink anything but orange juice."

It didn't occur to Evelyn that someone had added anything to the juice, neither did it cross her mother's mind. She left Evelyn slowly sipping tea to return to her angry husband. When they sat down to lunch, he asked why Evelyn was not eating with them.

"She's still sick, Wes. I want her to stay in bed."

"Sick, my eye. She was drunk last night and now she's keeping out of my way. She's shamming. She needs a good thrashing, that girl does."

"She's too big for that, Wes. You know that I won't let you do it, so get that idea out of your head. I had a chat with her. She swears that she didn't touch any alcoholic drink."

"And you believe her?"

"Yes. She's always been honest with me."

"She's lying. We raise a girl to obey God's Commandments, then we send her to a university and she comes back a liar and a drunkard, and who knows what else."

"That isn't so, Wes. She's a good girl. She says that she didn't drink any liquor. Her word is good enough for me and it should be for you too."

"You're a fool, Sara, a fool." Wes was shouting now. "She came in here last night, stinking of alcohol, so drunk that she couldn't stand on her feet. I saw her with my own two eyes and so did you. I'm not going to pay for her education this year. She can give up that nonsense and get a job here in Renmark, where I can keep an eye on her."

Evelyn heard his shouting as she lay in bed, sick and crying. She hated that bully of a man, her father.

Bully Brown didn't return to the party. Judy, the girl he had dumped for Evelyn, would probably be there and might take him back with open arms. Women were like that — treat them rough and they desired you. But he was in a mess and so was his car. He couldn't go back to the party. Tomorrow he could resume his sport with one of them. He took off his clothes and, leaving them in the wash basin, showered and went to bed. He too was up early, washing out his clothes as best he could, cleaning the interior of his car with copious amounts of water. It was a hell of a job. Flying vomit had splashed and penetrated everywhere. His 'shagging rug' was still at Evelyn's place. He wondered if they'd clean it for him. It needed a good cleaning. In its time it had soaked up a lot of body fluids. It needed a good wash.

It took him until noon to complete the job as best he could, working in the hot one-hundred-degree sunshine. The fetid smell lingered, so he left the windows open. No one would steal a car smelling like that. He wondered what to do. To give up on Evelyn and go back to his 'sure thing' if she'd have him, or have another crack at Gerald's girl. He decided on the second course. It was only decent for him to see if the poor girl was feeling better. He also wanted to know if she was mad at him.

At three he presented himself at the Robertson front door in clean fresh clothes, smelling of Lifebuoy and aftershave. He was lucky — Mrs Robertson opened the door.

"Happy New Year, Mrs Robertson. I called to see if Evelyn is feeling better."

Something in his voice, or was it his looks, made her feel ill at ease, but he was her daughter's friend. She treated him civilly.

"She's getting dressed. She's a lot better but still feeling a bit queasy. My husband wants to know what you gave her to drink last night."

"Drink, last night? Why, we only had orange juice."

His story corroborated what Evelyn had said, satisfying her mother that her daughter hadn't been drinking.

"No alcoholic drink?"

"No, only orange juice."

Now she knew he was a liar. She'd never heard of a party with young people without beer. The Robertsons might not touch the stuff, but they were probably the only people in the town who didn't, and she knew it.

"Evelyn said the drink tasted funny. Did it taste funny to you?"

"A little. I didn't drink very much."

"So it didn't make *you* sick? Listen, Mr Brown, my husband is convinced that our daughter was drunk last night when she came home with you. I'm inclined to believe my daughter. I'm going to get my husband. I want him to hear what you have to say."

She returned with a very angry-looking Mr Robertson. Later on, she regretted that she hadn't got rid of that man herself, but later was too late.

"Mr Brown, I want to talk to you. I didn't think you'd have the audacity to come here again."

"I had to find out if Evelyn was feeling better."

"Listen, Mr Brown. You brought my daughter home in a state of advanced intoxication last night. What have you got to say for yourself?"

"I think that you're mistaken, Mr Robertson. We only drank orange juice."

For the second time that day, Evelyn heard her father raise his voice.

"You're a liar, Mr Brown. You're a liar, and *both* of us know it. I want you out of my house before I get a stockwhip and thrash the living daylights out of you. I suggest that you leave Renmark. When I speak to your employer you won't have a job anymore."

"You're mistaken, Mr Robertson. Evelyn really was sick. The orange juice must have been bad. I had a bad stomach this morning, too."

"Don't lie to me, Mr Brown. I've seen drunks before. This isn't the big city, but we have our share of drunks in Renmark. I don't want my only daughter to be one of them. Get out of my house. You're not welcome here."

Evelyn, dressed and looking pale, burst into the room.

"Louis is a friend of mine. He came to see how I am. Don't you *dare* throw him out."

She had never spoken to her father like this before. She was surprising herself. She was surprising her parents.

"He came to see if you were still drunk," he shouted back at her.

"Sick, father, sick. I've never been drunk in my life and that includes last night."

"Be quiet, you wicked girl, and don't lie to me or I'll wash your mouth out with soap. Get out of my house, Mr Brown, and don't ever come back. Evelyn, go to your room!"

Louis Brown went dutifully to the door. When he reached it, he felt Evelyn join him and take hold of his arm. She went down the steps with him while her father bellowed at them from the front door.

"You get back inside the house. You're not to speak to him, Evelyn. Come back, I tell you."

"I'll speak to whom I please," she shouted back at him.

"You'll get it from me when you come back."

"*If* I come back."

She got into his car and waited for him to drive off, not looking at her father, who was still shouting from the veranda. They drove off towards the centre of town.

"Louis, what stinks in here?"

"Don't you know?"

"Should I know? It smells like vomit. Was I sick in here last night?" She remembered her mother's inquiries. "Louis, did someone put something in my drinks last night?"

"Like what?"

"Like alcohol. What was that bottle in the paper bag?"

"I don't know."

"Didn't you bring it, with the beer in your kitbag?"

"Oh, that was gin."

Evelyn didn't know much about gin, apart from a line in *Pygmalion* about gin being Mother's Milk, or was it Mother's Ruin?

"Do you think that father was right? Did someone put gin in my juice last night?"

"Why ask me?"

"You didn't do it?"

"No! If I find out who did I'll beat his brains out."

"I'll tell Dad that it wasn't you. I'll make him apologise to you."

"What'll happen to you when you go home?"

"I don't know, I've never stood up to Dad before. I'll ring from Deirdre's place and speak to Mom. I'm sick of being a prisoner in my father's house."

"What'll you do now?"

"I'll stay out and wait till Mom tells me it's safe to go back. If necessary I'll stay out until tomorrow. I'll go to work from Deirdre's place. I'll have to make peace with Dad or he won't let me go back to uni in April."

"He'd do that?"

"He said he would. You heard him. He never threatened me before, but then I've never crossed him before. It's all because some smart alec fixed my drinks. Was I really drunk last night?"

"I don't know. One minute you looked alright and then you started being sick."

"Where?"

That he couldn't tell her. He couldn't tell her that he'd taken her down to the landing to get even with Gerald and Richard for treating him like a shit.

"All over the place. I suppose you *were* drunk. Drunks always sick up all over the place."

"No wonder Dad was mad. I'd better stay away from him. I'd better spend the night away from home."

Louis Brown liked the idea of her spending a night away from home. Things were looking up.

"Have you eaten lunch?" he asked her.

"I had a piece of toast. That's all I wanted. I haven't had a proper meal in two days."

"You should eat to settle your stomach. I've got some biscuits and some fruit in my room. Later we can eat at a cafe when they open up. We can't sit around in this heat and in this smelly car for much longer."

"You can say that again."

They went into the boarding house where Louis was staying. Evelyn felt a little apprehensive.

"I hope no one sees us and tells Dad."

"There's no one about at this time of day. Everyone is still sleeping off last night."

Gerald rang again at four in the afternoon. Mr Robertson answered the phone, still boiling with rage at his daughter's defiance.

"Who's speaking?"

"It's Gerald Fisher. I'd like to speak to Evelyn."

"Who is it?" he asked again.

"Gerald Fisher, speaking from Adelaide. I rang earlier in the day. I want to speak to Evelyn."

"I don't know you. What do you want with my daughter?"

This was the third time he'd called. This time he listened to him.

"I'm Evelyn's boyfriend. She came to Adelaide to see me yesterday."

"That's news to me. This is Evelyn's father. My daughter doesn't have any boyfriend and doesn't want to hear from you, and neither do I."

"I don't understand."

"My daughter just left my house with another one of her Adelaide boyfriends. I don't know when she'll be back or if she'll be back, but she certainly won't be taking any phone calls from strange Adelaide men. Please don't call again."

He slammed down the handset.

"Who was that?" his wife asked.

"What does it matter. Your daughter has some explaining to do when she comes back."

"Was it Gerald? That's her boyfriend in Adelaide."

"So who is Brown? How many boyfriends does she have?"

Now he was sure that his daughter had been misbehaving herself in Adelaide. By his strict definition she had been, but not by the accepted community norms — not yet.

"Just Gerald. I've never heard of Mr Brown until I saw him last night. I don't like him any more that you do. I have a horrible feeling about him and about Evelyn going away like that with him. Wes, I'm sure that she only went because you were so rude to him."

"She'll be back. Tell me about the other boy."

"She went to see him but he wasn't waiting at the station and they had a fight over the telephone."

"You let her go to Adelaide just to see a boyfriend?"

"He's going into the army this week."

She wanted to add, that they loved one another, but Wes might get the wrong idea if she said that.

"So who is she out with now?"

"I told you, I don't know. Why didn't you ask him, instead of shouting and ordering him out of the house? Evelyn would probably be with us now but for your behaviour."

"They lied to me. There was drink at that party and she did come home so drunk that she couldn't stand up."

"Why should she lie if it was so obvious?"

"I don't know."

"Perhaps because she's so scared of you. You're always bullying her. She's a young lady, *not* a child any more."

"If she wants to be treated like an adult, she should behave like an adult and not a child."

"Behave like an adult! It's adults that get drunk, Wes, not children."

"I'll ignore that comment. Tell me, where is our daughter?"

He wanted her back under his control.

"I don't know. *You* shouted her out of here, not me."

"I did not. I spoke to the man who took her out, after I told her to stay home and then brought her back in the early hours, drunk."

"So now she's with him, probably getting drunk again. Is that what you want?"

"What do you want me to do, race after her, find her and drag her back here? If I catch her drinking again, I'll..."

"You'll do what — beat her?"

Mrs Robertson was in control of herself. Her husband wasn't. Evelyn's sudden exit had robbed him of a target for his anger.

"No, Sara, I won't beat her. What do you want me to do?"

The father was worried too. His only daughter was somewhere with an evil man, just because he'd shouted at her. He wanted her back. He wanted the words that he'd said to her back, too, but they couldn't be unsaid. It didn't show, but he was hurting, as was his wife.

"Talk with her, Wes. Sit and hear what she has to say. She's a good girl. Listen to her side of the story. You called her a liar. You told a friend of hers to get out of the house. Why were you rude to that man? I think that the very least you can do is say that you're sorry."

"Do you want me to condone her drinking?"

"Someone put liquor in her orange juice. That's the only explanation."

"Mr Brown?"

"Maybe, maybe not. Let's give him the benefit of the doubt."

"If he did, I'll have him arrested."

"It isn't against the law. Evelyn is over eighteen."

"There ought to be a law against selling the vile stuff in the first place."

"So you'll speak to Evelyn and not shout and hit her?"

"I wasn't going to hit her."

"I thought that you might. I'm sure that she did, too."

"I was very angry. I'm still angry."

"At our daughter?"

"Yes, but if she's been telling the truth... If she has, I'm sorry."

Mrs Robertson was pleased to hear him say that. It meant that there'd be peace in the house. But she wasn't pleased that Evelyn hadn't returned.

"She was telling the truth, Wes, she was. Go and see if you can find her."

"Do I have to go out? She could be anywhere."

The possibility that she was at Brown's lodging house was something that he couldn't even contemplate. That there was no other place to go in the summer heat occurred to Mrs Robertson, but she was too frightened to make such a suggestion to her husband.

"Ring up some of the people that she may have gone to. Tell her that you're not mad at her and to come home."

"Where might she be?"

This was a question that neither of them wanted to ask, or to know the answer. Evelyn had left with a big man from Adelaide. It was hot outside, unbearably hot. They wouldn't stay outside in this heat. Was she still with him and what was she doing? This was on their minds, but they couldn't speak of it together. They rang a close school friend of hers, Deirdre Williams. She spoke to her mother. Deirdre and Evelyn weren't there.

"If she rings or calls in, tell her that her mother called. Tell her to ring me urgently. Tell her that her father's cooled down."

"What happened?"

"Wes lost his temper. He's cooled down now and wants to say he's sorry. It was all a big misunderstanding. If she drops in, tell her her father's not angry anymore."

After eating half a dozen biscuits and a couple of peaches, Evelyn began to feel herself again. The colour returned to her cheeks as her hunger subsided.

"I'd better go, Louis."

"Home?"

"No, I'll drop in on a friend and ring up later on. If Dad's still mad I'll sleep over and face the music tomorrow."

Louis Brown had a better idea, but he kept it to himself. The poor girl could spend the night with him.

"I'll take you there when it's a bit cooler. If you like, I'll even speak to your parents. I'll tell them where you've gone and fix things up for you."

'He'd do that for me?' she thought. 'He is a good person, not the bad person that they say he is.' She felt close to him at this moment, lulled into a sense of security by his kindness, his lying kindness.

"What if you can't? What if Dad loses his temper again? He might hit you."

"No one hits Louis Brown. Why should he? I haven't done anything wrong. I won't leave until he hears the truth and believes it."

"You're sweet, Louis. I don't know what I'd have done today if you hadn't been here. Why do people hate you?"

"Jealousy. I'm big. At school I was captain of the football team. I used to play a rough tough game and sometimes hurt other players. It happens all the time in football, but because I was big they used to call me Bully Brown. What was I supposed to do, ease up and lose the game? I have friends. You can't be friends with everybody."

They sat together in his little room, silently, Evelyn on the chair and Louis on the bed, wondering how he could get her over there with

him, wondering how to make a move without frightening her off.
Most girls when they came to a man's bedroom expected action, but
she hadn't come for that. She'd come for comfort, for a refuge. She
sat thinking of the events of the last twenty-four hours. Over and over
she heard Gerald saying, "You make me sick. You make me sick."
Did he mean it? Why hadn't he called? She started to cry. Louis had
no idea why she was crying, but it was the opening he'd been looking
for. He moved across to her to comfort her. He took hold of her
hand. What she needed was a little loving.

He lifted her up from the chair and put his big warm arms about
her. It felt so natural that he should do this. When he kissed her
tenderly and comfortingly on the cheek, it was like a father kissing a
child. He held her tight, pressing his body close to her, holding her
neck in his hand, his other hand massaging her back making her feel
warm and wanted all over, making her feel feelings deep down inside
which both tingled and worried her. Her thin summer blouse pressed
against his chest; she could feel her nipples hardening, pressing into
him. He held his hand pressed against the small of her back and slid
one leg slowly between hers, pressing against the lower extremity of
her body, against her erogenous zone, with a devastating effect on her
whole being. She felt a sensation deep inside her which was taking
over her body, a sensation that stopped her from backing off, and she
pressed herself against him with all of her might, lest the sensation
cease. It didn't. He held her by the back of her head, kissing her
softly at first then brutally on the lips. At first she pulled back, and
then kissed him back, again and again, as they fell back onto the bed.
She was out of her depth and she didn't know what to do.

She tried to pull away but he held her, slowly sliding his hand
under her dress, and she felt him slowly slide it down past her thighs
into parts that no man had ever touched. She wanted to resist, but
was powerless under him. The effect of what he was doing was too
overpowering. There were two beings inside her — one telling her to
get up and run, and a second enjoying the feeling of being a woman.
As he removed her panties and started to stroke the most sensitive part
of her body, she gave in, moving with the never-ending sensation,
holding Louis by the shoulders, kissing him without stopping. She felt
him push and probe with a mixture of pain and pleasure and loss, as
his fingers entered her and she was no longer a virgin. 'Poor Gerald,'
she thought for a second and soon forgot him, as Louis removed the

192

last pieces of their clothing, placing her on the crumpled sheets. She
knew what was coming next but was unable to stop herself or Louis at
this stage, taking a quick look, watching with fascination and horror,
as the man on top of her quickly put on a contraceptive.

'Thank God,' she thought. 'Why didn't *I* think of that?'

Then he slid under the covers and took her into his arms. She
expected him to get on top of her at once and put the fearsome-looking
thing into her. She wanted to escape, but he resumed his playing with
her body, playing with her breasts, with her thighs and her genital
region until she felt aroused as she had the first moment he laid her on
the bed. She writhed with pleasure. She felt herself hot and moist.
He, feeling this, raised his huge bulk above her and descended deep
into the moist place waiting to receive him.

She hadn't expected this — not the pleasure, not the pain, not the
overwhelming *sensation*. She gripped his shoulders and flung her
head back and cried. He began moving inside her and she held on for
dear life as the sensations continued. They came simultaneously —
she crying out. Then she cried real tears, tears of joy, tears of
sadness. It had been so wonderful and it should never have happened.
As the sensation slowly went away she wondered how she could feel
like that with a man that she hardly knew.

Evelyn wanted to get up and go, but Louis held her to him, kissing
her and telling her that he loved her, and she was too exhausted to do
anything about it. He was feeling so pleased with himself. One
minute he'd been wondering how to get to her, then they were
embracing and he had her where he wanted her. 'Who would have
believed that this quiet girl would go off like that? Who would have
believed that she'd still be a virgin? Shame on you, Gerald Fisher,
not doing your duty by the girl. No wonder she went off like a
rocket; she was frustrated. Once more, and I'll have it made for the
rest of the summer. Fisher will be last year's garbage.'

Half an hour later they were still lying naked, side by side.
Evelyn was beginning to doze off, but she felt Louis sit up, go over to
the wash basin, wash himself and return to bed. She heard him
putting on another contraceptive and it frightened her. She made to
get up, but he pressed himself to her, starting the whole process of
arousing her again. At first she tried not to give in, but he was
persistent. Soon, she was all a tingle, wanting nothing but for him to
continue his massaging and stroking and probing. She eagerly awaited

his forceful entry, but he delayed until it was almost unbearable, and then he was on her and she was all his for the second time on that New Year's Day. "I love you," she whispered, and hated herself for saying it. He was her master and she his slave. Was this what love was all about? Later they spoke.

"Why did you make love to me, Louis?"

"Evelyn, I've admired you from afar all year. You're the most attractive woman I've ever known."

He didn't add that he wanted to get his own back on her friends. That wasn't a reason she'd like or understand.

"So what happened today?"

"Love's like that. It comes when you don't expect it."

"We hardly know each other. We only met last night."

"We met last April."

"I suppose so, but I scarcely knew you before."

"I wanted you, from the first day I saw you."

That was a lie. He hadn't noticed her standing next to the famous Meredith money and Meredith tits.

"When was that?"

"I saw you having your picture taken, outside the Bonython Hall."

"Did you really?"

He had, in fact, noticed Joan Meredith and gone after her. Evelyn suddenly remembered that day and having her picture taken with Gerald, and all the sadness of the previous day came back. Twenty four hours ago she was telling him on the phone how much she loved him and now he was gone and she'd given her body to this man, telling him she loved him in the midst of passion. It was too much for her — she turned her head to the pillow and cried. Soon she fell asleep.

She dreamed a wild dream that took her back to Adelaide where Gerald was waiting at the station, but the train didn't stop and Gerald spat at her as she passed by, and she called out to him and she saw him again, but he didn't see her. He had a stern look on his face, and as she called out to him to forgive her she realised that it wasn't Gerald but her father, dressed in black, like a minister, and cursing her. She woke up, terrified, and found Louis looking at her.

"What's the matter?" he asked. The room was dark now. She could just make out, in the dark, a few features in the room — the mirror, the window, the end of the bed — and the gleam in Louis's eyes.

"Who's there?" she said, pulling the sheet over her naked breasts.

"Your lover. Who did you think it was?"

Evelyn was confused. She was lying naked in bed. There was a man with her and yet it seemed alright. It was Louis and they'd made love before she fell asleep. It had been so wonderful, so frightening, and so wrong. She remembered the events leading up to their love-making. She felt so ashamed.

'Thank you, Father,' she thought. 'You brought this upon me. I so wanted to be good and be with my love, but now I'm this man's lover. I've gone off the tracks and you pushed me.'

Louis tried to take her into his arms and kiss her. She knew it meant more caresses until he made her lose control. That wasn't what she wanted. She slipped out of his hands, out of his bed.

"What's the matter?"

"Please don't. I don't want to do it again."

"Don't be silly, I love you. I want to make you happy."

"Please Louis, you've made me happy." That she had to admit — if sexual pleasure is happiness, he had given her some moments of happiness, so why deny it? But she wasn't happy now. She was anything but happy.

"I need to think, Louis. I've just had a bad dream."

She wanted to scream at him. She wanted to ask him why he'd taken advantage of her, but she couldn't. She felt that she was equally guilty. It was wrong to do what they had done. She didn't want to marry the man, so why let him do this to her? She felt dirty, she felt like a tramp.

"You should make love, after a bad dream. Come over here and I'll give you a good dream."

"Not now. Please, Louis, not now."

"Was I in your nightmare?"

"No, everybody but you."

"Good, if I had been, it would have been a good dream."

Evelyn had her clothes now and started to dress.

"Don't go." He reminded her of Gerald and her father.

'Why did men think that they owned you?' she thought. Evelyn found her shoes and was at the door.

"I'd like to see you again, Evelyn."

"Louis, I need time to think. Good-bye."

"Are you angry with me?"

"No, I'm not angry. I'm just confused. I don't think what we did should have happened."

When she left, Louis smiled to himself.

"She'll be back. This is a pretty dull town for a girl who shags like that. That girl is dynamite."

Evelyn arrived home at ten, and was met by her mother.

"Where have you been? We've been worried sick."

"I've been at Deirdre Williams' place. Is Dad still mad at me? I'll get my pyjamas and go back if he is."

Mrs Fisher knew that she was lying, but she was back. That's all that mattered. Evelyn didn't like to lie to her, but she couldn't tell her the truth either. From now on she would live a lie continuously.

"Your father's calmed down. You shouldn't have run out like that. Dad didn't mean what he said."

"Yes he did, or he wouldn't have said it."

She started to cry. It hurt where she'd made love, reminding her of an afternoon she wanted to forget.

"What's the matter dear?"

"Everything. Gerald and Louis and Dad. Why are men so cruel? I thought Dad was going to beat me."

"He won't, dear, not while I'm around."

"If he starts shouting and threatening me, I'll go away and never come back."

"He won't. I promise he won't. Tell me one more time. Did Louis know that you were getting drunk?"

"No, Mom, I'm sure that he didn't know. He's really a nice person when you get to know him."

'That was a lie, and yet he had been nice to me before I gave myself to him,' she mused.

"What happened to your nice young man in Adelaide? Does he know you're seeing Mr Brown?"

When she saw the look of horror in her daughter's face, she knew something was wrong. She had touched a raw nerve.

"Mom, I don't know what to do. I'm so confused. I don't know if he still loves me and I don't know if I really love him. I don't know anything anymore."

Evelyn felt soiled, like her ruined party dress. She took a long shower and went to bed without seeing her father that night. She woke late and only had time to say a quick 'good morning' before they both went to work. At lunchtime she sought out Deirdre Williams and asked her to cover for her by saying that Evelyn had spent the previous evening with her.

"Your mother rang yesterday. We were supposed to ring if you turned up. I told Mom that I was at your place!"

"So Mom knows that I was lying. I never wanted that. Well, there's no use crying over spilt milk."

"Where were you, Evelyn?"

"I had a big row with Dad and ran out of the house. It was all about the party the other night. It appears that I got home drunk and was sick as a dog."

"I know. I was a little pissed myself and so was Peter. The orange juice was laced."

"Did you see who laced the drinks?"

"No, but it happened *after* you arrived with Brown. He was supposed to be with Judy. She wasn't half shat off when she turned up and found Brown dancing with you. She was waiting at home and he didn't turn up. That wasn't right, after taking her out all December."

Deirdre should have said "after laying her all month", but Evelyn was a goody-goody girl — she wouldn't want to know that, but she should have known it. She should have known that Brown wasn't a lover, but just a Don Juan.

"Don't say that. Louis is a nice guy. I came back from Adelaide, sad and miserable, and he picked me up, waited until I got dressed, and brought me to the party. He went out of his way to cheer me up."

"Why? Were you in need of cheering up?"

"I wanted to stay in Adelaide, but I was too scared what my Dad would do that I came home, and Gerald said he was sick of me and I haven't heard from him since. I upset him. I was stupid and now I've lost him."

"Why don't you write and say you're sorry?"

"It isn't just that, Deirdre, there's something else."

"What?"

"I can't tell you. I can't tell anyone."

"Has it got to do with last night?"

"Please don't ask."

She could see that Deirdre didn't have to ask. She'd told her everything without saying anything. She felt tears coming so she turned her head away. Deirdre felt so sorry for her friend. She had seen Brown in action in the short time he'd been in town, and didn't like him at all. She also knew who had laced the drinks. She wondered if he'd done it to her when she was drunk. Knowing Evelyn as she did, he assumed that he had. She hated Brown for being such a bastard to two friends of hers.

That evening Evelyn made peace with her father. He did so at his wife's insistence. He was still annoyed at his daughter's behaviour and defiance. The fire of his anger was out, but it still smouldered like the ashes of a bush fire waiting for a wind to blow up and start a fresh conflagration. He told Evelyn that he believed her story, even though he didn't. There was also the story of being with Deirdre Williams that she'd made up.

Brown saw her each day as she finished work. Three days after their first love-making she again went to his room and became his regular lover. She made up tales of going to visit friends. She was ashamed of what she was doing, but she needed the love she'd lost, and Brown supplied her need.

Chapter Fifteen

January 1953

On New Year's Eve Richard rang his friend to see if he wanted a lift to the party. Mrs Fisher answered and called Gerald to the phone. He told him that he wasn't coming to the party, but didn't tell him why. When he rang off, Richard concluded that Evelyn was in town and that the two lovers wanted to be alone. He wished his friend good luck.

Richard spent the night with Sally, going from party to party. He ended up at Joan Meredith's poolside celebration. As the first light of dawn rose, high above the Mt. Lofty hills, a dozen of them were frolicking in the pool in wet undies or less. The *Truth* reporters would have had a field-day at this party if they'd dared to crash it. Then he took Sally back to her place at Handorf, spent the dawn hours making love, and most of the morning sleeping it off.

It was four in the afternoon, the same time that Evelyn was surrendering her body to Louis Brown, when he returned home from his blonde lover and thought about Gerald. He telephoned him.

"Gerald, Happy New Year. What did you do last night?"

"Nothing. We went to the Town Hall and then back here."

Gerald had hoped against hope that the caller would be Evelyn, but he was glad to hear his friend's voice.

"You and Evelyn?"

"No. Me and my parents. Evelyn didn't stay."

"Stiff shit. Why didn't you tell me yesterday? Why'd she do a thing like that?"

"I don't know. I don't know why the hell she came in the first place. I was so mad, I told her to go to hell."

"Is that why she went home?"

"Hell, no. I said that over the phone when she said she wasn't staying. I didn't say that, only something like it. I forget the exact words. I lost my temper."

"That was a bit silly, Gerald."

"I should have left work the moment she arrived. No one would have objected. I worked hard all bloody month for nothing."

"No use crying over spilt milk. Ring her up and tell her you're sorry."

"I did, but Mr Robertson told me not to ring again and hung up the phone. He won't let me talk to her. I probably upset her and now she doesn't want to hear from me. It serves me bloody-well right!"

"So write a letter."

"I'll do that. I'm so damn miserable. What a New Year. How was your evening?"

"So so." He couldn't tell his lovelorn friend what a fabulous night he'd had. "You missed a good party, several in fact. Why don't you come over here? There's no sense you moping about at home."

"I'll see if I can get the car."

Mr Fisher gave him the keys. In two days he'd be in the army. It was the least thing he could do for his son. He asked him not to get drunk — not that he was likely to — but he was worried that in his state of mind he might be tempted.

The first thing Richard did was to offer him a beer.

"Just one. Dad doesn't want the car wrecked. If I have more than one, I don't think I'll be able to stop."

"Come and see what I got for Christmas. It's a microgroove player. I also got five jazz records from Dad, 78s, Billy Holiday and Charlie Parker.

"78s? I thought you were going to spend all your wages on microgrooves."

"No sense doing that. I'll be away at Nasho until mid-April so they'd only be on the shelf gathering dust. I've decided to put the money into shares."

"Shares? Isn't that a bit risky?"

"I got a hot tip yesterday. One of Joan's friends was a little pissed and whispered something in my ear. It appears that this mining company has found a rich load of ore — Wolfram, I believe. If I buy shares when the market opens, they should double or triple by the end of the day. You got any money?"

"A hundred and fifty pounds."

"Want to double it?"

"I was going to buy Evelyn an engagement ring. I'll need most of it."

"You'll have three hundred pounds by tomorrow evening."

"Are you sure? What if this guy was bullshitting?"

"We checked him out. He's a geologist and his father runs the mining company."

200

"How are we going to do this if we're in the army?"

"Through a broker. Dad has one. I'll ask him to buy first thing and sell the next day after the news breaks. He's also buying."

"How many people know about this?"

"I don't know. We were chatting when the guy told me. He asked me not to spread the word about and specifically not to tell anyone else at the party. I don't think anyone else heard him. He was frightened that the Merediths would get wind of it, buy big and raise the price before the announcement. Then questions would be asked. A few people always buy before an announcement, those in the know, but if the information got out and too many people bought, those who leaked it might get into trouble."

"I thought that the stock market was a mug's game."

"It is if you don't get information. With tip-offs, it's a mint. The brokers often get good tips, but they only give them to selected clients. If you're in good with a good broker, you make a profit: if not, you contribute to other peoples' profits."

"This isn't a trap, Richard? Do you think you can trust this geologist guy?"

"There's no reason why the guy should lie to me. Gerald, I'm putting all my money in this. Dad's doing the buying for me and also buying a few shares. Do you want to come in with your one hundred and fifty pounds?"

Gerald finished his beer and put down the glass.

"I can't get it to you in time, it's in the bank."

"I don't need the money. You don't pay the broker until settlement day. If you sell before that at a profit, you don't pay a thing."

"So what's to stop you buying a million pounds worth?"

"A broker won't accept it unless he knows you can pay. You have to establish a credit rating before he'll take buying orders. That's why my father can buy and you or I can't. You follow?"

"Put me in for the full one hundred and fifty pounds. Who knows if Evelyn will want my ring now?"

Gerald wrote to Evelyn and she received the letter on the fifth. In it he apologised for shouting at her and he told her that he wanted to see her on his first leave. He told her that he'd write to her again as soon as he knew the date and asked her to write to him, care of his parents as he didn't know his army address.

Evelyn had been in the middle of a letter to Gerald on the first of January, when her father had shouted at Louis and she'd gone off with him and he'd taken advantage of her. Try as she might, she had never managed to write another word. The half-finished letter stayed on her table, pricking her conscience whenever she saw it. How can you write to a man, who may or may not love you, when you're going to bed with another man and enjoying it? Evelyn looked forward to seeing Louis, and the moment he touched her hand or kissed her she was his, and the moment she got home she felt ashamed and hated herself for being so easy. Louis was so warm and loving. She couldn't help it. She wanted his loving.

When Gerald's letter came, it was like a bolt from the blue. She'd been so sure that he'd meant what he'd said and didn't love her anymore. Now that she had given in to another man's desire, she knew, or thought she knew, what he felt when she'd taken the train. All her old feelings for Gerald returned. She locked herself in the room and cried.

Why hadn't he called? Why did he let her go to another man? Why didn't I trust him? Trust! What will he think of me when he finds out what I've been doing? If he was mad at me for not staying, what will he do if he finds out about Louis? For a moment she thought of not telling him, but she knew that he'd have to know. As much as it would hurt him, she could never hide such a thing from him. But she couldn't tell him either. She looked for words to write and tell him, but couldn't finish the letter. She knew how much he wanted to hear from her, but she couldn't write. She couldn't tell him of her infidelity and she couldn't not tell him.

Louis picked her up at the factory the next day. He asked her to his room, but she asked him to take her home. He could see in her face that she wasn't happy and suspected that she wanted to end the affair. Instead of driving her home he drove past the house out into the countryside.

"Why did you do that?"

"You look upset. I thought we should talk."

"Yes, I suppose we should."

She told him that she'd decided that they should stop meeting in bedrooms and sleeping together. She didn't tell him why, and

Gerald's name never came up. In all the time she was with Louis she never mentioned him and never would. Perhaps if she had mentioned his name, she might have had the strength to resist him, but she didn't. She felt awful and on the verge of crying. He insisted on embracing her and once reluctantly in his arms, he persisted. His brute strength overcame her efforts to resist him, and she gave in to him, letting him bring her to a state in which she wanted him. They made love, outside on the recently-washed rug as the stars came out. Then he took her back to his room and she spent the night with him. Nothing had changed. Gerald's letter was left unanswered, Brown made love to her whenever he wanted and Evelyn learned to live with her conscience, Deirdre Williams covering for her. Then, in mid-January a second letter came, one that she had to answer.

Dearest Evelyn,

Please write to me and tell me that you still love me and have forgiven me for hurting you. I'm getting my first leave on Australia Day Weekend, three whole days. I'm coming to see you. Don't worry, I'll make my own hotel booking. I'll sleep out if I have to. There's this guy from Renmark in our Company and he thinks he can get me a lift and I can even stay at his place if I need to. Why haven't you written to me? The other guys get letters from their girlfriends. I die every time they get letters and there's nothing for me. You still love me, don't you?

Nasho isn't that bad. The food's plain, but there's plenty of it. So far no maggots in the meat. We spend all our time marching and getting fit. Then there's weapons training and range practice. It's great fun shooting at targets. I just hope that I never have to shoot at a living person. Richard's in my platoon. He sends regards. He made a lot of money on mining shares just before we were called up. I tripled my meagre savings too, so I'll be able to buy you a nice present when I get out of here. I think of you every night. I can't wait for my leave. I'm dying to meet your family. I hope your father likes me. He shouted at me over the phone when I tried to call you. I'm sorry I was rude to you. I so much want to make it up to you.

It's hot here, but the nights are terrific. The stars are so bright. Are they bright over Renmark too? We get up early and go to bed early. This is the life. All I miss is you, dear. I can't wait until Friday week when I can hold you in my arms and kiss you.

All my love,

Gerald.

The day the letter arrived Evelyn met Brown after work and stayed out late. She went for another drive to the lonely landing on the river bank, and as the sun set, Brown spread out the rug and the cushions and they made love, half-dressed, under the stars, lying together lovingly, until it was late. She didn't have a care in the world. It was so nice to be made love to, to lie in this man's arms, looking up at the gum trees and at the stars. When she arrived home still in a state of after-love-making euphoria, her parents were asleep and Gerald's letter was placed on her pillow. Her mother suspected that she was out with Louis that evening, and hoped that the letter would shock her enough to come to her senses. Shock her it did, but to her senses it didn't.

She saw the army envelope, quickly opened it, and rapidly read the letter. Then she wept. She hated herself. She wanted to die.

"What have I done to you, Gerald? You're serving your country, loving me all the while, and I'm sneaking out with another man and I can't help myself. There you are thinking of me and I'm not fit to lick your boots. I'll never be able to look you in the face again. What can I say? Gerald, I've been sleeping with Louis Brown. I'll stop if you'll forgive me. And if he won't forgive me? Why should he? I've done him the most unforgivable injury that I could. If I wanted to hurt him I couldn't have found a better way, but I never wanted ever to hurt him. I wish I was dead."

Evelyn took up her pen and scribbled a short note to Gerald. She found a stamp and envelope and took the letter to the post box. This was one communication that her father wouldn't prevent. She regretted her haste as soon as it fell inside the box. Then she walked out of town, a long walk to the bridge that crossed the Murray, and stared for a long time at the black water running under it, before slowly walking home. Her sleeping parents never knew how close they came to losing their daughter that night. At the last minute she remembered that look on the face of Jonny's mother at the graveside. She couldn't do that to her mother. It wouldn't be the last time that

Evelyn would look death in the face. 1953 had started badly for her, but the worst was *yet* to come.

At breakfast her mother asked her about the letter.

"Yes, Mother, I had a letter from Gerald."

"What did he say?"

"He wanted to come for the long weekend. I wrote and told him not to come."

"Evelyn, *that* wasn't very nice. Why did you do that?"

"Mom, it's all over between us. I wrote and told him."

"You told me that the two of you were in love, 'very much in love' was what you said."

"I know better now."

"Is it because you've been seeing Louis?"

"Partly. Mother, I can't be in love with two men and I can't string Gerald along. I decided to make a clean break."

"What if you meet him next term and your feelings come back?"

She wished her mother wouldn't pry. She couldn't be open with her any more. She picked at her breakfast.

"Mom, what's over is over."

"Are you and Louis in love? Is that what you're trying to tell me?"

That was the last thing her mother wanted.

"Mom, I *don't* know."

There was a tremor in her voice, and tears in her eyes.

"I thought that Gerald and I were in love once, but now I'm not sure of anything. I don't think I'll see Louis again. If he calls or rings, tell him I've got a headache. I want to be by myself and think for a while."

That day Evelyn had her period. It was the first time since she began to have intercourse, and she was never so glad in her life when it came on time. So was her mother. It also gave her an excuse to stay out of Brown's bed for a week. He might have taken her to the pictures or they could have sat and talked, but he just stayed away. It should have been a warning sign to her, but it had the opposite effect. When on Friday the twenty-sixth he asked her out, he also asked her if her period was over, and when she said it was, he took her back to his room where they renewed their relationship.

As the long weekend drew near, Gerald's spirits rose. Soon he'd be seeing Evelyn and they would renew their love. He intended to propose to her, and when she said "yes", he would ask her father. All December she had written to him regularly and it was with a sense of relief that he received his first letter from her in January. When he read the contents his happiness ended.

Dear Gerald,

These last few weeks that we've been apart I've had time to think about our relationship. I'm afraid that I don't feel for you the way that you feel for me. I thought that I loved you, but now I think that I was mistaken. I think that we should both go out with other people. Please don't come here next weekend. Stay in Adelaide. Go out with someone more deserving of your love. It was great knowing you. You'll always have a little corner in my heart. Let's part friends, before one of us gets hurt.

Love,

Evelyn.

There were blotches on the letter where her tears had fallen and made the ink run.

Richard watched as the smile on his friend's face disappeared, his features changing to that of a man in pain.

"Bad news?"

"She doesn't want me to come for the weekend. She says it's all over."

Richard took the letter and read it.

"She's got another guy, Richard. The bitch has dumped me for another guy, and all because I told her I was sick of her. I must have been off my bloody rocker."

Richard knew his friend was right, but didn't say so.

"That's quite a letter."

"In three days I was going to ask her to marry me."

"You have to go and see her."

"You read the letter. She says not to come."

"Gerald, women never mean what they say, especially in letters. I don't know why she wrote what she wrote, but you mustn't accept it. Her father's probably giving her a hard time. Ignore the letter and go to her. Take a bit of money. We made enough out of the Wolfram shares. Give her a good time. Book into a hotel and take her back there and make love to her. You should have done that a long time ago. Then when you've straightened out your love life, you can come back here and play soldiers again."

"You really think I should go?"

"If it was me, I'd go AWOL this afternoon. I think going is mandatory. That letter read like a 'come on' to me, not a 'put off'. Show her father that you're as good a man as he is. When she sees you in your uniform, she'll be so impressed that she'll drop everything and run to your arms. There's nothing like a uniform for impressing a sheila."

On Friday the twenty-sixth Gerald got a lift in the back of a utility all the way to Renmark. The drive there took a lot less time than the train and he expected to get there at seven. At Berri, the last town before Renmark, they picked up a couple of hitch-hikers, two young men, who piled into the back with Gerald. One was a stranger, the other a man whom he knew from the university.

"Good day, soldier boy. When did they let you out? Great to see you, Gerry."

"Hi, Charlie. What are you doing up here?"

"We're picking fruit. There's about thirty of us from the uni here. We're having a wacko time."

"Anyone that I know?"

"Ted Ford, John McIntosh, Jim Parker, and Bully Brown."

"Louis Brown?"

He didn't like it, Brown so near to Evelyn.

The stranger, hearing Louis's name, joined in, "You know Bully Brown? Lucky bugger's been getting the best sheilas in the town. First he gets this shop assistant, hot as bloody mustard, and now he's shagging the arse off this girl in the Canning Factory."

"Brown's no friend of mine and I'm not interested in what the animal does. You a local lad?"

"No, I'm an Adelaide boy too. I'm waiting for the next call-up in April."

"So what brings you to Renmark, Gerry?" his friend asked. "This isn't your home town."

"My girlfriend lives here, Charlie. You know Evelyn, don't you? She's a science student."

"No, I don't think I've seen you since the night on the river when poor Jonny died."

"So you don't know my girlfriend, Evelyn Robertson?"

The other man looked up at the sound of her name.

"*That's* the girl Brown's been shagging," he said thoughtlessly to Gerry, who reacted violently.

"*Listen*, mate. You watch what you're saying. I think you're making a mistake."

Gerald felt his stomach turn over and his heart start to pound. He remembered her writing that they should see other people. He was stunned.

"I stay in the same lodging house as Brown. He told me on New Year's Day. You'd think he'd won a double at the races. He told me he'd just finished shagging this virgin and he'd never had it so good. I've seen them together almost every day. Her name is Evelyn Robertson and she works in the laboratory at the canning plant."

So there it was. Gerald now knew why Evelyn had told him to stay away. It was too horrible to hear it from a stranger and in such a filthy way. He wanted to tear the man's tongue out, but it wasn't his fault.

The last few miles into Renmark were unbearable. He felt like he was going to his execution, being transported into Aushwitz. The thought of his Evelyn naked in bed with that horrible person tore at his insides. It was as if someone had plunged a bayonet into his belly. What would he say to her or to Brown if he saw him? He wanted her so much that he couldn't comprehend what he'd heard. If he'd been able to see her alone he might have pleaded with her to come back to him, forgetting and forgiving what he'd heard, but it wasn't to be.

He got down from the utility, dazed. The other two men went their own ways, feeling sorry for him. What a thing to happen to a guy on his first leave. Gerald set out for Evelyn's house, walking like a wounded man. Evelyn's mother came to the door.

"I'm Gerald Fisher. Is Evelyn in?"

He was calmer now. He promised himself that he wouldn't scold her. He'd ask her to come back and if she said "no," he'd go back home.

"Oh, so you're Gerald? I've heard so much about you. Come in."

Mrs Robertson was so glad to see him. She knew that her daughter had written to him not to come, telling him that they were finished, and was so pleased that he hadn't been put off by this. He'd bring her to her senses and she'd stop seeing that horrible Brown man. One thing worried her. Evelyn hadn't been out with Brown all week, but tonight she hadn't come home. She'd rung to say that she was going to spend the evening with her girlfriend. Was she at the Williams house, or with Louis Brown? Mrs Robertson was concerned.

"I'm on leave until Tuesday morning. Where's Evelyn?"

"She's at her girlfriend's. I'll telephone and tell her to come back."

"I have to find a hotel room. I'll book in and go there myself if it isn't far. I want to surprise her."

"Gerald, you can stay with us. I wanted to invite you for Christmas, but we had relatives. Evelyn should have told me that you were coming. Gerald, she hasn't been herself of late. Your visit should do wonders for her."

Mrs Robertson sent Gerald to Deirdre's house. When he told her who he was, she went white and couldn't answer him. Finally she told him to go back to the Robertsons and she'd tell Evelyn. She'd be straight home. As soon as he was out of sight she ran to the boarding house where Brown lived, found his room, and pounded on the door.

"Who is it?" called out Louis. He hadn't been with Evelyn for over a week, and they were in bed. They were on the verge of having sex, he having slowly and patiently broken down a little reluctance on her part. This knock on the door couldn't have come at a more inopportune time. Now he would have to start all over again.

"It's Deirdre. Is Evelyn there?"

"What if she is?"

"She has to go home at once."

"What's the matter, Deirdre?" It was Evelyn's voice.

"Your soldier boy's here."

"Gerald?" At first her heart jumped for joy, until she realised where she was and what she'd been doing. Thank goodness that Deirdre had come now and not a minute later. She grabbed her clothes, ashamed of her nakedness, and dressed as fast as she could. Brown too got dressed.

"What's the big hurry?" he asked.

"Gerald's here." Saying that name had broken the spell. "That's what's the matter. I have to go home at once."

"Stay here and go home when he's gone. He can't stay for ever."

"He can. Mom likes him and she doesn't like you. Besides, he came all the way from Adelaide just to see me. I have to go."

"Tell him to go away."

Evelyn didn't answer. She didn't like Louis's attitude and she didn't want to tell Gerald to go away. She wanted him to rescue her from herself, to forgive her.

"You'll tell him to go?" Louis asked.

"I don't think so. You stay here."

"I'll take you home."

He could feel her hostility to him. He had to do something, or his summer sport would be over.

"I can manage. God, I feel terrible."

"I said, I'll take you."

"No."

"I'll go by car and get there first."

"Do what you bloody-well like."

They left the room together.

"Hop into the car and I'll take you."

"Then you'll go?"

"Yes."

At the Robertson house he didn't go. Evelyn ran up the front path and he followed. Her father was also on his way home and the three of them entered the house together. Before Evelyn knew what was happening, they were all standing in the living-room confronting Gerald and Mrs Robertson who had been sitting and talking. She looked at him in his khaki uniform. She wanted to say something, to go to him, but she couldn't, not in front of her father and Louis Brown.

"Hello, Evelyn," he said.

"Hello, Gerald. This is my father. Father, this is Gerald Fisher. He's doing his National Service."

She didn't have to introduce him to Louis Brown. She pretended that he wasn't there. Why didn't he keep his word and go away?

Mr Robertson looked at Gerald. He seemed a fine young man. He was soon to change his opinion.

"Evelyn, can we talk? Is *he* the reason that you didn't want me to come?" He nodded in the direction of Brown.

Before she could answer, Brown stepped forward.

'Why doesn't he keep his promise and go away?' Evelyn wanted to scream out.

Brown came so close to Gerald that when he spoke, the others in the room didn't hear all of what he said.

"On your way, soldier boy. You've been replaced by a *real* man, you queen. Get back to your box with all the other toy soldiers. Evelyn's *my* woman now."

There was something sordid in the way he said 'my woman'.

Gerald forgot where he was and shouted at Brown, "Shut your bloody mouth, you filthy shit."

Gerald was red in the face and shouting at the top of his voice. The shock of hearing about his love's lover took hold of him, and he lost control.

"I want to talk with Evelyn," he screamed. "Evelyn, *what* is going on? What is this bastard doing here? What in hell's name has he been doing to you? What's happening?"

Evelyn's parents were stunned by the boy's anger and rage. So was their daughter. She couldn't answer his accusation, not in front of her father.

"Listen, Fisher..." Brown put his hand on Gerald's shoulder. He was going to tell him to get lost, but didn't get the chance. Gerald responded like a startled deer. All of the frustration and pent-up anger he'd been feeling for the past hour suddenly burst out. He hit Brown with all the force he could muster, putting his whole body behind the punch. He hit him in the stomach and felt him buckle up under the sudden punch. Before he could recover he smashed him in the jaw while he was still doubled over.

Had the big man been prepared he would have killed Gerald. Gerald was fit, but Brown was big and heavy. As it was, the two punches were enough — two punches from an enraged man. All the force he could summon up together with the force of his anger sent Brown reeling. He collapsed on top of the coffee table, smashing it, sending cups and saucers and tea everywhere. He lay there moaning in the mess, blood coming from a split lip. Mr Robertson leapt forward.

"Have you taken leave of your senses? This is a decent, Christian household, not an alley behind a public house. You come into my house to see my daughter and you act like a barbarian. Get out of here before I throw you out."

He made no move to throw Gerald out. He didn't want to tangle with the mad soldier. The two women looked wide-eyed, not knowing what to do. Brown was about to get up and hit his assailant, but he suddenly realised that he could do better by pretending to be injured, so he just lay there and listened to what was happening. He knew that Mr Robertson wanted Gerald to go, and so did he. If he got up now, he would share Gerald's fate. If he pretended to be hurt, they couldn't throw him out.

"Get out of my house. Evelyn, go to your room."

"Don't worry, Mr Robertson, I'm going. I've seen enough. I came here to ask you for your daughter but I wouldn't have the whore now if you begged me to take her. Filthy bloody whore, that's what she is. You can keep the dirty bitch. Here's money for the cups and the table. As for this useless lump of shit, tell your whore to throw it in the river."

He was pointing to Louis Brown.

"Get out of my house!"

"I'm going, you poor bastard. I won't stay in this brothel a minute longer than I can bloody-well help it."

He kicked Brown in the backside.

"Get up, you shit. You make the place look like a dog's dunny."

Then he turned and went out. Evelyn, tears streaming down her face, moved to follow, but her father grabbed her by the elbow and she didn't have the strength to break free. Gerald put on his hat, shouldered his duffel bag, and cursing to himself walked back to town.

Chapter Sixteen

January 1953

Gerald wandered aimlessly into town. He was thirsty, in need of a drink, but it was well past closing time. He passed a pub and noticed that there was a light in the saloon bar. The door was open, so he went in.

"Any chance of getting a beer, mate?"

"If you sign the book."

"What book?"

"The Bone Fide Traveller's book. You don't look like a local. Where you from, soldier?"

"Adelaide."

"Good, sign the book and we'll get you a beer."

Gerald didn't know it, but he was the only *bone fide* in the pub. The rest were locals and the few other names in the book were all bogus. He signed his name under Ned Kelly and Roy Rene, had a couple of beers, bought a big bottle of Chateau Tanunda Brandy and went out into the night. Half a bottle later he found himself on the bridge. He went to the middle and, standing near the place that Evelyn had stood ten days earlier, cried into the river. The river was low and the water smooth, reflecting the light from the bridge and the houses along the river bank. Gerald thought of Jonny Marco.

"Jonny, Jonny. Was it a woman that made you do it? Was it Evelyn? Or was it a bastard like Brown? God, I know how you must have felt."

He took a swig from the brandy bottle and then another one. He stood in the middle of the bridge and shouted, "I'll get you for this, you bastard Brown, and I'll get you for Jonny Marco too. I know you killed him. I don't know how, but I know you did it, you bastard."

He was standing there when a car started to cross the bridge. It stopped as it reached Gerald and the driver called out to him, "Want a lift, soldier boy?"

"Where are you heading?"

"Adelaide."

"Good. I hate this bloody town, it's a whorehouse."

Gerald got in. He had the back seat to himself. He was glad to be with people. Being alone on the bridge had scared him. He didn't want to be left alone with his thoughts after what had happened and what he'd said at Evelyn's house, what he'd said about her in anger. There were two men in the front, and the three of them chatted and sang songs all the way to the city. They were also fruit-pickers and were on their way from Mildura to Adelaide for the long weekend. Gerald talked about National Service and told them about his trip to Renmark and how the bastard Brown had stolen his girlfriend. The brandy had loosened his tongue. He told them how he'd hit Brown and got thrown out.

"Pity you didn't go there with a 3-0-3 and put a bullet up his arse. You'd have done the nation a service."

"You're well shot of that sheila, mate. Any girl who'd shag with another bloke when her boyfriend's doing Nasho ain't worth a pinch of shit. You're well shot of her."

"I just can't believe it. I could understand it if he was a nice guy, but to do it with the biggest turd in Adelaide — that's *too* bloody much. Of all the people in the world, she had to pick Louis bloody Brown."

"Or he picked her. Women are stupid, mate. They always fall for the biggest ratbags in town. Take my advice, mate. Stop being a nice guy. You want a girl — treat her like shit, and she's yours. Put her on a pedestal, and she'll piddle on you from a great height. You gotta beat up a woman from time to time to keep her from strayin'."

"I came as close as I'll ever come to hitting a woman tonight. If I didn't tonight, after what she did to me, I don't think that I ever will. I'm not a caveman."

"Don't let the clothes we wear, the posh cars and houses fool you. Basically, we're all cave men and cave women."

"I wanted to marry that woman."

"Well, you've had a lucky escape. Just think what you'd have done if you found out that she was shaggin' somebody *after* you married her? What if you didn't find out? You might have spent your life working to bring up someone else's brat. You might never know what was going on and who was doing it. You had a lucky escape, mate. Go and dip your wick somewhere else. Don't get married until you know how to handle a woman. You're living at home, aren't you?"

"Yes."

"So what's the hurry? You're getting fed and getting your washing done. Have your fun and don't get married. Why buy a book when you can join a library?"

It was good being with other men, but when they dropped him off in Victoria Square just after midnight, the pain returned. The city was its usual dead self, the pictures and the theatres all closed, together with the shops and restaurants. The trams had stopped running and the streets were deserted. There wasn't a taxi in sight. Gerald found a bench in the square and took a big swig at the brandy bottle. At first it burned and then it warmed him as it went down. He took another and another. The pain went and sleep came. The next thing he knew was that it was morning, he was in a police cell, a military police cell, and he felt lousy.

He was brought before the officer-in-charge and fined ten pounds. He put his hand into his pocket, but there was no money. He looked in all of his pockets.

"I think I've been robbed, sir."

"What did you expect, getting drunk in a public park. Where's your base?"

"Woodside, sir."

"Your leave's cancelled. We're sending you back there this morning. Remember: when you're wearing the Queen's uniform, we expect you to conduct yourself like a gentleman."

"Yes, sir."

An hour later he and two other miscreants were on their way back to Woodside. They spent the remaining days of the weekend doing menial jobs — sweeping, cleaning, kitchen duty, and guarding. On Tuesday morning he was released to join his platoon. By this time he was completely demoralised — by his visit to Renmark and his subsequent detention. Richard was shocked by his appearance.

"Shit, Gerald. What happened to you?"

Gerald told him of his lost weekend.

"Hell! That shouldn't happen to a dog. You really hit Brown and knocked him down?"

"I was mad, Richard, mad as a bull. I haven't been in a fight since I was in primary school. I lost me block and hit him as hard as I could, right in the guts!"

"You're lucky that he didn't kill you."

"Do you think I care? I might be better off dead. It was a stupid thing to do. I went there to make a good first impression on her parents and got myself chucked out."

"What did Evelyn do?"

"Nothing. She thought I was going to hit her too. For a moment I wanted to, until I saw the look on her face. She'd been sleeping with him and was with him when I turned up in town. You should have seen the look on her face."

"How do you know she was sleeping with him?"

"Some ratbag I met told me. I told him that I was her boyfriend and he told me that Brown was bragging about how he'd... I can't say it. To hear it like that from a total stranger. Why did he have to tell me? Then when I saw the two of them together and I saw her face... She couldn't look me in the face, she was so ashamed. A least she had the decency to tell me not to come. Four bloody weeks ago she told me how she loved me and then she went straight home and hopped into Brown's bed, New Year's bloody Day — the bitch."

"If it had been someone else and not Brown, would it have made a difference?"

"No... Yes, it would have. You know what a shit he is. I warned her against him. The bastard even whispered to me that Evelyn was *his* woman. He did that to provoke me."

"Well, she's been a bloody fool and so have you, Gerald. You went there to speak to her and you shouldn't have left until you did. Write to her, tell her that you're sorry for doing what you did, and saying what you said. Tell her that you still love her, no matter what she's done."

"Do I?"

"Yes, you do. If she wants to come back to you, in spite of what she's done, you'd welcome her with open arms, wouldn't you, Gerald?"

"Yes, I would, damn it, I would. I want her so much. It's all my fault. Why did I say such hateful things to her?"

Richard didn't know what to tell him. He couldn't understand why a nice girl like Evelyn should get involved with a Brown. He thought that she was gone for good because of his friend's stupidity, but he didn't tell that to Gerald. That wasn't what he wanted to hear.

"Write to her," he told him.

"I don't know what to write."

"Imagine that you're with her. What would you say?"

"I'm not going to crawl to her."

"That isn't necessary. Ask her if she prefers Brown to you and tell her that you didn't mean what you said, again."

"And if she says she prefers Brown?"

"Any girl as stupid as that, you can forget about."

Gerald didn't like that reply.

"Your talking about my Evelyn."

"Gerald, she's his Evelyn right now, unless you write one hell of a letter. You're young, Gerald, and the world is full of women. You'll get over this one. Women are like that, Gerald. They fall in love and they fall out of love again. Remember Dawn — how she wanted me to marry her? She's in love again and getting married next month. She even sent me an invitation to the wedding.

"Evelyn will probably lose interest in Brown too. Give it one more try and if it doesn't work, forget about her. Find yourself another girlfriend, or better, several women."

That night Gerald wrote to Evelyn. He told her how he knew about her and Brown. He told her what Brown had said to him, why he lost his temper. He told her that he still loved her and that, if they could, they should both forget the past and forgive each other. He wanted to see her and try and regain her love. It was a letter that she would never read.

Then he was caught up in the daily army routine. Every day, several times a day, he thought about Evelyn and hoped against hope that she would send him a favourable reply. He wasn't prepared for the response when it came.

When Gerald ran out of the Robertson house after knocking down Louis Brown, Evelyn tried to run after him, but her father grabbed her by the arm and stopped her. Then she ran to her room and fell onto the bed, leaving her parents staring at the big man, who was lying on the floor moaning faintly. Mr Robertson wanted to kick him out of the house and his wife also wanted him as far away as possible, but he seemed to be injured.

Brown played possum for all it was worth. Mr Robertson turned him over and saw the nasty cut on his lip, which had been squashed between Gerald's fist and his own teeth. It was quite bloody. At a glance he could see that the damage was minimal, no teeth were broken. He and his wife helped him to the sofa and Mrs Robertson picked up the broken tea cups.

"Fetch me a wet face towel, Sara. If that soldier comes back, call the police."

Mrs Robertson thought about Gerald. 'The boy's got guts hitting a big man like that. I can't blame him. He's in the army and this horrible man comes and takes his girlfriend away. Oh Evelyn, what have you done with that young man's heart? What have you been doing with that brute of a man when all the time you've been telling us lies?'

"Don't just stand there staring, Sara, can't you see this young man's hurt? Go and get Evelyn back here. This is her friend. She brought him here. The least she can do is look after him."

"Leave her alone, Wes. She's had a terrible shock."

"So have I. Who was that madman?"

"He's been Evelyn's boyfriend for the past year."

She whispered this to her husband, not wishing Louis Brown to hear her.

"Well, she's well rid of him. Did you hear what he called our daughter? He called her a—"

"Please, Wes, *don't* say it. I don't ever want to hear that word in this house again."

"Why did I ever let her go to Adelaide? You bring up your daughter to be good and clean and decent, and she brings home filthy-mouthed hooligans to brawl and swear in your living-room. Go and get Evelyn. I want her to help me get this other lout back to where he lives."

Louis Brown wasn't ready to go home. Mr Robertson went into the kitchen to sit and think, and Evelyn was brought out, crying. She and her mother attended to Brown's wound and his needs for another hour, then Evelyn helped him into the car and accompanied him home.

His room was still a mess from their interrupted love-making. She tidied up and put him to bed. Louis was really pleased with himself. He was being mothered by the girl who he had almost lost to his rival. Unknown to her, he had provoked Gerald into hitting him, a small price for total victory, and he had seen him banished from her house.

Evelyn was in a state of shock over what had happened. She'd been having a dirty affair at the very time that the man who'd declared his true love to her had come to see her. She felt ashamed and she felt unclean. He had called her a whore. It wasn't an insult, it was a statement of fact. He knew what she'd been doing, Gerald knew! How in heaven's name did he know? She hadn't wanted him to find out, not from another person.

'Why didn't I go after him?' she asked herself, despairingly. 'Why did I let Daddy stop me? If he had hit me too, it would have been what I deserved. I wanted so much to talk to him, to try and explain, to tell him that I didn't mean to do what I did. I went to bed with the first man I met, while he was fulfilling his duty to the nation. I'm a whore and he doesn't want me, and I can't blame him. I want Gerald. I love him.'

Evelyn went home, knowing that she still loved Gerald but not knowing what to do about it. She was too ashamed to write and tell him how sorry she was. It was left to him to write. A letter came from Woodside a week later. Mrs Robertson put it on the hall stand, but Mr Robertson found it. When he saw who the writer was, he wrote on it "Return to Sender" and took it to the post office. That evening Evelyn asked if there was any mail and before her mother could tell her that there was, her father said that there *wasn't*. Later Sara asked him what he'd done with the letter.

"I mailed it back, that's what I did."

"Why, Wes? Why did you do that?"

"I was going to tear it up, but I thought that if he gets it back, he won't write again. I don't want him to write to her."

"Wes, that was a *rotten* thing to do. The girl's heartbroken. She cries herself to sleep every night. How *could* you be so heartless?"

"I did it for the girl's own good, Sara. That boy's no good, Sara. She'll soon forget him."

"Do you prefer the other man, the one who came and stole her away from him?"

"She's our daughter, not a piece of baggage to be given and taken."

"She's a woman, Wes, and she needs love. I'm going to tell her about Gerald's letter."

"Don't you dare. I forbid you. I won't pay her college fees if you do. I don't want her to have anything to do with that man again or the other man, the one who got her drunk. She's not to see him either."

"Wes, sometimes you frighten me, you really do. You can't control Evelyn's life. You have to trust her and let her live her own life."

He wasn't convinced. Evelyn had to buckle under if she wanted to go back to Adelaide. He was the provider of this household, not Mrs Robertson.

"She's had a year's freedom and she's brought back her newly-found friends. She's been associating with all the riff-raff of Adelaide. If she wants to study, I'll go along with that; but if she wants to go out with every Tom, Dick and Harry, I think she ought to get a job here where we can keep an eye on her."

"Wes, she got a good pass last year. She has a scholarship. What do you want from the girl?"

"I just want a daughter that I can be proud of. We're respectable church-going people. Why does she have to study? Why does she have to go out with trash? Why can't she find a nice Renmark boy, get a job here, and settle down?"

"She did find a fine decent boy in Adelaide, and would have settled down with him eventually if you hadn't thrown him out of our house."

"I had to, Sara. You saw what he did and what he said. He swore at us like a—"

"Like an Australian man does when he gets angry. Do you think that I've never heard the way men talk?"

"Not in my house."

"You've never used bad language, have you, Wes?"

He had, but he hadn't known that his wife had heard him.

"I may have forgotten myself — once or twice."

She thought that she had him now, and tried again.

"Wes, tell Evelyn about the letter."

"No, Sara. I've already posted it. A man who can't control his temper and uses his fists is not a suitable companion for our daughter. Just as well that he left his rifle at his camp. He might have killed all of us. I don't want her to hear about that letter. I'm the breadwinner, Sara. I have to pay her college fees. I'll decide who she sees and who sends her letters."

"It's Evelyn's life, Wes. *Don't* spoil it for her."

"I know what I'm doing, Sara, as God is my witness."

Mrs Robertson knew that she couldn't move her husband, and whilst she didn't agree with him she decided against telling Evelyn about the letter. It would only upset her. Either he'd write again, or, come April, things would sort themselves out. If not, there'd be other young men. She thought that she'd stop seeing Louis Brown after what had happened.

On the last day of January one hundred and twenty-eight people died when a car ferry, the *Princess Victoria*, foundered in the Irish sea on a trip from Scotland to Northern Ireland. The rear car doors had not been secured. In February over a thousand people drowned in Holland as a storm surge breached the dikes. There was heavy loss of life in floods that ravaged eastern counties of England from Lincolnshire to Kent.

After a couple of weeks and no letter, Evelyn stopped hoping that Gerald would write. She also stopped telling Louis Brown that she was too busy to see him and renewed the relationship. She was lonely, tired, and beaten. It was better to be with Brown than no one at all. The thrill had gone from their meetings, but it was a way of forgetting her misery, and it helped. She looked forward to April when she would return to Adelaide and the university. Mrs Robertson noted a change in her daughter. She had lost her sparkle. She used to be such a lively girl and now she was quiet and subdued, like a broken filly. That terrible Friday night had taken its toll. Evelyn was a shadow of her former self.

Louis Brown didn't come to the house again. They met after work, going to his room, and she again made up stories to explain where she'd been. Again her mother knew that she was spending her evenings with that man, and now she wept secretly for her daughter but did nothing to stop her. She'd seen the effect of her husband's interference, and she lived in fear of him finding out what was going on and of what it would do to the family. She tried to get her daughter to confide in her, but she wouldn't. Evelyn didn't like what she was doing or know why she was doing it, so how could she tell her mother about it? She did, however, confide in Deirdre Williams. One afternoon, when she really did visit her friend, she discussed the subject with her.

"Tell me, Deirdre, did you say anything to Gerald? He knew about Louis and me. You didn't say anything, did you?"

"No, but I think that he was suspicious when you weren't at my place."

"I don't understand it. *How* did he find out?"

"Evelyn, the whole town knows. How many people have seen you walking with him or going into his place or coming out? You haven't been very discreet, have you? There are lots of students. Any one of them could have told him."

"I suppose so. I just hope that no one tells my father. If he finds out, God only knows what he'll do to me."

"Evelyn, I think I'm pregnant. I'm three weeks overdue."

"When did it happen? You must feel terrible."

"New Year's Eve. We were a little drunk and Peter forgot to take precautions."

Evelyn was shocked, but not amazed. Deirdre and Peter were always cuddling and kissing, not like her and her lover, doing it on the sly, like adulterers.

"Does Peter know?"

"Yes and he's going to marry me."

"Is that what you want?"

"You bet! And I want the baby too. I love Peter and I know that he loves me too. If it wasn't for this, we'd probably have had a summer romance, then he'd have gone his way, leaving me miserable. Now we're going to get married and I'm going to have his baby. Isn't life wonderful?"

"I hope it doesn't happen to me. I don't want to get married or have a baby, certainly not Brown's baby. I think I'll stop doing it. I'd die if it happened to me. Don't you feel bad about trapping Peter?"

"No. I didn't do it on purpose. Peter's quite pleased, if you must know. He's proved his manliness and he's marrying someone he loves. Evelyn, I'm so happy."

"If you two love each other, why would you have broken up at the end of summer? Couldn't you have come to some agreement?"

"Like you and Gerald did?"

"I was a fool. I should have known better."

She didn't say it, but she regretted that she had never slept with Gerald, now that she knew what love-making was all about. It must be wonderful, she thought, to be in love and give yourself to your lover.

"I shouldn't have said that, Evelyn. What are you going to do?"

"Nothing. There's nothing that I can do. The next move is up to Gerald. I have a feeling that he'll never speak to me again. I'll get over it in time. Time heals all wounds."

"Why are you still seeing Louis?"

"I have to, Deirdre. I couldn't bear to be alone. After April it'll be over. That much I owe to Gerald, even if I don't make up with him. Louis and I don't love each other. For two weeks in January I thought that we might, but now I know we don't. I suppose that it was love on the rebound. When I'm back in Adelaide with my real friends, it'll be different."

Gerald waited for a reply from Evelyn. The last thing he expected was to get his letter back unopened, but it didn't occur to him that anyone but Evelyn would have returned it. He showed it to Richard and tore it into little pieces.

"I guess that she's still mad at me. What did I do to her? She owes me an explanation."

"What did you do? You called her a whore. Can you think of a worse insult?"

"If it's the truth, it isn't an insult."

"You're wrong, Gerry. The best way to insult a woman is to tell her the truth. Never tell a woman the truth."

"God, Richard, you're one hell of a cynic."

He threw the letter remains into a bin and took up his 3-0-3. It was clean, but he decided to clean it again for something to do.

"Gerry, I know a lot more about women that you do. That wouldn't be very difficult, but believe me, I'm still pretty ignorant. With women you're always learning and always wrong. I thought that I had Evelyn figured but I was wrong. She's been behaving like no woman I've ever known. Something's very wrong with her, something fishy. I smell a rat there, Gerry."

"The rat is Louis Brown, a big brown rat."

Richard knew in his heart that Brown had used Evelyn to hurt the two of them. He felt sorrier for her than he did for his friend.

"Remember, Gerry, when Jonny died and how we smelt a rat then? I smelt it then and I smell it now, the same rat."

"So do I. Do you think he'll hurt her, drive her to her death too?"

"He almost drove you to it, pal. I gather it was touch and go with you for a while."

"If he hurts her, if she kills herself, I'll *kill* the bastard with my own hands. What can I do to get her away from him, Richard?"

"Nothing. You could go AWOL and go there and see her again and then go to jail afterwards. And what if you go there and she doesn't want to see you? I wouldn't risk it, not after she returned your letter. It's over, pal."

Gerald knew that he was right. That didn't make him feel any better.

"So what do you suggest?"

"Forget her, Gerald, and when we're back in civilisation, go out with other girls. It's the only cure."

"It won't be easy, Richard. If it was anyone else but Brown, I could accept it, but knowing what a shit he is I just feel sorry for her all the time."

"Your trouble is, mate, that you feel sorry for yourself. Have you ever thought about Joan Meredith?"

"Yes."

"What have you thought about Joan Meredith?"

"I'm too much of a gentleman to say."

"Good. There's still hope for you. Go and have a fling with Joan Meredith."

"She's the richest girl in Adelaide."

"That's an asset, not a liability. She's also one of the sexiest and one of the most experienced for her age."

"She has a boyfriend, a law student."

"She's available; she has other boyfriends. You should have seen her on New Year's Eve, swimming in her undies."

"New Year's Eve, I thought I had my own girlfriend. What makes you think she'll go out with me?"

She had come to see him in the store. Joan must think something of him.

"Gerald, she's a fellow student. You'll see her almost every day. You'll have plenty of opportunities to speak to her. We're bound to be studying something together."

They were cleaning their rifles, pulling *four-by-two* through the barrels as they spoke.

"But what if she doesn't want to go out with me?"

"Think positive. What if she does? Think what a time you'll have."

A smile came over Gerald's face.

"Tell me, Richard. Have you ever done it with Joan?"

"No."

"What stopped you?"

"Nothing. I just didn't feel the need. I was with my physio at the party. You should see Sally in wet undies. But I have thought about Joan. I've been saving her for a rainy day. Well, it's *your* rainy day. You will ask her out, won't you?"

"If I don't settle things with Evelyn."

"Gerald, you are hopeless."

He lifted his rifle and looked through it. The rifling spiral stood out in the shining barrel. Satisfied, he replaced the bolt as Gerald continued wiping the black metal.

"I can't help it. If it's finished between Evelyn and me, I'll give Joan a go."

"She'd be flattered to hear that. Dear Joan, I love someone else, but as she's dumped me and if you're not too busy, I'd like to have a crack at you until I get her out of my system or she gets jealous and comes back to me. Be gentle with me, I'm a frustrated virgin."

"Maybe I'd better forget about Joan Meredith too. We've still got two months of Nasho. I might steer clear of women altogether until I graduate."

"That, my friend, is easier said than done. I couldn't live without them, mate."

"I don't think I could either. It's been too long as it is, Richard."

He remembered that last night with Evelyn, lying on their living-room floor. He had had his chance and he'd missed it. He wouldn't make that mistake again.

"Let's see if there's a ping-pong table in this camp. We both need a bit of sublimation."

Later in the week they went to the rifle range.

"Men, you've all been here before. You know what we want. Don't fire until you receive the order and hold your rifle up when you've finished firing. Check that there are no more rounds in the breech. Take your time and fire your five rounds. Then we'll examine your targets and adjust your sights accordingly. Then you'll all get five more rounds and we'll see who can shoot and who can't."

They lined up again, fired off five rounds, and examined their targets. The officer wasn't pleased.

"Bloody awful, men, bloody awful. I hope you bastards are better at your learning than you are at shooting. God help the country if we have to rely on you buggers. You'd be better throwing books than bullets. You're supposed to put the five rounds as close together as possible, not spread them around like piddle on a wall. This time I want you to concentrate, line up the sights with the target, hold your breath, steady yourself, and squeeze the trigger. Imagine that someone you hate very much is there in the centre of the target. Imagine it's Uncle Joe Stalin or your mother-in-law."

"The Vice-Chancellor," someone shouted.

"Bob Menzies."

Richard turned to Gerald, "Louis Brown."

Gerald went back to the mound. He waited for the order, pulled back the bolt, pushed it forward to drive a round into the breech, and took aim.

"Alright, Brown, this is for Evelyn."

Then he put five rounds slowly and deliberately into Louis Brown, checked that the rifle was empty, and held it up. Richard, lying alongside, did the same, thinking of the same human target. The targets were recovered and examined.

"That's more like it, men. Some of you buggers must really hate somebody. Fisher, bloody good grouping. You could be a marksman. I want to see some of you on the range tomorrow, and if you can do it again, I'm signing you up for the marksman's course. Fisher and Flynn, good shooting — collect all the empty shells. The rest of you, fall in. We've got a job to do before lunch."

They marched them out of the camp, a little way down the road. There was a truck waiting there with a few NCOs who handed the national servicemen shovels and trenching tools. They spent two hours under the hot midday sun clearing a fire break alongside the road to Oakbank, collecting all the dead leaves and branches, rubbish and weeds, and making piles on the road, which they shovelled into the truck. They were late back for lunch. Hot and sweaty and dirty, they flaked out on their beds for a quick nap, only to find that they had to go out and do it all over again. The stupid sergeant had got them to clear the wrong side of the road.

The next day Richard appeared with a large, brown envelope which he held aloft proudly.

"What's that for?"

"You'll see."

Next time they were told to fall in, Richard held up the envelope and ran off.

"Where are you going, Flynn?"

He just showed the sergeant the envelope and made off, as if he had something urgent to deliver. The sergeant assumed that it was something he'd been asked to take somewhere. Richard found a pile of mattresses behind the cinema screen and went to sleep. All day long he carried the envelope. Whenever an officer approached, he held up the envelope and ran. No one ever asked him who had given it to him and where he was supposed to take it. He never stayed long enough for that. From time to time he changed the item that he carried, using other envelopes or folded pieces of paper. He completed his National Service as an envelope carrier, reading Mickey Spillane on the pile of mattresses.

Gerald took his service seriously when he was selected to do the marksman's course. He and the others in the group spent day after day on various ranges, and were spared the drudgery of marching or digging fire breaks. He found that he liked guns and was good at shooting, that he had an aptitude for it. At the range he forgot about Louis Brown and Evelyn, concentrating on becoming a marksman. He won the rifle shooting prize for the intake. Nasho may have spoiled his holiday and his love life, but it hadn't been a *complete* waste of time.

Chapter Seventeen

March 1953

Joseph Stalin died on Thursday, the fifth of March. Uncle Joe, as he was known in the west, was mourned by a nation, most of whom, it must be assumed, loved their great war leader. At this stage very few Australians knew what a butcher this man was. Even in Russia his misdeeds were only spoken about in whispers and at great risk to the whisperer.

On the seventh of March elections were held in South Australia. Labor, with fifty-one percent of the popular vote, won fifteen seats. The Liberal/Country coalition with thirty-six and a half percent won twenty seats. Tom Playford retained his premiership. One of the youngest members to be elected was the new Labor member for Norwood, Don Dunstan, a reformer who was to become Premier for the decade of the seventies and change the city in many ways. The National Service trainees at Woodside were too young to vote in State or Federal Elections.

Evelyn's break with her father came in mid-March. It should never have happened. She didn't want it to happen. It was such a stupid, unnecessary calamity. Her involvement with Louis Brown had continued, a routine mechanical affair, with little feeling on either side. She felt it was coming to an end. She only went to his room as a refuge from her father's daily reproaches and her mother's questioning sadness. Brown's presence in town had split the family into three.

Making love had lost its thrill, Louis didn't bother to try and arouse her as he had done at the start, or perhaps he'd lost the ability and she was losing interest in him. She kidded herself each time that next time would be better, but it wasn't. She thought a lot about what she was doing. Gerald was right, she *was* a whore. She was letting Brown use her body in exchange for the pleasure of his company. She felt that he was getting the better part of the arrangement.

Louis had his supplementary exam at the end of March and decided to return to Adelaide two weeks before this to study. Evelyn intended to return to St Ann's on the first of April, a week before lectures started. She was looking forward to returning to Adelaide.

She hadn't enjoyed the vacation, in spite of her affair with Louis. The rows with her father and her break with Gerald had been a nightmare. The break with her father added to her black summer.

Mr Robertson wasn't spying on his daughter. Since the night he threw out the soldier boy she'd been a dutiful daughter, so what happened this night came as a complete surprise to him. He noticed Evelyn leaving the factory and was going to join her, intending to walk home with her, when he saw Louis Brown come up and take her by the arm. He watched the two of them set off down the roadway. Instead of heading for home they moved off into town. As he watched and followed at a distance, he saw them go into Mrs Evan's lodging house. He began to get hot under the collar.

"My daughter going into a lodging house with a man, with a man that I forbade her to see! What's she doing in there?"

He followed them inside and sought out the landlady. The moment she saw him she knew why he was there. She knew what was going on between his daughter and one of her lodgers. He saw the look of apprehension on her face and it told him exactly what he didn't want to know.

"My daughter just came in here with a Mr Brown. I want you to take me to her."

"Are you sure it was her, Mr Robertson?"

"Don't fool with me, Mrs Evans. I want my daughter out of this house at once. Where are they?"

Mr Robertson was getting angry. Mrs Evans didn't know what to do. She complied with his request.

"I'll see if she's here. Will you wait here?"

"No, take me to the room."

Evelyn was saying good-bye to Louis after a summer of passionate love, gone sour. She'd miss this strange, selfish, terrible man, but it would be a relief to know that he was gone. They would sit and talk, and then go to bed and make love for the last time. She hoped that this time it might have the magic of that first seduction. Louis passed her a glass of sherry and she was about to take a sip when there was a commotion outside. They listened, expecting it to go away, but there was a loud knock on the door. Louis unlocked it and peeked out. The door was pushed out of his grasp and Mr Robertson was inside the door. Evelyn tried to back away, but he grabbed his daughter, dragging her out into the corridor. The sherry glass fell to the floor and broke, sending the aroma of the wine into the air. As he left the room Mr Robertson struck out at the hated sherry bottle, knocking it to the floor where it poured out over the rug.

He faced Mrs Evans.

"I'm taking my daughter home and then I'm coming back. If Mr Brown is still here, I'm going to break every bone in his body." It was a vain stupid threat.

Then he left, dragging Evelyn with him. She was too terrified to resist.

Mrs Evans looked at her lodger.

"When are you leaving, Mr Brown?"

"I had intended going in the morning."

"Make it tonight. You've done wrong by that man's daughter. I want you gone before he comes back. I don't interfere with my lodgers, but what you've been doing with that girl, and the other girl before her, is despicable. You'd better go and pack."

'That girl's for it,' she thought 'She used to be one of the nicest girls in town. What *happened* to her?'

Mr Robertson didn't let go of his daughter until they were inside their living-room. He dragged her all the long way home, down the highway, in full view of everybody, workers on their way home. He was red in the face and she was crying. It was so humiliating. Evelyn's fear was changing to hurt and hate.

He sent her to her room and told Mrs Robertson what had happened. Then he called her back to the living-room. She came back like a convict awaiting the sentence, death, or penal servitude in the colonies. Her wrist was bruised and hurt from his vice-like grip.

"Sit down, girl, and explain yourself."

She didn't answer.

"What were you doing in that man's room?"

Still no answer.

"*What* were you doing?"

"Saying good-bye."

"In a *man's* bedroom?"

"Yes."

"And drinking wine?"

"Yes."

"And you've been there before?"

"Yes."

Evelyn had never been to a law court, but she felt like a prisoner in the dock. As least he hadn't found them in bed.

"Many times?"

Evelyn didn't answer. She couldn't say "no", and not answering was as good as saying "yes". She and her mother started to cry.

"I see. I thought I told you not to see that man again or, for that matter, the soldier."

"I haven't seen Gerald."

"But you've been seeing Mr Brown in his room and drinking with him?"

No answer.

"And what else have you been doing, you little whore, when you said you were at the Williams or with Sally Thomas? Were you in his bedroom *every* night?"

No answer. How could she answer such a question?

"Damn you, Evelyn, I want to know where you were."

Mrs Robertson could see how upset he was. He had said "damn!"

"I was with Louis."

"You little whore. Does he intend to marry you now that he's ruined you?"

Again she didn't answer. In her eyes she wasn't ruined.

"I asked you if he intends to marry you, or are you just his whore, to be discarded now that he's leaving town?"

Mrs Robertson couldn't take any more and tried to stop her husband. It was she, and not her daughter, who was crying now.

"Wes, stop bullying the girl! Stop saying things like that. Stop it, Wes!"

"Sara, if you'd kept an eye on the girl, none of this would have happened. Did you know what was going on?"

"No, Dad." Evelyn stepped in to defend her mother. "Mother didn't know. I'm sorry. I didn't do anything bad. I was lonely. I'm sorry. Tonight I was going to see him for the last time."

"You deceived us! You lied to us! Well, you can forget about going back to Adelaide."

"Wes!"

"Don't interfere, Sara. I'm not paying for my own daughter's debauchery. I'm going to write a letter to the principal of St Ann's and ask her what kind of a place they're running. I hoped that a

Christian girl's college would protect my daughter's morals. I didn't think that they'd turn her into a tramp."

Evelyn had had enough. She shouted back at her father, "I am not a tramp! Why does every person I love call me names?" Evelyn was beginning to fight back.

"You *are* a tramp, and if you weren't my daughter and my responsibility, I'd throw you out on the street."

"You do that! I'd be better off on the street than in this prison. If I can't go back to university, I'll go to Adelaide and get a job. I *won't* stay in this prison."

"You'll do what I tell you to do, my girl."

Mrs Robertson tried to stop the fight.

"Wes, please calm down."

"Sara, I've made up my mind. She's not going back to St Ann's or anywhere in Adelaide. She's going to stay here in Renmark."

Evelyn didn't say another word. She wiped her tears and went to her room, hoping that her father wouldn't follow her there, hoping that he hadn't read her mind.

"Come back here," her father called to her. "I didn't say that you could leave the room."

At first she wanted to cry, but there wasn't much time. Her suitcase was half packed, ready for her return to Adelaide. She dragged it out from under the bed and threw into it the last remaining things she could find. While her parents were arguing about her she slowly slipped out of the back door and crept out quietly into the street through the back gate. She wasn't a moment too soon. Brown was loading up his car when she joined him. She looked back down the street. It was empty. They hadn't discovered that she had gone.

"Louis, I'm coming to Adelaide with you."

"What happened? Did you get a thrashing?"

"No, but we'd better get going. If Dad finds out I've gone, we'll both be for it. I've left home."

Louis put her suitcase in the boot and got in the car. He expected her father to appear any minute with a stockwhip. He got in and they were on their way out of town. Once underway they were able to relax.

Mrs Robertson went to see Evelyn. She found a note on her table:

> *Goodbye, Mother. I'm going to Adelaide. I can't take*
> *any more bullying. I'll write to you, Mother.*
> *love,*
> *Evelyn.*

She showed the letter to her husband. "Please stop her, Wes. Tell her you didn't mean what you said."

They rang Mrs Evans.

"Is Mr Brown there?"

"No, he just left in his car."

"Was my daughter with him?"

"I don't know. I didn't see her."

Mr Robertson put the handset back on the phone and sat down by his weeping wife.

"He's gone, Sara. She may be with him."

"Are you sure?"

"No."

"Go out and find her. She might still be here."

"No, Sara. If she wants to leave, I can't stop her. Brown just left. I'm certain she went with him."

"She was going to say good-bye to him, that's all. Now you've pushed her into going away with him."

"Sara, I found them together in his room."

"You drove our daughter out of our house."

"She went of her own accord. If she's lucky, he'll do the right thing and marry her."

"Is that what you want?"

"No, but that's what I expect him to do."

Mrs Robertson couldn't believe her ears. How could he want their daughter to marry that dreadful man?

"She doesn't love him, Wes."

"Are you crazy, Sara? She as good as admitted that she's been his..."

He couldn't bring himself to say "lover."

"...She's been visiting him in his room all summer."

"Wes, if she'd been in love with Louis, she'd have told me. I know what she was doing was wrong and so does she. She needed help to straighten out her life, not your shouting. Let me go to Adelaide and tell her she can go back to St Ann's and resume her studies. Don't crush the girl, Wes. She's our only daughter. She's all we've got."

"Go to Adelaide if you want, and bring her back if that's what you want. Then she stays in Renmark."

"Wes!"

"*No* college. She has to stay in Renmark."

"She's our only daughter, Wes."

"So why do you want her living a life of sin in Adelaide?"

"I'll go and see her and I'll talk to her. She'll listen to me."

"But not to me! You tell her to get back here and forget about Brown and her other men friends. If, on the other hand, she decides to marry her lover that's OK by me, but I don't intend to support her any more."

"She's got a little money of her own. She took her bank book."

"She'll come back when she's spent it."

That was the last straw. She had never expected him to adopt this attitude.

"You're a bastard, Wes. That's our daughter you're talking about."

"Don't you swear at me. I know what I'm doing. You go and get her back or let her stew in her own juice."

"You're a bastard, Wes. I wish I'd never had a daughter for you to bully."

"If she doesn't come home quickly, we won't have a daughter. I'll disown her."

Mrs Robertson had had enough. She went to her room and cried. For the first time in twenty years of marriage she thought about leaving her husband, but she knew that she couldn't. She had no money of her own, no place to go to, and no profession. All she knew was how to look after his house, look after him and their daughter, her daughter, that she might never see again. She had a little housekeeping money. The rest of their funds were in his account. After twenty years of marriage she didn't have enough money of her own to help her daughter if she needed it.

'Will she be forced to live with Brown because her father won't give her the money to stay in college? Will she have to get a job to support herself? Perhaps she'll write to us and Wes will change his mind. Perhaps she'll meet Gerald again and forget all about Louis. I hope so. Where will I write to her? Will Wes hide her letters from me and return them unopened, if she does write?'

When her husband came to bed, she pretended to be sleeping, but he could hear her sniffling and hated himself. But he didn't change his mind.

'I only did what a father has to do,' he thought. 'I'm right and I know it. I have God on my side.'

On Sunday they went to church. Sara Robertson prayed for her daughter's safety. Wesley Robertson prayed for support and his daughter's soul. If God heard their prayers, he was slow to respond.

It was late and the road to Adelaide was almost empty. Louis Brown drove fast. Evelyn sat in silence and he didn't intrude on her thoughts. They were both deep in thought — he wondering what to do with her when they arrived in the city, and she wondering what would become of her with her limited funds. Would her father stick to his guns and withdraw all support? Would she see Gerald and would he forgive her? He would still be doing his National Service, his damn National Service that had kept them apart. She blamed it for what had happened. She blamed her father and her own weakness. She didn't blame the real snake-in-the-grass, the man at the wheel of the car, the man driving her away from her family.

Why hadn't Gerald written? She decided to find herself a room of her own and then contact him when he came back to Adelaide. Someone had to break the ice. He might tell her to get packing and if he did, she'd only herself to blame. She cried a little. Brown noticed a tear fall down her cheek, but said nothing. He wondered what had happened between her and her father that evening, if he'd beaten her. Would she have marks on her? He felt sorry for her.

It was after midnight when they got to Adelaide.

"It's late, Evelyn. You'd better come to my place. You can find somewhere to stay tomorrow."

He took her home, woke up his mother, and she took them both inside.

"Mom, this is Evelyn. She needs a bed for the night."

"Why didn't you tell me that you were coming? I'd have fixed up a room and made up a bed for your friend."

"Sorry, but we left Renmark in a hurry. Can't Evelyn sleep in the spare room?"

"She'll have to, won't she? It needs a good cleaning, but I can't do it in the middle of the night. I'll bring some sheets. You help her with her things."

"I'm sorry to be such a nuisance. I wanted to find a hotel room, but Louis thinks it's too late."

"You from Renmark?"

"Yes, but I'm studying at the university."

"You're a bit early, aren't you, dear? Louis has an exam in two weeks time. Have you been studying for it, Louis?"

"Yes, Mom."

He was lying, he hadn't opened a book all summer.

Evelyn was grateful for the bed and that Louis stayed away from her that night. She was up early in the morning, had breakfast with Mrs Brown, and looked in the *Advertiser* for accommodation. She estimated that she'd have enough money to live in a cheap room and feed herself for about six months. There was a weeks wages due to her at the cannery. She would have to ask her mother to get that for her, and hope that they didn't give it to her father. When her money ran out, she could apply for a living allowance to go with her scholarship, or go out and find a job. It wouldn't be easy trying to study and support herself. She'd have to work as a waitress in the afternoons or evenings. She hoped that her father would relent and let her go back to the college when he saw how determined she was, and when he calmed down. She would have to apologise. If it meant a promise never to see Louis Brown again, she was more than willing.

She was thinking about this when Louis appeared in his pyjamas, unshaved and barefoot, joining them at the breakfast table. She had hoped to be out of the house before this.

"You're up early, Louis."

"I have to study, Mother."

"And I have to find a room," said Evelyn. "I think I'll try the student accommodation service at the SRC."

Evelyn returned at four. The Browns were having tea and cake, so she joined them.

"How did you make out?"

"I looked at a few places. Nice, but too expensive. I've two more addresses to go to, but they're on the other side of town and would involve me in a lot of travelling. Do you think I could stay here another night?"

"Evelyn, I've been thinking. We often rent the spare room to students. It's only a fifteen-minute walk from here to the university. Would you like to rent the spare room?"

"I couldn't."

She wanted to tell her that she couldn't stay in the house with her son, but she didn't want to offend them.

"I can't afford to pay much rent. So far, the people want a lot of money. I'll be living off a shoestring until Dad and I settle our differences, if we do."

On the one hand Mrs Brown realised that if Evelyn stayed, she'd be placed in temptation's way with Louis, but she also fancied Evelyn as a possible bride for her son, so she really wanted Evelyn to stay. She didn't need the thirty shillings a week, as her late husband had left her well provided for, but Evelyn seemed such a nice girl. She had ambivalent feelings about her. What was the relationship between her son and this young woman? She watched them as Evelyn chatted with Louis and helped him prepare for the exam. She liked Evelyn. Later she heard them talking in his room late at night and wondered if they were still studying or doing something more intimate. If Louis had a fiancée, he might pass his exams. Mrs Brown wanted this girl to stay. She wanted her here to make a man of her son, she wanted her company. She wanted her as a daughter-in-law. More than anything in the world, she wanted her son to get married and settle down.

Chapter Eighteen

April 1953

Louis Brown had failed Bacteriology I and was studying for a supplementary exam on the thirty-first of March. Evelyn hadn't studied the subject, but as she had nothing better to do and because Louis asked her, she helped him study for the exam, testing him on each day's material. He didn't know the work, he was a slow learner, so she soon realised that he'd be very lucky to pass the exam. She herself had learned enough in two weeks to pass it, but he hadn't. Quite often, after they'd spent the evening together, Louis persuaded her to come to bed with him. The night before the exam he insisted once more to help him relax before the paper. He sat for the exam, handing in a worse paper than he'd done in November.

Evelyn accompanied him to the university in the morning and waited for him. She wandered into town, looked at all the goods that she couldn't afford to buy in Myers and John Martins, then went back to the campus and the Refectory. The place was full of Freshers. She sold some of her first-year books to one of them. She'd wanted to hang onto them, but needed the money more than the books. Evelyn met a few friends who all asked the same painful question.

"Where's Gerald?"

"He's finishing Nasho. I haven't seen him," was her standard reply.

Joan Meredith turned up in the red Mercedes and joined her for coffee and scones. Joan ate, while Evelyn ordered nothing. She couldn't afford such luxuries. Evelyn felt annoyed. Joan had money to burn and she had barely enough for the next six months. She ate one of Joan's left-over scones.

"You back at St Ann's, Evelyn?"

"No, I'm living out this year."

"Good for you. You'll be able to stay out as long as you like. I don't know how you stood for it. Is that why you moved out?"

"Partly that and partly because of the cost."

"Gerald for one will be pleased. Does he know?"

"We've split up. I haven't heard from him."

Joan wasn't able to conceal her surprise. Evelyn saw it in her face.

"What happened? You two were so close."

"I'd rather we didn't talk about it, Joan."

Evelyn was upset by their break-up. Some guys didn't know when they were lucky.

"Never mind, you'll find someone else."

"I don't think that I want to, just now. I have to find a job after lecture hours."

"Why?"

"I left home against my father's wishes and he won't pay me any allowance. He didn't want me to continue this year. I have to support myself."

'What a shit of a father!' thought Joan.

It was good to talk to someone, another woman like herself. She'd never felt close to Joan, but now she seemed so sympathetic. Evelyn had thought of her as a woman of loose morals, thought that she was better than Joan, but now she was wiser. She, Evelyn, was the same, she had been sleeping with Louis Brown. She vaguely remembered Gerald telling her that Louis had been Joan's lover last year. She listened as Joan told her what she thought of Mr Robertson.

"After you passed? What a bastard! Don't worry, Evelyn, he'll change his mind when he sees that you're serious about studying. What did you do to make him do that?"

"I can't tell you. We had a big row and I was partly to blame. But I have to study, with or without his blessing."

"Don't worry. It'll turn out alright in the end."

"Thanks, Joan. I have to go now. I'm meeting someone."

Evelyn got up and left the Refectory. Joan, curious, got up and followed her to the door and watched as she walked over to Brown's car, his new car. He was waiting for her. She got in and they drove away.

'So that's how the land lies. Who left whom and why? She says she doesn't want anyone, so why is the fool seeing Louis Brown? Silly little bitch. How could she dump Gerald for such a big shit? God help her.'

She wanted to warn Evelyn, to tell her what a bastard that man was, but she was in Brown's car, heading back to his place, heading into a sea of troubles.

Evelyn spent the afternoon looking through recent newspapers. Tito had been in London for talks with Winston Churchill — the

British were still protesting about the loss of a Lincoln bomber that the Russians had shot down, flying the Berlin Corridor. In Kenya the Mau Mau had murdered two hundred men, women, and children. She turned to the Amusements section. *Kiss Me Kate* was coming to the Theatre Royal. If she made up with Gerald, he might want to take her. She didn't have the money to go there by herself and she didn't want to go with Louis. She put on the radio. Eddy Fisher was singing *Lady Of Spain*. She suddenly thought:

'What am I doing in this house? What will Gerald think if I'm still here when he comes out of the army?'

She had two and a half weeks to find a room of her own.

Louis had gone straight to his room when they got home. At four he re-emerged holding a university examination book, the kind used for writing in one's answers. Without any explanation of his reasons, he abruptly asked Evelyn to come with him for a drive. She was having afternoon tea with his mother. She didn't want to go for a drive.

"Where, Louis?"

"Not far. I'll show you when we get there."

They drove three blocks to where Steven Meredith, the lecturer in Bacteriology, lived, parking outside his house. Evelyn knew the house well, it was just down from St Ann's and she'd often passed it on her way to and from lectures. Louis put the examination book into her handbag, closing it.

"What's all this about, Louis?"

"I didn't tell you the truth this morning. I made a mess of the exam. I couldn't remember anything. I just checked my answers against my lecture notes and saw what a mess I'd made. I smuggled an answer book out of the exam room this morning and I rewrote the exam. Meredith took them home with him after the exam. Now he's at the uni and we can substitute the paper for the one I did this morning."

"That's cheating, Louis."

Copying from her practical book was one thing, switching examination books was a different kettle of fish.

"Evelyn, I have to pass that exam. Besides, everybody cheats. If I don't pass now, I'll never get my degree."

"It's still cheating, Louis."

"Everybody cheats, I said."

He was adopting that bullying tone he used when he wanted her to go to bed with him.

"No they don't. I don't cheat and my friends don't."

"Only because they're frightened that they'd get caught. Evelyn, we haven't got much time. Dr Meredith gets home just after five."

"I'll walk home. I hope you get caught."

She tried to get out of the car, but he stopped her.

"That wasn't nice after all I've done for you."

"How do you intend to change the papers over?"

"You're going to do it."

"Me?"

'The man's mad!' she thought, 'and so am I to be here with him.'

"It's simple. Meredith has lots of girlfriends. You go up and say that you're expected. While you're waiting, you'll be able to find his briefcase and change over the exam paper. I've already put it in your handbag. Up you go."

"I can't break into his house."

"You don't have to. He has a housekeeper who'll let you in. Get going, we've only got half an hour. You should be able to do it in ten minutes, but the sooner you go the sooner we'll be out of here."

He held her by the wrist, the wrist that had been sore for a week from her father's grip. He squeezed it until she consented.

"You're a bully, Brown. After this we're finished."

"As you like, but hurry."

Evelyn went up the steps and knocked on the door of the old house. She was scared, scared of what she we going to do and scared of Louis Brown, down there behind her.

"Is Mr Meredith in?"

"No, he'll be back after five."

"Oh. I'm afraid that I'm a little early. Can I wait for him inside?"

"Is he expecting you?"

"Yes."

"Come in. You can wait in the library."

As soon as the housekeeper left, Evelyn got up and started looking for the briefcase with the exam papers.

"I must be mad," she said to herself. "What am I doing for that bully?"

Meanwhile the housekeeper telephoned her employer.

"Mr Meredith, there's a girl come to see you. Were you expecting anyone?"

"No, what does she look like?"

The housekeeper went to take another look at Evelyn, saw that she wasn't in the library and finally found her in Steven's study. She watched as she changed over the exam paper and rushed back to the telephone.

"Mr Meredith, I think she's a thief. I just saw her taking something out of your briefcase. I'll call the police if you like."

"Don't. I'm coming home at once. There's only exam papers in that briefcase. Keep her in until I get there."

It was about a five-minute drive from the university to his house. Steven did it in four. Evelyn had put Brown's morning exam paper into her handbag and was ready to leave, when the housekeeper came back to the library.

"Would you like a cup of tea while you're waiting?"

"No, I think I'd better go. I'll come back after five."

"Now that would be silly. It's almost five. Steven will be here in another half an hour. I'll make you a nice cup of tea."

"I think I made a mistake. I..."

She couldn't think of an excuse on the spur of the moment.

"Mr Meredith will be upset when I tell him you've gone."

"I'll be back in thirty minutes. I want to change my shoes. I'm a nurse from the children's hospital."

This was all going wrong. She could see that the woman suspected something, that she wouldn't let her go.

"Would you care to leave a note? I'll bring a pen and paper from the study."

"No, just tell him that Joan was here, Joan Fisher."

It was the first name that came to her mind and she hated herself for using Gerald's name. She ran to the front door, but Louis's car wasn't there. She saw it moving away, driving up the street. There was a big black Buick in its place and a well-dressed tall man with black hair coming up the steps, Steven Meredith, Joan's brother.

"Thank God you're here," said the housekeeper. "I couldn't keep her any longer."

He pushed Evelyn back from the door, closed it and locked it. The bruise he gave her was the least of her worries.

"This is Miss Joan Fisher, Mr Meredith. She said that you were expecting her."

He dismissed the housekeeper and turned to the frightened girl.

"Miss Fisher? I don't think that I've had the pleasure."

"Would you excuse me, I shouldn't be here."

"Oh, but you are. What are you doing here?"

"I made a mistake. Can I go now?"

He looked a lot like his sister. They both had the same black hair and hazel eyes. He was taller and broad in the shoulders. If only Joan were here, she'd help her. She could tell by the look on his face that he was very angry. He looked at her with a cruel look that made her shake with fear. Why didn't Louis come back to explain? This was *his* affair, not hers.

"What are you doing here?"

"I told you, I made a mistake."

"What kind of mistake?"

"I came to the wrong house."

"No you didn't, you asked for Mr Meredith. That's me! Listen, young lady, I don't know what your game is, but my housekeeper saw you open my briefcase and interfere with my papers. Show me what you've got in your handbag."

Evelyn *knew* that the game was up. For the second time in the three long months that she had known Louis Brown, he had put her in an impossible position, first with her father and now with Joan's brother.

"Leave my handbag alone. Let me go. You can't keep me here."

"Yes I can. I can hold you and call the police. Then you'll have to open your handbag for them."

"Alright, have a look in my handbag."

She handed him her handbag, watched as he opened it, took out the examination paper and read the name on it.

"Louis Brown. Is he a friend of yours?"

There was a wicked smile on his face, as if someone had just told him a dirty joke.

"Yes." She should have told him that he *had been*. Now he was anything but a friend. He was, in fact, her enemy now.

"Are you a student, too?"

"Yes."

"You've got a bank book here. You don't have much money. I also see that your name isn't Joan Fisher, it's Evelyn Robertson, or did you steal this book, too?"

She started to cry.

"I'm not a thief."

"Oh, yes you are. You stole this examination paper. Did he give you one to replace it with?"

She nodded.

"Well, I'm not going to read it. I'm going to fail Louis Brown and have him expelled from the university and you too, Miss Robertson."

"Please don't have us expelled."

Steven wasn't angry. He had caught Louis Brown and he had a pretty woman at his mercy. He was enjoying himself as he feigned indignation, like a little boy pulling the wings off a grasshopper.

"I have never heard of such a thing. You break into my house and tamper with exam papers. I've never heard of such a thing."

"Can I go, now?"

"No, you'll go when I decide what to do with you."

"You've already decided to report me. I wanted so much to study. You've just ruined my life."

"*I* ruined your life? You ruined it when you decided to become a cheat and a thief. You ruined it, as you say, for a ratbag, a lazy fool of a man. I watched him all year, sitting on his arse in practical classes, doing no work at all. Why on earth did you let him talk you into this?"

"I felt a little sorry for him and he pushed me into doing it. Louis can be very persuasive."

She rubbed her sore arm.

"You felt sorry for him! That's the weakest excuse that I've ever heard. You did it because he's your lover."

That she wouldn't admit. Once for a couple of weeks he had been her lover; now he was just a terrible mistake, something that she was ashamed to acknowledge.

"Please don't have me expelled. My scholarship is all I have. It's everything to me. My father's mad at me. I can't even go home."

"Because of Louis Brown?"

She nodded . She was a pitiful sight. He couldn't hurt such a soul in distress, but she was a pretty young woman, Brown's woman. To Steven Meredith women were commodities.

He had just caught this commodity committing a felony. She was his commodity now, not Brown's.

"Evelyn Robertson, you are a silly cow. I'm going to fail your lover. I'm going to have him expelled too. I can't do that without involving you. You're my witness to his villainy."

"Please, Mr Meredith."

She was clinging to his lapels and crying.

"It's late, I can't do anything about it until tomorrow and I can't let you go out in your state. Shall I ask Brown to come and fetch you? After we wipe away those tears of yours?"

"Louis will want to know what happened. How will I tell him?"

He was fooling with Evelyn. He was having fun. It wasn't every day that a pretty woman like Evelyn was at his mercy. It gave him a sense of power, like his money gave him.

"To hell with Louis Brown. Was that him driving away? Let him suffer. Come and tell me all about yourself. First, I think we should have a glass of sherry."

"I don't drink."

"Nonsense, a small glass of sherry will put the colour back in your cheeks."

"You're playing with me. Is it fair to tease me when you're going to ruin my life tomorrow?"

"Don't worry about tomorrow until tomorrow comes. *Che serà serà*. Stay and have dinner with me."

"So you can watch me and gloat? You're as big a bastard as Louis is."

"That's your lover you're calling a bastard. The truth is, I haven't quite decided what to do with you. You're a very attractive woman even though you've been crying. I don't have a heart of stone, but as an employee of the university I have to decide if what you've done is a felony."

"Why don't you leave that to the Vice-Chancellor?"

"Is that what you want?"

"No."

She almost shouted. If Meredith went to the VC, she'd be back in Renmark with an angry father.

"Good, so we'll have dinner together. Just let me make a phone call and cancel a prior engagement and tell my housekeeper. I'll be right back."

"Do I have any say in the matter?"

"I'm afraid not."

'The bastard,' she thought. 'He's playing with me like a cat plays with a mouse. If I manage to get out, he'll disgrace me. If I don't, God knows what he'll want from me. Well, Mr Brown, look where your bullying's got me. You and I are now really and truly finished. What does Meredith want with me? He obviously likes me. Perhaps he wants to ask me out. Perhaps he wants me to dine with him and nothing more. Fancy me dining with Joan's brother. What else will he expect me to do? I might as well leave now and return to Renmark to eat humble pie and forget all about studying and making up with Gerald. If I caught a train, I could be home by midnight. But I'd be so miserable there, I'd die.'

Evelyn was crying again when Steven Meredith returned with two glasses of ice-cold champagne. He offered her a glass.

"This is the best French Champagne, pre-war. Drink up and you'll feel better."

"Mr Meredith, I think I'd better be going."

"Nonsense. I won't hear of it. I've ordered dinner for two. Drink up your champagne and tell me your story."

She put the glass to her lips and sipped it slowly. It was cool and refreshing, but the bubbles got up her nose. She thought of what her father would say, but the champagne tasted so delightful and her father was so far away. Steven was right, the drink did make her feel better. Talking with somebody had the same effect. She told him about her first year at university, of Gerald, her return to Renmark, and the events of the disastrous summer. She cried as she told him.

"You're still sleeping with Louis Brown?"

She nodded.

"And you want to leave him?"

"Yes."

"You weren't in love with him?"

"We spoke of love at night when we were together, but when we were apart, I knew that we'd been kidding ourselves. Who knows? Perhaps he was kidding me and I was kidding myself. You see, I had to have a reason for sleeping with him other than that I couldn't help myself."

"You, lady, were a sitting duck. Pity I wasn't around at the time. I'd have treated you better than Brown. If he cared for you at all, if he was a man, he wouldn't have driven off when I came, or at the very least he would have come and extricated you and taken all the blame. What about your boyfriend, the one that you cuckolded?"

'Does he have to speak to me like that, use such an expression, he, Adelaide's number-one Casanova!'

"Do you have to rub it in? Haven't I suffered enough for what I've done?"

"I like to call a spade a spade. You did do the dirty on your soldier boy."

"I suppose so."

It was no longer a comfort, talking to this man who held her future in his hands. He was grinding her into the ground and they both knew it. She put her head down.

"What about him?" Steven asked, grinding her down another notch.

"We're finished. He called me a whore and I haven't heard from him since."

"What did you expect — a medal, a box of chocolates?"

"I didn't want him to find out," she sobbed. "You should have seen the look of hatred in his eyes. Why did he have to find out? Why did I do this thing to him?"

"Would you have told him?"

"Eventually. I'm a bad liar. I always get caught."

"What did you expect? He'd have been hurt whenever or however he found out. Men don't like to be cheated."

"But they're allowed to cheat."

'Who was he to lecture her on morality?'

"What would you have done if you'd been in his place, if the roles had been reversed?"

All the time he was looking at her, examining her from head to toe, like a commodity, a side of beef. Steven Meredith liked what he saw, she looked like a good lay. He pictured her naked, wondering what she'd be like in bed.

"I don't know, I've never thought of Gerald sleeping with other women. I never thought that I'd do what I did. This summer has been so awful."

"It's time for dinner, I smell the beef cooking."

Steven was quite pleasant over dinner. He steered the conversation away from her troubles and Louis Brown. He was charming, very charming. He didn't press her to drink the wine and she remained sober and clear headed. Instead he called for a carafe of Perrier water, Adelaide tap water would never do. They spoke about books and music. Steven was well read and had a superb record collection, as well he could afford to have. He was the most eligible bachelor in the city. The candles flickered on the table and the flower arrangement gave off a faint perfume. It was as elegant a table as you would see anywhere in the city.

It was a romantic setting and Evelyn would have loved to relax and enjoy herself, if she hadn't been a prisoner at this man's table. This tall young millionaire had her in the palm of his hand together with her future, hers and Louis Brown's too. This would be a fateful night for the two of them and for others as well.

'Louis can take what's coming to him,' she thought. 'He made me come here and ran out on me. Maybe, after dinner, this man will let me go and forget my part in it. He is being ever so charming.'

She didn't know Steven Meredith and his appetite for women. She didn't know that she was dealing with as big a rat as Louis Brown, probably a bigger one.

After dinner Evelyn decided that it was time to try and leave.

"What's the hurry? I'm having such an enjoyable evening."

"It's late and I haven't got a house key."

"You can't go now. I'm just getting to know you."

"Some other night."

"No, Evelyn, tonight."

His voice had suddenly turned cruel again, as it had been when he'd found that examination paper in her handbag.

"What are you trying to say, Mr Meredith?"

There was no sense beating about the bush. Evelyn wanted out and she wanted out now.

"Don't be naïve, girl. You know what I want."

"Yes, I suppose I do, but I don't want what you want."

"You're a fool, girl."

"Why, because you're Steven Meredith, son of Meredith Beer and you are filthy rich?"

"So you've heard of me?"

"Yes, but I still don't want you."

She should have mentioned that she was a friend of his sister. Then what followed might have been avoided.

"Why not?"

"Because I have a boyfriend. Why should I sleep with you?"

"To get your boyfriend off the hook."

"I wasn't referring to Brown. He's not worth it."

"Am I so repulsive?"

"No, Steven, you're quite handsome. It's just that I don't love you."

"Love? What has that got to do with it? Do you love that big slob you've been sleeping with?"

"I thought I did. The fact is, he got me to do it in a moment of weakness."

"You seem to have had a lot of weak moments."

"I know better now..."

She thought, 'What a vindictive bastard he is.'

"...I'll never sleep with him again."

"Terrific. I hate sharing a woman. Evelyn, you're a very attractive woman and you're growing more attractive every minute. What can I do to convince you to spend the night with me, to be my new romance?" She wanted to throw up, to do to this man what she'd done to Brown on New Year's Eve.

"If you want me to be your mistress, Steven, forget it. I'm just getting out of one mess and I don't want to get into another. I want my freedom and my self-respect."

"Stay with me tonight. I'll let you go in the morning."

"No."

"Evelyn, I cancelled my date to be with you tonight. Don't spoil my evening."

"It'll do you good to sleep alone."

"Maybe, but it won't do you any good."

The warm dining-room suddenly changed into a torture chamber. The candles flickered and Steven's face grew harsh.

"If that was a joke, Mr Meredith, it was in bad taste."

"I'm not noted for my sense of humour."

"What about your sense of decency?"

"You should talk. You came to my house to commit a crime."

"I told you, it was all Brown's idea. I didn't do it for myself. I did it for him. I didn't come voluntarily."

"And now you want to go back to his bed?"

He hadn't listened to a word she'd said.

"I don't want to go to anyone's bed but my own. Please let me go."

She was again on the verge of tears.

"No."

"And forgive me my trespassing. I've learned my lesson."

"Amen! Spend the night with me and I'll wipe the slate clean. Leave me alone to my own devices and there's no knowing what I may do."

"That's—"

Steven stopped her from saying the word, "blackmail".

"Don't say it. If we're going to spend the night together, we should only say nice things."

"You want me to be nice to you. How can I, when I'm being forced? Give me a choice."

"You want me to agree to wipe the slate clean and then you'll decide whether or not you'll stay?"

"Yes."

"I'll say one thing for you, Miss Robertson, you sure are plucky. I've never had a girl stand up to me like you're doing, not even a virgin. Damn it, girl, you've been sleeping with a creep, a cheating rat, so why won't you sleep with me?"

"I was sleeping with someone I *now* know to be a creep, I admit it. I just don't want to sleep with another one."

"That does it. I'm going upstairs. When you're ready, come up. The bedroom is the second on the right. I'll leave the door open, or would you prefer to accompany me now?"

"No, I want to go home."

"Pity. A bright girl like you should study. It'll be a pity to lose such a good student."

He left the room, but didn't leave the door open. He locked it, imprisoning her. Evelyn lay down on the floor and cried. If she was expelled from the university, shame and disgrace would follow her. She'd either have to look for a job and forget about her friends and studies at the university, or go back to Renmark and her father's anger. How would her father treat her when he heard of her latest misdemeanour? He'd never let her out of his sight again. He'd force her to marry the first man that could be found, just to get her off his hands. One thing, she decided, she wouldn't go back. In no time she'd be a housewife like her mother, a husband's property, having babies, washing clothes and having sex when and if her husband wanted it. Last year had been such a good year, such a happy year. Why did this Meredith man want to deprive her of this?

'I could go back to Louis,' she thought. 'We'd both be in the same boat. Why should I? He's the rat that ran out on me and got me into this mess. If only Gerald were in town, I might have someone to turn to. He'd help me, he or Richard, but they're still in camp at Woodside. I could ring his mother. Would she hang up on me when she heard my name, after what I did to her son? What can I do? Now I know what went through Jonny Marco's mind before he jumped off the bridge. Is this what Louis Brown brings people to? Oh, Gerald, why didn't I listen to you and Richard? My life is a mess before it's really begun.'

She was glad, in a way, that the door was locked. If it had been open and she'd gone out, the world outside would have had no room for her. She had run out of alternatives.

She didn't hear the key slowly turning in the lock. She felt the soft touch of Steven's hand on her shoulders. She let him pick her up like a sack of potatoes and carry her out of the room. At the foot of the stairs he set her on her feet, kissed her gently on the forehead and with one arm around her waist, helped her to the top, then into the bedroom. He locked the door behind them, took the key with them to the bed, which had been pulled back to receive them. He placed the key under the mattress. She felt nothing. The hour spent by herself with her thoughts had broken her. She stood, standing shakily before a huge ornate four-poster bed.

"Why did you lock the door?"

"I don't want you to change your mind at the last moment or run away crying afterwards. It's for your own good. Relax, Evelyn. Most women in Adelaide would give an eye and a tooth to be where you are tonight."

'An eye for an eye,' she thought.

Evelyn said nothing. Louis Brown had always locked the door to keep people out, people like her father. Being locked in made her apprehensive but resigned, which was his purpose. She'd have to let him do what he wanted to her. It would be an experience, but she couldn't relax and enjoy it. Could it be any worse than sleeping with Louis?

'It looks like I'm spending a night with Steven Meredith whether I like it or not,' she thought, saying nothing to him. 'Get it over with. Get it over, I'm guilty as charged. I'll take my punishment like a man. What a funny expression — like a man.'

Having stowed the key in a safe place, Meredith turned to his quarry. He whispered in her ear how beautiful she was and kissed her there. She shuddered. Then he showered her with kisses as he slowly undressed her, caressing her with his hands. If another man had done this to her, a man she loved, it might have been magical, but his hands gave her goose pimples. When she was completely naked he stood back and admired her.

"Not bad, not bad at all. Nice tits, a bit skinny but then you're young, you'll fill out. Too good to waste on Louis Brown."

Evelyn felt sorry for Louis. Everybody spoke badly of him when he wasn't around to defend himself. But she now hated him for getting her into this predicament. She quickly got under the sheets to cover her nakedness.

"Please put out the light."

"That's what I like. It always feels better in the dark."

He put out the light and Evelyn was spared having to see him undress. Then she felt him slide under the sheet, cold and clammy like a toad, next to her.

"Steven, please take precautions. I don't want to have a baby."

"Don't worry, neither do I."

She heard him fumbling in a drawer.

"Here we are — lucky, last one. Must have some more in the other bedroom."

She felt the bed wobble as he prepared himself and steeled herself for what was to follow. She was being forced to do this, this most wonderful of all activities, but she was determined not to let herself go and make sure Steven Meredith knew it. She hoped that he wouldn't arouse her as Louis had done. She didn't want to give him that satisfaction.

He put his mouth to hers, but she didn't kiss him back. He played with her breasts, but it had no effect on her. Finally he touched her down below.

"You're dry. I'll have to use some Vaseline."

He made love to her and she bit her lip until it bled, trying to get away from the sensation of it. He came quickly and she was spared any more of this indignity, as he rolled over and lay next to her.

'Thank God, that's over,' she said to herself. It had been a horrible experience, paying for her misdemeanour with her body. Louis was so much better than Steven would ever be. She was grateful. If he'd been a considerate lover, she'd have responded like a woman, and she didn't want to do that with a man who had forced her into bed with threats. Now she could resume her life and studies. It hadn't been so bad after all.

"What time is it, Mr Meredith?"

"Between ten-thirty and eleven."

"I'd like to have a shower and go."

"You'll go when I tell you to go. Wasn't that great?"

"You enjoyed it?"

"Yes, didn't you?"

He knew she hadn't, but his pride wouldn't admit it.

"No, it was like eating broccoli. You do it because you're told it'll be good for you, but it tastes bad."

"You were tense. You should have come to bed willingly. Next time will be better."

"Mr Meredith, there won't be another time. You can't blackmail me all of my life."

"I just thought, now that we've been intimate once we could do it more often."

"No Steven, I don't love you. I don't even like you."

That was an understatement. She was almost falling out of the huge double bed, trying to distance herself from him.

"So you only make love, for love?"

"Yes, I once thought that was the only reason."

"It's a good reason, but the real reason is because of one's urges, one's needs. Love is hormones, chemicals that make you want to copulate and so preserve the race."

"So you just make a little love whenever you have the need or the urge to fulfil a craving, like eating a ham sandwich?"

"We call it a hair sandwich. Why do you do it with Brown? Do you love the big bastard?"

Evelyn didn't answer. She hated him for reminding her of her weakness. What Brown had done to her was a confidence trick. She knew that now.

"Tell me why you shag with Brown?"

"At first he did things to me that aroused me. You reach a state where you can't stop yourself. You lose control."

"You call that love?"

"I didn't know what to call it. It was all so nice and loving and he was so gentle, I thought it was love. He said he loved me and in the heat of love-making I believed him. He may have meant it. Somehow, now I think not. I needed to be loved and he was there. I fell for him. I suppose you call it a craving but it was for love, not for sex. Now look where it's landed me. Look at what I've just done."

She didn't mean to offend him. They both knew that he'd forced her to do what they'd just done.

"Stop saying that, woman. You make me feel like a nobody. I'm Steven Meredith. I'm somebody."

Now it was Evelyn's turn to rub it in. This beast had feelings after all.

"Being a Meredith doesn't make you anything but rich. I'm in bed with a nobody. I just let a rich nobody have my body so I can stay at university. I'm respectable again, but I've lost my self-respect. I feel like a whore."

"All women are whores!"

Evelyn moved as far from him as she could and covered herself all around with the bedclothes.

"If they are, it's only because men like you make them whores. Is your sister a whore?"

"Joan? You know Joan?"

"Yes, is Joan a whore?"

"Joan, my dear, is a nymphomaniac, not a whore. She loves rooting. She does it for nothing. She loves rooting like a drunk likes booze."

"The way you like it, Meredith. Why shouldn't a woman like making love?"

"You don't. You just said that you didn't like it."

"I didn't say that. I didn't enjoy what you just did to me. I didn't enjoy being blackmailed and locked in a room and humiliated like a slave in a harem."

"If I'd let you choose, would you have come to my bed?"

"No. From now on I'm going to be bloody particular who I go to bed with. No more Brown or his kind again. Next time it will be for love, mutual love. I'd rather be a nun than your kind of woman. Now, if you aren't going to unlock the door, be so kind as to let me get some sleep. I have to move house tomorrow."

"Go to sleep, damn you!"

Evelyn felt a little better. The animal had got what he wanted from her, but she had crushed his ego. It gave her some satisfaction. After what he'd done he couldn't get her expelled. He was also breaking the rules.

"What are you going to do?" she asked him as he got out of the bed.

"I've wasted an entire evening with you. I'm going to mark some papers, then I'm going back to my own bedroom."

"Isn't this your bedroom?"

"No, this is the guest room. The master bedroom is down the hall. This is the mistress's bedroom. There's a bathroom over there. Pleasant dreams. I'll see you in the morning."

He put on his pyjamas and bathrobe and taking the key from under the mattress, let himself out. To Evelyn's annoyance, he locked the door from the outside. He showered in his own room and went down to the study.

Evelyn lay back on the bed and thought. The cloud of expulsion was lifted from her head, the sex act with Meredith hadn't been all that bad and was now in the past. In three weeks time Gerald would be back in town. Louis was also a thing of the past. Tomorrow she'd find herself another room and put her life back on the right track again. She relaxed and fell asleep.

Steven Meredith left the locked bedroom feeling angry. He was angry at himself for letting that woman get the better of him. He had conquered her body but not her spirit. He had to let her off the hook, if he had her expelled she'd tell the authorities what he'd done to her. He went down stairs to his study to mark the papers and calm down.

There were only three students who sat for the exam, three students who were given a second chance of passing. The first two passed easily. That left Dr Meredith with the two papers that Brown had written, one with the other papers and the one he'd taken out of Evelyn's handbag. He marked the morning effort and gave him forty percent, a failing grade. Then he looked at the second paper out of curiosity. He gave it fifty-four, a rather poor pass. He put both papers in his briefcase and went back upstairs. He hadn't decided what to do about Brown. Now that he'd had his fun with Evelyn he couldn't expose him for cheating, but he could fail him. That's what he deserved. That would teach that woman to call him a nobody. He didn't know that it would have pleased her sense of justice to have him fail.

As he left his study he played with the key to the guest room and thought of the naked body lying there in the four-poster bed. Steven never supplied his ladies with night garments. He thought, 'Why sleep alone, when there's so much room in the big bed and such a beautiful occupant?'

Climbing the stairs, he slowly opened the door and sneaked in, like Tarquin seeking Lucretia. He locked the door again, leaving the key in the lock. Then he slowly slid into bed. He had a feeling that he'd forgotten something.

Evelyn went to sleep thinking of Gerald and the last night they'd spent together at the end of the term, the night that they'd so much wanted to make love, but ran out of time.

'It won't be easy,' she thought, 'telling him that I've jumped the gun, that I went to bed with another man, which he already knows, but I have to tell him and tell him how sorry I am and make it up to him. We'll probably become lovers, like we were meant to be, if he'll have me back. Now I know why he was so mean to me at the station. He wanted to make love to me so much, and I went away, went away to Bully Brown. What would it have been like with Gerald? I can't tell him about Meredith, he mightn't understand why and how it happened. I don't know, myself, why I ever let Bully Brown get me into this.'

Later she dreamed that she was in the Bonython Hall and Gerald was at her side and they were both called up to receive their degrees and then he kissed her and put a ring on her finger. They walked over the footbridge and looked down into the water. They dragged out a body. It was Louis, but he was alive and ran after them. "That's my girl now," he was calling out and chased them to the gates of St Ann's. They ran inside, Brown stopping at the gates, shouting at them, "That's my girl now!" Then she was alone with Gerald in front of the gas fire and they were lying on the carpet, their bodies close together, kissing, endlessly kissing. He was holding her so close that it made her body tingle.

Slowly she realised that she wasn't alone in bed, she was with a man and it wasn't the man she loved. There was a foreign body with one hand on her breast and the other touching the moistness between her legs, the moistness of the dream. She was moving as she woke to the sensations coursing through her body, making love to her dream lover. Before she realised that it was neither Gerald nor Louis, the dark shape had raised himself onto her and with his mouth to her lips, entered her, deeply and forcibly. She was moist, very moist, and she was now wide awake, aware where she was and who was doing this to her. He held her tight and the more she tried to stop him, the more the sensations rose inside of her. She was being taken advantage of, and she couldn't stop him or stop her own instinctive response. In a few minutes it was too much for her and she felt herself climaxing as she had done with Louis on the first occasion, as she hadn't in recent months.

She flopped back, hot and sweaty on the bed, feeling Meredith continue and then grow momentarily stronger, throb, and spurt as he spilt his genes into her. It was only when he withdrew, soft and moist and sticky, did she realise that he wasn't wearing anything. Evelyn, tired by her experience, screamed at him, "You bastard, you bloody bastard. What have you done to me?"

"I meant to get them, but I forgot."

He was lying, he just couldn't bother going into the room down the hall.

"You raped me!"

She hit him with all her might across his face. She would have hit him again, but he leapt up and ran out of the room. She followed him to the door, closed it and locked it. Then, weeping, she went to the bathroom. There was a bidet and she tried to use it, but she knew that her efforts were as good as useless. Time would tell if the worst had happened, if his sperm was on its way to a fateful meeting with one of her ova. Only time would tell. Tired as she was, she showered and went back to bed. She went to sleep, knowing that this time she wouldn't be disturbed.

At eight she was awake, thinking about the terrible night that had just ended. If she'd had bad times in the last three months, they were nothing compared to this night. She remembered that she now had the key and wasn't in any immediate danger. Then there was a knock on the door.

"Are you alright, Evelyn?"

She didn't answer.

"Are you alright. Can I come in?"

"I'm getting dressed and going home."

"I want to talk to you."

"I don't want to talk to you. Leave me alone."

He didn't answer. He waited, and when she came out of the room, he took her by the hand. She lunged at him, missing, and he let go of her.

"Let go of me if you don't want your nose broken. You've had your pound of flesh."

"I want to talk. I'm sorry for what I did to you."

"Not as sorry as I am. I'd have been better off if you'd called the police."

"Sit down with me for a minute. I'll drive you home."

"One minute. Then if you ever touch me again I'll defend myself. You are a madman, Mr Meredith. Do you often rape your house guests, the female ones?"

He didn't answer. Evelyn wasn't the first girl he had had to lock in a bedroom to seduce. They sat down at the breakfast table.

"You're a sadist, Meredith."

"All men are sadists, and all women masochists."

"Amen. The Gospel according to Saint Steven of Meredith. Men are decent playboy sadists, and women are disgusting masochist whores, with the exception of rich women who do it for free, they're called nymphomaniacs."

"That's been my experience. Women like a bit of rough stuff."

"Well, *I* don't."

258

"You too are a masochist. That's why you've been sleeping with Brown and came to my house on his behalf. You're your own enemy, you poor cow."

"If I thought that, I'd put my head in the gas oven. You're the real poor cow, not me. You've got everything, Meredith — money, brains, education, even good looks and more money — but you're crazy. Steven Meredith, your mind is warped, sick rotten. Last night I hated you, but now I pity you. Have you ever loved anyone or been loved in return? How many times have you lain with a girl and told her that you loved her, knowing it to be a lie, and how many women have done the same to you, hoping to catch you and all your money? You can't buy love with all your money. You're the tin man, with no heart. Go and seek out the Wizard of Oz, see if he has one for you. While you're at it, get a brain for Brown."

He knew that Evelyn was telling the truth. He had never been in love and never would be, for all his love-making. If he ever married, it would be to provide the heir that his parents wanted so much. This girl was a possibility. She was sexy, intelligent and spirited. Why not?

"I could fall in love with *you*, Miss Robertson. Could we meet again?"

"If you were the last male-sadist on this earth, Meredith, and I the last nymphomaniac, I'd start a convent. I find your suggestion revolting. I want to go now."

"I'd like you to know that I'm forgetting your trespass, and giving Brown a pass."

"And I'd like to tell you that I'll never forgive you your trespass, your vile use of my body, and that Brown can go to hell with you."

"You won't tell anyone what happened?"

"Do you think that I could? I'm ashamed of what happened in this house. As for complaining to the police or going to the newspapers, I've got more to lose than you have. What a pity. *Truth* would love to hear my story, and I could do with the money they'd pay me for it."

"You'd never go to the newspapers. You're too proud. Besides, the papers wouldn't print anything wrong about a Meredith. The reporter might write all about my sexual appetite, my many conquests, and set it up for page one, but the editor would throw it out. They need the beer ads."

He laughed as he said this. He was pleased with himself. He regarded his second assault on Evelyn as a triumph. Against her will, he had forced an orgasm into her body. That was quite a victory.

"What about the university. Raping a student is sufficient grounds for dismissal."

"Dad's donating a building to the university. You'd only get yourself expelled. I'm safe. The university wants its Meredith Building. Dad isn't going to donate a building to an institution that dismisses his son."

"Meredith, this is all academic. I'm leaving this house and never coming back, not for all the Browns in the world."

She went looking for her handbag, finding it in the library. Next to it was a Paris Edition of Durrell's *The Black Book*. She assumed that it was a banned book. There were other Paris Editions on the desk, *Tropic Of Capricorn*, a book by D. H. Lawrence, somebody's lover. Another person could be arrested for having a bookshelf full of banned books, but not a Meredith — their money placed them above the law.

Looking inside her handbag, Evelyn found a folded piece of paper. It was a cheque for a hundred pounds. She went back to the kitchen and put it into the gas flame on the stove. Then, slapping Steven Meredith across the mouth, Evelyn left his mansion, the house in which an unspeakable cruelty had been done to her. She met the housekeeper entering as she left. It made her feel like a whore leaving a whorehouse. The woman went to see her employer. She'd seen more young women leaving Chez Meredith than she could remember. Her employer paid well, it was no concern of hers how many tramps spent the night with him.

"Did you have a nice evening, Mr Meredith?"

There was a red mark on his face, but she didn't recognise it as a slap-in-the-face-mark. There was a smell of burning paper and ashes on the floor.

"The dinner was excellent, particularly the last course. I bought a few things that should be delivered this week: my new doctoral gown and hood, a trunk and some suitcases. Also a new suit and a warm coat. It'll still be cold when I get to London. Have them put everything in the room next to mine. One other thing. I used the guest room last night, you'll have to have it tidied up. I won't be home for lunch. I'm dining with Father and the Vice-Chancellor at the Adelaide Club. The family are donating a building to the university."

Chapter Nineteen

April 1953

Steven Meredith's house was just down the hill from St Ann's. As she left the Meredith house Evelyn imagined that hundreds of eyes were watching her. She hoped against hope that no one would recognise her, emerging from that house as she walked quickly through the gardens and over the footbridge to the university. Here in the sunshine amidst familiar surroundings she felt better. It was Orientation Week and the place was full of new students. She heard someone calling her name and turned to see Joan Meredith getting out of her car. Joan waved to her, but Evelyn kept walking. The last person she wanted to talk to was his woman. It would be impossible to hide last night from Steven's sister, so she pretended not to hear her. Evelyn wondered if the fiend would tell his sister about last night.

Evelyn made more inquiries about accommodation and went looking for a place to stay. She decided to rule out North Adelaide, which although it was very close to the university was too close to Louis and the Meredith mansion. The girl didn't want to run into either of them on a dark night. She finally decided on a room off Kensington Road, Rose Park, near the racecourse. She'd have to travel by bus, but if her money ran out she could walk it in about forty minutes. It was two pounds a week including breakfast. The room was bare but clean and had a large window that let in the sun. She went back to the Browns to get her belongings.

When she arrived, Mrs Brown was quite anxious.

"Where have you been all night, Evelyn? Louis was quite worried. We both were."

'Louis was worried!' thought Evelyn. 'So why didn't the coward come and rescue me?'

"I've been hunting for a room and I found one. I'm moving out today."

"Why, Evelyn, don't you like it here?"

"You're very nice, Mrs Brown, but I can't stay in the same place as your son. My parents are old-fashioned. I ran away from home because of Louis. I want to mend my bridges and I can't do that if I stay here. I need my parents."

Mrs Brown saw the logic in her argument.

"I'll be sorry to see you go, but I think you're making the right decision. I was worried about you when Louis told me that you ran away and your father treated you so badly, but I'm sure that your parents love you. You should try and make up. There's a letter here for you from Renmark. It's probably from them."

"How would they know that I'm here?"

"It says "Please Forward" on the envelope. Haven't you written to them?"

"No, I was waiting until I had another address."

The letter was from her mother:

Dear Evelyn,

Why did you leave without saying good-bye? I suppose because we would have stopped you. I'm sorry that it came to this. I cried when I read your note. You've made things worse with your father. I might have talked him into changing his mind about your studies, but your running away has made him unapproachable.

Why didn't you write? I obtained Louis's address from Mrs Evans. I hope this letter gets to you.

Evelyn, you were wrong to lie to us and visit this man as you did. If he wanted to see you, he should have come to the front door like a gentleman and not steal you from us like a thief in the night. I can't stop you from seeing him if you want, but he isn't a nice person. I'm sorry, but that's my opinion. If I'm wrong, I'm sorry. I'm willing to be proved wrong. If I'm right, God help you, my daughter. Come home before it's too late.

Your father hasn't changed his mind about your studies. He's a proud man and expects obedience from his family. You hurt him and his pride and he won't forgive that in a hurry. If you need money write to me. I haven't much, but I've decided to economise and put a little money aside from the housekeeping money. I hope that your father doesn't find out.

Write to me dear. I worry about you. Remember I'm your mother. I carried you in my womb nine months and nursed you on my breast. One of these days you'll marry and realise what a wonderful thing it is to be a mother. I know that you want to study, but you're a woman, and women have their lives to live and can't be like men.

Don't be afraid to come home if things don't work out. I'll see that your father doesn't bully you.

I spoke to Mrs Williams the other day. Did you know that Deirdre's married? Her mother told me and we cried here in my kitchen. She's in her third month. She's living in Adelaide, in Norwood. I'll write the address at the end of the letter. Her married name is Roper. Her mother would like you to go and see her. Look after yourself, and please write,

Love,

Mother.

Evelyn put the letter in her handbag and went to pack. She hoped that she could get out of the house before Louis came home, but just as she was closing her suitcase she heard his car in the driveway. He came straight to her room, entering it without knocking.

"Where the hell have you been? I've been searching all over the place for you."

"I'm moving out, Louis. I called to get my things."

"You never told me you were moving. What happened?"

She didn't like the way he spoke to her. He was adopting that bullying tone again.

"I can't live in this house with you. It isn't right."

"Of course it is. We've had other female boarders."

"And did you sleep with all of them? Louis, please don't stop me. I have to go."

"It'll make sleeping together difficult."

Couldn't the idiot see that that was her intention?

"Louis, we aren't going to do that any more."

"Come off it, you like sleeping with me."

"I did, but not any more. Let's part friends."

"Is it anything I did?"

Evelyn wanted to scream at him. Didn't he know?

"You ran out on me yesterday. Have you forgotten?"

"No, what happened?"

Evelyn wasn't vindictive by nature, but she wanted Louis to share some of her suffering.

"Meredith caught me. I spent the night in the lockup."

She didn't tell him it was Meredith's lockup.

"What happened? Does he know about me? Did you manage to change over the exam papers?"

"Wait and see. Meredith may press charges, he may not. You may find yourself being called to see the Vice-Chancellor today. You might have ended your days as a student. Your future is in Meredith's hands, Louis. What you made me do was unnecessary and despicable. Yesterday I saw the real Louis Brown for the first time and I didn't like what I saw. Goodbye, Louis, I'm going."

He stood in the doorway and she had to push past him, as he remained blocking her way, sullenly. She had no way of knowing what was going on in his mind. She said good-bye to Mrs Brown, who kissed her as her mother had so often done. Then she went to catch a tram, lugging the heavy suitcase. A taxi was out of the question and she didn't want to ask Louis for a lift. She didn't want him to know her new address.

The first thing she did after unpacking was to write a short note to her mother, telling her where she was living and that she had stopped seeing Louis. She hoped that this would pacify her father, but it didn't. Then she went to see Deirdre. It took her twenty minutes to walk there. It was so nice being free and walking in the sunshine, through tree-lined streets and gardens full of flowers. School was coming out and she passed groups of boys or girls, neatly dressed in their uniforms, with their coloured caps or felt hats. She arrived at the Ropers in a happy frame of mind.

Mrs Roper, Deirdre's mother-in-law, came to the door, and took her to see her friend. She was sitting at the *Singer* making pillowcases.

"Evelyn. I asked Mom to get your address for me. How did you find me?"

"Your Mom spoke to my Mom and I got a letter from her today. How are you? When did you get married?"

"Two weeks ago, just after you ran off. Peter wanted to get it over with quickly, so we had a quiet ceremony just before he finished working and left Renmark. I told you about Peter, he's finishing his apprenticeship and then we can look for a place of our own."

"You're definitely pregnant?"

"Come and feel my tummy. You can see it when I haven't any clothes on. I got pregnant on New Year's Eve when that boyfriend of yours put gin in the orange juice. You weren't the only one to get pissed that night. Well, I was rather upset when it happened, but it meant that I got to stay with Peter, so it turned out alright, didn't it?"

"Did you say that it was Louis who laced the drink? He swore to me and to Mom that he didn't do it. You remember what happened to me when I got home?"

"He lied to you. Peter saw him doing it. He thought it was funny at the time. Men have funny ideas of what is funny. Are you still seeing the big bastard?"

Yesterday morning Louis was a friend that she wanted to distance herself from, this morning she hated him, now she wanted to kill him. Was there no end to his bastardry?

"Not any more."

"Because of what I just told you?"

"No, but I wish you'd told me when it happened. I wouldn't have had the row with Dad, if I'd known. My father isn't as stupid as I thought he was."

"Sorry, Evelyn. I thought that you guessed. He did bring the bottle with the beer, didn't he? I had my own troubles, as you know. Thank God they're over."

"Deirdre, how do you know when you're pregnant?"

She couldn't forget waking in the middle of the night, finding Steven on top of her, dripping semen as he left her, not caring what he did to her.

"When your period doesn't arrive, silly."

"I know that, but how can you be sure?"

"When you're about a month overdue, you go to a doctor. He sends a sample of your pee to a lab and tells you the result in a couple of weeks. It's probably quicker here in the city. You really don't need the test, as by the time you get the result you feel changes in your body. You know that you're pregnant."

"So, you knew by the end of February?"

"I told Peter of my suspicions in January. We got married ten days after the lab test confirmed it."

"Why so quickly?"

"Evelyn, the baby's due in September. We had to get married in a hurry."

"What if Peter hadn't agreed?"

"Peter not agree! He's crazy about me. He didn't hesitate. Secretly, he's proud of himself. Some men have doubts about their ability to make children, you know."

"Do you love each other?"

"Of course we do. Do you think I'd go to bed with a man I didn't love?"

"It wasn't just the gin in the orange juice?"

"No. We were doing it before that night."

"I hope you'll always be happy."

"Thanks. What about you and Louis?"

"I told you, Deirdre, the man is no good. He's a liar. He was such a bastard and I didn't see it. Well that's all over and I can start to put my life together again. Gerald will be back in two more weeks."

"Evelyn, I saw him the night that he came to Renmark. He knew all about you and Louis before he came to my place. Are you sure he'll forgive you and take you back again?"

Deirdre had asked the question uppermost in Evelyn's mind. She wanted Gerald back, but he had called her a whore. He hadn't written to her. What would he do, what would he say next time he saw her?

"No, but I have to see him. I'll admit everything and tell him that I know I was wrong. He loves me. He'll forgive me."

"It isn't that easy with men. You've been sleeping with another man. Not only that, but a man he knows and hates. You two hurt his pride, his manliness. How can you be sure that he still doesn't hate you? Has he written to you?"

"No, but I haven't written to him either."

"So don't expect him to forgive you. He loved you for your purity and your innocence. You gave that to another man. It's the worst thing you can do to a man."

"You don't have to tell me. That was two months ago. He can't still be angry."

"He may have another girlfriend."

"He's been in the army."

"Good, he'll be starved for a little love."

'Like I was on New Year's Day,' she thought, 'when I went to bed with Louis.'

"Be careful when you see him. Don't end up like me."

She patted her tummy and they laughed.

That night Evelyn enjoyed the freedom of sleeping in her own room without Louis or Meredith or her father to bother her. It was a small room with floral wallpaper, a wardrobe, bed, table and chair. There was also a dressing-table with a round mirror in it that wouldn't stay where it was placed. The room was just what she wanted, nice and cosy and private.

The third of April was Good Friday. Evelyn went to church for the first time since leaving home. On Saturday she went window shopping and walked over to the racetrack, where she watched the races from the field outside the enclosures. It was free and it was fun, but she couldn't see the finish from where she was. She imagined telling her father that she went to see horses racing. Another step on the way to hell. After the races were over she went to see Deirdre again and met her husband. She didn't remember him, but Peter remembered her.

"I'm not surprised that you don't remember me. You were drunk when we met. Come to think of it, so were we."

He patted his wife's tummy. She took his hand and wouldn't let it go.

Evelyn suggested that they put a sign up, "Watch this place for developments."

It was nice to have a close friend living nearby while she waited for Gerald's return.

Back in her room she consulted the calendar. Sunday the eleventh lectures started. Friday the seventeenth the boys came back from Woodside. There was another important date that troubled her. Wednesday the fourteenth her period was due.

On Tuesday Evelyn went to the library. It was almost empty as lectures hadn't started. It took her some time to find the book she wanted, a book on human physiology, but she finally found what she wanted to read, and opened it at the chapter dealing with human reproduction. She read about how hormones govern a woman's cycle and about ovulation and fertilisation. The more she read the more it worried her. She read that the ovum is released on the thirteenth or fourteenth day of the cycle and, if fertilised, becomes imbedded in the wall of the uterus within a day or two and grows into an embryo. Fertilisation takes place between the thirteenth to the sixteenth day of the cycle, and if this doesn't happen, the wall of the uterus breaks down, bleeding occurring on the twenty-eighth day. Evelyn sat back in her seat and took a deep breath. What she'd read confirmed her worst suspicions.

"Meredith raped me the night of the first of April, fourteen days into my cycle and right in the middle of my fertile time. Today is the seventh. If I don't get my period in a week's time, I'm in trouble. Then *what* do I do?"

The next seven days went by like a life sentence for Evelyn. She was glad when lectures started on the eleventh and she had to think of something else. She was surprised that Gerald's name wasn't on the roll cards in any of her subjects, but supposed that it would be added later. She didn't know that he'd changed subjects to avoid the unpleasantness and pain of being in the same class with her hating him. She expected to see him on the twentieth and was longing for that day to arrive.

Thursday the sixteenth came, but Evelyn's period hadn't, not on that day or on Friday, Saturday, or Sunday. On Friday the boys returned from National Service and marched through the streets of the city. Evelyn read the *Sunday Mail*, which her landlady bought; Joan Meredith was on page three at a pre-Commencement Ball party, next to a photograph of Gerald in his army uniform. Evelyn got a thrill when she saw that Gerald received a prize for marksmanship. She was so proud for him, but so worried about her period. It still hadn't come. She'd never been three days late before. She went to the phone to ring Gerald, but her courage failed her, and she went back to her bedroom and cried.

Joan rang the *Sunday Mail* and ordered a glossy of her press photograph. As an afterthought she asked for two copies of Gerald's picture — one to give him, one for her collection. He looked handsome in his uniform, handsome and available.

On Friday, when Gerald got home, he quickly showered, put on civilian clothes and took the car to St Ann's. He asked to see Evelyn. If it wasn't too late he wanted to ask her to the Commencement Ball if Brown wasn't taking her, damn him.

"Evelyn Robertson didn't come back this year."

"Do you know where she's staying?"

"No."

"Does anyone know if she's come back."

No one was sure, but someone thought that she'd seen her. She wasn't certain.

Gerald got back in the car.

'It's all my fault,' he thought. 'Her father stopped her allowance and now she can't study, and it's all my fault for being selfish. No wonder she won't write to me. She must hate me.'

Then he reconsidered.

"That bastard Brown did this. If he hadn't interfered, this wouldn't have happened. I bet he did it just out of spite. I'll kill that bastard one of these days."

He drove to Richard and told him about Evelyn.

"Stiff shit, Gerry. Have a beer."

"No, Richard, getting drunk won't help."

"Have a beer. Don't have half a dozen. What are you going to do?"

"What can I do? I don't know where she is. I can't go to Renmark and drag her back here like a caveman. I don't know what she thinks. I haven't heard from her in months."

"Do you think she's still seeing Brown?"

"Don't rub it in, Richard. You know what it did to me to see them together."

"Knowing that, do you still want her back?"

"Yes, damn it, and I can't have her. She doesn't love me any more."

"Gerald, find another girl. Girls are like tramcars. If you miss one, there'll always be another. I'll find you a blind date for the ball tomorrow."

"No, they might be there. I don't want to see her with him. I'm not going to the Commencement Ball. I don't want to see him with her."

His friend understood him. The thought of that girl with that man made him want to vomit.

"Damn it, Richard, I know you're right. I'll make the effort to meet other girls. It isn't going to be easy. Evelyn's not the kind of girl that'll be easy to replace. I don't think I'll ever stop loving her."

"You'll fall in love again."

"I suppose so. Next time nothing will get in my way — no father, no army, and no Louis Brown."

"That's more like it. Did I tell you the story about the guy who took his girl for a drive and ran out of petrol? When he was pushing it home, someone stole the car. Gerald, you go home and get a good night's sleep, between clean sheets on a soft mattress. Tomorrow I'll see if I can rustle up a couple of girls and we'll go out on the town. It's probably too late to get tickets to the ball."

The following Wednesday they were eating their sandwiches in the Refectory when Evelyn walked past under the far cloisters. Richard noticed her and turned to Gerald. "Look, Gerry, she's back after all."

Gerald took off like a startled kangaroo, across the sunken lawn and got to her by the door of the Lady Symon Hall. He called to her and she turned, looked at him in horror, turned away from him and ran down the basement steps to the toilets where he couldn't follow. The look on her face was a look that he'd never forget. Where was the joy of their previous meetings? He waited at the top of the stairs. She'd have to leave this way and then she'd have to speak to him. Richard came over. It was getting close to the afternoon lecture time. He stayed for five minutes before going to the lecture, leaving Gerald behind. Joan Meredith came out of the building and asked him what he was doing.

"Evelyn's down in the toilets and I want to speak to her. Would you hop down and tell her?"

"Sure."

Joan found her sitting on a toilet, her face a mess from crying. She told Evelyn that Gerald was waiting to see her.

"I don't want to see him," she answered, tears running down her face. "Tell him to go away."

"Can't you tell him yourself?"

"I can't, I can't face him."

"Why? You used to be friends."

"I think I'm pregnant."

Joan was stunned. What a calamity! The worst thing in the world to happen to a single girl. Joan knew that feeling so well.

"Shit, Evelyn. He's the one person that you should see. You have to tell him. Come, I'll take you to him."

"He didn't do it. I've never been intimate with Gerald."

Now Joan was doubly-stunned.

"No wonder you don't want to see him. I'll get rid of him, then I'll come back for you."

"Haven't you got to go to a lecture?"

"I can miss it. I have to take care of a friend."

Joan went up to Gerald. This was going to be difficult.

"Is she down there?" he demanded.

"Yes, Gerald. She won't come up until you go. She doesn't want to see you. I'm going to take her home. She isn't feeling well. I'll call you tomorrow and try and explain things to you."

"I want an explanation now."

"Evelyn will not come up while you are here. Are you dense or something? Go to the lecture and make a copy for me. I'll see you tomorrow."

"What's the matter with her?"

"I don't know. Go away or I'll never find out."

She watched him turn around and walk away. Then she returned to Evelyn.

"Has he gone?"

"He's going. Boy, have you got some explaining to do."

"Don't lecture me, Joan. You don't know what's happened to me."

She wanted to add, "what that bastard brother of yours did to me," but Joan was a friend and Evelyn was in need.

"Come on. My car's nearby. I'll take you back to the college, and you can tell me."

"I thought I told you. I'm not at the college. I can't afford it."

"What happened? Did your father lose his job?"

"I ran away from home. I rented a room."

Was this the quiet girl from the country who wouldn't say 'boo' to a goose, running away from home and getting herself in the club? What was the world coming to? She had to get to the bottom of this. She had to help her. Joan helped her dry her face and took her to her car. Gerald watched them go. He watched as Evelyn and Joan got in the car and drove away. He went late to the lecture, but he might as well have stayed away. He didn't hear what the lecturer was saying. He wanted to know what was wrong with Evelyn.

Meanwhile the two women drove out of the city.

"What makes you think that you're pregnant?"

"I'm a week late."

"Well, don't give up hoping. Have you any other reason to think that you're pregnant? You did have sex, didn't you?"

"Yes, right in the middle of the month and he didn't use anything."

"And you let him?"

"No. He said he would, but he didn't."

"What a rat! Listen girl, never trust a man. Get your own contraceptive device and use it. Who is this bastard?"

"I can't tell you, Joan."

"Do I know him?"

She didn't answer. There was no way she could tell Joan what a bastard she had for a brother. It was a pity. Joan knew all about Steven, she had known him all her life. She might have been much more understanding if she had known. Evelyn had a sympathetic friend to share her troubles with, but she missed the opportunity because she was ashamed of her own part in her own tragedy.

"That means that I do know him. Tell me, Evelyn, don't keep it to yourself. You don't owe him anything."

"I can't tell you."

"So that's the reason that you hid from Gerald Fisher. Well, I can understand that. Never mind, he'll keep. You can see him when you get over this. He's wants to see you."

"I don't understand that. I thought he hated me now. He was horrid to me and never wrote to me."

"That's not the way I saw it."

"What if I am pregnant?"

"You'll get rid of it and go back to Gerald as if nothing happened."

They arrived at Evelyn's place and sat talking in the car.

"What do I do now, Joan? How do I know if I really am pregnant?"

"Go to the student medical service, or if you prefer you can see my gynaecologist. He's expensive."

"I'll see the doctor at the university."

"He'll tell you when to take a urine sample and where to take it. If it turns out positive, you have to tell the guy who did it to you. I take it you don't want to marry him."

"I'd rather die."

Joan gloated. She was sure that Brown had done this to her friend. Now they had something in common, they both hated that bully. What a pity she couldn't spread the word about, but that would hurt Evelyn more than that monster. Still, it was a pity.

"So you'll have to get rid of it. We'll discuss that when the time comes. Then you can go back to your real boyfriend."

"If he'll have me."

"I know Gerald. He's not going to let a little thing like a pregnancy and abortion come between you. I'll tell him what happened to you and help you through the rough."

"Please don't. I think that I should tell him."

"When?"

"When it's all over — one way or the other."

"That could be four or five weeks."

"So I'll keep out of the Refectory."

"What'll I tell Gerald tomorrow?"

"Don't tell him where I'm living. Tell him there's another person in my life and I have to decide who I really love. Tell him not to pester me."

"You're making a big mistake, Evelyn. You should go to him, tell him and go through this together."

"No, not while I might have another man's child in me."

"You'll see the man who did this?"

"When I know for certain."

"Cheer up, you probably aren't pregnant."

"Joan, I don't need any rabbit test. I know what I feel in my body."

Joan knew this feeling. It created a bond between the two of them.

"You'll be alright. Do you need any money?"

She took out her purse. Evelyn stopped her before she could get to the money.

"No, I'm going to find a part-time job as soon as I get over this."

"Ring me if you need anything, or if you need someone to talk to."

"Thanks, Joan. I don't know what I'd have done without you, today. Please don't tell Gerald."

"I won't tell a soul."

"Do I have your word on that, Joan?"

"You have the word of a Meredith. What could be better than that?"

When she got inside there was a letter from her mother waiting for her. It was a nice letter. She asked about Deirdre and if she was showing. If this was meant as a warning to her, it was too late. She was glad that Evelyn had a place to stay, meaning she was glad that she wasn't staying with Louis. Her mother wished her good luck in her studies. She didn't mention her father, which meant that he was still angry with her.

The letter and the talk with Joan had a calming effect on Evelyn, but her problem was a real one, and it was growing bigger every day.

Gerald rang Joan at six. He couldn't wait until the next day. Joan was beginning to feel like "Dear Dorothy Dix".

"What's the matter with Evelyn, Joan?"

"She isn't sick, but she says she can't see you."

"Forever?"

"No, she didn't say that. Gerald, let me do the talking. Evelyn has been seeing another man. I think she wants to stop it and make it up with you. S he won't see you until it's over."

"Is that what she told you to say?"

"Yes, those were her words."

"I want to speak to her. I want her to tell me, herself."

"Gerald, her father didn't want her to come back to Adelaide so she ran away from home. She's trying to end an affair and, believe me, that isn't easy. She's also trying to attend lectures. She's got enough troubles. Leave her alone. She'll contact you when she's ready. She knows that you want to see her."

"It's Brown, isn't it?"

"Louis Brown?"

"Yes, I know about it. He was seeing her in Renmark."

Joan didn't say anything. So it really was that bastard. Although she knew it, she was too shocked to speak.

"Joan, is it still Louis Brown?"

"Gerald, she didn't mention any name."

"Are you being honest with me?"

"Meredith honour, for what that's worth."

"Who is she having this affair with?"

"She didn't say. I asked, but she wouldn't tell me."

"Well, Joan, I'll tell you. It is Louis Brown."

"I can't believe this. Evelyn's got too much sense to have anything to do with that shit."

"Joan, I saw them with my own eyes. He's been after her for months. It's my fault. I told her I was sick of her, but I didn't mean it. I regretted it the moment I said it. I don't know what came over me."

Joan was shocked. She thought it was all Evelyn's fault.

"Gerald, you're a bloody fool."

"I know."

"Are you certain it's Brown?"

"That's why I haven't heard from her. I knocked him down in her living-room."

Joan couldn't believe her ears. This was the best news that she'd heard in years.

"You knocked down Louis Brown?"

"Yes."

"Gerald, I could kiss you. I'd have given my right eye to have been there."

"Well, I'd give anything not to have done it. It wasn't a clever thing to do. I went to ask her to marry me and got myself chucked out of her house. Joan, she hasn't spoken to me or written to me for three months. Do I deserve that?"

"Of course you don't, Gerald. Have a little patience and you'll see her. I'll speak to her again. Please don't pester her. That'll only make things worse."

"Just once. If she says she loves Brown and doesn't love me any more, I'll understand. Is she living with him?"

"No, she's got a room in a boarding house. Have you any message for her?"

"Tell her that I love her and I want her back. I don't care what she's done."

"I'll tell her."

"Where is she living?"

"I can't tell you. She doesn't want you to know."

In *Nature* on the twenty-fifth of April there was an article written by two young Oxford scientists, Watson and Crick, postulating that DNA, the genetic material of all cells, was made of a double helix.

All that long month, Gerald pestered Joan for news of Evelyn. She pleaded with her friend, but couldn't persuade her to see him. Time passed and they were now sure that she was pregnant. Then the rabbit test came back positive. Steven's DNA had fused with hers and was growing inside her.

"Now you have to tell Gerald."

"Soon, there's somebody else that I have to see."

"You go to him. He'll have to pay for what you need."

Evelyn looked at her with those sad eyes of hers, eyes that had once sparkled.

"Tell me, Joan, what do I need?"

"An abortion, you silly girl! You can't have the baby!"

"Isn't that illegal? And dangerous? I could get infected and die."

"Evelyn, you don't go to a woman in a dirty basement. You get it done by a doctor under sterile conditions. It's easier than having a tooth pulled."

"How much does it cost?"

"The doctor takes fifty pounds. He's also taking a risk."

"He put a cheque for a hundred in my handbag."

That didn't sound like Louis Brown.

"Good, you'll be up fifty pounds."

"I didn't take it."

"Well, you go and get it again. Why did you do that?"

"I don't take money for that. I'm not a prostitute."

"Well, this is different. You go back to the bastard and make him pay. It's a pity he couldn't suffer too."

"Joan, how do you know so much about this?"

"Can't you guess? Isn't that why you came to me?"

"I didn't come to you. You came to get me out of the Lady Symon toilets. Have you been pregnant, too?"

"Three times. The first time when I was almost sixteen."

"What happened?"

"Let's put one down to inexperience; the second, the less said about it the better; and the third, to too much drink."

She couldn't tell her friend that the second pregnancy was due to her brother's lust and carelessness. Evelyn wouldn't understand. Joan didn't know how wrong she was.

The next day, Saturday, she was looking at some papers that her landlady was about to discard. Newspapers were a luxury that Evelyn couldn't afford. She noticed a picture of Joan in a group and standing next to her, Steven.

TRAVELLING TO LONDON ON THE ORONTES

The Meredith family gave a shipboard farewell party at Outer Harbour today for their son, Doctor Steven Meredith.

Doctor Meredith received his Doctor of Philosophy degree at last month's commemoration ceremony at the university. He is setting out on a tour of Europe and plans to work in the USA. His sister Joan is starting her second year of a science course after a brilliant first year.

'Well,' she thought, 'so much for his help. I'll have to pay the fifty pounds out of my own money. There goes two months of my budget. I wonder what he'd have done if I'd seen him before he left. Offered to marry me? I doubt it. He'd have paid up. He's probably done it before. I couldn't see me as Mrs Meredith, honeymooning on the Orontes. I'd die before I'd marry that rat. I hope the bastard falls overboard.'

Chapter Twenty

May 1953

On Sunday evening Joan took Evelyn to see the doctor. She didn't see the name on the door or the address, but it was somewhere in Parkside near the Asylum. He listened to her story, asked her numerous questions, and examined her. Then, taking her back into his office, he told her. "Listen, young lady, Miss Meredith here tells me that I can trust you. I'm prepared to help you because I feel that you need help and I don't want you to go to someone who'll botch the job (he didn't mention the fifty quid). I don't know how you got into this situation, but I suppose that it isn't entirely your fault. I hope that you learn from this. I don't recommend abortion as a method of birth control. Be here at eight o'clock on Wednesday. You'll be out in an hour. Joan will stay with you during the night.

"If you have any problems or bleeding, you're to go at once to the Royal Adelaide Hospital. Tell them that you have vaginal bleeding, but for God's sake don't tell that that you've had an abortion. Act dumb. They'll understand and look after you. It hasn't happened to any of my patients yet, so I don't expect it will happen to you. That's just in case. Don't be brave or scared to go, and don't tell them anything. They'll know what to do so, you mustn't incriminate yourself, or me for that matter."

"How could I? I don't know your name."

"That's the way it should be. You know that it'll cost fifty pounds. Bring it with you in cash."

Joan arranged to call for her at seven-thirty and took her home.

"You can spend Wednesday night at my flat. Then on Thursday we'll return you to Gerald. You won't be able to do anything for a while."

"Don't worry, Gerald isn't like that. We have a barrier of confidence to break down before we'll try anything new. Then I have to make it up to him for what I've done."

"Just be careful. You don't want to make a habit of this. It can't be good for you, you know."

She was supposed to go on to the Ropers, but she didn't go. She couldn't see Deirdre, now that she was going to terminate her pregnancy.

Evelyn found herself getting tense during the days that followed. Tuesday night she didn't sleep, Wednesday she had no appetite and couldn't concentrate in lectures. She went home, skipping afternoon classes. She read and reread her mother's letter that reminded her how she'd carried Evelyn in her womb and nursed her at her breast. How could she ever face her mother again?

When darkness came, together with the time for the abortion, she started going out of her mind. The room was closing in on her. It seemed that there were people, a room full of fathers all around her, whispering and pointing fingers at her. Ten minutes before Joan was due to collect her she left the house.

Joan arrived five minutes early and went to Evelyn's room. She asked her landlady if she'd seen Evelyn.

"She hasn't eaten a thing all day. Came home early. I think I heard her go out a few minutes ago."

Joan went back to her room.

"Shit, she's chickened out. I'd better go and find her."

Then she noticed a note on the table and read it:

I can't go ahead with this I can't kill a baby I can't live with this I can't do this and go back to Gerald This is too much for me

Evelyn

Joan ran to her car and drove down to the main road. There were a few shops there, so she asked the occupants if they'd seen Evelyn. At the third shop the man said he had.

"She came in here about ten minutes ago."

"What did she buy?"

"Nothing very much, just a packet of razor blades. She didn't know what brand she wanted so I sold her Gillette. I hope that's what her husband wants."

"She's not married. Which way did she go?"

"Razor blades! What does Evelyn want with razor blades?" Joan knew the answer to that question.

"That way," said the shopkeeper, pointing to the racecourse. Joan drove over there, parking by a section where the fence was low and she could get inside.

"She'd better be here. If I don't find her quickly, it'll be too late."

She ran onto the track near the stands, calling Evelyn by name. Between calling, she listened. Finally she heard a movement in the stands. She ran to the fence, climbed it and calling to her, ran up into the stand. Then she stood still and listened again. She heard a whimper and headed in the direction of the noise.

"Evelyn, I'm coming. Everything's going to be alright."

"Go away. Leave me alone."

Joan picked her up from where she was lying between the seats. She felt her wrists for blood. As she did the blades fell out of the open packet onto the floor. They left them there, Joan walking Evelyn down the steps, to the car.

"Why did you come after me? In a few minutes I'd have been free of this tainted body and there'd be one less bastard to be born into this world. Where are you taking me?"

Time was running out. Joan had to get her to that doctor. She didn't want Evelyn to miss her appointment.

"We have a meeting with a doctor. Did you get the money?"

"No."

"I'll pay and you can pay me later."

"No you won't. I'm not going. Take me home."

Evelyn dug her heels into the ground and Joan couldn't budge her.

"Evelyn!"

"Take me home. I'm beginning to think again."

Joan took her back to her room and closed the door.

"Joan, I'm not going to have the damned abortion. I know I'm mad, but I can't go ahead with it."

The lady brought them a pot of tea and some cake. Joan persuaded Evelyn to eat while they continued to talk.

"Well, Evelyn, one thing's clear to me. If you aren't going to go ahead with the abortion, you have to have someone to look after you. Why didn't you wait for me? It isn't such a bad thing. Lots of women have abortions."

"If you hadn't interfered we'd both be dead by now and we wouldn't be a burden to anyone."

"Why Evelyn? Why won't you get rid of it?"

"I'd rather die."

"You wouldn't be killing a real person. There's no baby inside you. It isn't formed yet. At two months it isn't alive. You can't kill what isn't alive."

"Joan, if I do this I won't be able to live with myself. I thought that I could, but I can't. If the doctor had done it at once, before I had time to think, I might have felt differently. I'm glad he didn't. I don't think I could live with myself if I killed my baby. I'm glad I didn't do it."

"What are you, a Roman Catholic?"

She knew that Evelyn came from a religious family.

"No, it isn't a religious belief; it's how I feel. I don't want a helpless being removed from my body and destroyed."

"It isn't a being. It hasn't a brain. It's nothing at this stage."

"Joan, to you it's nothing. Logically, you're right. I could have lots of children to make up for it, but I can't kill this one. It's part of me."

"You're crazy."

"I suppose I am. I was, when I agreed to get rid of it. Look at what it drove me to. I was so crazy that I wanted to die a few minutes ago. Now I want to live and have my baby. You can leave me now, Joan, I won't kill myself. I want my baby to live."

Joan had never felt like this. When it had happened to her, she couldn't wait to get rid of it. The funny thing was that Evelyn seemed calmer now than she had seen her for over a month. If this was what she wanted, let her have the baby!

"What are you going to do?"

"I'll finish this year at university, then I'll go back home and have the baby."

"And then?"

"My father will scold me every day and people will talk about us and my mother will not be invited to other people's houses, not that she'll care. Neither will I. I'll be alive and I'll have the baby."

"You're willing to do that?"

"I don't want to do what you want me to do."

"Evelyn, let's think this over."

"There isn't anything to think about. I won't have my pregnancy terminated."

She hadn't touched her tea. Joan put it in her hand.

"Will you have the baby adopted?"

"I'd like to see someone try and take this baby away from me."

"You're going to regret this. Last week, you couldn't wait to get rid of it."

"That was before I met that doctor. Then I started to realise what I was doing. The more I thought, the more I got myself into a corner that I couldn't get out of. When it became dark I lost my mind. I was trying to get the razor blades out of the packet when you found me. I didn't even remember that I have my own razor in my Botany kit."

"Thank God. You wouldn't have had the nerve. You wouldn't have done it."

"I don't know. You saved my baby, Joan."

"Can't you think of yourself? Forget about the baby, as you call it. Are you trying to make me feel inferior, because I've had abortions? I know what I did was right."

"For you, Joan, but not for me. I'm not against other women terminating their pregnancy. Joan, I know that I'll probably live to regret what I'm doing, but I know for sure that if I do what you want me to do, I'll regret it for sure. This way I'll be at peace with myself. It's all over. I'll go home and face the music."

The two women sat silently for a few minutes. It was Joan who broke the silence.

"Listen, Evelyn. I have to make a phone call. You'll be here when I come back?"

"Joan, I told you to stop worrying. I want to live and I want my baby to live. Go and make your phone call. I'm going to have another cup of tea." Evelyn heard Joan on the phone in the living room. She was having a long animated discussion, but she didn't try to listen. Joan's affairs were not her concern. She looked in the mirror. She was a mess. She began to wonder how she'd spend the rest of the evening. Joan returned and they both had a second cup of tea. Ten minutes later there was a loud knock on the front door. She heard the landlady going to open it. Then she appeared at the bedroom door.

"Evelyn, there's a young man to see you."

'Gerald,' she thought and rose to meet him. 'Joan called Gerald and he's come to look after me.'

Louis Brown appeared in the doorway. She turned to Joan.
"Did you call him?"
Joan didn't like the look on her face.
"No, I called Mrs Brown. She wants to see you."

She felt the sense of panic coming back and grabbed Joan by the arm.

"Don't leave me, Joan. Take me there. Don't leave me alone with him."

"I won't hurt you," said the bully, but Evelyn now knew him to be a liar. She would never trust him again.

Joan took her in her car; Louis took his car. He lost them, racing ahead of them, heading past the brewery and up Hackney Road.

They arrived to find Mrs Brown standing in the doorway with her son behind her, big and menacing. She put her arm around Evelyn and took her inside.

"Thank you, Miss Meredith. You don't know how grateful I am that you called. We'll look after Evelyn now."

Evelyn felt safe with Mrs Brown. She knew what she wanted of her and although she was being led like Isaac to the altar, she felt calm. She kissed Joan and said she could go, that she'd be alright. Then Mrs Brown took her into her old room and closed the door, leaving Louis out of their conversation. Mrs Brown began to cry and so did Evelyn. They hugged each other for comfort. She was a good woman.

"Why didn't you tell us, Evelyn?" she sobbed. Louis is a good boy, he'll do what's right and you're a good girl, Evelyn. Another girl would have found the easy way out."

'My God!' she thought. 'Joan's told Mrs Brown that her son's got me pregnant. What am I going to do?'

"I wanted to take the easy way, Mrs Brown, but it wasn't easy, not for me. I couldn't do it."

"Did Louis tell you to do that?"

"No, I didn't tell him about it."

Evelyn realised what was happening. Joan had told the woman that her son had made her pregnant, that Evelyn was carrying his child. She wanted to disillusion Mrs Brown, but she couldn't. For Louis's mother it seemed like the answer to all her prayers, not the disaster that it really was. She couldn't tell the poor woman about Steven Meredith and how Louis had pushed her into that man's house.

"Well, he knows, now. I love my son, he's a good boy, but I know that he's no saint. I'll see that he looks after you. As long as I'm alive, I'll look after you, Evelyn. How far are you?"

"Eight weeks."

"Eight weeks. You left us eight weeks ago. That was the first of April."

"I think that's when it happened."

"Well, I don't know why you left when you did and I don't approve of what you were doing. I knew that you were doing something, but you're young adults so I didn't say anything. Perhaps I should have. We'd better get Louis in. The sooner you two get married the better."

'But I don't want to marry Louis, I want to marry Gerald,' she thought. 'I'm being forced to do what I don't want to do again. Why does this always happen to me? Does Gerald know what happened to me? Does he hate me for what I've done? Is the baby worth this? It has to be and I have to give up Gerald. I have to choose between the baby and Gerald and I want them both. It isn't fair. It isn't a fair choice. I can't decide against the baby. I shouldn't have to decide like this.'

When Louis came in with his mother, neither of the young people could look at the other. If he had, he would have seen that she, like his mother, was crying. It was up to Mrs Brown to break the ice.

"Louis, I've waited for the day that you'd bring back a girl and tell me that you wanted to marry her. I thought when you brought Evelyn back from Renmark that she might be the girl and I was disappointed when she left. I never thought that I'd have to send you out to rescue her and have to ask you to marry her this way."

"Honest, mother, she didn't tell me. I only found out tonight when you told me. Mother, I don't know how this happened. We took precautions."

Louis was angry. Some damn chemist had sold him faulty merchandise.

"I'm not interested in that. I want to know what you intend to do?"

"I'm prepared to marry her."

She hadn't been too bad in bed, better than lots of girls. She'd been kind to him. He also knew that his mother wouldn't let him off the hook.

"You don't sound too enthusiastic."

"I want to talk to her alone."

"No!" Evelyn screamed.

"What's the matter, dear?"

"Don't ever leave me alone with him, Mrs Brown. If I have to go through with this, I'll do so under my conditions."

"Your conditions! You're in no condition to be making conditions," he shouted, as if he already was her husband.

"Shut up, Louis. I want to hear what Evelyn has to say."

"I want my own room. I'll pay for it. I want to continue studying and I want him to stay out of my room and my bed."

For a moment, you could have heard a pin drop in the room. Mrs Brown hadn't expected this. It was Louis who broke the sound barrier first.

"You don't expect me to agree to that. When I get married I'll expect my wife to know her place, and that includes the kitchen, the laundry, and the bedroom."

"Good. That's what I expected to hear from you. For once Louis you're being honest. Would you please call me a taxi. I want to go home."

Mrs Brown agreed with her son. Evelyn's conditions were no basis for a happy marriage, but she didn't want the girl to go away with her grandchild inside her.

"Evelyn, please don't go. Why must you have a separate room?"

"Why, Mrs Brown? I'll tell you why. I don't love him and he doesn't love me. I don't want to marry him and he doesn't want to marry me. I never wanted to sleep with him in the first place. I must have been mad. If you want us to go through a ceremony for the sake of the baby, that's alright by me, but afterwards I want my freedom."

"And what am I going to do?" he asked.

"If you mean for sex, Louis, that's your problem. I don't intend to sleep with a man I don't love just to provide for my child. If you find another woman who is prepared to share your bed, that's alright by me. If you want a divorce, I won't stand in your way."

"Evelyn, Louis, we're talking about marriage. Don't talk about a divorce at the same time."

"Mrs Brown, we aren't talking marriage, that's for people who love each other. We're talking about a ceremony to prevent a child being born out of wedlock, and that's what's going to happen if he doesn't agree to my conditions. I'll do anything for the baby inside me, but I won't sleep with him anymore."

"Why not, you slept with me all through the summer?"

286

"You lied to me, you laced my drinks, you seduced me, pretending to be my friend."

Evelyn felt sorry for Mrs Brown, but she had to say this. She had to know what Louis had done to her. He had committed every kind of abomination short of getting her pregnant. The truth was, for all she knew it *was* Louis's baby. They night before Meredith forced himself on her, Bully Brown had come to her bed, damn him.

"You destroyed my home life and my private life and you almost got me expelled from the university. I see it all now, quite clearly, especially how you drove a wedge between me and my father."

"You did nothing, I suppose?"

"Yes, I helped you. You can be a charming bastard, Louis Brown, but not anymore. What's it to be — my conditions or good-bye?"

"I'll call you a taxi."

Mrs Brown sat silently, stupefied by the violent verbal intercourse. Her son's suggestion woke her up.

"You'll do no such thing, Louis. Evelyn, it's late and I don't want you to go. I've made your bed. Go to sleep and we'll continue this discussion in the morning."

Evelyn locked the bedroom door when they were gone. She remembered that Louis had put the lock in the morning after they returned from Renmark, so they wouldn't be disturbed when they were in bed together. She'd never locked it when she was on her own. She did tonight.

'Well,' she thought. 'Tomorrow I'll go home and tell my parents that their daughter intends to be an unmarried mother. My father will scold and my mother will weep. I'll get a wedding ring and we'll tell people that I'm separated from my husband, or he died on the honeymoon, but it'll be better than being Louis's private prostitute, giving my body for my food and lodging. Poor Mrs Brown thinks the baby's her son's. I hate to deceive her, but on the other hand she likes the idea. Why not give her the pleasure of a grandchild? Louis doesn't seem to want to do that for his mother. It is his fault that I'm pregnant. He took me to Meredith's and left me there with that pervert. He did this to me as much as Meredith. I saved his neck. Let him share the punishment that I received. *He's* the guilty one.'

With Evelyn safely in bed, Mrs Brown spoke to her son. "Louis, I lied when I told that girl that you're a good boy. You've behaved badly before. You've brought girls home to your room and you've stayed out all night. You haven't even had the decency to hide your carrying on. I've seen those discarded things in the rubbish. You could have wrapped them so I wouldn't have seen them. You really did it tonight. Tonight you really excelled yourself."

"I don't want to marry the stuck-up bitch. What's wrong with that?"

"I'm sad to hear you say that, Louis. It isn't that simple. There's a baby on the way, your baby, my grandchild. I want to see that baby and I don't want him brought into this world a bastard and I won't have that girl ruined for the rest of her life. Louis, I want my grandchild."

"Good, you marry her. You don't need me any more. I've done my bit."

"You talk to me like that and I'll send you packing and find the girl a husband and give them your inheritance. I am going to look after that girl whether you like it or not."

"You won't send me packing. I'm your son, your own flesh and blood."

"So is her baby. Right now that means more to me. Louis, I'm not asking you any more, I'm telling you. If you won't give your name to my grandchild, Louis, you can pack your bags and get out. She's a pretty girl. She won't have too much trouble finding a husband."

"I'm not good enough for her!"

"Louis. I heard what she said. You haven't treated her like a lady, have you?"

"Don't believe it, Mom. She isn't the sweet innocent girl she makes out to be."

"I'll be the judge of that. A girl in her position who's prepared to have a baby — that speaks for itself. She's all I ever wanted as a daughter-in-law. If you won't marry her, I'll take her in as if she was my daughter and you, dear boy, will have to fend for yourself. I'll need our money for the child's upbringing."

Louis knew that his mother meant what she said. He was being asked to chose between the devil and the deep blue sea. Why couldn't she do the right thing and get rid of it?

"What child?" he said, "There isn't any child, she's only two months gone."

"Louis, you are a fool. You'd better start looking for a job and a place to stay. Why don't *you* take Evelyn's room before it gets taken? If you're old enough to father a child, Louis, you're old enough to look after yourself."

"Mom, I'm your son. Who the hell is she?"

"She's a helpless woman who needs a home for herself and my grandchild, which just happens to be inside her."

"You really intend to give her all of my money?"

"Not give her, spend it on her and the child."

"So, I've got to marry her?"

"You should be happy. She's such a nice girl."

"She hates me, Mom. She thinks she's better than me, she and her snobby friends. They all treat me like shit."

"Why did you seduce her and make her pregnant, if you didn't like her? To teach them a lesson?"

Louis said nothing. He knew that his mother was right. He'd have to give up uni and the car, even do his own laundry. He had no profession and no money of his own. He was up shit-creek, without a paddle.

"You ruined a young girl's life when she had everything to look forward to, out of spite, to hurt your fellow students?"

"Fellow students! I hate them all. They treat me like a fool because I failed a few exams. Only Evelyn was nice to me, only Evelyn."

"So you had to ruin her life, the only girl who was nice to you? No wonder people don't like you. No wonder Evelyn hates you."

"And you want to give her my money?"

"My money, Louis, it isn't a lot and it'll never pay for the wrong that you've done to her."

"Do you still want me to marry her?"

"I want you to go through with the ceremony and give the child a name. Then you can go your way."

"Do you want me to move out afterwards?"

"No, not as long as you behave yourself and don't drive her away."

"You prefer her to me?"

"No, I want to love both of you. You're a man, Louis, and sooner or later you'll go. I so much want to look after this girl and the baby, when it comes."

"What about my allowance? When I'm married, I should get a bigger allowance. I'll be able to study too? I won't have to leave the university?"

"You won't need a bigger allowance. I'll see to Evelyn's needs. It'll cut into my savings so I mightn't be able to be so lavish with you. You'd better make sure you pass this year and don't fritter all your time away. I won't be able to support you for ever."

"What about my car?"

"We'll see. You'd better look after it. Don't go losing it in the river again. We won't be able to afford a new one. The next car you'll have to buy out of your own earnings. Louis, seeing how you two feel about each other I think that Evelyn's conditions are reasonable. Can I tell her that you'll accept them?"

"Yes, mother. You've got me by the balls and I know it. I hope you realise that if my wife won't fulfil her obligations, I'll have to get other women to oblige."

Poor Mrs Brown! Her son may not have treated other women properly, but he'd never spoken to his mother this way. She was too concerned to be shocked.

"As you please, but I don't want another repeat of tonight's events. Stay away from decent girls until you're divorced and mature enough to settle down."

"You're the boss, mother."

Louis Brown was mad that night, mad and frustrated. If he could have got at Evelyn, he would have broken every bone in her body, hers and Joan Meredith's as well. She was the interfering bitch that brought this calamity to their house. She had promised him revenge for killing Jonny Marco. Was this part of her vendetta against him? It was. Joan thought she was helping Evelyn, but her real reason for calling Mrs Brown was to make Brown pay for his sins, past and present. She was playing God. And why not? She was a Meredith.

Joan didn't go straight home, but dropped in on Richard on the way there.

"Richard, I've just had the most harrowing experience. I have to talk to you. But first give me something long and stiff. Get that look off your face, I want a drink! This isn't a social call. I've got bad news."

'What a pity!' he thought as he brought her a brandy, lime and soda. For a moment he thought that this might be his lucky night.

"I've just come from the Browns."

"From where?"

"I'd better start at the beginning. I've been seeing Evelyn. Gerald asked me to act as a go-between, to get her to come back to him. I tried, but she wouldn't see him and now she definitely won't. She's going to marry Louis Brown."

Richard took the drink he had just handed Joan and gulped at it. He poured her another one.

"That's impossible. Why would she do a silly thing like that?"

"Because she's pregnant. She's having Brown's baby."

"That's terrible."

He couldn't have been more shocked if Sally had told him she was pregnant. He downed his drink and took another, this time without the lime and soda. Evelyn was his friend, not just his best friend's love. It was the worst kind of news.

"That's what's happened. You remember that day in the cloisters when she wouldn't come out of the toilets until Gerald went away. That was because she thought that she might be pregnant but wasn't sure at the time. The poor kid didn't have an idea what to do and was terrified that Gerald might find out. I helped her and we were going to have it got rid of tonight."

"Nothing happened to her?"

"No."

"So why is she is getting married to Brown?"

"She chickened out and I found her in a hysterical fit. She was going to cut her wrists. I found her with a packet of Gillette blades in her hands. If I hadn't found her, she'd be dead by now over at the racetrack."

Richard remembered helping drag a limp body out of the Torrens.

"Joan, it's Jonny Marco all over again. Brown makes people suicidal. Thank God you got there in time."

"I'm glad I did. I might have helped Jonny, but I didn't. This time I think I got it right. I don't understand the girl, Richard. She'd kill herself rather than terminate the pregnancy. I rang Mrs Brown and took Evelyn to see her. She's a lovely woman. How could she give birth to such a monster? When she heard about Evelyn's condition she took her in and said she'd look after her."

"How could she live with Brown? I tell you, Joan, she isn't out of the woods. She'll kill herself yet if he doesn't kill her first."

"No, she won't. She's over that stage. She wants to have a baby and keep it. This is the only way."

"Does she want to marry him?"

"Richard, I don't know. I think she will for the baby's sake. I'm sure that it won't be much of a marriage."

Richard had always regarded Joan as a spoilt, over-sexed over-rich pain in the neck. Tonight she was gaining his respect.

"She's our friend, Joan. She's my best friend's girlfriend. We have to stop this."

"She made her choice, several times. She didn't have to sleep with him. She could have had the abortion tonight and left Brown. She may yet leave him. The only thing that I know is that she is going to have the baby. I'll say one thing for her, the girl's got guts."

"She's making a big mistake."

"She made it two months ago. Now she's paying for it."

"What are you going to tell Gerald?"

"I can't tell him, Richard, not after what I've been through tonight."

"It'll break his heart, what's left of it. The poor bugger's been miserable ever since Brown butted in."

"What did happen? I came back to uni and I saw the two of them together. I nearly died."

"That's the effect Brown has on people. It was touch and go with Gerald too. He was suicidal when he found out. Joan, I don't know what happened, and Gerald doesn't either. For that information you'll have to ask Evelyn and if she doesn't know, ask Svengali himself. Neither Gerald nor I have spoken to Evelyn in five months."

"She won't see him now, either. She's too ashamed."

"So I have to tell the poor bastard. What am I going to tell him?"

"You're a good talker, you'll think of something. Don't tell him about the abortion plan or the razor blades. Tell him the barest facts, that she's getting married. Don't even tell him that she's pregnant. He'll see that for himself if he sees her later in the year. They'll get married soon and that'll be that. He'll accept it as a *fait accompli* and he'll get over it."

"Do you think I should see Evelyn too?"

"No, I'll be seeing her. It won't be easy. You know that Brown and I are enemies. It was really terrible tonight. By the look in his eyes I could see how he hated me. If looks could kill—"

"Brown's a shit, Joan. How can we let her marry him?"

"It's her choice."

Joan wasn't lying. She just assumed that by deciding to have the baby, she wanted to marry its father, whom she assumed was Brown. It was a fair assumption.

"Tell me, why are you and Louis such enemies? You were good friends once."

"For one unfortunate week last year and then he used me. It wasn't just for you-know-what — that was mutual — he used me to hurt someone. I did something unforgivable under the influence of Brown. I can't tell you what it is, but it was a watershed in my life. I'm not the stupid girl that I used to be."

"Yes, I think that I noticed the change."

'So they did do something to Jonny,' Richard mused. 'I *knew* it! What could he have done to drive him insane?' But that was in the past. Now the bastard was going to marry Evelyn. He liked Evelyn almost as much as Gerald.

"I have nightmares when I think of it, Richard. It worries me to think of that poor girl living with him."

"Isn't there *anything* we can do?"

"No, she wants to have his baby. Do we send her home? Do we ask Gerald to marry her, knowing that she's carrying Brown's baby?"

What would she have done if she'd known that Evelyn had her own niece or nephew in her womb? Would she have left it and its mother in the care of the man that drove Jonny Marco to his death?

"I don't know, Joan," said Richard. This was too much for him. "Gerald ought to know what's going on."

"I'm not going to tell him. I'm not going to ask him if he still wants her. What would you do in his place?"

"He'd probably shoot himself. He's good with guns. He hasn't much money and neither have his parents. If he had to get married and support a child, he'd have to give up university. Then how would he tell his parents that the child isn't his? Imagine, they'd have to live in the Fishers' house, all close together and all knowing that she's brought a little cuckoo into the nest. They couldn't keep the secret from his family if they tried. Gerald was in Nasho when it happened and hasn't seen her for months. He couldn't tell his parents that he was responsible, even if the poor bastard was so much in love to do such a thing. I don't even know if he'd be prepared to play father to Brown's child and I don't think I'm prepared to ask him."

"So, she's better off where she is?"

"God only knows. She must feel something for Brown, if she wants to have his baby. I'll never understand women, Joan. Perhaps we're worrying about nothing."

Joan didn't say anything. She knew that Evelyn was entering into a relationship that was doomed from the start, but she couldn't tell Richard. There weren't many options open to Evelyn, so Joan decided to let Richard and Gerald think that things were better than they were.

"When will you tell him, Richard?"

"I'll be meeting him tomorrow."

"Good. I'll join you for lunch. You'll probably need some moral support."

Richard thought of the previous year when they also ate together as a trio and a lump came to his throat. It would be Joan instead of Evelyn. Joan might be the right medicine for Gerald's illness.

The two boys met as usual to play table tennis, but instead Richard told him that Evelyn was getting married. *He took it like a man, swearing and banging on the table, calling her names over and over again.*

"I'll never speak to the bitch again and I'll never trust any woman again."

"You'll get over it."

"To think that I haven't touched another woman in six months while that bitch played me for a fool. I should have stuffed that girl instead of letting Brown get to her first."

"Forget her, Gerry. She did try to tell you in January, but you wouldn't listen. Take out other girls. Don't get involved in a hurry. Learn from this."

"I'll never love anyone else."

"You will. I've been in and out of love half a dozen times."

"I'm not like you. I don't like one-nighters. I want a girl that I can take out every week and marry when I graduate. That girl was Evelyn."

"No it wasn't. You'll find some one much nicer than her, Gerald. This won't be the only time that you'll be disappointed. Life's full of disappointments."

Richard was planning a little merriment, so he decided to involve Gerald in it to take his mind off of Evelyn.

"Gerald, we're having Biochemistry this afternoon. We're going to have a bit of fun."

"You're joking. Nothing could be less fun than Biochem. Practical."

"Not today. Today we'll piss ourselves laughing. Wait 'til I show you what we're going to do."

Evelyn got up early and, unlocking her door, went to say good-bye to Mrs Brown.

"I'm going now. I have to write and tell my mother and then go to lectures."

"Please sit down and have some breakfast."

"I'm not hungry."

"You have to eat, your baby needs food, you know. Evelyn, Louis and I had a long talk after you went to bed. I admit that at first I was a little taken aback by your conditions, but in the light of my discussion with my son I think that not only are they reasonable, but in the circumstances, quite sensible. You don't love one another."

"I hate him. I'm sorry, I know that he's your son, but that's what I feel."

"I don't blame you, Evelyn, after what he's done to you. You two don't have to cohabit if you don't want to."

She saw a look of disgust on the girl's face and it hurt her, but she didn't let it show.

"You can have your own room with a lock, if you want it, but it won't be necessary. I want you to finish your studies this year and if it's possible next year too. I'd love to look after the baby while you're at the university. I'll give you a small allowance too."

"Why are you doing this?"

The woman was a saint.

"We owe it to you. You might have got rid of the baby. I think it's a terrible crime, but it's your body. I can't force you to have the baby."

295

"It is a terrible thing to do. I didn't think much about it until I had to have it done to me. I never thought that I'd ever get into such a situation. If a girl doesn't want a baby, I don't think she should have it. If a baby isn't wanted, why bring the poor thing into the world? I didn't want a baby, right up until the time that I thought I was going to lose it. I know now that I can't part with this little piece of life growing inside me. It's a part of me and I'll die before I'll hurt it."

"No one's going to hurt it or take it away from you."

"Mrs Brown, I have a mother in Renmark who loves me very much. I feel that I'm getting another such mother."

"What about your father?"

"He loves me too, in his way. He loves to tell me what to do and what not to do. When he hears about my condition, he'll feel so good that he was right and I was wrong. He used to be so loving, but this summer he's kept me at arm's length, as if I offended his nostrils."

"Evelyn, I've only had the one child. I wanted more. I wanted more, but I wasn't well when I had Louis, and God took my husband, with the help of the Japs. I want you to be the daughter that I wanted and never had."

"How can I go when you say things like that? I'll stay, but I'd better get going now or I'll be late for lectures."

"I'd better wake Louis and tell him that he's getting married after all, and he'd better get going too if he's got lectures this morning. He's not such a bad student. He did pass his supplementary examination."

Poor Mrs Brown. If she only knew how Louis passed that exam, and how much that pass was costing all of them.

"I don't want a church wedding."

"Why not, Evelyn?"

"My folks take their religion seriously. If this is going to be a mock wedding, I don't think it should be in a church. It would be blasphemy. When I get married in a church, it will be for keeps."

"And then I'll lose my daughter?"

"No, Mrs Brown. You've just saved my life. I may leave your son, but I'll always have a place in my heart for you. I'm the daughter that you never had, remember?"

Evelyn sought out and found Joan after the morning lecture.

"It's going to be alright, Joan. I've been made Mrs Brown's honorary daughter and I'm marrying her son under my terms. These include my remaining here and completing my degree. It won't be easy, but it'll keep my mind off other things. I'll be able to have the baby and keep it. Now, all I have to do is tell my parents. I'm going to telephone Mom this afternoon when Dad's at work. I don't want him to answer the phone."

"You certainly sound like a different person today. Did you have a good night's sleep?"

"The first in three days."

"Are you going to be alright?"

"If you mean am I going to do anything silly, you've got nothing to worry about. The only silly thing I'm going to do is get married, but I'll get over that too. I can't say it's going to be a bed of roses, but I'm getting what I want, except for one thing and I know that I can't have him, so I'll have to live without him. Have you told him?"

"No, I couldn't. I asked Richard to do that. He's his best friend. He told him this morning."

"Joan, I've written him a letter. Give it to him."

"I'll be seeing them this afternoon. Boring Biochemistry Practical. We're doing urine today."

"Tell me how he takes it, Joan."

"I'll ring you tonight."

Evelyn left and Joan felt terrible.

"She still loves him. What have I done to her? I wish I had a better solution to this, but I don't. This is so wrong, so unfair and so damned inevitable."

She gave Gerald the note while they were having lunch. He read it quickly, rolled it into a ball, and threw it into a nearby bin. He said nothing, but it was plain to her that he was hurt by the contents. Shortly afterwards he left with Richard. As soon as they were gone she retrieved the letter from the bin and read it.

Dear Gerald,

I know that I owe you an explanation for what I've done and I want to give you one, but I can't. There is no explanation. If there had been one, I'd have given it to you a long time ago. I cannot explain my actions or justify them. I never meant to do it or hurt you in any way. It just happened. I wish it hadn't but it has. I'm sorry. Please don't hate me. God knows you have every right, but please don't.

I'll never forget the times that we shared together. They were happy times. Last year was the happiest year of my life. Knowing you was one of the nicest things that ever happened to me. I'm sad it's all over.

Forget me, Gerald. Go and find another girl who won't break your heart. Please don't try and see me. I don't want complications in my life. I see that you changed classes. It was a good idea and will make parting easier. I'm going to be alright, Gerald, so don't worry about me. Joan's been a tower of support for me. She's the good Meredith.

I can't say any more. Soon it will be clear to you why I've done what I've done. Please forgive me. Thanks for all the good times. I'm sorry it wasn't to be. Fate was against us.
E.

Joan felt her eyes water as she read the note, and her mascara ran. She put the note in her handbag and went to the washroom to freshen up. She changed into her lab coat and arrived late for the practical class, looking composed as usual. One phrase in the letter stuck in her mind and puzzled her.

Why did she write: 'She's the good Meredith'? Why such a strange phrase in the letter? If there was a good Meredith, it implied that there was a bad one too.

It didn't occur to her or to Gerald that this was a hint that another Meredith had contributed to her situation and that she couldn't tell him about it. As far as Joan was concerned, Evelyn had never met her brother, Steven. Joan saw in the letter a cry for help, but Gerald didn't. She didn't tell him. It was a private letter that she'd read.

The Biochemistry laboratories in the Darling Building were some of the most dismal in the university. Both the large room used by the second-year medical students and the room above it, used by the science students, were tall rooms with narrow windows and glass that one couldn't see through, and calcimined walls that collected dust and cobwebs. The benches were undertaker-black, as were the shelves and plumbing. The lighting was poor and it was almost impossible to see the colours of the solutions on rainy days, or in winter when the sun went down early.

The practical work matched the decor. The first part of the year was taken up with examination of biological materials, sugars, carbohydrates, proteins and lipids. Then they advanced to biological materials such as blood and urine. It was clinical biochemistry, following the practical text book written by the Professor, and detested by students, especially of Medicine. This probably accounts for the words in the student song, sung to the tune of *Lili Marlene*:

> Night upon the Torrens, we were doing Med.
> The Nurses were all up, the students all in bed.
> When I was in second year I condemned,
> The SCM and Biochem,
> And all I passed was water,
> When we were doing Med.

On this day they were doing tests on urine and measuring its urea content. As soon as the preliminary lecture was over, all the class took beakers and went *en masse* to the toilets, bringing back samples of urine, light yellow to rich amber in colour. There was a lot of joking. It appeared that the larger the sample the greater guy you were, as if micturition had something to do with virility.

They soon settled down to their task. This involved pipetting a measured amount of urine into a flask and measuring the carbon dioxide formed when the urea was broken down. Richard took his beaker and, followed by a couple of Agricultural Science students, went into the midst of the girls who were busily pipetting. One of them noticed the boy standing there, sucking up the frothy amber coloured liquid, and instead of stopping at the mark on the pipette, sucking it up slowly like a milkshake through a straw.

"Look at him! He's *drinking* it!"

"I'm gonna be sick!"

At once, all the girls standing there turned and watched as Richard, Gerald, and three other students drained their beakers, making horrible sucking noises at the bottom. Most of their exclamations consisted of guttural sounds of disgust. Someone called out, "I'm going bring up my dinner!" Richard returned with a second beaker, containing at least half a litre and proceeded to pour it over Joan Meredith's permanent wave. She screamed for a second and then a smile came to her face:

"You bastard, Flynn. That isn't piss, it's *beer*."

The smell of it rose from her warm body and the look of shock on everyone's face turned to merriment.

"That's for putting alcohol, you-know-where, Joan. Now for the test. What brand is it?"

"Well, it isn't *West End* or *Southwick*, and I don't think it's *Cooper's Ale*, so I guess it's Daddy's. It's *Meredith*, isn't it?"

"That was too easy."

"I'm soaked to the skin. I smell like a brewery, but I won't need a beer rinse this week."

"Can I help you out of those wet things?"

"No thank you, Richard Flynn. Some other time. Anyone got a spare lab coat?"

Gerald offered her one of his. He noticed how the wet lab coat clung to her, how her full round breasts in her black lace bra were outlined and pressed against the wet fabric. It aroused him. He hadn't felt that way about a woman in months. Then, when she came back wearing his lab coat, he couldn't help noticing the famous Meredith tits, which couldn't be entirely hidden by the cut of his lab coat.

"I'm going to skip next week's class, boys."

"What's the matter, Joan?"

"Look at the book, we're doing faeces next week. That's shit, in case you don't know, and I don't trust you guys. I won't be there to see what you're going to do."

"There's this shop in Adelaide Arcade that sells magic tricks and fake objects. They've got the cutest turds and mock vomit. Do you remember the mouse in physics last year? That came from there. If you're scared, we won't do anything."

The demonstrator told them to clean the beer off the black floor and to get on with the work. Later Joan wanted an eraser and called out across the partition to Richard.

"Richard, got a rubber on yer, Dick?"

He threw it at her while several people sniggered. It wasn't a new joke for Richard.

Ten days later it was end of first term and Evelyn married Louis Brown at a registry office. Joan was there, standing next to the bride's sobbing mother who came down from Renmark, without her husband's blessing. The bride wore no special dress, no jewellery and didn't have her hair done. She wore no make up, wanting to look as plain as she could, even refusing to have her picture taken. They did not kiss after the ceremony or hold hands during it. She shuddered when he put the ring on her hand and she took it off soon afterwards, never to wear it again. She didn't care what people thought, just so long as the baby wouldn't suffer.

"Where are you going for the honeymoon?"

The look that Joan got when she asked this question, told her all she didn't want to know.

"The honeymoon is over, Joan, a long time ago. Joan, there's one thing that I want to tell you that I have to tell someone. I haven't told it to another living soul."

They sat in the privacy of her car and Evelyn told her,

"This is really going to shock you, Joan."

"Go ahead, nothing shocks me."

"Louis didn't make me pregnant. Someone else did."

"Shit, Evelyn, you've really shocked me. Are you sure?"

"Yes, he always used a contraceptive."

"So it leaked. Why do you think he isn't the father?"

"There was someone else who didn't use anything."

"Who?"

"I can't tell you."

"Do I know him?"

"I don't know." To say that she couldn't tell would mean "yes", and she didn't want Joan to know.

"It can't be..."

"Gerald? I wish it was. God, I wish it was his baby. I would want nothing else in the world. Then I could have gone back to him and not be ashamed. Even if he told me to go away, I'd be happier than I am now. If it were Brown I still could have gone back to Gerald, have waited until he could marry me, but this is too, too terrible."

"Evelyn, You aren't the girl that I thought you were. How many men have you been sleeping with?"

"Louis was the only one. The other man forced me against my will."

Joan was reeling. It was one damned revelation after another. She was a sexual novice compared to this girl.

"Why didn't you report the bastard? Someone raped you and you did nothing about it?"

"It isn't that simple. Louis is to blame. He made me go to the man's place."

"You're losing me. Brown forced you to go to a man's place to have sex with him against your will?"

"No, Joan. I can't tell you what happened — it's too painful and I'm too ashamed. Louis made me go to the man's place when he wasn't at home and pretend that I was a friend of the man. I didn't want to do it, but Louis insisted. I don't know what possessed me to do it. Louis, you may not know, can be very persuasive."

"Don't tell me, Evelyn, I've been his victim too."

Joan should have turned him in in 1952. Was there no limit to that man's bastardry?

"Well, the man came home and Louis left me. He was going to hand me over to the police and that would have been better than what he did. Instead he locked me up for hours and made me submit to him."

"Did he use force?"

"No, only mental pressure and a locked door. After several hours of incarceration I was too weak to resist. Then he raped me as I slept. That was when it must have happened. I know it. I couldn't go to the police. I went to his house. You can't do that and cry 'rape'."

"What were you doing for Brown?"

"Something really rotten. I can't tell you."

This was only too familiar to Joan. What a pity they couldn't share their stories, she thought.

"Why didn't you go to this man and tell him he's going to be a father and ask for future child support?"

"He isn't in the country anymore. I'm glad in a way. I'm going to have the last laugh on him. I'm going to have his child and he'll never know about it. Joan, I didn't want this to happen. It's messed up my life and lost me the man I love, but I'll have a child to love and he won't. So, all in all, I haven't come up empty-handed."

"Your crazy, Evelyn, but in a nice way. I hope you have your baby and he grows up and appreciates what a good mother he's getting. I hope too that you get out of this mock marriage and find a nice father for the baby."

Joan didn't say "Gerald" and wondered why. Was it too much to hope that they'd ever get together again?

She liked Gerald and felt sorry for him, but she also found herself attracted to him, all the more so now that he was unattached. Gerald wasn't going to wait for Evelyn, now that she'd married Brown. Love, when treated cruelly, turns into hate.

"Why did you make us believe that Brown knocked you up and make the sucker marry you?"

"He's more to blame than the real father. He lied to me, seduced me, made my father drive me away from home and lost me my boyfriend, all for spite; and if that isn't enough, he took me to that man's house. I'm not ashamed to make a sucker out of him. It's nothing to the suffering that that man's caused me. Do you think that I like doing it? I have to do it. It was that or go back to my father and have an illegitimate child. I never said that Louis was the man. You all assumed it. I never said so to him either. Well, I haven't got a lot of options. Between you and me this wasn't such a good idea, but no one came up with a better one."

"I won't tell anyone what you told me. If I did, they'd think I was mad. It's just too incredible. Evelyn, I won't be seeing you so often now. I'm not welcome in Brown's house. Ring me if you need help."

"Joan, you've been a brick. Come and see me when I have the baby. Mrs Brown's going to look after me and Mom says I can come home for holidays, so I have people to talk to now. I'll see you at university too. You saved my life, Joan. I'll always be in your debt."

Joan went away feeling relieved. Evelyn was going to be alright. She'd have her baby and sooner or later she and Brown would go their own ways. Evelyn would make a fresh start. Joan thought of telling Gerald to wait for her. He was so madly in love with her, he might just do that. On the other hand it might drive him to distraction. Better say nothing about her and comfort him instead.

Chapter Twenty-One

June 1953

At what stage Joan decided that she wanted Gerald is hard to say. She herself didn't know. Acting as a go-between, she'd got to know him, to see his inner feelings, and she liked what she saw. No man had ever felt like that for her. She envied Evelyn. Also the experience had brought her very close to Gerald. They understood one another.

Joan wasn't the kind of person to steal another girl's boyfriend, not in recent years, but Gerald was fair game now that Evelyn was married. He was also a lonely man, without a girlfriend. If Joan didn't step in some other girl would. Human nature abhors a vacuum.

One thing bothered her. Why did she ring Mrs Brown that fateful night and not Gerald? Was she already subconsciously getting rid of a rival? Why hadn't she told Gerald that Evelyn was pregnant and let him decide what to do? He'd have taken care of her, the lovesick fool, no matter what. The two of them would have stopped studying and lived like a couple of church mice.

"I could have supported them both and not seen the difference in my bank account, but I did nothing. What's the use in blaming myself? All Evelyn had to do was to pick up a telephone or hop into a taxi and she could have told Gerald herself. I told her to go to him, but she didn't want to. It's all over now, there's no sense crying over spilt milk. I comforted her, now I'm going to comfort him."

It wasn't hard to attract Gerald. It wasn't hard for Joan to attract any man. She had an attractive face, a beautiful body, and money to spend on clothes to display it as a lure for a lonely male. He was lonely and vulnerable. She didn't have to throw herself at him, she was with him almost every day and had already replaced Evelyn in the trio, studying together in the libraries, eating together in the Refectory or on the lawns. They were studying the same subjects, so it was natural that they should spend a lot of time together. Soon Richard dropped out, deliberately to leave the two of them alone together at her request. He played Cupid by default. Joan always wore perfume and either a tight sweater or a loose blouse with one or two buttons open. It was difficult for Gerald to concentrate on the work and not think about the woman sitting next to him or opposite, leaning over the table offering a delightful view down inside her blouse. He didn't stand a chance, but he also came to her willingly, driven to distraction by her sexuality.

In Bacteriology they sat together and were partners, sharing the same samples as they worked together. This had been the subject that her brother used to teach. She was glad that he wasn't there this year, as she didn't like the idea that he'd be her lecturer and see how she was getting under Gerald's skin.

Their practical work usually meant staining and examining slides. Joan hated staining slides. No matter how careful you were, the stains got on your hands and they stayed red or purple for weeks, so Gerald did the staining for both of them. She could do it, but only did when she had rubber gloves. Most of the time she let him do it while she looked over his shoulders, resting the "Meredith tits" on them. Once or twice she noticed stirrings under his lab coat and chuckled to herself, as she saw him wriggling uncomfortably in his seat. At first he found the feel of her, warm and soft pressing down on him, disconcerting, but soon he got to like it. He began to have fantasies about her, lying in bed at night, removing her blouse and lacy bra and making merry with the contents.

The day after Evelyn's wedding, Joan took the bull by the horns. It was the day of the Coronation, the day the conquest of Everest was announced, that she undertook her conquest of Gerald Fisher. She invited a group of students to a party at her place, all couples, except Gerald and herself. She wore a very low-cut dress and a strapless platform bra. The other girls couldn't herd their guys out of the party fast enough, leaving Gerald and Joan alone together just before midnight, Gerald without a lift home. Joan had danced with him for most of the evening, and he was more than ready to make a pass at her and glad to find himself alone with this delightful creature. He'd had a few drinks, not enough to make him drunk, but enough to reduce his inhibitions. Richard hadn't been invited to the party, but he had told his friend what to do if he found himself alone with the party giver. He gave Gerald a house-key so he wouldn't have to walk home.

Joan locked the door, drew the curtains and put on a record. What was the more seductive: Billy Holiday's *So Easy To Love*, or Edith Piaf's *La Vie En Rose*? She chose Billy Holiday. The only light in the room came from the fire in the fireplace, and it was just enough to help her find her quarry and draw him to her, with the pretence of dancing with him. Dancing alone in the fireglow with only their

clothes keeping them apart, she waited to see what he would do —
whether he'd be bold enough to take what she was offering him or too
afraid to accept the challenge.

Gerald might have been inexperienced, but he wasn't a fool. He
was well aware that Joan was there for the taking, and she expected
him to accept what she was offering. He knew that this was a come
on, in big, bold letters. He also knew that he wanted what she was
offering, a meal to a starving man. They were alone in her flat and
she herself had locked the door. That said "I don't want to be
disturbed". It was now or never. If he didn't accept the challenge,
he'd insult her and that's the last thing he wanted to do. She was so
soft and lovely, her body so close to his was so arousing, her bosom
so exposed and so inviting. He didn't know what to do first, take a
handful of her breasts, bursting to be free of their enclosure, or start
conventionally with a kiss. He chose to be conventional. They were
dancing close, very close. She was tall, almost as tall as he was, so it
was a small movement to bring his lips to hers. After the first gentle
kisses, she began to kiss him back passionately and they quickly sank
to the soft thick angora rug in front of the sofa. He began to kiss her
on the neck and made for the soft round breasts that had caught the
eyes of all the guests all evening. Joan arched her back with the thrill
of his touch, easing herself out of the dress, so he was able to kiss
first one breast and then the other. The famous "Meredith tits" were
his, so round and warm and soft. He kissed them and put his lips to
the nipples, making Joan sigh with the pleasure of it, holding his head
to her body like a baby. Then she rolled over and lay above him,
smothering him with them all over his face, as the record finished
playing, the pickup arm went back to its place, the turntable stopping
with a click. Gerald's heart was beating fast. He was about to become
a man.

She got out of her dress and started to undress him, slowly,
sensually, touching his taut muscles as she did. Three and a half
months in the army had brought him to the peak of physical fitness.
When she got to his underpants, it was too much for him. He *shot his
bolt*, spilling his seed as she started to remove them. He felt acutely
embarrassed, like a child who has just blotted his copybook.

"Never mind, Gerald. I take it as a compliment. I bet you've got
plenty more where that came from. Go and wash yourself down and
come back. Bring a bath-towel with you."

Gerald returned, head bowed, with a towel wrapped around his waist, which Joan quickly removed. She lay back on the towel and he lay next to her just touching. For a while they looked at the fire and deciding that he should take the initiative, Gerald drew her to him, resuming his exploration of her body, starting with her head and lips, renewing his acquaintance with her breasts. As he felt his organ recover from its earlier *faux pas*, he removed Joan's thin black lace panties to reveal between her wide child-bearing hips, a tuft of jet black pubic hair.

As she took his hand, showing him what delighted her, he remembered the packet of Durex that had remained unopened in his wallet since he bought it on the last day of 1952. He remembered what a fool he'd been that day. As he reached for his pants, Joan realised what he wanted and pulled him back.

"That isn't necessary. I put my diaphragm in while you were washing *little Richard*. I see he's feeling better. Don't go in just yet. A little more play and then it's all up to you."

Gerald did as he was bid and they mutually aroused each other. In a couple of minutes Joan was ready for him and he for her. Then they joined their bodies. Gerald, making love to a woman for the first time, had no trouble in doing what comes naturally. He didn't realise that it could feel so good, or that a woman would be so active, meeting his every thrust with hers until, gripping him tightly, she climaxed and he felt himself doing the same, as she put her lips to his, kissing so hard that she almost drew blood.

Later she told him she wanted him to spend the night with her and they went to bed. Joan fell asleep at once, with her arm and one breast lying on his chest, and he lying back, thinking about the experience and the evening that led up to it. He was flattered that Joan had chosen him for a lover and wondered how long he'd be *number one*.

'If after this night she never wants me again, that's alright with me. I've broken the ice and it's been a wonderful experience. But why should she throw me over now? I think she enjoyed the love-making; if not, she certainly can fake it. She's been throwing herself at me all week. I don't know how long we're going to be lovers, but it's just what I need, a nice unemotional sexy relationship. Richard, you were right, as usual.'

He thought of getting on the phone and telling Richard where he was. The phone was next to the bed. It would be worthwhile waking him up to tell him the good news, but that wouldn't be nice, to make love and tell, with your lover sleeping by your side. He extricated himself from Joan, turned over and went to sleep.

In the morning he opened his eyes and saw a pair of beautiful hazel eyes looking at him from the sweetest face and blackest hair. It was Joan. It was a sight that he'd never forget. Long after the winter of 1953 and the fateful spring of 1956, the memory of waking with Joan that morning came back, a photograph of the mind.

"I've been looking at you for fifteen minutes, Gerald. I could look at you for the rest of my life."

She snuggled close to him, pressing two soft warm breasts to his hairy chest and he knew that he must make love to her again, which was precisely the reason that she'd been watching and waiting. She'd already put another lot of Ortho-gynol cream in herself just in case. She desired him, she wanted him to father her children, but not at this time, not until he wanted her the same way.

"What are you planning to do today?" she asked him when she got her breath back and was relaxing in the after-glow of love-making.

"I was going to study at home. I'd better go soon."

"When I'm getting to know you! Spend the day here. Spend a few days here. It's a long weekend. We can study together."

"I've got no clothes. Besides, my parents should know where I am."

"Ring them. If you want clothes, Steven left some things upstairs in his room. You're about his size. I'm going to shower and then I'll get dressed, go upstairs, and get us breakfast. I'll get you a pair of Steven's underpants. Come and have a shower."

They showered together, with Gerald soaping her beautiful body and pressing her, soft and slippery, against him. This was an experience that he savoured more than anything else. On later occasions they made love under the shower, a mixture of soapsuds, water and gymnastics.

When Joan went upstairs, Gerald rang home. It was Sunday and they didn't even know that he wasn't home in bed.

"Mom, I'm staying with a fellow student and we're going to study today. I might be back tomorrow; if not, I'll go straight to uni and see you in the afternoon."

Joan returned with their breakfast of steamed Scottish kippers and butter, with a pot of tea, toast and marmalade.

"If you want a steak to replenish your protein reserves, I'll have one sent down."

"No, I haven't had a good kipper like this in ages. You can order them for me every time."

"You're pretty sure of yourself. Who says that there'll be a next time?"

"Are you telling me that we won't do this again, Joan?"

He looked like a little boy who had just lost his bag of marbles.

"No, Gerald, I was just kidding. Once, I never invited a guy back a second time, but I'm a reformed woman now. You, Gerald, are welcome here whenever you want to be here."

"And in between, will there be someone else?"

"Not if you don't want. I want you to be my boyfriend, lover, whatever you want to call it. If I'm presuming too much, tell me. After a night like we've had, I think we don't need to hide our feelings. I like you, Gerald, I like you a lot. I won't look at another man as long as you want me. Trust me, Gerald, I'll never let you down."

That was what he wanted to hear. This was his lucky day.

"Joan, I believe you. You're the only woman that I've ever slept with. Last night was the first time for me. It shouldn't have been, but it was. Joan, it was all I'd ever expected it to be. I couldn't imagine it could ever be better. You are a sexy woman, Joan, with a body that dreams are made of. What do you see in me?"

"I see a man of character, intelligence, and for a man doing it for the first time, you're not bad, not bad at all. Heaven help me when you become an expert, and you will if you stay with me. You're also the best shot in the regiment."

"But what if some bigger, sexier guy comes along and sweeps you off your feet?"

"Gerald, I went through the stage of being swept off my feet, literally swept off my feet, two, three years ago. I don't go for the Robert Mitchum, Errol Flynn type any more, or for Mr Atlas types. At present I feel attracted to you and I think that you are to me. Am I correct?"

"I suppose I am. I definitely am. I suppose sooner or later I'd have asked you out. Now that we've made love, I'm sorry that I didn't do it sooner. You've been teasing my prick for a while, haven't you, you seductress?"

"Gerald, I know that expression, and I assure you that one thing I have never been, ever, is a prick tease. I've always delivered the goods."

"Tell me, Joan. How can you make love to a person that you don't love?"

Gerald was worried. He was having sex with a woman. It was great. But what did it all mean?

"I would have loved to fall in love with the first person that aroused me so much that I let him take my cherry, as they say, but he didn't feel anything for me. Sometimes I've made love because I loved the man, but most of the time it was because I was attracted to him and he aroused me right from the start, or I was alone with him and he touched and petted me until I wanted him to make love to me. Then there were other times when my date or my boyfriend insisted and I was neither aroused nor did I enjoy it. I made love because I'd done it before and it was expected of me. Last year I took a good look at myself and now I'm almost virtuous. Do you know that I haven't had a man in over a month?"

"Is that a long time?"

She laughed, and her breasts shook under her lace negligée.

"Gerald, you are a scream. I've been saving myself for you. Finally I gave up hoping that you'd ask me out so I invited you over. If you'd resisted me, I think I'd have upped and raped you last night."

"Can a woman rape a man?"

"If she's strong enough or she has a gang and he's really a man. Well, thank goodness I didn't have to try. Gerald, I'm glad we're lovers. Here's to us. May every time be the best time."

"I'll drink to that. Now, are we going to study together or what?"

"Get out the books."

"And put on something less provocative. Loose, buttoned to the neck and no perfume. Otherwise, I'm going to study with Richard. What the hell, I can afford to miss a day's study. Let's go back to bed. It's raining outside and there's nothing better than staying in bed on a rainy day. I can't study today with you, and if I go home, I'll think about you, so let's have a good time."

He picked up Joan and carried her back to the bed.

"Gerald, you catch on fast. Tomorrow we'll organise our study plan to fit in with our love and social life. I want to see *Annie Get Your Gun* if it's still on."

"Do you want to show everyone that we're going together?"

"No, Gerald, I want to see Annie. Next month I want to see the Womens' Revue — some of my friends are in it. Are you worried about being seen with me?"

He was, but he wouldn't admit it — not to Joan, not to himself. Joan and her boyfriends attracted a lot of talk, and people made snide remarks about who was getting his bit.

"Worried? of course not. It's a great honour that you want me to take you."

"Cut the bullshit. I'm rich and people will say you're after my money. It isn't true and we both know it, otherwise you would have asked me out long before this, so don't think about it. You're after my body and that's expected of a young man, even in Adelaide."

"Just don't expect me to be affectionate in public. I always think that people like that are phoney."

"You're the boss, Gerald."

"Well what are you waiting for? Get that nightie off."

Louis Brown also spent the night with a woman that wasn't his wife. His new wife spent the evening listening to the radio with her husband's mother, then studying alone in her bed until one o'clock, and after breakfast again settled down with her text books. Mrs Brown, senior, listened to the Coronation Broadcast from London, saddened by the knowledge that her son hadn't come home all night. She still clung to the hopeless hope that he and Evelyn would be reconciled.

Monday was a public holiday. Tuesday Gerald arrived in Joan's car at the university, dressed in his best suit. Richard noticed the suit and commented, "Going somewhere later on?"

"No, I'm going home to study."

"So why are you wearing a suit? Your sports coat and pants at the cleaners?"

There was a strange grin on his friend's face, replacing the grim look of recent weeks.

"Richard, I haven't been home for three days. I've got a girlfriend."

"Anybody I know?"

"She invited me to a party on Saturday night and you weren't invited."

"Joan? She invited you to a party, just the two of you?"

He was joking. He knew all about the party.

"No, but we were when the others left. Richard, don't tell a soul, but we just came from her flat. We're going to see more of each other."

This was a red-letter day. Gerald had done it!

"A long weekend with Joan Meredith and you're going to see more of each other. What more is there to see?"

"Richard, do me a favour. Joan's thick-skinned, but don't give the slightest hint that I told you. We're going to the theatre together next Saturday night, so everyone will know that I'm the new consort, but it's worth it. She's a great girl."

'So Gerald's finally a man!' he thought. 'Whacko-the-didle-oh! What a way to go!'

"She's also a rich one, Gerry."

"I'll try not to think about it."

"Don't you want to share in the Meredith Millions?"

"Richard, I'm doing what you wanted from me. I'm taking out the girl that you think will get me back on the tracks. We're good friends, that's all, extremely good friends. Joan's experienced and I've never been to bed with another woman. I felt inadequate."

"Do you still feel that way?"

"No. I didn't know a woman could be so understanding."

"Stay with her, Gerry. She's a good woman and she likes you. If it's only for a month or a year, so what? Remember the good times, and find yourself another girl."

"Richard, you don't have to worry any more about me. I won't make the same mistake twice."

It took Gerald a month to settle in to his new situation. He and Joan were now inseparable. She sat next to him in the George Murray Hall, holding his hand, as future leaders of the community debated the topic, "That this House Prefers Bertrand to Joan", squeezing his hand at every *double entendre*. When one speaker said, "3-D movies gave the audience the opportunity of seeing Miss Russell while sitting in the front row under the balcony", she almost sprained Gerald's wrist.

They went to the Curzon to see Lawrence Olivier in *Hamlet* and Orson Welles in *Macbeth*. They went out to many more parties than he ever used to go to, and to show after show. He liked the parties, but couldn't wait to leave them and Joan's friends so he could make love to Joan. After the theatre she always went with her companions for coffee, or supper and dancing at "The Paprika", a small upstairs restaurant with continental food, continental records, and lighting so dim that you could hardly see the faces of your companions. It had a dance floor that was small, on which they danced close to romantic music, crushed by their neighbour-dancers. It was an oasis in the Adelaide provincial desert. Often Joan invited her friends back to her flat and they stayed late.

Joan found Gerald a good lover. He couldn't wait to be alone with her, to get away from parties, to get her away from her panties. He couldn't wait for her guests to leave them so he could caress her and take her to bed. It made her feel good to be desired, a feeling not new to her, but always refreshing, especially in someone that she also desired.

Slowly, after a month's "honeymoon", they got back to studying together or separately. Sometimes they arrived at her flat, studied from five until midnight and then, and only then, made love. Gerald told his parents that he was studying with a girlfriend, but didn't tell them her name, they knew he studied late and spent the night at her place. They didn't ask if he had his own bed, and as he was a young man they didn't want to know. They were delighted that he was over his long period of misery and that he had another girlfriend. It was a bit sad, Evelyn had made a good impression on them. She hadn't seemed like the kind of girl that would desert a man during his army service. Gerald hadn't told them very much about the break-up.

It was inevitable that Joan and her new escort would appear in the social pages. Both his parents and Evelyn found out who his new girlfriend was by seeing their picture in the papers. If they went to a ball or to the theatre, one or all of the social photographers would be there. Miss Meredith and friends were first choice to be photographed.

Evelyn first saw them in the *Sunday Mail* and it made her cry. She was intensely jealous, but felt that as she had to give him up, why not to a good friend like Joan? She'd told him to forget her and find himself another girlfriend. But it hurt her to think that when she got free of Louis, Gerald wouldn't be waiting for her. If only there was a way, but there wasn't. Joan had a reputation as a sexpot, her own brother had called her a nymphomaniac, so she and Gerald must be lovers. If only she could change places with her. She wanted Gerald so much. She could feel a little mound of a tummy and she clung to it for consolation. They had been meeting almost weekly at the university, Joan and Evelyn. She stopped coming and Joan knew why. Under the circumstances they could no longer be close friends.

Gerald's parents also saw the photograph. Was Joan Meredith his new girlfriend? They knew that she was a friend of his and studying the same subjects. Gerald was taking out the beer heiress, staying at her place nights and weekends. Had he fallen on his feet or tumbled in, beyond his depth? She was a pretty girl, so they felt happy for him. When he saw the picture on his mother's dressing table, he told her about Joan, that she was his new girlfriend. As for the nature of his relationship to Joan, that was his business and they didn't discuss that. Mrs Fisher didn't have to be told, she used her intuition to guess that they were lovers.

"One thing that I don't have to worry about is what happens if she gets pregnant. They'll be able to live like lords if they want to."

Richard still managed to find more good tips on the stock market. He was in with a group of student investors and they regularly made moderate to substantial winnings. He bought to the limit of his credit, adding to his capital which grew to twenty-five thousand pounds and continued to use this as an investment stake.

He let his friend in on several tips and his savings also grew. Gerald needed the money. He insisted on paying his way with Joan and his allowance couldn't cover his new expenses. He finally bought a dinner suit, a necessity if one goes to balls. There were theatre tickets, ball tickets and suppers at "The Paprika". The only concession he made was that they often used her car. She let him drive it, quite an experience after the Minor. When he was spending the weekend with her, he couldn't race off home to borrow the car, if it was available, on a Saturday night. Somehow he managed to avoid meeting her parents, but they must have seen him coming and going or seen his picture with Joan in the papers. So long as Joan didn't want to him to meet them, he didn't care.

This was a time of great change in Europe and indeed the world. In March Joseph Stalin, the man most feared since and before Hitler, had gone wherever atheists go, having sent millions of his fellow Russians there ahead of him. The impact of his life and death would have ramifications for months, years, even decades to come. The truth of his infamy might never be known as he destroyed the evidence together with the witnesses. He would long be remembered as the leader of a people who bore the brunt of the Nazis and in doing so, gave the rest of the world a chance to recover from defeat and in turn, defeat Hitler.

Stalin, who had been both God and the devil, would be a hard act to follow. In the darkest days of the cold war Malenkov came to power and Beria, hated head of the KGB, was sacked, later to be put on trial. It must have given joy to many a joyless Russian to see him getting some of what he'd meted out to others. In Berlin there was a two day uprising in June with workers chanting, "Ivan, go home". In July there were reports of unrest and possible uprisings in other Soviet satellite countries, firstly in Poland, also in Hungary and Romania. The reports soon ceased. Malenkov announced that the Soviets possessed the H-bomb.

The news from Korea was better. After three years of war a cease-fire was announced from Panmunjon. On the twenty-seventh of July, at ten o'clock Korean time, the gunfire stopped and troops in the front lines stood as the silence fell, breaking it with their cheers. There was cheering in the streets of Teheran in August, as the Royalists threw out the left-wing Prime Minister, Mossadeq, who wanted to take over Western oil assets. In Kenya the RAF bombed concentrations of Mau Mau terrorists. Their-leader, Jomo Kenyatta, was in jail.

West Berlin hosted a hundred thousand East Berliners when they distributed free food: milk, flour, fat, dried vegetables, and tinned milk were given away — food stocked in Berlin since the Blockade. The police were powerless to prevent them going across the border for the handout in pre-wall Berlin.

The same month the United States announced they had confirmation that the Russians had indeed exploded an H-bomb and that they had measured the resultant radioactivity released into the atmosphere, as it floated freely around the globe.

Joan went with Gerald and Richard to the Science Association Dinner, enjoying it better than the previous year. Neither Brown nor his new wife were there. Gerald drank a lot to blot out the memory of the previous dinner, which he regarded as the beginning of the end of his relationship with Evelyn, the first night that Brown tried to get his hands on the woman whose memory still haunted him.

On Friday the thirty-first of July they went with Richard and friend to the Women's Revue, *Too Darn Hot*, which, as the reviewer subsequently wrote in *On Dit*, was "hot and amateurish". It starred some of the prettiest girls on the campus, *Hell's Belles*, delighting an enthusiastic audience with the *cancan*, and the male compere dressed as Mephistopheles.

The highlight of Procession Day, a fortnight later, was the visit to Adelaide of the 'Peruvian Ambassador'. When the Express arrived from Melbourne, a large group of officials, reporters and onlookers were assembled to greet him. The red carpet was laid out, and the 'ambassador' in fancy uniform stepped off the train, with his wife and uniformed entourage. They had boarded further up the train, quickly uncovered their fancy dress, and moved down the carriages to the red carpet and welcoming committee.

On the platform they inspected a platoon of soldiers from the University Regiment, including Gerald and Richard, and were escorted to their cars behind two pipers in tartan and kilts. The official convoy of two Daimlers behind a motorcycle escort, executed a U-turn, stopping the traffic as they did, and drove fifty yards to the State Parliament, where they were welcomed by the Premier's representative, dressed like the Captain of the Pinafore, and blessed by the 'Head of the South Australian Peruvian Church'.

They then called at the Town Hall and Government House. On the way out of the stone gates the ambassador was 'assassinated'. The student actors and the crowd returned to the campus. There were other stunts during the morning. The Myer Emporium had its windows pasted with *Sale, Everything Half-Price*. An 'explosives truck' caught fire in King William Street, and a policeman bravely ran out to warn the drivers, only to find boxes filled with smokebombs. A zebra crossing was drawn across the road leading from the exclusive Adelaide Club.

After the parade a beer drinking competition was held in the cloisters. Teams of five lined up behind glasses of beer, chins on the table. At the word "start" the first team member downed his glass, and slammed it down on the table, and so on down the line. The women's union team was one of the first to be eliminated, as they went through the heats, the semi-finals and the final. Reporters from *Truth* tried to sneak in and photograph the tournament, but were caught and escorted out of the gate. Nevertheless, they reported the competition on page one, a lurid story of hundreds of beer-crazed students on the rampage, threatening the free press with violence.

In the August holidays, the Coronation Year University Drama Festival was held in Adelaide at the Tivoli Theatre. Seven universities presented plays, including *Pygmalion, Blithe Spirit* and *The Glass Menagerie.* Adelaide won the competition, staging a massive production of Shelley's *The Cenci*, with a stunning performance by Darlene Johnson in the heroic role of Beatrice, the unfortunate daughter of the bestial Count Cenci.

Evelyn asked her mother to send her train fares for the two term holidays. Her father told her mother, "Tell her to get the money from that husband of hers."

Her daughter didn't go back to Renmark all that dreadful year. She went alone to see the plays, sitting high up in the gallery, slipping out quickly after each performance to avoid showing herself to old friends. Her companions of 1952 sat in the stalls with their girlfriends.

In August the English cricketers defeated Australia, winning *The Ashes* for the first time in 20 years, since the *bodyline* tour.

In September, Joan, Gerald and Richard went to a recital at the Town Hall to hear the young American pianist, William Kapell, play Moussorgsky's *Pictures At An Exhibition.* On Saturday, they went to the Grand Final of the football to see West Torrens beat Port Adelaide by seven points. On Monday in the newspaper, next to the football results, was the news of an air crash. A British Commonwealth Pacific Airlines DC-6 crashed in fog into a hillside in San Francisco with the loss of all on board. The young pianist whose playing they had so much enjoyed was one of those lost. His loss was felt by everyone who had heard him play.

The first Tuesday in November is one of the most important days of the Australian calendar, Melbourne Cup Day. In the capital city of

Victoria it is a public holiday. The entire nation stops work just before the race to listen to it, offices, factories, schools, everybody.

The day fell a few days after lectures had ceased, two weeks before the annual examinations. The Barr Smith Library, full fifteen minutes before race time, began to empty, first a trickle and then a flood, as students found themselves friends with portables, or gathered around cars with radios. Almost everyone clutched a ticket, or several tickets, with the name of a horse written on it, their share in the thousands of sweeps organised by groups from primary school to the big betting or social clubs. A flutter on the Melbourne Cup wasn't gambling. It was "being in it". If you won, good on you and if you didn't, better luck next year.

Hydrogen, who was the favourite and supposed to go like a bomb, was beaten by a horse named Wodalla, at the end of the two mile race. Australians collected their winnings if they were lucky and went back to work. The Barr Smith Library filled up again.

No sooner was he back in his seat in the library, than Gerald noticed a plump woman at the counter, taking out a text book. He noticed her at first because pregnant women weren't a common sight on the campus. Then he noticed who she was and buried his head in his book. Joan looked where he'd been looking, and she saw Evelyn pick up her books and leave the library. Later Gerald asked her, "Did you know she was pregnant? She looks enormous. Joan, was she pregnant before she got married?"

Joan told him most of what she knew, omitting the part about the other man and that the couple weren't in love, that the marriage was only to give the baby a name. She didn't tell him that Evelyn hoped to get a divorce. Gerald was hers now and she didn't want to lose him.

"Why didn't you tell me about this before?"

"I wanted to, but she made me promise that I wouldn't. Gerald, it isn't the kind of thing that a girl likes people to know about."

"I wasn't *people*, damn it. I cared for her."

"I know, but she insisted. Gerald, I took her to a doctor who would have given her a safe abortion, but she didn't want that. She chose to have the baby and get married. I think she made the wrong decision. You know what I think of that man. I did my best for you, Gerald. I did my best for both of you."

"I know you did. Seeing her today with his baby inside hurt me, it hurt me a lot, but I'm glad she's having it. It somehow seems the right thing to do. I wouldn't have wanted it destroyed just for my sake. If that's what it takes to get happiness, is it worth it? Thanks for telling me. It makes me feel better."

Poor Joan, she had her man, she possessed his body, but that poor pregnant, Mrs Evelyn Brown still had his love. She wondered if, when they lay together in bed, he thought of her. He didn't, but there was a part of him, the part of him that she wanted, his heart, his undivided love. She wondered if it would ever be hers.

On the 9th of November, in a New York hospital, a Welsh poet who was at the time rising from obscurity to fame, died of alcohol poisoning. His name was Dylan Thomas and his master work *Under Milk Wood* had just been completed.

Exams began on November 17th, lasting for two weeks. Towards the end of the fortnight, the three friends discussed summer jobs. There were plenty of these, especially for those who finished early. Gerald decided to return to the store, but Richard decided not to look for employment.

"I'm learning to fly, and I'm also spending a lot of time wheeling and dealing. I can make more money in a minute than I'll make the whole summer if I'm around when there's a good bit of information. I have to see friends, people in the know, and be at the broker early in the morning when I'm onto something good. I don't want to miss a good tip because I'm working in a store."

"Don't forget to buy in for me. I could do with a little extra brass. Taking out a Meredith can be bloody expensive. Now that term is over, we'll be out every night."

"Would you like me to go Dutch?" asked Joan. "At least you get your breakfasts and your beer for nothing. How would you like to work in a brewery, Gerald?"

"Great," said Richard. "Why didn't you ask me?"

Joan made a rude sign.

"You pay for your beer from your wheeling and dealing, Dicky Flynn. Are you interested, Gerald?"

"I think I've got a job, they want me at the store."

She didn't want him to go back to the store. She wanted him to work for her father. Joan wanted Gerald to take the first step up the ladder, so she persisted.

"The pay's good. There's plenty of beer and overtime and it's scientific work. What's more, you'll be able to work, if you still want to, when term starts."

Gerald was suspicious. What did she want from him?

"Is this something special that you've obtained just for me because we're going out together?"

"No, they always take on a few students each summer. Some stay on after they graduate."

"What would I be doing?"

"All kinds of jobs. Output goes up in December for the holidays and the summer. There're jobs in malting, brewing, bottling and dispatch. There're also lab jobs that would be right up your alley."

"Where do I apply?"

"Through the usual channels. I'll give you a reference, if you like."

"He's not looking for that kind of job, Joan."

It was Richard's turn to make a rude gesture.

"Richard, go plait your shit! One more remark like that and you won't be invited to my New Year's Eve party."

"I don't mind. I wasn't invited last year, but that didn't stop me from being there."

That afternoon Joan rang the head brewer at the brewery.

"George, I want you to do me a favour. You're taking a few students into the lab this summer, aren't you?"

"Two or three, if they look good to me."

"I told a very good man to apply. His name's Gerald Fisher. Write down the name and be a dear and see he gets one of the positions. You won't regret it. He needs the money, his girlfriend likes to go out a lot. Be nice to him, George, who knows, one day you might be working for him."

"Yes, Miss Meredith."

As she expected he reported the conversation to her father next time he spoke to him, Gerald got the job, and Charles Meredith got to hear about the man his daughter was hoping to marry.

In November 1953, an ex-employee of the magazine for men, *Esquire*, put out volume one of a new magazine, *Playboy*. He used all his savings to print in it that famous calendar nude picture of Marilyn Monroe. All 53,000 copies were sold. Its editorial was indicative of things to come. "We believe we are filling a need only slightly less important than the one just taken care of by the Kinsey Report."

In 1953 Kinsey published his second report, *Sexual Behaviour in the Human Female*, snippets of which filled the daily press and popular magazines. Half of the women questioned admitted to premarital sex, a quarter of them to adultery after marriage, two thirds of married women complained of sexual dissatisfaction at some stage of their marriage. Both Kinsey Reports were bought by most major libraries in Australia, *Playboy* was banned.

Evelyn was finishing the eighth month when she sat for the exams. It was hot and uncomfortable, she could hardly reach the table in order to write. When the baby kicked it ruined her concentration. She was dreading the end of the exams, when she'd have nothing to do but sit around, waiting for the baby's arrival.

Exams over, she spent much of her time trying to help Mrs Brown, endlessly talking with her, and listening to the radio. She didn't speak to the man she had married, or he to her. When he was in the house, she stayed in her room and read her books, behind the locked door. He either stayed out or kept to his room. Since Evelyn's return his mother preferred her company to his and he felt like an intruder in his own home.

The day that the exams were over Louis told his mother, "I want to build my own room outside, complete with toilet and shower."

"What on earth for? What's wrong with your room?"

"It'll be noisy when she has her baby. I want a room separate from the house."

"We can't afford it."

"I'll build it myself with the help of my mates. The materials won't cost that much and I have a summer job to pay for it."

"What kind of a job?"

"Builder's labourer on a housing project. I'll be able to learn while I work. It'll help me with the room I'm going to build. I'll build it weekends and evenings with my mates. Here, I've already drawn up the plan."

"What about Council approval?"

"Who needs it? You won't be able to see it from the road so how are they going to find out? Besides I haven't got time to wait, or money to waste on getting approval."

A week later he started digging the foundations. During the day, Evelyn would wander out to see the progress in the yard, fascinated by it. By December 10th, the foundation was dug and the concrete poured. Ten days later, the walls were half up, a double row of bricks with a cavity, and the window and door frames were set in place. The walls were complete before Christmas and Louis, with his carpenter friend, started on the roof timbers on Boxing Day. To do this, he had to remove part of the old roof and join the new frame to the old section. This left a hole in the rafters, but Adelaide has a Mediterranean climate, so there was no likelihood of rain. If anything, it made the house cooler.

Evelyn was in the last weeks of the last month of her pregnancy. Before the hot December sun rose high over the hills, she went out every day that Louis went to work to look at the construction. It was interesting and she didn't have much to do. She was impressed that Louis could do this work. 'Why was he struggling to get a poor degree when he works so well with his hands? He could work for a while, set himself up and be his own boss. He'd probably make more money and be happier than he'd ever be as a scientist.' She told Mrs Brown what she thought, but whether or not she told her son, she never found out.

There was something strange about the design of the room. There were two long windows, squat windows set high in the wall. Evelyn soon worked out the reason.

'He wants to entertain here and with such high windows it will be impossible to be observed. The driveway will pass alongside the new door, making a separate entrance straight from his car. He wants to have his cake and eat it, have his girlfriends over and not be caught. That means he doesn't want to give me a divorce. What's the use? Gerald's got Joan now. So much for my dreams of a quick divorce and a return to my old love. Well Louis can have his lovers. Better that than having him pestering me.'

On December 2nd, a group of professors from the university protested against the new Anti-obscenity Bill, being debated in the State Legislature. Meanwhile the proposer of the bill quoted a local school teacherm, "Once these kids start reading obscene comics, I fear for them."

The professors claimed that under the proposed legislation, many books of classical and artistic value would be banned, and that many existing texts would have to be removed from public and university libraries. On December 3rd the Bill was amended to exclude books of artistic merit. Another amendment, proposed by the Labor member for Norward, Don Dunstan, that the age limit at which young people could buy unsuitable material be lowered from 18 to 16, was rejected, but another amendment, that the fine for *ringing doorbells* be reduced from ten pounds to six pounds, was accepted.

The Bill was passed and had little effect on Adelaide life. Copies of *Lady Chatterley's Lover* circulated with paper covering and schoolboys sniggered at pictures of Asians making love, in the corners of playgrounds or under the grandstands where they rolled their cigarettes and smoked secretly. The pubs closed at six and only the churches opened on Sunday. For peace, quiet and sobriety, the city was hard to fault.

In London, 'the man nobody wanted to hang' received a reprieve from the gallows. He had been sentenced to death for the mercy killing of his 24 year old imbecile son. 4,500 people signed a petition asking that he not be hung.

At midday on the 3rd, Richard received the best tip that he would ever get. He rang Gerald who had only been at the brewery for a few days and told him the news.

"Gerald, oil's been discovered at Exmouth Gulf. How much are you in for?"

"When do I have to decide?"

"Now. This is a big one. I'm buying £50,000 of shares."

"Have you got that much money?"

"I've got half so I'm covered if this is a false alarm, but it isn't. I got a call from someone in the lab. She's seen the first samples and the test report."

"Put me in for £500 and Dad for another £200. It's all the profits from your other tips so we're ahead, whatever happens."

"Gerald, you know me. I only bet on sure things."

Richard phoned his broker and went to the stock exchange to see how things were going. Others must have heard the news as the stocks rose a few points. Then early on the next day the news broke. Even before the papers were out the stock market went wild. West Australian Exploration shares doubled in value and kept rising, dragging other oil and mineral shares with them. The *News*, put out a special edition, "OIL STRIKE IN EXMOUTH GULF" in big black letters covering almost all of the front page. On December 4th, Richard gained over £150,000, Gerald and his father showing a profit of £1,500 and £600 each. Gerald could, if he wanted, buy a brand new Holden deluxe car.

That night they dined out at the Gresham Hotel. It wasn't anything spectacular, but then there were so few places to eat out in Adelaide, apart from milk bars, dingy restaurants and fish and chip shops. Opposite the wholesale market there was a Chinese café but only the Chinese from the market seemed to eat there. Only the hotels served liquor, so if you wanted to eat like a civilised person you dined out at one of the better hotels.

Gerald looked at the other people in the dining room.

"We aren't the only ones celebrating. I wonder how many of them had oil shares?"

"Daddy didn't. He was furious when he heard that you had a tip off and didn't tell him."

"He's got enough money, Joan. Besides he'd have bought so many shares that people would have smelt a rat and my source might have lost her job."

"You've got enough money to really have a good time, Richard. What are you going to do with it?"

"Well, Joan my dear, I have several options."

Richard leant back in his chair and elucidated. He had made a lot of money and felt like a lord. It showed.

"I could buy a house with a swimming pool, or get one built for me. And I could buy an aeroplane. I've always wanted my own aeroplane. I could, on the other hand, take a trip all over the world. I could also put it in securities and live off the interest. Then I could stay at the university for ever. But that's not what I'm going to do. I have decided that I want to be a millionaire and with today's windfall I think I will be by, say 1958, in five years' time. Then I'll really start making money."

"Why?" asked Gerald, "Isn't what you've got enough? My father doesn't make what you made today in a hundred years."

"It's my destiny, Gerald. I have a flair for turning money into more money. Why fight it? Don't worry, I'm not a miser. I'll spend it on things that I need when I need them. I don't need a house just yet, so why buy one? I can hire a plane whenever I want. One of these days I'll build the Flynn wing at a hospital, or Flynn Gardens in the parklands, but first I have to make the money so I can donate it.

"Now that I've got a little capital I can involve myself in other projects and not wait for inside tips. I think I'll move into real estate. Thousands of immigrants are coming to Australia, millions. The city is growing. I think I can buy the right land cheap and develop it for housing. Bankrupt companies and factories can also turn over a nice profit if they can be rehabilitated. I don't think I'm being over-optimistic if I say I'll make my first million by 1958."

Joan put down her glass of wine and asked Richard, "Are you trying to emulate my father?"

"No, Joan. Your old man got his money from his old man, who got it from his. For him it was easy. Money makes money. I'm doing all this all by myself like your once poor ancestor did. You'll see, one of these days I'll be as big as the Merediths, maybe bigger."

"Wouldn't it be easier to marry the boss's daughter?"

"Would you have me, Joan?"

"No, I'm happy with the man I have, thank you very much, but I know of a few other good catches."

She mentioned a few names. Richard made a face for every name.

"I'll introduce you, to all of them if you like."

"No, Joan, if I can't have you, I'll just have to get rich the hard way."

"Gerald, should I marry Richard?"

"Sure. Be my guest. This is the time of the year that I usually change partners."

Richard changed the subject.

Gerald enjoyed his new job working in the laboratory. It was so different to university practical work. It was bright and clean and the equipment was well cared for. There were a lot of tests to do and it all seemed so important. Batches were waiting for his tests, for the beer to be bottled, raw materials to be released and finished goods to be sold. He learned more and more tests daily and was expected to provide quick accurate results. Sometimes he went into the brewery to bring back samples from the malting sheds or brewing rooms. He loved the smell of malting barley and of freshly brewing beer. The laboratory and quality control area had a huge cold room, full of icy-cold beer samples and there was plenty to drink. They had a glass with their lunch and a few at the end of the day, cold unpasteurised beer, so cold that the outside of the glasses clouded in a second. Gerald finished work every day slightly intoxicated. He'd never seen so much beer in his life.

Chapter Twenty-Two

December 1953

The 1953 Nobel Prize for literature was presented to Winston Churchill on December 12th. George Marshall won the Peace Prize.

On the 17th Joan came to visit Gerald in the laboratory an hour after his return from lunch.

"Do you know what day it is?"

"No, what day is it?"

"The seventeenth. They'll be putting up the results any time now."

"You go and make some notes. I'll see you at 5.30."

"No, you're coming now."

She went to the Chief Brewer's office.

"I'm taking Gerald, George. Do you need him for the rest of the day?"

"Not if you need him."

"They're posting the examination results. It would be a pity not to be there."

"Off you go. Tell him he can have the afternoon off. He'll have to buy his own beer today."

"It's 90 degrees outside. What about a glass, George, before we go?"

He told Gerald to get them a bottle and the three of them had a drink together. Then they went to the car.

Gerald was annoyed. All the lab staff stopped working and watched as he went away with the boss's daughter, Joan, who was looking lovelier than ever, in one of her low cut summer frocks and her broad sunhats. Gerald felt like one of her employees, summoned to carry her parcels or clean her car. He didn't like it but he didn't say anything.

There was a large crowd gathered waiting for the results to be posted. They were listed by subject, the credits according to merit and the passes in alphabetical order. There was a second list with the names of all students who had passed at least one subject. Gerald looked at the second list. High above the heads of the crowd he noticed the name Brown, Louis, pass in Inorganic Chemistry 2. At a subject a year, he would need nine years to get a degree.

"Where was Brown, Evelyn? Why wasn't her name there? Don't tell me she didn't get a single pass."

Then he looked down and found his own name, Fisher, Gerald. Three passes, with a credit in Bacteriology. Richard's name was below his, also three passes and a credit in Organic Chemistry. Gerald pushed his way to the front and found the name he was looking for, Robertson, Evelyn. Three passes, credits in Botany 2 and Zoology 2. His heart quickened and he felt relieved. Then he remembered Joan. She was pulling his arm and shouting.

"I passed! I passed! You passed, we all passed!" Gerald looked at the subject list and stood back from the crowd, as Joan continued to look at the results, discussing them with people she knew. Then, he heard some students talking at the edge of the crowd.

"There'll be trouble at the Browns tonight. Evelyn Brown showed up that ratbag husband of hers. Two credits and a pass to his one lousy subject and I bet he cheated to pass that one. I wouldn't want to be in her shoes when he finds out. He doesn't like to be shown up."

"Do you think he beats her? She's ten months pregnant, if she hasn't had it by now."

"I wouldn't put it past him. She had no right to pass more subjects than he did."

"They're a strange couple. They never meet at all here at the university. He doesn't even drive her home. I haven't ever seen them together."

"Well they must have got together to get her the way she is. You know they had to get married. He was too damn stupid to take precautions. Serve him right. I feel sorry for her, but it's her own fault. I don't know how she stomachs him."

"Well, she won't be back next year. She'll be too busy with the baby and looking after his needs. It's a pity he doesn't have the baby so she could study. Look at how well she did. Poor girl, clever but stupid when it comes to men."

Gerald went across to Joan. He was upset.

"Drop me off at the brewery if it's convenient. I want to go back to work."

"Don't be silly. George said to take the day off."

"Listen, Joan, let's get things straight. I may work for your father, but you don't own me. Are you taking me back to work or do I have to walk there?"

Joan didn't want an argument so she did what he told her to do. She arranged to pick him up after work and he agreed. As they left the two students that had been discussing the Browns noticed them.

"That's Evelyn's ex. She dumped him for Bully Brown. There's no accounting for taste, is there? He's certainly fallen on fertile ground, lucky bastard. Do you think he heard what we were saying?"

"What if he did? He's better of with what he's got. Money, brains and sex. She's slept about a bit, but I'd park my boots under her bed any day."

"And you'd get a bullet up your arse for your pains. Gerald Fisher's the best shot in the regiment."

"Well it's a pity he didn't shoot Bully Brown before he stuffed his previous girlfriend."

Richard came to see the results half an hour later. He rang Gerald at the brewery and then Evelyn at home to tell her the results. It was good to hear that she'd passed. It was good to hear Richard's voice and know that she hadn't lost all of her old friends. He said he'd come to see the baby when it came and wished her an easy birth.

The day after he finished his exams, Richard went up to Parafield and enrolled in a flying course.

'What a pity,' he thought, 'that I didn't apply to join the airforce for Nasho and get into a pilot's course. I might have saved a bit of money and not wasted my time last year.'

He flew solo for the first time two days before Christmas, flying in a Tiger Moth, and got his licence in January.

Gerald was angry at Joan and upset by the conversation he had overhead when the results had been posted. By five thirty he had a bit of work under his belt, a belly full of beer and was feeling better. When he saw Joan after work, he was his usual self. He wondered if she'd be upset at the way he had spoken to her, but he didn't care. If she wanted to run his life, she could go to hell. He didn't need her or her bloody money and if he lost the job, so be it. If being her boyfriend was a prerequisite, he didn't want the bloody job.

Gerald thought a lot this month about his relationship with Joan. She took him for granted and organised his life. She knew what he liked, plenty of sex, good theatre, concerts and films, so he let her make plans for both of them. He didn't assert himself just to prove a point, but when she came to his boss and told him that she wanted

Gerald for the rest of the day, that was taking a liberty. Joan hadn't reacted to his going back to work, so he soon forgot the incident. She continued to make decisions for both of them and he continued to let her.

What troubled Gerald was that he compared Joan and his feelings towards her with what he'd felt for Evelyn. The two relationships were so different. With Joan it was sexual right from the start, with Evelyn it ended just when they were getting around to sex. He didn't feel the emotional yearning that he'd had for Evelyn, especially during their separation and the months when she wouldn't see him. It distressed him to have felt so strongly for his former love and very little for this woman with whom he was having an active sex life. If she told him that she wanted to end it, and she might, would he be upset? He didn't think that he would be, but he didn't want it to end either.

Seeing Evelyn's name on the notice board had given him a thrill and he felt so happy for her, much more so than for Joan. He rationalised, Joan had so much, she didn't need a meal ticket, but Evelyn had done so well and her studies meant so much to her. He felt sorry that she'd come so far only to throw it all away with one more year to go.

The day he'd been dreading was coming up, Christmas Day. Joan had invited him to have dinner with the family and he was to be presented to them at last. Joan picked him up from the brewery on Christmas Eve. It was just as well that she did. The annual Christmas party was held that afternoon. Copious quantities of beer were quaffed down, together with open sandwiches and pasties that George's wife prepared, as she did every year. Joan drove him to the Meredith's summer mansion, "Boronia", up in the Mt. Lofty Ranges. Without a car or a taxi he would never have made it. It was two miles from the nearest town.

"Boronia" was the family estate of Joan's grandfather, Sir William Meredith who lived there with his widowed daughter, Violet Meredith, whose husband had died of Spanish Flu at the end of the First World War and had not remarried. That left Joan and Steven as the last of the Meredith line. Steven resented that fact that the Meredith name depended on him having a son and heir, a fact that he couldn't care less about. He'd marry, if and when he met the right girl and if that didn't happen, he'd remain a bachelor. He hadn't met the woman yet that he was prepared to live with to the exclusion of all others, here or in America, and the only thing that he liked about babies was the man's role in their creation.

So a week before Steven's accidental impregnation of Evelyn was about to bear fruit, unknown to his family, Joan brought a potential son-in-law to meet the family and with him the hope of a future generation of Merediths. Perhaps they could call any future son, "Meredith-Fisher", to keep the name alive.

The estate was set in an area of dense forest, partly natural, partly planted. It lay two miles by winding road from Cherryville, close to Marble Hill where the Governor's summer residence was also situated. They were almost neighbours. Gerald knew the area well. He had taken Evelyn for a drive through Cherryville in the only spring they had known together, to see the fruit trees in blossom.

The house was built of Murray Bridge sandstone, squat and solid with arched windows and a minimum of ornamentation. Built in 1890, it contained 11 bedrooms, a big dining room, drawing room, library and a small art gallery. There was a kitchen and staff quarters under the back of the house. Joan's grandfather and his daughter collected Australian Art which was displayed in the art gallery. For a small collection, it contained many famous artists, some dead, some contemporary. They had two Namajiras, acquired as were most of their paintings, before the artist became popular.

When Charles Meredith married and took up residence in the Glen Osmond Estate, his father and Violet Meredith moved up to "Boronia" on a permanent basis. Every member of the family had their own room in each of the two houses, including Joan and Steven. The Merediths were a small family with large houses.

Joan showed Gerald to his room which was dominated by a huge, beautifully carved four poster bed. She closed the door and kissed him, letting his hands explore her willing body, hungrily. He was still half drunk from the party and would have made love to her, if she had let him.

"No dear. We have to dress for dinner. It's formal with cocktails at a quarter to seven. I'll order orange juice for you or you'll pass out before the meal. Don't be late. We can try the four poster tonight."

"I've never seen such a bed before. Do you know what Confucius says about such a bed?"

"No, you tell me."

"Confucius say that girl who sleep in four poster bed, should beware of fifth column."

"Not me. I adore your fifth column. Look, you can pull the curtains and be closed up like in a cocoon. It's ever so intimate, like a wall to wall mattress. I'm going to send you up a cup of black coffee. I hope it helps you sober up a little. See you at 7.45. I'll come and collect you so you won't have to face the family alone."

"Thanks. I'd hate to have to make a solo appearance."

The Merediths went out of their way to make Gerald feel at home. Joan had hinted that this was the man she wanted to marry and while he wasn't of their status in society, her parents were anxious that their daughter settle down. An undergraduate, with one year to go towards his degree was good enough for them. Her father had spoken earlier in the week to his head brewer and George had spoken favourably about Gerald. With Steven showing no interest in his father's business interests, Charles Meredith had plans for this young man, if he should marry Joan. He kept these thoughts to himself as he made Gerald feel at home.

Gerald was impressed but not overawed by the opulence and amused at the mundane things that they talked about. It seemed out of place to talk about such topics in such a fine home. He wondered what the Queen and Prince Philip discussed at the dinner table or what Bob and Pattie Menzies discussed over the lunch at Yarralumna. Still, as the evening dragged on, it was a strain, so he was glad when Joan said that she was tired and that Gerald probably was too, and they retired for the night.

She told him not to lock his door. He showered and got into the huge bed with a novel, waiting for her to join him. Twenty minutes later Joan tiptoed in through the door, locked it and got into the bed. Before lying down she closed the curtains, shutting them off from the outside world. Then she took his Evelyn Waugh and, switching off the light, snuggled close to him. There was a little moonlight coming through the big window, just enough to outline the bed frame as their eyes got accustomed to the light. Inside the curtains all was cosy intimacy. Joan nuzzled close to her man.

"This is quite a bed, Joan."

"It's Steven's. This is his room. He has one of these beds in both of our houses and two in his own house. They're antiques. He had an agent who found them in old homes being sold. Steven's the playboy of the family."

'And you're the playgirl!' he thought, but didn't say it. 'God, these Merediths are oversexed. I'm sure glad that this one is.'

"You'd think that with all these beds and bedrooms, there'd be a lot more Merediths about."

"Oh, there will be! I intend to have lots of children."

"Why doesn't big brother do his bit and keep up the family name?"

"Steven? He's too selfish. He wouldn't be seen dead with anyone who'd marry him. Any number of silly girls would marry him tomorrow, just to live like a Queen, but he'll never settle down. If he has to sleep with the same woman twice he thinks he's hard done by. If he does marry, his wife is going to have to let him carry on as usual while she looks after his children. I wouldn't wish that on a dog."

"You don't like Steven, do you?"

"As a brother, yes, but not as a person. He'll be back in a couple of years, then you'll see what I mean. It breaks my parents' hearts that Steven doesn't want to settle down."

"You want to make them happy, to have lots of kids?"

"It just so happens that my wishes and their wishes coincide. Sometimes I feel that I'm wasting my time at university. I'll probably marry and have babies and never use my degree at all. Don't worry for now, I've put my thing in and I can tell that you're dying to do the same, so let me help you out of your pyjamas."

"Terrific, but no babies until we graduate. I do want to work in my career and not just be fresh genetic material for breeding Merediths."

Gerald woke late the next day, alongside Joan in the huge bed, their night attire alongside it on the carpet. It was strange lying there with three curtained walls alongside, like a compartment of a train. After a while he pulled back the curtains to let the cool morning air enter. When Joan woke up he took her naked body into his arms and gave her a big Merry Christmas kiss. She rolled over covering him with her breasts and they closed the canopy to make merry of the Christmas morning. Joan sat astride her lover as he supported her, kissing her lips and bosom until it was over and she collapsed, exhausted, on top of him. They lay entwined for another twenty minutes.

"I'd better go, Gerald. People will be stirring. I'm going to rest for a while and skip breakfast. I feel well and truly shagged. You can go down and I'll see you later."

It was 9.30 when Gerald arrived at the breakfast table and joined Joan's father. He ordered breakfast for Gerald and the waiter brought him a huge sirloin steak, with onions, fried potatoes and an egg. Gerald felt that he was a lamb being fattened up for the daughter. He needed plenty of calories and protein to keep Joan Meredith in the manner to which she had become accustomed.

Gerald imagined that at any moment the man sitting with him would ask him what his intentions were towards his daughter.

'Why don't you ask your daughter what her intentions are towards me?' he thought.

Instead, Mr Meredith started the ball rolling slowly.

"You're a fellow student of Joan's, I hear."

"Yes."

"In the same year?"

"Yes."

The food was delicious.

"And studying the same subjects?"

"Yes. "

Not bad, three questions successfully answered. As an afterthought he added, "We study a lot together."

"You've been seeing a lot of my daughter?"

That was the statement or question of the year! There was a lot of Joan to see and Gerald had seen the lot. Less than a hour ago, he'd been smothered by it.

"Yes, I suppose you could say that we've been going steady for six months."

Gerald wasn't giving away any secrets. He braced himself for the next question, "What are your intentions?" but it didn't come. Instead Mr Meredith spoke to him like his father might.

"Listen, my boy. Young people these days take their time deciding what they want and I think that it's a good thing. I don't believe in hasty decisions. You're a man. You have to think about your career and get your degree. Then you'll have to decide where you're going to work and how you're going to make your living. You'll want interesting work and prospects of advancement.

"We're on the look out for young graduates in Meredith Industries. The days are gone when a company employed a chemist to do a few tests and an engineer to run the plant. Now we're taking on dozens of graduates, lawyers, economists, but mostly engineers and chemists. I'd like to take on some food technologists, but the university doesn't produce them. They turn out thinkers with little practical knowledge and expect industry to train them on the job. I've taken steps to remedy that. When the Meredith building is opened, there'll be courses in Food Science. We can't call it Food Technology, that might lower the standards down there."

Gerald knew what he meant. Technology was a dirty word in that white tower of a university.

"My son Steven, who I don't think you've met, is studying Food Technology in California and, as he doesn't want to come into the business, I hope he'll come back here and start up the new course. He'll be head of our companies one day but if he doesn't want to take on the job, it might fall to Joan's husband if he's suitable. I don't think a woman could handle such a task."

'Joan's husband!' Gerald braced himself. 'Had they married him off last night, under the influence?'

"I suppose you think that I'm jumping the gun, Gerald, but I've heard about you from George down at the brewery and although you haven't been there long, he's pleased with your attitude and ability. When you graduate, Gerald, I think there's a place for you in my organisation. We're in the middle of a big reorganisation and expansion and I'll be needing bright young graduates to train as future executives. I'd like you to be one of them."

"Are you telling me this because I'm Joan's boyfriend? Would you still want me if our relationship came to an end?"

"I think that I would. Are you two planning to end your relationship?"

"No, but neither have we decided to make it permanent. As we can't marry before I graduate and we're not too sure of ourselves, I wouldn't want to mislead you into seeing too much in our relationship. We'll probably get married, but I want to be certain before we do."

"That's between the two of you. Better to be sure than sorry. I felt that you ought to know that my son-in-law will have a place, Joan's place, on the board that I'm establishing to run the business. Not at once, but as soon as he's ready. Eventually, when I retire, the chairman will be Steven if he wants the position or you, if you do decide to marry my daughter."

"Thank you, Mr Meredith. That's quite a sobering thought."

"As for the job for next year. The offer stands, whether or not you decide to marry Joan."

"Mr Meredith, I want to make my own way in the world. I don't want to live off my wife's money. It may be the one thing that makes me hesitate."

"Don't worry, boy. If you come to work for me, you'll earn your keep. It isn't easy running one company let alone a dozen. You become an executive with Meredith and Joan'll be complaining that she doesn't see enough of you. You'll come home at night too bloody tired to do anything."

'And get up in the morning, too bloody tired to go to work!' contemplated Gerald.

"I'll bear that in mind, Mr Meredith. It isn't easy being Joan's boyfriend. Supposing that I want to buy her a present. What can I give a girl who has everything?"

"You can give her what money can't buy, love and happiness."

"I'll try."

"I hope so. I think she'll give you the same in return. She likes you a lot, you know."

Gerald finished his breakfast thinking about this conversation. With Joan's father promising him exhausting days, and Joan exhausting nights, he wondered if he could live up to Meredith expectations.

Later the whole family went to church together with the inhabitants of Marble Hill, the Governor and his family, and Gerald was able to see the residence with its extensive garden full of tall pine trees, and its spacious lawns.

Gerald noticed that a firebreak had been cleared all around "Boronia", but that weeds were already growing in it and dead leaves accumulating. There was a shed at the back of the garden with fire fighting equipment, but without a firebreak it would be useless.

Joan also had a large bed, not as big as the four poster, but large enough for the two of them. That evening the family retired early and it was Gerald's turn to put a dressing gown on over his pyjamas and cross the corridor into Joan's room.

Gerald told Joan about his discussion with her father.

"What's going to happen with us, Joan?"

"You're the man, you make the decisions."

"And you'll go along with any decision that I make. If I decide that we get married, you'll agree and if I decide that we should live together out of wedlock, with or without children, you'd still agree?"

"Don't talk rubbish. If you want to marry me I'll agree. You won't ask me to live with you in sin, so I don't have to agree. You're too straight-laced."

She had him figured out and he knew it. All she had to do to get Gerald to the altar was to stop taking precautions.

"I'm not ready to make a decision. Do you mind?"

"No, I can wait."

"How long? What if I feel the same way in a year's time?"

"What do you feel, Gerald?"

"I feel terrific, especially when we're making love."

"So do I."

"But it's what I don't feel. I think I should feel more involved. I should feel deep emotion, but I don't."

"I feel deep emotions for you."

"We never talk of love."

"I love you. I'm always telling you that I love you."

"Yes, but saying's easy. I want to feel it too."

"I feel it."

"Since when?"

"I don't know. Quite a long time. I think of you all the time, all day long."

"That's because you do nothing all day long. You should get a job."

She needed a job, like an Eskimo needed an ice-box.

"It's because I love you and I'm scared of losing you. I want to be with you forever."

"Well, Joan, don't worry. I'd be a fool to leave you. You may get your clutch of little Fishers yet."

"Well that is good news. I can hardly wait."

"Well you'll have to, for at least another year."

When Joan fell asleep, Gerald stayed awake thinking. Here he was lying next to Joan and he was undecided whether he loved her, whether he wanted to spend the rest of his life with her. She was perfect in every way, beautiful, sexually satisfying, intelligent, good

natured and considerate. Making love with her was more enjoyable
than he could ever have imagined. She wanted to have his children,
lots of them, and she was as rich as Midas. The last wasn't
important, but it was a fact and couldn't be ignored.

'Why me?' he thought. 'Why has she chosen me? She doesn't
need me, yet she wants me and nobody else. It sure makes you feel
good to hear a woman like Joan say that. When am I going to wake
up from this dream?

'Why don't I feel anything? Is there something the matter with
me? I don't think I'd hesitate to go back to Evelyn if she was free. It
isn't fair. She left me and I can't feel for Joan the way I felt for her.
I want to love Joan, I need her love, but I still feel more for a woman
that I haven't spoken to in a year. I must be crazy.'

What he couldn't get over was the thought that Evelyn had chosen
Brown and not him. Now that she was married to him and having his
baby she was forbidden fruit. He never mentioned her to any of his
friends, but when he was left alone she often filled his thoughts.
There was no longer any pain, just concern. Was she happy? Did she
ever think of him? Did she love her husband or was she just another
victim of a man's carelessness?

Chapter Twenty-Three

December - January 1954

Evelyn was due to have her baby at the end of December and December was coming to an end. Mrs Brown had given her some new books to read and she'd finished two of them, *The Cruel Sea* and *Doctor In The House*. The third book, *The Devils Of Loudon* by Aldous Huxley was a bit too gruesome for her so she went to sit with Mrs Brown in the living room and listen to the radio. Stan Freberg's *Saint George And The Dragonet* was on the air again.

On the 28th they listened to the Davis Cup from Melbourne. It was a bad day for Australia, with Seixas and Trabert thrashing Hoad and Rosewall. The second day Australia kept the match alive by winning the doubles in straight sets.

Evelyn went to see her doctor. The baby was low down, it could come any day now and was kicking like a mule.

The next day, Evelyn stayed in her room. She slept a little, read a little and wrote a letter to her mother. It was hot. She was big and very uncomfortable. She cursed Steven Meredith and Louis Brown for doing this to her. As much as she hated that pair, she longed to see the baby and hold it in her arms, to put it to her breasts that were so big and ready to nourish it. Soon she'd have someone of her own to lavish love upon and the two of them could go to hell. She'd have the last laugh. Mrs Brown called out to her to come to the living room.

"Listen, Evelyn. Hoad's beating Trabert. It'll be two matches all. We could win after all."

"What's been happening?"

"In the first set, all games went with service, they're both powerful servers. Then Hoad broke Trabert's service, and won 13:11. Then Hoad went to a 4:1 lead and won the second 6:3. It's been raining and they've had to go off a couple of times. Typical Melbourne weather."

Soon Evelyn was caught up in the drama taking place at Kooyong. Trabert took the next two sets 6:2, 6:4 and the Americans were a set away from regaining the Davis Cup. Mrs Brown held on to her seat and Evelyn to her tummy. There was some more light rain at the start of the fifth set. This set was a thriller like the first set, going from

three-all to four-all and then five-all. Hoad held his service to lead
6:5. Then suddenly he had three match points on his opponent's
service. Trabert served at love-40, Hoad returned and Trabert let it
pass. It fell in. Hoad won the set 7:5 and the tie was drawn at 2 all.
Mrs Brown came over and gave Evelyn a big hug. It was too late to
play the second of the reverse singles, so it had to be played on the
31st. It would be a hard match to win, Seixas had beaten Rosewall
the last time that they'd met, so the American was the favourite.

The next day, the last day of 1953, was a tough day for Evelyn.
She woke up, remembered the last New Year's Eve when all her
troubles began and tears came flooding down her face. Not since
she'd been a baby in her first year of life, had she cried so much in
one year. One decision, to take the train back to Renmark, and the
walls had come tumbling down.

If only she'd stayed with Gerald and they'd become lovers. Now
he was Joan's lover and he must have forgotten his former love.
From the kitchen she heard Doris Day singing on the radio, singing
Secret Love. It brought tears to her eyes.

She was apprehensive. She had high expectations for this baby.
Would he live up to them? Would she still love him when she had to
care for him and put up with his crying? She'd sacrificed a lot for
him, had almost died rather than be parted from him. Why 'him'?
He might be a she. How would she cope? How would Louis react?
Would she be able to keep the baby away from him, or would he want
a share in the child? Would he want to play father to the child that he
hadn't fathered, that he didn't want and thought she should have
destroyed? If he didn't want it then he'd better not want it now!
Evelyn decided to leave the Brown household as soon as she could.
That wouldn't be easy. Her father had washed his hands of her,
denying her the fare to return home for holidays. She was dependant
on Mrs Brown for everything.

She thought again about Gerald. If he had called her a whore,
what was his new girlfriend? His affair with Joan mightn't last, or
had he lowered his standards? If it didn't, she'd contact him again.
There wasn't much chance of that. Joan Meredith was a formidable
rival.

It was early in the afternoon that she had the first contractions.
She told Mrs Brown and when she was sure that the contractions were
regular, not isolated like she'd had earlier in the week, they called a

taxi to take them to the hospital. Mrs Brown wanted to get Louis to take them, but Evelyn wouldn't hear of it, although the taxi took ages to come. She told him where they were going, but he didn't answer. He and his mate were busy finishing the roof frame. They continued, as the women went away in the taxi. The driver had a radio and they heard the last part of the Davis cup. The last thing that Evelyn heard on the drive was that Rosewall, the underdog, had won in four sets and the Davis Cup was to stay in Australia. It was a happy note on which to enter the hospital, a good omen for 1954, nine hours away.

Louis continued working after the taxi left, to the surprise of his mate. "We can finish this tomorrow, Louis. Don't you want to go with your wife?"

"I hope the bitch dies, the kid too. That woman isn't my wife. She's the bloody bitch that Mom made me marry."

He hammered in a nail, with all the force of his hatred for Evelyn.

"That's stiff shit."

"Yes mate. You can't trust women and you can't trust French letters either. Why do you think I'm moving out to this little place? So I can get me end in, have a bit of carnal when I want to without her finding out."

"You'd better be careful."

"Why? They can't make me marry a second time."

"That's a fact. That reminds me. Did I tell you about the man who sold facts?"

"No, get on with it."

He stopped hammering and listened to his mate.

"This bloke set up a stall in the Central Market with a big sign - I SELL FACTS. A crowd gathered and a policeman came along and spoke to him."

"Just what's going on here?"

"I'm selling facts, constable."

"Well, you'd better close up and get on your way. You can't sell facts."

"Oh yes I can."

"Well, sell me one, or I'll run you in."

"OK, constable, put this in your mouth and give me five bob."

"The policeman put what he was given into his mouth and immediately spat it out."

"That's shit!"

"Yes, constable. That's a fact! Now you owe me five bob, copper."

They finished the roof frame just before five and decided to call it a day. Tomorrow afternoon they'd be able to start putting up the tiles. Then there was the floor to be nailed down, the ceiling to be set in place and the room would be almost finished. Louis estimated that he'd be in his own room by mid-January. Meanwhile it was New Year's Eve. He cleaned up and went out.

Louis had his usual good luck at the party. He found a good looking girl who liked his piano playing. She seemed to be on her own, so he asked her to dance.

"I know you, I think. What's your name again?"

"Louis Brown."

"I met you two years ago when I was a student nurse. You used to date my roommate, Jacky."

They went over to the bar.

"You've got a good memory. How is your old roommate?"

"Fine. She's going to marry a doctor in March."

"Good for her. What's your name?"

"Yvonne. I'm a qualified nurse now. I'm working at the Royal Adelaide. I've got to work tomorrow, New Year's Day. Wouldn't it make you mad."

"Well, you better have a drink. What'll it be, beer or orange juice?"

"I wouldn't say no to a brandy."

By midnight they had all consumed enough booze to welcome in 1954. Everybody kissed everybody and Louis, who had spent most of the evening attending to Yvonne with all of his charm, gave her a long kiss. She responded warmly. He knew he'd struck pay-dirt.

"Let's go for a drive," he suggested, holding her close to him, her soft round bottom in his large hands. She said nothing, so he took her by the hand and she followed him willingly. Brown had selected a willing playmate. He drove to one of his favourite "shagging spots", a field close to the upper section of the Torrens, where he could drive off the road, well away from any houses. Louis had a thing about river banks. They embraced, Yvonne letting Louis undo the buttons of her dress from top to bottom, and when this was done, opening it up to reveal her in bra and panties. He removed her bra quickly, and a few minutes latter suggested that they lie on his rug, outside under the stars.

There in the open, he satisfied his carnal needs with this woman whom he had met just a few hours earlier. The air was warm and dry, but it cooled their almost naked, sweaty bodies as they lay together, the tall gum-trees on the riverbank forming a black arch above them. Yvonne closed her eyes, Louis caressing and kissing her body where he knew it would stimulate her. As he moved onto her, bringing their bodies together to unite them, she looked into his face and at the stars beyond.

"The stars, Louis, they're so beautiful."

"I'll take your word for that. I'm in no position to know."

Then he lowered himself into the soft, moist warmth of her body, as they mutually gratified their sexual needs.

They lay side by side for a while looking up through the trees at the Southern Cross and the Milky Way.

"Will I see you again, Louis?"

"Sure, we should do this more often. I'm building a room of my own. Perhaps you might like to help me christen it. It'll be ready in a fortnight, shower and all."

"It sounds nice. We'd better be going. I have to be at work at eight. I'd better get some sleep."

Louis threw the contraceptive into a hollow tree. They dressed and he dropped her off at the hospital. It was then that he remembered that his wife was in there, having or having had a baby. He recalled their chance meeting a year ago and her being sick all over him. He thought for a while that he'd had the best of that encounter, but looking back it seemed that Evelyn had fought back and was now winning, having that bloody baby with his money. He, like Evelyn, wished that they'd never met. And that Fisher bastard was now rooting Miss Money-bags Meredith. Instead of hurting the bugger, he was going to get his mitts on the rich bitch's millions! Damn him! Damn the both of them!

Later, Yvonne met her ex-room mate Jacky, signing off as she signed on.

"Hello, Jacky. Guess who I met last night? Your old boyfriend, Louis Brown. He hasn't lost any of his charm."

"Yvonne, I only went out with the bastard twice. I wouldn't sleep with him, so that was that. I wouldn't advertise that you've been out with him. *Mrs Louis Brown* is in maternity. She had the first baby of the year. Why don't you say hello to her? Tell her how her old man is. I'm sure she'd like to know."

Yvonne paled.

"That's impossible. I've been... We've... "

Jacky didn't have to be told what they'd just done.

"Well, you're a fool, just like she is. I told you two years ago the kind of person he is. Since then I've heard several stories about him. Don't you listen when the girls are gossiping? The only reason he married that girl was because he had to."

Yvonne thought how nice it had been lying with Louis under the stars. All the time he'd been enjoying himself with her, his wife was in hospital having a baby. It gave her the shivers. She'd have to attend to her and the baby, knowing what she had been doing with the poor woman's husband. She felt like an intruder and cursed him, all the feeling of pleasure that she had felt during their union turning to disgust.

Evelyn was ready to have the baby two hours before midnight, having been in labour for eight hours. She spent another two hours in the delivery room. Shortly before twelve, the baby started its quick, painful passage into the world. Fifteen minutes into the new year, he made his first cry and Evelyn heard it, with the news that it was a boy.

"Hello, Jonny, my new love," she whispered as she relaxed after the strain of her labour and the pain of giving birth. She fell asleep.

Later in the day, the baby was brought to her, all wrapped up with his little red face just visible and head covered with fine black hair. Evelyn remembered that Meredith had black hair, whereas Louis had brown, like his name. What did it matter, the baby was hers, not either of theirs? Now that she could hold him in her arms, she loved him even more than she had when it was an unknown quantity, growing and moving inside of her.

Her first visitor was Mrs Brown. She asked her how she was feeling.

"Tired, very tired. Have you seen him? He's a cute little boy and such a fine baby and he's got hair too."

'Had she noticed its colour?'

"We'll call him John Mark."

344

She didn't mention his surname. That, she would have to change.
The nurse came to take the baby.
"Nurse, when will I be able to feed him?"
"Not yet. Towards evening. Get some more sleep. You'll need it, so you'll have plenty of milk."
"I think I have. I'm so big."
"This evening you can feed the baby."
"Thank you, nurse. What's your name? Mine's Evelyn. Evelyn Robertson."
"Yvonne."

When Yvonne told the other nurses that she'd been at a party with Evelyn's husband while she was here giving birth, they weren't at all surprised. Louis Brown was not unknown to many of them, his reputation having gone before him. She felt sorry for Evelyn and made up her mind never to go out with her husband again. Yvonne wasn't to know that Evelyn didn't care what Louis did, as long as he left her alone with the new male who had entered her life, to the exclusion of all others, little Jonny Mark.

Mrs Evelyn Brown was a celebrity. When it was visiting time, the press came to see her. They wanted pictures of the mother of the first child born in South Australia in 1954 and of the baby. They asked for the father, but had to settle for mother, baby and grandmother.

Mrs Brown took a taxi home at one in the morning and, as Louis wasn't home, couldn't tell him the news. She got up early and finding his door locked, assumed that he was asleep in his room. Leaving a note to tell him that he had, as she thought, fathered a boy, she went back to the hospital.

She was glad Evelyn had chosen John for the baby's name. John was her late husband's name. Louis's father had been a doctor. They had met and married shortly after his graduation in 1930. He enlisted in 1939 when Louis was seven, served in Egypt and then on hospital ships in the Pacific. He lost his life when the hospital ship, Centaur, was torpedoed in May 1943 by the Japanese, off the Queensland coast. Louis was 12 at the time and from that day he hated the Japanese, a hatred that he extended to all Asians, blacks and non-Australians in general. Perhaps he became a bully out of a desire to make someone pay for the loss of his father. Perhaps it was the lack of a father. Mrs Brown was left with the house, her War Widow's pension, some money that her husband had inherited or saved, and her memories. Legacy helped with Louis's education, but it couldn't replace the boy's father or pass exams for him at the university.

She telephoned Renmark to let Mrs Robertson know that she had a healthy grandson and that her daughter was fine and feeling well. Evelyn's mother decided to come down to see them the following day. She told her husband, but he expressed no desire to visit his daughter. Evelyn had only been married six months. He knew this would happen the night that he'd dragged her out of Brown's bedroom and she'd run off with him. It didn't matter that he had driven his daughter away, she had let him down and he wasn't interested in her, her baby, or that wicked man she had run away with.

Mrs Brown met Sara Robertson's train and walked with her along North Terrace to the hospital. They could have taken a tram but it was a nice day and a pleasant walk.

Evelyn cried tears of joy when she saw her mother. Nothing was mentioned about her father, his absence spoke for itself. He looked at his daughter's picture in the *Advertiser*, reading it alone at the breakfast table while his wife was on the train. Mrs Brown had a copy of the paper and gave it to Evelyn, leaving mother and daughter to themselves.

"I've got a famous daughter. I'll have to start a scrap-book. When do I meet the proud father?"

"Mother, Louis isn't proud." She would have loved to have said, "Louis isn't the father," but that would take a lot of explaining. "Jonny's my child and mine alone and I want it to stay that way. Jonny has no father, for now. I haven't seen Louis. That's the best birth present that he could have given me."

Mrs Robertson was, and wasn't, shocked. She shared her daughter's hatred of the man who had had to marry her.

"Is there no hope, Evelyn?"

"Mother, the only hope is that I'll soon be free of him, that I can get out of this mock marriage. As soon as I can, I'm going to see a divorce solicitor."

"How will you live?"

Her mother was a slave to her husband. She assumed that the same fate awaited her daughter.

"I might have to wait until I graduate. Yes Mother, I'm going back to study this year. When you see Daddy, tell him that all he did by stopping my allowance was to leave me to the mercy of others, and that I'm finishing my degree without him. Mother, if he wants to patch things up between us, tell him that I need money so I can leave Louis. He never wanted me to live with him in the first place. Boy, was he right and I wrong. It'll take time to get a divorce, so the sooner that I leave him the better."

"How have you been?"

"Fine, just fine. You saw my examination results. I've only got one more year to go, Mother. Louis's mother looks after me almost as well as you did. I'd never have made it without her. I'm going to hate leaving her when the time comes. She'll look after Jonny, when uni starts in three month's time. Without her, Mother, I'd have returned, probably unmarried with no prospects of marrying or of studying. She's made it all possible. All that she wants in return is Jonny. I have to share him with her, but that'll be a pleasure, she's so nice to me."

"Evelyn, you aren't serious about studying this year?"

"I am, Mother. What else will I do all day?"

"Look after the baby."

"Mother, a baby sleeps most of the time. The first year will be the easiest. How I'll manage after that, I don't know. I've gone over it with Mrs Brown. I'll buy a bicycle and I'll be home in ten minutes. I won't be away from the baby for such a long time. I'll be able to feed him, morning, noon and night. I want to breast feed for as long as I can. I might have to miss a lecture now and then, but I know I can do it. I want that degree, almost as much as I wanted the baby. I'm going to get it, Mother. Then Dad will be proud of me and I'll be able to work and support the two of us. I won't have to come begging to Dad, ever again."

Sara Robertson saw some of her husband's stubbornness in her daughter. She liked what she saw.

"You're determined, aren't you?"

"I can't live off the Browns all my life and I don't think Louis will ever be able to support us, not that I want him to, so it isn't just being stubborn. I need to be able to earn a living."

"What about the boy's father? He should be made to look after both of you."

"Jonny's father! That's a laugh! What kind of father wants his own flesh and blood killed before it's born?"

She had told her mother about Louis, how he had wanted her to get rid of the baby, and how Joan had tried to talk her out of getting married, what they wanted her to do.

"He probably feels differently now."

"Listen, Mom. I'm sure he doesn't, and I'm glad he doesn't. I am through with him. I have been for nine months and two days. Dad may be a little rough around the edges, but he knew what he was talking about when he told me to stay away from Louis Brown. Why in heaven's name didn't Dad try using a carrot instead of a stick? Mother, I want to come home for a holiday. Can I come, just before term starts?"

"Whenever you want. Come home every holiday. It'll be like old times. I'll pay for the fares from my own money."

Mrs Robertson stayed with Mrs Brown until Evelyn left the hospital and three more days after that. The two women had a great time together, organising the baby's things and mothering their mutual daughter. Evelyn's mother went shopping in the city, looking for new things for the baby. Apart from the quick trip for Evelyn's wedding, she hadn't been to Adelaide for years. Mr Robertson had to look after himself for a few days, something he hadn't done since the birth of Evelyn.

Her mother soon saw that Louis really wasn't interested in Evelyn or the baby. She spoke to him once, but he didn't have anything to say to her. He worked late into the night, nailing down floorboards and, when he'd finished this, putting tiles up in the shower and toilet. The day Mrs Robertson returned to Renmark, Louis moved his bed and belongings out into his room. He rang Yvonne, but she told him that she didn't want to see him again, so he had to wait a few days until he found another woman, to launch himself into his new self-contained life in his self-contained room with its separate entrance.

Louis never forgave Evelyn her implied insult and humiliation, making him agree to non-cohabitation. If he had to marry her, let them at least try to make a go of it, let him at least get the benefits and privileges of having a wife. She was a very desirable woman. To be shunned, to be locked out of her bedroom, was the worst injury that she could do to him, especially as she had given herself so willingly to him when they were lovers. He remembered the good times he had had with her and not the injuries he had heaped upon her. He still wanted her as he lusted after many a woman, and her being in his house, hiding behind his mother, irritated him. Once in his own room, it would be as if he was in a different house. If he couldn't have his wife, he would have other women under their very noses and they wouldn't know anything about it. One of these days his mother wouldn't be around any longer and no locked door would keep him away from what was rightfully his.

January 3rd. Richard and Joan visited Evelyn, bringing flowers, chocolates from Rundle Street and presents for the baby. It was a tense meeting with the spectre of absent Gerald, ever present. No one told him about the baby. Joan saw him with the *Advertiser* containing Evelyn's picture in it, so he didn't have to be told. He was obviously upset by the picture and it hurt her too, that Evelyn still had the place in his heart that she felt should be hers. Joan didn't tell him she was going to visit her and neither did Richard.

Joan didn't stay long. There was a barrier between her and Evelyn now, a barrier that couldn't be ignored. Richard stayed, telling her about his latest deals, and how he was progressing with his flying lessons. She told him of her mother's visit and how she intended to return to university, he promising to keep in touch. One of the nurses thought that Richard was her husband and congratulated him. Richard took her hand and told her, "I'm just sorry that I'm not, Evelyn. I'd have been proud to have been in that picture the other day."

When he left, she felt lonely and let down. She only perked up when the baby was brought to her and she was able to feel and hold him. Holding Jonny to her breast made her feel wanted. He was so small, so helpless. All he could do was suck with powerful little lips at her breasts heavy with milk, and wave his little hands about aimlessly, but it was Jonny and Jonny alone that made life worth living.

The next day, she had another visitor, Deirdre Roper. Evelyn felt ashamed. She hadn't contacted the Ropers, not even when Deirdre had a baby girl.

"I saw your picture, Evelyn. Why haven't we seen you?"

She now knew why. That Brown bastard had got her pregnant. Now that she knew, she came to Evelyn to comfort her. She had a husband who she loved, who loved her. Evelyn was married to Louis Brown.

Chapter Twenty-Four

January 1954

As soon as Richard had his flying licence, he invited Gerald to be his first passenger and they went flying one Sunday morning. Gerald had never flown, not even in a commercial plane. When he saw the yellow Tiger Moth which looked like a World War I aeroplane, he had second thoughts.

"We're not going up in that? It's open, I'll fall out."

"You'll be strapped in. In any case, we won't be flying upside down. It'll be noisy up there, so we'll have to speak through an intercom. If you want to speak press the mike button. If you don't, I won't be able hear you. Don't forget to put on your headset."

"Where are we going?"

"We'll do a wide circle of the city, that's all."

They taxied across the rough grass. Gerald was surprised at how bumpy it was. Richard revved the motor, checked the controls and revved the engine again. Then he opened the throttle and they started rolling. The roar of the engine was deafening. The Tiger Moth gained speed and, as the tail lifted, Gerald felt his heart sink into his boots. Then the plane stopped bumping across the grass and was airborne. The sensation of moving forward gave way to that of moving upward, as if an unseen hand was pushing the plane from below.

Gerald looked to his right. They had cleared the field and were passing over the Adelaide road. Cars, toy cars, were passing below. Richard put the plane into a shallow bank, allowing Gerald to look between the wings at the farms below, scorched brown by the summer sun, and then once again they were flying level. They headed towards the foothills.

Richard spoke to him over the intercom.

"We're heading for Teatree Gully. Then we'll turn south and fly over Norton's Summit and Mount Lofty. After that we'll head for the coast and complete the circuit. How're you feeling?"

"Fine." Then he remembered to press the button. "Fine, Richard. I think I'm going to like this."

It was rather bumpy as they flew over the hills and the Torrens Gorge. The view was magnificent of the scenery below.

Their field of vision was restricted by the fuselage and the wings, but there was plenty to see. There were forests, green fields, and extensive orchards. Everything was greener here than the foothills. They saw cows grazing in grassy fields edged with hedges and trees, fruit trees, everywhere.

They had a brief glimpse of "Marble Hill" and Gerald looked in vain for "Boronia", which he knew must be near. A few minutes later they approached the twin tops of Mt. Bonython and Mt. Lofty with its thin white obelisk.

Using this as a turning marker, Richard banked, giving them a clear view of the greenest and highest part of the hills, stretching down to the Adelaide plain below. They flew west over Belair National Park, above the people playing cricket, heading towards St. Vincent's Gulf. Now, as they crossed the southern suburbs, Gerald could, for the first time, see the whole of Adelaide spread out like a map. The roads radiated out from the city like a spider's web. The city itself was ringed by park lands, yellow in the rainless summer, with the Torrens a tiny ribbon of water.

The twin towers of the Town Hall and Post Office could be clearly seen in the middle of the city, away from the taller office buildings at the far end of King William Street. Ahead there was a thin line of sand and the sea beyond.

Richard made straight for the Centre of Glenelg, passing Morphetville racecourse, where Brown had tied Jonny Marco to the tram tracks, and then over the beach. People put their hands over their eyes, looking up at them as they crossed overhead. Turning over the mouth of the Patawalonga Creek they flew up the coast, over the shallow green water. He pointed to Gerald where the new Adelaide Airport was being constructed at West Beach.

Looking down Gerald saw another place he immediately recognised, the Metropolitan Sewerage Treatment plant. Their school science teacher had taken the class there. Gerald remembered the manager holding up a glass of effluent from the line leading to the sea, crystal clear water, and asking them to taste it, assuring them that it was germ free. No one was game, no one wanted infantile paralysis. Why take a chance? The manager had drained the glass. Afterwards they wondered if the water was really effluent or tap water. They had no way of telling.

Instead of flying towards Port Adelaide and Semafore Beach, Richard gained height and flew out over the Gulf. Then he spoke again to Gerald.

"Want to take the controls?"

"Are you crazy?"

"Go on, there's no one down there to hurt."

"What about us?"

"Do as I say, and we'll be alright. Take your stick and do exactly as I tell you, and let go exactly when I say. I can take over, quick-smart, whenever I want to. You game?"

"Alright, just as long as you don't expect me to land the bloody thing."

For ten minutes Gerald had control of the aircraft, climbing and descending, banking and flying straight. He even managed with a little help from his friend, to turn the plane around and head back to Glenelg.

Richard took over again, cutting back across North Adelaide to have a closer look at the city. Over Montefiore Hill, with its statue of Colonel Light, they took a last look at the river, the gardens, the university and the public buildings. He saw the Meredith Brewery, where he was working for Joan's father, a mass of buildings on West Terrace.

Contacting the Airport, Richard asked for permission to make his approach. Then he put the plane into a glide and descended across the Northern Suburbs back to the grassy runway at Adelaide Airport.

When he'd taxied past the big aluminium airliners and cut the motor, Richard asked Gerald how he'd liked his first flight.

"Terrific, let's do it again sometime."

"Why don't you take up flying?"

"It wasn't that terrific."

"Next time I'll try and get an Auster. It's closed up, with high wings and you get a better view. Bring your camera and we'll do some aerial photography. Did you hear that another Comet crashed? Pity, it looks like there's something wrong with the design. Now the Yanks will have the skies to themselves with their Boeing Jets. Have you read *No Highway* by Nevil Shute?"

"No."

"It's about a scientist in an aeroplane, flying over the Atlantic who realises, during the flight, that the tail could fall off at any second because of metal fatigue."

"So what happens?"

"I'll loan you the book. Funny, I wonder if Shute knew what he was writing about. I wonder if metal fatigue caused the Comets to crash?"

"Richard, I've just flown in a plane for the first bloody time. Let's talk about something else."

January 16th. Marilyn Monroe, at the height of her film career, married Joe Dimaggio. With two great films, *Gentlemen Prefer Blondes* and *How to Marry a Millionaire* made in 1953, she was the undisputed top box office attraction and sex symbol. Her photograph replaced that of Eartha Kitt in *On Dit* in the column *ABREAST OF THE TIMES*. At a news conference she told the press that she'd have plenty of children, but no more calendar photographs.

"Joe doesn't like that sort of thing."

On the 21st, Mrs Eisenhower launched the Nautilus, the world's first atomic submarine. On the 26th there was a meeting of the big four foreign ministers in Berlin. On the 12th of February, the British Standing Committee on Cancer stated that there was a link between smoking and lung cancer. On the 16th Maurice Chevalier was refused a US visa. No reason was given for the refusal.

The big news in the Australian press at the start of 1954 was the Royal Tour. The Queen was on her way to New Zealand and Australia, having cancelled her visit in 1952 when her father, King George the sixth, died.

Australia was catching Royal Tour fever.

Australia is a continent with no active seismological areas, unlike its neighbours, New Zealand and New Britain. One of the few destructive earthquakes to be recorded in Australia struck Adelaide at 3.40 in the morning on the first of March, 1954. It wasn't a major quake, no buildings fell and no one died. That was luck, considering the damage. Falling bricks and masonry fell on empty beds and a chimney crashed through the roof of the South Australia Hotel onto an empty veranda. The GPO clock face was cracked and many thousands of homes damaged, a few beyond repair.

Evelyn had to get up and feed the baby at three. She'd just put him back to bed and was returning to sleep herself, when she heard the sound of the earthquake that preceded the shaking. She sat up in bed wondering what the sound was, when the house started to shake. She stopped wondering and grabbed Jonny. Evelyn knew it was an earthquake and feared that any second the whole house would fall down. Many people had this fear. She got under the table, as it was the only solid thing in the room. Twenty seconds later the shaking stopped and she sat there in the silent darkness. The quake had filled the air with fine dust, making her cough. Then she heard Mrs Brown calling, "Evelyn, you alright?"

She ran to the door, unlocking it and turned on the light. They looked about the room. Plaster had come away from the ceiling at several places and bits of it had fallen onto her bed. That seemed to be the extent of the damage. They inspected the rest of the house. The other rooms were similar. Louis didn't stir and his door was locked, so they didn't bother him. They went outside where they saw other neighbours inspecting their houses. Dogs were barking and howling all over the city. Mrs Brown remembered the radio.

They went inside to turn it on. The voice of the 5KA announcer was that of a shaken man in more ways than one. He repeated the news for thousands of South Australians turning on their sets.

"We've had an earthquake, folks. Believe me, I was as shocked as you people. I thought that the antenna mast had fallen down. Well, we're still on the air. I suggest that you check your houses for damage. We've haven't had any reports of injuries, but we'll keep you informed. Please don't call the station for information. You'll get that over the air. We need the lines open for reports. I repeat, Adelaide has been stuck by an earthquake. Damage in the city appears to be light. There was greater damage to the south of the city. There are no reports of injuries. Keep tuned to this station and do not telephone unless you have important information to tell us."

Satisfied that the danger was over, Evelyn put Jonny back in his cot and she too went back to sleep.

Gerald was sleeping at home for a change. He got up, went outside, inspected the house and turned on the radio. He remembered Joan and, concerned for her safety, telephoned her. There was no answer. He began to worry. She lived in the southern suburbs. Finally she answered the phone.

354

"Who's calling?"

"Gerald. Are you alright?"

"What time is it, Gerald?"

"Four. Are you alright?"

"I was alright, until you rang. What's the big idea, ringing me in the middle of the night?"

"You didn't feel the earthquake?"

"Gerald, darling, not without you. What say you go back to sleep and you can make it quake tonight. Save your jokes for the first of April. Goodnight, love. See you tonight."

She put down the phone and went back to sleep. Gerald felt like an idiot. In the morning she heard about the earthquake. The conversation with Gerald had been forgotten and only when he told her about it did she vaguely recall it.

On the same day, five US Congressmen were shot and wounded in the House by Puerto Ricans, calling for independence.

The Adelaide earthquake was insignificant compared to the Hydrogen Bomb that the US tested at Eniwetok Atoll. It exceeded the expectations of the scientists and rained radioactive ash over a large area, contaminating a Japanese fishing boat, *Lucky Dragon*, whose unfortunate crew were down wind of the blast. Radioactive ash fell on Japan four days later. The Japanese also complained about fallout from Soviet tests.

During the month of March, Richard noticed that several properties in the foothills along the fault line, went on the market and he was able to purchase them quite cheaply. Being on the edge of the suburbs, he knew that in a year or two he could get the farmland rezoned for housing. It wasn't as quick as the stock market, but the yields would be much higher. Richard was reaching out for his first million.

On the first of March Evelyn took Jonny for his first train ride, to visit his grandparents in Renmark. They caught the early train, arriving shortly after noon. She was met by her mother and together they wheeled Jonny home in the pram. Mr Robertson didn't take time off from work. He wasn't going to kill the fatted calf for his prodigal daughter. Her room was much as she had left it, except for the cot that her mother had borrowed. She breastfed the baby while her mother unpacked their things, put him down to sleep and joined her mother in the kitchen for a cup of tea. Shortly after five Mr Robertson returned from work.

"How are you, Father?"

"Fine, thank you, Mrs Brown. Have you brought your husband with you?"

"No Father. Please call me by my name, Evelyn. I've come with your grandson, Jonny Mark."

Later in the week she told her parents that she wanted to get a divorce from Louis as soon as she could. As she expected, her father objected.

"You know that I don't approve of divorce. You made vows when you married Mr Brown. You can't throw them aside."

"I made no vows before God. We were not married in a church, as you commented upon at the time. You know why we had to get married. You were right about that man, Father. I admit to my foolishness and to my mistakes. I offer no excuses. That doesn't mean I have to stay tied to him. I went through a civil marriage to make all you respectable people happy, and so people wouldn't call me a whore and your grandson a bastard. I didn't have to do that. I could have come back here and had the baby, unmarried, or done something that is better not discussed. I want to divorce Louis, which won't be too difficult and, God willing, meet and marry a man who will be a real father to Jonny."

It was the longest speech she had ever made to her father. It fell upon deaf ears.

"What's wrong with his real father?"

"Plenty. Let's just say that we dislike one another."

'Poor Dad,' she thought. 'What would he do if he knew what really happened? Would he go and get a horsewhip and seek out Steven Meredith, or say that I put temptation in his way? He's a man, like those two rats who ruined my life.'

"You seemed very much in love with Jonny's father last summer. Have you forgotten that?"

"Thank you for rubbing my nose in it, Father. So I behaved badly, stupidly. Do you have any idea how I've had to suffer for what I did? I may have hurt you, but what you had to put up with is nothing to what I've had to suffer."

"You break God's laws, you have to pay for it."

Not for the first time in recent months, she wanted to swear at her pompous pater.

"What about the men who break God's laws, night after night and get off Scot free? Why is it that stupid girls have to do all the paying?"

"They'll get what's coming to them in the next world. Evelyn, don't disobey me again by divorcing your husband."

"He hates me, Father. He has other women."

"And you?"

Now her father had gone too far. He knew it.

"Is that what you think of me, Father?"

Evelyn knew it was no use talking. He father wasn't going to change his mind, but he'd have to hear her out.

"I have my baby and he's the only man in my life at present. When I'm free of Louis, I hope to resume my life and learn from my mistakes, yes and marry again. I can't afford to mess up my life again like I did last summer. I have a child who needs me. Father, will you help me when I'm on my own? I want to move out and obtain a legal separation."

"You want me to support you and that man's child?"

She noticed that he couldn't look her straight in the face.

"I only want what you would have spent on my allowance, until I can support myself."

"With a young baby? You'll never be able to do that."

"I'll be entitled to support from Louis. I'd rather try and do without that. I'll graduate in a year and then I'll get a job."

"That's out of the question. A mother's place is with her baby. You won't be able to work until he's in school and then only part time."

"Mrs Brown will help me if you don't. I don't see why you won't help me. You saved my allowance and college fees last year and now you want to save it for a second year. You won't be happy until that husband of mine kills me and then you can say, 'I told you so'. Do you want me to come back and stay with you? What do you want?"

"I want a little respect from my daughter. I also think that you should go back to the man that you chose to run away with, and love, honour and obey him, as a dutiful wife should. Give up your talk of divorce and I'll give you all the money that I'd intended to use for your university expenses. That should make your husband happy."

"I don't want to make him happy," she shouted at him. "Thank you, Father. Don't waste your money on us. It was you and your threats that drove me out of this house in the first place, and you seem determined to keep me a second class citizen like my mother. I'll stay with Mrs Brown. She'll be the parent that you don't want to be. I'm going to university and I'm getting out of this marriage too, Father. I'm not doing it to spite you, Father. I'm doing it for me and for Jonny, your grandson. We'll be gone in a few days and I suppose that we'll see you again this year if your son-in-law doesn't break down our door and murder us in our sleep. Thank you, Father. Every time that I lock my door, I'll remember you."

Evelyn went to her room, boiling with rage. She had hurt her father this time, gotten to that hard heart of his. Evelyn could see it in his face. But she had upset him, not moved him. Mr Robertson didn't speak to Evelyn for the rest of her visit. Her mother tried to effect a reconciliation, but didn't have a chance. It was unpleasant for Mr Robertson, too. He was an outsider in his own house, with the two women in one camp and him out on a limb. He was right and he knew it, so paid no attention to his wife's pleadings or his daughter's silence. When they returned to Adelaide father and daughter shook hands and said "good-bye".

On the 17th of March, the city was lit up, as the illuminations for the Royal Visit were turned on. Two days later the Queen and the Duke of Edinburgh were in Adelaide. On the 24th the Queen attended a gathering of Adelaide women at the Bonython Hall. It was by invitation only. Joan's mother received an invitation, but not Joan. The university grounds were closed to anyone who didn't work or study there. It was a fine Autumn day with a clear sky and a few small clouds. Evelyn decided to go and see the Queen. She took Jonny with her and Mrs Brown. At the Union gate they were stopped by an attendant.

"Sorry ladies. Students and staff only."

"I am a student."

She showed the man her pass.

"You can come in, but not the lady."

"I need her to help me with the baby. How am I going to get this pram up the steps?"

"In you go. Better hurry, the Queen's due in another five minutes."

North Terrace was a mass of people waiting for a glimpse of the young Queen. Inside the grounds it was completely different. A hundred or so students, many with cameras, had plenty of room. Queen Elizabeth 2nd arrived in an open topped Daimler, without Prince Philip. He was touring the Weapons Research Establishment at Salisbury. A little girl presented the Queen with a bouquet of flowers while a hundred cameras clicked. Then she entered the hall where the VIP ladies of Adelaide were waiting to greet her.

The two mothers went down to the Refectory for a cup of tea. Friends and strangers came to look at the baby and wish mother and son well. Then they went back up and waited by the Elder Hall for the Queen to emerge from the meeting and drive past in the Daimler. For a second, as the car drove slowly past them, they were a mere six feet from Her Majesty. Then the car was gone into the crowd-filled streets of the city and on to the garden party at Elder Park. Joan and her parents attended this function but Gerald wasn't included in the invitation. He too was at the university, where he noticed Evelyn and the pram from a distance. He turned away so she wouldn't see him. He had no wish to see Louis Brown's baby and couldn't forgive Evelyn for having it. Had he seen the beautiful baby, who knows, he might have seen it in a different light and forgiven its mother.

On the 26th, Gamel Abdul Nasser, the strong man behind the ousting of the Egyptian Monarchy, retired for the first time. William Holden and Audrey Hepburn received Oscars for their roles in *Stalag 17* and *Roman Holiday*. Frank Sinatra won one for his supporting role in *From Here to Eternity*, the film that won the Best Film Award. On the 29th, Nasser came out of retirement and took over leadership of Egypt.

Winston Churchill, Prime Minister of England, defended the development of the Hydrogen Bomb in the House of Commons, saying that it was the greatest deterrent against the outbreak of World War Three.

On the 10th of April, Joan and Gerald went to the Annual Commencement Ball in the Refectory. Evelyn left the baby with Mrs Brown and, for the first time in six months, had a night out. She went with Deirdre and her husband to the Regent to see *How To Marry A*

Millionaire, starring Marilyn Monroe. She thought of Gerald. Was he going to marry his millionairess? Louis Brown spent the evening with one of his girlfriends in his new room. He couldn't go to the ball with a woman who wasn't his wife.

The following Monday lectures started for 1954. Evelyn who had two third year subjects to complete her degree was enrolled in Zoology 3 and Botany 3. She cycled to the university, returned to feed Jonny at lunchtime and cycled back for the afternoon classes. She wanted to breast feed as long as possible. Her studies and the baby were her whole life, feeding the baby comforted Evelyn for her lack of other love. For company, she had Louis's mother.

Mrs Brown looked after the house with a little help from Evelyn and took care of Jonny for the hours that Evelyn had to be at the university. She also had to look after Louis, but it was clear that he now had third place in her affection. He was repeating two second year subjects and had a light lecture load with exemptions from part of the laboratory work. He found his popularity at a low ebb. Most of his friends from earlier years had graduated or left and other students talked and joked about him. The story of how he had stolen Gerald's girlfriend while he was in National Service was well known and regarded as a low act. That he'd got her pregnant and had to marry her, was spoken about him behind his back. In addition, the fact that he was a married man chasing girls and a no-hoper of a student made him a person to be avoided and ridiculed.

At the start of the academic year, the fact that Brown was a parent was made known by a notice in *On Dit*, which congratulated *Father Brown*, as it called him. It was written by a non-well-wisher, one of Joan's friends, and made no mention of Evelyn, who continued to call herself Evelyn Robertson and didn't wear a wedding ring. The name *Father Brown* stuck to Louis and he failed miserably with the fresh batch of female students. Father figures had fallen from fashion, so Brown had to throw his net further afield.

Three days before Easter, Australia's great spy scandal, the Petrov Affair, broke. Vladimir Petrov, a Third Secretary in the Soviet Embassy in Canberra, sought and obtained political asylum. It was a planned defection, he brought with him thousands of secret papers from the embassy. To the Menzies Government, which had lost a referendum to ban the Communist party in 1951, Petrov was a godsend, even if he had come from atheist Moscow. A scandal involving the Communists might embarrass the left wing of the Labor Party and disclose hidden sympathisers and fellow travellers. The Petrov affair was to become a minor witch hunt with many unproved allegations, but without the excesses of the McCarthy era in the United States.

The day after Easter, Soviet secret police escorted Mrs Petrov to Mascot Airport and onto a BOAC Constellation to take her back to Russia. An angry crowd at the airport tried to stop them. There were scuffles as they boarded the aircraft. The agents and Mrs Petrov left as scheduled on the flight, only to be taken off the plane at Darwin, where the Russian secret police were relieved of their guns and their prisoner. Whatever they thought about her husband, Mrs Petrov had the sympathy of millions of Australians. Four days later, the Soviet Union broke off diplomatic relations with Australia, a break lasting five years. This happened the day before Anzac Day, when Returned Soldiers march through all the major cities, in memory of those who fought and fell at Gallipoli in particular, and all wars in general, among them Louis's father and Evelyn's uncle.

The Petrov affair dragged on for months. A Royal Commission was set up to investigate if any Australians where involved in spying. Although no spies were found, it was caviar for the Liberal-Country coalition. It helped them win another election on May 29th, when Menzies' popularity was flagging. It contributed to the split in the Labor movement that was to keep them out of office for over a decade.

May 1954 saw the French besieged in the north of Indo-China, at the town of Dien Bien Phu. On the 7th, the outpost fell to the Vietminh Communist forces of Ho Chi Min. Viet Nam would now be divided into a Northern Communist State, and a Southern state with Saigon as its capital. On the 14th, Communist China was admitted to the 1956 Melbourne Olympic Games. Nationalist China withdrew its team.

On the 24th of May the International Business Machines Corporation (IBM), announced that it was manufacturing an advanced calculating electronic brain, capable of 10 million arithmetic calculations an hour, a thousand fold advance on existing machines. It had advance orders for 30 machines.

Joan, Gerald, and Richard chose Organic Chemistry, as one of their two third year subjects. The course was given by Professor MacBeth, this being his final year before retirement, and by his successor to be, Dr Badger. The former was known to students as the author of the first year text book on Organic Chemistry. Dr Badger gave most of the third year lectures. He was a good lecturer.

These lectures were interesting, especially when he enlivened them with details about the deadly poisons, there were many of them, and how they were used to kill people down the centuries, from Socrates to Crippen. There were compounds like mescaline, which Aldous Huxley experimented with, and Indian Hemp which in those days wasn't known on the campus, and drugs like morphine, and cocaine, which were curiosities that people in far off countries used, or doctors administered to relieve pain. They had to know how the formula for such compounds was elucidated and how they could be synthesised.

Professor MacBeth lectured to the class on other naturally occurring compounds, terpenes, plant oils such as turpentine, eucalyptus oil and citronella. They also included compounds recently found to be important in biochemical synthesis of vitamins and steroids.

The Professor didn't use a blackboard as other staff members did. He used a large black optical device, which, as he wrote on a clear celluloid, projected his writing onto the white wall behind him. The celluloid formed an endless page, and he wrote in copper-plate handwriting, while the class copied furiously. At the end of each line, the image of his handwriting frequently disappeared behind the shadow of his ear, at which stage, the students made noises of protest.

"We can't see the writing, Sir."

Professor MacBeth would stand back from the machine, and look at the wall, where his shadow had been a second before.

Then he'd turn to the class, with a expression of puzzlement.

They were copying the uncovered words, as fast as they could.

"It's all perfectly clear to me."

"What's the last word in the third line, Sir?"

"Pyrolytic".

"I was paralytic last Saturday, after the pubs closed," murmured a student at the back of the class. The professor resumed his writing. As he spoke the words while he wrote, it wasn't too hard to guess the words behind his ear. The machine was nicknamed, the *Balshazzar-scope*, the device that created the writing on the wall.

One day the roll of celluloid ran out, and Professor MacBeth, presented it to one of the girls in the front row, as an almost complete lecture course. She had to promise not to sell it to a publishing house. Then as no other roll was available, he continued the lecture on the blackboard.

In Organic Practical classes, the students put into practice some of the syntheses that they'd learned about in lectures. Sometimes they were successful, and handed in the compound they were expected to make, sometimes it didn't work. Joan did a Friedl-Crafts reaction three times, starting with naphthalene, and ending with naphthalene, before she realised that the aluminium chloride catalyst was moist and therefore useless. It took her a week to get the smell of naphthalene off her skin and out of her hair.

Gerald almost fainted when someone lit a cigarette next to the hydrogenation apparatus, which was full of hydrogen, and bleeding the excess gas into the air. He asked him quietly to keep his distance.

They all decided that Organic Chemistry wasn't for them.

"I like the theory, it's interesting, but playing around with dangerous chemicals is not my idea of a worthwhile profession," said Gerald one day.

"Last week, someone left the bromine tap open, and a burette full spilled all over the floor. I damn near coughed up my lungs," said Joan. "Then yesterday, Ted was shaking benzene with sulphuric acid to dry it, and forgot that it gets hot. Off went the cork, and half of the mixture flew into the air. One minute later, three of us girls found our nylons disintegrating. It also made holes in my blouse."

"They say that benzene rots your bones, or gives you cancer, or makes you sterile."

"Probably, all three. Carbon tetrachloride rots your liver, and methanol your eyes. You can't even drink the alcohol here, it's contaminated with benzene."

"I had to use 20 percent peroxide last week. That's nasty stuff. If it gets warm, it can blow the lid off the bottle. It can blind you if you get it in the eye."

"Don't talk to me about hazards," said Richard. "For the last two weeks I've been trying to add a ring to a benzoic acid compound. I started with a hundred grams, and one of the first things that I had to do was make the nitrile. That involved adding a cyanide group, and steam distillation of the nitrile. I used the best quickfit glass, but I almost shat myself during the distillation. I had visions of the flask breaking, and showering me with broken glass and cyanide. I got my nitrile, not very much of it, and tried to clean up the reaction flask.

"It was full of black tar, set like a rock. After two days, I gave up and threw it in the bin. I wonder what happens to the rubbish? I hope it doesn't end up on some dump, where kids go looking for goodies. I hydrolysed the nitrile, and got about 20 grams of compound. Then I lost it in the next reaction, when I couldn't get anything to crystallise out of the mixture. Two weeks work down the drain. I wonder what it's like in a big organic chemical factory. All you need is a burst pipe, or a boil over, and out comes the cyanide, and a factory full of people are lying on the floor, all going blue and twitching."

"Last year at the brewery, a fork lift smashed a refrigerator line, and let out a stream of ammonia. The driver was killed, and several others had narrow escapes."

"Ammonia! Why don't they use freon, or one of the other fluorochlorocarbon compounds, Joan? They aren't poisonous."

"You tell them, Gerald, you're working there, not me."

On the 3rd of April, a fifth Comet crashed 90 miles south of Naples, again as it was nearing maximum height. Later it was discovered that metal fatigue had caused this aircraft to disintegrate and probably the earlier tragedies.

May 5th. Roger Bannister ran the mile in 3 minutes, 59.4 seconds at Oxford, breaking the four minute barrier.

On the 17th, the US Supreme Court declared racial segregation in schools to be unconstitutional, ordering desegregation to proceed with all possible speed.

At the beginning of May, the Union Cloisters were the scene of Tragedy. The Drama Society staged Shakespeare's *Romeo And Juliet* under stars, on one side of the area, with the audience sitting on the grass or the paths around. They played for four nights and every seat was sold. The setting might have been made for the play, with its covered open arches and the black star-studded sky above and behind.

The Boravansky ballet came to Adelaide in June. Gerald and Joan were invited to share a box in the theatre, together with her parents, to see excerpts from *Swan Lake* and *Symphony Fantastique*. Gerald had a fine view of the theatre from the box, and almost three quarters of the stage. The section close to the box couldn't be seen.

Throughout the winter months the Petrov affair dragged on, together with the fighting in Indochina. In July a peace settlement divided Viet Nam into Communist North Viet Nam, with Hanoi as its capital, and South Viet Nam, ruled from Saigon. On the 27th the *Advertiser* carried banner headlines:

NO WAR ANYWHERE IN WORLD.

The Science Association organised a number of lunchtime meetings, the highlight being a symposium on July 14th, in the Lady Symon Hall. They invited three speakers to talk on Beauty, Brains and Sex.

The first speaker, a biochemist, spoke about beauty, comparing it to music, art or mathematical analysis. Then the Professor of Anatomy, a popular speaker, if you weren't a third year medical student, spoke on the second subject.

"Some people have beauty, some brains, all have sex. Some more than others! While some of us use beauty, or sex to get what or where we want, in the long run brains wins the day." He gave examples.

Then he went on to ask why it was that women wanted sexual equality. Women were better off in a man's world, than they would ever be, in a woman's world. Since women were given the vote (and South Australia had been in the forefront, giving voting rights and little else to women in 1894) there had been two world wars, Russian Communism, and the atom bomb.

The third speaker gave three reasons for the puritanical attitude to sex in the community: jealousy, the attempt of frustrated men and women to frustrate the pleasures of others, and thirdly, totalitarianism. He quoted from the book *1984*, comparing *Big Brother* and his thought police, and their society without sex, to Malenkov and his secret police to God and his Angels. "In that country, young people are taught that sexual intercourse is like an enema, something to be endured for a good outcome, in this case the production of more people to go to work for the state."

The "REDEX" Round Australia Trial cars reached Adelaide on July 20th, and stayed overnight at Morphetville Racecourse. Richard and Gerald were among the hundreds of spectators that welcomed in the leading cars. Leading the field came the immaculately polished

1948 Ford Mercury of *Gelignite* Jack Murray. Jack got his nickname from a story, unsubstantiated, that he threw lighted sticks of gelignite at any car that tried to overtake him. He went on to win the race without loss of points, in spite of a *horror stretch* on the final stage of the race.

The Merediths were members of the Adelaide Oval, and had tickets to the Members stand. This year they loaned them to Joan and Gerald to see the football Grand Final. Gerald was a Port Adelaide supporter, living in their sector, and Port Adelaide were the favourites. West Adelaide had a 25 point lead just before half time, when there was an ugly incident. The West captain knocked down the Port centre, Davie Boyd, in a hard tackle just before the half time whistle. When the players went off the field for the break, several hot-heads in the crowd attacked the West players, and punches were thrown. One of the West Adelaide room stewards lost three teeth, when he took a blow meant for one of the players. Afterwards he said that he hadn't even seen it coming. Port went on to win by 13 points.

July 7th in Berne, Germany came back from 0-2 down to beat the favourites, Hungary, 3-2 in the World Cup. The Boeing 707 made its maiden flight over Seattle on the 15th. Elvis Presley cut his first disc on the 19th, *It's All Right, Momma*. Oxford English Professor, John R.R. Tolkein published *The Fellowship Of The Ring* on the 26th.

In August, the Brazilian President shot himself after the army forced him to stand down.

Evelyn took Jonny to Renmark for a holiday before the final term and the third year examinations, all that she needed to pass for her Science Degree. As she expected, her father was cool to her, speaking only when it was necessary. She for her part kept the peace. It was so good being with her mother that she enjoyed the visit in spite of him. In three months she would pass her exams and find work. Then he would see that she had succeeded without him.

When she returned to the house in North Adelaide, Evelyn found Mrs Brown sick in bed, with her head propped up with two pillows, and her neighbour in attendance. She immediately noticed the worried look on Evelyn's face.

"Welcome home, Evelyn, I've missed you and the baby. I'm not as bad as I look. It's just a little kidney infection. I've had them before. The doctor gave me some sulpha drugs, and I'll be up and about before you can say Jack Robinson."

Evelyn took over from the neighbour. It was several days before Mrs Brown felt better. Evelyn cared for her and looked after the house, in addition to looking after Jonny. She even cooked meals for Louis. Three days after her return, the doctor came to see how his patient was progressing. After examining her, he spoke to Evelyn in the sitting room.

"So you're the daughter-in-law? How was your holiday?"

"Fine until I returned and found my mother-in-law in bed, sick. I got quite a shock when I arrived back."

The doctor had a grim face, grimmer than that abortionist doctor, whose services she hadn't wanted. He took her to the living room, out of earshot of his patient.

"Mrs Brown. I'd like to talk to your husband."

"Why?"

"I think he ought to know about his mother."

'God,' she thought, 'she has cancer!' She could tell that the doctor had bad news.

"I'm estranged from Mr Brown. I was going to leave at the end of the year. Can I get Mrs Brown to tell him to call you? What's wrong with her, Doctor? I'm looking after her, now that I'm back."

"She's got a kidney infection, pyelonephritis, but that's only part of the story. She's also got chronic kidney disease and that's serious. She's got a form of Bright's disease, chronic glomerulonephritis, and she's probably had it for years. This acute infection hasn't helped things, but I'm glad to say that the sulpha seems to have gotten on top of it. After she's up and about for a month, I want her to have tests done. Then I'll know how bad it is."

"How bad? I don't follow."

Mrs Brown was her only friend. Evelyn couldn't afford to lose her.

"The illness is progressive and terminal. I can't tell you if she's got six months or six years, until I get the blood tests, and even with these I can't be too sure. I don't like the colour of her skin, and there's a faint smell of ammonia. Those are two bad signs. Haven't you noticed the colour of her skin?"

"No."

"It's grey. That's because her kidneys aren't eliminating all the poisons in her blood. Well, she'll be on her feet in a few days. She'll be a little weak, but she should get over it this time. Make sure she takes all the tablets, and drinks lots of water, and that she goes for the tests. Then, I want to see her with the results. You can come with her, if you want."

Evelyn stayed home and cared for Mrs Brown, missing the first week of third term. She telephoned a fellow student, who came after classes and gave her most of the material that she missed. She had no time to study, as she was too busy with her two dependants. When Mrs Brown was well enough to resume caring for Jonny, Evelyn went back to classes. One of the first things she did, was to look up Bright's disease in a medical textbook. It wasn't pleasant reading. Mrs Brown had a slowly progressive fatal disease. She could be close to death, depending on the extent of kidney damage. That evening Evelyn spoke to her.

"How are you feeling?"

"I'm fine. I feel so silly that we called the doctor for nothing."

"It may not be nothing. You have to have those laboratory tests done in a fortnight."

She could see the discoloration of her skin. It had happened gradually. That was why she hadn't noticed it.

"I'm much better now. Do I need to have the tests done?"

"The doctor was very definite about them. It's important to do them after a kidney infection."

"I haven't got it any more, it's gone."

"You've had them before? Why didn't you tell me?"

"Just what did the doctor tell you?"

"Enough to realise that the lab tests that he's asked you to do are important, particularly as you've had kidney trouble before."

"When I was a girl, Evelyn, I got a chill one day and rheumatic fever. Then I got it for the first time."

"A kidney infection?"

"Nephritis. I was fourteen at the time."

"And you've had it since then?"

"When I was pregnant with Louis. I shouldn't have gotten pregnant. I shouldn't have had children at all. I might have died. It's a strain on the kidneys, and mine aren't all that good."

Evelyn thought to herself that it was a pity that she hadn't taken the doctors' advice. Mrs Brown continued. "That's why we only had the one child. I got over it and I've been fine all these years. Do you think that I've got it a second time?"

"The lab tests will show us."

"Yes, I suppose that we've got to know the worst. Don't worry, Evelyn, I've provided for little Jonny in my will, and I'm transferring some money to your account, just in case something happens to me. You could find yourself without any money, waiting for the lawyers to carve up whatever's left after the government and the lawyers take their slice. My war widow's pension doesn't continue after I go."

"You're not going to die. Louis is old enough to look after himself and I will be at the end of the year, when I graduate."

They both wondered if she'd see that happen.

"And little Jonny?"

"You'll look after him for years to come."

"I hope so."

Evelyn took Mrs Brown to do the tests and to see a specialist when she had the lab results. He examined her and spoke quickly to Evelyn, while her mother-in-law was dressing.

"What is your relationship to Mrs Brown?"

"I married her son. How is she?"

"Do you know what Bright's disease is?"

"I looked it up in a medical book. I'm a third year science student."

"I want her son to know. Will you tell him?"

"I'd rather you wrote a note to him. I don't live with him any more."

"Mrs Brown's tests indicate that her kidneys are working at ten percent of their normal function. That's close to the lower limit, depending on what she eats. She already has a high blood urea, and a raised creatinine level. She has advanced Glomerulonephritis. She's got a year to live, probably less if she's unlucky, two years at the most."

"Is there any cure, or treatment?"

"Neither."

He didn't bother to tell her that doctors in America had transplanted a kidney into a uremic patient. That patient hadn't survived.

"I gathered that. What do we do?"

"She'll have to avoid any stress, or chills, and she must go on a diet. Salt free and low in protein. The thing to fear is another kidney or lung infection. She doesn't have the strength to survive that, or flu either."

"I'll look after her."

"Tell me, if you're separated from her son, why do you still look after your mother-in-law?"

"I'm not just the daughter-in-law to her, Doctor. Mrs Brown looks after me like a daughter, better than my own father in fact. I love her, Doctor. She helped me when I needed her and I'll stand by her, as long as she needs me."

"It won't be pleasant, especially towards the end. She'll be very ill."

"Will she be in a lot of pain?"

"She'll feel very ill. She may vomit a lot, and have headaches, and no appetite, rather than pain. A big risk is infection. She already has less resistance to infection."

Evelyn wrote a note to Louis telling him what the doctor had told her. In it, she said that if he wanted to speak to her about it, she didn't mind, they could talk in the garden, just so long as his mother couldn't hear them. He didn't answer her note. What he felt, he told nobody. Evelyn didn't tell Mrs Brown, but she knew the score. She had seen other people die of kidney disease, so she knew that she too was dying. She continued to mind Jonny during the day, and Evelyn managed to complete her final term, and sit for the November exams. She did miss a lecture that filled the Bonython Hall on October the 8th, when biologist Sir Julian Huxley was guest lecturer. She wanted to hear the famous scientist from that illustrious family, but she couldn't get away from those in her care.

There was trouble in the Australian Labor Party, which was coming apart at the seams. Dr Evatt, a High Court Judge who had returned to politics during the darkest days of World War II, tried in vain to hold the party together. Finally on October 6th, he made a speech attacking the right wing of the Victorian branch of the party, blaming their "disloyalty" for the loss of Victorian seats that cost them the May Election, accusing them of "using tactics similar to the Fascists and Communists" to infiltrate the party and attack from within. Dr Evatt, one of the greatest minds ever in the Federal

Parliament, the man that the UN General Assembly in 1948 elected to the post of President, could not save the party. Attacked from within, by Menzies and the press from without, it went on crumbling, heading for a long, lean time on the opposition benches.

The morning of the last class, the professor asked Evelyn to come to his office. He asked his secretary to bring them coffee and biscuits and told Evelyn that he wanted her as a post-graduate student.

"First, I have to pass, Professor."

"Pass! That's not the question. You're the favourite for a medal, Evelyn. I'd like you to do an honours degree."

"I can't. I have to find a job."

"I thought that we'd lose you at the end of last year, when you went to have the baby. It was a pleasant surprise to see you back last April. Why do you have to get a job?"

"Because I want to leave my husband, and because my arrangement for looking after my son, won't last for much longer. I'm going to have to support the two of us."

"What about your husband?"

"You know him. If I have to wait until he's able or willing to support us, I wouldn't need a baby-sitter. In any case, in all honesty, I can't expect to leave him and still live off of his money, and my father won't help me if I do leave him. My relationship with Louis Brown was a big mistake. It almost cost me my degree, Professor. Do you know of any available jobs, perhaps teaching Biology?"

The professor, who had never interviewed Evelyn before, but recognised her as his best student, warmed to this young woman. She was a remarkable person.

"Evelyn, I'm not completely ignorant of your situation. I'll try to get you a special grant, so that you can work towards a Master's degree and pick up a bit of extra money, demonstrating. I've never done this before, but then I've never had such a deserving student before. You've come through with remarkable tenacity, when anyone else would have given up. I want you back here, next year. You're worth ten of the other students, pampered, lazy, some of them, wasting their time and our funds, like that man you married. He should have been kicked out after he failed first year."

The professor knew that Evelyn's marriage had been one of the shot-gun variety.

"And I would never have met him. I'd be free of him."

The professor's words were the best thing that had happened to her in a long time.

"Well, we can't turn back the clock. Come and see me as soon as the results are out, and don't worry, dear. Don't judge all men by your husband. Some of us are quite decent. Now you'd better get back to your books and your baby."

She felt uplifted. On the way out she met Richard. This was a day of surprises.

"What are you doing here, Richard? Have you been waiting for me?"

"Yes. Everyone got out twenty minutes ago. I'd missed you."

"The professor just offered me a job, with a salary for next year. Richard, I can't talk now, I'm late. I've got to get home to Jonny."

"I'll walk part of the way with you. I just wanted to wish you good luck for the finals."

He gave her an affectionate peck on the cheek.

"Good luck to you too."

"How's it going, Evelyn?"

"So so. Jonny's a handful now that he's walking, and becoming too much for Mrs Brown to handle. She's going to die next year, Richard, and then I'll be on my own."

"On your own?"

"Yes, I'll have to find another place to stay."

"Why can't you stay where you are?"

"With Brown? Richard don't you know? I would have left him ages ago, but for Mrs Brown. I'll tell you about it after the exams. Give me a call."

"Evelyn!"

"After the exams."

Richard had always considered that Evelyn was happily married. He thought her a fool to have married Brown, but a happy fool. The revelation that she wanted to leave Brown came as a surprise to him. Richard's opinion of Evelyn took a quantum leap. He was curious. He wanted to hear more, but Evelyn was on her bicycle, pedalling home.

November 30th. Evelyn, Richard, Joan, and Gerald celebrated the end of their exams, each in their own way, feeling that they were going to pass, to graduate.

In England and the Commonwealth, the birthday of England's Prime Minister was also celebrated, with greetings from all over the world. It was Winston Churchill's 80th birthday, and his last before handing over the reins of Government to Sir Anthony Eden. He was still the best-loved person in the world, nearly ten years after the defeat of the Nazis.

Remembering what Evelyn had said, Richard telephoned her on December 1st.

"Evelyn, last time I saw you, you said we'd get together and have a chat after the exams. How'd it go, by the way?"

"I've done it, Richard. I know I passed. Now I can go back to Renmark, and crow a little when the results come out. I'd like to have a chat, but I'm going home in two days, and there isn't time. I can't invite you here. *He* might see you. Come and see me in the Department in January when I come back. I'll be working, if Mrs Brown's still alright."

"What's this about you leaving Brown?"

"I don't know. I wanted to do it before, but now I can't. It isn't as if we've really been married. I sleep in my own room with the door locked. Does that shock you?"

Richard considered his words before answering.

"No. To be honest, Evelyn, I was more shocked by the thought of you sleeping with him. Tell me more."

"When I come back from my holiday. What are you going to do next year?"

"I haven't made up my mind. I might enrol for another degree. See you in January."

On December 2nd, Senator Joe McCarthy was condemned in a vote in the Senate for action unbecoming a member of the Senate. The witch hunt was coming to an end. At the end of the year, America took its revenge on Australia, as Seixas and Trabert defeated Hoad and Rosewall in the Davis Cup.

Chapter Twenty-Five
December 1954

Throughout 1954 Gerald continued to work two evenings a week at the Meredith Brewery, from five to eleven at night. In March he bought a 1950 Hillman Minx and this made him independent of trams. After work he usually studied until one in the morning. Together with lectures, practicals, his social and sex life with Joan, he was busy all the time. He told George that he might have to quit the job later in the year, or take leave in October or November, but apart from a fortnight during the exams he didn't miss an evening's work.

Now with his final exams over, Gerald had to make some decisions. Joan's father had offered him a job in the company. For 18 months he had been the constant companion of his employer's daughter. It was expected, it had been long expected, that the couple would get engaged. While he was a student there was some excuse for not doing so, but now with the exams over the pressure was on. Gerald knew this and that he had to make up his mind. Was he in love with Joan, and did he want to marry her?

With Evelyn it hadn't been a problem for Gerald. Very early in their relationship he had felt that he loved her, wanted her, and he continued to do so long after the relationship was over. He wanted to feel the same way about Joan, but he didn't. Was it because it had been so easy with Joan? Did there have to be a challenge? He never went after Joan, she in fact had made him an offer that he couldn't refuse. They'd reversed the normal sequence of events, having gone to bed together before they'd started going steady.*p Logically he was mad not to love her but love isn't logical. She loved him and did everything to make his sex and social life wonderful, he desired her and couldn't wait to be alone with her, in her flat and that luxurious bed of hers. She was intelligent, fun to be with and never in a bad mood. Every time he thought about her and the future, it became more and more obvious. He would marry Joan Meredith.

The other thing that worried Gerald was Joan's money. It was great to know that as a millionairess-escort he'd never want for anything or really have to work. His only function in life would be to keep the young lady happy, in and out of bed, and father as many children as the Meredith dynasty needed, plenty in this particular case, if Steven didn't pull his finger out and shoulder his responsibility.

Joan's father had hinted that his son-in-law would get a substantial 'nest-egg' as a wedding present, so that he wouldn't have to ask Joan all the time for pocket money to keep her in the style that he expected his daughter to live in. He would also be groomed to move up in the Meredith companies, so that he'd be able to take Joan's place on the board. He intended to place a large block of stock in his daughter's name as soon as the reorganisation was completed.

This was all very nice, but he really didn't need it. He often wished that she wasn't an heiress. Then he could work for whoever he wanted and not be regarded at work as the boss's protégé, or around town as a gold-digger. People referred to her, behind her back, as Queen Joan and to him as Prince-Consort Gerald. He heard this and it annoyed him.

He often told Joan that he loved her, sometimes as they shared their bodies in bed, sometimes as they sat about studying, or having breakfast and he meant it whenever he said it. He loved her, that he knew, but he had loved Evelyn passionately. Why didn't he love Joan the same way?

On December 3rd with the examinations behind them, Gerald and Joan went to the Annual Recuperation Ball. They and their party dined before the ball at the South Australia Hotel and were photographed as usual by the photographer for the social page, who raced off to get it ready for the *Sunday Mail*. They arrived at the ball quite late. The Refectory was overflowing with students letting off steam after the stress of examinations. There were no alcoholic beverages served, but as usual, there was plenty under the tables.

Joan was sure that Gerald would finally ask her to marry him. This evening was the right occasion; however both she and her parents were disappointed. Another occasion came when on the 16th the exam results were posted. They both passed, but Gerald saw Evelyn's name on the board and this was more important to him than his own result. There it was again, Evelyn Robertson (why not Evelyn Brown?) with two credits, and a university medal. Joan saw that look on his face and knew that there'd be no love making that night, let alone any proposal. For the first time in their long relationship she was jealous. Her boyfriend was still in love with that girl she had married off. So much for out of sight, out of mind. Could it be that absence makes the heart grow fonder?

Louis Brown did not pass a subject in 1954. Joan noticed this and began to worry for Evelyn. Through no fault of her own, by being herself and working hard, she had once more humiliated her husband, and she knew what Brown could do to a person that he hated. Joan knew of their domestic arrangement and how they disliked one another. As much as she feared for Evelyn's safety, she did nothing. There was nothing she could do. Evelyn had her degree. She could leave Brown now and go back home. Joan forgot about her. Gerald, blissfully ignorant of the real situation, felt proud of his old love, wondering what she'd do now that she had a degree and a child to look after, while the man she loved had nothing. Surely Brown would now give up his attempts at studying and get a job. He had a wife and child to support.

On Friday 23rd while Australians were boozing themselves into a pre-Christmas stupor at thousands of parties all over the continent, Australia's leading Aboriginal artist, Albert Namatjira, was arrested on a charge of bringing beer into an Aboriginal reserve. The case was proved against him and then was dismissed. The same day, Adelaide's first drive-in cinema opened at West Beach, screening *Genevieve* and cartoons. In the evening Joan and Gerald went to see the annual Footlights Club revue.

The Jarrah building, unlike the rest of the buildings on the campus, was not named after a benefactor. There was no Sir Reginald Jarrah or Lady Margaret Jarrah. Jarrah was the name of the wood used in its construction. Commonly called *The Hut*, it was a low construction of wood and galvanised iron, a relic of the war years, used as the university theatre. Stage facilities were meagre, dressing rooms inadequate and the few people that could get into the auditorium had to sit on rickety benches. No one sat far from the stage. The lighting was usually augmented by borrowing equipment from the Physics and Electrical Engineering Departments. The standard of some productions may have matched the building, but the Footlights Revues in the last years of *The Hut*, were great, none being greater than the 1954 production of *Be Your Age*.

It opened with Jacques' *All the World's a Stage*, setting the theme of the revue, *The Seven Ages Of Man*, followed by a rousing number, *Be Your Age*, sung by the entire cast. Jacques came on again to announce the first age, "The infant, mewling and puking in the nurse's arms". This act contained two wise-cracking babies and concluded with the song,

We're a couple of Freudian Rabbits,
Leading a miserable life.
Burdened by such dirty habits,
Weighed down by sub-conscious strife.
We learn sublimation from things like our dummies,
Conceal our fixation for each other's tummies.
We long for the days when we're Daddies and Mommies,
We'd rather be dead than be babies.

We hate to be complex,
We'd rather be simple,
And stay away from sex,
Till the age of the pimple.
We long for the day that we lose our last dimple,
We'd rather be dead than be babies.

The Whining Schoolboy was a group of St Trinian's girls and their version of *Medea*, concluding with a song *Medea, The Scourge Of Ancient Greece.*

So it went for all seven ages, the fifth act being a parody of the Petrov Inquiry, with the judge telling key politicians to "Be Your Age!" As in the real inquiry, the leader of the Federal Labor party, Dr Evatt, was made to look ridiculous. This was as close as the student body got to making a political statement in the 50's.

Each act had an original song, the evening ending with the whole cast and a powerful closing number. It was a polished revue, it had rave notices in the papers and, best of all, a letter from the Vice Chancellor praising it, saying it was a creation that the university could be proud of. This was only a few years after he had asked the Footlights Club to censor a section of a previous revue, that he had found to be offensive.

The theatre critic in the *Advertiser* the following day headed his report on the show

FUN, GAMES, ENCHANTMENT.

After the show the actors cleaned off the greasepaint, piled into cars and headed for the nightly cast party. This night Joan Meredith played host, inviting everyone to a barbecue at "Boronia". Sir William Meredith and his daughter were on holiday in Hobart so Joan had the place for a week. There was a big clearing at the back of the house; they built a bonfire in the middle and set up two big oil drums cut in half with sheet iron on top for the barbecues. There was plenty of firewood, brought in from the surrounding forest. By midnight the sausages, steaks and lamb chops were sizzling, the beer and wine flowing.

The cast, stage hands, and helpers numbered about 50, their friends another 50. Another 70 acquaintances who had been at the theatre also came along. They sat around the bonfire, eating and drinking. As they finished with the food they either sang songs or disappeared, couples hand in hand to bedrooms or to well cared for lawns on the dark side of the house. The art gallery was locked.

Louis Brown had helped out backstage, making sets, painting and setting up the lighting. As such he was entitled to join in the fun. Joan and Gerald didn't even know he was there until they heard about it the next day, they were too busy looking after the interior of the house, attending to the needs of the party-goers, keeping an eye on the locked gallery.

Always on the lookout for new conquests, Brown had noticed what looked like an unattached female at the theatre, and asked her if she wanted to come along to the cast party.

"I'd love to, but I have to be at work at eight."

"I'll drive you straight to work after the party. Where do you work?"

"Royal Adelaide Hospital. I'm a nurse."

"Do you know a nurse about your height and age, a blonde called Yvonne. I forget her last name. I haven't seen her for almost a year. We used to be good friends."

"There's an Yvonne in maternity. She's a blonde."

"Give her regards from Louis Brown. Are you coming?"

"If it's all the same I think I'd better get back to the hospital. I can walk, it's not far."

"Come to the party. I'll bring you back early. What time do you want to get back?"

"One. Is it worthwhile going?"

"Make it two and it will be."

"Alright, two, but no later. My name's Robin."

"Let's get moving, Robin. The party's in the hills."

Louis didn't try anything at the party, not at Joan Meredith's place. With so many of Evelyn's friends there he couldn't risk one of them reporting to her what he was doing. He wasn't going to give her grounds for divorce if he could help it.

Those not engaged in amorous pursuits, stayed in a large group around the campfire, listening to records and singing. There were a few records of Eartha Kitt that were extremely popular, with songs from her film *New Faces*, *Santa Baby*, and *I Want To Be Evil*. This record was banned on the radio, because of its lyrics. They also played the Ruth Wallace records, *Long Playing Daddy*, and *Davey's Little Dinghy*, over and over. Then they started singing limericks:

I dined with the Duchess at tea,
The Duchess she sat next to me.
Her rumblings abdominal,
Were simply phenomenal,
And everyone thought it was me.

A policeman who came from Kew Junction,
Lost the use of his sexual function.
For the rest of his life,
He deceived his wife,
By the skilful use of his truncheon.

There once was a girl from Dakota,
Who lived in a Chinese pagoda.
And the wall of the halls,
Were lined with the balls,
And the tools of the fools, that had rode her.

There was a young man from Kent,
Whose penis was horribly bent.
To save himself trouble,
He bent the thing double,
And instead of coming, he went.

and so on, until almost hundred verses had been sung.

Then they went through the unwritten song book with *Poor little Angeline*, *Abdul Abulbul Emir*, and *Charlotte the Harlot*. Someone sang solo, *These Foolish Things*:

Three shades of lipstick on an old French Letter,
A case of Syphilis that won't get better,
And when I piss, it stings.
These foolish things, remind me of you.
A book on birth control with well worn pages.
A contraceptive, that's been used for ages,
Three broken sofa springs.

After that, some of the men sang the *Latrine Song*, the anthem of National Service, to the tune of *Begin The Beguine*. Richard called Gerald out from the kitchen to join in this song.

My Job is to clean an army latrine,
It's the type of latrine that everyone uses,
The paper is clean, on both sides the news is,
To read while you've been in my latrine.
I scrub it all day, I scrub it all night.
I keep it that way, just as you'd expect it,
And when it gets high I just disinfect it.
Terrifically clean, my latrine.
I scrub it again at four in the morning.
We polish the chain, my cobbers and I
And there am I scrubbing away for ever
And wandering if ever, I'll get out that stain,
I scrub it again.
Such motions of slime, such ruptures I've seen,
When a crowd comes along to destroy the work I've created.
They just sit and (pause) sit, don't care wherever they place it,
You can see what I mean, in my latrine.
If a man is a freak and must leak like a creek, make him pay.
Every seat is so neat and complete,
Underneath little wedges,
But it still gets all wet like an artist's palette, round the edges.

No they won't keep it clean, my bloody latrine.
Every seat is all smooth, for each base to establish connections,
But the clots all take shots in all directions.
But I still stand aloof, they can't hit the roof.
It's the one place that's clean, in my la-trine.

It was almost two and they were singing *Roll Me Over, In The Clover*, when Robin asked Louis if they could go. He'd come there with a packed car but that didn't matter. The rest could find their own way home. He took her by the hand and they went quickly to the car. To the strains of,

And this is number four and he's got me on the floor,
Roll me over, lay me down and do it again,

ringing out against the tall trees, they drove out of the drive and into the dark summer night. He didn't take the Norton Summit Road that lead straight back to the city, but continued on towards Crafers and down into Belair National Park. After 15 minutes Robin began to wonder why they weren't out of the hills.

"Louis, where are we? We didn't come this way."

"Don't worry. I'll get you back in plenty of time."

She didn't like the tone in his voice, it was harsh and frightening. Then he turned off the narrow road and drove across the grass playing field to the edge of the forest.

"Louis, it's late. Take me back to town."

He turned off the motor and the lights. They were all alone in the dark. Robin couldn't see a thing inside or out of the car. There was no sound save for his breathing. She felt the hairs on the back of her neck rise, as the nature of her situation dawned on her.

"Please, Louis. We can go out another time."

That was a promise she'd never keep, even if he started the car and drove her back at once. He had seemed such a nice person, why was he doing this?

He reached out in the dark and touched her hand. She pulled it away. He moved closer and put an arm around her. She was as furious as she was frightened.

"Stop it. I have to get back. Please take me back."

"Just a little kiss and cuddle. The sooner we start, the sooner you'll get home."

That told her all she wanted to know. It said, either you come across, baby, or we sit this one out. It was a blatant threat.

"I don't want to, I have a boyfriend. He'll get you, if you hurt me."

He'd heard this one before.

"Why wasn't he with you tonight?"

"He's a doctor. He had to work."

"You haven't got a boyfriend. Come here and stop wasting time. You aren't the only one that wants to get some sleep."

Robin got out of the car. She did have a boyfriend. She wanted nothing from this man.

"I'm walking home. You're a rat, Louis Brown."

"You'll be late for work."

She had a problem. She didn't know where she was and how she'd get to the hospital.

"I'm getting in the back. Take me back, please."

Louis leaned over and opened the back door.

"Why did you come to the party and lead me on all night, if you won't even give me a kiss? You're a damn tease, that's what you are."

"I hardly know you. If it's just a kiss you want, why come to this place? Take me back to the hospital and I'll give you a kiss there."

"I just want to get to know you better."

He got in the back seat and moved across. As he did, she opened the door and stepped out. Louis slid across the seat, stood up and grabbed her two shoulders, so that she couldn't get away. Robin then did what she'd been told to do in a case like this. She knew that she'd have to do it hard or she'd be in real danger. She let Louis draw her to him, pulled back her knee, then brought it forward and up with all the might she could muster. As she felt her knee crush him where it really hurts a man, she felt his grip on her tighten and then let go. She fell backwards as he fell forward, doubled up like an overgrown foetus.

She rolled over away from the moaning Louis, stood up and ran. Robin never ran as hard and as fast in her life. The second thing she'd been told to do, was to run like mad, because if a would-be rapist recovers from a blow to the balls, he's going to be madder than a fighting bull. Brown was cognisant of nothing except excruciating pain. As this receded, he became aware of the faint sound of Robin running down the road. Then the sound was gone.

Once back on the road, Robin stopped to get her breath back and think. They had come from the left, Adelaide must be to the right. She listened but heard nothing from the direction of Brown. Just in case he was close behind she ran as fast as she could. Five minutes later she heard the sound of a car starting and looked back across the playing field. She saw the car lights being lit, the car turn and head back towards the road. Robin walked into the trees, hid behind a tall specimen and waited until the car passed. It threw eerie, racing shadows through the forest for a couple of seconds, before it was gone. She watched as the red tail lights disappeared down the road, then stepping out of the trees, she started walking the same way.

There were no lights in the park. Robin's eyes slowly got used to the starlight as she walked along the road. She almost didn't see the car coming back. A flicker of light, a faint reflection from the chrome, made her stop and get off the road. There it was, coming slowly back with its lights off. Robin dropped down into the ditch and crawled behind a fallen tree. It was muddy there but she didn't care. Not knowing if he'd seen her or not, she listened as the car glided slowly by in the direction she had come from. When she could no longer hear it, she sat up. She was covered with wet rotting gum leaves. She'd lost a shoe and couldn't find it. She took off the other one.

Brown would be back, so she sat and waited. The car passed again, still without lights. Robin rightly assumed that he would abandon her now, so she set off in stockinged feet down the road. Without her shoes she would hear the car if it reappeared. What if he was sitting around a bend in the road waiting for her? What would he do if he caught her? That quick knee must have really hurt the bastard.

There were no other cars in the park. It was three o'clock in the morning and the park was only used during the daylight hours. It took Robin an hour and a half to make her way out and find a farmhouse on the fringe. A big dog greeted her and licked her fingers. It felt so good after the grip of Brown on her shoulder. She held the animal and cried over it. Then she knocked on the door of the farmhouse.

Only when the veranda light was lit and the farmer emerged, did she realise what a state she was in. There was brown mud and leaves down the front and side of her dress, her feet were cut and bleeding and her hair was splattered with mud. The farmer didn't ask her any questions. He just took her in and called his wife.

"I'm lost. I was coming home from a party and this man took me into the park and I had to run away."

The farmer looked at Robin. She looked as if she'd been rolled in the mud. He assumed the worst.

"Did he do anything to you? Let's call the police."

"No, I hid in the trees. I have to get to the hospital."

"Are you hurt?"

"No, I'm a nurse. I have to be back on duty at eight. What's the time?"

"Four fifty."

"I'm sorry I woke you up."

"Don't worry, I had to get up to milk the cows."

"Do you think you could call me a taxi?"

"No, you won't get one to come out here at this time. Go with the missus and get cleaned up and I'll take you home. You ought to go to the police."

"I'm alright. I want to get some sleep."

"You ought to report him. He may have a record. The police might be looking for him."

"I'll tell Matron. I'd better get going."

By the time that Robin arrived back at the nurses quarters, looking like something that the cat dragged in, the place was beginning to stir, with nurses getting up for the morning shift. By breakfast time everybody knew the story of Robin's escape from Louis Brown. She showered and tried to sleep for an hour. Yvonne, when she heard the story, came to see her and hear it directly. She went to work at eight, tired, dead tired from lack of sleep and the walk out of the park. At ten, Matron rang and called her down to her office. Yvonne was there and a policeman.

Robin told her story to the officer of the law and answered his questions. Then he spoke to her.

"You're a lucky girl, Robin. You probably escaped a sexual assault or worse. What you did was very courageous. You're lucky that he didn't catch you. I know that you want us to arrest Brown and put him on a charge. We can bring him in, question him and make a report. It may frighten him, frighten him enough not to try this sort of thing in the future. We'll have to see if he's wanted for any attacks on women and we'll let him know that he'll be a suspect in future investigations. That'll make him think. If as you say he's a student, he can't be all that stupid, although sometimes I have my doubts about them."

"Aren't you going to charge the animal?"

"On what charge, Matron?"

"Attempted rape, abduction, leaving her alone out there in the bush."

"Attempted rape? I can't even charge him with assault, indecent or otherwise. Robin, I'm glad to say, was too quick for him. You've heard her story. She assaulted him before he could assault her. If he'd molested her or torn her clothes or confined her in any way, we'd have a case, but he didn't. You have told us exactly what happened? You wouldn't care to change your story a little bit? No, that wouldn't do, I'd have to call the farmer and his wife to testify so you can't change your story. He hasn't committed a crime that he can be charged with. He behaved like a rat. That's a social misdemeanour, not a crime."

"That's that?"

The Matron and the two nurses were disappointed. In their eyes, Brown was a criminal on the loose. The least the law could do was to put him away and throw away the key.

"Yes, Matron. We'll talk to him and we'll make him think that we're going to throw the book at him. He probably doesn't know the law. We'll also inspect his car. There's bound to be a few things that need fixing, brakes, tires, perhaps a missing globe. The traffic boys will find a way to take away his wheels for a while."

Louis was lying in his bed. It was two in the afternoon and he lay awake, feeling the damage that Robin had caused to his genitals. It still hurt. He wondered if he'd need medical attention, but it would be embarrassing trying to explain his injury. The football season was over. Hit by a cricket ball? Not at that angle. Finally, he decided that he was going to live, he was just about to get up and ask his mother for lunch, when she knocked on his door.

"Get dressed, Louis," she called through the door. He put on a pair of shorts and a shirt, then unlocked the door. Two policemen pushed it open and stepped inside. He knew that they had come about Robin and wondered for the first time since he woke up, what had happened to her, if she'd found her way out of the park.

They told him to put on proper clothes and marched him out of the house, without a word of explanation to him or to his mother. She asked them what he'd done, but they just told her that he was wanted for questioning. They left her crying and thinking how lucky it was that Evelyn wasn't in Adelaide to witness his arrest. Then she tidied his room.

Louis saw a policeman examining his car. He told him that he intended to impound it, as he'd found some faults.

It was after seven when he left the police station. They had left him in a cell for three hours and then questioned him for another hour and a half. When he went to the university for the last performance of *Be Your Age* he was met by some of the men at the backstage door, who told him that his help wasn't needed and asked him to leave. Robin's story mightn't make the pages of *Truth*, but it was spreading fast. It was common knowledge among the cast of the Footlights Club. Joan heard about it at the cast party later that night and so did Gerald. He was furious and frustrated at his inability to do anything about it. Poor Evelyn, married to this monster. They left the party early and Gerald went home to sleep alone in his own bed. Joan wondered if he would ever belong to her. While her lover lay awake thinking of another woman, Joan cried herself to sleep longing for him, cursing the memory of Louis Brown.

Chapter Twenty-Six

January 1955

Joan and Gerald went to "Boronia" for a few days, again on January 1st, straight from an all night party. It was very hot with a steady north wind blowing so they had to stay indoors most of the day. The heat woke them up. At four they put on the lawn sprinklers, got into their bathing costumes and played about on the lawns. They could have worn nothing, the staff were not in the house. They had the big house and the grounds all to themselves. Now that he had had a good look at the place he was reminded of Hetton Abbey or Brideshead as he imagined them in Evelyn Waugh's books, with lots of rooms that would never be used.

"Why don't you put in a swimming pool up here?"

"Why don't you suggest it to my father?"

"Why don't you? You're his daughter."

"When you're lord of the manor, you can have it put in."

"If you're afraid to suggest it, get your big brother to do it for you, when he comes back from the States."

"It was your idea, Gerald. You do it."

"You could put it where we had the bonfire, or behind the trees if you think it might spoil the view. When is big brother returning?"

"When they finish building the Meredith Building for Food Sciences."

The water felt good in the hot sunshine. But it would have been nicer if they could go for a swim.

"Big brother's going to be a professor?"

"Eventually. He'll start off as Lecturer-in-charge and later on they'll have to make him a professor."

"I thought that he was a bacteriologist."

"He was, but he's been doing post-doctorate work in Food Technology. It's to enable him to keep a eye on Dad's interests without having to run them. It's a compromise, so Steven can have his cake and eat it too. He'll be able to leave the mundane work to Dad and tell him what he's doing wrong. Dad's funding the department just to get him to settle in Adelaide."

"What if Steven doesn't get the job? Won't they have to advertise it?"

"He'll get the job. They'll advertise it as a lectureship and no one important will apply for it, and then, when Steven builds up the department, his status will be raised accordingly and according to the size of Meredith donations to the university."

"Who planned all this, Steven or your father?"

"Dad. Steven doesn't know what's going on, well not everything. Dad doesn't want him to stay overseas or come back to live in Sydney or Melbourne."

'Why does she dislike her brother?' he thought. 'You'd think that having so much money, they'd have nothing to fight about.'

"And what plans has father made for you?"

"Nothing, I'm just a woman. I'm useless. I too, am expected to settle down close to home, and produce grandchildren. Dad seems to like you, Gerald. Now that you've graduated he wants you to do an executive training course."

"I know, he's told me. I have a meeting with him next week."

"You're also invited to dinner next Sunday."

He was now a regular at Charles and Diana's dining table, as if he was already a son-in-law.

"Your parents will want to know when I'm going to make an honest woman out of you."

Joan came out from under a sprinkler and looked him straight in the face.

"Well, if you were my father wouldn't you expect that the man who took his daughter out of circulation for a year and a half, would either marry her or step aside and give the other fellows a chance? You must admit they have been most understanding. Most fathers don't let young men sample the merchandise."

'That's not fair,' thought Gerald. 'I didn't rob her of her virginity. She did it to me!'

"And most men do it in spite of them. You did buy me the Kinsey report for my birthday, and we did read it together, didn't we? Plenty of girls tell their parents that they're with a friend and they're really in bed with their boyfriend. We're not doing anything that other young people the world over aren't doing."

"Gerald, we have been lovers for a long time. I'd like something more from our relationship. I want to have a baby."

He pretended to be shocked.

"Joan, we're not married!"

"If we were, we could start a baby right away."

"You are still taking precautions?"

"Don't worry, I wouldn't trap you, barring accidents, but don't make me wait too long. I mean it when I say I want a baby."

This was another offer he couldn't resist. Like the man in *Annie Get your Gun*, his defences were down. How could he resist her standing there, under the sprinkling water, her black hair wet against her hazel eyes?

"Soon, Joan. I like the idea of being a father."

"Are you worried that I won't be faithful?"

"No. I was at first, but not any more."

"That you won't be?"

"No."

"I want to have a baby with you, several babies. Doesn't that mean anything to you?"

"Joan, I do love you, but I can't think if you pressure me all the time. Tell me, am I the first man that you've proposed to?"

"Yes. Every other time they wanted to marry me."

"If I'd have proposed to you back in those winter nights in 1953, would you have rejected me?"

"I'll answer that question on our honeymoon."

"Have you got the suite already booked and the church?"

Joan hated Gerald's obstinacy. She had learned to control men from an early age, had controlled Gerald to a certain extent, but it was the part of him that she couldn't dominate that intrigued her, made her want him so much. Would he still hold such fascination for her, when he gave in and asked her to marry him?

That night the wind strengthened and brought with it all the heat of the Red Centre. They had to close up the entire house and sleep in the cooler, but stifling air, stored within its walls. There were no coolers up here and air conditioning was still a rarity in Australia. In a day or two, the wind would change and they could once more enjoy the cool night air of the hills. They showered before and after making love and again upon waking up on *Black Sunday*.

On the second of January 1955, the city temperature was 100 degrees by nine in the morning and reached a maximum of 109. No sunshine reached the settled area. A huge cloud of dust covered the plains and the hills, ahead of the depression that brought scorching air all the way down from Alice Springs, and the surrounding desert. The airport was closed and the tops of the city buildings couldn't be seen from the street. No one but Mad Dogs and Englishmen would go out on such a day. It was Sunday and most people stayed at home, lights lit because of the dust storm, listening to the radio, wondering when the promised change would come. It was a day of extreme fire hazard.

The fires started in mid-morning, hidden by the dust storm, spread by the gale force winds into a flood of burning grass, blazing trees and flaming undergrowth. This day was to be known as Black Sunday, a day of tremendous destruction of farmland, forest and homes. Two people died in the fire, but the death toll among residents and fire-fighters could have been more. Many people had narrow escapes.

The State Governor and the Premier were among those people. The Governor, his family and staff spent two hours trapped in a garden against a terrace wall, while his home was destroyed and the fires formed an impenetrable wall around them. The Premier, Tom Playford, was with a group of fire-fighters caught when the fire approached. He stopped them from running away and being enveloped by the flames, making them lie down in a ploughed field, where they all survived. It was a lucky escape for South Australia.

Gerald woke up at seven. He showered, put on a pair of shorts and went outside. It was hotter than it had been the previous evening. The dust got in his throat and nose, making him sneeze. He had to squint to see. As quickly as he'd come out, he returned to the house. Then he went to the kitchen to make himself a little breakfast and listen to the radio. At eight o'clock the forecast was for gale force northerly winds and extreme fire hazard, with relief coming in the evening. He took breakfast to Joan which she ate sitting naked in bed, the toast crumbs falling on her wondrous breasts. When she was finished Gerald removed the tray, and the crumbs with his tongue. Then he took off his shorts and got back into bed.

At nine thirty, they heard the fire alarm siren coming from Cherryville. Gerald got out of bed.

"I'm going to see if I can help. They'll need every volunteer they can get. You get dressed and listen to the radio. Connect up all the hoses, just in case the fire comes this way."

"Don't worry about me. This place is quite safe. You be careful, Gerry."

"I'm taking the car. See you when it's all over."

Gerald joined the locals and volunteers at Cherryville. There was a fire out of control several miles to the north. It was coming their way. They were set to work clearing fire breaks in its path. Gerald took a rake and started collecting dead wood and leaves. It reminded him of his Nasho days.

Soon the smell of smoke came in together with the dust. It made them work faster. Then the man in charge was called to the phone. He came back and gathered the fire-fighters together.

"It's coming this way boys, up from Teatree Gully. There's nothing for it but to burn back. I'll light the fires and you keep them from getting out of control. Some of you get on the other side of the road and put out any fires that start from flying ash. Run to the town if the fire crosses the road and try to save the houses."

He didn't tell them that they had no hope of holding back the fire. The experienced men knew that.

The sky was dark and menacing with grey smoke carried by the wind. The men tended to the fire as it slowly crept back into the bush to meet the fire raging up the hill. The sky turned red before the advancing fire front with sparks and cinders racing overhead. When they heard the fire roar and saw it glowing through the trees they grabbed their tools and ran back to the road. They all knew that the wind would carry the fire over their futile work and stood by helpless, before retreating to the town to try and save the houses.

Gerald remembered Joan, alone in the big house two miles away. He decided that he had to go and get her out and drive her to safety, ahead of the conflagration. He told the leader of the fire-fighters and leapt into the Hillman, before the man could stop him. Then he turned into the road where the fire was coming up like a sunrise.

As he left the town, he saw the fire burst into life in the trees on both sides of the road and advance behind him. The fire moved in a straight line, ahead of the gale; Gerald, by contrast, had to drive along two miles of winding road. He turned the first bend and the fire was all around him, racing in the direction of "Boronia" and "Marble Hill". He was driving in a tunnel of flame. High eucalypts, their leaves full of oil, exploded like shells on either side of the road. It was only two miles, but it was hilly and there were curves to negotiate. He drove fast, following the white line in the middle, not knowing or caring if a car might suddenly appear ahead of him. Any moment the heat might stall the engine, vaporise the petrol, ignite the tank, or shatter the windows protecting him from the intense heat.

He was almost there, with one turn to go and knew he could make it, when burning branches started cascading out of the fiery canopy and a tree began to fall just ahead of him. He put his foot down and lowered his head, as if the car had no top. The burning trunk of the tree hit just over the back seat and slid down the back of the car. Gerald drove on, pushing a pile of burning branches ahead of him. He turned into the gate, a burning arch of wood, and into the clear path ahead. Then he leapt out into the oven around him and ran to the front door where Joan let him in. As she did, the Hillman exploded.

"Gerald! Why did you come back? You might have been killed."

She held his hot body close to hers, looking over his shoulder at the burning car. It was still cool in the house, especially after running the gauntlet from the car. Joan brought him a wet towel to rub his face and hands. He was slightly burned. The heat around the car had been intense as he jumped out of it. He embraced her and kissed her over and over. She felt so good. She was fresh and cool, her bra-less breasts round and soft through her thin blouse.

"I wanted to get you out of here, but we can't go now. We'll just have to try and hold out here. We're surrounded by the fire. Joan, if the house catches fire, we've no escape."

Gerald was in a panic, but not Joan. This house had stood here for 75 years. It wasn't going to burn down.

"Have a shower. You're covered with sweat and ashes."

"Did you connect the hoses?"

"Yes".

Joan suddenly remembered something. She stopped and corrected herself.

"Oh-Oh. You can't have that shower. The water's off."

"Wouldn't it! We can't do anything if the house catches fire."

"The phone's off too. Daddy rang 10 minutes ago and asked if we were alright and what it was like up here and right in the middle the phone went dead. That was just before you got here."

"The lines probably go through Cherryville. What about the power?"

She held up her arms.

"Same thing. It went off just after the phone."

"Joan we're in a spot here. I'm going to inspect the house and see if we're in any danger."

"Good, that'll keep you out of my hair. I'll be down in the kitchen if you want me."

Gerald quickly went around the ground floor. The house was made of stone and the walls would keep the fire out. Then he went upstairs to inspect the upper rooms. Finally he went about listening for sounds of fire in the roof. He caught a glimpse of Joan dragging something across the hallway towards the kitchen. It looked like a mattress.

Gerald continued his inspection of the upper storey. He went into Joan's bedroom at the northern side. There were two tall pine trees close by, both burning. Gerald pulled down the curtains away from the window which had already cracked from the heat outside. As he did, he heard something ominous. There was a crackling sound in the ceiling above, and as he looked, whisps of smoke began to emerge through the plaster. The roof above was on fire. The fire must have spread from the pines. The roof and guttering were probably covered with dead leaves and this must have set the eaves and the rafters alight.

Mr Meredith tried to call back to Joan. The exchange told him that all lines in that area were down, burnt down. He rang the police. Finally he found someone who could tell him what was happening.

"The fire went through Cherryville and Marble Hill an hour ago. Marble Hill is on fire and there are people trapped up there, including the Governor and his family."

"'Boronia's' right next door. Do you know anything about 'Boronia'?"

"No. Only that the whole area's cut off and burning."

Joan's father went to tell her mother what was happening. He told her to prepare for the worst. There was nothing he could do, but wait and pray for their safety. If he drove up there, he'd be in the way. All the hill roads were closed, except to fire-fighters and emergency vehicles, those not closed by fire.

The fear that gripped Gerald in the car returned to him. He raced downstairs and called out to Joan. She came out of the picture gallery with two paintings under her arms.

"Joan, 'Boronia's' burning. We'll have to get out."

"Gerald, don't worry. Grab a couple of paintings and bring them down to the kitchen."

"Are you mad? This isn't the Forsythe Saga, this is a bloody fire! What are we going to do?"

"We've got plenty of time. These paintings are Grandpa's pride and joy. Help me get them downstairs."

"You're crazy."

"The fire's up there in the roof and we've got lots of time before we're in any danger. I am not going out into that inferno outside. Grab those Drysdales and then the Dobell on the far wall. They're too heavy for me."

"Where are we taking them? Aren't you worried that we may die in this fire?"

"Just bring those paintings and follow me."

Joan put them down by a big iron door in the kitchen. Then off she went for more paintings. Gerald followed. The noise of burning was quite loud now and a pall of smoke hung above them at the top of the stairs. Joan hurried back with two more paintings and Gerald did likewise.

"What's behind that iron door?"

"The wine cellar. Here's the key. It's deep down under the back garden. We'll be safe as houses there."

Gerald stopped hyperventilating. They took the last of the pictures down as the fire broke through the ceiling and parts of it rained down onto the stairs, setting the carpet alight. The kitchen was below the ground floor, made of stone. It wouldn't catch fire, but might fill with smoke. The two of them took the paintings down below, watching the door at the top of the kitchen stairs as they did. Soon smoke started to creep under it too as the rooms above them burst into flames. Crashing noises could be heard as roofing fell inwards. Gerald decided it was high time they closed themselves into the wine cellar. He told Joan to come with him.

"You go, I just want to get something from the fridge."

Gerald joined the paintings and the wine in the cold air of the wine cellar. There was a candle lit in an empty bottle, giving the place a medieval appearance. Joan followed him down, closed the iron door and put her goodies on the table next to the candle. There was a roast chicken, a salad and a bucket of ice.

"Fetch a bottle of champagne from the bin next to you. If we're going to be locked in we might as well enjoy ourselves."

"Can we breath down here? Shouldn't we blow out the candle to preserve the air? We could be here a long time."

"There's enough air for days, there are ventilation ducts to the surface too and enough drink for a year. Do you want me to go up and see if I can get some more food? There's no power, it'll only spoil up there."

"No, you stay here. When do we eat?"

"As soon as the champagne is cold. It's French Champagne, pre-war too. Grandpa was saving it for my wedding, but after all the paintings we saved he won't begrudge us a bottle."

After the meal, Gerald went to the door and looked out. The kitchen was full of smoke and there was a fire raging at the top of the stairs. He wet his shirt with claret and pushed it into the crack under the iron door. Then he rejoined Joan. She touched his bare chest and put her arms about him. The champagne had made her light-headed.

"Gerald, the candle will finish soon. We'd better make ourselves comfortable until help comes, or we can get out by ourselves."

He kissed her and she pressed her body to his. She wasn't wearing a brassiere. He put his hands under her blouse, taking her breasts into his hands, grimy with smoke, chicken and claret, and lifted the blouse over her head.

"Did I see you dragging a mattress down here?"

"Yes. It's only a single one, so we'll have to snuggle. The floor here is cold, even on a day like this."

"Is there anything that you didn't bring?"

Joan remembered the little ring of rubber which she took out when Gerald went to fight the fire, and the contraceptive cream. It was still in the bathroom, if there still was a bathroom, which wasn't the case. She told Gerald, "I'm willing to take a risk."

"Me too, Joan. I want to marry you as soon as you want."

"First things first. Let's make love before the house falls down. If we're going to die, let's go out with a bang."

She was undoing his belt.

"Seriously, Joan. On the way back, I thought that I'd never see you again. I thought I mightn't get through the fire. Again when I heard the fire in the roof I thought that we were for it. When I thought I might lose you, I knew that I needed you. It took a bloody bushfire to make me make up my mind. Joan, will you marry me?"

"Yes darling. Now come over to the mattress before the candle burns out. I don't want you breaking your neck now that we're finally getting engaged."

Three hours later, they were still in each others arms, lying on the mattress in the dark, when they heard noises in the kitchen above.

"Gerald, do you think the house is falling in?"

"No. The roof caved in when we were making love. You were coming when it happened, you probably didn't notice. It does sound like people up there. I'm going to get my pants on and take a look."

"The kitchen has an outside door. We might be able to get out now."

They crept up the steps to the door. It wasn't hot and when they opened it, there wasn't much smoke. Gerald called out into the kitchen.

"Anyone there?"

A man in a breathing apparatus came back in the kitchen door. He lifted his face mask and called out, "You people alright? Better come quickly. The building isn't safe."

They didn't wait to be asked twice, but ran through the kitchen out into the yard. Then they looked about them. The forest had been transformed into a cemetery of blackened tree trunks standing in a field of ashes. The garden trees were similar, some of them fallen and some still burning. The house was a collection of stone walls with fires burning where there had been rooms. In the driveway a red fire truck stood next to the burnt out shell of Gerald's Hillman. Gerald noticed that Joan had a bottle in her hand.

"What's that you're carrying, Joan?"

"Something cold for our rescuers, Gerald. Help me get the cork out. Come on guys, cold champagne. Sorry but we don't have any beer or any glasses. Come and have a drink, boys. We're having a celebration!"

Gerald popped the cork and they all swigged at the champagne. Fire fighting is thirsty work. Then they got into the fire truck and drove up to Marble Hill. The Governor's residence, like "Boronia", was a shell with a few small fires still burning inside, the blackened tower still standing in one corner. As they sat in the truck and watched, a sash cord must have fallen and with it, a blackened shattered window slowly opened.

"The Vice-Regal party were trapped over there in the garden. They got out about an hour ago. Before that, you couldn't move on these roads."

The firetruck dropped them off in Cherryville and went on its way. The orchards and fields all around were burnt, a number of houses too. Gerald stood looking down at a grey piece of metal, three foot square with a square hole in it, wondering what it was. Then he remembered. The public telephone had been here, bright red with a red roof and glass sides. All that remained was the concrete floor, the roof and blackened pieces of glass.

The gale force wind had dropped and was now variable, with puffs of cool southerly air from time to time. The sky was clearer, overcast with much less dust and smoke. It was getting cooler by the minute and a few drops of rain fell followed by a steady drizzle. They left the hills as darkness fell. All around, where the day before tall forests of eucalypts had stood, there were black tree trunks stripped of their foliage. Here and there they were still burning, hollow trees with sparks rising out of glowing interiors, like Roman candles.

They telephoned Joan's home as soon as they managed to get to a phone. Her parents were worried out of their mind; they knew that the house had been gutted, but in all the confusion, didn't know that the couple were safe. Joan told them how the house had burnt down and how they'd survived and that they'd rescued the paintings. Mr Meredith rang one of his workmen and told him to send a truck right away to salvage the paintings and the wine. Then he got in the Bentley and came down to pick them up.

When they got to the house in Glen Osmond Joan told him, "Daddy, Gerald's got something to ask you. Gerald, ask him."

She wasn't letting him off the hook.

"I want to marry Joan if that's alright by you, Mr Meredith."

"Alright? Of course it's alright. An hour ago Diana and I were preparing ourselves for a funeral, but we're getting a wedding instead."

"Sorry that I kept you waiting so long."

"Nothing to be sorry about, my boy. You've been busy with your studies. I understand that. Gerald, my boy, I want to replace the car that you lost in the fire."

"Thanks, Mr Meredith, but it was insured, so I really didn't lose anything."

Monday's papers were full of the fire. One of the most dramatic stories was that told by the Aide who was trapped with Governor and Lady George. He described how they were watching the smoke, when the fire roared up the hill and trapped them in the house. Then when the house caught fire, they had to flee with wet blankets over their heads and huddle against a low bank by the side of the road, while the fire raged all around them.

"South Australia is lucky to have its Governor today. We were nearly all incinerated."

The story of Gerald's dash through the flames to rescue Joan Meredith was also reported in the papers. They gave him full credit for the idea of hiding in the wine cellar, presenting him as a romantic hero going to the rescue of his love. It made a good story. Their engagement was announced in the article and the phone didn't stop ringing at the Meredith house all day. Joan also told her family that it was Gerald who suggested saving the paintings.

Those people who thought that Gerald was after Joan's money were now convinced of the depth of his love for her. His dash back to "Boronia" showed that.

Richard, who had also gone to help fight the fires, came to congratulate them the next day. They hadn't spoken for over a week.

"So you finally popped the question? What held you up?"

"It's strange, Richard, when you have something, or in this case somebody, you don't value her, you take her for granted. But when you are threatened with losing her, you suddenly begin to think. I have never been so scared, scared of losing my life and of losing Joan. Richard, first I thought that the fire would get Joan, then me, and then the both of us. It's a terrible feeling when you think that you're going to die. Funny, it takes a disaster to make you think straight. What say we go out together to celebrate? You got anyone that you want to bring?"

"I could find someone. Why not just the three of us?"

"As you wish."

"I don't feel like bringing along a stranger."

The exams had lead to a hiatus in Richard's love live.

"What have you been doing with yourself?"

"A bit of flying, a bit of business. I sold some land and bought some. Some of my land got burnt out yesterday, but don't worry, we were going to have it cleared anyway. It'll save us part of the cost. It might help us get some of the other land rezoned too. I'll save a choice plot for you and Joan. When are you two getting married?"

"Soon. Joan's father's keen on sending me to Boston to attend an executive training course. It's for a year. It's funny what snobs Australians can be. If you say you've just come back from the States, people think you know something and Meredith can give me a managerial job that he could never justify if I stayed here and really worked."

"So you're giving up science too?"

"No, I'm going to apply it in manufacturing. I might do a course in Food Science when Steven Meredith starts up. You've seen the Meredith Building on Frome Road? It should be finished some time this year."

Richard had seen the big "Meredith Building" sign next to the construction site. He didn't know that the family were putting it up for their son.

"The Food Science Department? Food is a science?"

"Richard, people might wear less or stop buying new cars when they're short of cash, but they always eat and drink. You ought to get into the food business. Are you still playing the stock market?"

"Only when I know I can make a quick buck. I'm sticking to real estate, land and bankrupt companies. What you said about the food trade makes sense. I wonder if there are any food companies for sale."

Richard was looking for something to invest in, something to diversify into and spread his risk.

"What about a job, Richard?"

Richard looked at him as if he'd given him bad beer.

"The stock market isn't that bad! I may return to uni next year to do an Economics or Commerce course."

"Do you need it?"

"I like being a student."

"Still trying to make the first million?"

"I'm only 21, Gerry. I'll make the million before I'm 25. It all depends on when the land I've bought is rezoned. It has to be, Adelaide is expanding and my land is right in the path. Then I'm going to move up into the Meredith league."

"So we'll be competitors, perhaps enemies?"

"No, just two sharks in an ocean full of fishes. There'll be plenty of fish for the both of us. When are we going flying again?"

"Not next week. I'm eating with my future in-laws. How about the Sunday after?"

"Good. I'll book an Auster. Bring your camera again. The last photos you took were great. This time we can look at the bushfire damage."

"They're starting a bushfire relief fund. Joan's father's on the committee. He's also giving a big donation to commemorate his daughter's rescue."

"And his acquisition of a son-in-law. To think that I'm racking my brain to make a million and you're getting it all on a silver salver."

"Richard, you know me. I come from a working class family. We never went hungry but I never had more than a few pence in my pocket. I've got a degree and a job and, thanks to you, almost £4,000 in the bank. That's a lot more than most couples have when they get married. I wouldn't mind a little more, but the wealth of the Merediths, shit, that's overwhelming."

"Don't look a gift horse in the mouth, especially when it comes with such lovely lips as Joan Meredith. Remember, they need you as much as you need them, more so. Old man Meredith needs a son-in-law to hand the business to and to carry on the dynasty."

"You make me feel like a prize bull."

"You'll be expected to produce quickly. Big brother Steven is a confirmed bachelor."

"Do you think he's funny or something?"

"No, just the opposite. He's the randiest ram there ever was, a regular Henry the Eighth. What with his cars and his mansion and his money, he gets more roots than you and I will ever get. Where is the shagger these days?"

"California."

"Adelaide wasn't big enough for him? He shagged all the local talent, now he's rooting his way though Hollywood?"

"You're talking about my future brother-in-law."

"Hasn't Joan told you about big brother?"

"She doesn't like talking about him."

"Well, if he wasn't a Meredith, he would have been kicked out of his job as a lecturer for immoral behaviour."

"Can't a staff member shag any woman he likes?"

Gerald didn't mean any woman, just any single, willing woman, over the age of consent.

"What about seducing students?"

"That's different. Has any girl complained?"

Richard had heard a few complaints, but then he met more women than Gerald, whose experience was limited to two.

"Girls don't brag about losing their cherry or being seduced, or about guys who make all kinds of promises in the night and forget them in the morning."

"I don't feel right about marrying into such a family."

"Gerry, you're marrying Joan. You won't have to sleep with Steven. You are the luckiest man in Adelaide. Do you know what my bank manager says about marriage? He says it's just like going to a bank. You put it in, make a little deposit, but when you take it out you lose interest."

Chapter Twenty-Seven
January 1955

Evelyn started working at the university on the tenth of January. The first thing that she noticed on her return from her holiday, was Louis's car in pieces in the garage.

"What happened to the car?" she asked his mother.

The moment that she asked the question she realised that something was wrong. Mrs Brown had tears in her eyes as she tried to explain.

"The police were here and they took the car away. They told Louis that he'd have to fix it and made him get it towed to a garage. The man at the garage thought that most of what they wanted fixed could wait a year or two, but if he wanted to drive that car he'd have to do it and prove to the police that it had been done. He wanted £90 for all the repairs. Evelyn, I haven't got that kind of money and Louis hasn't saved that much from his earnings. It meant that we'd have to carry out the repairs and sell the car, or scrap it. The car's only worth a hundred pounds. Louis decided to repair it himself. It'll cost about £30 to do it and I decided to split the cost with him. It isn't fair for the police to do this to him."

"Why are the police down on him?"

"I don't know what to say to you, Evelyn. I didn't want you to know."

"Why? Is it to do with other women? You know that I don't care what he does."

"It was a nurse from the hospital."

"Did he hurt her?"

"No, thank God, he didn't, but he did behave badly. I can't tell you how badly. The police came and took him away for hours. I thought that he was going to jail."

"Did they charge him?"

It wouldn't have surprised her if they had. She knew that Brown was capable of anything.

"No, the girl ran away before anything happened. What's the matter with Louis? He was such a nice boy."

"Mrs Brown, he's your son. I don't want to tell you bad things about him. You know that I don't like him any more. He preys on young women for his own selfish enjoyment. He's good at it, too damn good, and there's something in his nature that makes him hurt people. It frightens me. That's why I keep my door locked. I don't know what I'd do if you weren't here to protect me. I know I'd go."

"I won't be here much longer."

"I know. It worries me. Do you know the girl's name?"

"Robin Turner. She's a nurse."

"Not Robin! She was one of the nurses that cared for me after I had Jonny. She's a sweet girl."

It wasn't pleasant to know that he'd done something terrible, she didn't know what, to that girl.

"You know her?"

"Yes. I must go and see her."

"Why, Evelyn?"

"I don't know, Mrs Brown. I just feel that I must."

The following afternoon she took Jonny in the stroller and walked across the playing fields to the hospital. Robin was in her room. She came to the door.

"Robin Turner?"

"Yes?"

"I'm Evelyn Robertson. I'd like to talk to you. I brought my little boy. I hope you don't mind."

"I remember you! You had the first baby of 1954. This is little Jonny? Isn't he cute? Where did he get those hazel eyes? Tell me, why do want to see me?"

"Can I come inside?"

"Sure. Pull up an armchair."

"I heard about what happened to you. I'm sorry."

"You're sorry? Why should you be sorry? You aren't the bastard that tried to rape me."

She knew now. Just as she had dreaded.

"He tried to rape you?"

"I think so. Offered me a lift home and took me to a lonely place and went for me."

Evelyn was, and wasn't, shocked. She knew what some men were capable of doing. She'd often seen that look in Brown's eyes, that said, don't let me catch you with mother away and your door unlocked.

"I'm sorry."

"Mrs Robertson, why do you keep saying you're sorry? What is this to you?"

"I don't use my married name because I'm ashamed of the man I married. The man who tried to rape you is the man I married, Louis Brown."

"Oh."

Robin had been holding Jonny. She put him down in the stroller. She wasn't to know that this wasn't Brown's baby.

"That is, we went through a civil ceremony together. The truth is, I haven't had anything to do with him since the night that Jonny was conceived, two months before I had to marry him. Our marriage wasn't one of those made in heaven. It was arranged for Jonny's benefit. The only thing that keeps me in the house is his mother. She looks after us. Jonny's the only bit of happiness that Louis has brought her in recent years. She's terribly upset about what happened to you. Poor Louis is an outsider now, in his own home."

"Poor Louis? Poor me! He's a madman and should be locked up in Parkside. I think he'd have killed me if he'd caught me."

"I know how you feel. Only Mrs Brown stops him from hurting me. I want to see a solicitor next week. Will you tell him your story? It might help me in my divorce proceedings. He may have tried something with other nurses."

"Listen, Mrs Brown..."

Evelyn stopped her.

"Please don't call me that, call me Evelyn."

"Listen, Evelyn. Some people think that we nurses, because we see and treat people without their clothes, are easy going sexually, immoral perhaps. It just isn't so. We certainly have a better sex education than most girls, but we aren't any different. We're women like all other women. So some nurses sleep around, just like other women do, but most of us have steady relationships and want what most women want out of life, a proper respectable marriage. We don't like married men, cheating on their wives, pretending that they're single, or guys out for what they can get, or guys who ply you with alcohol so you don't know what you were doing the night before, guys like you know who."

"It's not only nurses that bastards like him prey on. I wasn't a nurse."

"When I was in first year in nursing school, one of the girls got pregnant. She said the guy loved her and wanted to marry her. He said that he wanted to have a doctor check her over, and before she realised what was going on the doctor had performed an abortion on her."

"That's criminal."

"She was too scared and ashamed to complain. Beside she was so upset that the guy had lied to her, that she locked herself in her room for days and we all had to comfort her. They didn't even ask her! Then he took her away for a few days and gave her £500 in cash, you might say for services rendered. That was the last she heard of him."

"£500! That's a lot of money. He must have been rich."

"Rich, I'll say. His father owns the brewery."

Evelyn said nothing. She paled as if she'd seen a ghost.

"What's the matter? I shouldn't have told you that story. I'm sorry."

"I'm just glad it wasn't me, that's all. I've heard many a story about Steven Meredith, but that beats them all."

"How do you know his name? I didn't mention it."

"Don't ask me. It had to be Steven Meredith. He's as low as his father's wealth is great. He and my boy's father are two of a kind. Sometimes I hate men."

"Some nights I can't sleep, thinking about what happened to me and what might have happened. I haven't been out with my boyfriend since that night."

Suddenly Evelyn remembered that she hadn't been with a man since the conception of her child. In her case it wasn't trauma, it was her situation that robbed her of the company of men. The company she wanted was engaged to Joan Meredith.

"Robin, I want your help. Do you think you could ask some of your friends if they know of others girls who might be prepared to testify against Louis?"

Evelyn went to the student advisory service and they found a young solicitor to advise her and help her get a divorce. She arranged for him to interview Robin. He listened to her story and then spoke to her.

"I can't use you, Robin, not as a main witness. I'm glad that he didn't hurt you, but although his intention was to be intimate by persuasion or by force, I'm glad to say that nothing occurred. You can't get a divorce on the grounds of intent. Had he been charged with attempted rape, that may have been relevant. As it is, no adultery was committed."

"Thank God," said Robin. This man's questioning was making her feel ill at ease.

"Evelyn, you'll have to provide evidence that your husband has been intimate with another party or was alone with her in a place such as his home, a bedroom or hotel room, or was seen in the act."

"Robin, do you know anyone else who could help us?"

"No, Evelyn. I know Louis was friendly with Yvonne, but she isn't prepared to testify against him. She doesn't want the publicity and she's scared that Louis might do something to her. To tell you the truth, I'm worried that he might still want to hurt me after what I did to him."

Robin left at this point, leaving a disappointed Evelyn with the solicitor.

"We'll have to get evidence against him, have him followed and catch him at it. That'll cost money."

"I haven't got much money. Besides, he can drive right up to the door to his room inside the yard. You won't be able to see who's coming and going. Or he goes parking in some lonely field. There's another complication. Louis's mother is dying and I don't want to hurt her. When she goes I'm moving out, but until then I don't want to do anything."

"How long is she expected to live?"

"About six months ago, I was told about a year."

"So, you'll wait?"

"Yes, I'll wait. I owe it to her."

"You'd better be careful. Don't give him grounds to divorce you."

"What do you take me for?"

"I'd be failing in my duty if I didn't warn you. He could then get married and ask for custody of the child."

"But it's my child, not his. I brought him into the world. I look after him. He never wanted me to have him in the first place."

"He's the legal father, whether he wanted him or not, he has rights. The law usually favours the mother unless she's declared unfit."

"Don't worry, that won't happen. I have a job and he hasn't. Thanks for the warning. I haven't any intention of committing what the law calls adultery, but now that I know that I could lose Jonny, I'll be purer than Caesar's wife. Jonny's the only man in my life for as long as necessary, maybe longer."

January was a bad month for fires in the Adelaide Hills. On the 10th, fires broke out again in the Morialta Falls Reserve and at Norton Summit. The fires were thought to have been deliberately lit. Again on the 15th the fire-fighters were out, this time on the Mt. Barker Road.

Across the world in Scotland, by contrast, heavy snow blanketed the country. Helicopters were used to rescue stranded people and drop food to isolated communities in the north west. People blamed the H-bomb for the vagaries in the weather.

On the 18th the USS Nautilus, the first submarine powered by a nuclear reactor, started its sea trials.

On the 26th Evelyn had a welcome visitor who called on her at work. She was busy reading by herself in the departmental library, when Richard entered and said, "Hello."

"Richard. What are you doing here?"

"I was in the area, so I called in."

"How did you know that I'd be here?"

"I asked. How are you?"

"I'm busy. I'm reading up on my research topic."

"You've got time to join me for lunch?"

"I was going home. Mrs Brown's expecting me."

"Ring her. Tell her that you're eating in town."

"Richard, what do you want?"

He sat down opposite her. She was pleased to see him. He could see it in her smile.

"We're old friends, Evelyn. I know how things are with you. I meant to contact you for Jonny's birthday, but it was such an inconvenient day."

"No one sent you to see me?"

That was a strange thing to say. Evelyn didn't know why she said it. Neither did Richard. Did she know that Gerald was engaged to Joan? Surely she must have read the bushfire rescue story in the paper.

"No. My other friends have their own life to live now."

"I know, I read the papers. They're lucky to be alive. I guess that I'll see them at graduation."

"No, you won't. They're going to Boston in March. Are you going to have lunch with me?"

"Alright. I'll ring home and then get changed. I'll meet you at the front steps in five minutes."

They walked across the path to the Refectory.

"Let's eat here, it's almost empty at this time of the year and we can talk. Tell me, Evelyn, how long are you going to keep up this farce of a marriage? You know that man tried to rape a nurse last month?"

"I know. I've been to see her. Richard, I've been to a solicitor. We're working on it. I don't want to do anything positive while his mother is dying."

"That's a strange way of organising one's life. You could be stuck with him for years."

"I wish it wasn't so, but it'll be about a year. When my own father deserted me, she and only she came to my help. How do you think I was able to complete my degree and survive? Without her I'd be an unmarried mother working in a cannery, with all the noses of my home town turned up at me, and my sanctimonious father chiding me daily for my sins."

"How is your reverend father?"

"He's not a reverend. He's deeply religious, that's all. I just didn't measure up to his ideals. He contributed to the mess that I got myself into, but I still respect his beliefs. I wish that I had his religion sometimes."

"You don't go out much, do you?"

"No, now that Mrs Brown is in such bad health, I don't go out with her, except for short afternoon walks. I haven't been out at all since I came back from Renmark."

"Perhaps we could go out together."

Richard felt close to Evelyn, closer than he'd been with any woman, and he'd been as close as a man can be to several. But with Evelyn he could speak his mind, she was a friend like Gerald. But unlike Gerald, she was young, attractive and a woman. What a pity she wasn't available.

"What do you want from me, Richard? I'm a..."

"Don't say happily married woman, or even married. Those two words don't apply."

"So why are you asking me out? You know I can't afford to get involved."

"Can't two good friends go out together?"

"No, not when one of them is trying to get a divorce."

"Evelyn, I know your situation. I'm not stupid. I don't want to have an affair, not that there's anything wrong with you."

He wasn't being completely honest, not to her and not to himself. Deep down, Richard would have loved to have an affair with Evelyn, not a sordid affair, but a proper love affair, if that was what she wanted.

"There is something wrong with me, Richard. I'm married to a first class bastard who hates me and hates you too. He only seduced me out of spite, to hurt Gerald. Do you know that he tried it first by getting me drunk? I sicked up all over him. He denied it and I like a fool took his side."

"We warned you to keep away from him."

"Yes, you were right and I was stupid. I don't blame Gerald for hating me for what I did."

"He didn't hate you. He was upset. He blamed himself, he said a few things he didn't mean, but he didn't hate you, not even when you returned his letter unopened, not even when you..."

Richard saw her react to his words. What had he said to shock her?

"What did you say?" she asked.

"When you returned his letter unopened. I was with him at Woodside. What's the matter? Have you seen a ghost?"

"I have, Richard, I have. I waited day after day for a letter. You don't know how I waited."

"You don't know what it did to him, Evelyn."

"What it did to *me*, not to receive it. That was Dad, dear, church-going, Christian, Dad. He drove Gerald away. Thank you, Dad. Did God tell you to do that? Did God tell you to wreck my life?"

Evelyn was upset. Her life had been messed up by one vicious interfering act, perpetrated by her father. She sat silently for a minute before continuing,

"I don't want you to tell Gerald about this. I don't want to wreck his life, Richard."

"That's up to you. It's not too late, he's not married."

"But I am. Richard, I've hurt him enough. Let's let sleeping dogs lie."

"I'll go along with that."

Richard wasn't happy. They ought to tell Gerald, let him talk to Evelyn, let him make up his mind who he wanted to live with for the rest of his life. But Gerald had taken his time and Richard knew that he was in love with Joan. Evelyn had missed the boat, and all because her father had sent back a letter, the interfering old bastard. He changed the subject. "You haven't answered me. Can we take in a show or two?"

"First, tell me what your motives are."

"Alright. In the first place, I feel sorry for you and think you deserve a bit better. I also think that you're good company. That's all."

"Nothing more, no other motive? Richard, I can't refuse your offer. I need a friend more than ever now with Mrs Brown dying. As for romance, I don't think it could ever be, now or in the future. Gerald would always be there. When I'm free of that bastard I married, I want to get away from here and all the old memories. I might go to Melbourne. Adelaide is too full of memories, some happy, some terrifying. I don't want to be in the same city as Jonny's father. How come you haven't got a girlfriend of your own?"

"It's quite simple. My best friend took the pick of the crop. Evelyn, don't worry about me. I'll settle down with the right girl at the right time."

"What are you doing? Do you have a job?"

They had been out of touch for a long time.

"A job! Not me, I'm a capitalist. I do a little flying and have my business interests. Last Spring I took a few days off from studying and flew up to the Flinders Ranges. I intend to study again this year. I like being a student."

"Do you still play the stock markets?"

"Sometimes, when I hear of a way to make a quick profit and get out. I'll let you know next time I have a good tip, you and your mother-in-law."

"Leave her out of this, she's a sick woman and she hasn't got money to lose."

"I don't lose. What about your parents?"

"If you mean Father, he doesn't speculate. Gambling's a sin, like swearing, drinking, or having babies and boyfriends. He's never had a ticket on the Melbourne Cup."

"He'd better be careful. They might call him up before the *UnAustralian Activities Commission*."

Richard had never met the man, but he knew all about him. A good man, but a bugger to have for a father.

"What are you going to study this year, Chemistry?"

"No, I've finished with Chemistry. There's no money in it. My only regret is that I didn't study Geology. There's money in minerals. Evelyn, don't tell anyone, but in the last few years I've made more money speculating than most scientists make in a lifetime, tax free too."

"But you could have lost it all, couldn't you?"

"Speculating wasn't the right word. I only invested in sure things. There are rules that a speculator has to follow, only bet on a certainty, play big, and don't bet on horses."

"I'll pass the word on to Father, about the horses."

"I told you, I don't gamble. I do it scientifically. I research and I invest. I had to learn how and where. You don't find that information in the Barr Smith. I have a group of friends and we share information and we all do quite well. Most of them are small fish. I've outgrown them. I do better because I work harder and take time looking for profitable investments. Evelyn, I know things are hard with you. If you need money, don't hesitate to ask."

"Richard, I may be poor but I'm not a charity case."

"Who mentioned charity? I'll lend you the money. You, my dear, are a damn good risk. Who else would have had the baby and got a degree and a job?"

Hearing Richard talk made Evelyn feel good, better than she'd felt in a long time. He was a smooth talker, but unlike the man who she married, his words came from the heart and she knew it. Here was one man she could trust. She felt close and safe with Richard. Why hadn't *he* seduced her and not that Brown bastard? He hadn't because he was a man of honour and loved her as a friend, as his best friend's friend, a woman to protect from the Browns and Merediths of this world. It was good to have him back, to sit and talk with him. It restored her opinion of the opposite sex.

"You sound like my professor," she said, "the day he offered me the job. I wanted to kiss him that day, he was so nice. Richard, you don't know how good it is to be working and not a student any more. They're all so nice to me in the department. That reminds me, I'd better be getting back to work. By the way, have you heard the news today?"

"No, what happened?"

"Professor Mitchell's yacht sank off Kangaroo Island."

"The Grelka? Serve him right for writing that boring practical book of his. Was he hurt?"

"No, he wasn't on it, only the technical staff of the department. The engine exploded, setting the yacht alight, and they had to get into the dinghy. They had about four inches of boat above the water and an 18ft. shark alongside. The dinghy itself was only 10 foot long. When the outboard motor failed, they threw it at the shark. They finally rowed to the island. A Navy survey ship saw the burning yacht and found them, otherwise they'd have spent the night on the rocks. It's all in the *Advertiser*."

"Lucky bastards! There was a boy killed in Sydney Harbour by a shark last week."

"This shark was a huge white-pointer. Lucky it was calm and the shark didn't overturn the boat, otherwise the Biochem Department would be looking for fresh technical staff."

That afternoon Evelyn thought about Louis and about the technical staff. He needed a job and he wanted to try and complete his degree. He was good with his hands, she had seen for herself how he built the room and repaired the car. Why didn't he do that kind of work and forget the degree? If he had to keep trying, why not get a technical job on the campus? He could get time off for lectures. She told this to Mrs Brown and went to the University Employment Office to see what was offering. They tried to employ students who were poor, even poor students like Louis Brown.

There were jobs in the fitting out of the Meredith Building and later there would be jobs for technicians. Evelyn took down the details and told Mrs Brown, who told her son. She couldn't tell him directly, but he was pleased to hear that it was Evelyn who had made the inquiries. It meant that she did think of him sometimes. He had thought that she'd be glad to see him leave the university and look for an outside job. He applied for and got a job working as a handyman, enabling him to enrol for two of the three subjects that he needed to complete his degree. As he'd done the practical classes, he was exempted from these and only had to attend lectures and the exams.

February was a wet month in Australia, unusually wet. On February 9th, Adelaide was drenched with two inches of unseasonal rain, flooding the beach suburbs. On the 28th, New South Wales was deluged, with heavy loss of life. 50,000 people were evacuated as the town of Maitland on the Hunter River was inundated. The town centre had to be relocated. There was also flooding in the Darling River System, which fed into the Murray River.

March wasn't any better. There were flood rains in the Centre. Two people died when they were swept away with their jeep in the middle of the usually dry Todd River in Alice Springs. Two days later a tropical cyclone hit Central Queensland. The month ended with another deluge, flooding the Brisbane River and low lying parts of the city.

The international scene was just as stormy. In the Gaza Strip, 37 Egyptian soldiers were killed in a clash with Israel, with both sides blaming the other. The Baghdad pact was signed, uniting Britain, USA, Turkey and Iraq against Soviet expansion. Later Iran and Pakistan joined them.

Churchill again warned of the danger of the H-Bomb, "Global War Would Mean Global Annihilation", he said as part of his "defence by deterrence" policy speech.

There were rumours in the British press that Princess Margaret was planning to marry a divorcee, Captain Peter Townsend, and comments from the church to the effect that if she did, she would have to renounce her claim to the monarchy in the unlikely event that this should fall to her.

In Canberra Dr Evatt attacked the Santa Maria Movement inside the Australian Labor Party, accusing them of McCarthyism, which he said would only help Communism instead of defeating it. The movement was expelled from the Victorian branch, forming a breakaway party, the Democratic Labor Party, a split which was soon to spread and keep the Federal Labor Party out of office for another 17 years.

Australian troops were sent to Malaya to help in the fight against Communist insurgents. Recent trainees like Gerald and Richard had a worrying time, until it was stated that no National Servicemen would be sent. That doubtful honour was left to the next generation, and Viet Nam.

In Saigon, Communist-free Saigon, three South Vietnamese militias fought for control of the city. The former rulers of Indochina, the French, looked on saying that this was a purely internal affair. Most Australians didn't know where Saigon or Viet Nam was and didn't care.

On April 6th, Winston Churchill resigned his position as Prime Minister of Great Britain and was succeeded by Sir Anthony Eden.

Evelyn accepted Richard's idea to go out together, but only in the company of other friends, in order to protect herself from any action if Louis decided to sue for divorce. He didn't call for her at the Brown house or drop her off. He asked friends to do this or sent her home in a taxi.

One celebration that Richard did not attend with Evelyn was the wedding of the season, Gerald and Joan's wedding at which he was best man. The day after the wedding, the newlyweds flew to Sydney, then by Constellation to London for ten chilly days and on to New York. By the end of March they were settled into an apartment in Boston and Gerald started his course in business management for science graduates. Joan learned to play golf.

That year the Science Association organised a Graduation Ball on Commemoration Day, March the 30th. Richard arranged a party of friends and included Evelyn in the party. The day before he told her, "Before the degree ceremony there's another commemoration that I want to do and I'd like you to join me."

"Tell me what it is."

"Today is three years to the day that Jonny Marco died. I think that in our hour of glory we should remember him."

"What do you suggest? Float a wreath under the bridge?"

"No, I would like to place one at the graveside."

They arrived at one o'clock and quickly found the grave with the stone bearing his name. There were fresh flowers that his parents had put there earlier in the day. Richard placed a wreath and Evelyn a bouquet of roses. Then they stood in silent prayer before driving back to the university.

"You know, Richard, I remembered Jonny in my own way. I named my son after him, Jonny Mark. I did it to keep that bastard away from my son. I somehow imagine that the spirit of Jonny will protect his namesake from that man."

"That's a smack in the eye for Brown. I still think he was involved in Jonny's death, Evelyn."

"Don't I know it! Why do I live behind locked doors?"

"But surely, as his father he must want to play with him, like any father?"

"No, as far as I know he's never touched him or picked him up, or so much as looked in his pram. He hates me and he hates my boy too."

"It isn't natural."

"I don't blame him. Jonny's cost him a lot, his freedom to some extent, his mother's love and most of his mother's money that should have gone to him. His allowance has been cut and he can't afford to change his car. Jonny and I have been living off his inheritance. But it's a drop in the ocean to what he's cost me, Richard."

"Why doesn't he find a job?"

"He has. He's working in the new building on Frome Road as well as repeating a couple of subjects."

The grave-yard was empty, they had the hillside to themselves. It would have been so easy to embrace, to kiss and become lovers. No one would have known, and they did have strong mutual feelings, love for one another. But people were waiting for them back at the university. There were degrees to be conferred on them. This was a great day for Evelyn, a great day for the two of them.

They met Mrs Brown by the Hall together with Evelyn's parents, both of them. Mrs Robertson didn't get her own way very often, but she did insist on her husband accompanying her down to Adelaide to see their daughter graduate and receive a University Medal. In a way she was rubbing his nose in it. He wouldn't admit it to a living soul, or to the Almighty, but he was proud of his girl, his stubborn Evelyn.

The new graduates wandered around the vicinity of the Bonython Hall in black gowns and hoods trimmed with their faculty colour, gold for science, white for arts and so forth. The PhD's had a second hood, trimmed with red and the staff wore their graduation hoods and gowns as well, the majority from foreign universities.

Richard returned Evelyn to her parents and then came back with a press photographer.

"What are you doing, Richard?"

"You're news, whether you like it or not. A young mother graduating and getting a medal as well."

"You called the press over?"

"Yes, I too know who's who in this town. With no Meredith to photograph they have to take pictures of we plebeians. Go and get little Jonny from Mrs Brown and smile for the camera."

The photographer took a series of pictures of Evelyn with her parents and with Jonny. Mrs Brown was left out. She was rather tired and sat on a nearby bench, enjoying the joyful atmosphere. She thought of how her husband had graduated such a long time ago, and how she'd hoped that her son would also do so. If he did it would be too late for her to attend. During the degree ceremony she sat outside with Jonny, and Richard drove all of them home soon afterwards as she was very tired. It would be one of her last outings.

Meanwhile Evelyn was angry with Richard.

"You shouldn't have called the photographer over. You embarrassed me. I'm here with no husband and everyone knows that Jonny was born early, a mistake, the reason I had to get married. Do you think that I like having my nose rubbed in it in the newspapers?"

"On the contrary, Evelyn. You're standing up for all womanhood, for the rights of women. You, Evelyn, are a heroine. Emmeline Pankhurst should be here today. Hold your head up, Evelyn Robertson. You have nothing to be ashamed of."

It was good to hear his words; Richard knew how to turn a girl's head. If he'd proposed to her after uttering this last compliment, Evelyn would have accepted him.

She saw her parents off home on the train and returned to get ready for the ball. Her mother had made her a new dress, which she wore to the graduation and to the ball. Not one person asked about Louis. It was marvellous. They went to a party after the ball and Evelyn wasn't home until after two. Mrs Brown wasn't asleep. She suffered from insomnia brought on by the poisons accumulating in her body. Evelyn told her about the evening, making sure that she realised that she'd gone out in a party and not as someone's partner which wasn't strictly correct. If Richard hadn't invited her she wouldn't have gone. Then she locked herself in her room with Jonny. She gave him a gentle kiss, making sure she didn't wake him. As she undressed, Evelyn cried a little, only this time it was tears of joy.

Two years to the day, two years after Brown had almost got her expelled, she had her degree and a companion. She was alive again.

In the morning Mrs Brown showed her the *Advertiser* with the picture on page one, of Evelyn, her parents and her son, Jonny Mark. Richard brought her a set of glossy pictures a week later, with a second set for her parents in Renmark and kept one picture for himself. He had enjoyed the ball, and the day spent with Evelyn.

Chapter Twenty-Eight

April 1955

1953 had been a bad year for Evelyn, the worst year of her life. She'd spent the second half of it trying to hide her growing tummy, ashamed of it, wondering if it would all be worthwhile. In 1954 when she had her son she knew that it was, but it had also been a busy year and a tiring one. She'd breastfed Jonny for six months and between attending to his needs and studying, she had had no time for student activities. Now as a graduate she had a little more time. Richard, who had lots of time, helped her make new friends and renew old friendships. He also kept his word. He didn't bring about any situation that might tempt or compromise her.

It was difficult. Evelyn was as attractive as ever and it would have been so easy to start something. He sometimes thought of taking her to some place where they could be alone together and no one could spy on them, but he knew that once he did this there would be no going back and it would only lead to difficulties. It wasn't worth ruining such a close friendship. Richard knew that, lonely as she was, Evelyn didn't want a clandestine relationship and he respected her wishes, knowing that she was right. That didn't make it easier, there were occasions when both of them had doubts about this.

Evelyn drove all thoughts of love and love-making out of her mind, which wasn't easy. She was as vulnerable now as she'd ever been. She showered Jonny with all the love and affection that she felt for Richard. She had a child to love and only her sick mother-in-law to look after him. She was also trying to get free of her husband. Jonny was now a handful and it took all of Mrs Brown's meagre strength to manage him while Evelyn was at work. Without Jonny to keep her busy Mrs Brown would have stayed in bed all day and slowly died.

On April 7, Richard, Evelyn and friends went to see the Ice Frolics. It wasn't the skating that interested Richard, it was the presence on stage of Graeme Bell's Dixie Band. Having heard them on the radio and on record, Richard had to see them in the flesh.

On the 24th of April, 29 African and Asian countries met in conference in Bandung, Indonesia. They represented a nucleus of nations dissatisfied with the lack of consultation in world affairs, particularly by the Western nations.

Richard received a letter from Gerald written in London, and another from New York describing his first few days in that city. Early in May he opened another letter, this time written by Joan. It was a cheerful letter, he could tell that she was very happy.

Boston, 25th April, 1955.

Dear Richard,

Happy Anzac Day. Gerald asked me to reply to your last letter as I was bored and he has to study. It's cold here and we have the central heating on. There was snow in London and snow here when we arrived. It's melted down town, but there's still plenty in the hills. At first we thought it was wonderful, but you soon get sick of it. I was going to play golf today and wouldn't you know it, it's raining cats and dogs.

Most weekends we go down to New York. Dad has an apartment overlooking Central Park and we have it whenever we want. I go down on Thursdays to look around the stores and Gerald takes a train after lectures on Friday. Tell me, Richard, do all men hate shopping? I found this downtown record store and I bought a stack of records. All the latest rock and roll. I bought you a few jazz records and some for Gerald's father too. Have you heard of Dave Brubeck? He's all the rage on the West Coast.

I intend to see at least a show a week while I'm here. We saw Tennessee Williams' "Cat on a Hot Tin Roof" with Burl Ives in it. Remember his recording of "The Foggy Foggy Dew" was banned in Australia? We also saw Harry Belefonte in a revue. He was that sexy singer in "Carmen Jones". I bought a copy of the film. I bought a movie camera and projector. I want it for when we have kids.

Talking about sexy actors, have you seen James Dean in "East Of Eden"? His eyes do things to me. The chicks here are mad about him. Burl Ives is in the picture too. Next time I'm in New York I'm going to buy some of his records. He's got the cutest beard, hasn't he? The other big movie here is "Blackboard Jungle", all about violence in school.

You wouldn't believe the things people say about the blacks here, and the racial discrimination. It's as bad as South Africa. There are parts of Boston and New York that white people don't visit and towns on the South that have "whites only" cafés and buses. My golf club doesn't admit Jews, let alone niggers. Gerald wants me to find another place that's less snobby, but I don't see why. He doesn't ever go there. We Aussies are lucky we have the White Australia Policy. It saves us a lot of trouble.

Shopping here is something unbelievable. I bought Gerald a new rifle, over the counter, like a bottle of beer. I spend hours in the supermarket. Do you know they have cake mixes? I made a Betty Crocker cake last week and Gerald ate it. I want Dad to make them. Then they have frozen vegetables, and frozen meals too. Anyone can be a cook here. We eat out a lot. So far we haven't been to the same place twice. These Americans eat like civilised people. You can get wine or a beer with your meals. They have beer in cans!

We have Television. It keeps me busy when Gerald's studying. We've seen Nat King Cole and Erroll Garner on it. He's a favourite of yours isn't he? I love his "Misty". Gerald thinks he's the cat's pyjamas. Also Count Basie and his band. I booked a table to see them at Birdland next weekend. When are you getting Television in Adelaide? I want to bring a set back when we come next year. My parents are buying us tickets for the Melbourne Olympics. Do you want to join us? Mum's coming in June to see me. I knew she couldn't stay away. I'll send you a copy of Playboy with Mom. I hope the customs don't find it, or Mom for that matter. I'm not going to tell her. I'll just hide it in with all the records.

You heard about Einstein dying last week. Funny thing, no one understands what he did, but he was mourned like a head of state. He must have felt terrible seeing atom bombs destroying cities, based on his relativity work, and now the Hydrogen bomb. They're all building fallout shelters here.

They are planning to inoculate millions of children in America against Infantile Paralysis, and then almost the entire population with the new Salk vaccine. Remember Bill Gordon, the guy who got it in first year? My children will be luckier with this new vaccine. They're also developing a new contraceptive pill, not that I'd use it now that I'm married. It's going to make a difference to us women.

How's your love life? Getting any? Who did you take to the Graduation Ball? Anyone I know? Why don't you take a trip when it's summertime here and visit us? We want to go to the Newport Jazz Festival in June, and drive up to Canada and across to Niagara Falls in July. Do you remember that film with Marilyn Monroe?

Gerald sends his love. I'm dragging him out tonight to see "Guys And Dolls". I just hope that the bloody rain stops.
Yours truly,
Joan Fisher.

Rugby season started in Autumn. Louis Brown turned up for practice and for the first Saturday game against Woodville, a good hard opening game to the season. He had no idea what was in store for him.

At the kick-off, the big lock-forward caught the ball. As the Woodville forwards charged up the field, all big men, men as big as Brown, the lock handed it to Louis, catching him flat footed. Before he knew where he was, three men tackled him, two high, one around the hips. They hit him with all their might, smashing him to the ground. In the ensuing ruck, nobody kicked at the ball. While the backs prevented the man in white seeing what was happening, a dozen men put their boots into the man on the ground, as the ball lay loose in the melée. He was kicked and mauled in the face, the ears, all the way down the body. Spectators called for the game to be stopped. Finally the whistle was blown. The two sets of forwards stood back and the St. John's man raced onto the field. Brown was a mess of blood and torn flesh.

He was placed on a stretcher and carried off the field. The Woodville captain leaned down to speak to him. It seemed like a nice gesture.

"Can you hear me, Brown? You go near my Robin or any other of the nurses again, and we won't wait four months to get you. This is nothing to what we'll do next time."

They put on a substitute and went on with the game. Brown went to Royal Adelaide where they were expecting him in Casualty, with their iodine, blunt needles and surgical thread. He never went to Rugby practice again.

In a macabre incident in May, Karen rebels north of Rangoon, invited local Burmese Communists to a friendly soccer match, then massacred the entire team.

June came in with a series of cold winter storms and there were floods all over the state. In the shelter of the Town Hall, a lady of great talent, insight and humour took the stage, Anna Russell.

June 9th. Don Dunstan was guest speaker at the University Labor Club. The same night the University Film Society screened Griffith's classic film, *Birth Of A Nation*.

Mrs Brown constantly listened to the radio, her favourite program being a BBC comedy-drama *A Life Of Bliss*, in which young Mr Bliss was always getting tongue-tied and constantly in trouble with his girl-friends and his boss. She also never missed the midday out-back serial, *Blue Hills*, on the ABC, or the two big quiz shows with Bob Dyer and Jack Davey on the commercial networks. During the day, when there was nothing better to tune in to, she listened to Parliamentary Proceedings from Canberra. On June 11th she called out to Evelyn, who had returned from work. "Come quickly, there's a big fuss in Canberra. I've never heard the likes of it."

It appeared that certain Sydney businessmen were trying to blackmail and bribe a local Member of Parliament. One of them, known as Mr Big, had published a series of libellous articles about MPs in a local paper. This was brought to the attention of the party leaders, the two men were arrested and brought to face charges before the House of Representatives. With speed unknown in the Capital city, they were tried and convicted of "Contempt of Parliament" by a vote of four to one. Such speed and consensus were known only for the granting of Parliamentary pay rises.

Before sentencing the miscreants, they were allowed to speak on their own behalf. Mr Big mumbled an apology and grovelled an inaudible plea for mercy. His co-conspirator gave a speech like that of Mark Antony, after the death of Julius Caesar. For 15 minutes he told his accusers, the assembled politicians and the radio audience what he thought of the Parliament and their processes of justice. He accused Prime Minister Menzies of organising a "Kangaroo Court" and a personal vendetta against him. In the end both men were sent to jail for three months in the first and only time that Parliament acted as a court of law, accusing, trying and sentencing the two men in a couple of hours.

The following day, June 12th, was a black day in the history of motor racing. During the 24 hour endurance race at Le Mans, a Mercedes exploded after being in collision with a smaller Austin Healey. The wreckage of the Mercedes ploughed into the crowd, killing 84 people, with others severely injured in the crash. Mercedes withdrew from the race and subsequent Le Mans races.

Australia's Wimbledon hopes for 1955, Lew Hoad and Joan Staley wed on the 19th. Joan went back to Australia and Lew Hoad didn't win Wimbledon until the following year. That prize went to Tony Trabert of the United States.

The "Big Four", Eden, Faure, Bulganin and Eisenhower met in Geneva from the 17th to the 24th. At the end of their meeting it was announced that complete agreement had been reached about future steps to ease world tension. The first day of the conference saw the release, in Budapest, of Cardinal Minszenty who had been sentenced to life imprisonment in 1949. The months and years following the Geneva conference saw increased tension, increased spending on arms and newer techniques for global warfare.

Meanwhile a declaration was published urging nations to renounce war and the use of nuclear weapons. Organised by Bertrand Russell, it had been signed by eminent scientists, including the late Albert Einstein.

On the 18th, Disneyland was opened at Anaheim, 22 mile from Los Angeles. Theatregoers walked out of the London premier of Samuel Becket's play *Waiting For Godot*.

August 5th was the annual procession and rag day at the university. In addition to the procession and the collection for charity, the students arranged a 'Big Four Meeting' in the entrance to one of the bank buildings in King William St. As hundreds of students and people attracted by the crowd looked on, carloads of delegates arrived, the 'Americans' and 'Russians' in big cars with security men in trench coats, the 'English' in a Morris Minor and the 'French' on bicycles. At the end of the meeting, they issued a statement of optimism to the press, posed for photographers and departed with each other's wives.

At the annual flour bomb fight, the student pharmacists laced their bags of flour with powdered dyes so that when their opponents went to shower the powder dissolved, staining the showerers with malachite green, gentian violet, or mercurochrome red, colours which remained for several days.

The only thing keeping Mrs Brown alive with her failing kidneys was her love for her grandson, Jonny, and her efforts to look after him and let Evelyn continue in her job. But love cannot keep a person alive and working in the face of such an illness. Mrs Brown went to the hospital in mid August and returned in an ambulance, as ill as when she went there. Evelyn stopped working, to be a full time nurse and mother.

When Richard heard the news he came to her aid by finding volunteer nursing aid and student baby sitters, so that she did manage to work some days in August. He warned them to stay away from Brown. Louis sat with his mother afternoons and sometimes on the weekend, but flatly refused to do so of an evening as he didn't want Evelyn to have the evenings free. He had noticed that she was going out now. He didn't know who she was seeing, but he wasn't pleased. He still regarded her as his property, property that his mother was preventing him from having, property that would soon be his again. He knew his mother's days were numbered.

Richard paid most of the 'volunteers' and baby-sitters out of his own pocket without telling Evelyn. If she'd known she mightn't have accepted this help.

Friday and Saturday, August 12-13th, the university held a Conversazione, an open day when the public was invited to see what went on in those red brick buildings down by the Torrens. All departments put on displays, trying to explain the research work being carried out and collect funds for the Union Building Appeal to enlarge the Union buildings and build a theatre. The most popular exhibit was 'Ivan The Terrible', a machine that looked like a candelabra, set up to smoke ten cigarettes at a time in the Organic Chemistry Department. This was part of Professor Badger's demonstration explaining the work he was doing, and world-wide research into the connection between smoking and lung cancer.

Evelyn had to withdraw from her part in the Conversazione because of Mrs Brown's illness.

At the end of August the scientific community in Australia converged on Melbourne for the annual meeting of the Australian and New Zealand Association for the Advancement of Science. The needs of her child and her dying mother-in-law came first and Evelyn was also unable to go to Melbourne for this meeting.

After returning from the hospital, Mrs Brown did not leave her house except to sit in the garden for short spells on the few sunny days left to her. She couldn't sleep and was very weak. She was as thin as a Belsen Camp inmate from not eating. When Evelyn did manage to get a spoonful of food into her, she as often as not brought it up. Her skin was grey and her breath vile. Her room smelt of ammonia. A month after her return from the hospital, she was unable to get out of bed, complaining of failing vision and then complete loss of her sight. Two days later she drifted into a coma. Evelyn called the doctor and when he came, they called Louis in to hear what he had to say.

"Your mother's got only hours to live, Louis, a day at the most. I could have her removed to hospital, but it won't change the outcome. There's no treatment for kidney failure."

Louis said nothing.

"Call me when it's over," he told them.

Evelyn showed the doctor out and then went to her room. She quietly turned the key to lock the bedroom door, then packed the last few things in the suitcases that she'd started to pack a few days earlier. She was reliving the exodus from her parents' home, the difference being that this time she was running away from the man she ran away with that fateful, hateful night. She put Jonny in the stroller and, leaving Louis sitting by his unconscious mother, went for a walk. She found a phone and called Richard. She'd told him what was about to happen and how she needed him to help her.

"Richard, this is Evelyn. I'm packed and ready to go."

"Fine, I've got a room for you with a young couple in Unley. They're old friends of mine; well, she used to be. I only met Bruce at the wedding and again when they had the baby. You'll like them, they're both nice people. They could do with the rent money and they have a spare room. It isn't close to uni but it's away from Brown which is what you want, isn't it? Dawn has a little girl Jonny's age."

"Richard, I hope you aren't going into match-making."

"No, but you'll be able to pay her to look after Jonny and go to work. I told her that you'll baby-sit for her from time to time too. She warmed up to the idea."

"Richard, I could kiss you."

"So, when do you move out?"

"I wanted to wait until Mrs Brown dies but I'm scared to be alone in the house with Louis. I want to go right away."

"I'll send a taxi for you, one with a driver bigger than Brown. Then we can go right over to Dawn's place. I'll call her before I order the taxi. Where are you calling from?"

"A phone box round the corner from the house. I'm packed and ready to go. I'll wait for the taxi in the front garden and then I'll tell Louis. And then I'll run for my life. He's not going to like my leaving any more than he welcomed my coming in the first place."

When the taxi came, Evelyn put her bags in it and told the driver to mind Jonny while she went in to say good-bye. She found Louis where she'd left him, still sitting in an arm chair beside his mother, who was quite still save for the faintest breathing, in a deep predeath sleep.

Evelyn spoke to him from the door.

"Louis, I'm going. I'm moving out."

"Why are you going?"

He looked at her with a lost expression on his face. For the first time she noticed the scars on his face, results of the mauling he'd suffered on the rugby field.

"Louis, I looked after Mom as long as I could. I can't do anything for her. I have nothing to do here anymore."

"My mother's dying. I need you. I want you to stay."

"You'll be alright. If you don't want to be alone call someone to keep you company."

"What's the matter with you? Are you afraid I'll hurt you or something? Where are you going?"

"I'll call you later."

"Go and piss off. Good riddance to you. Just like a rat, leaving a sinking ship."

Evelyn was out of the room and the house before he'd finished his last words. Louis didn't need her, he was himself again. Half an hour later Richard took her to the house of his friends, Dawn and Bruce Grover, to an old house with a stone front, brick walls and a large veranda, with lawns front and back. Dawn showed her her room and letting the two children play on the carpet, they sat down to get acquainted over a cup of tea.

That afternoon she rang the doctor and told him where she was staying, asking him to notify her when he found out about Mrs Brown's death.

She asked him not to tell anyone where she'd taken refuge.

Three days later she stood by the graveside with Louis on the opposite side, the last time that Mrs Brown would be there between them. She spoke to him, telling him of her sorrow at his mother's death, but he didn't answer. At this stage he didn't know the content of his mother's will, that left him the house, but most of her money to her grandson, or the child she thought was her grandson. Had he known, God only knows what he would have done to his run-away wife when he saw her at the funeral.

Jonny was at home with Dawn, so after the funeral Evelyn went back to the university to work.

The arrangement with the Grovers worked well. Richard was able to call and talk with Evelyn in the living room or out in the garden, sometimes playing with Jonny whom he really liked. He was beginning to speak and called Richard "unka ichard", sounding like one of Donald Duck's nephews, when he said it. At the Browns', Richard had never set foot in the street let alone the garden or house, but here he could come and go and it was all perfectly respectable. Shortly after the move, he brought up his favourite topic.

"Evelyn, you're still married to that man. What are you doing about a divorce?"

"It takes time, Richard. Louis won't agree to give me grounds. I left him, not the other way around. If we go before a judge, he'll say that he wants me to come back. It could take years."

"What happens if you meet someone in the meantime and you want to get married?"

"I don't know."

"Evelyn. You need a different solicitor. I want you to talk to my solicitor."

She looked at Richard with a puzzled look on her face.

"Your solicitor? Why do you have a solicitor? Who are you divorcing?"

"Solicitors don't only handle divorces. They are a necessary evil when you buy and sell property, and they also draw up business contracts."

"I can't afford a different solicitor. Most of my salary goes to Dawn for my room and looking after Jonny."

"This guy won't cost you a penny, I'll see to it. I've given him a lot of work and he knows that there's a lot more coming his way. I'll invite him over and we'll discuss your problem over dinner and get some free advice, which is something that lawyers almost never give. He is, I've heard, a very astute divorce lawyer."

The following Sunday Richard brought his friend to see her. They were dressed in whites, having just come from playing tennis.

"Evelyn, this is John Higgins. I told him all about your problem on court. Tennis court, that is. Now he wants to meet you. It won't cost anything. John doesn't take money on Sunday, but see him tomorrow and he'll ask for a king's ransom."

"Yes, but I should warn you that free advice usually isn't worth the money you pay for it. Tell me, what's a pretty girl like you doing in a situation like this?"

Evelyn blushed. "Trying to get out of it."

"Good. I've heard a bit about the other party. The best advice that I can give you is to try and get a divorce on the grounds of his adultery, either with his assent or by getting him observed. He seems to be a man who leads a full sex life, so there'll be plenty of occasions. All we have to do, is catch him at it once. Alternatively, have you or your solicitor asked him to give you grounds?"

"He doesn't want the divorce, I do. He doesn't want me to be free of him any more than he wanted to marry me in the first place. He promised when we got married that he'd let me go when I wanted to go. It was one of the conditions that I demanded and he agreed to. He hasn't kept that promise. Did Richard tell you why we got married?"

"The law doesn't recognise such an agreement."

"We haven't cohabited all the time we were married, does that count?"

She shuddered when she said the word "cohabit". The thought of having sex with the man who had introduced her to it, gave Evelyn the shivers. The solicitor continued. "It might have if you didn't have a child. The law doesn't recognise miraculous conceptions."

"I conceived before the wedding. It was a marriage in name only."

"You were living in the same house. Can you prove that you didn't cohabit? Have you any witnesses?"

"No, the only witness was Louis's mother, but she recently died."

"Perhaps she wrote something down before she died."

"She was his mother. She wouldn't have written anything that would hurt him."

"That's a pity. You should have got something in writing. Did he hit you? Was he cruel to you in any way?"

"No, he had his room and I had mine and his mother was in between."

"So that's it. You have to catch him with another woman or prove that he spent some time with one, in conditions and location where one would expect intimacy to have occurred. That shouldn't be hard to do."

Evelyn described the layout of Louis's house. John frowned when she described Brown's room at the back.

"I don't like the set up. He can drive up and park under the car port roof, and it'll be so dark that the observer won't be able see anything unless he uses a flash camera and gives the game away."

"He built the place himself. It has high windows and wooden shutters on them."

"Evelyn, how anxious are you to get a divorce? Is there another man waiting for you, Richard perhaps?"

She looked at Richard before replying. "No, John. Richard and I are just good friends."

"I seem to have heard that line before. You aren't thinking of taking up a screen career? Listen, Evelyn, wait a bit. You've just left his house, so he's going to be suspecting something for the next few months. Then I'll give you the name of an ex-cop that I know who does a bit of observing still. If your man is playing around he'll get the dirty on him."

"Why does it have to be so sordid?"

Evelyn imagined how Louis would behave if confronted with evidence, pictures perhaps, of him being intimate with one of his women.

"Because guys like your husband are such bastards and so damn stupid. They think that they have the right to hold on to their wives and fool around with any silly sheila that they can get into their bed. By refusing to come to an arrangement, which by the way we aren't supposed to do, but it's what reasonable people do, he leaves us no choice. Have your solicitor contact him and give him one more chance, and then we'll wait a few months. When he's forgotten about the last warning, we'll put my ex-cop onto him. It'll cost a bit of money but it'll be money well spent."

'Damn it,' thought Richard. 'I told him not to mention money.' If there were bills to be paid, he wanted to pay those bills.

"Another thing, don't worry about the boy. If he tries at any stage to get custody of him we'll get that Robin girl to testify, the one who kicked him in the knackers. They wouldn't give him custody of a mule after that. If you want, you two can get together. Just do it discreetly, that's all."

"Thank you, John," said Evelyn. "Up until the last suggestion, I liked your advice. I'll let you know if I need your ex-cop."

Richard dropped John off at his home and came back to talk to Evelyn.

"What did you think of my friend?"

"He seems to know his divorce law. Some of his advice was quite good. I'll let Louis cool off a bit and then try again. When I left the day his mother went into the coma, he was so mad I was afraid that he'd come after me."

"I hope John didn't annoy you with his final comment. He's so used to being a lawyer, he thinks I have a motive in helping you."

"Have you, Richard?"

"Evelyn, I don't know the answer to that question. I do know that we've been friends for three years and that itself is sufficient reason. Let's leave it at that."

"Thanks, Richard. I do want to be free of that man before I get involved again. It's only a couple of weeks since Mrs Brown died. I'm still getting over that shock. Next time that I get married, I'll play it by the book, father's way."

"Are you and he reconciled?"

"Yes and no. He almost admits he was wrong trying to keep me in Renmark and I know I was wrong in my behaviour with that man, so we've called a truce. One of these days we may even make peace. Sometimes I think he wants me to make penance. He thinks that if I went back to that man as a dutiful wife, I'd save my soul from the eternal damnation that I'd incur if I got a divorce."

"Amen."

"What do you think?"

"I don't believe in heaven or hell, definitely not in hell. I'm willing to give heaven the benefit of the doubt."

"Hell to me is being married to Louis Brown. I know one thing; look at my boy, Jonny. He'll be two in three months time. If I'd have taken the easy way out and gotten rid of him, then what would I be? That to me would be hell. To me that would have really been a sin."

"What do you mean by a sin?"

"Don't get me wrong, Richard. I'm referring to my sin, not anyone else's. I'd have had to live in my own hell all my life."

"Your sin! Why do you keep referring to yourself? What about the doctor who would have done it, or the man who got you pregnant in the first place?"

"They don't concern me. The doctor's only doing what he's asked to do. If he can live with that, so be it. He is doing some poor girls a favour. It's a bit like the man who pulls the handle at an execution, the difference being that one kills the guilty and the other the innocent. If Joan Meredith had an abortion and can live with it, that's her business. If brother Steven can't bother to put on a contraceptive and prefers to use an abortionist, and can sleep soundly at night, that's his business. I don't think that we should call down the wrath of God on them."

"Why bring the Merediths into this? Are you mad at Joan, perhaps jealous at her being married to Gerald?"

Evelyn hid her reason for mentioning Steven Meredith. She regretted her slip of the tongue. This still wasn't the time to tell Richard about him. She wondered if he knew that Joan had had abortions, whether Gerald knew this part of his bride's past. She answered Richard. "I have mixed feelings about Joan. I always feel that she gave me the worst advice for the best reasons, and yet I think that she meant well. I just want to say that what was right for Joan, was wrong for me. As for being jealous, what if I am? I'm only human. She's got Gerald and I've got my boy. I never was in a position to have both. It's sad, but that's the way it is. Nothing's going to change the way things are."

September 1st saw an outbreak of fighting in the Middle East. Following the murder of 15 Israelis by raiders from Egypt, Israeli troops attacked their bases in the Gaza Strip in another of the never ending series of attacks and counter attacks on this border. In a dogfight over Kibbutz Yad Mordechai two Egyptian Vampire jets were shot down.

The party of deposed King Norodam Sihanouk of Cambodia won that country's first election on September 11th.

On the 19th armed forces in Argentina ousted Juan Peron, claiming that the country was on the verge of bankruptcy. The President was sent into exile.

Saturday the 24th President Eisenhower was hospitalised following a heart attack, spending the next few days in an oxygen tent. Vice-President Nixon was in attendance in Washington, but Ike recovered and presidential powers remained with the President. Political pundits assumed that he would not seek a second term.

The 28th was Flower Day in Adelaide, with large displays of flowers and floral pictures near the War Memorial in North Terrace and in Victoria Square.

Saturday, September 30th was Grand Final Day. Port Adelaide won, this time by a walkover, beating Norwood 15:11 to 5:8. The same day James Dean, star of the film *Rebel Without A Cause*, was killed, driving his Porsche to a race meeting, in a crash that completely demolished his car.

The Old Vic Shakespeare Company came to Adelaide in October, playing *The Merchant Of Venice* with Katherine Hepburn in the part of Portia and Adelaide-born Robert Helpman returning to his native city to play Shylock.

At the Curzon, crowds flocked to see Gina Lollobrigida in *Pane, Amore E Fantasia (Bread, Love and Dreams)*.

On the 1st day of November, Buckingham Palace announced that Princess Margaret's romance with Group Captain Peter Townsend, a divorcee, was over, as she had decided to place her country before love, while he went home without commenting to the pestiferous press.

"Mindful of the church's teaching that Christian Marriage is indissoluble, and conscious of my duty to the Commonwealth, I have resolved to put these considerations before all others. I have reached this decision entirely alone."

The Archbishop of Canterbury denied on BBC TV that he had put any pressure on the Princess.

Mr Robertson cut Princess Margaret's statement out of the paper, asking his wife to send it to their daughter in her next letter, but she burned it in the kitchen stove the same day. Like many Australians she felt sorry for the Queen's sister. If her uncle, the Duke of Windsor, could marry the person he loved, why couldn't she? If

Evelyn didn't love her husband, why shouldn't she have a second chance too?

There was another big clash on the Israel-Egypt border on the third of November, with 50 Egyptians killed and 40 captured, as the Israelis drove them out of Israeli territory. The Israelis lost 4 soldiers killed.

In November, Kim Philby was accused of being involved in the defection of the spy-diplomats, Burgess and Maclean. He denied the charges, challenging his accuser to repeat his accusations outside Parliament. According to evidence published by Vladimir Petrov, the two defectors were recruited when they (and Philby) were studying at Oxford.

On December 9th, Richard watched from the top of the Shell building as the brand-new Comet 3 flew low over Adelaide, on a proving and publicity flight from England.

The 10th was Federal Election Day. Menzies remained Prime Minister after a close race for the Senate. Dr Evatt's seat of Barton was in doubt at the end of counting, but he scraped in by 226 votes when preferences were allocated.

In December the Sun Record Company sold its recording rights to 19 year old Elvis Presley to RCA for $40,000. With his first cheque of $5,000 Elvis was reported to have gone out and bought a pink Cadillac. He had just been voted most popular Country and Western artist in a DJ poll.

In Montgomery, Alabama, Mrs Rosa Parks was arrested for refusing to give up her seat to a white man passenger on a bus. The next day the 50,000 black inhabitants of Montgomery began a 54 week boycott of the buses, lead by a young black clergyman, the Reverend Martin Luther King.

Evelyn decided to stay in Adelaide until Christmas Eve this year. Now that she was employed she didn't have four months summer holiday. She went to see the Footlights Club Revue, *Count Your Chickens* the day before she went home.

Afterwards she told Richard, "That's the first University Revue I've seen, apart from the Women's Revue in first year which I didn't enjoy, because I didn't understand the dirty jokes. I was still a prude then. Are end of year revues always as good as this?"

"Last year's show was as good if not better and 1953 wasn't too bad either. The guys who put this together have been doing it for years and got it down to a fine art. It's a pity they have to play in such a lousy theatre."

"There'll be a new theatre soon. The appeal is getting in a lot of money. Why didn't the Merediths give money for this instead of that place they're putting up for their son?"

The Meredith Building was almost finished, and the man who was going to rule inside it, had been appointed to the post. The man Evelyn feared was helping fit it out for the man she hated more than Brown, for Jonny's progenitor.

"I was in Melbourne last week and saw the Christmas Revue with Barry Humphries. He does this drag act, impersonating an elderly rich Toorak bitch, Dame Edna Everage. Talk about funny. I laughed till the tears were running down my legs. He's so real that you think it's really a rough Australian dame."

"Sounds right for Australia. I couldn't see the English going for that sort of thing."

The 1955 Footlights Club Revue the smash hit, *Count Your Chickens,* was the story of one man, *That Man*, and his many romances. It was full of original songs, including a mini opera to the theme of the Marlon Brando film *On The Waterfront*. The *Advertiser* on the day following the first night wrote,

BRILLIANT COMEDY IN VARSITY REVUE.
FUNNIEST IN YEARS.

Evelyn returned home for Christmas in a happier mood than she'd been in for years. On January 1st 1956 the Robertsons, all of them, celebrated Jonny's second birthday. Grandpa played with grandson, as his wife and daughter watched him enjoying himself being a grandfather. This time Uncle Richard's present came with her in her suitcase. Again there was no present and no birthday card from Mr Brown. It wasn't missed.

On the 29th of December, Soviet Prime minister, Bulganin, announced that the USSR possessed a rocket capable of carrying a Hydrogen Bomb 4,000 miles.

In 1955 no Nobel Peace Prize was awarded.

Chapter Twenty-Nine

January 1956

The holiday period was a lonely time for Richard Flynn. Although he had many friends, lady friends and business friends, those whom he really liked were away, Evelyn in Renmark and Gerald in Boston.

The 8th of January he went alone to Elder Park to hear an all Tchaikovsky Concert and two weeks later he was again there for another concert in the open air. The Central Command Band, dressed in bright red uniforms, joined the Orchestra for an evening of light music, ending with the 1812 Overture. There were six army guns which fired over the water during the final battle theme, filling the park with light from the flashes and smoke which drifted back in front of the stage.

Evelyn was back in Adelaide and at work two days later. Richard took her and Jonny to the beach together with the Grovers on the 30th, Australia Day holiday. They looked like two young couples out for the day, each with their firstborn.

"Did Jonny like the present from his Uncle Richard?"

"Yes. I'm sorry you couldn't come to the party."

"How was the holiday?"

"Boring. Dad played with Jonny, I sat around with Mom, but after a week I wanted to come back to Adelaide."

"I think Adelaide is boring, but then I've never lived in the country. I went to a few parties and a couple of concerts by the river. I should have gone to Sydney. This town gets duller every year."

The truth was that he missed having her to look after, but he wasn't ready to admit that to Evelyn.

"We missed you, Uncle Richard."

"You, or Jonny?"

"Both of us. What's new? Have you heard from the Fishers?"

Richard was surprised to hear her mention their name. That was a good sign. She hadn't asked about them before.

"Since when are you interested in the Fishers? Let me see, Joan's shat off because hurricane Dianne knocked down most of the trees on the golf course last August, and she couldn't play golf for a few weeks. The fact that 200 people died doesn't seem to matter to her. They saw the show *Can Can* and Joan saw Hoad and Rosewall win back the Davis Cup at Forrest Hills, also last August. They saw

Miles Davis at Newport, Joyce Grenfell and Maurice Chevalier on Broadway and David Oistrakh in Carnegie Hall. Joan's been buying trunkloads of clothes, household goods and lots of records. In the last letter Gerald was raving about the autumn colours in the forests and the first snow. I guess that it's below freezing up there now. He joined a rifle club where they shoot clay pigeons. Do you know what's strange? Joan hasn't written a word of late. It isn't like her."

"Knowing you, you probably offended her. Try and recall what you wrote."

"Offend Joan Meredith! Come off it, Evelyn, she's as rough as bags. She used to embarrass me every time that she asked for..."

"I know, an eraser. When I first heard her, way back in '52, I almost died. And what about the alcohol in your pants! Was she trying to sterilise something?"

"Did you know what a rubber was then?"

'God,' she thought before replying. 'Those were my happy, innocent days.'

"I didn't know that 'Dick' had another meaning then."

"So, why doesn't Joan write to me any more?"

"Perhaps she's pregnant. Women get funny when they're pregnant. I did."

"Maybe. You'd think that they would have told me."

"When are they coming back?"

"Gerald finishes the course in March. Then they're flying to Italy and Greece and should be back here by the beginning of May. Brother Steven stayed with them for a few days. Reading between the lines I don't think that Gerald likes him, or Joan for that matter. He's on his way back and should be here next month. What are you making faces for? You look as if you sat on the rough end of a pineapple."

Evelyn hadn't meant to frown. She tried to smile. So Jonny's evil father was coming back. That was a man she loathed, as much as she loved his child.

"Sorry, I just thought of something not very nice. Now I'm back in Adelaide I guess that I'll have to see the solicitor. I don't think Louis is going to agree to anything, so we'll have to go after evidence. I hate doing this to him. It'll only humiliate him and that makes him angry and that makes me scared. Have you seen the scars on his face? I never knew that rugby was so rough."

Richard knew what had been done to Brown. He hadn't told Evelyn, she'd only feel sorry for the bastard. She must be the only person on campus who didn't know. His only regret was that he hadn't been there to see it happen.

"If Brown gives you any trouble, or threatens you in any way, let me know. Don't forget, he probably doesn't know where you live. You haven't been telling anyone, have you?"

"No, I have everything but my parents' mail addressed to the university."

Again, Evelyn spoke to her solicitor and he spoke to Louis who told him, "Get stuffed. If that bitch wants a divorce tell her to pay me back all the money that she stole from my mother that was coming to me. I want £5,000 and not a penny less."

Louis came to see Evelyn on the first of March. She could see that he was angry and it made her apprehensive.

"You got me fired, you little bitch, just because I wouldn't play ball with your lawyer."

"Louis, I don't understand. Who fired you?"

His scars were paler now, just faint stitch marks.

"You know. The head technician told me, this morning. He told me to go at the end of the week."

"Why would he do that? Did you do something wrong?"

"Evelyn, I've never worked harder in my life. I like the work. Why did I get the sack? If you didn't do it, who did? Who else wants to hurt me?"

"Tell me the name of your boss and I'll go and see him. If it's at all possible, I'll get you your job back."

"Why should you help me?"

That was a good question. Why *should* she help him?

"It may make you think better of me. If I get you your job back will you speak to my lawyer?"

"Did you get me sacked so you could do this?"

"Louis, believe what you like. I don't know what I can do for you. I don't know if I can help you at all. For all I know, you may have seduced the man's wife or his daughter. I wouldn't put it past you. You say you've done nothing wrong. I'm prepared to believe you. Do you believe me when I say that I had nothing to do with it? Do you want me to try and get your job back, yes or no?"

That was what Louis didn't like in Evelyn. She talked too bloody much. What did it matter, he wanted that job back.

"Go ahead. I'm so upset I don't know what to think."

When he left, she rang the head technician.

"Hello, my name is Evelyn Robertson. I work in the Benham building. I'd like ask you a question."

"Go ahead."

"Why did you fire my husband, Louis Brown?"

"I was told to fire him. He isn't employed on a contract. He can be fired on a weeks notice."

"Are you firing all workers who haven't got contracts?"

"No."

"So why did you fire Louis? Was he a bad worker?"

"Listen, Mrs Brown, I wanted to keep him. He's a good worker. The new boss told me to get rid of him. He didn't give me any reason."

"Who is the new boss?"

"He's the big boss, lady, he can fire whoever he likes."

"You mean, dislikes. What's his name?"

"Dr Meredith."

She should have known. The man who had brought disaster on her head was due back. That she knew. How she hated him, how she loved the child he'd forced into her.

"When did *he* get back?"

"Last week. He saw Brown's name on a staff list and told me to get rid of him."

Evelyn hesitated before asking the next question.

"Where is Dr Meredith at present?"

"He's in his office."

"Thanks, and where's Louis?"

"I don't know. He went out of here in a huff."

"Don't give his job to anyone else. I'm going to see Meredith and get it back for him."

It wasn't easy for Evelyn to go and see Steven Meredith, face to face, the man who in one night had turned her life upside down. She didn't change out of her laboratory clothes, as she wanted him to know that she too was a staff member and that she could talk to him as an equal. She quickly walked over to the Meredith Building and sought out Dr Meredith. The place was full of electricians and carpenters getting the place ready for the first influx of students. She saw Steven Meredith talking to some workmen by his office door. It took her a few seconds to get up the courage to face him. He didn't recognise her.

"Dr Meredith, I have to talk to you."

"I'm busy now. See my secretary if you want an appointment."

"This can't wait."

"I told you that I'm busy."

Evelyn stood her ground.

"And I told you that this can't wait."

"OK., make it snappy. What do you want?"

"It concerns a man that you had fired today. I want you to give him his job back."

Steven suddenly knew Evelyn. He started to remember the circumstances of their meeting. He realised that he didn't want her to speak her mind in front of the men, so he dismissed them and took her past the secretary's office into his own inner sanctum. He closed the door, but as he went to sit at his desk, Evelyn opened it. She had a fear of Meredith and closed doors.

"If you don't mind I'd like you to leave the door open."

"What do you want with me?"

His first thought was money. Women always wanted to get at his Meredith money.

"I want you to give Louis Brown his job back. He's done nothing wrong, nothing that deserves being sacked."

"What's he to you?"

"He's my husband and we need the money. We have a child and unlike you, we need every penny and we're prepared to work for it. Not everybody gets their money and their employment from their Daddy."

Evelyn hated to admit that Louis was her husband, but it was the only way that she could explain her position.

"Let's forget him for a while and talk about you. Aren't you the girl who tried to cheat for him and to change over the exam papers? What are you doing now?"

Evelyn didn't want to change the subject. She wanted to get what she wanted, Louis reinstated, then she wanted to get the hell out of Meredith's building.

"Let's *not* forget about Louis," she told him, raising her voice. "I want you to give him his job again."

"He's lazy and dishonest. I don't want such a person working for me."

"Dr Meredith, how many times do you want to punish him for what he did? You got your pound of flesh from me, you bastard. He may be a lousy student, but your chief technician is satisfied with his work. Let him decide if he's lazy or not. He wants him to stay."

"I don't. I'm head of this department."

"You fire him and I'll go out of this office, and tell the Vice Chancellor that you locked me up in your house and raped me."

Dr Meredith sat upright. This Brown woman was threatening him.

"That's quite an accusation. Why did you wait three years?"

"I waited for you to come back. I'm willing to risk the publicity. I'll tell the story to the editor of *On Dit*. They don't print beer ads. I'll also find the nurse that you got pregnant and made have an abortion. You won't be able to buy a lectureship from Tasmania to Timbuktu."

He was shocked by that last threat. Steven Meredith turned pale. How did she know about that?

"That's blackmail."

"Yes, and you are a black-hearted male who deserves to be exposed. I'll tell my story to your brother-in-law and Joan, and the man who was best man at your sister's wedding, Richard Flynn. All three of them are friends of mine. They'll know that I'm telling the truth. You'll be an outcast in your own family, if you aren't already."

"You've been checking up on me. Am I your research project or something?"

"No, I found out about your nurse by chance. The story is no secret. They tell it at the Children's Hospital at midnight when the moon is full, to frighten the first year student nurses. If someone really took the time to do some research, I'm sure she could write a regular Kinsey report on you and your behaviour."

"I'm warning you, young lady, I'm a powerful man."

"That's why I insisted on keeping the door open. I don't want another confrontation with you. You may win or you may lose. We both might lose. Change your mind about sacking Louis and let me get back to my work. Then with a little bit of luck, I may never set eyes on you again."

Steven knew he had to give in. It made him angry, but he had to get this virago out of his room and shut her up.

"Go and tell him that he's got the job back."

"You tell him, you owe it to him."

"I owe it to him?"

"Yes, you black bastard. For what you did to me that night. If he knew, he'd kill you."

With that she got up and left. Louis came to see her the following day. He was in a good mood.

"How did you do it, Evelyn?"

"Louis, I have friends in high places. I did a little name dropping. If I were you I'd find another job. Meredith is a bastard, a bigger bastard than you. Stay away from him. And Louis, don't forget. I got you your job. Give me my divorce."

That evening she rang Richard and told him about Louis.

"I don't know how you did it, but you did well. Ring the solicitor and get him to see Louis before he changes his mind. What have you got over Steven Meredith?"

"I told him that I was a friend of his brother-in-law, and I also mentioned your name. I don't think he knew who you were, except that you were best man at his sister's wedding."

"He'll know who I am, one of these days. Just as well Joan and Gerald aren't in town. They wouldn't have helped you. They'd have seconded his sacking of Brown. I think that Joan hates him more than you do."

"I don't see why. I have more cause than she has. You know, Richard, she got a kick out of her part in making Louis get married. I don't know if she really did it to help me or to hurt him. She knew what a blow it would be to him, having to get married to me. That was pure revenge."

"I could think of no greater pleasure than being married to you, Evelyn."

"You cut that out, Richard Flynn. You know that flattery will get you somewhere. You know that Louis and I aren't living together."

"That, I agree, is fitting punishment for him."

Louis remained at work in the Department of Food Sciences. He proved himself not only a good worker, but Steven Meredith got used to him. They were birds of a feather and once they got to know one another, they became quite friendly. Steven had a research project which he wanted to get started as soon as possible, industrial microwave vacuum drying of foods. Louis was just right for the job of setting up the equipment. He had to work with the electricians, carpenters and fitters, as the oven was big and the equipment needed to operate it quite extensive.

Most vacuum drying ovens use steam or electric heating to replace the heat lost during drying. Steven had the idea that microwaves would do the same thing and produce a better product that would be tastier and if necessary, easier to dissolve. If it worked, there would be hundreds of applications. His father's factories alone could benefit, and would have first use of the new technique. Steven intended to use the money and facilities that his father had donated to benefit Meredith Industries.

Dr Meredith brought back with him from America plans for making the new oven and parts that would not be available in Australia. He set about building it, with Louis as his chief assistant. The oven had to be placed in an isolated room surrounded by radiation shields. Not much was known of the effects of microwaves on human tissue, but indications were that it was very harmful. They designed the oven to be operated by remote control, not taking any chances with microwave radiation. Safety devices were installed so that it couldn't be operated with the shields covering the magnetron tube removed, or if anyone was in the room.

Louis worked long hours, skipping lectures and putting in unpaid overtime. He forgot about Evelyn and his promise to her to help with the divorce. He wanted money from her, more than she could ever pay. When, later in the year Steven came to him with a plan to make a lot of money, hurting Evelyn, he aided him, forgetting that it was Steven who'd sacked him and Evelyn who'd gotten him his job again.

1956 was a year of increasing tension in the Middle East. The new Nasser Government was flexing its muscles, with the help of the Soviets who were moving in, replacing the British and the French in Egypt and Syria. Egypt was receiving vast amounts of arms from Russia and Eastern Europe, with the declared intention of going to war with Israel.

On the 4th of March, Tom Playford won another state election.

The crying crooner, Johnny Ray, was mobbed by fans in Sydney. His two most popular songs, which he sobbed rather than sang, were *Cry* and *The Little White Cloud That Cried*. They called him "The Prince of Wails."

The following day that little white cloud burst over Adelaide and cried, flooding Glenelg and surrounding suburbs.

On the 9th, the guardians of public morality had a good day at Sydney's Mascot Airport. They searched the baggage of the Conductor of the Sydney Symphony Orchestra, Sir Eugene Goosens, and charged him with bringing into the country forbidden material, pornographic pictures. Sir Eugene was found guilty, received a fine two weeks later and left Australia two months after that. It was a sad day for music lovers and Sydney Concert-goers. Mrs Meredith's luggage wasn't searched when she returned from visiting her daughter. If it had been, they might have taken exception to the magazine that Joan had sent for Richard.

On the 11th, the French Government accused Nasser of helping the rebels fighting against them in Algeria, of giving them French arms for use against Frenchmen.

On March 18th, Pravda disclosed to the world the content of a speech by Soviet Communist Party Secretary Nikita Kruschev, in which he accused Joseph Stalin of being responsible for a reign of terror, torture and mass murder. It was strange that this was such a big disclosure in Russia, seeing that it was old news in the West and must have been common knowledge in Russia. But in Stalin's day to mention it might have meant death or transportation to Siberia.

March 1956 was the month that the University of Tasmania dismissed the Professor of Philosophy, Professor Orr, for alleged misconduct, for having had a sexual relationship with a girl student. The speed of his sacking was rapid in comparison with what followed in his attempt to fight against this decision. The Professor went to the courts with his claim of wrongful dismissal, backed by students and staff from universities throughout the nation and beyond. It took the University of Tasmania ten years to admit that, in their treatment of the Professor, there may have been a denial of natural justice.

The first student meeting of 1956 was held in the Refectory to discuss the Orr case, as the other two meeting halls were too small to accommodate the large crowd interested in hearing a representative from the Tasmanian Students Association.

The speaker got up to tell the Adelaide students why he supported Professor Orr.

"I think you should know that the dismissal of Professor Orr has been condemned by the Students' Union and the Staff Association. We feel that the real reason for the man being sacked was because of his stand in university politics, and not because of what he did or didn't do with the girl in question, for which we only have her word. Professor Orr was involved in university politics and spoke out against the conduct of the university administration. He was a thorn in their side, not just a trouble maker, but a man concerned and working for the good of the university. He upset some of the leaders and pillars of the community and they didn't like it. That is the real reason for his dismissal. Late last year we discovered that the administration were asking around, sending their spies into our midst, looking for anyone who might have had a sexual relationship with Professor Orr. In other words, they were out to get him before there was anything against him, a strange thing to do to a senior staff member. When it was known that they were specifically asking for the name of any girl student who may have had sexual relations with the Professor we decided to do something. We collected the names of all the girls at the university on a petition stating that they all hadn't had sex with him, all except one. She was going to sign too, we think, but she went home and told her father about the petition. He told her not to sign.

"Her father is one of the big shots, who is in with the administration and wanted to get rid of Professor Orr. You've probably heard of her testimony, the press reported it in detail, how the poor innocent was seduced by the nasty professor. It's his word against hers. Either he's lying, as he denies everything, or she is. Considering the way she came forth some time after the alleged seduction and how convenient it was for those who wanted to get at him, to get rid of him, and that she is the whole case against the man, we think that her testimony is suspect and not enough to constitute a case against Professor Orr.

"On the other hand, why should a young girl admit to a sexual relationship that she never had? On the surface it seems improbable. We feel that she perjured herself to help her father and his cronies and now she has to stick to her story whether she likes it or not. We don't say that he lied or she lied. Unless someone admits that they lied we'll never know. What we are saying is that the case for Dr Orr's dismissal is flimsy and that he was wrongly dismissed. We'd like your support. Your staff association has given their support."

The speaker sat down and the chairman asked if there were any questions. Evelyn who had felt empathy for the girl and anger against the Professor, was now unsure how she felt. She wanted to get up and say, "I know nothing about Professor Orr, but I do know about a real lecher on this campus." Then she would name Steven Meredith and ask if there were other girls in the audience who had had experiences similar to hers, suggest that they make out a list. She didn't have the nerve, and she had made a pact with the devil to get Louis back his job. Another student got up to speak.

"I would like to know why a twenty year old girl would admit to being seduced, whatever that is, by a middle-aged professor if it didn't happen?"

"The real question is why would any girl come forth and tell about what must have been a very personal, intimate love affair, if it in fact happened? If the girl's story is true, and I don't think it is, she was a willing participant. Her family connections make her a biased witness. We question her honesty. Her evidence alone cost a man his job."

"Why question her honesty?" a second student asked.

"Professor Orr denies that they had sexual relations. Either he or she is telling the truth. Without corroborative evidence, you might as well toss a coin. But she hasn't been sacked; he has, because of her statement. There is a doubt as to who's telling the truth. Why not give him the benefit of the doubt? Next question."

"Who gives a damn whether he slept with her or not, as long as he didn't rape her or get her drunk or something? Are we going to fire all staff members who have extramarital sex or exclude students for doing the same thing? We'd have nothing but wowsers in the universities. I don't suppose that many of you have had a chance to read the Kinsey report yet. I managed to have a look and it makes interesting reading. Do you know that three out of ten married men have a bit on the side? Let's sack 30 percent of the staff.

"Perhaps we should restrict student entry to clean livers only and get the health service to install chastity belts on all freshettes and unmarried female staff members. The Refectory could put bromide in the tea and coffee. It would probably improve the taste."

He stopped for a round of applause.

"Why stop at the university, why not go the whole hog and clean up Parliament? I can hear question time."

The student went on to act a one man parliament.

"*Mr Prime Minister. I have a question without notice. Are you an adulterer?*

If the honourable member would table the question, I'll have my secretary look up the information, or perhaps, *I have a question without notice to the leader of the opposition, Dr Evatt, do you perform abortions?*

The right honourable member should know that I am a Doctor of Law.

Dr Evatt, if you won't answer the question we can only conclude that you have something to hide.'

"We could ask President Eisenhower if he ever had a WAC when he was supreme commander of Allied Forces in Europe. If we're going to dismiss every man who sleeps with a woman that he isn't married to, or every homosexual, there'll be no one left on the staff. What does it matter if the professor did whack it to her or didn't? Let him have his job back."

The questioner received a round of applause and the meeting voted to support Professor Orr. It didn't help. Professor Orr went from court to court seeking justice, but the courts believed the girl and not him. Staff associations world wide placed a ban on the chair of Philosophy at the University of Tasmania and it remained empty. In 1966 they finally admitted that there may have been a denial of justice, too late to help Professor Orr. He received a substantial settlement but died the same year a broken man.

Chapter Thirty

April 1956

Joan and Gerald returned to Adelaide at the end of April. Richard went to visit them the day after their return, in Joan's old flat. He was met by a grim faced Gerald. He put down the rifle he had just unpacked, as Richard asked him, "What's the matter, Gerry? Had a lousy plane trip?"

"No, it isn't the trip, Joan's a bit upset, that's all. She's upstairs talking to her Mom."

"What's upset her? I thought she'd be thrilled to be home again."

"Her Mom asked her why wasn't she pregnant. It wasn't a very bright thing to ask, that's all."

"Why not? That's the kind of question I'd have expected from her mother. Did she ask you too?"

"Joan had a miscarriage last November when she was in the second month. Then a gynaecologist told her that she couldn't have babies. Her mother didn't know, but she could have used a bit of tact. Apparently the lining of her womb is damaged and won't accept a fertilised egg."

"From one miscarriage?"

"No, from several. Joan has had three abortions. Now she wants a child and can't have one."

"When did that happen?"

"When she was younger. The first when she was 15. I think she had an infection once and that made it worse."

"Are you angry?"

"No, I knew who I was marrying. I knew about the abortions. Neither of us knew that it would stop her having babies afterwards. It's a bigger blow to her. She blames herself and goes about the house crying. She's better than she was. When she first found out she was in a terrible way. I had to stay with her day and night for a couple of weeks. We almost came home in December."

"Have you had a second opinion?"

"We're going to see a specialist next week. I don't think he'll be able to help. The gynaecologist in Boston was a famous specialist."

"How do you feel about it?"

Gerald didn't reply at once. He suddenly realised that he didn't have an opinion. Since marrying into the Meredith family, no one had ever asked him for his opinion.

"I haven't been able to afford the luxury of my own feelings. I've been too busy looking after Joan. She's used to getting everything she wants and can't accept this. It's like being caught by the only honest policeman in town. She feels she's being punished and doesn't know why."

"Shit, Gerry. Adopt children."

"That's what I told Joan. If the doctor confirms her condition, that's what we'll probably do. I think that it goes against the grain for a Meredith to have to adopt a child. They can't get used to the idea that some little bastard, the child of goodness-knows-who, will be brought into the family and inherit all their millions."

"Poor Gerald," he thought, "no longer Gerald Fisher, just Charles Meredith's latest acquisition."

"You never know, with Steven back in town, you may end up with one of his wild oats."

"Is he such a lecher?"

"They say that he has two big four-poster beds and some nights he alternates like a dentist with two chairs, as in the limerick,

There once was a lady called Joan,
Who went to the dentist alone,
In a fit of depravity,
He filled the wrong cavity.
Now she's nursing her filling alone."

Gerald closed the door quickly.

"You recite that in front of my wife and I'll kill you."

"Sorry. A few years ago she would have recited it to me. Remember that bonfire up at 'Boronia'?"

"Yes, and the one we had a week later. I was preparing to meet my maker and Joan's getting out the champagne, chicken and the mattress. Now all she wants is to make me a father. I think we'll have to get her a psychiatrist."

All around them there were suitcases. Gerald was doing the unpacking, as Joan wasn't up to it. The place looked like a bargain basement.

448

"It's a pity that you couldn't find a female who could have your children like Joan could, by artificial insemination if you were infertile. Imagine if you could have her fertilised ova placed in another woman's womb and when she gives birth, you get the baby. You'd have to pay her for the use of her body."

"It doesn't sound too ethical. You've been reading too much science fiction. Is that a John Wyndham idea?"

"No, have you read his latest book, *The Kraken Wakes*?"

"About melting the polar ice and flooding London?"

"Yes."

"That's about as probable as transferring eggs from one woman's womb to another woman's."

"Don't be such a sceptic. It's not such a long time ago that Rutherford said that we'd never harness the power of the atom. Any day now the Americans are going to launch an artificial moon. They'll be able to look down from space and see who's kissing who up at Windy Point."

Richard picked up Gerald's new rifle. It was a beauty. He looked through the telescopic sight, focusing on one of the lights around the swimming pool. Then he gave it to Gerald, who put it in a cupboard. Then he picked up a couple of books, reading the titles aloud.

"*Lolita!* That I want to read! *Casino Royale, Moonraker?* Who is Ian Fleming?"

"They're all for you: James Bond's a Super-spy, the Mike Hammer of the 50's. We bought them in London. I somehow think you'll like them, Richard."

"Much obliged, Gerry."

"About Joan and our problem. We're praying that the guy she's going to see this next week will disagree with the other doctor, or that he'll be able to treat her. It hasn't been a wonderful homecoming. That's enough talk about Joan and me, how's your love life?"

"So so. I've been seeing a lot of a certain woman, who's separated from her husband and trying to get a divorce."

"You're having an affair with a married woman?"

"No. I'm helping her get rid of her husband. She married him because she was pregnant and didn't want to get rid of the baby."

'Lucky woman,' Gerald mused. 'She has what my wife wants and can't have.'

"And now she's fallen in love with you?" he asked.

"No, she loves her baby and wants to get out of a terrible marriage. When she gets her divorce I'll be able to see more of her, without looking over my shoulder to see if someone's spying on us."

"Do you love her?"

"It would be so easy, Gerry, but she's a bit traumatised. I'm waiting to see what's going to happen."

"This isn't like you, Richard. This woman has really gotten to you. It doesn't worry you that she has a child?"

"The boy adores me. He calls me Uncle Richard."

"What about his mother, does she adore you too?"

"Gerald, she trusts me, I'm a friend and I helped her when she didn't have a friend to turn to. She wants her freedom and then she wants to start a new life. We've got an agreement not to get involved until she gets a divorce."

"But you've told her that you're interested?"

Richard was beginning to regret telling all this to Gerald. But why shouldn't Gerald know about it? He'd have to find out sooner or later. He didn't want Joan or some other person to tell him.

"I've been spending a lot of time with her."

"You said that you were worried about being spied on."

"We meet with friends, all nice and kosher."

"I hope it turns out alright."

"You aren't interested in who she is?"

"I think I know."

"You do?"

"It's Evelyn, isn't it?"

He was glad that Gerald knew. Now he wanted to know what Gerald felt about it.

"And you still give it your blessing?"

"If you take her away from that animal I'll always be grateful to you."

"I'll tell her that, some day."

"Some day we might all be friends again, the four of us, but not just yet. Joan's got to get over this problem first. If she sees Evelyn she'll get the wrong idea. This inability to have a baby has shattered her confidence. I didn't think that anything could do that."

Richard picked up a record. Bill Haley and the Comets.

"Tell me, Gerry. You into Rock and Roll?"

"Sure."

"What do you know about it? Where does it come from?"

"Everywhere. Jive, Country and Western, black music. The negroes have been playing R and R for years. They call it Rhythm and Blues. A white guy like Elvis Presley picks it up and sells millions of records. The blacks get bugger all. That's what it is, negro music played by whites. It's like Jazz was once. The Negroes invented it, but for every Satchmo there's a dozen Gene Krupas and Tommy Dorseys."

"So you think Rock and Roll is here to stay?

"We like it, but I prefer Charlie Parker and Miles Davis or the latest Dave Brubeck. That you can listen to."

Mrs Meredith took Joan to a tall building on North Terrace, to see one of the foremost gynaecologists in Adelaide. He listened to her story and read the report that the doctor had given her in Boston. Then he examined Joan and told them what he thought. He said that he agreed with his colleague in Boston, that he held the same opinion. He told her that she might be lucky but in his opinion there was very little chance of her bearing a child. If she did get pregnant, she would probably miscarry at an early stage.

She didn't feel like returning home, so she walked across the street to the university to see Steven. She told him what the doctor had said, put her head down on his desk and cried. Then she looked up at her brother.

"You know, Steven, this is going to affect you too. Mom and Dad are going to pressure you to get married and have a family. Ever since I got married they've been on my back, not that I cared at the time, but now that we can't have children, you'll have to have them."

"Joan, you know that I'm not the marrying type."

"Steven, your parents want grandchildren."

"It's my life, not theirs. I enjoy being a bachelor."

"You enjoy being difficult. Don't you want a wife and children, Steven?"

Joan was right. No one, not even his parents, told Steven Meredith what to do. Evelyn had been the exception. She had a hold over him.

"I have yet to meet a woman I wanted to the exclusion of all others. As for children, I couldn't care less. I have no wish to be a father. If Dad doesn't like that he can cut me out of his will. I have my position here and my salary."

"Dad got you your position here."

"So what? It's mine. No one can take it away from me. In a few years I'll be Professor Meredith."

There was a knock on the door. Steven opened it and spoke to Louis Brown about the microwave equipment, then returned to Joan who was annoyed to see her enemy in the department.

"What's he doing here?"

"Brown? He's my research technician. He was working here when I took over and he's very good with his hands. He's still trying to get his degree."

"Get rid of him. He's rotten to the core."

"I did, but his wife made me take him on again."

"Evelyn?"

"Yes, she said she was a friend of yours and Gerald too. She wasn't lying was she?"

"I was at her wedding. She was two months in the club at the time. Steven, it's not fair, she's got a baby that she didn't want, and I want babies and I can't have them. How did she make you rehire Brown?"

She didn't tell him that she married Evelyn's boyfriend.

"It appears that Brown needs the money to pay for her and the boy."

"Of course he does, they're married aren't they?"

"Not for long, she's left him. She's got a job over in Botany or Zoology I think."

"So she finally got out. Good on ya, Evelyn! She hates him as much as I do. How'd she manage to get you to give him back his job? You aren't easily persuaded."

"She threatened me. In view of what happened to Professor Orr, I thought it best to give in."

"What has the Orr case got to do with you and Evelyn?"

"Sit down, sister, and I'll tell you an interesting story about Louis Brown and his wife."

Steven told her of the phonecall he'd received from his housekeeper, how he'd trapped Evelyn and seen Brown driving away. He told Joan that he wanted to take her directly to the police, but that she'd pleaded and "offered herself", if he'd let her go and give a passing mark to her lover. He said that he'd "reluctantly agreed" and that Evelyn had spent the night with him, in exchange for getting Brown a pass.

Joan was surprised by the story, she thought it was either a pack of lies or not quite the truth. She knew Evelyn, and felt that she wouldn't sell herself to Steven just to help Brown pass an exam. Evelyn was probably pregnant at the time and she already hated Brown, Joan thought. Why would she do what Steven said she did? Steven continued telling Joan about Evelyn.

"Not only did I accept the offer and sleep with her, I falsified his exam results to pass Brown. Think of the scandal that there'd be if this got out, aiding and abetting cheating in an exam for a night in bed with a student. Not all the beer ads in the world would keep that out of the papers, Joan."

"Did she threaten to blackmail you, Steven?"

"She did. She also accused me of dismissing Brown without a good reason, which was the truth. She said she had a close friend who would support her."

"Do you know who her friend is?"

"A guy called Richard Flynn. He's supposed to be a friend of your husband. He's also a financial genius. He's made a lot of money recently, he and his company. He has the knack of buying very cheap rubbish and selling it as gold. He's done very well with real estate, I'm told."

"Dick Flynn! He is Gerald's best friend. He sold us the land for the house we're planning to build. He was at school with Gerald and was best man at our wedding. He's a nice guy. Evelyn used to be Gerald's girlfriend, until she had a mental aberration by the name of Brown, and had to get married. I'm not surprised that she and Richard are friends. We all were, in first year. What's Dick been up to of late?"

"Your friendly genius made a fool out of your father last year. Dad's still mad about it. He tricked Meredith Foods out of a quarter of a million pounds."

"Shit! A quarter of a million? How'd he do that?"

"There was this fish cannery in the old part of Finsbury, the old munitions plant. January last year, when you and Gerald were planning your wedding, your best man Flynn put a bid in for the cannery and word got out. He probably leaked it himself to draw in the big fish. You know that we're always on the look out to buy into anything in the way of food processing. Dad put in a counter bid and ended up paying three times what the factory was worth. I'm sure that Flynn got the owner to hold out and ask for a ridiculous price. Dad should have given up at this stage, but your friend knew just how to sucker him in."

Joan didn't know what to think. She had mixed loyalties. She was pleased that her friend had pulled a swift one, but concerned that her father had been the sucker.

"That doesn't amount to a quarter of a million."

"I haven't finished. We signed the contract and got the builders in and started to reconstruct the whole place. Then, last November with half a million invested and another million planned, we get a letter from the owner of the adjacent block. He wanted to build a warehouse on his land and asked us to remove the sewer that he'd allowed the previous owner to run through his land. Your father's engineers hadn't known that this block of land wasn't ours. They'd neglected the first rule of factory planning, getting rid of your sewerage."

"Oh." She was beginning to see the funny side of this.

"It was an easy mistake to make. The previous owner had spread out and used the empty block next to him to store his junk, wooden boxes, pallets, old machinery, so it looked like part of the place. The sewer line ran under it and they thought that part was owned by the local council, but it wasn't and there were no other sewer lines that we could connect to. You can't push shit uphill. Richard Flynn owned the company that owned the empty plot and we couldn't operate the factory without his consent. He'd planned this trap a year in advance and our Daddy fell in."

To Steven's annoyance, he noticed that Joan was getting a kick out of this. So much for her family loyalty.

"Poor Daddy! I hope he had a shower afterwards. Steven, it could have been someone else. If the engineers had done their job, they'd have seen that we needed the plot in the planning stages and not bought the factory without it. What happened? Did we pay through the nose for the land?"

"No, Flynn held out for a share in the factory, claiming that he bought the land and was going to buy the factory next to it when we muscled in. At one stage we put the factory up for sale and Flynn put up the only bid. He'd have got the factory for peanuts. Finally we made a deal. Richard Flynn owes 25 percent of the factory, £250,000 worth of shares and I think he paid £8,000 for his plot of land. The factory, when it starts operating, should operate at a handsome profit and be worth a lot more in a few years' time. Dad has a new partner and doesn't like it a bit."

"Don't remind him that Dick's a friend of ours. I don't want him to think that Gerald or I are involved. You must admit that Dick's a smart cookie. If Dad was smart he'd bring him into the business, put him on the board. But then Richard wouldn't come in. He doesn't need Dad, when he can make a quarter of a million from £8,000."

"I know. I had a lawyer prepare a dossier on him."

"You spied on Dick Flynn?"

"No, we researched him. His company owns a lot of farming land in the Adelaide Hills and a lot of land that's being developed. What with bushfires and drought, the farmers are glad to sell him the land. When the land he owns gets rezoned for housing he'll be worth millions."

"Will it be rezoned?"

"Yes, sooner or later. He's already converted some of the land to home sites and he's getting fantastic prices. It seems that everyone wants to look down on the city and build under the gumtrees."

"Gerald bought a parcel of land from him before we got married. We've got an architect drawing up plans now."

"I suggested that Dad invest in land the way that Flynn does, but he wasn't interested. He only wants to invest in food. I think he's wrong. I think we should invest where the profits are and, at present, land is the best investment. They aren't making it any more."

This was one of the things she hated about her brother. He wasn't prepared to help their father, only comment and criticise him from the sidelines. At least Gerald was prepared to go into the business.

"Why don't you take all your money out of the bank and put it in land?"

"Because I don't need more money. I'll never be able to spend a fraction of my wealth, so why waste time making more money? For kids that I don't intend to have? I have my work which I like and my four poster beds which, thanks to my money, I have no trouble filling. I'll leave the money making to Dad and Gerald when he grows up.

It's funny Joan, but I can't see Gerald running Meredith Industries. You should have married Flynn."

'And left Gerald for Evelyn,' she thought. 'It's too late now. I can't have a child, like she had, poor cow. The only thing I want, she's got.'

"When did you have the pleasure of her company?" she asked her big brother.

"Just before I went overseas. April Fool's Day."

Joan went home and sat alone in her flat. Gerald was at work and she had nothing to do but think. She thought about Steven's revelation that he had spent April the First with Evelyn and tried to remember what she had told her. One thing stuck in her mind, the memory of Evelyn telling her on the day of her wedding that Louis wasn't her baby's father, but that he was the cause. She now had the solution to that enigma. If that was the case, Louis by leaving her at her brother's house had gotten her into the situation that led to her getting pregnant. Steven must be the father! Holy shit! No wonder Evelyn had kept his identity from her!

Steven's story that Evelyn had offered herself to save Brown had seemed far fetched. Why hadn't Steven taken precautions? Then she recalled how Evelyn had told her of being locked in the room and being raped in the middle of the night. Now she had two reasons for hating Steven. She recalled how he'd gotten her pregnant when she was younger, and how she'd gotten unpregnant, impairing her fecundity in the process. Joan had put together the puzzle. She couldn't believe it possible, but all the pieces fitted into place. She remembered Evelyn telling her that the man was no longer in Adelaide. Steven was in America. The boy was her nephew.

"My brother raped my friend, and I made her get married to a monster, all because of his lust and his thoughtlessness. Now the laugh's on us, because she has a genuine Meredith baby. I've got a barren body and can't have what she has. I've got the man she loves and she's got our baby!"

From that moment she thought of nothing but Evelyn's baby, the baby that her brother must have fathered. From the day that Jonny was born Joan had been slightly envious of Evelyn, but now her envy became an obsession. The one thing that she wanted belonged to that woman. She had once held Gerald's love, now she had the Meredith's child. Joan had that love, now she wanted that child.

That evening she told Gerald what the doctor had told her, without any tears, and she told him that she wanted to adopt a child. He told her that he thought it a good idea. She seemed in a better mood.

As the days passed Joan settled down and became more like her normal self. Gerald stopped worrying about her and forgot about having a psychiatrist examine her. They talked about their plans to build a house. When Richard came to dinner the next day, Joan took him aside and questioned him about Evelyn.

"Richard, I heard that Evelyn's left Brown. I'd like to see her. Where is she staying?"

"You can see her at the university."

"I'd like to see Jonny too. I haven't seen him since he was a day old. Do you think Evelyn would mind me going to visit her?"

"Joan, she's staying with friends of mine and no one but her parents know her address. We don't want Brown to know. I'll invite them all over to my place one day and you can drop in."

"I'll come by myself, without Gerald."

"Yes, I'd do that."

A week later he invited the Grovers to afternoon tea with Evelyn and the two children. It was a sunny day and they were able to have tea on the back lawn. At four Joan called in as planned on an unannounced visit. Richard introduced her to his friends.

"Joan, meet Dawn and Bruce Grover. Evelyn, Joan wants to see Jonny."

"You call him over. He comes quicker when you call him."

Joan at once noticed that the three of them were like mother, father and son. Then she took a good look at Jonny and any doubts that she might have had about who his father was, vanished. Looking into his face was like looking into a mirror. There was the same black hair and hazel eyes. He was a miniature of herself, of Steven, a Meredith. Evelyn, looking at the two of them, also noticed the likeness. For the first time in her life she felt worried about this, and wondered if anyone else would notice, especially Joan. She was glad when Joan left. She felt uneasy in her company, uneasy and frightened.

"Richard," she asked, "did you know that Joan was coming over this afternoon?"

"Yes, she wanted to see you and Jonny, so I invited you all and she just dropped in. The truth is, I asked her to. You don't mind, do you? I didn't want her visiting you where you're staying."

"You shouldn't have done that to me. Why was she so keen to see Jonny?"

Richard had never heard her speak like this. Evelyn was upset and she was angry.

"Because she can't have children of her own."

"The poor thing." She forgot her anger. "No wonder she made me feel strange. I can't comfort her, I suppose she wouldn't want me to know."

"They want to adopt children. Do you know any children who want to be millionaires?"

"May I ask another question? Who can't have children, Joan or Gerald?"

"Joan had a miscarriage. Does that answer your question?"

She was sorry for Gerald, that he'd never have the joy of parenting a child, a joy that she herself had once hoped to share with him. He was still her first love, Joan Meredith couldn't take that away from her. She could frighten her, she could upset her, but Gerald had loved her first, Joan had been his second choice. It was cold comfort.

"Richard, please don't arrange any meetings like this again. Don't even ask me. I don't want Joan Meredith coming and gloating over me. Richard, I think I'll go to another state and to hell with Louis and the divorce and the Merediths."

She didn't say 'The Fishers'. Then Evelyn said something strange, a slip of the tongue. "I suppose the inability to have a child isn't grounds for divorce, is it, Richard? It must impose a terrible strain on a relationship."

"They'll get over it."

Richard took them all home. The young mother was quiet and so was he. Joan's visit had been a dark cloud over their friendship. She had used him and hurt them both, but that wasn't Joan's intention. She just wanted to know if Jonny was Steven's child and now she knew.

Richard was annoyed at himself for being used, but he couldn't understand the purpose of her visit. It wasn't to gloat, she had nothing to gloat about any more, but it had a purpose. He was sure of that. He was sure of another thing. Evelyn was wondering if Gerald might want to leave Joan. He was glad that he hadn't come with his wife. It might have opened old wounds.

1955 and 1956 were great years for Rock and Roll and for Elvis Presley, but neither phenomenon was welcomed by the press. On May 14th, Elvis gave a press conference and was portrayed as a near-illiterate who spent most of his time in amusement parks and spoke in a corrupt dialect of English. *Time*, on June 18th, reported on a Bill Haley Rock and Roll Concert, "It does for music what a motor-cycle club at full throttle does for a Sunday afternoon. The results bear a passing resemblance to Hitler mass meetings." *Newsweek* commented similarly on the same concert.

John Osborne's play *Look Back In Anger* opened in London in May, upsetting conventions of middle-class English Drama. It received mixed reviews.

On the 2nd of July the papers were full of the story of Marilyn Monroe and Arthur Miller's wedding. They were an odd couple, she the sexy *Dumb Blonde* and he the playwright, the *intellectual*. It was the type of romance that Hollywood screenwriters might conjure up. Marilyn Monroe had to travel back to London where she was making a film, but the US State Department held up his passport application, apparently because his play, *The Crucible*, was an allegory of the McCarthy Communist witch hunt. Arthur Miller got his passport, but was also given a fine and a jail sentence for refusing to denounce his friends, a verdict that he successfully appealed against.

Flood waters were sweeping down the Darling and Murray River systems from earlier torrential rain, threatening the fruit growing areas of Victoria and South Australia. Troops were sent to reinforce the river banks in Evelyn's home town. A flood tide was slowly coming down the river towards Renmark.

Hoad and Rosewall returned to Wimbledon and met in the men's final, Hoad winning in four sets.

July 27th. Nasser nationalised the Suez Canal. There was singing and dancing in the streets of Cairo and anger in Great Britain and France, the co-owners of the canal. The canal was not just the property of the Canal Company, it was a strategic waterway, the route taken by tankers bringing Middle East oil to Europe. Egypt was receiving military help from the Soviet block. Anything could happen.

In July, Boris Pasternak, Russian poet and author, survivor of Stalin's purges, submitted his novel, *Dr Zhivago*, to the literary magazine *Novy Mir* for publication. It was rejected.

In July, Jim Laker took 19 Australian wickets in the fourth Test played in Manchester, a feat never performed in first class cricket.

Joan Fisher did not go to find out about adopting a child, as she'd told Gerald she would. Instead, she stayed home brooding about Evelyn and her son, fathered by her brother. Finally at the end of July she went to see him in his office in the brand new Meredith Building.

"Steven, do you remember telling me in this very office that you spent a night with Louis Brown's wife?"

"Yes, but she wasn't his wife then."

"On April 1st, 1953?"

Steven had to think. He didn't know the date he slept with every girl. This was easy, it was a date that he could remember, six weeks before he went to California.

"Yes, I think it was April Fool's Day."

"Well, big brother, April Fool! It looks like you are a daddy. Jonny Brown was born nine months to the day, on New Year's Day 1954. Why didn't you take precautions?"

"I can't remember. You think that I'm the boy's father and not Louis Brown? That's a laugh."

She could have killed her brother for that laugh.

"Yes, you bastard, just before you went overseas. I was with her when she missed her period and I had to help her. I heard her story, but she didn't tell me it was you. She didn't offer herself to you. That's a lie, isn't it?"

"Do you think that I forced myself on her?"

"She told me, Steven. She didn't tell me who, you told me that. Did you force her to go to bed with you?"

"Let's say that I persuaded her."

"You threatened her?"

"A little."

"You locked her up?"

"A little."

Joan wasn't shocked. She knew her brother. He used to prey on her friends, until she stopped him. It was just as she'd expected it.

"I've heard enough. You also raped her while she was asleep. I hope that you're pleased with yourself. I stopped her from killing herself two months later."

"I'd have helped her, with money, that is."

"And I thought at the time that Brown was responsible."

"The coward ran away and left her."

"To another bully. Because you found her in your house, it gave you the right to lock her up, rape her and impregnate her? No wonder you aren't married, Steven Meredith, you're a woman hater and a sadist. Do you rape many women? I've hated you for years for what you did to my friend, not knowing your identity. Now that I know that it was you, it makes me sick. The funny thing is, that she's quite happy. She's got a fine little boy and she loves him and you've got nothing. If it's any consolation, Steven, your son's being well looked after."

"She had no right to have the baby. It's as if she stole my sperm!"

'Damn him!' she thought. 'What right does he have to object?'

"You should have kept your sperm to yourself. Steven, I want that child."

"What do you want me to do?"

"You're his father. Get him for me."

He thought Joan was joking, but Joan wasn't. She wanted that little boy. It was his turn to be shocked.

"Why that particular child? You could adopt or even buy a baby from an unmarried mother."

"I don't want another baby. I want that boy. It has our blood in its veins. It looks like us. It's a Meredith."

"Not in the eyes of the world. It's Jonny Brown, the son of Evelyn and Louis Brown."

"I've seen him, Steven. He's a Meredith. Go and acknowledge that you are the father and buy the boy back."

"For me? I don't want the child."

"For me, your sister."

"What do you mean, buy back the child?"

"Pay her whatever she wants, just get me the child. I'll see that you get the money back."

'God,' he thought. 'She really wants that child.'

"How much?" he asked.

"I don't care. The child is our child, so money doesn't mean anything. We're worth God knows how many millions. What is the money worth if some other woman has our child? I'd give all my wealth to have that boy."

"A million pounds?"

Steven was joking. She wouldn't pay that much for the baby.

"I've got more than that if we need it. I've got the shares Daddy gave us when we got married."

"You want me to offer Brown's wife a million pounds for her son? What if she won't take it?"

"Offer her two million, ten million."

"Have you got ten million?"

"No, but you have. I'll have to pay you back. When we have a child, Daddy's bound to give us some of my fortune. Steven, please do this, I'm relying on you. I want that boy."

"What are you going to tell Gerald? He'll want to know what happened to the money."

"He couldn't care less. He doesn't give a damn what I do with my money. He won't know about it. He wants a child to play with, when he comes home from working for our Daddy."

"What about Brown's wife? She's your friend, isn't she?"

"With the money she'll be able to buy her freedom from Brown and marry and have more children. I think I know who'll she marry, too. Better hurry and buy the child, before he pays off Brown and it's too late."

Richard wouldn't want to adopt Brown's baby. Joan was kidding herself. She had seen him playing with Jonny. There were flaws in her plan.

"OK., sister, I'll buy the boy, if that's what you want, but I think you're out of your mind."

"What if I am? I'm going to have a real Meredith child by a fine mother. What a pity I can't tell Mom and Dad and Gerald. Gerald! He's the last person who must find out. Perhaps we can get Evelyn to move to another state."

As long as Evelyn was in Adelaide she was a threat to Joan's happiness. She had her man, now she wanted her child. She was forgetting what Evelyn went through to keep Jonny.

Chapter Thirty-One

August 1956

Steven Meredith thought for a few days before he spoke to Louis Brown. Joan wanted Evelyn's boy, his own son that he could never admit to fathering. Good, he would get him for her. She was prepared to pay a million pounds, more if necessary. What if Evelyn wouldn't sell, not even for ten million? Steven knew that she hated him and that she wasn't in dire straights. She had a job and she also had a friend, Richard Flynn, who with all his land and his share in the cannery was worth almost a million. Joan was crazy. Evelyn wouldn't part with the boy willingly. Brown, his legal father would. He'd sell his mother if he had one. He sold out Evelyn for a lousy examination paper, the miserable bastard. Steven decided to get Brown to give him the boy.

One evening a man employed by a solicitor followed Evelyn home from the university, noted down her new address and passed it on to Steven Meredith. He told this solicitor what he was planning and got him to prepare a set of adoption papers to trick Evelyn into signing away Jonny. Then, he called Brown into his office.

"Louis, how would you like to make a bit of money, £15,000?"

He had Brown figured for a sucker. That was a bad mistake.

"Very much, Dr Meredith. What do I have to do?"

"My sister wants to adopt your child. I want you to get your wife to sign adoption papers."

Brown thought that he was joking.

"She'll never do that. What do you really want?"

"Louis, my sister Joan wants to adopt little Jonny."

"I'm separated from my wife. I don't even know where she lives, not that I care."

"I have her address."

"Give it to me."

He had no plans to go to her, to hurt her, but she was his wife. He had a right to know where she was living.

"I thought you didn't care. I'll tell you when we have an agreement. I want you to persuade her to sign adoption papers."

"You want to buy my child for a lousy £15,000?"

Brown knew he was dealing with a multi-millionaire. Meredith wanted something from him. He decided to milk him for as much as he could get.

"He'll be brought up as one of the family. He'll be a millionaire before he leaves school and be my sister's heir. What can you provide for him?"

"I don't understand. Why doesn't Joan have a baby of her own?"

"She can't."

"That's a laugh. Tell her if Gerald Fisher isn't up to it, I'm willing to step in again."

He hated Joan's husband as much as he hated her. He'd smacked him in the face and got away with it.

"You watch what you say, Brown."

"No deal, Meredith. That stuck-up bitch isn't going to part with the kid for a mere £15,000. Make it a million and you can have the brat tomorrow, with or without her consent."

"Do you think that she'll sell us the kid for a million?"

"No, but I will."

"A million is out of the question. How about £15,000 for each of you?"

"Chicken feed. What's so special about the kid?"

For a moment, Steven suspected that he knew about Jonny. It wasn't an unreasonable supposition. He didn'ant swer the question truthfully. Instead, he made one of his private jokes. "His parents. His mother's quite intelligent and his father's *brilliant*. We don't want to adopt just any child. Let's make it a round £50,000."

"Each? That's a little better."

"You'll get me the boy for £50,000 each?"

Steven had taken Brown to be a fool. He was learning that Bully Brown wasn't as stupid as he'd thought him to be.

"First I'll tell you what I'm going to do. My dear little bitch of a wife won't part with the brat willingly, so we'll have to trick her. Make her think I'm signing the brat over to her, or I'm signing divorce papers. That'll do it. I reckon she'd do anything if she thinks she's getting free of me. Then slip in the paper that she has to sign among the rest of the papers. Then we'll have to get the boy away from her. It isn't going to be easy."

"We'll have a meeting with my solicitor. He's an expert in shady deals. He's got me out of some scrapes with women in the past and he traced your wife for me. If the two of you take the money and sign the papers, she'll never see the kid again."

"I want my money in cash, when you get the kid. After I get the kid for you I want to piss off, get out of town. If your plan misfires, I could go to jail."

"It won't misfire, my solicitor will see to that, but I agree, you should leave Adelaide."

"I think with a quarter of a million, I could live comfortably in Rio. I want £100,000 for her and 150,000 for me. A quarter of a million in US dollars or sterling, whichever takes less space, cash on delivery."

"We agreed to 100,000."

Louis Brown laughed at him. He had once dismissed him. Now that he wanted something from him, Brown was taking him for a ride.

"No we didn't. If you don't want to pay our removal costs, then go and talk to her yourself. Better still, I'll go over to the Benham Building now and tell her all about your generous offer, Dr Meredith. I wonder how much *Truth* would pay for a report on our conversation."

Steven wasn't worried about the newspaper, but if the boy's mother was alerted, they could kiss Jonny good-bye.

"I'll pay. Why are you so keen to leave the country?"

"Because, when we take the *tin lid* away from my *trouble and strife*, I don't want to be around, that's why."

"She'll make a fuss?"

Brown knew she would, but he didn't want Meredith to know that.

"I just don't want to be around."

"That suits me. I don't want you around either. We'll meet tomorrow with the solicitor and then we'll get Joan her little boy."

The following Monday Evelyn had a call from a solicitor.

"Mrs Brown, I represent Louis Brown. He's prepared to sign divorce papers and relinquish all rights to your child. Can you come and see me at my office, tomorrow 12:30?"

Evelyn couldn't believe what she was hearing.

"Why the sudden change in mind?"

"Can we discuss that tomorrow?"

"Sure. I'll be there at 12:30."

Evelyn told Richard the news. They were both elated. He promised to come around the following evening to hear how it went. He wondered how she'd feel towards him, once the impediment of her marriage no longer existed. She began to hope that she could enjoy a normal life again. For the first time in three years she longed for someone to hold her close and kiss her. She expected that man would be Richard.

When she arrived at the solicitor's office, the man greeted her like a long lost cousin. That alone should have put her on her guard. Then he put on his coat and picking up his briefcase, ushered her out of the office.

"I've got the papers here. Come with me and we'll have them signed in no time."

"Where are we going?"

"To sign the papers with your husband. It's his signature that we need."

"Why can't we sign them in the office? Why didn't he come to the office?"

"I'm afraid that I told him that we'd come to him. If it isn't convenient I'll arrange a meeting next week."

'Next week he mightn't want to sign,' she thought and fell into the trap. When she saw the car passing the university and heading to North Adelaide, she asked, "Why isn't Louis at work?"

"It's his lunch-hour."

"Why does he want a divorce now? Does he want to get married to someone else?"

"No, I convinced him that you could go ahead and claim maintenance and take a big slice of his earnings. You'll agree to make no such claims, Mrs Brown?"

"What about the £5,000 he wanted me to pay?"

"He knows that you haven't got that kind of money. If you both waive all claims, we can get a hearing quickly and you'll both be free in no time."

"It seems too good to be true." It wasn't.

Evelyn entered Louis's room for the first time in her life. She shuddered as she crossed the threshold and saw Louis sitting down at the table waiting for her. She was glad that there was a third person in the room and that the entrance door was open. The room was like a prison with all the outside shutters closed. The main feature in the room was Brown's big bed. It, more than anything else in the room, frightened her. She sat with her back to it, at the table, facing Louis. One of his ears was badly scarred, where he'd been lacerated and sewn up by a medical student.

The solicitor put his briefcase on the table and removed from it a thick pile of papers. He quickly explained what each group of papers was and asked Louis to sign, after which Evelyn had to witness his signature with her own. The first paper was a statement by Louis admitting he'd been intimate with an unnamed girl on a specific date and place.

There were three sets of papers like that. Evelyn wondered if a judge would accept such statements. It sounded too much like collusion to her. She made a mental note to ask her own solicitor, scolding herself for not contacting him and bringing him along to the meeting.

Then Louis signed papers agreeing to make no claims and she signed a similar paper. Her solicitor may object, but this was what she wanted, a clean break with that man. Finally they signed papers in which she was told that Louis agreed to give total custody of Jonny to her. What she didn't know was that when she thought that she was witnessing his signature, there was a space for a typist to add a line saying that she too was relinquishing her right to her son. There was room to add the name of Mrs and Mrs Gerald Fisher as the recipients, the foster parents of John Mark. Evelyn hadn't signed away her son. She had read the papers, and they were, when she signed them, what they seemed to be. An hour later they would be changed by the solicitor himself, and Jonny would belong to Gerald and Joan.

When the papers were signed, they all got up to go and Evelyn followed the solicitor to the door. He stepped out, and Louis stepped into the doorway, blocking her exit. Evelyn could see that he had her where he wanted her, alone in that room of his.

"Wait, please wait for me," she called out, but the shyster was gone. Louis pushed his long-lost wife inside. Then he closed and locked the door.

Evelyn felt panic grip her. No man had locked her in a room since that night with Steven Meredith. It was the one thing she dreaded. She was trapped by Louis Brown at the very moment that she thought that she was to be free of him.

"Louis, open the door. I have a job to go to."

"You're not going back to work today."

"Louis, please let me go."

"Did you enjoy signing the papers?"

"Not very much. It was a bit of a bore. Now can I go?"

"No, you're staying here, Mrs Brown."

Now she knew what he wanted, or she thought she did.

"Louis, we're legally separated. You can't keep me here against my will. Why did you sign those papers, if you intended to kidnap me?"

"Those papers! Those divorce papers aren't going anywhere. The other ones are. You signed away your little boy, Evelyn, your pride and joy. You signed adoption papers."

"No, I read them. You signed custody to me."

'This is all a nightmare,' she thought, 'This isn't happening. Pray, God, it isn't happening.'

"That solicitor is a crook. All he needed was your signature on the document and it'll be changed to read that we both signed over our s tono Mr and Mrs Gerald Fisher."

It couldn't be, not Gerald, not Joan, unless she knew whose son Jonny really was.

"You're lying."

"Have you ever known me to lie?"

He must be joking!

"Louis! The gin in the drinks! The exam papers! When haven't you lied to me?"

"Well, Joan is buying our little boy. That is no lie."

"You bastard. I'll fight it. It can't be legal. I'm going straight to my solicitor as soon as I get out of here."

"No you won't. You're going to stay here and rot in the room that I built."

"What do you mean?"

There was a wicked grin on his face. He had her where he wanted her, and this time he wasn't playing games, he wasn't lying to her.

"Look around the room. I built it to keep nosy people like you out. It was my own special private room, where I could have women over and shag to my heart's content without anyone else knowing. No one will know that you are here. You'll never be seen again."

"You're mad, Louis. I'll scream and someone will come."

"Who'll hear you? The land here faces the parklands on two sides and there's a telephone exchange on the other side. Besides with the shutters on the windows, someone would have to be standing in the backyard to hear you. You are going to die in this room, Mrs Brown."

She could tell that he wasn't joking. Louis was a potential killer. Richard had told her that a hundred times. He had warned her not to get into a situation like this.

"Where will you be? They'll hang you if you kill me."

"I'm going to get £250,000 as soon as I hand over my son to his new family. While you're dying here, I'll be over the seas and far away. They might even blame Joan and Gerald Fisher for your death and take the boy away from them. I hope they hang them! I've got my plane tickets in my pocket and my bags in the car."

"I'll be missed. People will search for me."

"Yes, but will they find you in time? They certainly won't find me."

"I'll survive, Louis Brown. I don't give up that easily."

"I should kill you and put you out of your misery, but that's not the way I do things."

"No, you drive people to their death, like you did to Jonny Marco."

"You shut up."

He didn't like Evelyn bringing that up.

"What did you do to him, Louis? It must have been something terrible."

Evelyn had to know. She didn't know if she was going to live or die, but she had to know what happened to Jonny Marco. She was also playing for time.

"It was terrible. At first I was sorry. I only wanted to frighten him, have a bit of fun at his expense. The truth is, now I'm glad I did it. I'm just sorry that I can't do it to Joan Meredith. She deserves to die more than you do. You should have asked Joan what happened to Marco, she was there. I used her as bait."

He looked at his watch.

"Well, my love, it's getting late. I have to see Mrs Grover now and collect little Jonny Fisher. That'll be his new name now. I promised to give him to Joan and then her big brother would give me my money. It's funny, Mrs Brown, tonight you're going to give your love a child and you've never slept with him. Our son's going to be a millionaire."

"How could you sell your own child?"

"For half a million I'd have sold him into slavery. One thing puzzles me. Why are they willing to pay so much money for our child?"

Evelyn tried to hold back her tears but couldn't. Brown continued, "I'm glad that the rich Fishers can't have children of their own. Serves them right! It rather makes you feel proud that they want our little boy."

"You're lying. Neither of them would take Jonny away from me."

"You're giving him to them for old times sake."

"So why won't you let me go?"

"So you can go there and get him back? I'd have to return the money and look for another job."

"Let me out of here, Louis!" she screamed at him.

"No, I don't want you to be found, Mrs Brown, until I'm in another country."

"So what are you going to do with me?"

"I'll be back as soon as I deliver Jonny to Joan and then, Mrs Brown, you are going to make up for all the nights you've kept me out of your bed, and what I paid for when I married you. Today, my dear, we're going to have a long delayed honeymoon and then it's good-bye for ever. I'm going to leave you to die here."

He meant it. He meant to rape her and leave her to die. She would never see her son again. She asked him, "Why?"

"For what you did to me. For that contract you made me agree to in front of my mother. For stealing my mother away from me, and my birthright too. All the money that should have come to me. It wasn't much, it wasn't the wealth of the Merediths, but it was all I had, and you and that brat of yours took it away from me. When you got pregnant, how I'll never know, you made me marry you and then wouldn't share my bed. You had to add that humiliation. In front of my mother! Well this afternoon I'll do the humiliating. It's going to be like old times on the river bank and the boarding house. You might even enjoy it again. Be nice to me and I might consider taking you to Rio with me."

Evelyn said nothing. She didn't want to anger him. She had to keep calm and get away from him. At least he didn't know the real reason that the Merediths wanted Jonny. They must have found out that Steven was his real father. Evelyn had noticed something when Joan picked up Jonny at Richard's place. She must have wanted to confirm her suspicions. What upset her most was the thought that Joan, and especially Gerald, could do this to her. It was that idea that was driving her out of her mind.

Slowly she took grip of herself. She stopped crying and looked around the room. She saw the telephone outlet, from which the phone had been removed, and noticed that there were no electric appliances in the room either. She also saw that steel bars had recently been placed inside the windows. Louis had planned her incarceration in advance.

Her silence annoyed him. He wanted her to beg and grovel. He had her at his mercy. Why was she so silent? What was she thinking? Was she still despising him? But he had to go; the sooner he went, the sooner he'd get back and make up for privileges denied.

"*Au revoir*, Mrs Brown. I have to go now, but I'll be back soon. I have to deliver a child. I want to do it before the men folk get home. Then I'll be back to show you that I haven't lost my touch. The bed's over there. Make yourself comfortable, but don't begin without me."

Then, locking the door behind him, he left.

Evelyn sat in her silent prison. She estimated that she had an hour and a half to get out. She looked about the room. Louiwas s right; she could shout her lungs off and no one would hear her. She tried the doors. They were both locked and too solid to break down or to lift off their hinges. Then she looked at the barred windows. They offered no way out. She went into the bathroom and looked at the small window. It too was barred. The cupboards were empty. She tried to get a drink from the tap, but the water was turned off. So was the electricity. Even the toilet cistern had been emptied of its water. She was to be denied drink, so that she'd die of thirst in a few days. Evelyn knew that she was in trouble. Louis was serious about leaving her to die, deadly serious.

There was no escape through the doors or windows. The floor was hardwood and even if she had tools it would take days and a lot of strength to tunnel out. That left the ceiling. Evelyn remembered how the roof and ceiling had been constructed. If she could break the plaster, she could get into the roof cavity and crawl through it into the old part of the house. There was no time to lose. She looked around the room. There was Louis's old piano by the wall, but its casters were rusty and it wouldn't move.

She climbed onto the table that they'd used for signing the documents, and felt the plaster ceiling. She scratched at it and beat it with her hands. It was too strong. Then she took off a shoe and hit it with the heel. It made a small hole.

Evelyn got down from the table and pushed it over near the inside wall. Then she pulled the bedclothes and the mattress off the bed, upending it next to the table. She climbed on to the table again, onto the end of the bed. It swayed and for a moment she thought that she was going to fall. Steadying herself against the wall, she hit out against the ceiling with her shoe. Soon she had a hole she could get her fingers into. She pulled out a handful of plaster and began enlarging the hole with her hands, exposing the lathing and the roof frame.

Breaking a piece of lathing, she stood up on the bed with her head and shoulders inside the roof space, and looked around. There was light coming in through the tiles and she could just see the frame of the old house. Taking her shoes with her, she lifted herself up into the space above and crawled onto the timbers. Then she squeezed between the timbers of the old roof into the space above the kitchen. She could have pushed out roofing tiles and called for help, but she didn't know that. Evelyn had a better escape plan.

She slowly crossed above the room until she reached a brick wall at the other end of the kitchen. She had to go around this, where the roof was high and she could stand up. Then she walked above what she thought was the corridor. It was easy to determine where the rooms started and ended, she could see the tops of the walls. Evelyn crossed into the space above another room and pushed a hole in its plaster with her foot. Looking down she saw as she had expected, her old room with her old bed in it. She made another hole over the bed, enlarged it, and throwing her shoes onto the floor, dropped down onto the bed.

Somehow the old room made her feel more confident and satisfied now that she'd escaped from Louis's prison, but there wasn't time to gloat. Louis was at this very time giving her son to her friends, her Judas friends who had betrayed her. There was a lump in her throat when she thought of Gerald conspiring to steal Jonny from her. He had reason to hate her, but not to do this to her. As for Joan, why did she want the baby that she'd told Evelyn to get rid of? She was playing God again. Joan liked playing God with other peoples' lives. Evelyn was sure that Richard would help her, old friendships or not. He knew right from wrong.

Closing the door, Evelyn locked her room and put the key into her handbag. She pictured Louis looking for her escape hole and his frustration at finding the door locked. There was a telephone in the kitchen, but Evelyn was too anxious to get out of the house to use it. She couldn't unlock the front door, so she let herself out of a window and ran as fast as she could away from the house into the heart of North Adelaide. Finding a hotel, she went into the lobby and asked if she could make a phone call. There was a public telephone outside, but she wanted to be inside among people, just in case Louis came looking for her. Her first call was to Dawn.

"Dawn, is Jonny alright?"

"Thank heaven you called, Evelyn. Your husband came twenty minutes ago and took Jonny. He was asleep and he didn't even get him dressed. I told him to go away and leave Jonny, but he's a big man. What could I do?"

"Dawn, don't worry. He won't hurt Jonny. I know where he's taking him and I'm going to get him back."

"I rang you at work, but they didn't know where you were. Richard rang too and he's terribly worried."

"Did he say where he is now?"

"Yes, you're to call him at home. Shall I call the police?"

"No, if we need them we'll call them ourselves. I'm going to call Richard now. Don't worry, I'll get Jonny back, and I'll let you know all about it later."

She was calm when she spoke to Dawn, but when she heard Richard answer the phone, she broke down and cried.

"Richard, He's taken Jonny. Richard, come and help me."

"Where are you?"

"In the lobby of a Hotel, on the corner of O'Connell and Tynte St. Gerald's taken my baby."

"Evelyn, sit down and relax. Order a drink. I'll be there as fast as I can. If you're in any danger call the police."

"Come quickly, Richard. I'm scared."

The lady at the desk brought her a glass of sherry.

She'd overheard what Evelyn had said and thought the drink would help her.

"Here, love. This'll steady your nerves. What's the matter?"

"I'm separated from my husband and he found out where I live and took my child away."

"Look at yourself, you're covered with dust."

"He locked me up and I had to crawl out through the roof. I came in here in case he comes looking for me. He's a big man, over six foot."

"Well he won't touch you here. We've got some big men working here. If you see him, call out."

"Someone's coming to fetch me. He should be here soon. He's got a new, blue Holden. Don't set your men onto him."

"Drink up and wipe your face. The drink's on the house."

The lady stayed with her until Richard arrived. Evelyn thanked her and got into the car with him. She looked about, but there was no sign of Louis. It was comforting to be with Richard. As they drove away she told him from the beginning what had happened to her, about Louis and the day's infamy.

"He told me that he was going to sell Jonny to Joan and Gerald for money and leave me locked up in the flat to die."

"Evelyn, I spoke to Gerald last night. He told me that Joan was adopting a child. He was as pleased as Punch. I'm quite sure that he didn't know that it would be Jonny. He would have told me. You know him, Evelyn, he would never get involved in such a scheme. He would never do anything to hurt you."

"But they're taking Jonny away from me!"

"I'm going to drop you off and then I'm going over to the house. I'll get to the bottom of this and I'll get Jonny back. Pack your bags. I don't think you should stay with the Grovers with Brown on the loose."

"Where can I go?"

"We'll decide that later. First things first. I think that Joan's behind this. She's been a bit crazy ever since she discovered that she can't have children. Gerald wanted her to see a doctor. Then a few weeks ago she wanted to see Jonny. What's so special about Jonny?"

"Richard, I had a secret that no one knew. It's rather complicated, but I'm not entirely to blame. Louis isn't Jonny's father, Steven

Meredith is. I never had a love affair with him, what I did I didn't do willingly. That's why they want Jonny."

Richard forgot where he was. He almost had an accident. At the last minute the other car, in the right, gave way.

"Holy shit! I thought Brown was Jonny's father. That's why he married you, wasn't it?"

Evelyn told him the story of the night that she spent with Steven Meredith.

"She knows, Evelyn. I even noticed the likeness, when she came to see the boy. Gerald doesn't know about that visit, she asked me not to tell him. She's doing this behind his back. Listen, Evelyn, I have to be quick. Brown will go back to the house and when he finds you gone, he might come back. I want you out of here by then."

They pulled up outside the Grovers' house and the two young mothers embraced. Richard made a phone call and returned.

"I'm going to get Jonny. Get your things packed. Dawn, when will Bruce be back?"

"Not until five thirty."

"Call him, tell him you'll be at your mother's place. I'll take you there when I come back. Tell the neighbours to keep an eye on the place. If Brown comes back, tell them to call the police. I'll see you later. Don't worry, someone's coming to look after you."

Richard ran to the car and drove off.

Ten minutes later there was a knock on the door. Evelyn looked out of the window and saw a car in the driveway. It was an English Sports Saloon, brand new and sparkling. Unless he'd stolen it, it wasn't Louis.

"Who's there?"

"Evelyn, it's Gerald, let me in."

Evelyn told Dawn to open the door. Gerald came in carrying a rifle, which he propped against the wall.

Evelyn cried out to him hysterically. "What have you done to my baby? Where is he?"

He hadn't known what to expect, least of all Evelyn's outburst. If he hadn't put up his hands, she would have struck him.

"Evelyn, I've seen him. He's with Joan and her mother. He's alright. Richard told me over the phone that he's your boy. Evelyn, I had no idea. I had no idea that Brown brought him, or that you were in any danger. I came straight away."

"You stole my baby!"

"No, Evelyn, no! I wouldn't buy a child from anyone. Joan told me that he was legally adopted. Is that beautiful child yours and Brown's?"

She felt better. Gerald's presence and his protests had a calming effect. Evelyn had to know that Gerald wasn't in on the conspiracy.

"He's my Jonny. Brown and some crooked lawyer tricked me into signing papers. He was going to kill me."

"I wouldn't have let them get away with this. I couldn't do this to you, Evelyn. I love you."

"No you don't. You married Joan Meredith."

"Evelyn, I love you. You rejected me and married that monster. What was I to do? Joan wasn't my first choice. We'll get you your boy back and then I'll go away, if that's what you want. I can't go back to that house again, after what Joan did today. I'll go away."

That was the last thing that she wanted. He had just told her that he loved her. She had never expected to hear that again.

"Don't Gerald, I couldn't bear to lose you again. I still love you."

They embraced and kissed, forgetting that Dawn was with them. She went to pack a bag for herself and her daughter. Reunited, Gerald spoke to Evelyn.

"What are we going to do, Evelyn? I can't go back to Joan after what she's done to you."

"Brown wants to kill me."

"Don't ever leave me. This time we're staying together."

"I was mad to let you go, Gerald."

"You didn't let me go! I messed up, not you, Evelyn. I'm going to marry you this time."

"That's what I want, Gerald, but we're both married to other people. I have a son, don't you remember?"

"Yes, and when we're married I'll adopt him and bring him up as my son, legally. Richard's bringing him back."

"What if he can't?"

"He can't? A Meredith is no match for Richard Flynn. Did he tell you how he took them for a quarter of a million? You know, he's terribly fond of you. He hinted to me that he wanted to court you, as if he had to ask me first."

"What did you say?"

"What could I say? I had mixed feelings. That old pain came back, but I would have been overjoyed to think that you'd found a nice person and gotten away from that overgrown turd. I didn't know that you still loved me."

"You doubted my love?"

"Evelyn, of course I did. You returned my letter, refused to see me, married another man and had his child. I never knew why, but I was sure that you'd stopped loving me."

"Yes, I did all of that, except for returning your letter. That was Dad's doing. I wanted a word from you. I was sure that you hated me. Then when I knew that you still loved me, it was too late, I was pregnant. Gerald, I never meant to go to bed with Louis. I thought that you didn't want me and he took advantage of me. I never meant it to happen. I never meant to hurt you."

"It's all over now. I wasn't blameless, was I?"

"I'll make it up to you, Gerald, but you'll have to love my son. He's cost me so much, but without him I wouldn't have survived."

"Evelyn, I blame myself for what happened to us. It's I who have to make up for the past. I said things that I shouldn't have. I'm so glad that we're getting a second chance. I hope Richard comes back quickly with our son. Evelyn, I'll be the best of fathers to him."

'Poor Richard,' she thought. 'I know he loves me. He hinted so often that he'd marry me when I was free. We'd have been happy too. I hope he won't be hurt now.'

But she knew Richard. So did Gerald. He was a survivor.

Chapter Thirty-Two

August 1956

After delivering Jonny to Joan, a very distasteful meeting for both of them, Louis Brown went to collect his money. Steven wasn't going to part with such a large sum immediately. He told Louis, that he wanted to check up with Joan, and that he'd give him the money first thing in the morning. Louis was disappointed. He had wanted to show the money to Evelyn, to gloat a bit as he renewed his acquaintance with her. He had a plane to catch the following afternoon in Sydney, so he'd have to get the money and catch the first plane in the morning. Brown went back to his house looking forward to getting what was due to him from his wife.

As Steven went to see his sister and meet his son for the first time, Brown went to rape his recaptured wife. Louis switched on the electricity to his room and unlocked the door. When he turned on the light that feeling of utter humiliation came back. Evelyn wasn't there. He looked around the empty room and flew into a rage. He wanted to hurt her, but she wasn't there to be hurt.

He looked at the ceiling, remembering how he had put the plaster up with his own hands and helped the craftsman attach it to the cornices. Now the ceiling was holed and the cornice cracked. It had survived an earthquake, to be smashed by that bitch of a wife. The ceiling would never look the same. He liked his house and the thought of abandoning it, without even selling it, had rankled. But he couldn't have sold it, not with his wife starving to death in it.

Louis unlocked the inner door and raced from room to room looking for Evelyn. When he found her door locked, he knew that she'd locked it. He knew that she wouldn't be inside, but he had to be sure. He battered at the door until the frame gave way and he could look inside. He looked at the hole in the ceiling and he saw red. She had tricked him and locked the door just to put the boot in. Then he found the open window through which she had fled. He ran out to the car to chase her, not knowing where to look. He knew that the money which he should have received wouldn't be coming to him now. With no thought to the consequences, he set out to get his revenge on those who had humiliated him. He drove to the Meredith estate.

When Richard arrived at the Merediths, he asked to see Joan. She
received him in the spacious lounge room.

"Joan, where's Evelyn's boy? Where's Jonny?"

"Richard, I haven't the faintest idea what you're talking about.
Was it you that called Gerald before?"

"Yes, Joan. I told him what you did to Evelyn and he's furious.
How could you? Are you out of your mind?"

"What I've done? What did you tell him?"

How did Richard find out? If Gerald knew what she'd done to
Evelyn, she could tear up her marriage licence.

"Evelyn's boy was kidnapped and brought here. Gerald described
him to me, so I know he's here. Evelyn's at her wit's end. Brown
locked her up in order to silence her, but she escaped. I've come to
bring Jonny back to her."

"She signed adoption papers giving him to me."

"Bullshit! She was tricked by a solicitor who altered the papers
that she signed. He'll be disbarred if this gets out. The papers won't
hold up in court."

"Oh yes they will. We've got the smartest lawyers in the
country."

"Joan, you're making a big mistake. Bring me the boy or I'll go
from room to room looking for him."

Richard moved towards the door, to show her that he meant what
he said.

"And I'll get the servants to throw you out."

"Joan, be reasonable. I'll come back with Gerald and Evelyn, the
three of us will search the house. We'll bring the police if necessary.
You can't keep the child. A lawyer can't arrange an adoption, you
have to do it through the courts. You can't buy children, not even
with your money."

"Who said we bought the child?"

"Brown was supposed to get a quarter of a million pounds. He
was going to kill Evelyn and take all the money. You would have
been involved in her murder, and he would have gotten away with the
money to South America."

Joan had met her match. Richard knew everything.

"I told them to give her a million, more if she wanted it. I didn't
want her hurt."

"Because Steven begat him? I think 'fathered' too nice an

expression for what that shit of a brother did to her."

"You know?"

"Evelyn told me. Only Brown, the fool, doesn't know."

"Was he really going to kill Evelyn?"

"That, and other things."

Joan had spent a lot of time with Evelyn and a little time with Louis Brown. She pictured him killing her. She knew the thrill he'd get doing it. She broke down.

"Oh my God! I wouldn't have wanted that on my conscience. Not another death."

Richard showed her a small packet of razor blades that he'd taken from his own bathroom, before he picked up Evelyn. He knew how it would affect Joan if he showed it to her.

"Joan, I took this packet of Gillette blades away from Evelyn when I went to get her today."

It was a dramatic prop, a good one.

"Oh my God! Richard, take the boy! Take him quickly back to her. What have I been doing?"

Richard put the packet back into his pocket and followed Joan, sobbing, to her mother's room, where she was trying to comfort Jonny who was also crying, "I want my Mommy. I want my Mommy."

When he saw Richard, his eyes lit up.

"Unca 'ichard, where's Mommy? When can I see Mommy?"

"Joan, who is this Uncle Richard?" her mother asked.

"Mother, Richard was best man at our wedding!"

"Oh yes. How are you, Mr Flynn?"

"Mother, Richard's taking Jonny back to his mother."

"But, I thought you were adopting this child."

"There's been a mistake. His mother wants him back."

"Well the little fellow wants his mother too. Joan, what kind of mistake was made? You said that you had adoption papers."

"His mother didn't realise what she was signing. I'm just glad that she didn't wait until we got attached to him. The sooner he gets back to his mother the better."

"Joan, there'll be other babies. Where's Gerald?"

"He's out, Mother."

"Does he know about this?"

God, this was painful. Richard could see it and felt sorry for Joan. She was the victim now.

"Yes, Mother. Gerald's with the child's mother now."

Mrs Meredith turned to speak to Richard.

"Are you the Richard Flynn who owns Lumen Holdings and Glenside Developments?"

"They are some of my interests."

"I expected that you'd be older. I believe that you are now a shareholder in Meredith Canning. Are you the Richard Flynn that raided our Finsbury acquisition?"

Was she going to praise him or scold him?

"No, Madam. Meredith raided my attempted acquisition. I just stuck in there."

"You're a smart businessman. Why don't you join Meredith Industries?"

"I'm already in partnership with Meredith, in the Finsbury factory. Thanks for the offer, but I intend to take over Meredith, before I retire."

"You certainly have ambition."

"I've got youth on my side, and time. But I have to run now. This young man has to be restored to his mother."

Richard took Joan's mother aside and whispered to her, "Stay with Joan tonight. This has been quite a shock for her."

"What about Gerald?"

"He's not coming back. An adoption should have helped their marriage, but taking this particular child away from his mother has brought the house down like a pack of cards."

"I don't follow you, Mr Flynn."

"Today Joan opened Pandora's box. She can't put the lid back on. This could end badly."

"I don't understand."

"I can't explain. Gerald will be back, but not to stay. Meanwhile don't ask Joan to explain. If she feels like talking, listen to her. Look after her. She wanted that child so much. She'll need all the comfort you can give her."

Joan looked at them. He had never seen her look this way. She looked like the walking dead.

"Why are you whispering to my mother, Richard?"

"I asked her to look after you."

"Can I come with you and make my peace with Evelyn?"

"No, Joan, not tonight. Another day, soon. Louis may be looking for her. You'd only be in the way."

"When will I see Gerald?"

"I don't know. I'll get him to ring as soon as we get to my place."

"What are you going to do?"

"We'll have to get Evelyn and Jonny out of Adelaide to a safe place and then we'll tackle Brown."

He carried Jonny to the front door. He met Steven who was just coming in. He'd heard a lot about this man. Now for the first time in his life, Richard was face to face with the devil himself.

"So that's my son. Is he worth a quarter of a million?"

Richard wanted to throttle the bastard, but he had Jonny in his arms and didn't feel like putting the little guy down.

"To his mother, he's priceless. He's going back to her. He almost cost you your freedom, Dr Meredith. If Brown had killed his mother you'd have been an accessory. Joan might have been, and that lawyer shit too. Did you pay Louis?"

"No, I was going to pay him tomorrow. I wanted to make sure everything was done properly."

"Well it wasn't, you black-hearted bastard. You and your little plan has stirred up a nest of vipers by the name of Louis Brown. I suggest that you give him the money and make sure he leaves the country. If he stays in Adelaide, none of us will sleep in our beds at night, you, Joan, Evelyn, Gerald or me. He'll kill one or all of us. He killed Jonny Marco. He's a maniac and we've made a fool out of him. So pay him and hope that he never comes back again."

"You want me to pay protection money, blackmail money? I'll see him in hell first."

"You'd better pay. You raped his wife and put a cuckoo in his nest. You're not an innocent party."

"Does he know that?"

"He isn't very bright, but I think that sooner or later he'll figure it out, if he stays in Adelaide."

"I won't pay unless we get the child."

This bastard was unbelievable.

"Up yours! The boy goes back to Evelyn and Gerald."

"What do you mean Evelyn and Gerald?"

"Yes, your dirty dealing has cost you a brother-in-law. It looks as if Gerald will be Jonny's father after all, but Joan won't be his mother. The rest of your plan's gone up the spout."

"I wanted the boy for my sister."

"Joan? Your mother's looking after her."

"What's wrong with Joan?"

"This morning she had a loving husband and was expecting to adopt a child, her nephew in fact. Tonight she has neither. She's a sick woman."

"I suppose this is your doing?"

He hadn't been introduced to the man but Steven guessed that he was dealing with Dick Flynn.

"I'm going now, Meredith. Be sure to pay off Brown tomorrow. If you don't you'll regret it."

"The bludger's outside. He's parked opposite the drive."

"Wouldn't you know it! I should have taken Jonny and got out sooner. Is there another way out?"

"There's an exit further up the street. You'll have to pass by Brown as you go. It's a dead end street."

"Good. I'll be able to flash past him before he can turn around. He is facing into the street?"

"Yes."

Richard rang Dawn and asked for Gerald.

"Gerry, I want you to drive Dawn and her girl to her mother's place. Brown knows Dawn's address. He may go there. I'll meet you and Evelyn there. I'm bringing Jonny. If you encounter Brown, drive to police headquarters in Angus Street. I'll do the same if I can't give him the slip."

Richard started the car and drove out of the upper drive. He was past Brown's car, before Louis realised what was happening. As Richard turned the first corner he saw the other car turning in the narrow street, and knew that he could easily lose him. He turned into Glen Osmond Road and then left into the first side street. This was home territory. He drove quickly to Dawn's parents house while Brown drove down Glen Osmond Road looking for him, knowing that he'd been tricked again.

Meanwhile Gerald and Richard were deciding what to do.

"We have to hide Evelyn and Jonny somewhere, Gerald."

"Yes, but where? The Meredith mansion is probably the safest place, but we can't go back there after what's happened. What about your place or my parents' place?"

"Not safe enough. It's a pity we can't smuggle her into St. Ann's. Brown could never get in there."

"Renmark! I'll take her home to her parents. Tomorrow Steven will pay the bastard and when we're sure he's left the country, she can come back to the Grovers."

"Good, you've got a fast car. If you see Brown, head back this way, lose him, and then head north again. Make sure that he doesn't see you heading north. We don't want him to know you're going to Renmark."

"Why don't we call the police?" asked Evelyn.

"They'd have to find him. Besides there's no law against abducting your own child, or wife for that matter. If you want to stop him, you'd have to get a restraining order from the courts and then you could go to the police. They don't know that he's a homicidal maniac until he kills someone. That's why I'm taking you to Renmark."

"I'll pay him myself to go away if Steven doesn't. I don't trust him," said Richard. "How was your reunion?"

His two friends were as close as a couple can get, in company. He didn't have to ask that question.

"Thanks, Richard, for bringing Evelyn and me back together. I know it seems callous, but I've fallen out of love with Joan like a shooting star. Even if Evelyn hadn't taken me back, I couldn't go back to her after what she did. I was angry when I heard about it, but not any more. It feels so good knowing that Evelyn still loves me, that I can't be angry with Joan. I only wish I could help her. It's going to be rough on her."

"I thought that you and Joan were both trying to steal Jonny from me," said Evelyn. "I wanted to spit in your face. I hated you this afternoon, Gerald. I should have known better, but Brown is such a good liar. I felt like Caesar must have felt when Brutus stabbed him."

"Joan really thought that she could buy him."

"She knows that I went through hell for our Jonny. I was just seeing the light at the end of the tunnel and she tries to take him away. She's crazy, Gerald."

"No, Evelyn, Joan's sick. I just hope that she lets me go and doesn't try to keep me away from you."

"Don't you start feeling sorry for her, Gerald. I'm the one that needs you. Joan had you for three years and I've had three lonely years. I need you, Gerald."

Richard was standing by, as he had been at Gerald's wedding to Joan. Gerald turned to him.

"You didn't have to ring me today, Richard. I know that you've been spending a lot of time with Evelyn and you're more than just friends. You could have left me with Joan and looked after Evelyn yourself."

"He's right," said Evelyn. "When I rang you, Richard, you were the only one I could turn too. In my emotional state I'd have been an easy catch, and a willing one too, but I'm glad that you called Gerald. I suspected him of conspiracy with Joan. I'm glad that I was wrong."

"Don't think that it didn't occur to me to take advantage of the situation, but look at the consequences. Gerald would have found out the truth and that would have wrecked his marriage to Joan. Then sooner or later, you'd find out that Gerald wasn't involved. I'd have taken advantage of both of you. I don't intend to contemplate what would have happened. Gerald, I had to be sure that you weren't involved in this kidnapping. If you had been, it would have been the end of our friendship."

"I don't deserve her, Richard. It was you who looked after Evelyn while I was living with Joan."

"You're wrong, Gerald. Evelyn looked after herself."

Evelyn knew he was right, but she had help when she needed it, first Mrs Brown, bless her soul, and Richard for the last year.

"You helped me a lot, Richard. I was very happy seeing you, this last year."

"So was I. If today hadn't happened, I was going to ask you to marry me."

"I know. I'd have accepted you, after the divorce."

"So what's stopping you two. I know when three's a crowd. I'll go back to Joan."

"Do you want to?"

"No."

"Evelyn, are you still in love with Gerald?"

"Yes, Richard. He came back just in time."

"Just in time. We hadn't reached the passionate stage."

"Poor Joan," said Gerald. "Who's going to comfort her?"

Evelyn shook him, "Gerald, you can't help her."

"She's right, Gerald. Let the Merediths get a doctor for their daughter. We're going to get you two divorced and married to each other as soon as it can be done."

"Richard, you're preaching to the converted. If I want to get a quick divorce from Joan, I have to be nice to her. That doesn't mean that I have to live with her. I'll have to do this in a civilised way or her family will crucify me. Can I stay with you when I come back from Renmark?"

"I was going to suggest it."

"Thanks. We'd better go. Did you ring home, Evelyn?"

"I tried to but the post office said the lines were cut by the floods. We'll just have to turn up unannounced."

"Don't worry, Evelyn. I'll behave myself this time."

They drove towards town, down Fullarton Road, intending to continue around the parklands to the Sturt Highway. At Glen Osmond Road they had stop for cross traffic. As they waited, Evelyn looked out of the window and saw the face of Louis Brown who was waiting, parked in the other road. She slid down out of sight and told Gerald what she'd seen. As they moved across the road, he watched Brown's car, as it started up and turned into the street, following him. When he increased speed so did Brown.

"He's following us."

"What are you going to do?"

"I'm heading for the cop-shop."

Driving fast enough to keep ahead of Brown's Ford Prefect, Gerald turned back towards the city and five minutes later pulled up in a "police only" parking zone in front of the police station in Victoria Square. He sent Evelyn and Jonny inside and locked the car. As he did, he noticed Brown pull up and stop half a block away in Angus Street, just past the tramsheds.

Inside Evelyn told a couple of police officers that she wanted protection, that her husband was following her and that he wanted to kill her and her boy. Gerald confirmed the story, telling them that he was Charles Meredith's son-in-law, just to try and pull a little weight. He asked them to arrest Brown.

"We can't arrest him unless he's suspected of committing a crime. Did he try to run you off the road or something?"

"No, he just wants to find out where his wife is so he can murder her in her sleep. Isn't that a reason to arrest him? Why the hell do you think he's following us?"

"Because she's his wife. He has a right to know where she's going."

Evelyn went over to the counter and pleaded with the policeman.

"I'm separated, legally separated. He has no right to follow me. Are you going to stop him from following me?"

"You'll have to get a restraining order."

"She could be dead by then. He threatened her."

"We can't arrest every man who threatens his wife."

"He kidnapped my boy this afternoon."

"He's the boy's father. That's a matter for the courts."

"He followed us here."

"If that's the case, he may think you've complained about him and that we can do something. He won't know that we can't arrest him. It'll probably scare him off."

Gerald wasn't convinced. Brown had been hunting them for over two hours. He knew where they were. Why was he waiting outside?

"Not him, he's a madman. Thanks for the help. We'll try and give him the slip."

"Where are you going?"

"To Renmark. They'll be safe there."

"Be careful. We've had some recent reports that part of the town is flooded. The main road's still open, but mightn't be for long. The flood peak is expected in a couple of days."

They went to the door and looked out. It was starting to get dark.

"What are we going to do, Gerald?"

"Lose him. We'll head back towards Richard's and lose him on the other side of town. When we've done that, I'll take the fastest way to Renmark."

Gerald drove down Angus Street with Brown following at a distance, turned left and continued around the park into Rundle Road, into the heavy after work traffic. He increased speed, watching in the mirror Brown's Prefect drop back and then speed up in an effort to stay with him. Turning the corner into Dequetteville Terrace, Gerald put the gas pedal down and shot out down the long wide road heading towards the racecourse, leaving Brown back at the corner of Rundle Road.

"Gerald, slow down. This isn't a race track."

"It is now. How far back is he?"

'All we need now is a bloody copper,' he thought.

"I can't see him. There he is. He's way back, just passing Prince Alfred College. He's coming down the wrong side of the road. He'll never see us if we turn now."

They were approaching the intersection of five main roads. Ahead lay Fullarton Road leading to Richard's place and the Meredith Estate where they appeared to be heading. Gerald cut across the traffic into the left lane and turned sharply, in an almost U-turn into the north section of Fullarton Road, pulling up 30 yards from the intersection. He switched off his lights. They both turned around and watched as the stream of cars passed by, Brown racing down the middle lane with them. Soon he was lost in the traffic heading south. Gerald moved off and they headed north, across and out of the city.

Chapter Thirty-Three

August 1956

Louis Brown didn't know why he was following the other car, except that his wife was in it, that she was his and he wanted to get her back. He wanted to punish her, he wanted to kill her. It was she who had robbed him of his mother's money and again cheated him of the money that was due to him today. When they went into the police station it had worried him. He was deciding whether to go away or keep on following her, when he saw her emerge with Gerald and the boy and get back into the car. He burned inside at the sight of Gerald. What was he doing with his wife? When they drove off, he followed, with murder in his eyes.

"God, how I hate them. I wish I'd never met her. I should have got up off the floor and killed that boyfriend of hers when he hit me. I should have left her with her father in Renmark. Bringing her back to Adelaide was the biggest mistake of my life. I should have thrown her into the river. If I could only get my hands on them and that child of hers. Yesterday he was worth a quarter of a million to me. Now if I catch him I'll kill him with that know-it-all mother of his. Why did Meredith want that boy?"

This question continued to nag him. Something else was worrying him. Ever since he'd given the boy to Joan and he'd seen them together for a second, before he left that hated woman, there was something at the back of his mind, but what it was wasn't clear to him. He had seen the similarity, but couldn't guess the reason. All he could think of was the money that he wouldn't be getting, the humiliation of it and the five people who must now be laughing at him.

He drove after Gerald, but his Ford Prefect was no match for Gerald's sports saloon and he lost them just before the racecourse. He thought he saw them again and drove as fast as his car could, until he saw that he was mistaken. Then he drove first to Richard's house, but there was no car there, so he continued on to the Merediths. From the road, he couldn't see which cars were inside, so he turned the car around and parked across from the drive. Not knowing what to do, he just sat there staring at the house.

Half an hour later Richard arrived, after having waited for Bruce Grover to come to Dawn's parents' home. He'd suggested that they spend the night there and expressed his regret for their inconvenience. As he turned into Meredith's drive, his eyes met Brown's. It was an unpleasant experience for the two of them. The arrival of Richard made Louis confident that Gerald had also driven there. He must have hidden his posh car behind the house, the house where he'd slept with Joan and taken Jonny for that fateful *initiation,* three years earlier. He, like Joan, wished that terrible dawn had never happened.

Now he began to feel beaten. The house had servants and probably guards and guns. He sat there and waited, no longer knowing why he was there.

At seven, a police patrol drove up.

"What are you doing, Sir?"

"Just sitting."

"Do you live in this street, Sir?"

"No."

"Then why are you sitting here?"

"I was just sitting."

"Can we see your driving licence, Sir."

He showed it to the officer.

"Listen, Mr Brown, as you haven't any business here I suggest that you go back to North Adelaide where you belong."

Louis took the policeman's suggestion. His one meeting with the police had taught him that it pays to take notice whenever they suggest something. The Merediths had sent for them and the police did things for people with money. As he drove off he watched the policemen walk up to the house.

'They're probably getting their payoff for getting me to go. They'll probably come and reinspect my car tomorrow.'

Back at his home, he straightened up the room. He went into the kitchen, took a couple of bottles of beer out of the fridge and got himself slightly drunk. Then he switched off the light and tried to go to sleep. All the time he could see the hole in the ceiling, even with his eyes closed. He could see Evelyn's face up there like a Cheshire Cat, grinning, and gloating and mocking him. Finally, he could bear it no longer. He ran out of the room with the hole in the ceiling and went to sleep in his mother's room.

Richard found Joan and Steven alone in her old bedroom. Joan was in bed and he was talking to her. He told them about Brown trying to follow him and that he was parked outside. When he didn't go away, they called the police. He also told them of Gerald's departure for Renmark and that he'd be back the following day. He didn't say that he'd only be back for his belongings. He could say that for himself.

Joan asked him if there was any danger that Brown would come in the middle of the night and kill them all.

"Not in this big house. But I suggest that you sleep up in your mother's room tonight and not in the flat. Steven should also sleep here tonight. Do you think you can find a bed for me? Do you have any guns?"

"Yes," said Steven. "There's a pistol that Dad keeps and our shooting rifles."

"Good; you and I and the servants will keep guard all night, taking turns, at the top of the stairs. Then tomorrow you pay the bastard. We can't do this for the rest of our lives, Steven."

"Richard, the Merediths didn't get rich by giving money to madmen."

That was the last thing that Richard wanted to hear. Brown wanted to kill them, the police couldn't do anything about it, and Steven was being difficult.

"You're a bloody imbecile, Steven. How did they ever make such an idiot into a department head? How did you ever get a degree? Did Daddy buy it for you?"

Richard could see that Steven wasn't used to direct face to face insults. He was getting hot under the collar.

"You watch what you say, Richard Flynn."

Richard continued as if Steven hadn't spoken.

"I don't know how old Great-Grand-Daddy Meredith got all his loot, but I bet he wasn't as stupid as you are. He'd have paid off a rat like Brown, or had him buried at the bottom of a mine shaft. You could probably get an underworld killer over from Melbourne for a tenth of the money, but don't say I put you up to it. I'm for paying him."

That was easy to say. It wasn't Richard's money.

"It isn't as if you're so lily-white, yourself, Meredith," he continued. "You conspired with him to get you the boy. You're in it up to your neck.

"You're also the boy's father, Dr Meredith. You should pay up for that alone, for raping his girlfriend as she was at the time. Imagine what he'd do to you for that little episode and to her too, if the big gorilla finds out that she made a monkey out of him. He paid for what you did to Evelyn out of his own pocket, or rather his mother's pocket-book. You ought to be emasculated for the safety of the race for what you did to her, Dr Meredith."

Richard said "Dr" contemptuously. He didn't care very much for the man or his title.

"I caught her in my house, swapping exam papers for that lazy bugger boyfriend of hers."

"Yes, and you punished her, cruelly and unnaturally and sadistically, like the Japanese did to our nurses in Malaya."

"I was a soldier too, you know."

"I bet you never left Australia."

Steven didn't answer. By the time he got to Darwin, the Japs were on the run.

"Well, have I convinced you, *Doctor* Meredith?"

"Yes, I'll pay the lazy bugger tomorrow."

Richard gave a sigh of relief. He was glad that he'd made his point. He wanted Brown as far away as possible.

"Let me know what happens. Find out when he's leaving the country and on what plane. Make sure that he catches the plane, here and in Sydney. Then you might use your influence and get the local embassy there to keep an eye on him. I'm sure that they'll want to know what kind of animal we've landed them with. He'll probably end up in jail or get shot by a Latin father or husband."

"Gerald's mad at me isn't he?" asked Joan.

That was all she cared about now. She didn't want Jonny any more. She wanted her husband back.

"Joan, we're not mad at you. We were, when we found out what you were doing, all three of us. I'm mad at your brother for his part in this. He should have known better, but you, well I don't think that you knew what you were doing. We're mad at Steven for stirring up King Kong out there. I get mad when my life and that of my friends is endangered. Gerald, if you must know, is very happy and so is Evelyn. Some good has come of all this, Joan."

"I've lost him."

"If it's any consolation, Joan, he wouldn't have left you without a good reason. He wouldn't have even looked for a reason. He hoped that I'd marry Evelyn if you must know. I would have, if you'd have left her alone."

Poor Joan, she now knew that she was the victim of her own machinations.

"How is Evelyn?" she asked.

"She's happy that she got Jonny back."

"And Gerald, too?"

"In that order."

"What an idiot I've been."

"Joan, three years ago when you called Louis's mother, you should have called Gerald. We both should have."

"Richard, I thought that I was doing the right thing."

"You knew Brown. How could you really believe that?"

"You don't think I had my doubts?"

"Doubts! Joan, try and explain those doubts to Gerald. If you didn't want to be his go-between, you shouldn't have taken on the job, or stopped when it got too tough for you."

"Don't make me tell him about that night. I saved her life, Richard."

Richard decided to go easy on her. She couldn't undo what she'd done.

"I won't, but don't make things difficult for him and for Evelyn. Think of what that girl's been through and make it easy for them."

"I'll try. If only Evelyn had confided in you from the start and not in me, none of this would have happened."

"Joan, don't blame yourself. The real villains in all this are your brother and Brown. God, I hate men like that. Joan, one other thing. Tell me what happened that night with you, Brown and Jonny Marco. The three of you were together the night he lost his mind, weren't you?"

"Yes, but I had nothing to do with it. I tried to stop him. I'll tell you everything, but not tonight. Mother gave me a tablet and I'm so tired. He killed him, Richard. That I have to tell you. I have to tell someone."

Joan lay back and fell asleep. Steven spoke to Richard as they left the room.

"You hate us, don't you, Flynn?"

"Cut the royal plural, Steven. You, I hate, Joan I quite like. We've been friends for four years. I'd like to think we'll remain friends. As for Meredith, the money pile, I regard that as a business rival like any other business. I'd like to own it one day."

"Do you think that Brown will still want to hurt us after a good night's sleep?"

"Yes, and if I were in your shoes I'd carry a gun and meet him in a solicitor's office. The shyster you used today should be fine. And you can tell that crooked lawyer that if I don't get each and every paper that he, Brown and Evelyn signed today, I'll press criminal charges against him. Do that. I'd hate to have to drag the Meredith name through the courts. Those papers are just what Evelyn lacks. Brown's confession will have her free in no time, especially as he won't be here to defend the case. Tomorrow night we'll all sleep confidently in our own beds again."

Once on the open road, Gerald put his foot on the gas. There wasn't much traffic, he had a fast car and he was a good driver. Jonny soon fell asleep in the back and Evelyn told Gerald her story, with occasional interruptions from Gerald, clarifying what had been happening to him at the same time. In the main it was her story and a grim story at that. She sat close to him, touching his hand when she thought what she told him might upset him. She kept nothing from him, hard as some of it was to tell, or explain, or justify. He felt bad, because he had misjudged her and had made her miserable, as he had been too. But more than that, he felt that he had let her down, thrown her to those two wolves.

She cried as she told him of the three months with Brown, months in which she'd doubted Gerald's love, months that she now loathed and was so ashamed of, months that she couldn't explain. There was the bullying of her father ever present, his interference and then the Brown snake in their Garden of Eden. Gerald cursed him and Steven Meredith. Only when she got to the part where Jonny came into her life could she smile again and Gerald felt warmth in the touch of her hand and serenity in her words.

"Gerald, be careful what you say when we get home."

"I've grown up a little, love. I don't shoot my mouth off any more."

"So have I. Dad doesn't bully me the way he used to, and he has been known to listen to what I have to say. Mom made him come down to the big sinful city when I graduated. She didn't tell him that I was going to a dance in my graduation dress that night."

She left for last the story of the night when Joan stopped her, when she was contemplating killing herself.

"You should have come to me. I would have married you. You knew how much I wanted to marry you."

"You're sure you'd have married me?"

"Sure, I'm sure."

"Would you have, three years ago?"

"My pride would have been hurt, but it had already taken a battering by then. I was shattered when I saw him at your place. I thought that you preferred him to me. I could have died."

"I never did, not for a moment."

"Why didn't you tell me?"

"I was so ashamed and such a fool at the time. I thought that you didn't love me any more and when I found out that you did, I was pregnant. Gerald, I thought that you'd never forgive me for that."

"You were wrong. You were a part of me, like my right hand. When you married that animal it was as if you'd been torn out of me. God, how it hurt."

"It hurt me too. When you started going out with Joan, I felt so miserable, sitting all alone, growing bigger every day. I knew how sexy she was and it made me mad to think of the two of you together, and all the time we wasted when we too could have enjoyed ourselves."

"That's what I felt when I heard about you and Brown."

"I think that you had the better time."

Gerald laughed. They both laughed. Now that he was hers again, Evelyn could joke about Joan.

"Yes, I was happy with Joan, but I wasn't in love with her the way I was with you, the way I am in love with you. It took a bushfire, when I almost bought it, to make me pop the question to Joan."

"You were a regular hero. Why didn't you stand your ground when you knocked Brown down?"

"With your father screaming at me? It wasn't just that, it was everything together. It was you and him, that's why I left. I thought that I'd come where I wasn't wanted. Evelyn, I don't want to go to

Renmark tonight. Let's find a place on the way. I'm going back to Adelaide in the morning. I want to spend this night with you."

"I do too, Gerald, but would it be wise?"

"I don't want to be wise, Evelyn, I want to be with the woman I love."

"What if Louis is following us?"

"If he is, he'll be miles behind us. We'll drive to a town off the road. He can't look in every room in the north east. I've got my rifle here if we need it. I'm sure that he doesn't know where we've gone."

"I'm convinced, Gerald."

"You know the district better than I do. You find us a place to stay."

An hour later they found a small room in a small hotel, in a small town off the highway. Gerald even found a garage for the car, while Evelyn borrowed a cot for Jonny. He woke up and played for a while, enjoying the luxury of having two adults looking after him. They rigged up a screen between the cot and the bed, so that he wouldn't see his mother with his father-to-be in bed together.

They undressed in the dark and came together as lovers in the strange springy bed. It was one of those beds that were common in hotel rooms, a bed that sagged deeply in the middle, so that the sleepers rolled together into the centre, whether they liked it or not. They lay together, lips together at first, just feeling each other's presence and feeling good after such a long separation.

"How did you sign the registry, Gerald?"

"Mr and Mrs Miller."

"Miller, why Miller?"

"I remembered Marilyn Monroe and Arthur Miller."

"Thanks for the compliment, but I'm no Marilyn Monroe."

"To me, you are."

Slowly, very slowly, they touched each other, not letting their passion take over, but wishing to savour the reunion, which they had thought would never happen and which might have to last them over another lean period, while they both disentangled themselves from their marriage partners. Gerald was no longer the inexperienced boy or Evelyn the apprehensive maiden, but being together in bed was something new to both of them. More than that, they both felt responsible for their partner's sorrows and each wanted to make it up to the other.

Gerald was as determined as Evelyn that this night should be a memorable one. When he felt that their touching had aroused her, and him too, he whispered for her to relax, kissing her young breasts and stroking the soft white skin between her thighs. For three years, not since Steven Meredith, had a man touched her. All the feelings that had been suppressed, poured back into her and she whispered to Gerald "I love you", over and over again, until he entered he and she could only hold on to him, letting her body meet his, letting it speak for her. They were together as one and nothing else mattered any more.

"We're going to be very happy together, Evelyn," he told her as he lay beside her, still in the intoxication of having just made love.

Evelyn said nothing, but kissed him on the side of the cheek, a kiss that signified her agreement. Then, as he kissed her back, she fell asleep in his arms and he too drifted into sleep in that hollow of that double bed.

As they drove the last few miles left to Renmark, Evelyn asked Gerald, "Why did you decide to make a stopover?"

"Evelyn, people and circumstances have conspired to keep us apart. Today I'm going back to heaven knows what. We needed a night together to give us the strength to carry on."

"It's been three years since I made love. I'd almost forgotten how nice it could be."

"I've never made love until last night. I know that isn't fair to Joan, but our love was nothing compared to what I feel for you. I've had a surfeit of sex."

"You seem to have thrived on it."

She gave him a dig in the ribs.

"I don't know what we'll do while we're getting out of our marriages."

"I'll wait. This time, Gerald, I'll wait. It'll be easier now that we've spent one night together."

"You can go back to your room at Dawn's as soon as Brown goes away. If I can reach an agreement with Joan that she doesn't bother us, Mr and Mrs Miller might be able to meet on a regular basis until we become Mr and Mrs Fisher."

Evelyn didn't reply. For answer she stroked Gerald's thigh. It told him that she liked his suggestion.

Travelling by daylight, they could now see the extent of the floodwaters. Most of the traffic on the road was confined to trucks taking workers and troops to build up the levee banks, or rescue stranded people and stock. When they had to cross the river, before Barmara, the water was lapping the river banks just below the top and just below the bridge span. Low lying land was flooded as far as the eye could see, and at other places the road ran like a ribbon through the water on both sides. The Murray River seemed to be spreading everywhere.

Renmark itself, normally a busy shopping centre during the day, was like a ghost town. Every able-bodied man was out of town, helping wherever he could, driving tractors and bulldozers, shovelling dirt and mud, or filling sandbags while the women kept them supplied with sandwiches, cake and plenty of hot tea, day and night.

Evelyn directed Gerald to her house and took him inside. He carried his rifle, as he wasn't in the habit of leaving it in the car and old habits die hard. Mrs Robertson hugged her daughter and Jonny. Then, she noticed Gerald.

"Mom, do you remember Gerald? Mom, we're back together again. We both have to get divorced now, but after that I'm going to marry him. Mom, isn't that grand?"

This was the greatest joy she could have given her mother, better than the happiness she felt when Evelyn told her she had left Louis. Any person that would strike that evil Brown man was a hero, worthy of her daughter's hand in marriage.

"Gerald! Thank God! Now I know that my little girl is going to be happy. Come in and have a cup of tea. I'm baking cakes for the men. I just hope the power lasts until I finish. The phones went yesterday and the road could be cut too. The flood peak hasn't hit the town yet. Why did you bring Jonny back at such a time, Evelyn?"

"Mom, Louis is after me. He wants to kill me and little Jonny. We had to run for our lives. It isn't safe for us in Adelaide. We'll be staying until it is."

"All three of you?"

"No, Mrs Robertson, I'm going back soon. I hope I can come back for Evelyn in a few days. What do you feel about me marrying your daughter?"

"I'm delighted. From the moment that Evelyn first told me about you that's what I've wanted. I tried to stop her getting involved with that horrible man, but my husband, he always had to be right, even at the cost of a daughter. She's a good girl, Gerald. I know that you'll both be happy."

"I'd like to see Mr Robertson, before I go back."

"He's over at the hospital, helping out. You can't get there without a boat. I'll tell him the news, when I see him. He mightn't be back for a day or so. He won't say anything, but don't talk about getting a divorce. He's against divorce on principle. He won't start an argument, so don't you. The days when Evelyn and Wes fought like cat and dog are over. It's live and let live in this house now."

"Tell him that I'm sorry for what I said and did that night. I behaved le ika fool."

"I can understand you hitting that man. We all wanted to hit him. I'm only sorry that you didn't stay."

"So am I," said the two young people together and the three of them laughed. After a cup of tea Gerald kissed Evelyn good-bye and set off back to Adelaide. Then Evelyn sat down and told her mother some of what had happened to her in the last 24 hours. She told her of the whole plan to sell Jonny. She couldn't explain to her that Jonny wasn't Louis's son, that would have been too much ttoell her mother. The simplified story was enough of a shock to her.

"You must have left Adelaide very early to get here when you did, Evelyn."

"We left last night, Mother. We haven't spoken to each other for so long, we needed a little time together."

Her mother knew what that meant. She wasn't shocked. If anything, she was pleased for her daughter. She was glad that she was happy again.

"Gerald could have stayed tonight. Your father probably won't come home."

"Thanks, Mom, but he should be back in Adelaide."

"Aren't you worried about him?"

"A little. But, it's Jonny we have to look after. Gerald will be back in a day or two. Brown's leaving Australia today."

"Praise the Lord," her mother replied.

Meanwhile, Gerald was heading down the Sturt Highway towards Adelaide. High above him a Convair 240 headed for Sydney without one passenger who had booked a ticket. Louis Brown wasn't on the plane. He wasn't going to catch his flight to America.

Chapter Thirty-Four

August 1956

Louis Brown woke up the following morning, still very angry. He had a ticket in his wallet for Sydney and other tickets to South America that he couldn't use. He didn't have the money to go with them, so he decided to go to work and see if he still had a job. He still hated his wife and child, her two friends and the Merediths, but his desire to hurt them had subsided. He was only concerned with his own well-being. Sleep had calmed his rage. His meeting with Dr Meredith would reawaken it.

Dr Steven Meredith was a person who hated people giving him advice and hated acting upon such advice. That was why he couldn't bear the thought of working for, or with his father and of marrying. This department of his own had been ideal for him. He was his own boss and didn't have to listen to anyone. Even when Richard and Joan told him that he had to pay Louis to get rid of him, he had other ideas.

"Flynn might have fooled Charles Meredith and all the company over the Finsbury factory, but he wasn't going to tell Steven Meredith what to do," he said to himself.

He asked his secretary to see if Brown was at work and to send him in to see him. To his surprise he came.

"Mr Brown, come in and close the door. We had a little deal going didn't we?"

"Yes, I was to sign certain papers and see that my wife signed them and bring the boy to your sister, for which I was to get a quarter of a million pounds."

"And you did what was required of you?"

"Yes."

He began to perk up. Was it possible that Meredith was going to pay him? He didn't know, not yet, that the department head was having some sadistic fun at his expense.

"And now I suppose you want the money?"

Louis Brown thought that Steven intended to hand over the money. He couldn't believe what he was hearing, until Meredith changed his tone.

"Well, Louis, you delivered stolen property. That's a criminal offence, you know."

"You told me to take the boy. He was my boy. You knew that his mother wouldn't agree."

"You're her husband. You should have made her agree."

"The bitch got away. I should have silenced her when I had the chance."

"Then we'd all be facing a murder charge, all except you, with my quarter of a million pounds, in Rio."

Brown knew that. Why hadn't the smart-arse Doctor thought of that when he started the ball rolling?

"You thought that you could hold on to the boy if my wife signed the papers. What happened, Dr Meredith?"

"You let her go too soon."

"Do I get the money?"

"Louis, I paid you £5,000 in advance. I'd like it back if you don't mind."

Steven could be just as sadistic as Brown, more so, he was rich.

"Don't be a shit. I spent most of the money. I had to buy the plane tickets. I had to put bars on the windows. I should have put chains in as well and tied her up."

"If you hurry you can still catch your plane to Sydney."

"I'm not going without the money."

"You want me to pay you to go away?"

"Yes. I brought the boy, didn't I?"

"Well I'm not going to. You can clear out of this department too. You're fired. Don't go and ask your wife to get you your job back. She's gone home and she's not coming back until you are out of town. You'll get paid until the end of the month. What did you mean by coming to my house last night and intimidating my friends?"

"I was angry last night."

"Are you still angry?"

"A little."

That was a lie. He was very angry and getting more so by the minute.

"Why?"

"You all ganged up against me."

"You were going to kill the boy's mother."

Louis said nothing. Steven had expected him to get rid of Evelyn.

"You were going to leave her to starve to death while you took her share of the money."

"She would have taken the boy back, as she did, didn't she? I had to get her out of the way."

"Louis, is that the way to treat a woman who was willing to help you cheat to pass your exams? Do you remember running out on her that evening?"

Again Louis had nothing to say. He knew he should have stayed. It had been a bad night for him too.

"What did she tell you about that night?"

"She said she spent the night in the lockup. Then you dropped the charges."

Steven thought that funny, but it didn't show in his face. He was too busy making this oversized worm squirm.

"She lied, she spent the night with me in my lockup. It was like what you did to her yesterday, only she didn't escape from me. She paid for her foolishness, for your stupidity and your cowardice. If it's any consolation to you, she didn't do it willingly."

"Why are you telling me this?"

"She never told you what happened that night?"

"No. You forced my wife? Did you do something to her?"

He was lighting a fire in the man's brain, a fire that would burn Steven, and all for a moment of sadistic satisfaction. Richard had warned him, but Steven Meredith listened to no man.

"She wasn't your wife at the time, she was your lover, I think. I don't think that I actually forced her. Let's say I pressured her. I can't remember exactly what happened. It was a long time ago."

"Now I know why she was so mad at me. She never forgave me for leaving her at your place. She hasn't let me near her or the kid since I did that. Yesterday was the first day that I touched my kid."

"Did you notice anything, Louis?"

"Yes I did, but I don't know what it was. There was something about that brat and your sister, the hair."

"Do you know why Joan wanted the brat, as you call him?"

He didn't know when to let sleeping dogs lie. Steven had to humiliate this poor wretch. He'd already done that, but he had to drive home the last nail.

"Because he looks like her. So people will think it's her child."

"I too have black hair."

Louis Brown saw it all now, what had been bothering him since yesterday. Steven was smiling at him and telling him what he must have known all the time. It wasn't a faulty contraceptive, but this rich playboy who'd saddled him with his kid. His mother had made him marry the bitch who surely knew that he wasn't responsible.

"I'm not the boy's father?"

"Don't blame the girl. She wasn't to know. It could have been either of us. You were her lover, weren't you?"

"She should have told me about you."

"Would you have married her?"

"No, not for all the mothers in the world."

"She couldn't have come to me. I was in California."

Louis suddenly remembered that call, after which his mother told him to go and get his future bride!

"Your sister put her up to it. They conspired against me. They both knew that you're the father and not me."

"I'm sure she knew. I think she even told Joan."

He was enjoying himself, watching the suck serquirm.

"When did she know?"

"Ask her."

"Don't worry, I will."

"You'd better stay away from your wife. She has two young men looking after her now."

"Stuff them. Dr Meredith, I want my money. That bitch took all my money to pay for herself and your child. I couldn't even get her to sleep with me. She took the lot and gave me nothing in return."

"Serves you right for leaving her at my place."

"She can't pay up, so you'll have to. You owe me what I had to pay to look after your kid. I want my money."

"I suppose that you want your job back too."

"No, I want the money. I want to go to Sydney or Melbourne."

"I thought that you were going to Rio."

"That was yesterday, when I thought I'd be rich. I can't go there without money."

"Yesterday you were going to leave your wife to die. You didn't want to be around when they found the body?"

Louis looked at the other man with hate in his eyes.

"You were going to leave her to starve to death, without food or water, and now you want me to pay you? Get out of here, you bastard. I'm not giving you a penny. I hope that she goes to the police and they put you away. Go and clear out your locker before I call the police."

Louis left the office, but not the building. He went to his workbench to lick his wounds and think about what Meredith had told him. It was a shock to find out that he hadn't gotten Evelyn pregnant, but that Meredith had. Yesterday's anger was nothing to today's rage which was rising within him. This time the main focus of this anger was the man who had just dismissed him. No one had ever spoken to him this way and no one had ever hurt him like he had done, not even Evelyn, the other focus of his anger, nor Joan. He hated all of them, but it was Steven whom he hated the most.

Louis had seen some preliminary results on microwave heating with the new equipment. He only vaguely understood what he'd been doing for Dr Meredith, but he concentrated, read through the results and made an estimate of how long it would take to kill a man standing next to the oven. Two minutes without the protective guards would heat a man's brain seven degrees. That would do it, if the other effects of the intense radiation didn't kill him first.

Two hours after his meeting with Meredith, Louis was in the microwave room, removing the protective covering from the experimental oven, exposing the magnetron tube. He placed Durex-tape over the safety switches and connected wires to short the other protective devices. The door to the room had an inside knob which, when pressed, released the outer lock. He pushed a pencil shaped wedge into this and tried it out. The knob would no longer work. Once the door was closed it could only be opened from outside. Louis placed a three foot dish of wire and aluminium foil upside down over the oven, gluing it to the walls with more tape. It would focus the radiation at head level. Then he hid in the outer room and waited.

As he'd expected, Steven came to look at the equipment just before twelve. Now that Brown was gone, he'd have to find another assistant to look after it. He looked through the metal and glass door and noticed that the oven was partially dismantled. It was second nature to him to put it back together. He fell into the trap set for him. Steven Meredith went inside to reassemble the microwave oven. As he did, Brown came out of hiding, grabbed the door out of his hands and slammed it closed.

Steven turned around and saw the grinning gorilla. When he pushed at the knob and it wouldn't open, a wave of fear passed through him. His one consolation was that there was a door between him and Brown. He looked up and saw the metal reflector above his head. He knew what was going to happen to him if he didn't get out of the room.

"What are you doing, Louis?"

"Where's my money?"

"Let me out. You've gone too far."

"If I don't get the money, you'll be your next experiment, Dr Meredith."

"You can't operate it with the covers off."

"I can, and I have my hand on the switch. Would you like a little test?"

He was sweating. Steven remembered how he'd humiliated Brown. He knew that he'd said too much. This man had plenty of reasons for flicking that switch.

"No! Don't touch it. I'll give you the money."

"And you won't report this?"

"Just let me out."

"When I get the money. Where is it?"

"In the boot of my car."

"And where are the keys?"

"On my desk."

"Good."

"Now, will you let me go?"

Louis Brown shook his head. He knew that he couldn't trust that man in the microwave oven room. If he got out, it was good-bye to the money and good-bye to his freedom. Steven knew what he was thinking. He knew that the man on the outside of the cage didn't trust him.

When Brown closed the door on him he'd felt fear. Now he felt it again and felt it grow as the man outside, with his hand on the switch, looked at him with a wicked grin and said nothing. Brown was getting a thrill out of watching another man facing death. Not since Jonny Marco had he had a thrill like this. This was a moment to be savoured, to be stretched out. He watched beads of sweat form on Meredith's brow. He wanted to reach out through the glass and wipe them off. But more than that, he wanted him to die.

Steven wondering whether the maniac outside was going to release him, but knowing there was little chance of this, tried to think how he could save himself. He noticed in the corner of his eye the scotch tape on the microswitches. If one was released he'd be safe, the equipment wouldn't work. He leapt across to the oven.

As he moved, Steven heard the click of the switch followed by the noise of the oven switching on. As it came to life, pain came to him, intense pain all over his body, but mainly in his head. He couldn't move his arm and hung for a few seconds like a dancer, before collapsing onto the floor, into unconsciousness.

Louis left the oven on for a full four minutes before entering the room. He put on rubber gloves and felt Steven's pulse. Nothing. He wasn't breathing either. It reminded him of Jonny Marco. But this time, he didn't want this man to recover.

At 12:30 the secretary went home. She only worked half a day. When the other staff members left for lunch, Louis checked the area and finding it free of people, carried the dead Dr Meredith to his office, putting him in his chair with his head down on his papers. He helped himself to Steven's keys and closed the door. In all probability he would sit like that until the secretary returned the next day. Then Louis went back to put the microwave room as it should be, removing all evidence of the fatal trap that he'd sprung on the departmental head.

Louis took the bunch of keys and went outside. Steven's car was parked in a special place by the back entrance in Frome Road. He waited until there were no people passing in the street, quickly opened the boot, took out a briefcase from inside and transferred it to his car. Then he drove to a field near the Torrens Gorge where he hid the money and the keys in a hollow tree. This done, he went home to await developments. They came for him quicker than he thought they would. At 6 pm he was arrested on suspicion of murder.

Dr Steven Meredith died on the morning of August 9th, Student Day. There were no lectures and no other classes that day. No one entered or left his office after Louis Brown, no one saw him remove Steven's briefcase and drive away. Most people were up on North Terrace watching the procession, which returned down Frome road shortly after Brown left the university with the money.

Later in the day there was the annual flour fight, rugby match and a few student stunts, the chief one being a mock visit by Marilyn Monroe and Arthur Miller. Some students staged a mock underworld shooting in the city for which they were widely criticised. They apologised for this stupid act.

Arriving back from Remnark, Gerald went to Richard's home where he found his friend waiting for him.

"You took your time."

"Did you expect me to drive there and back last night? Richard, we didn't get there until this morning."

His friend slapped him on the back.

"Why did you hurry back?"

"I knew you'd approve. We needed a little time together. It's crazy up there, flood waters everywhere. I was lucky not to have to swim out. What's going on here? Has Brown left yet?"

"Steven was supposed to ring me. I don't suppose he will. He's a surly bastard. Do you want to ring him?"

"I'd like to ring his bloody neck. That is one Meredith that I'll never speak to again. You've heard Evelyn's story? I'd like to put a bullet up his arse."

"Join the queue! I told the bastard what I thought of him last night. I also told him to contact me, but I haven't heard from him. Wouldn't you know it. I'll ring up Joan."

"Let me. I'll have to go and see her later."

Joan was happy to hear his voice.

"Gerald, where are you?"

"I'm at Richard's. I'll be over later. Have you heard from Steven?"

"No."

"Did he pay Brown to go away?"

"I haven't spoken to him since last night. I slept late. I'm sorry about what Steven did to Evelyn. I didn't know until recently. I didn't know it was him."

"Where is the bugger?"

"I don't know, Gerald."

"Ring every place that he might be. We want to know if Brown's left. If not, Richard wants either to go to the police or get a private detective to watch him. That'll cost money. Brown's a psychopath."

"I know. You look after yourself, Gerald."

"We're both keeping our rifles loaded and close to us. Steven should carry a gun too."

"I'll ring you back when I've spoken to him."

Later she rang back. Richard answered the phone.

"He isn't at home and there's no one answering at the department. I don't know where he is."

At five she rang back, crying.

"Richard, the cleaner found Steven in his office."

"Found him? Is he dead?"

"Yes."

"Did Brown kill him?"

"Richard, there was no sign of any violence. It was as if he'd fainted or had a heart attack."

"Joan, keep calm. We'll be right over. One thing's sure, Brown did it. How, it's up to the police to find out. Tell your father to ring his friend at the CID and get them to arrest Brown. Tell them that he's planning to leave the country. Tell them that he threatened Steven and was waiting outside your house last night. Tell him about the meeting planned for this morning, and the money. The sooner that they catch him, the happier I'll be."

The two of them went across to the Meredith house where they joined Joan and her grief stricken parents. When they could, they spoke to Joan alone.

"Did Steven give Brown the money?"

"I don't know."

"Was there a meeting this morning?"

"I didn't see Steven this morning."

"So we don't know what happened."

Her eyes were red and her cheeks wet. He might have been an evil man, but he had been her brother.

"Not unless Brown tells us."

"We'll stay here until we hear any news about Brown, all night if necessary."

"How are you, Joan?" Gerald asked sheepishly.

"How do you expect? I lost a husband yesterday, a brother today. I wonder what I'll lose tomorrow."

"We're still your friends."

"You shouldn't be. I wasn't very nice to Evelyn."

"She forgives you too."

"Don't worry, Gerald, I won't keep you away from her. I know when I'm beaten."

"Thanks, Joan. I still love you a lot, but with Evelyn it's part of me. Yesterday it came back to life. It isn't the way I wanted to treat you, but I hope you understand. Yesterday morning, nothing would have pleased me more than to see Evelyn marry Richard here, as I think she would have done. You shouldn't have interfered."

"I was crazy, Gerald. It was temporary insanity that made me do it. Perhaps it was fate, Kismet, a heavenly plan to bring you two together, and I was just a pawn in a celestial chess game."

At six thirty they received a call from Captain McInnes. The police had found Louis Brown in his house and were holding him for questioning.

"Why don't they charge him with my brother's murder?"

"They will, Joan," said Gerald, "But first they have to determine the cause of death. My guess is that he was poisoned. Meanwhile we can sleep in peace, knowing that he's locked up. When he's charged with the murder I'll be a lot happier. I won't get Evelyn back until that happens."

"What if they release him?"

"It'll be a crime, Joan, a bloody crime."

It was late Monday before the pathologists discovered the cause of Steven's death. At first they thought that he'd died of a massive stroke. There was bleeding and tissue damage in the brain, but it was inconsistent with that expected from a CVA. No known poisons were found.

Microscopic examination revealed damage of a kind that no Adelaide pathologist could recognise. They sent more tissues to the toxicologists. Finally, late on Monday, one of them looking in a recent publication, found what he was looking for. The brain damage was similar to that suffered by technicians killed while working too close to powerful RADAR transmitters.

At first, this was a baffling discovery. There were no RADAR installations in the Meredith Building and Steven had not, to anyone's knowledge, ever been near such an installation. Then, someone remembered the microwave oven. That was what he worked on and the microwave radiation was the same as RADAR. Now all they had to do, was link the murder weapon to the suspect. A team of police technicians and detectives descended on the department and the microwave oven.

Another possibility arose. The equipment might be faulty and Steven's death may have been accidental. A team of physicists checked it and declared it to be safe. This meant that the case remained a mystery. Dr Meredith had been killed by a harmless machine three rooms away from where his body was found.

Gerald, Richard and Joan went down to her flat to discuss developments.

"This time tomorrow, Louis Brown will be free if they don't find any evidence," said Gerald.

"I know he did it and he took the money too. I'm sure Steven had it with him."

"It was his money, Joan. If your brother didn't give it to him, he contributed to his own death and he also put us in danger. They probably took Brown's passport away. I wish I knew what went on at that meeting between them on Friday."

"He's dead," said Gerald. "Brown killed him. Don't make it any harder for Joan. Let's see if we can come up with any ideas and help the police before they let the bugger go."

"I was talking to the forensic people today. The machine isn't dangerous with its radiation guards in place, but it can't be operated without the guards, so Brown must have found a way to circumvent that. That wouldn't be hard. Then he'd need a way of locking the door. It opens in, so it couldn't be barred from the outside. The lock had to be jammed. A pencil could have done that. This is alright in theory, but without proof it isn't enough to charge him, let alone convict him."

"What prevents the machine from working with the cover removed, Richard?"

"Two microswitches and an internal switch. The first two could be plastered down and the other switch shorted out. They were all clean and it's impossible to find any trace that they'd been put out of action."

"What about the door mechanism?"

"There were traces of sawdust in it, but there were traces of the same kind of sawdust in other parts of the room. The shelves and a pump cover were made of the same type of wood. It's a kind of hardwood, very common."

"It could have been the piece of wood that locked Steven in when he was killed. And why was the place so clean?"

"Where was Brown when Steven died?"

"He says he was watching the procession, but he can't prove it. He has no alibi for the time after he left Steven, and before one o'clock, when a neighbour saw him arrive home. He's still a prime suspect. He had motive and opportunity. There's one other thing. Above the door and over the oven there are marks in the dust made by sticky tape. Something was stuck up there recently and then removed. It must have something to do with Steven's death, I'm sure of it."

"Joan, you're the one who knows Captain McInnes. Go along to the department tomorrow, tell whoever's in charge that you're a friend of his boss and see what you can find out. Then have a look around the place. See if you can find the pencil he used for the door and the sticky tape. The rubbish bins were checked, but it wasn't in there. He either took it away or it's still in the department somewhere. You might also look out for whatever it was that he stuck up over the door. Look for something with tape on it."

"There's something I have to tell you," said Joan. "It's something that you asked me to tell you several times. If only I told you when it happened, I might have saved some of us a lot of suffering."

Joan told Gerald and Richard of the night that Louis Brown tied Jonny Marco to the tram lines.

"If I'd told the story the next day, Brown would have been arrested then and thrown out of the university. Jonny may have received the proper treatment and lived. Evelyn would never have met Brown and Steven would be alive too, and all because I was frightened of having my name mixed up with what Brown did. Do you think I should tell the police now?"

"He's done something much worse. They'll have to nail him for this first. After that, what happened that night is rather academic. Did he tell you why he did it, what he had against Jonny Marco?"

"No, but it happened when they were at school. That would have been two years earlier."

"They didn't go to the same college. One went to St. Peters and the other to Prince Alfred."

"So it must have been on the sporting field. They were both footballers, weren't they?"

"Jonny was a good runner too. He once held the schools record for the hundred yards, still does I think."

"Steven went to Brown's school, Joan. Did he get the school magazine after he left?"

"Yes. However I think I've got something better than that. He used to film the intercollegiate matches for the Old Boys' Association. What year would we want to see?"

"Brown's last year at college was 1949."

"Jonny would have been 15 then. Wouldn't he have been too young to play in the match?"

Joan took them upstairs to Steven's old room. In the bookshelves she found the College Year Book and looked for the page reporting the intercollegiate match.

"Here it is. Brown was captain and fullback. They lead all three quarters, and then lost in the last by eight points. Here it is, 'congratulations to Jonny Marco, declared Best and Fairest Player of the match, and scoring the winning goals. This young player should go far.'"

Then she flipped the pages, looking for Intercollegiate sports day.

"Brown first in the shot putt and the broad jump. The relay team came second. I bet I know who was on the winning side. Help me set up the projector. I think that we have a film of both events."

Joan found the two reels of 16mm film, dusted them off, and put the football one in the projector first. For the first half Steven must have concentrated on the other goal, as very little was seen of Louis. His team seemed to be scoring all the goals. There were one or two shots of Brown defending his goal, but mostly he was away from the field of play. Steven was filming for his college and photographed his team players. Once or twice they saw Jonny who played rover, and seemed to be doing good work gathering up the ball around the ruck.

Steven must have realised that the boy was brilliant, and took some more shots of him in the second half. He was swift and kept getting away from the other players to get at the loose ball and pass it up field to his team-mates. Early in the last quarter, the captain rested him on the front left pocket and they used him as a path to goal. Twice he outpaced Brown to the ball and not waiting for the free kick, ran around the big guy to put in six points. The third time the ball came their way, Brown moved out of goal to anticipate Jonny and keep him away from the ball. It came in high and Jonny got up above the bigger man, preventing him taking the mark. It only remained for the full forward to snap it up and run it into the goal, where Brown should have been. After the match they carried Jonny off shoulder high.

They had to watch an hour of sports day before they came to the relay race. They couldn't make out anyone during the first legs, they were too far away. Only in the last 40 or 50 yards did they see Louis Brown, puffing like a steam engine coming down to the line, ahead of his smaller opponent who was running straight and effortlessly. As the camera panned to cover the finish the boy overtook the giant, breaking the tape with a yard to spare.

Joan sat looking with tears streaming down her face.

"I held him like a baby after we untied him. I wanted to mother him, to love him and make him better. I wanted to love him but he went and killed himself. Ever since that night I've wanted to love somebody. I so much wanted a baby. I'm going to be so lonely when you go, Gerald."

"What can I say? I never thought this would happen. You're making me feel like a heel. I'm happy at what's happening to me, but because of it you have to suffer."

'She'll soon forget him,' thought Richard, and wondered if he might help her, as he'd promised himself in first year. They'd both suffered a loss.

"I feel that I'm returning stolen property. I've told my mother about us. She knows it's because of little Jonny, but not why I was so anxious to get him. She told me what a bloody fool I was, as if I don't know it. I told her we want a quick divorce."

"Thanks Joan. Evelyn and I have been apart too long."

He kissed her, a short affectionate kiss.

"You were together the other night, weren't you?"

"Is that a guess, or do you know something?"

"My late brother told his solicitor to make a check of the hotels on the way. He told me. There aren't that many hotels, Mr and Mrs Miller. I'm glad, Gerald. I'd have been disappointed in you if you hadn't."

"You're not jealous?"

"Gerald, I'm a good loser. I had a good run for my money. Sorry, that's a bad way to put it. I've only got myself to blame. I played God with your lives and hurt both of you. Evelyn, I hurt a lot. I want you to make it up to her. Now, all I want is to see the man who killed Steven get what's coming to him. I hope they hang him. I want to see you and Evelyn married and having the babies that I can't give you. Are you going to keep working for us?"

"Probably not. I'll stay on for a while, if your father wants me to."

"Let us get over Steven's death before you go. My parents loved him. They didn't know about his attitude to women or his being Jonny's father. I want them to have only good memories of him."

Chapter Thirty-Five

August 1956

The following day Richard took Gerald to meet the solicitor who had tricked Evelyn and left her with Louis Brown. Gerald's adrenaline was up at the start of the meeting, as it had been the night he hit Brown, but he calmed down when he saw how shaken the man was by his client's fate. They told him that his action had contributed in no small way to the chain of events leading to Steven's death. They also told him that they were considering pressing charges against him, for his part in the plot to kidnap Jonny, and for aiding Brown in his incarceration of Evelyn, knowing of his intention to harm her.

They asked him to hand over all of the papers that Evelyn had seen and signed. When he refused, Richard picked up the phone and put in a call to Captain McInnes. Richard told the solicitor that they would wait with him until a policeman came to prevent him destroying the papers. Knowing that there was no point in further delay, the man gave them all the papers and told them where they had been altered after Evelyn had signed them.

"We'll keep the adoption papers, Gerald, as evidence against this guy, but the useful ones are Brown's signed admission of adultery. That together with her story of the way he locked her up should get her a divorce, *toute suite*. Now, Mr Lawyer, I'd like a statement from you in writing, that you took Evelyn to Brown's house, that she didn't want to go, and that you raced out leaving her there, although she asked you to wait and that he locked her in there with him."

"I'm not going to sign that."

"It's all true, isn't it?"

"Yes."

"Good, write it all down as it was and sign it. It'll be used against Brown, not you. If you won't do it, we'll call in the police. Put in a description of the room in the statement, the bars and all that."

"You won't report me?"

"Let's put it this way. If you co-operate with us, we mightn't, if you don't we will. Co-operate with us and you're still on the map. Don't and you're history."

He started to write. It wasn't easy. He couldn't keep his hand steady.

"I could be disbarred, even go to jail."

"That's just what you deserve. If Brown confesses, we'll forget all about you, but then if he does he might dob you in. If he does confess, he'll probably blacken every name he can, especially the Merediths."

"Do you think he'll confess?"

"Only when they have a case against him, and so far they haven't. He's due to be released this afternoon if the police don't find out how he did it."

They met Joan and had lunch with her at the Richmond. She had been with the police during the morning.

"Have they found anything, Joan?"

"They've been all over the building, but they don't know what they're looking for. The microwave room and Steven's office and the corridor where he must have carried Steven, haven't yielded a thing. The money and his keys are still missing. They haven't found them in Brown's car or in his house.

"They were fascinated by the holes in the ceiling. I told them how they got there. They sent a man up to search every inch of the roof. That was a waste of time. The holes were too small for Brown to get up there. He might have thrown something into the hole, I suppose."

"Did you tell them what to look for?"

"A pencil sized piece of wood, a few inches of Scotch tape and something nondescript, five feet across with Scotch tape attached to it. He probably got rid of it with Steven's brief case."

"It's a reflector of some kind," said Gerald, thinking out loud. "He stuck a piece of metal above the microwave source to reflect the microwaves down."

"You mean silver paper?"

"Yes, Richard, metal, iron, tinplate, aluminium foil, chocolate wrapping, Sisalcraft perhaps. It would act like a concave mirror and concentrate the waves. Then instead of them being dissipated into the walls, they'd be focused, probably at head level. Sorry, Joan, but that's what I think happened to Steven. It explains why he suffered brain damage and little other damage to tissues."

"Do you think my brother suffered?"

"Probably not," said Richard, but he felt sure that it must have been an agonising, but thankfully swift death. It was the work of a cunning, sadistic killer. Louis Brown wasn't the fool they had thought he was; he waa s lot nastier.

"I think we ought to tell the police about our reflector theory and ask them to hold onto Brown while they look for it. I'll go ring Captain McInnes when I get home."

"I'm going back to the building. I'll poke around where the police let me and see if I can find any foil or, who knows, maybe the reflector itself."

"You be careful, Joan. Brown could be back on the streets at any time."

"Get Dad to ring McInnes. He'll make them hold onto him. Tell him about Jonny Marco and some of the other things he's done."

"And you get out of the department when the police leave and go straight back to the house."

"I hope you don't intend to order Evelyn around like this, Gerald. She isn't used to taking orders like I am."

"Why don't you become a Mormon or an Arab and keep both of them?" said Richard.

"Richard, you've always been a good friend of mine. Why don't you do me a favour and look after Joan? You've always lusted after her tits."

Joan looked at Richard. She wasn't surprised. She knew men and she knew her husband's best friend.

"Richard, I never would have thought it of you. How'd you like to be a co-respondent with me in a divorce case?"

"Don't tempt me, Joan. I've just been disappointed in love. I guide Gerald through the wilderness and I have to spend all my time comforting the women he's finished with. Sorry, Joan, I don't think that either of us want an affair just now. I think we're both past that stage. But we both need a good close friend, now that Snow White's been rescued by Prince Charming and they don't need us any more."

'Perhaps,' thought Richard, 'when she's seen a doctor and given Gerald his divorce, I might have a wild sexual weekend with Joan. Neither of us are exactly virginal. It could be fun. I might even learn something.'

"That's enough, you two. If Joan's going to get anything out of the Meredith Building today and get out, she'd better get moving. I think we've got time to walk her down there. You'll be secure there with the police."

They took the long way, walking past the Institute of Technology and down Frome Road under the long arch of plane trees, a lattice of winter branches above their heads, down past the hospital and Bacteriology Department, where Steven had once lectured. They went through the gate opposite the Medical School to the red-brick Meredith Building, where they left Joan talking to the detectives. She couldn't be in safer hands. Another person the police would have told to get out, but she was Adelaide *royalty* and her father a pal of the Captain. They let her go inside.

Joan didn't ring or come to see them at five as she'd promised. At 5:30, they went over to her house. Mr Meredith was there with Captain McInnes. Neither of them had seen or heard of Joan. He had disconcerting news for them. Brown had been released at three.

"I'm sorry, we couldn't hold him without evidence. We have a man following him in the hope that he may lead us to the money and any other evidence. If he does the man has orders to arrest him or call for help if he needs it."

"What if he tries to kill someone?"

"Our man will prevent him. He has a radio-car. Don't worry, we'll get this guy. He'll slip up, they all do. I don't think that this one's very bright. Cunning he is, but not very bright. If it takes us a year, we'll get the evidence and put him away."

Gerald was upset. Brown was out if jail, and no one knew where Joan was. He spoke his mind.

"We haven't got a year. Joan could be in danger at this very minute. She was with your men at the Department."

"I'll ring in and see if they know anything. Does she have her car there?"

"Yes, a Cream 1956 Mercedes Sports. Do you want the licence number?"

"No, your description is quite sufficient."

He returned from telephoning a few minutes later. From the expression on his face, the others could see that something was wrong.

"Bad news. The man trailing Brown was found dead beside his car in a field, just out of town. He was probably attacked with an axe. We've put the entire police force on this and cancelled all leave. The officer was killed at least an hour ago, maybe two, soon after Brown's release. We're looking for Brown and his car. Joan's car is still outside the Meredith building. The officers left there at four-thirty, but as they hadn't seen Joan, thought that she'd left the building. The caretaker locked up after them."

"She could still be inside. We'd better go and get her." Gerald went for his car keys. Joan's father stopped him. "Let's ring, it's quicker. I have the numbers on my desk." Charles Meredith led the way, as they followed him into his office, where he rang the department.

Joan answered the first number that they tried.

"Daddy, is that you, Daddy? Daddy, I'm locked in here."

There were two phones in the room. Gerald had the other receiver in his hand and answered her.

"Are you alright?"

"Brown was here. I hid in the library inside a cupboard. He was looking for me. He knows that I'm in the building."

'Her car!' thought Gerald. 'He's seen her car!'

"Hold on. I want to send help. Captain, she's there, and so is Brown. There's a second phone in Joan's flat. I want to keep her on this line. Joan, the cops will be there in a few minutes. Can you stay on the line?"

"Yes. I think Brown's gone, but he's locked all the doors. I was on my way to Steven's office when I heard him coming. I had to hide. He locked the door and now I can't get in or out. I think he's gone, but I'm not sure."

"Help will be there in a few minutes, so will we."

"Gerald, I found the evidence. It was in the cold room. There was this piece of estafoam in the bin and it looked the size of a briefcase, so I thought that the briefcase must be where the estafoam came from. That led me to the coldroom because estafoam's used in insulating cold rooms. I've seen it at the brewery. I looked inside and found a screwdriver on the floor. I started removing panels, it was cold work, I damn near froze my fingers off, but finally I found it behind the third panel, the foil reflector, folded up inside the wall. I was on my way to the phone when I saw Brown and ducked into the library cupboard. He must know that I found it."

"Terrific, Joan. Why didn't you get out with the policemen?"

"I was in the coldroom, looking for the hiding place. I didn't hear them going."

"Joan, Brown killed a policeman this afternoon, the man sent to watch him. He doesn't care any more about evidence. When the cops come, stay close to them."

"Gerald, there's something else. I smell gas."

"Joan, can you get to a window?"

"No."

"Can you get back to the coldroom?"

"Yes."

"Well get inside, quick. Grab a lab coat to keep warm. You won't freeze. We'll have you out of there in no time. Good-bye. I have to ring the fire brigade."

Gerald did this. Then he ran out to the car with Richard. Soon they were racing down towards the city, wondering what Brown had done and if the police could get Joan out in time. He'd told the fire brigade where she was. They could break in and get her out. They didn't need keys.

The police arrived at the Meredith Building at five to six, five minutes after they were summoned by Captain McInnes. The whole area was cordoned off and a vain search made for Brown, who was now hiding a mile away, in Steven Meredith's garage with an axe and a rucksack full of dollars, having let himself in with Steven's keys.

The police gained entrance to the Meredith Building, only to be driven back by gas from the pipe that Brown had opened. The place was a gas bomb waiting for a spark to ignite it. They found the main, closed it, and went around the building smashing windows to let the gas escape. Almost at once the fire brigade arrived and two men in rescue gear made for the area of the building where Joan was trapped.

Gerald had just crossed Greenhill Road, when he saw the north sky light up for a second. He didn't hear anything, the sound of the gas explosion came later, and the car was making too much noise. He knew what that flash was and drove fast, recklessly fast, almost hitting a car at the intersection.

He arrived at the Meredith Building to find it a burning shell, with its tiled roof scattered over the area and a fire raging in the interior. It reminded Gerald of "Boronia", when he had had to leave it.

He quickly worked out where Joan had been, in the corner opposite the Medical School. He was relieved to see that the firemen were directing their efforts at putting out the fire there and that a rescue team was getting ready to go in. He also noticed several injured firemen and policemen, with three ambulances in attendance. Mr Meredith and Captain McInnes joined them as they watched the rescue team enter a window, in the wake of men with hoses making a path for them.

The cold room was made of concrete blocks, lined with several layers of foam and an inner aluminium wall. The gas explosion had demolished all other internal walls and shattered every piece of glass in the building. The walls of the coldroom had withstood most of the blast, but one wall had cracked allowing the estafoam to ignite at this place. Joan was extricated from the wreckage, in a semiconscious state, suffering from smoke inhalation. She was given oxygen on the short ambulance ride across the street to Royal Adelaide, while her father and Gerald watched helplessly.

"Is she going to be alright?" he asked the ambulance man. He wondered if Brown was there somewhere, watching, and who his next victim would be. Watching Joan being carried away, he began to worry for Evelyn and the boy.

"I can't tell. They'll tell you at the hospital."

Then the door was closed and the ambulance drove up to Casualty in North Terrace. Gerald and Richard followed in the car. They watched as the doctors treated Joan who was now unconscious, and followed as they wheeled her to the Respiratory Ward, where she was placed on a breathing machine. Gerald stayed close by together with her parents. Richard accompanied Captain McInnes back to police headquarters where the Captain took charge of the hunt for the killer. Richard told him what he thought Brown's next move would be.

"Four days ago all he wanted to do was go and make a new life for himself. Now he wants to kill those he hates and try and get away with the money. I think he killed Dr Meredith because he wouldn't give him that money and because he treated him like shit. He's out to get his wife too. He hates her more than he hated Meredith or Joan, so I think he'll try and get to her. He won't go after Gerald or me. It's Evelyn that we have to protect."

"If she's in Remnark, you couldn't have found a safer place. It's completely cut off by floodwater, with only boats and amphibious vehicles getting in or out. It could be that way for days. We'll alert area police, just in case he doesn't know about the flood and heads there. I think the only coppers in the state not looking for Brown will be the ones in Renmark. They'll be too busy helping with the floods. Their radio is the only way of contacting the town."

Richard thought of Evelyn and the boy. Had she heard of Steven's death? That would have been on the radio news, even if there were no newspapers in the town. Was she worried about Gerald? It was just as well that there was no telephone. What was happening in Adelaide was too much to burden her with at this time.

Gerald was thinking about Evelyn as he sat in a draughty hospital corridor with Joan's parents, when Richard suddenly appeared close to midnight. He took Gerald aside.

"We're flying up to Renmark just before dawn. Brown's heading that way. I've arranged to take an Auster."

"Why don't we go right away?"

"I can't land in the dark. We'll try and get there just before sunrise. Did you know that Steven had a boat?"

"Yes, he kept it in the garage in North Adelaide. He used it for water-skiing."

"He also had a Chevrolet there in the garage. Brown took them earlier in the evening. He went south through Strathalbyn, crossed the Murray on the Wellington Punt and is out east heading for Renmark, unless he's decided to make a run for it in the direction of Melbourne or Sydney. But then why take the boat if he wasn't going to Renmark? There aren't enough police in the state to find him out there at night. He could reach Renmark by a dozen different routes.

"If he wants to launch the boat, he can only do that on a narrow stretch of the river. There are locks that he'd have to pass through, and they're not operating during the flood peak. In any case he won't try and launch the boat at night, so we should be able to get there before him."

"Where are you going to land?"

"There's bound to be a road or a field above water. I'll show you on this army survey map. I've got a few landing sites marked out."

Gerald pointed at the map.

"This is close to the house. It's between the town and the bridge."

"We'll have to have a good look first to see if there are any power lines. That would make Brown's day if we got ourselves killed."

"It wouldn't help Evelyn either."

They said good-bye to Joan's parents and went to prepare for the flight to Renmark.

Chapter Thirty-Six

August 1956

Gerald and Richard drove to Parafield and loaded the plane. Each took a rifle, a little food and a thermos of hot coffee. They drank and got into the plane at four thirty, the coldest part of this cold winter night. At least the weather was clear. Bad weather would have made what they had to do even more hazardous than it already was.

There was no one manning the control tower, nobody was supposed to take off at this time, but they had a good reason so they bent the rules. Richard put the nose of the plane into the wind and went through his pre-flight checks.

Satisfied, he released the brake and, giving the engine full throttle, let it roll along the dark field. He took off, turned north, keeping well away from the hills and climbed to 5,000 feet in the black, star studded sky. Then he set a direct compass course to Renmark. Ahead of them the sky was already light with the Morning Star bright in the eastern sky. Half an hour later they crossed over the Murray at Swan Reach, wide and meandering below, reflecting the faint light of the sky. Instead of following it they flew straight on over the dark desert, intending to meet the river again as day dawned, near their destination.

It was light when they reached the river a second time. Gerald who was following their progress on the map, pointed out the towns and the highway, leading to Renmark. Here the river made a loop to the south, and turned back north to Renmark and the Victorian Border. It wasn't the river that was on the map, but a series of wide flood-lakes and islands around the main river course. There was an airfield down there, between Berri and Renmark. Richard could land there if he couldn't put the plane down in the town, but he'd need a boat to make it the rest of the way. He put the Auster into a glide, heading for the road bridge crossing the river to the east of Renmark.

They took a good-look at the eastern side of the flood, as Brown had last been seen on that side heading east. It was a huge basin of muddy water three miles wide, north of the bridge, covering the western approach road. If, as they expected, Steven's killer had turned north he would have to launch the boat from a narrow reach of the land, opposite the town, above Lock Five and the bridge. In the half-light, they scanned the flooded fields for Steven's Chevrolet and the boat trailer. Suddenly they both saw it on a dirt road leading up from the water's edge. The car was standing a few feet behind the trailer, which was itself standing on a half submerged road. The boat was not on it.

Richard flew across the wide lake-like river searching for the motorboat. There was a clump of gum trees just down from the town and in this the boat could be hidden from them. He circled low over the town, looking for a place to land, as Gerald detected Evelyn's home, on the highway. He came in again, over the river bridge, landing on the main road and taxi-ing along it, up to the Robertson house. Grabbing their rifles, they jumped out and ran to the open doorway. The house was empty. The inhabitants had left in a hurry. There were bedclothes thrown on the floor and the electric kettle was boiling. Gerald turned it off.

They ran next door. A lady in a dressing gown was standing there with a shotgun and levelled it at them as they approached.

"Stop right there!"

"Where are the Robertsons?"

"Who are you?"

"I've come to protect them from Louis Brown. He's a killer. Where are they?"

The woman lowered the gun.

"Missus and the boy are here. He just took Evelyn. He's going down to the river. He's heading for those trees."

Gerald ran ahead of Richard as they hastened in the direction shown. He had a glimpse of Brown, wading knee deep in water a half a mile ahead. He was pushing Eveyln in front of him across a flooded stretch of road. Gerald couldn't shoot for fear of hitting her, so he ran after them.

They reached the flooded section as Brown drove Evelyn ahead of him into the trees on the river bank, a long island in the flood. He was only a few yards away from a landing pontoon, floating high above the water. Steven's motorboat was beyond. Gerald stopped and took up his rifle. By the time they could cross the stretch of water it would be too late. They were halfway across the pontoon, Evelyn in her pyjamas, and Brown with an army rucksack on his back, an axe pushed through the top of it.

Gerald pulled back the rifle bolt, pushed a bullet into the breach, took aim and squeezed the trigger. Brown pushed Evelyn into the boat. The warning shot whistled past his head, shattering the boat's windshield.

"What a lousy shot," he muttered, bending down to pick up the mooring rope.

Back at her neighbour's house, Evelyn's mother heard the shot. What did it mean? Had anyone been shot? She'd seen that the boys had rifles. Had they shot Brown? And what about Evelyn? She'd seen the axe that Brown carried.

Gerald quickly reloaded as Brown slipped the rope off the bollard. He took the axe out of his rucksack. It gleamed in the morning sun. They wouldn't keep shooting if he held it over Evelyn. As he jumped into the boat, axe in hand, Gerald fired a second shot. The bullet smashed into his shoulder, knocking the axe out of his grasp and Brown off his feet.

It wasn't a fatal wound, it wasn't meant to be. Gerald already had a third bullet in the breach for that purpose, if it was needed. The second bullet had in fact destroyed Brown's right shoulder, splintering the head of the humerus and the surrounding joint. It would have taken an orthopaedic miracle to restore it if Brown ever got to a doctor, but at the moment he had other problems. He was holding on to the pontoon with his good left hand, the other dangling in the widening gap between deck and the mooring, as the flood-waters took hold of the speedboat. His legs were sliding across the polished decking, his body a gangplank over the muddy water.

Brown wasn't aware of his situation or he would have let go and stayed on the boat. All he felt was the pain in his shattered shoulder. His wounded arm was dripping blood. At last his body could no longer bridge the gap and he collapsed into the water, losing his one-handed grip on the mooring bollard. Coming up, he was supported by the rucksack full of dollars. He floated after the speedboat and Evelyn, as the current carried them away from the pontoon and the levee. A few minutes later, Gerald and Richard arrived there. They called out to Evelyn, across 50 yards of water.

"Start the motor."

"I can't. He has the key."

She pointed to Louis, who was slowly sinking as the rucksack filled with water. He was struggling to get ashore with one arm, failing and floating further out into the current. Gerald and Richard followed them along the river bank. They were too concerned about

Evelyn to pay much attention to Brown. They weren't going to risk their lives to bring him to justice. The three of them watched as the water filled the rucksack and instead of supporting him, the water soaked money dragged him down. He made an attempt to free himself and then disappeared forever with the money, into the brown swirling flood to feed the Murray cod. Evelyn was moved, but not to tears.

Gerald and Richard ran down the river. They couldn't go very far, the levee bank didn't exist past the clump of trees.

"I'm going to swim out to her, Richard."

"Don't, Gerald. You won't make it in this current and you'd never make it back with her. We have to find a boat or get help. She isn't in any danger."

"Yes she is. There's a weir at the next lock. It's probably a cataract now. The boat will never negotiate that. It'll be turned over."

Gerald, stripped to his underpants, dived into the cold brown water and struck out for the boat. He too was caught by the current. It was the motorboat or nowhere.

Evelyn looked on silently. Somewhere in the water, under Gerald, was her drowning husband. What if he suddenly surfaced and dragged Gerald down with him? She didn't know what was happening to Brown or where he was. The water was thicker than Brown Windsor soup. She took up the water-ski rope to throw to Gerald as he swam on towards her. This wasn't Glenelg or the River Torrens. There were branches and other things floating down the river with him. He swam on.

Gerald had one thing in his favour. Both he and the boat were floating at the same speed. Now he could hear Evelyn calling to him. He headed for that sound. Behind him, he heard the sound of rifle fire.

Richard was worried about Gerald. Even if he did get to the boat, could he start it and stop them being carried over the weir? He picked up his rifle and emptied the magazine into the air, high across the river. He did the same with Gerald's rifle. Then he reloaded and did it again.

As he finished he saw that Gerald was going to make it, at least to the boat. What would happen to them after that was anybody's guess.

Evelyn threw the rope and Gerald grabbed it; she pulled him in and he climbed over the stern. They embraced quickly, the muddy water on his face mixing with Evelyn's tears. Evelyn was shivering. He too felt the cold. He tried to open the dashboard and start the motor.

Gerald couldn't get behind the dashboard. There were four screws holding the panel down. They searched for tools. There weren't any. Evelyn remembered her nail-file, but that was back in the house in her hand-bag. The land was slipping past them. Richard let off a volley of shots. Then they heard another sound.

"What's that?" asked Gerald.

"A tractor?"

"No, that's an outboard motor."

Richard didn't have any more bullets. The boat was now a mile down stream. Suddenly he saw his friends stand up in the stern and wave frantically. He couldn't see around the bend in the river. He couldn't see why they were waving. Then the boat disappeared around the bend. As it did, he too heard the outboard motor.

Gerald called back to Richard, but he was out of earshot, so he pointed down stream. He pointed to a dinghy containing four policemen armed with rifles. They headed straight for Steven's boat and took it in tow. Then they towed it back against the current, around the bend in the river, to the pontoon. Richard went back there, both rifles over his shoulder. He helped them out of the boat. They turned to meet Captain McInnes, emerging from the other boat.

"You came along at the right time. How did you get here?"

"We drove up last night and came into Renmark in this boat. We were about to land, when we heard the shooting."

"I hoped it would bring help," said Richard. "It was all I could do."

Captain McInnes looked at the speedboat.

"Is that Meredith's speedboat? Where's Brown?"

Richard answered with a phrase from the *Goon Show*.

"He fell in the water."

It broke the tension, but nobody laughed. Gerald told how he'd shot Brown, defending Evelyn. He showed the axe to Captain McInnes. Then Evelyn told them of Brown's arrival in Renmark that morning.

"Mom heard the sound of the motorboat. She was up making a pot of tea. She went to the back door and saw Brown coming across the field. She woke me and told me we had to get away. I grabbed Jonny and we tried to get out. Louis was already at the front door, so we ran out the back with Louis running down the hall. I gave Jonny to Mom and told her to run to the neighbours. Then I ran the other way. I knew that he'd run after me. He caught me and dragged me back to go after Jonny.

"When we got to Mrs Sim's house, she poked a shotgun out of the door and told Louis to let go of me. Instead, he held me in front of him and started walking up to the house. Then a plane flew low over overhead. Was that you, Richard?"

"Sorry we couldn't make it a little earlier."

"Brown must have been scared by the plane, so he made me go with him to the boat. I didn't know you were following until I heard the rifleshots."

"Neither did he. Do you know that he killed Steven and a policeman, and Joan's in hospital in a bad way?"

"I heard about Steven. What's this about Joan?"

Gerald told her.

"It was horrible watching him drown like that, but God knows, he deserved it. That poor policeman and Joan. We can go back to Adelaide now. I'd like to see Joan."

Evelyn remembered her mother. She grabbed Gerald's arm.

"We've got to get back to mother and Mrs Sims. She must have heard the shooting. She must be terribly worried."

A group of men drove up in a truck through the shallow water and got out of it. Gerald recognised one of them as Evelyn's father. He wore mud-splattered work clothes and a three-day growth of beard. As soon as he saw his daughter clad only in pyjamas wet up to the waist, he went to her.

"Are you out of your mind? You'll catch pneumonia!"

It was cold. He was right. Taking a coat from one of the policemen he covered her. Then he continued,

"What's going on? What was that shooting we heard? It sounded like World War III."

"Mr Robertson, I'm Gerald Fisher. I was shooting. I just shot your son-in-law. He fell into the river and we saw him drown. Then Richard fired off the guns to attract attention. I know this isn't a good time, but I want to marry your daughter, Mr Robertson. We just saved her from Brown. He wanted to kill her."

Evelyn's father remembered who he was. He was the man who had punched the Brown lout. Now he'd just shot him! He didn't know whether to be glad or sad.

"Mr Fisher, we've met haven't we? You have a very strange way of obtaining a bride. Who do you think you are, King David?"

He turned to his daughter.

"You don't seem too sad at becoming a widow, Evelyn. This is all beyond me. Am I missing something? Let's go back to the house and get Evelyn into dry clothes. Then you can tell me what's going on. Bill, can you drive us home? I'll be over to help as soon as I can. It isn't every day I lose a son-in-law like Mr Brown."

They piled onto the already overloaded truck and drove back from the pontoon to the house, leaving Brown's axe next to the mooring bollards and the two boats. Quiet returned to the riverbank.

When the truck pulled up next to the aeroplane, Mrs Robertson ran out to greet her husband. She had heard a lot of shooting and it worried her. The men who went to Evelyn's rescue had rifles, but maybe Brown too had a gun. What if Evelyn got hit by a stray bullet? Evelyn opened the car door and ran down to her.

"I'm alright mother, I'm alright."

Gerald dropped down from the back.

"Mrs Robertson, Evelyn's safe. He can't hurt her now."

"What happened?"

"Mother, Gerald's a marksman. He wounded him. Then we saw him drown, Mother. It was terrible, but it couldn't be helped. Mother, he killed a policeman and tried to kill Joan. He came here to kill Jonny."

Mrs Robertson took Gerald by the hand.

"Thank you, Gerald, and if I'm not mistaken, you must be Richard. I met you at Evelyn's graduation. You're the pilot, aren't you? Thanks for flying up here and saving my girl. Now let's get back in the house. Wes, will you get Jonny back from Mrs Sims? Tell her to come over. I want to thank her for sheltering us this morning."

Captain McInnes went into town, coming back half an hour later with the local police officer. The ladies were dressed and everyone was seated at the kitchen table, warming their insides with hot porridge. There was a frying pan with sausages in it sizzling on the stove, next to the porridge pot. The men had lit and attended to the fire, while the women were dressing and Mr Robertson sat back, listening to the story of Brown's last days of homicidal madness.

He felt quite pleased that his first estimate of Louis Brown had been the right one, but was still ignorant of the fact that it was his bullying of Evelyn that had driven her to seek Brown's company in the first place. He had warmed up to Gerald and was pleased that he wanted to marry Evelyn. He didn't know that he was married or that his wife was fighting for her life in an Adelaide hospital.

The police questioned Evelyn, her mother and Mrs Sims to get the complete story, then Gerald and Richard. They had to sign statements at the police station before they were allowed to leave the town. Gerald wanted to return to Adelaide with Evelyn. As there wasn't room for all of them in the plane, Richard returned alone, refuelling first at the nearby airport. The others left at noon by boat with Captain McInnes, who then drove them back to the city.

On arrival they went straight to the hospital where they rejoined Richard and Joan's parents. Richard took Jonny, who was pleased to see him and go with him. Joan had regained consciousness but could not speak because of the machine pumping oxygen into her burnt lungs. She could only communicate with eyes and touch. Evelyn sat by her side and took her hand. Richard had told her of Evelyn's rescue and of Brown's fate. When she saw Evelyn, tears came to her eyes, to both of their eyes. Gerald kissed her on the forehead and stood next to Evelyn's chair.

A few days earlier she had hated Joan. She had been mad at her for taking Jonny, but now she told her how that was all in the past and that she must get better so they could be friends again. She asked Gerald to get Jonny and the doctor let them bring the boy in until he became a little too noisy and Evelyn had to take him outside, where she wept on Richard's shoulder. Then Gerald came out and told her that he was going to stay at the hospital with Joan.

Richard took Evelyn and Jonny back to his place. They rested and waited for Gerald's return. He arrived at six and lay down on the couch, exhausted.

"She's dying, Evelyn. I'm going to have a nap and go back at ten. I don't think she'll last the night."

Evelyn stood up and put her arm around the man she shared with a dying friend.

"What's the matter?" she asked him. "She regained consciousness. Wasn't that a good sign?"

"It isn't her brain that's damaged, it's her lungs. They were burnt and poisoned in the fire. They're filling with water. She's drowning in her own fluids."

"That's horrible. Is she in pain?"

"They've given her morphine, but that just puts her to sleep. It's awful seeing her fight for breath, seeing what the doctors are trying to do for her, knowing that they're losing the fight and that she is too."

"Do you want me to come back with you?"

Gerald adjusted a pillow and lay down. It had been along day. He hadn't slept for two days.

"No, love, you've made your peace with her. For what it's worth I think she was glad to see you. At least she knows that Brown is not going to hurt anyone else, that her killer has been killed. Few murder victims live to have that satisfaction."

"I wonder if she cares."

"She cares, if not for her sake then for Jonny Marco and her brother and that he can't hurt us. Let me take my nap. I hope he won't haunt my dreams."

Joan was still asleep when he returned to the hospital, and she died in the early hours of the morning. Gerald drove the grief stricken parents home and spent the rest of the day with them, resting and trying to comfort them for the second time in less than a week. He spoke to Evelyn during the day and went back to Richard's house in the evening. He spent the night with Evelyn but they didn't make love. It didn't seem the right thing to do.

Gerald spent every day with his in-laws, helping them arrange the twin funeral. Joan was buried next to her brother in a section of the cemetery that was owned by the Merediths, where their recent ancestors were buried, next to the plot that Sir William had selected for himself. He never thought that he'd live to see his grandchildren laid to rest before himself. Gerald felt terrible at losing a person whom he had so dearly loved, and that he, in the midst of mourning was looking forward to his next marriage. Evelyn came with Richard and stood in the back, well away from the principal mourners. They were lost in the huge crowd attending the funeral of both Meredith children. Joan's picture was featured on page one of the newspapers for the last time, with a picture of Gerald placing a wreath on her grave.

Before leaving, Evelyn and Richard placed flowers on Jonny Marco's grave.

"Jonny, you can sleep in peace now," she whispered, "Louis isn't going to hurt anyone any more."

Chapter Thirty-Seven

August 1956

Charles and Diana Meredith were a broken couple. In the space of four days they had lost a son and then their daughter, both murdered by a maniac that they had never heard of before. They were pleased that Gerald and his friend Richard had gone after the killer, but didn't understand why Brown had gone to Renmark and what was the role of Evelyn Robertson in all this. They knew that she was the mother of the boy who Joan had said she was adopting, but they didn't know that baby Jonny had been stolen from her, so they resented Evelyn. They thought that she had agreed to the adoption, but felt that by changing her mind she had in some way brought about their childrens' death. Gerald couldn't tell them the truth about the adoption scheme.

He didn't talk with them about Brown and the deaths of Joan and Steven. It was a painful subject. Steven's evil role was kept from them and so was Joan's compulsive action in demanding Jonny. Gerald spent many afternoons and evenings with the Merediths, but stayed with Richard or his own parents. He made a point of finishing work at five and calling for Evelyn whom he took back to Dawn's house, where she continued to live during this hiatus in their lives, while Gerald mourned the death of a woman that he had loved for three years. He wasn't just doing this for appearances, Joan's death had been a blow to him. They both felt it and decided to observe the propriety of mourning for a month and not to get married until the following year. Evelyn for her part did not mourn for Louis Brown. Nobody did. His body was never recovered.

The day that Richard and Gerald returned from Renmark, the day that Joan died, they spoke briefly to the reporters, and at length to them the following day. Gerald, as Charles Meredith's son-in-law, spoke to the editors of the leading newspapers, telling them that he and only he would represent the Merediths, and that he'd speak for Evelyn and her family too. They weren't pleased as they were anxious to interview her, but bowed to his wishes, all except one reporter who decided to bide his time. Gerald and Richard gave them such a story that they could readily forget about the other smaller fish.

A few days after the funerals, Gerald received approval for the house that he and Joan had been planning to build. His first impulse was to scrap the idea, but he told Evelyn autbo it and showed her the plans.

"When would it be ready, Gerald?"

"Richard knows a builder who could have it done in five months."

Evelyn looked at the plans. She knew Gerald wanted to scrap them, but she saw nothing wrong with them. She liked them. They'd need a house when they got married.

"We could move in at the end of January."

"So when do we get married?"

"February, Gerald. When we come home from the honeymoon we can move into a new house."

"I was going to sell the land. It's enough for a dozen houses. Won't you feel funny moving into the house that Joan and I planned?"

"That's up to you. We did make up, before she died. If you have to replan and buy another plot of land, we might have to rent for a year. I thought that you'd have planned a bigger place with all that Meredith money."

"I intended to build it with my money and live off my salary. There's another plan showing how it can be extended up the slope."

"But you are being paid a good salary."

"I earn it. I'm working with Charles Meredith now."

"And all of Joan's money will come to you too!"

"Yes, as of last week's funeral, what the government doesn't want will come to us. You'll be able to stop working, Evelyn."

"In a pig's eye, Gerald. I worked bloody hard for my degree. I'm not stopping work until I get my Master's Degree and then only when I'm pregnant. I think that I've earned the right to take it easy for my next pregnancy. Then when the kids go to school I want to go back to work."

"When do we start *our* baby?"

"Let's see. I expect to finish my work by December and I'll be writing my thesis after that. That'll take a few months. We could start enlarging the family after that."

"I think that Charles Meredith wants to make me his heir. I might have to name any male children Meredith-Fisher. They want their name to be remembered."

Evelyn put down the plans and stood up. She raised her voice a little.

"Over my dead body! You know, Gerald, I've had enough of your in-laws. Are they going to rule our lives?"

"He's my employer, Evelyn."

"So far you've managed to stand on your own two feet. Do you like the prospect of being Charles Meredith's understudy, waiting in the wings like a Prince-of-Wales, until he can't make an appearance, and then taking over the lives and livelihood of a thousand people, sacking a hundred here if they aren't making a profit and buying up a plant from a poor widow for half what it's worth? If I wanted to live with a wheeler-dealer, I would have chosen Richard."

"I didn't choose this life. It was thrust at me. I can't throw it away or even give it away. I knew it was a mistake marrying all that money. It's funny, you spend all your life dreaming of being a millionaire, but when it happens, you're not prepared for it."

"I'd give the lot to charity and just keep enough for our immediate needs and our old age."

"And throw thousands of workers out of their jobs?"

"You used to be a socialist. Give it to the workers."

"I haven't got it yet."

Gerald didn't like this bickering over money, over Meredith money. Neither did Evelyn. She told him so.

"I can see us living like lords and spending the next fifty years fighting over money. Then we'll buy little Jonny a university and he can be Vice Chancellor, or vice everything else, like his father was."

"I'm his father now, or I will be next February."

"I'm frightened, Gerald. I don't want our kids to end up like their kids were."

"That's up to us. All rich kids don't turn out bad."

"I hope so. The irony of it is that Jonny's going to get his birthright and only we'll know it."

"Evelyn, I have a request. Something that's important to me."

"I'm devoted to fulfilling all your requests, my love."

"Good, let's not refer to Jonny's father ever again. It hurts me and I know that sometimes it could hurt you. Let's bury the past. Let's not talk about Brown either."

Evelyn liked his suggestion. If he hadn't done it first, she was going to make the same request.

"And Joan too, only when we have to. That suits me, and if you want to scrap the house plans and start afresh I'll understand. But I do like them, Gerald."

"I'll tell the architect to proceed. He did the planning. We left the whole thing to him. You can come and see the site next week. The wattle's in bloom, I think, either that or the almond trees. The site's quite pretty. It's a pity to disturb it. We'll have to remove most of the trees or it'll be a firetrap in a bushfire. That I don't want to experience again. Meanwhile I can't stay with Richard until we get married. I'll have to find a place to rent. I don't want to go back home apart for the odd night, and I can't go back to the flat."

"When do I meet your parents? I want to see them, Gerald, but I hate to think what they must think of me. What did you tell them? I wanted to speak to them at the funeral, but I couldn't."

"They didn't know what to say to you either. I told them about your father returning my letter to you and not saying that I rang, and how I'd said horrible things that I didn't mean. You're back in their good books again. They'll even treat Jonny as their own grandson. My brother and his wife are expecting a child later this year. Come to dinner, Sunday week. They want to see you again."

"So where are you going to live until our house is built?"

"I'll rent a place somewhere near you. I want to keep an eye on you."

On the 3rd of September, Australia's Prime Minister, Robert Menzies, flew to London and Cairo to try and mediate in the growing row that was developing over Nasser's nationalisation of the Suez Canal. After talks with the colonel, he returned, acknowledging that his mission had failed.

"Fancy sending Pig Iron Bob to Cairo. We're lucky he didn't start a war. He's got about as much tact as a Sherman tank," commented Richard.

"I wonder if he offered Australian Troops to the British like he did in 1940?"

"If there's a war, Gerald, your father-in-law can feed the troops again. How are they getting over what happened?"

"They aren't. Mrs Meredith hasn't left the house and her husband makes the odd appearance at the office. We're thinking of setting up an office at his house."

"Who's running the organisation?"

"It's hard to say. He used to run everything himself."

"You might be the chairman before you know it, Gerry."

"I'd be a lot more confident flying one of your aeroplanes, Richard. I've had it, mate. I spend all day reading reports and looking at accounts and bloody production reports. I understand it but it bores me to tears. I preferred working in the Brewery lab."

That night the three of them went out together, the first time that Gerald and Evelyn had gone out since the death of their respective spouses. They went to the Theatre Royal to see a new Australian play, one that the whole country was raving about, Ray Lawler's *Summer Of The Seventeenth Doll,* a play about Queensland cane cutters, enjoying their holidays and their hard-earned wages with their girlfriends.

September 22nd saw another atom bomb test at Maralinga in the north of the state. Australian troops were stationed five miles away from the blast centre and it was stated by the Federal Minister in charge of the tests that there was no risk to them or to anyone else, now or in the future.

On the 29th, Gerald and Richard went to the Football Grand Final and watched Port Adelaide win again.

On October 18th in Canberra, the Prime Minister was asked in Question Time, if Elvis the Pelvis was coming to Australia, and if so couldn't the money wasted on such a visit be spent buying life saving medicines for people who couldn't afford them? The Prime Minister was puzzled by the question and asked, "Who is Elvis the Pelvis?" He promised to look into the matter. Elvis did not visit Australia.

At Wests, *Rock Around The Clock* was screened amid mob scenes as hundreds of teenagers were turned away from the cinema. Bill Haley records were on sale in all the record stores, *See You Later, Alligator* on a 45, and an LP for 61 shillings. Elvis's *Heartbreak Hotel* and his version of *Hound Dog* were on salelo ang side Louis Armstrong and Garry Crosby's *Lazy Bones.*

The Hungarian Revolution broke out in the last week of October with street fighting in Budapest on the 24th, the day after Hungarian troops and police refused to act against a crowd of 200,000 demonstrators. Hundreds of people were killed by Russian troops in the next few days, until a cease-fire was declared on the 27th by

Prime Minister Nagy, which lead to the withdrawal of all Russian troops from Budapest on the 31st.

There had also been a cease-fire on the Egyptian-Israeli border but no peace. The Arab nations, in particular Egypt, were arming for another war. Israel mobilised its civilian army in the last days of October, and President Eisenhower advised American citizens to leave the Middle-East. Late on the evening of the 29th, Israeli paratroops landed east of the Mitla Pass, the start of a pre-emptive war to destroy the threat again Israel and eliminate the *fedeyin* terrorist bases close to the border. The military operations in Sinai were considered a threat to the Suez Canal and gave the British and French a reason to try and re-occupy it, hoping to topple Nasser and restore their influence in Egypt. They failed. Israel got the Egyptians off their backs, but the canal was closed. Prime Minister Menzies gave his full support to the British action.

The Russians threatened to come to the aid of Egypt, but went into Hungary instead, suppressing the revolution as thousands of Hungarians fled into Austria before the border was again closed.

In the United States, Ike was elected to a second term, beating Adlai Stevenson in a landslide.

In Australia, it was decided to go ahead with the Melbourne Olympic Games, threatened by world turmoil, and to take in 3,000 Hungarian refugees. November saw Professor Orr lose his court case against the University of Tasmania for wrongful dismissal, but not the end of the fight.

Prince Philip opened the 16th Olympic Games at the rebuilt Melbourne Cricket Ground on the 22nd of November. It was seen in and around Melbourne on television, which had been introduced in time for the games. Television was yet to come to Adelaide, so people had to listen to the events on the radio or wait for the newsreels to come to the cinemas.

Gerald and Richard went to Melbourne for the Olympics. The Merediths also had tickets for themselves and their dead children and these went unused. They were good games for the Australians, with Betty Cuthbert and Shirley Strickland excelling in the sprint races, with Australian swimmers led by Dawn Frazer and Lorraine Crapp winning most of the swimming medals. The 10,000 metres was a magnificent race with two world champions, Gordon Pirie and Vladimir Kuts running away from the field early in the race. The

Russian set a blistering pace. It was all over four laps from the end when the English runner wilted. Kuts made it a double, when he won the 5,000 metres gold medal.

The Russians met the Hungarians in the final of the water polo, while Russian troops were still putting down the revolution in their country. The enmity of the streets of Budapest entered into the contest, which was marred by fighting and which Hungary won 4-0. 29 members of the Hungarian Olympic Team defected after the games, with most of them deciding to stay in Australia.

After the closing ceremony on the 9th of December, Richard decided to stay in Melbourne to help the committee formed to look after the Hungarian athletes wanting to stay, and the Hungarian refugees expected to come to Australia. It was uncertain whether he was attracted to this philanthropic activity by his desire to help a group of people in need, or his desire to get to know a certain Hungarian swimmer who, while she wasn't a match for the Aussies in the water, was pretty as a picture out of it.

Richard made a bee line for her and cut her off from the bunch. At first she was wary of the handsome young Australian, but soon accepted his invitations to go on outings, to Healesville to see the collection of Australian Wildlife and to Frankston to swim in the placid waters of Port Philip Bay. *The Argus* printed a picture of the young defector and her Australian escort. When Richard returned home she was with the small group of Hungarian athletes electing to settle in Adelaide. He introduced her to Gerald and Evelyn.

"I want you to meet my Hungarian refugee, Anika, or Anna if you prefer. She was part of the Olympic team and hopes to enrol at the uni for an arts degree. You can talk to her, Anika speaks four or five languages including English."

"I suppose you're homesick, Anna, and worried about your family?" Evelyn asked.

"I think my family ran away to Vienna. I'm not sure. Some of my team-mates have had news, but I haven't. Someone's going over there next week to try and get news of our relatives."

"I'm going with them," said Richard.

Later when they were on their own, Gerald asked him, "How did you get in on the act, Richard?"

"I offered to help by employing a few skilled refugee men on my home building projects and I said I'd pay my own fare to Vienna. I'm going to be in charge of finding employment for the refugees in Adelaide and I expect that Meredith will employ a few. What about it, Gerry?"

"I'll do what I can, but it isn't going to be easy. Meredith may be putting off employees."

Richard looked at his friend. He knew that expression. Gerald had something on his mind.

"Aren't you selling enough beer?"

"The brewery's the one bright spot. The mills are just breaking even and the cannery's a dead loss."

"It's a good thing I got out of it last July. What's the matter?"

"Charles Meredith. Meredith Industrial has been a one man show for years. My father-in-law doesn't seem to have it any more. He's made a few disastrous decisions of late, or not made them and that sometimes is worse. Meredith Industries needs a new manager."

"You're his son-in-law. Get up there and help him."

"I don't think that he wants my help. Sometimes the managers try to get me to speak to him, but he doesn't like that, so I told them that they'd better deal with him directly. Two managers left us for other companies. When his children died, Meredith Industries died with them."

All this wasn't news to Richard. Adelaide was a small place. News travelled fast.

"Where does that leave you?"

"Richard, I don't know and I don't care. I've got the land you sold me and a house going up on it and money in the bank. Evelyn and I are getting married in February. If Meredith snaps out of it, good, if he doesn't I'll find another job."

"Do you want to see him fritter away the whole show?"

"No, but if he does, I'm not going to lose any sleep over it. It's their money."

'What would I do if I was in Gerald's shoes?' thought Richard. Then, 'I'd make Meredith pay attention to me.'

"Aren't you his heir now, Gerry?"

"I might be. I suppose that I must be. There may be some second cousins somewhere. I've never met them."

"So get in there and do something."

"Richard, he resents me. I think he resents the fact that I'm alive and Joan's dead, that somehow I let her down. I'm thinking of looking for another job."

"So what's stopping you?"

"The old man would regard it as an affront to him. Now I know why Steven didn't want to work with his father. He doesn't think anyone can do anything. He knows the whole lot and there's no room for other people's ideas and with him in prolonged mourning, the organisation is standing still or sliding backwards."

"It's a pity. I haven't got nearly enough to put in a take-over bid, Gerry. I might put in a bid for the canning factory when I come back from Vienna. I think I could put it on its feet."

"When are you going to Vienna?"

Gerald was glad that he'd changed the subject.

"Soon. The first week in January. You look after Anika for me. See she doesn't get lonely and keep the Browns away."

"What's with you two, Richard?"

Evelyn had told him Richard was in love, but he didn't believe her.

"I'm going to marry the girl. That's why I'm going to Vienna. I want to bring back her family."

"Anna seems a nice girl. She's pretty too. Don't be gone too long."

"I won't be. I'm relying on you and Evelyn to keep the Go-annas away."

Again in 1956 no Nobel Peace Prize was presented.

Richard flew to Vienna with a group of Australian officials on the third of January 1957, promising to be back for his friends' wedding on February 16th. Before leaving, he and Anika announced their engagement.

Neither Gerald nor Evelyn saw the article in *Truth* and although some people who knew them did, they said nothing. Diana Meredith showed the article to her husband.

MURDERER'S WIFE TO WED VICTIM'S HUSBAND.

Mrs Evelyn Brown, widow of the triple murderer, Louis Brown, is to wed Gerald Fisher whose wife was killed in the fire that Brown maliciously caused last August 14th. Thus, in a curious twist of fate, the murderer's child may some day be the heir to the Meredith millions. Not only did Brown kill Mrs Joan Fisher, but also her brother Steven Meredith, co-heir of the Meredith family. Gerald Fisher in the absence of other claimants, is expected to take over Meredith Industries some day, and be declared heir to the Meredith fortune.

Readers of this paper will remember that it was Gerald Fisher who shot the murderer, Louis Brown, after a dramatic chase in the Renmark flood with his pilot friend, Richard Flynn, thus preventing him from getting away with his wife and money stolen from the Merediths. Neither the money nor the murderer's body have been seen since the three people saw Brown disappear into the Murray River. The man who shot the murderer, saving the State the expense of a trial, is now to wed the woman he widowed. The wedding, a small family affair, is to take place on February 16th in Renmark, the place where the groom shot the husband. We hope the young couple have better luck this time. At least they won't have financial worries.

The newspaper editor was away on summer holiday when the reporter got the article past the deputy editor. When he returned he was furious, expecting any day a summons from Charles Meredith. The summons never came. Neither did any more advertising from any Meredith companies. The damage had been done. Charles Meredith summoned Gerald Fisher at work and showed him the article.

"My wife showed this to me. Have you read it?"

Gerald looked at the paper. The article was on page one, next to a semi-naked picture of Brigitte Bardot from *And God Created Woman*. He got very angry at the uncomplimentary references to Evelyn, especially that she had been going away with Brown. He quickly saw that although it was malicious it was essentially factual, even if there was distortion and omission of some of the facts. He took his time before answering his father-in-law and employer.

"I don't read that paper. I find that article upsetting and in very bad taste."

"If it isn't true, I want you to take them to court. I don't like that paper either. I want them taught a lesson."

"If what isn't true?"

"About you and Mrs Brown."

"Please don't call Evelyn by that name."

The way Gerald said "Evelyn" confirmed Charles Meredith's fears. He was seeing Mrs Brown.

"Is it true? Are you engaged to this woman?"

"Yes, I am going to marry Evelyn. I was going to tell you this week. I was going to invite you to the wedding."

"Of all the women in the world, why do you have to marry this one, the wife of the man who killed Joan?"

Gerald didn't like the way his employer referred to the woman he loved. He spoke in her defence.

"She also was a victim of his. He tried to kill her. She wasn't going away with him, she went to Renmark to escape from him. I took her there. None of this would have happened if your son hadn't provoked Brown in the first place."

"Are you forgetting that he killed my son in such a horrible way? He planned the whole thing and killed him. Premeditated bloody murder! God, I'm glad you shot him."

"Steven would have been alive today and Joan too, if he'd only have listened to us. We told him not to fool with Brown. Well, he did and he got himself killed, and Joan and that poor policeman too. If you must know, that madman would have killed Evelyn if we hadn't stopped him. When Joan was dying in the hospital I brought Evelyn to see her. She was her friend too, you know. Joan knew that I was going to marry her and she was pleased."

"How do you know? Joan wasn't able to speak."

"She was able to communicate. Believe me, I know what I'm talking about."

Charles Meredith was astounded. While his daughter was dying, his son-in-law was carrying on with another woman!

"I don't believe this, Joan's dying and you're introducing her to your next wife? Explain yourself."

Gerald was calm now, but not his father-in-law.

"We were all friends once, until Evelyn married Brown. Listen Mr Meredith, Evelyn's marriage was a disaster. They were separated almost from the wedding day."

Gerald didn't want to tell him why they got married.

"She has a son. Are you going to adopt Brown's child?"

Gerald hated the way he said "Brown's child", as if the sins of the father were passed down to the son.

"Yes I'm going to adopt Evelyn's boy when I marry her."

"I don't like it."

"What don't you like?"

He was adopting an angry tone, that Charles Meredith thought lacked respect.

"Gerald Fisher, I don't want my son-in-law adopting the child of the man who killed Joan and Steven."

"Come off it, Mr Meredith. He's a three year old boy."

"His father murdered my children."

Gerald, for a second was tempted to tell Charles Meredith the truth about Jonny, but he'd sworn to Evelyn that he'd never tell the Merediths. In any case why should he disillusion the man? He was beginning to develop an intense dislike for Charles Meredith and his wife, who was undoubtedly behind this.

"He's a little boy and his mother loves him. I love him too. I wish he was my natural child, but I intend to treat him as my own and treat his just the same as any other children we have."

"You know that you are to be the main beneficiary in our wills now that our children are gone, Gerald?"

"I didn't know."

"If you marry that woman and adopt that murderer's boy, we may have to modify our wills to exclude his benefiting by his father's crime."

It took a lot of restraint on Gerald's behalf not to tell the gentleman to stick his will where it would cause him a lot of constipation.

"That woman is Evelyn Robertson, soon to be Evelyn Fisher, and I don't like her son being referred to as a murderer's son. Mr Meredith, I expect that from this bloody newspaper, not from you, Sir."

"I'm sorry, but I had to express our feelings."

"Well, I wish that you'd feel differently. I have a wedding invitation for you. I hope that you'll open your heart to Evelyn and her boy and we can all be family again. I'm sorry about Joan. I loved her too, you know."

"If you did, why did you race off to that other woman, when she was dying in hospital?"

"If you must know I asked Joan to divorce me the night before Steven was killed, for reasons that I can't tell you. She agreed and we would have parted friends. I repeat, Sir, friends. I went to Renmark as you bloody well know to save Evelyn and the boy from the man who killed your children. I didn't go to hunt Brown, that was police business. I went to protect Evelyn and Jonny. The boy that isn't good enough for you was also going to be killed by your daughter's killer."

"Why? Who would want to hurt a little boy?"

"Exactly. Now if you don't mind I want to go now. I'm taking that little boy and his mother out for an ice-cream."

Evelyn was still living with the Grovers although she now spent more time at Gerald's house. They considered her moving in with him completely, but Dawn looked after Jonny during the day and with only a month to go it wasn't much of a problem. Gerald picked up Evelyn from the university, they collected Jonny from Dawn and went back to Gerald's house. They walked down to the corner shop, bought three ice creams and returned to the house. Then they played with Jonny on the grass until the sun went down. Gerald listened to the radio, while Evelyn fed Jonny and prepared a couple of steaks for the two of them. Gerald did the dishes and put Jonny to bed, while Evelyn worked on her MSc thesis. They played *Que Será Será* and *Love Me Or Leave Me* on the radio, Doris Day recordings, and a selection from *High Society*. It took his mind off the *Truth* article.

At eleven she came out and spoke to him.

"What happened at work today? You haven't complained about the place all evening. If I didn't know you, I'd have thought that you spent the day at the cricket."

"Nothing happened."

He didn't know how to tell her.

"Gerald, what's the matter? You didn't say anything all the way to the Grovers and you picked at your steak and you haven't bothered me at all this evening. You're not having a male period are you?"

"I am a bit tired, that's all."

"You're not getting cold feet about the wedding?"

"I'm sick of working for Charles Meredith."

"If you want to find another job that's alright by me. How are you going to tell Charles? Did you invite him to the wedding?"

"Yes, but I don't think he wants an invitation."

"Oh. That sounds ominous."

He had to tell her. He had to tell her about Charles and Diana Meredith. It concerned her too.

"Evelyn, they found out about the wedding from another source. Our wedding plans came out in last week's *Truth*. Charles Meredith called me in today and expressed his displeasure at my choice."

"He disapproves of me?"

"No, your son. He doesn't like Jonny's father."

"Neither did I. That's a laugh. Does he know who Jonny's father was?"

"No. Do you want me to tell him?"

"Gerald, if I'd had an affair with Steven, if we'd loved one another, I'd tell them, but I'm not prepared to tell them what really happened and I'm not prepared to lie to them. What do you want to do?"

"Move to Sydney or Melbourne where people don't know what happened. Adelaide's too small. Everyone knows everyone else here. I want to sell the house and cut myself loose from the Merediths."

"Charles isn't going to like that, Gerald."

"Charles and Diana Meredith can plait their shit. They want to put a proviso in their wills specifically excluding Jonny from their wealth. I don't see how they can do it without excluding me too, so I'm going to tell them that I don't want to be a beneficiary. I want Joan's money to go to charity. I have £15,000 that I've saved and got back from Richard's investments. With that and the house and the land around it, we can buy a house anywhere in Australia and still have money in the bank."

"And we won't have the spectre of Joan and Steven behind us whenever we go to the bank. Pity, I was thinking of buying father a cathedral for his next birthday. It looks like he'll only get a hymn book."

"So when do we move?"

"Not for a few months, Gerald. I've got my thesis to submit and we want to be here for Richard and Anna's wedding and you have to find a job. Have you got that paper cutting?"

"Yes, but I'd rather you didn't read it."

"Gerald, I want to see it."

Evelyn read the article and then tore it into little pieces. Then they went to bed and were especially nice to each other.

January 14th. Humphrey Bogart died. He was 56 years old. On the 23rd, Princess Grace of Monaco gave birth to a girl, Princess Caroline.

Five months after his wedding to Evelyn, Gerald went to work as assistant laboratory manager in a large food factory in Melbourne, while Mrs Eveyln Fisher, MSc, stayed home to attend to home, garden and Jonny Fisher. She didn't look for a job for herself. There was no point. She was expecting a second child in November.

Chapter Thirty-Eight

April 1988

The letter came on the 20th of April, 1988. It was from Adelaide. It had the university crest on the envelope.

Dear Dr Fisher,

As you know, we have received a grant to establish a Chair of Ecology at the University of Adelaide. We have advertised this position and the Senate is ready to appoint the new professor.

I took the liberty of adding your name to the list of candidates as I believe you are the right person for the job, even though your candidature wasn't received. The Senate's choice is you, Dr Evelyn Fisher.

All that remains is for you to tell me that you will accept the position and we will announce your appointment. We hope to commence courses in Ecology for the academic year 1989, so your early acceptance is desired. I hope you accept the appointment.

Yours faithfully,

Dean of the Science Faculty.

Evelyn showed the letter to Gerald,

"I told him I wasn't interested. Why is he persisting, Gerald?"

"What if I also got a job in Adelaide? Why don't you want to go back?"

"You like your job, I have a job here too. We don't have to move."

"I've got news too. Our new owner came to see me today. You know we've been taken over. He wants to reorganise."

"Are you telling me that you'll be losing your job?"

"The opposite. We've just been taken over by Lumen Industries."

Evelyn put down the letter. She was beginning to realise what was happening.

"That's Richard's company. You're working for Richard?"

"He wants me to run the brewery."

"But he hasn't got a brewery in Melbourne. Don't tell me he's bought Fosters?"

"Merediths."

A cold chill went through Evelyn's body. That was a name that they hadn't used in years.

"They have a new name now. Richard's been buying up the Meredith empire, what was left of it."

They both thought back to those terrible days in August 1956, remembering the double funeral, when the future of a dynasty was laid to rest.

"You knew about that professorship, Gerald. Did you ask Richard to fund it so I could accept?"

"He told me he funded the chair. That's all I know about it."

"So I'm getting it by graft. I don't want it."

"No, he did a little research, found out that you stood a good chance of getting the chair, and gave the Dean the money he needed. He didn't influence the senate, but the Dean might have. You know he wants you back."

Evelyn thought for a while. The professor was still a good friend of hers, he never came to Melbourne without coming to see her. She knew she had the qualifications and she was ready for the job. But was she ready to return to Adelaide?

"Do you want to work for Richard?"

"I am working for him, he's my boss's boss."

"Do you want to manage the brewery?"

"It was either that or become his personal assistant. That would have meant a lot of travelling."

"A brewery. It's just as well Dad isn't alive to see this. His only daughter married to a brewery manager!"

"We're flying to Adelaide with Richard next week. That'll give us time to have a look-see and make up our minds. We're staying with them. You don't have to go if you don't want to."

"Of course I'll go, Gerald. Isn't Anika going to Europe?"

"They're both going in May. Richard is looking at investment opportunities in Hungary. Anika wants to do something for the land of her birth."

Anzac day, the 25th, they packed. In the evening Evelyn read the paper. Bob Hawke wanted to lower tariffs. The Duke of Edinburgh, speaking in Perth condemned apartheid. The Queen was in Hobart. In the US a 77 year old woman was jailed for prostitution.

There was an article on sex in the Soviet Union. Evelyn read it. What a place! Contraceptives were unobtainable, homosexuality a crime, the highest abortion rate in the world, sex education rudimentary. She wondered if it was all true or just anti-Soviet propaganda.

On the overseas page, there was a report of a car bomb in Lebanon, 50 dead and 80 injured in Tripoli. No wonder there were so many Lebanese fruiterers in Melbourne. Gerald had the sports section. She could see a headline, "The Second Coming of MacEnroe." She wondered what that meant.

On the 28th they flew to Adelaide. Richard left the controls to his pilot and spent the flight talking with his friends. Gerald and Evelyn did most of the listening, as their old friend told them about his latest acquisitions and what he'd planned for them in Adelaide.

He didn't tell them about his biggest surprise. When the plane landed at West Beach, Anika was waiting for him and with her was their son, Jonny Mark Fisher, MD, FRCOG.

Evelyn ran to her firstborn, kissing and hugging him.

"Why didn't you write and tell me that you were coming?"

"Sorry Mother. Uncle Richard wanted it to be a surprise. You know Uncle Richard, he always gets what he wants. He's becoming another Alan Bond."

Gerald embraced his adopted son, who was supposed to be in London. Evelyn gave Richard a friendly hug.

"Why are you always interfering with other people's lives? And why are you so good at it?"

He drove them to the old railway station. They went through the hall, where the Science dinner had been in 1952, over highly polished granite, up an escalator, through the gambling casino to the restaurant.

"I've read about it, but I never thought I'd see it with my own two eyes. A gambling Casino! Drinks with our meal! A smorgasbord! What next?"

"We have Lite Beer, nude swimming at Maslin beach, and a terrific Tandoori restaurant on Unley Road."

Evelyn spoke to her son.

"How long are you staying, Jonny?"

"Two weeks. We're here for the 200 year celebration."

"So why didn't you tell us you were coming?"

"Richard rang me two days ago. Said he had a plane ticket for me. That's not all, Mom, I'm going for a job interview. They're opening an IVF unit, and Richard got me an interview."

"Here in Adelaide?"

Evelyn looked at her old friend, Gerald's old friend, with a look of suspicion.

"Did you put up the money?"

"Adelaide women want babies as much as Melbourne women."

"If my son would have been an abortionist, would you have funded an abortion clinic?"

"Your son wouldn't be an abortionist. Besides, there seems to be enough money for abortions."

Richard knew that Jonny didn't do abortions. They all knew that as a gynaecologist, this was part of his job, but he knew how his mother felt about abortions, so he went into In-Vitro-Fertilisation instead. It was also more interesting.

'It's funny,' she thought. 'If IVF had been available in 1956, and surrogates, Joan would have become a mother, and I'd be married to billionaire Flynn.'

The next day they all went for a tram ride to Glenelg. Down there nothing had changed. *The Buffalo* sat above the fish and chip and souvenir shops. They walked along the beach front. Where the Patawolonga Creek had emptied its smelly water into the sea, there was a new marina full of yachts and simmering reflections. Then they walked out on the breakwater in the bracing breeze, where they could look back at the beach and the distant hills.

Later, Evelyn and Gerald strolled through Central Market and down King William Street to Rundle Mall. They spent an afternoon threading their way in and out of arcades, looking at menus in restaurant windows. Jonny took this opportunity of cornering Richard. There were things he wanted to ask him.

"I know I'm adopted, that Gerald isn't my biological parent. He's been the best of Dads, but I do get curious. I'd like to know who my real father was. They won't even tell me his name."

"And you want me to tell you?"

Jonny noticed Richard frown. That told him what he already knew. He had asked for forbidden fruit, for classified information.

"I'm 35, Richard. I'm a gynaecologist. It isn't as if I could be shocked or amazed. Why won't they tell me?"

Richard took a deep breath. This wasn't going to be easy, like acquiring the Meredith companies had been.

"Jonny. You've put me on the spot. If your parents don't want you to know, their reasons have to be respected. I know the reasons, they're valid reasons. The only person who can tell you about your father is Evelyn. Please don't ask her. If you let me think, I'll tell you what can be told."

Richard hesitated. They sat down on a park bench, he considering what to tell this man about his birth.

"The truth, Jonny, is relative, depending on who tells the story. It never gets to the thoughts and the reasons, what happens in our minds when we blunder."

"Was I a mistake, a blunder?"

"Would it hurt you to know that you were?"

"No. Most children aren't planned."

"OK, first, the bad news. Your father was a bad man, clever, but rotten to the core. He came from a good family, so we can safely say that there wasn't anything in his genes that made him the man he was."

"Is he dead?"

"He is."

Richard was thinking of Jonny's two fathers, Steven, who preyed on women and Brown, the mad killer who also preyed on women. If anybody deserved their fates, those two men did. How could he tell Jonny about them and how he'd been conceived?

"How did he die?"

"Violently. Jonny, I think we'd better stop here. It's all in the newspapers, and it isn't. You can read what happened, but not why it happened. Forget about the past. It was a very traumatic time for your mother."

"Why did she have me?"

"Because she had guts. It takes guts to do what she did. At the time, I didn't think she should have had you, not that I was consulted. I'm glad I was wasn't."

"And my father?"

"Gerald wasn't consulted. He and your mother were very much in love. She married another man to give you a name and a home. I hope you appreciate what she did for you."

"Are you kidding? I'm alive. I could have been washed down the toilet."

"Don't tell them that we had this conversation. And forget that you ever had another father, because Gerald's the only father that you ever had and your mother's only love."

For as long as he could remember there had been a present from Uncle Richard for him on New Year's day, even in far off London. This man loved him as much as his parents, as much as his wife and his own children. He had listened to him and he was satisfied. He knew all he wanted to know.

The next day Richard flew them all to Canberra for the Royal opening of the new Parliament building and later in the week to Brisbane for Expo 88. On the flight back they read about a Hawaiian Boeing that landed with part of its roof missing. It wasn't pleasant reading that in an aeroplane.

Gerald and Evelyn decided to make the move. Richard took them house hunting. Jonny took the IVF job. Before he flew back to London to tell his wife the good news, they went to the cemetery. They put flowers on Jonny Marco's grave. Gerald put flowers on Joan's grave. There were two fresh graves in that section, Charles and Diana Meredith. He put flowers on their graves too. Evelyn shuddered as they passed by Steven's grave. That man had hurt her, but he had given her Jonny. He hadn't meant to, but he had given her a son to love, of whom she was proud. That son didn't notice his father's grave. It wouldn't have meant anything to him if he had. Jonny was thinking of his namesake, the boy after whom he'd been named, the boy who'd died in his first week at university.

'What a terrible waste of young talent,' he thought.

THE END.